Janet Evanovich's Stephanie Plum Novels

ONE FOR THE MONEY

TWO FOR THE DOUGH

THREE TO GET DEADLY

FOUR TO SCORE

HIGH FIVE

HOT SIX

SEVEN UP

JANET EVANOVICH

THREE PLUMS IN ONE

ONE FOR THE MONEY,
TWO FOR THE DOUGH,
THREE TO GET DEADLY

SCRIBNER
NEW YORK LONDON TORONTO SYDNEY

SCRIBNER
1230 Avenue of the Americas
New York, NY 10020

This book is a work of fiction. Names, characters, places, and incidents either are products of the author's imagination or are used fictitiously. Any resemblance to actual events or locales or persons, living or dead, is entirely coincidental.

Text set in Bitstream Dutch 823

Manufactured in the United States of America

ISBN-13: 978-0-7432-1639-5
ISBN-10: 0-7432-1639-3

ONE FOR THE MONEY

This book is for my husband, Peter—with love.

The author wishes to acknowledge the invaluable assistance of the following people: Sergeant Walter Kirstien, Trenton P.D.; Detective Sergeant Robert Szejner, Trenton P.D.; Leanne Banks; Courtney Henke; Kurt Henke; Margaret Dear; Elizabeth Brossy; Richard Anderson, Gilbert Small Arms Range; David Daily, Fairfax County P.D.; and Roger White. With special thanks to my agent, Aaron Priest; to Frances Jalet-Miller; and to my editor, Susanne Kirk, and her assistant, Gillian Blake.

CHAPTER 1

There are some men who enter a woman's life and screw it up forever. Joseph Morelli did this to me—not forever, but periodically.

Morelli and I were both born and raised in a blue-collar chunk of Trenton called the burg. Houses were attached and narrow. Yards were small. Cars were American. The people were mostly of Italian descent, with enough Hungarians and Germans thrown in to offset inbreeding. It was a good place to buy calzone or play the numbers. And, if you had to live in Trenton anyway, it was an okay place to raise a family.

When I was a kid I didn't ordinarily play with Joseph Morelli. He lived two blocks over and was two years older. "Stay away from those Morelli boys," my mother had warned me. "They're wild. I hear stories about the things they do to girls when they get them alone."

"What kind of things?" I'd eagerly asked.

"You don't want to know," my mother had answered. "Terrible things. Things that aren't nice."

From that moment on, I viewed Joseph Morelli with a combination of terror and prurient curiosity that bordered on awe. Two weeks later, at the age of six, with quaking knees and a squishy stomach, I followed Morelli into his father's garage on the promise of learning a new game.

The Morelli garage hunkered detached and snubbed at the edge of their lot. It was a sorry affair, lit by a single shaft of light filtering through a grime-coated window. Its air was stagnant, smelling of corner must, discarded tires, and jugs of used motor oil. Never destined to house the Morelli cars, the garage served other purposes. Old Man Morelli used the garage to take his belt to his sons, his sons used the garage to take their hands to themselves, and Joseph Morelli took me, Stephanie Plum, to the garage to play train.

"What's the name of this game?" I'd asked Joseph Morelli.

"Choo-choo," he'd said, down on his hands and knees, crawling between my legs, his head trapped under my short pink skirt. "You're the tunnel, and I'm the train."

I suppose this tells something about my personality. That I'm not especially good at taking advice. Or that I was born with an overload of curiosity. Or maybe it's about rebellion or boredom or fate. At any rate, it was a one-shot deal and darn disappointing, since I'd only gotten to be the tunnel, and I'd really wanted to be the train.

Ten years later, Joe Morelli was still living two blocks over. He'd grown up big and bad, with eyes like black fire one minute and melt-in-your-mouth chocolate the next. He had an eagle tattooed on his chest, a tight-assed, narrow-hipped swagger, and a reputation for having fast hands and clever fingers.

My best friend, Mary Lou Molnar, said she heard Morelli had a tongue like a lizard.

"Holy cow," I'd answered, "what's that supposed to mean?"

"Just don't let him get you alone or you'll find out. Once he gets you alone . . . that's it. You're done for."

I hadn't seen much of Morelli since the train episode. I supposed he'd enlarged his repertoire of sexual exploitation. I opened my eyes wide and leaned closer to Mary Lou, hoping for the worst. "You aren't talking about rape, are you?"

"I'm talking about lust! If he wants you, you're doomed. The guy is irresistible."

Aside from being fingered at the age of six by you-know-who, I was untouched. I was saving myself for marriage, or at least for college. "I'm a virgin," I said, as if this was news. "I'm sure he doesn't mess with virgins."

"He specializes in virgins! The brush of his fingertips turns virgins into slobbering mush."

Two weeks later, Joe Morelli came into the bakery where I worked every day after school, Tasty Pastry, on Hamilton. He bought a chocolate-chip cannoli, told me he'd joined the navy, and charmed the pants off me four minutes after closing, on the floor of Tasty Pastry, behind the case filled with chocolate éclairs.

The next time I saw him, I was three years older. I was on my way to the mall, driving my father's Buick when I spotted Morelli standing in front of Giovichinni's Meat Market. I gunned the big V-8 engine, jumped the curb, and clipped Morelli from behind, bouncing him off the front right fender. I stopped the car and got out to assess the damage. "Anything broken?"

He was sprawled on the pavement, looking up my skirt. "My leg."

"Good," I said. Then I turned on my heel, got into the Buick, and drove to the mall.

I attribute the incident to temporary insanity, and in my own defense, I'd like to say I haven't run over anyone since.

During winter months, wind ripped up Hamilton Avenue, whining past plate-glass windows, banking trash against curbs and storefronts. During summer months, the air sat still and gauzy, leaden with humidity, saturated with hydrocarbons. It shimmered over hot cement and melted road tar. Cicadas buzzed, Dumpsters reeked, and a dusty haze hung in perpetuity over softball fields statewide. I figured it was all part of the great adventure of living in New Jersey.

This afternoon I'd decided to ignore the August buildup of ozone catching me in the back of my throat and go, convertible top down, in my Mazda Miata. The air conditioner was blasting flat out, I was singing along with Paul Simon, my shoulder-length brown hair was whipping around my face in a frenzy of frizz and snarls, my ever vigilant blue eyes were coolly hidden behind my Oakleys, and my foot rested heavy on the gas pedal.

It was Sunday, and I had a date with a pot roast at my parents' house. I stopped for a light and checked my rearview mirror, swearing when I saw Lenny Gruber two car lengths back in a tan sedan. I thunked my forehead on the steering wheel. "Damn." I'd gone to high school with Gruber. He was a maggot then, and he was a maggot now. Unfortunately, he was a maggot with a just cause. I was behind on my Miata payments, and Gruber worked for the repo company.

Six months ago, when I'd bought the car, I'd been looking good, with a nice apartment and season tickets to the Rangers. And then *bam*! I got laid off. No money. No more A-1 credit rating.

I rechecked the mirror, set my teeth, and yanked up the emergency brake. Lenny was like smoke. When you tried to grab him, he evaporated, so I wasn't about to waste this one last opportunity to bargain. I hauled myself out of my car, apologized to the man caught between us, and stalked back to Gruber.

"Stephanie Plum," Gruber said, full of joy and faux surprise. "What a treat."

I leaned two hands on the roof and looked through the open window at him. "Lenny, I'm going to my parents' house for dinner. You wouldn't snatch my car while I was at my parents' house, would you? I mean, that would be really low, Lenny."

"I'm a pretty low guy, Steph. That's why I've got this neat job. I'm capable of most anything."

The light changed, and the driver behind Gruber leaned on his horn.

"Maybe we can make a deal," I said to Gruber.

"Does this deal involve you getting naked?"

I had a vision of grabbing his nose and twisting it Three Stooges style until he squealed like a pig. Problem was, it'd involve touching him. Better to go with a more restrained approach. "Let me keep the car tonight, and I'll drive it to the lot first thing tomorrow morning."

"No way," Gruber said. "You're damn sneaky. I've been chasing after this car for five days."

"So, one more won't matter."

"I'd expect you to be grateful, you know what I mean?"

I almost gagged. "Forget it. Take the car. In fact, you could take it right now. I'll walk to my parents'."

Gruber's eyes were locked halfway down my chest. I'm a 36B. Respectable but far from overwhelming on my 5' 7" frame. I was wearing black spandex shorts and an oversized hockey jersey. Not what you would call a seductive outfit, but Lenny was ogling anyway.

His smile widened enough to show he was missing a molar. "I guess I could wait for tomorrow. After all, we *did* go to high school together."

"Un huh." It was the best I could do.

Five minutes later I turned off Hamilton onto Roosevelt. Two blocks to my parents' house, and I could feel familial obligation sucking at me, pulling me into the heart of the burg. This was a community of extended families. There was safety here, along with love, and stability, and the comfort of ritual. The clock on the dash told me I was seven minutes late, and the urge to scream told me I was home.

I parked at the curb and looked at the narrow two-story duplex with its jalousied front porch and aluminum awnings. The Plum half was yellow, just as it had been for forty years, with a brown shingle roof. Snowball bushes flanked either side of the cement stoop, and red geraniums had been evenly spaced the length of the porch. It was basically a flat. Living room in front, dining room in the middle, kitchen at the rear. Three bedrooms and bath upstairs. It was a small, tidy house crammed with kitchen smells and too much furniture, comfortable with its lot in life.

Next door, Mrs. Markowitz, who was living on social security and could only afford closeout paint colors, had painted her side lime green.

My mother was at the open screen door. "Stephanie," she called. "What are you doing sitting out there in your car? You're late for dinner. You know how your father hates to eat late. The potatoes are getting cold. The pot roast will be dry."

Food is important in the burg. The moon revolves around the earth, the earth revolves around the sun, and the burg revolves around pot roast. For as long as I can remember, my parents' lives have been controlled by five-pound pieces of rolled rump, done to perfection at six o'clock.

Grandma Mazur stood two feet back from my mother. "I gotta get me a pair of those," she said, eyeballing my shorts. "I've still got pretty good legs, you know." She raised her skirt and looked down at her knees. "What do you think? You think I'd look good in them biker things?"

Grandma Mazur had knees like doorknobs. She'd been a beauty in her time, but the years had turned her slack-skinned and spindle-boned. Still, if she wanted to wear biker shorts, I thought she should go for it. The way I saw it, that was one of the many advantages to living in New Jersey—even old ladies were allowed to look outlandish.

My father gave a grunt of disgust from the kitchen, where he was carving up the meat. "Biker's shorts," he muttered, slapping his palm against his forehead. "Unh!"

Two years ago, when Grandpa Mazur's fat-clogged arteries sent him to the big pork roast in the sky, Grandma Mazur had moved in with my parents and had never moved out. My father accepted this with a combination of Old World stoicism and tactless mutterings.

I remember him telling me about a dog he'd had as a kid. The story goes that this dog was the ugliest, oldest, most pea-brained dog ever. The dog was incontinent, dribbling urine wherever it went. Its teeth were rotted in its mouth, its hips were fused solid with arthritis, and huge fatty tumors lumped under its hide. One day my Grandpa Plum took the dog out behind the garage and shot it. I suspected there were times when my father fantasized a similar ending for my Grandma Mazur.

"You should wear a dress," my mother said to me, bringing green beans and creamed pearl onions to the table. "Thirty years old and you're still dressing in those teeny-bopper outfits. How will you ever catch a nice man like that?"

"I don't want a man. I had one, and I didn't like it."

"That's because your husband was a horse's behind," Grandma Mazur said.

I agreed. My ex-husband had been a horse's behind. Especially when I'd caught him flagrante delicto on the dining room table with Joyce Barnhardt.

"I hear Loretta Buzick's boy is separated from his wife," my mother said. "You remember him? Ronald Buzick?"

I knew where she was heading, and I didn't want to go there. "I'm not going out with Ronald Buzick," I told her. "Don't even think about it."

"So what's wrong with Ronald Buzick?"

Ronald Buzick was a butcher. He was balding, and he was fat, and I suppose I was being a snob about the whole thing, but I found it hard to think in romantic terms about a man who spent his days stuffing giblets up chicken butts.

My mother plunged on. "All right, then how about Bernie Kuntz? I saw Bernie Kuntz in the dry cleaner's, and he made a point about asking for you. I think he's interested. I could invite him over for coffee and cake."

With the way my luck was running, probably my mother had already invited Bernie, and at this very moment he was circling the block, popping Tic Tacs. "I don't want to talk about Bernie," I said. "There's something I need to tell you. I have some bad news. . . ."

I'd been dreading this and had put it off for as long as possible.

My mother clapped a hand to her mouth. "You found a lump in your breast!"

No one in our family had ever found a lump in their breast, but my mother was ever watchful. "My breast is fine. The problem is with my job."

"What about your job?"

"I don't have one. I got laid off."

"Laid off!" she said on a sharp inhale. "How could that happen? It was such a good job. You loved that job."

I'd been a discount lingerie buyer for E.E. Martin, and I'd worked in Newark, which is not exactly the garden spot of the Garden State. In truth, it had been my mother who had loved the job, imagining it to be glamorous when in reality I'd mostly haggled over the cost of full-fashion nylon underpants. E.E. Martin wasn't exactly Victoria's Secret.

"I wouldn't worry," my mother said. "There's always work for lingerie buyers."

"There's *no* work for lingerie buyers." Especially ones who worked for E.E. Martin. Having held a salaried position with E.E. Martin made me as appealing as a leper. E.E. Martin had skimped on the palm greasing this winter, and as a result its mob affiliations were made public. The C.E.O. was indicted for illegal business practices, E.E. Martin sold out to Baldicott, Inc., and, through no fault of my own, I was caught in the house-cleaning sweep. "I've been out of work for six months."

"Six months! And I didn't know! Your own mother didn't know you were out on the streets?"

"I'm not out on the streets. I've been doing temporary jobs. Filing and stuff." And steadily sliding downhill. I was registered with every search firm in the greater Trenton area, and I religiously read the want ads. I wasn't being all that choosy, drawing the line at telephone soliciting and kennel attendant, but my future didn't look great. I was overqualified for entry level, and I lacked experience in management.

My father forked another slab of pot roast onto his plate. He'd worked for the post office for thirty years and had opted for early retirement. Now he drove a cab part-time.

"I saw your cousin Vinnie yesterday," he said. "He's looking for someone to do filing. You should give him a call."

Just the career move I'd been hoping for—filing for Vinnie. Of all my relatives, Vinnie was my least favorite. Vinnie was a worm, a sexual lunatic, a dog turd. "What does he pay?" I asked.

My father shrugged. "Gotta be minimum wage."

Wonderful. The perfect position for someone already in the depths of despair. Rotten boss, rotten job, rotten pay. The possibilities for feeling sorry for myself would be endless.

"And the best part is that it's close," my mother said. "You can come home every day for lunch."

I nodded numbly, thinking I'd sooner stick a needle in my eye.

Sunlight slanted through the crack in my bedroom curtains, the air-conditioning unit in the living room window droned ominously, predicting another scorcher of a morning, and the digital display on my clock radio flashed electric blue numbers, telling me it was nine o'clock. The day had started without me.

I rolled out of bed on a sigh and shuffled into the bathroom. When I was done in the bathroom, I shuffled into the kitchen and stood in front of the refrigerator, hoping the refrigerator fairies had visited during the night. I opened the door and stared at the empty shelves, noting that food hadn't magically cloned itself from the smudges in the butter keeper and the shriveled flotsam at the bottom of the crisper. Half a jar of mayo, a bottle of beer, whole-wheat bread covered with blue mold, a head of iceberg lettuce, shrink-wrapped in brown slime and plastic, and a box of hamster nuggets stood between me and starvation. I wondered if nine in the morning was too early to drink beer. Of course in Moscow it would be four in the afternoon. Good enough.

I drank half the beer and grimly approached the living room window. I pulled the curtains and stared down at the parking lot. My Miata was gone. Lenny had hit early. No surprise, but still, it lodged painfully in the middle of my throat. I was now an official deadbeat.

And if that wasn't depressing enough, I'd weakened halfway through dessert and promised my mother I'd go see Vinnie.

I dragged myself into the shower and stumbled out a half hour later after an exhausting crying jag. I stuffed myself into pantyhose and a suit and was ready to do my daughterly duty.

My hamster, Rex, was still asleep in his soup can in his cage on the kitchen counter. I dropped a few hamster nuggets into his bowl and made some smoochy sounds. Rex opened his black eyes and blinked. He twitched his whiskers, gave a good sniff, and rejected the nuggets. I couldn't blame him. I'd tried them for breakfast yesterday and hadn't been impressed.

I locked up the apartment and walked three blocks down St. James to Blue Ribbon Used Cars. At the front of the lot was a $500 Nova begging to be bought. Total body rust and countless accidents had left the Nova barely recognizable as a car, much less a Chevy, but Blue Ribbon was willing to trade the beast for my TV and VCR. I threw in my food processor and microwave, and they paid my registration and taxes.

I drove the Nova out of the lot and went straight to Vinnie. I pulled into a parking space at the corner of Hamilton and Olden, extracted the key from the ignition, and waited for the car to thrash itself off. I said a short prayer not to be spotted by anyone I knew, wrenched the door open, and scuttled the short distance to the storefront office. The blue and white sign over the door read "Vincent Plum Bail Bonding Company." In smaller letters it advertised twenty-four-hour nationwide service. Conveniently located between Tender Loving Care Dry Cleaners and Fiorello's Deli, Vincent Plum catered to the family trade—domestic disturbances, disorderlies, auto theft, DWI, and shoplifting. The office was small and generic, consisting of two rooms with cheap walnut paneling on the walls and commercial grade rust-colored carpet on the floor. A Danish modern couch upholstered in brown Naugahyde pressed against one wall of the reception area, and a black and brown metal desk with a multiline phone and a computer terminal occupied a far corner.

Vinnie's secretary sat behind the desk, her head bent in concentration, picking her way through a stack of files. "Yeah?"

"I'm Stephanie Plum. I've come to see my cousin, Vinnie."

"Stephanie Plum!" Her head came up. "I'm Connie Rosolli. You went to school with my little sister, Tina. Oh jeez, I hope you don't have to make bail."

I recognized her now. She was an older version of Tina. Thicker in the waist, heavier in the face. She had lots of teased black hair, flawless olive skin, and a five-o'clock shadow on her upper lip.

"The only thing I have to make is money," I said to Connie. "I hear Vinnie needs someone to do filing."

"We just filled that job, and between you and me, you didn't miss anything. It was a crummy job. Paid minimum wage, and you had to spend all day on your knees singing the alphabet song. My feeling is, if you're going to spend that much time on your knees, you could find something that pays better. You know what I mean?"

"Last time I was on my knees was two years ago. I was looking for a contact lens."

"Listen, if you really need a job, why don't you get Vinnie to let you do skip tracing? There's good money in it."

"How much money?"

"Ten percent of the bond." Connie pulled a file from her top drawer. "We got this one in yesterday. Bail was set at $100,000, and he didn't show up for a court appearance. If you could find him and bring him in, you'd get $10,000."

I put a hand to the desk to steady myself. "Ten thousand dollars for finding one guy? What's the catch?"

"Sometimes they don't want to be found, and they shoot at you. But that hardly ever happens." Connie leafed through the file. "The guy who came in yesterday is local. Morty Beyers started tracking him down, so some of the prelim is already done. You've got pictures and everything."

"What happened to Morty Beyers?"

"Busted appendix. Happened at eleven-thirty last night. He's in St. Francis with a drain in his side and a tube up his nose."

I didn't want to wish Morty Beyers any misfortune, but I was starting to get excited about the prospect of stepping into his shoes. The money was tempting, and the job title had a certain cachet. On the other hand, catching fugitives sounded scary, and I was a certifiable coward when it came to risking my body parts.

"My guess is, it wouldn't be hard to find this guy," Connie said. "You could go talk to his mother. And if it gets hairy, you could back out. What have you got to lose?"

Only my life. "I don't know. I don't like the part about the shooting."

"Probably, it's like driving the turnpike," Connie said. "Probably, you get used to it. The way I see it, living in New Jersey is a challenge, what with the toxic waste and the eighteen-wheelers and the armed schizophrenics. I mean, what's one more lunatic shooting at you?"

Pretty much my own philosophy. And the $10,000 was damned appealing. I could pay off my creditors and straighten my life out. "Okay," I said. "I'll do it."

"You have to talk to Vinnie first." Connie swiveled her chair toward Vinnie's office door. "Hey Vinnie!" she yelled. "You got business out here."

Vinnie was forty-five, 5' 7" without his lifts, and had the slim, boneless body of a ferret. He wore pointy-toed shoes, liked pointy-breasted women and dark-skinned young men, and he drove a Cadillac Seville.

"Steph here wants to do some skip tracing," Connie said to Vinnie.

"No way. Too dangerous," Vinnie said. "Most of my agents used to be in security. And you have to know something about law enforcement."

"I can learn about law enforcement," I told him.

"Learn about it first. Then come back."

"I need the job *now*."

"Not my problem."

I figured it was time to get tough. "I'll make it your problem, Vinnie. I'll have a long talk with Lucille."

Lucille was Vinnie's wife and the only woman in the burg who didn't know about Vinnie's addiction to kinky sex. Lucille had her eyes firmly closed, and it wasn't my place to pry them open. Of course, if she ever *asked* . . . that'd be a whole other ball game.

"You'd blackmail me? Your own cousin?"

"These are desperate times."

He turned to Connie. "Give her a few civil cases. Stuff that involves telephone work."

"I want this one," I said, pointing to the file on Connie's desk. "I want the $10,000 one."

"Forget it. It's a murder. I should never have posted bail, but he was from the burg, and I felt sorry for his mother. Trust me, you don't need this kind of trouble."

"I need the money, Vinnie. Give me a chance at bringing him in."

"When hell freezes over," Vinnie said. "I don't get this guy back, I'm in the hole for a hundred grand. I'm not sending an amateur after him."

Connie rolled her eyes at me. "You'd think it was out of his pocket. He's owned by an insurance company. It's no big deal."

"So give me a week, Vinnie," I said. "If I don't get him in a week, you can turn it over to someone else."

"I wouldn't give you a half hour."

I took a deep breath and leaned close to Vinnie, whispering in his ear. "I know about Madam Zaretski and her whips and chains. I know about the boys. And I know about the duck."

He didn't say anything. He just pressed his lips together until they turned white, and I knew I had him. Lucille would throw up if she knew what he did to the duck. Then she'd tell her father, Harry the Hammer, and Harry would cut off Vinnie's dick.

"Who am I looking for?" I asked Vinnie.

Vinnie handed me the file. "Joseph Morelli."

My heart flipped in my chest. I knew Morelli had been involved in a homicide. It had been big news in the burg, and details of the shooting had been splashed across the front page of the Trenton *Times.* VICE COP KILLS UNARMED MAN. That had been over a month ago, and other, more important issues (like the exact amount of the lottery) had replaced talk of Morelli. In the absence of more information, I'd assumed the shooting had been in the line of duty. I hadn't realized Morelli'd been charged with murder.

The reaction wasn't lost to Vinnie. "From the look on your face, I'd say you know him."

I nodded. "Sold him a cannoli when I was in high school."

Connie grunted. "Honey, half of all the women in New Jersey have sold him their cannoli."

CHAPTER 2

I bought a can of soda at Fiorello's and drank while I walked to my car. I slid behind the wheel, popped the top two buttons on my red silk shirt, and stripped off my pantyhose as a concession to the heat. Then I flipped open Morelli's file and studied the photos first—mug shots from Morelli's booking, a candid picture of him in a brown leather bomber jacket and jeans, and a formal pose in a shirt and tie, obviously clipped from a police publication. He hadn't changed much. A little leaner, perhaps. More bone definition in the face. A few lines at the eyes. A new scar, paper thin, sliced through his right eyebrow, causing his right eyelid to droop ever so slightly. The effect was unsettling. Menacing.

Morelli had taken advantage of my naiveté not once, but twice. After the scene on the bakery floor, he'd never called, never sent me a postcard, never even said good-bye. And the worst part of it all was that I'd *wanted* him to call. Mary Lou Molnar had been right about Joseph Morelli. He'd been irresistible.

History, I told myself. I hadn't seen the man more than three or four times in the past eleven years, and each time had been at a distance. Morelli was a part of my childhood, and my childish feelings for him had no place in the present. I had a job to do. Plain and simple. I wasn't out to avenge old injuries. Finding Morelli had nothing to do with revenge. Finding Morelli had to do with the rent money. Yeah, right. That's why I suddenly had this knot in my stomach.

According to the information on the bond contract, Morelli lived in an apartment complex just off Route 1. This seemed like a good place to start looking. I doubted Morelli would be in his apartment, but I could question his neighbors and see if he was picking up his mail.

I set the file aside and reluctantly squeezed my feet back into my black heels. I turned the key in the ignition. No response. I gave the dash a hard shot with my fist and let out a grunt of relief when the engine cranked over.

Ten minutes later, I pulled into Morelli's parking lot. The buildings were brick, two-story, utilitarian. Each building had two breezeways. Eight apartments opened off each breezeway, four up and four down. I cut the engine and scanned for apartment numbers. Morelli had a ground-level rear apartment.

I sat there for a while feeling stupid and inept. Suppose Morelli was home. What would I do, threaten to tell his mother if he didn't come peaceably? The man was up for murder. He had a lot at stake. I couldn't imagine him hurting me, but the possibility of being mortally embarrassed was extremely high. Not that I've ever let a little embarrassment stop me from forging blindly ahead on any number of dumb projects . . . like my ill-fated marriage to Dickie Orr, the horse's behind. The memory cued an involuntary grimace. Hard to believe I'd actually married a man named Dickie.

Okay, I thought, forget about Dickie. This is the Morelli plan. Check out his mailbox and then his apartment. If I got lucky (or unlucky, depending on how you looked at it), and he answered his door, I'd lie through my teeth and leave. Then I'd call the police and let them do the physical stuff.

I marched across the blacktop and diligently stared into the bank of mailboxes set into the brick wall. All were stuffed with envelopes. Morelli's was more stuffed than most. I crossed the breezeway and knocked on his door. No answer. Big surprise. I knocked again and waited. Nothing. I walked around to the back of the building and counted off windows. Four to Morelli and four to the apartment behind his. Morelli had his shades down, but I crept close and peeked in anyway, trying to see between the edge of the shade and the interior wall. If the shades suddenly rolled up and a face peered out, I'd wet my pants on the spot. Fortunately, the shades didn't roll up, and unfortunately, I couldn't see anything beyond them. I went back to the breezeway and tried the three remaining apartments. Two were no answers. The third was occupied by an elderly woman who had lived there for six years and had never seen Morelli. Dead end.

I went back to my car and sat there trying to think what to do next. There was no activity on the grounds—no televisions blaring from open windows, no children riding bikes, no dogs being rude on the lawn. Not the sort of place that drew families, I thought. Not the sort of place neighbors would know neighbors.

A sporty car pulled into the lot and swung wide of me, parking in one of the front spaces. The driver sat at the wheel for a while, and I wondered if this was an assignation. Since I had nothing better to do, I waited to see what would happen. After five minutes, the driver's door opened, and a man got out and walked to the breezeway next to Morelli's.

I couldn't believe my eyes. The guy was Joe's cousin, Mooch Morelli. Mooch undoubtedly had a real name, but I couldn't recall it. As long as I'd known him, he'd been Mooch. He'd lived one street over from St. Francis Hospital when he was a kid. Used to hang out with Joe all the time. I crossed my fingers and hoped old Mooch was retrieving something Joe had left with a neighbor. Or maybe Mooch was at this very moment jimmying a window to Joe's apartment. I was warming to the idea of Mooch doing breaking and entering when he popped out from behind the building, key in hand, and let himself in through Joe's front door.

I held tight, and ten minutes later Mooch reappeared carrying a black duffel bag, got into his car, and took off. I waited for him to leave the lot, then I pulled out after him. I kept a couple car lengths behind, driving white-knuckled with my heart drilling hard in my chest, dizzy with the promise of $10,000.

I followed Mooch to State Street and watched him pull into a private drive. I circled the block and parked several houses down. At one time this had been a fashionable neighborhood of huge stone houses and large, well-kept lawns. Back in the sixties, when block busting was a popular activity for liberals, one of the State Street homeowners sold out to a black family, and over the course of the next five years the entire white population panicked and left. Poorer families moved in, the houses deteriorated and were subdivided, yards were neglected, windows were boarded. But, as is often the case with a desirable location, the neighborhood was now in the process of being reclaimed.

Mooch exited the house after a few minutes. When he left, he was alone and without the duffel bag. Oh boy. A lead. What were the chances Joe Morelli was sitting in the house with the duffel bag on his lap? I decided they were fair to middlin'. Probably worth looking into. Now I had two choices. I could call the police right off, or I could go investigate on my own. If I called the police and Morelli wasn't there I'd look like a dunce, and the police might not be so anxious to come out and help me the second time around. On the other hand, I really didn't want to investigate on my own. Not a good attitude for someone who has recently accepted a job as a fugitive apprehender, but there it was.

I stared at the house for a long time, hoping Morelli would come sauntering out and I wouldn't have to go sauntering in. I checked my watch and thought about food. So far all I'd had was a bottle of beer for breakfast. I looked back out at the house. If I got this over with I could hit the golden arches and squander the loose change in the bottom of my pocketbook on a burger. Motivation.

I sucked in some air, shoved my door open, and levered myself out of the car. Just do it, I thought. Don't make a big deal out of something simple. He probably isn't even in there.

I strode purposefully down the sidewalk, talking to myself as I walked. I reached the house and went in without hesitation. Mailboxes in the vestibule indicated there were eight apartments. All apartment doors opened off a common stairwell. All mailboxes had names affixed to them with the exception of apartment 201. None of those names were Morelli.

For lack of a better plan, I decided to go with the mystery door. Adrenaline tripped into my bloodstream as I turned to the stairs. By the time I reached the second-floor landing, my heart was pounding. Stage fright, I told myself. Perfectly normal. I took a few deep breaths and without benefit of brain managed to motor myself to the appropriate door. A hand was knocking on the door. Holy cow, it was my hand.

I sensed movement behind the door. Someone was inside, looking at me through the security peephole. Morelli? I knew it with a certainty. Air stuck in my lungs, and my pulse throbbed painfully in my throat. Why was I doing this? I was a buyer for cheap lingerie. What did I know about catching murderers?

Don't think of him as a murderer, I reasoned. Think of him as a macho jerk. Think of him as the man who led you astray and then wrote the details on the men's room wall at Mario's Sub Shop. I gnawed on my lip and sent a wobbly smile of hope and insecurity to the person behind the peephole, telling myself no macho jerk could resist coming to the aid of that much guileless stupidity.

Another moment passed, and I could almost hear him silently swearing, debating the wisdom of opening the door. I did a little finger wave at the peephole. It was tentative, nonthreatening. It told him I was a piece of fluff, and I knew he was there.

The bolt slid back, the door was yanked open, and I found myself face-to-face with Morelli.

His stance was passive-aggressive, his voice laced with impatience. "What?"

He was more solid than I'd remembered. More angry. His eyes were more remote, the line of his mouth more cynical. I'd come looking for a boy who might have killed out of passion. I suspected the man standing in front of me would kill with professional detachment.

I took a moment to steady my voice, to formulate the lie. "I'm looking for Joe Juniak . . ."

"You got the wrong apartment. There's no Juniak here."

I feigned confusion. Forced a tight smile. "Sorry . . ." I took a step backward and was about to bolt down the stairs when recognition hit Morelli.

"Jesus Christ!" he said. "Stephanie Plum?"

I was familiar with the tone of voice and the sentiment behind it. My father used that same tone when he caught the Smullens' dog lifting its leg on his hydrangea bush. Fine by me, I told myself. Get it straight from the beginning there was no love lost between us. That made my job easier.

"Joseph Morelli," I said. "What a surprise."

His expression narrowed. "Yeah. Almost as surprising as when you nailed me with your father's car."

In the interest of avoiding confrontation, I felt compelled to explain. I didn't feel obliged to do it convincingly. "It was an accident. My foot slipped."

"That was no accident. You jumped the goddamn curb and followed me down the sidewalk. You could have killed me." He leaned beyond the doorjamb and looked the length of the hallway. "So what are you *really* doing here? You read about me in the papers and decide my life wasn't fucked up enough?"

My plan evaporated in a rush of pique. "I could care less about your fucked-up life," I snapped. "I'm working for my cousin Vinnie. You're in violation of your bond agreement."

Good going, Stephanie. Wonderful control.

He grinned. "Vinnie sent *you* to bring me in?"

"You think that's funny?"

"Yeah, I do. And I have to tell you, I really enjoy a good joke these days, because I haven't had much to laugh about lately."

I could appreciate his point of view. If I was looking at twenty years to life, I wouldn't be laughing either. "We need to talk."

"Talk fast. I'm in a hurry."

I figured I had about forty seconds to convince him to give himself up. Hit him with the heavy stuff right off, I thought. Appeal to his familial guilt. "What about your mother?"

"What about her?"

"She signed the bond agreement. She's going to be responsible for $100,000. She'll have to mortgage her house. And what will she say to everyone, that her son Joe was too cowardly to stand trial?"

The contours of his face hardened. "You're wasting your time. I have no intention of going back into custody. They'll lock me up and throw away the key, and in the process I stand an excellent chance of getting dead. You know what happens to cops in prison. It's not nice. And if you want to know more of the ugly truth, you'd be the last person I'd let collect the bounty money. You're a lunatic. You ran me over with a goddamn Buick."

I'd been telling myself I didn't give a hoot about Morelli and his opinion of me, but in all honesty, his animosity hurt. Deep down inside, I'd wanted him to hold a tender feeling for me. I wanted to ask him why he'd never called after he'd seduced me in the bakery. Instead, I yelled at him. "You deserved to get run over. And besides, I barely tapped you. The only reason you broke your leg was because you panicked and tripped over your own feet."

"You're lucky I didn't sue you."

"You're lucky I didn't put the car into reverse and back over you three or four times."

Morelli rolled his eyes and threw his hands into the air. "I gotta go. I'd love to stand around and try to understand female logic . . ."

"Female logic? Excuse me?"

Morelli turned from the door, shrugged into a lightweight sports coat, and grabbed the black nylon duffel from the floor. "I've got to get out of here."

"Where are you going?"

He nudged me aside, shoved an ugly black gun under the waistband of his Levi's, locked his door, and pocketed the key. "None of your business."

"Listen," I said, following him down the stairs. "I may be new at this apprehension stuff, but I'm not stupid, and I'm not a quitter. I told Vinnie I'd bring you in and that's exactly what I intend to do. You can run if you want, but I'll track you down and find you, and I'll do whatever is necessary to apprehend you."

What a load of bull! I couldn't believe I was saying it. I'd been lucky to find him this first time, and the only way I was ever going to apprehend him was if I stumbled upon him already bound, gagged, and knocked unconscious. Even then, I wasn't sure how far I could drag him.

He left through a back entrance and headed for a late-model car parked close to the building. "Don't bother tracing the plate," he said. "The car is borrowed. I'll have a different one an hour from now. And, don't waste your energy following me. I'll lose you. I guarantee it."

He dumped the duffel onto the front seat, started to get into the car, and stopped. He turned and straightened, hooked an elbow over the door frame, and for the first time since I'd popped up on his doorstep he took a few moments to actually look at me. The first rush of angry emotion was gone, and in its place was quiet assessment. This was the cop, I thought. The Morelli I didn't know. The grown-up Morelli, if such an animal existed. Or maybe it was just the old Morelli, looking for a new angle.

"I like the way you've let your hair go curly," he finally said. "Suits your personality. Lots of energy, not much control, sexy as hell."

"You know nothing about my personality."

"I know about the sexy as hell part."

I felt my face burn. "Tactless of you to remind me."

Morelli grinned. "You're right. And, you could be right about the Buick business, too. I probably deserved to get run over."

"Was that an apology?"

"No. But you can hold the flashlight next time we play train."

It was almost one when I returned to Vinnie's office. I slouched in a chair by Connie's desk and tipped my head back to get maximum benefit from the air-conditioning.

"You been out jogging?" Connie asked. "I haven't seen that much sweat since Nixon."

"My car doesn't have air."

"Bummer. How's it going with Morelli? You get any leads?"

"That's why I'm here. I need help. This capturing stuff isn't as easy as it sounds. I need to talk to someone who's an expert at this job."

"I know just the guy. Ranger. His full name is Ricardo Carlos Mañoso. Second generation Cuban-American. Was Special Forces. Works for Vinnie now. He makes apprehensions other agents only dream about. He gets a little creative sometimes, but hey, that's the way it is with a genius, right?"

"Creative?"

"Doesn't always play by the rules."

"Oh."

"Like Clint Eastwood in that Dirty Harry movie," Connie said. "You don't have a problem with Clint Eastwood, do you?"

She punched a number on her speed dial, connected with Mañoso's pager, and left a call-back message. "Not to worry," she said, smiling. "This guy'll tell you everything you need to know."

An hour later, I sat across from Mañoso in a downtown café. His straight black hair was slicked back in a ponytail. His biceps looked like they'd been carved out of granite and buffed up with Armour-all. He was around 5' 10" with a muscular neck and a don't-mess-with-me body. I placed him in his late twenties.

He leaned back and grinned. "Sooooo, Connie says I'm supposed to make you into a badass fugitive apprehension agent. She says you need to get the crash course. What's the rush?"

"You see the brown Nova at the curb?"

His eyes swiveled to the front window. "Un huh."

"That's my car."

He gave an almost imperceptible nod. "So you need money. Anything else?"

"Personal reasons."

"Bond enforcement is dangerous business. Those personal reasons better be pretty fucking good."

"What are your reasons for doing this?"

He did a palms-up gesture. "It's what I do best."

Good answer, I thought. More eloquent than mine. "Maybe someday I'll be good at this too. Right now my motive is steady employment."

"Vinnie give you a skip?"

"Joseph Morelli."

He tipped his head back and laughed, and the sound boomed off the walls of the little sandwich shop. "Oh, man! Are you kidding me? You aren't gonna get that dude. This isn't some street punk you're going after. This guy's smart. And he's good. You know what I'm telling you?"

"Connie says *you're* good."

"There's me, and then there's you, and you aren't ever gonna be as good as me, Sweet Thing."

At the best of times my patience was lacking, and this wasn't nearly the best of times. "Let me make my position clear to you," I said, leaning forward. "I'm out of work. I've had my car repossessed, my refrigerator is empty, I'm going to get kicked out of my apartment, and my feet don't fit in these shoes. I haven't got a lot of energy to waste socializing. Are you going to help me or what?"

Mañoso grinned. "This is gonna be fun. This here's gonna be like Professor Higgins and Eliza Doolittle Does Trenton."

"What do I call you?" I asked him.

"My street name. Ranger."

He reached across the table and took the paperwork I'd brought. He scanned the bond agreement. "You do anything on this yet? You check out his apartment?"

"He wasn't there, but I got lucky and found him in an apartment on State Street. I got there just as he was leaving."

"And?"

"He left."

"Shit," Ranger said. "Didn't anybody tell you that you were supposed to stop him?"

"I asked him to come to the police station with me, but he said he didn't want to."

Another bark of laughter. "I don't suppose you've got a gun?"

"You think I should get one?"

"Might be a good idea," he said, still beaming. He finished reading the bond agreement. "Morelli offed a guy named Ziggy Kulesza. Used his personal piece to put a .45 hydroshock between Ziggy's eyes at close range." Ranger glanced up at me. "You know anything about guns?"

"I know I don't like them."

"A .45 hydroshock goes in nice and neat, but when it comes out it makes a hole the size of a potato. You end up with brains all over the place. Ziggy's head probably exploded like an egg in a microwave."

"Gee, I'm glad you shared that with me."

His smile lit up the room. "I figured you'd want to know." He tipped back in his chair and folded his arms across his chest. "You know any of the background on this case?"

"According to newspaper articles Morty Beyers clipped to the bond agreement, the shooting took place late at night a little over a month ago in an apartment building on Shaw. Morelli was off duty and had gone to visit Carmen Sanchez. Morelli claimed Carmen had called him concerning a police matter, that he'd responded, and that when he got to Carmen's apartment, Ziggy Kulesza answered the door and drew on him. Morelli claimed he shot Ziggy in self-defense.

"Carmen's neighbors told a different story. Several of them rushed into the hall at the sound of gunfire and found Morelli standing over Kulesza with a smoking gun. One of the tenants subdued Morelli until the police arrived. None of the tenants could remember seeing a gun in Ziggy's hand, and the immediate investigation didn't turn up any evidence that Ziggy had been armed.

"Morelli had placed a second man in Carmen's apartment at the time of the shooting, and three of the tenants remembered seeing an unfamiliar face, but the man apparently disappeared before the police came on the scene."

"And what about Carmen?" Ranger asked.

"No one could remember seeing Carmen. The last article was written a week after the shooting, and as of that date, Carmen still hadn't surfaced."

Ranger nodded. "You know anything else?"

"That's about it."

"The guy Morelli shot worked for Benito Ramirez. The name mean anything?"

"Ramirez is a boxer."

"More than a boxer. He's a fucking wonder. Heavyweight. The biggest thing to happen to Trenton since George shafted the Hessians. Trains in a gym on Stark Street. Ziggy used to stick to Ramirez like white on rice. Sometimes Ziggy'd do some sparring. Mostly Ramirez kept him on as a gofer and a bodyguard."

"There any word on the street about why Morelli shot Kulesza?"

Ranger gave me a slow stare. "None. But Morelli must have had a good reason. Morelli's a cool guy, and if a cop wants to pop someone, there are ways."

"Even cool cops make mistakes."

"Not like this, babe. Not Morelli."

"So what are you telling me?"

"I'm telling you to be careful."

All of a sudden I had a sick feeling in my stomach. This wasn't just some slick adventure I was embarking upon to make a fast buck. Catching Morelli would be difficult. And turning him back in to the court would feel mean. He wasn't my favorite person, but I didn't hate him enough to want to see him spend the rest of his life in prison.

"You still want to tag him?" Ranger asked.

I was silent.

"If you don't do it, someone else will," Ranger said. "That's something you got to learn. And, you got no business making judgments. You just do your job, and bring the man in. Got to trust in the system."

"Do you trust in the system?"

"Beats the shit out of anarchy."

"There's a lot of money involved here. If you're so good, why didn't Vinnie give Morelli to you? Why did he originally give him to Morty Beyers?"

"Vinnie moves in mysterious ways."

"Anything else I should know about Morelli?"

"If you want your money, you better find your man fast. Rumor has it the judicial system is the least of his problems."

"Are you telling me there's a contract out on him?"

Ranger made a gun sign with his hand. "Bang."

"You sure about this rumor?"

He shrugged. "Just repeating what I heard."

"The plot thickens," I said to Ranger.

"Like I said before, you don't care about the plot. Your job is simple. Find the man, bring him in."

"Do you think I can do it?"

"No."

If he was trying to discourage me, that was the wrong answer. "Will you help me anyway?"

"Long as you don't tell nobody. Wouldn't want to tarnish my image by looking like a good guy."

I nodded. "Okay, where do I begin?"

"First thing we need to do is get you outfitted. And while we collect your hardware, I'm gonna tell you about the law."

"This isn't going to be expensive, is it?"

"My time and knowledge are coming to you free of charge because I like you, and I always wanted to be Professor Higgins, but handcuffs cost $40 a pair. You got plastic?"

I was all out of plastic. I'd hocked my few pieces of good jewelry and sold my living room sleep sofa to one of my neighbors to make my charge card payments. My major appliances had gone for the Nova. The only thing left was a small cache of emergency money which I'd steadfastly refused to touch. I'd been saving it to use on orthopedic reconstruction after the bill collectors broke my knees.

Well hell, it probably wasn't nearly enough money for new knees anyway. "I have a few dollars set aside," I said.

I dropped my new big black leather shoulder bag on the floor by my chair and took my place at the dinner table. My mother and father and Grandma Mazur were already seated, waiting to hear how it went with Vinnie.

"You're twelve minutes late," my mother said. "I was listening for sirens. You weren't in an accident, were you?"

"I was working."

"Already?" She turned to my father. "The first day on the job and your cousin has her working overtime. You should talk to him, Frank."

"It's not like that," I told her. "My hours are flexible."

"Your father worked at the post office for thirty years, and he never once came home late for dinner."

A sigh popped out before I could squelch it.

"So what's with the sigh?" my mother asked. "And the new pocketbook. When did you get the new pocketbook?"

"I got the pocketbook today. I need to carry some things around with me for this job. I had to get a bigger bag."

"What things do you need? I thought you were doing filing."

"I didn't get that job. I got another job."

"What job did you get?"

I poured ketchup on my meatloaf and barely restrained a second sigh. "Recovery agent," I said. "I've got a job as a recovery agent."

"A recovery agent," my mother repeated. "Frank, do you know what a recovery agent is?"

"Yeah," he said. "Bounty hunter."

My mother slapped her forehead and rolled her eyes. "Stephanie, Stephanie, Stephanie, what are you thinking of? This is no kind of work for a nice young lady."

"It's a legitimate, respectable job," I said. "It's like being a cop or a private investigator." Neither one of which I had ever considered to be especially respectable.

"But you don't know anything about this."

"It's simple," I said. "Vinnie gives me an FTA, and then I find him and escort him back to the police station."

"What's an FTA?" my mother wanted to know.

"It's a person who's Failed To Appear."

"Maybe I could be a bounty hunter," Grandma Mazur said. "I could use to earn some spending money. I could go after those FTAs with you."

"Jesus," my father said.

My mother ignored both of them. "You should learn to make slipcovers," she said to me. "There's always a need for slipcovers." She looked at my father. "Frank, don't you think she should learn to make slipcovers? Isn't that a good idea?"

I felt the muscles tense along my spine and made an effort to relax. Buck up, I told myself. This was good practice for tomorrow morning when I intended to visit Morelli's mother.

In the order of the burg, Joseph Morelli's mother made my mother look like a second-rate housewife. My mother was no slouch, but by burg standards, Mrs. Morelli was a housewife of heroic proportions. God himself couldn't get windows cleaner, wash whiter, or make better ziti than Mrs. Morelli. She never missed Mass, she sold Amway in her spare time, and she scared the beejeebers out of me with her piercing black eyes. I didn't think Mrs. Morelli was likely to snitch on her last born, but she was on my quiz list anyway. No stone unturned.

Joe's father could have been bought for five bucks and a six-pack, but his father was dead.

I'd opted for a professional image this morning, dressing in a tailored beige linen suit, complete with pantyhose and heels and tasteful pearl earrings. I parked at the curb, climbed the porch stairs, and knocked on the Morelli front door.

"Well," Momma Morelli said, standing behind the screen, staring out at me with a degree of censure usually reserved for atheists and slackers. "Look who's here on my porch, bright and early . . . little miss bounty hunter." She boosted her chin up an additional inch. "I heard all about you and your new job, and I have nothing to say to you."

"I need to find Joe, Mrs. Morelli. He missed a court appearance."

"I'm sure he had good reason."

Yeah. Like he's guilty as hell. "I tell you what, I'll leave my card, just in case. I got them made yesterday." I rooted through the big black bag, finding handcuffs, hair spray, flashlight, hairbrush—no cards. I tipped the bag to look inside, and my gun fell out onto the green indoor-outdoor carpeting.

"A gun," Mrs. Morelli said. "What is this world coming to? Does your mother know you're carrying a gun? I'm going to tell her. I'm going to call and tell her right now."

She sent me a look of utter disgust and slammed the front door shut.

I was thirty years old, and Mrs. Morelli was going to tell my mother on me. Only in the burg. I retrieved my gun, dumped it back into my purse, and found my cards. I stuck one of the cards between the screen and the molding. Then I drove the short distance back to my parents' house and used their phone to call my cousin Francie, who knew everything about everyone.

He's long gone, Francie had said. He's a smart guy and he's probably wearing a fake mustache by now. He was a cop. He has contacts. He knows how to get a new social security number and start over far away. Give it up, Francie had said. You'll never find him.

Intuition and desperation told me otherwise, so I called Eddie Gazarra, who was a Trenton cop and had been one of my very best friends since the day I was born. Not only was he a good friend, but he was married to my cousin, Shirley the Whiner. Why Gazarra had married Shirley was beyond my comprehension, but they'd been married for eleven years so I suppose they had something going between them.

I didn't bother with chitchat when I got Gazarra. I went right to the heart of the matter, telling him about my job with Vinnie and asking what he knew about the Morelli shooting.

"I know it's nothing you want to get involved in," Gazarra said. "You want to work for Vinnie? Fine. Get him to give you some other case."

"Too late. I'm doing this one."

"This one has a real bad odor."

"Everything in New Jersey has a bad odor. It's one of the few things a person can count on."

Gazarra lowered his voice. "When a cop gets charged with murder, it's serious shit. Everybody gets touchy. And this murder was especially ugly because the physical evidence was so strong against Morelli. He was apprehended at the scene with the gun still warm in his hand. He claimed Ziggy was armed, but there was no weapon found, no bullet discharged into the opposite wall or floor or ceiling, no powder residue on Ziggy's hand or shirt. The grand jury had no choice but to indict Morelli. And then if things aren't bad enough . . . Morelli goes Failure To Appear. This is a black eye to the department and fucking embarrassing. You mention Morelli in the halls and everybody suddenly remembers they've got something to do. Nobody's going to be happy about you sticking your nose in this. You go after Morelli and you're gonna be swinging on a broken branch, high off the ground, all alone."

"If I bring him in, I get $10,000."

"Buy lottery tickets. Your chances will be better."

"It's my understanding that Morelli went to see Carmen Sanchez, but that Sanchez wasn't there when he arrived."

"Not only wasn't she on the scene, but she's disappeared off the face of the earth."

"Still?"

"Still. And don't think we haven't looked for her."

"What about the guy Morelli says was in the apartment with Ziggy? The mystery witness?"

"Vanished."

I felt my nose wrinkle in disbelief. "Do you think this is odd?"

"I think it's odder than odd."

"Maybe Morelli went bad."

I could feel Gazarra shrug over the phone line. "All I know is my cop intuition tells me something doesn't add up."

"You think Morelli'll join the Foreign Legion?"

"I think he'll stick around and work to improve his odds on longevity . . . or die trying."

I was relieved to hear my opinion reinforced. "You have any suggestions?"

"None you want to hear."

"Come on, Eddie. I need help."

Another sigh. "You're not going to find him hiding out with a relative or a friend. He's smarter than that. The only thing I can think of is to look for Carmen Sanchez and the guy Morelli said was in the apartment with Ziggy. If I was Morelli, I'd want to get those two missing persons, either to prove my innocence, or to make sure they couldn't prove my guilt. I haven't a clue how you do this. We can't find them and chances are you can't find them either."

I thanked Gazarra and hung up. Looking for the witnesses sounded like a good idea. I didn't necessarily care that it was an impossible mission. What I cared about was that if I started running down leads on Carmen Sanchez, I might be following the same route as Morelli and maybe our paths would cross again.

Where to begin? Carmen's apartment building. I could talk to her neighbors, maybe get a line on her friends and family. What else? Talk to the boxer, Benito Ramirez. If Ramirez and Ziggy were all that close, maybe Ramirez knew Carmen Sanchez. Maybe he even had some ideas about the missing witness.

I took a can of soda from the refrigerator and a box of Fig Newtons from the pantry, deciding to talk to Ramirez first.

CHAPTER 3

Stark Street started down by the river, just north of the statehouse, and ran in a northeasterly direction. Crammed with small inner-city businesses, bars, crack houses, and cheerless three-story row houses, the street stretched close to a mile. Most of the row houses had been converted to apartments or rooms to let. Few were air-conditioned. All were overcrowded. When it was hot, residents spilled from the row houses onto the stoops and street corners, looking for air and action. At ten-thirty in the morning, the street was still relatively quiet.

I missed the gym first time around, rechecked the address from the page I'd torn out of my phone book, and doubled back, driving slowly, reading off street numbers. I caught the sign, Stark Street Gym, professionally lettered in black on a door window. Not much of an advertisement, but then I supposed they didn't need much. They weren't exactly in competition with Spa Lady. It took two additional blocks before I found a parking space.

I locked the Nova, hung my big black bag over my shoulder, and set out. I'd put the fiasco with Mrs. Morelli behind me, and felt pretty damn slick in my suit and heels, toting my bounty hunter hardware. Embarrassing as it was to admit, I was beginning to enjoy the role, thinking there was nothing like packing a pair of cuffs to put some spring into a woman's step.

The gym sat in the middle of its block, over A & K Auto Body. The bay doors to the auto body were open, and catcalls and kissy sounds drifted out to me when I crossed the cement apron. My New Jersey heritage weighed heavy, demanding I respond with a few demeaning comments of my own, but discretion being the better part of valor, I kept my mouth shut and hurried on by.

Across the street, a shadowy figure pulled back from a filthy third-floor window, the movement catching my attention. Someone had been watching me. Not surprising. I'd roared down the street not once, but twice. My muffler had fallen off first thing this morning, and my engine noise had rumbled off the Stark Street brick storefronts. This wasn't what you'd call an undercover operation.

The door to the gym opened onto a small foyer with steps leading up. The stairwell walls were institutional green, covered with spray-painted graffiti and twenty years' worth of hand smudges. The smell was bad, ripe with urine steaming on the lower steps, bonding with the musty aroma of stale male sweat and body odor. Upstairs, the warehouse-style second floor was no better.

A handful of men were working the free weights. The ring was empty. No one was at the bags. I figured everybody must be out jumping rope or stealing cars. It was the last flip thought I entertained. Activity faltered when I entered, and if I'd been uncomfortable on the street, it hardly counted at all to what I felt here. I'd expected a champion to be surrounded by an aura of professionalism. I hadn't anticipated the atmosphere to be charged with hostility and suspicion. I was clearly a street-ignorant white woman invading a black man's gym, and if the silent rebuke had been any more forceful I'd have been hurled backward down the stairs like a victim of a poltergeist.

I took a wide stance (more to keep myself from falling over in fright than to impress the boys) and hitched up my shoulder bag. "I'm looking for Benito Ramirez."

A hulking mountain of muscle rose from a workout bench. "I'm Ramirez."

He was over 6' tall. His voice was silky, his lips curved into a dreamy smile. The overall effect was eerie, the voice and the smile at odds to the stealthy, calculating eyes.

I crossed the room and extended my hand. "Stephanie Plum."

"Benito Ramirez."

His grasp was too gentle, too lingering. More of a caress than a handshake and unpleasantly sensual. I stared into his hooded, close-set eyes and wondered about prizefighters. Until this moment, I'd assumed boxing was a sport of skill and aggression, directed toward winning the match, not necessarily toward maiming the opponent. Ramirez looked like he'd enjoy the kill. There was something about the density of his eyes, black holes where everything gets sucked in and nothing comes out, that suggested a hiding place for evil. And the smile, a little goofy, a little sick in its sweetness, hinting of insanity. I wondered if this was a contrived image, designed to spook opponents before the bell. Contrived or not, it was creepy as hell.

I made an attempt to free my hand, and his grip tightened.

"So, Stephanie Plum," he said in his velvet voice. "What can I do for you?"

As a buyer for E.E. Martin, I'd dealt with my share of slime. I'd learned how to assert myself and still be pleasant and professional. My face and voice told Ramirez I was friendly. My words were more to the point. "You can release my hand, so I can give you my card," I said.

His smile stayed fixed in place, more amiable and inquisitive now than crazy. I gave him my card and watched him read it.

"Fugitive apprehension agent," he said, obviously amused. "That's a big title for a little girl."

I'd never thought of myself as little until I'd stood alongside Ramirez. I'm 5' 7" and rawboned from the Mazurs' good Hungarian peasant stock. Perfectly constructed for laboring in the paprika fields, pulling plows, and dropping babies out like bird's eggs. I ran and periodically starved to keep the fat off, but I still weighed in at 130. Not heavy, but not dainty, either. "I'm looking for Joe Morelli. Have you seen him?"

Ramirez shook his head. "I don't know Joe Morelli. I only know he shot Ziggy." He looked around at the rest of the men. "Any of you seen that guy Morelli?"

No one responded.

"I've been told there was a witness to the shooting and that the witness has disappeared," I said. "Do you have any idea who that witness might be?"

Again, no response.

I pushed on. "How about Carmen Sanchez? Do you know Carmen? Did Ziggy ever speak of her?"

"You ask a lot of questions," Ramirez said.

We were standing close to the big old-fashioned windows in the front of the room, and for no reason other than instinct, I shifted my attention to the building across the street. Again, the shadowy figure in the same third-floor window. A man, I thought. I couldn't tell if he was black or white. Not that it mattered.

Ramirez stroked my jacket sleeve. "Would you like a Coke? We got a Coke machine here. I could buy you a soda."

"Thanks for the offer, but I have a busy morning, and I really should be moving along. If you spot Morelli, I'd appreciate a call."

"Most girls think it's a treat for the champ to buy them a soda."

Not this girl, I thought. This girl thought the champ was possibly missing a few marbles. And this girl didn't like the climate of the gym.

"I'd really love to stay and have a soda," I said, "but I have an early lunch date." With a box of Fig Newtons.

"It's not good to go rushing around. You should stay and relax a little. Your date won't mind."

I shifted my weight, trying to inch away while I enhanced the lie. "Actually, it's a business luncheon with Sergeant Gazarra."

"I don't believe you," Ramirez said. His smile had turned tight, and the civility had slipped from his voice. "I think you're lying about lunch."

I felt tendrils of panic curl into my stomach, and I cautioned myself not to overreact. Ramirez was playing with me. Showing off in front of his friends. Probably stung because I hadn't succumbed to his charms. Now he had to save face.

I made a display of looking at my watch. "Sorry you feel that way, but I'm supposed to meet Gazarra in ten minutes. He's not going to be pleased if I'm late."

I took a step backward, and Ramirez grabbed me by the scruff of my neck, his fingers digging in with enough force to make me hunch involuntarily.

"You're not going anywhere, Stephanie Plum," he whispered. "The champ isn't done with you yet."

The silence in the gym was oppressive. No one moved. No one voiced an objection. I looked at each of the men and received only blank stares back. No one's going to help me, I thought, feeling the first licks of real fear.

I lowered my voice to match Ramirez's soft pitch. "I came here as a member of the law enforcement community. I came looking for information to help me with the recovery of Joe Morelli, and I gave you no reason to misinterpret my intentions. I'm conducting myself as a professional, and I expect you to respect that."

Ramirez dragged me closer. "Something you got to understand about the champ," he said. "First off, you don't tell the champ about respect. And second, you got to know the champ always gets what he wants." He gave me a shake. "You know what the champ wants right now? The champ wants you to be nice to him, baby. Real nice. Gotta make up for refusing him. Show him some respect." His gaze shifted to my breasts. "Maybe show him some fear. You afraid of me, bitch?"

Any woman with an IQ over twelve would be afraid of Benito Ramirez.

He giggled and all the little hairs on my arm stood straight out.

"You're scared now," he said in his whispery voice. "I can smell it. Pussy fear. Bet it making your pants wet. Maybe I should put my hand in your pants and find out."

I had a gun in my bag, and I'd use it if I had to, but not until all else had failed. Ten minutes of instruction hadn't made me a crack shot. That's okay, I told myself. I didn't want to kill anyone. I just wanted to back everyone up enough to get the hell out. I slid my hand over the leather bag until I felt the gun, hard and unyielding under my palm.

Reach in, get the gun, I thought. Take aim at Ramirez and look serious. Could I pull the trigger? I honestly didn't know. I had my doubts. I hoped I wouldn't have to take it that far.

"Let go of my neck," I said. "This is the last time I'm telling you."

"Nobody tell the champ what to do," he roared, his composure gone, his face twisted and ugly. For a split second the door swung open, and I caught a glimpse of the inner man—a glimpse of insanity, and of hellfires burning and hatred so strong it whipped my breath away.

He grabbed the front of my shirt, and over my scream, I heard the fabric tear.

In times of crisis, when a person reacts on instinct, that person does whatever is most comfortable. I did what any other American woman would do in a similar circumstance. I roundhoused Ramirez square on the side of his head with my purse. Between the gun and the beeper and the other assorted paraphernalia, the bag must have weighed at least ten pounds.

Ramirez staggered sideways, and I bolted for the stairs. I didn't get five feet before he jerked me back by my hair and flung me across the room like a rag doll. I lost footing and went facedown to the floor, my hands hitting first, skidding over unvarnished wood, my body following, the impact knocking the air from my lungs.

Ramirez straddled me, his butt on my back, his hand fisting in my hair, pulling savagely. I grabbed at my bag, but I was unable to get to the gun.

I heard the crack of a high-powered weapon, and the front windows shattered. More shots. Someone was emptying a clip into the gym. Men were running and shouting, looking for cover. Ramirez was among them. I was moving, too, crab style across the floor, my legs not able to support me. I reached the stairs, stood, and lunged for the railing. I missed the second step, too panicked to coordinate my movements, and half slid the rest of the way down to the cracked linoleum landing at street level. I dragged myself to my feet and staggered outside into the heat and blinding sunlight. My stockings were torn and my knees were bleeding. I was hanging on to the door handle, laboring to breathe when a hand clamped onto my upper arm. I jumped and yelped. It was Joe Morelli.

"For crissake," he said, yanking me forward. "Don't just stand here. Haul ass!"

I wasn't sure Ramirez cared enough about me to come charging down the stairs, but it seemed prudent not to hang around and find out, so I clattered after Morelli with my chest burning from oxygen deprivation and my skirt hiked up to my crotch. Kathleen Turner would have made it look good on the big screen. I was something less than glamorous. My nose was running, and I think I was drooling. I was grunting in pain and sniveling from fear, making ugly animal sounds and inventive promises to God.

We turned at the corner, cut through an alley on the next block, and ran down a narrow one-lane road carved out between backyards. The road was lined with broken-down single-car wooden garages and overflowing bashed-in garbage cans.

Sirens sounded two blocks away. No doubt a couple of cruisers and an ambulance responding to the shooting. Hindsight told me I should have stayed close to the gym and conned the cops into helping me track down Morelli. Something to remember next time I'm almost raped and brutalized.

Morelli stopped abruptly and jerked me into an empty garage. The double doors were cocked open enough to slide through, not enough for a passerby to see inside. The floor was packed dirt, and the air was close, smelling metallic. I was struck by the irony of it. Here I was, after all these years, once again in a garage with Morelli. I could see the anger in his face, hardening his eyes, pinching at the corners of his mouth. He grabbed me by the front of my suit jacket and pinned me against the crude wooden wall. The impact knocked dust from the rafters and made my teeth clack together.

His voice was tight with barely controlled fury. "What the hell did you think you were doing walking into the gym like that?"

He punctuated the end of the question with another body slam, rattling more filth onto the two of us.

"Answer me!" he ordered.

The pain was all mental. I'd been stupid. And now, to add insult to injury, I was getting bullied by Morelli. It was almost as humiliating as getting rescued by him. "I was looking for you."

"Well congratulations, you found me. You also blew my cover, and I'm not happy about it."

"You were the shadow in the third-floor window, watching the gym from across the street."

Morelli didn't say anything. In the dark garage his eyes were dilated solid black.

I mentally cracked my knuckles. "And now I guess there's only one thing left to do."

"I can hardly wait to hear this."

I shoved my hand into my shoulder bag, pulled out my revolver, and jabbed Morelli in the chest with it. "You're under arrest."

His eyes opened wide in astonishment. "You have a gun! Why didn't you use it on Ramirez? Jesus, you hit him with your pocketbook like some sissy girl. Why the hell didn't you use your damn gun?"

I felt color flooding into my cheeks. What could I say? The truth was worse than embarrassing. It was counterproductive. Admitting to Morelli that I'd been more afraid of my gun than I'd been of Ramirez wasn't going to do much to further my credibility as an apprehension agent.

It didn't take Morelli long to put it together. He made a disgusted sound, pushed the barrel aside and took the gun from me. "If you aren't willing to use it, you shouldn't be carrying it. You have a permit to carry a concealed weapon?"

"Yes." And I was at least 10 percent convinced it was legal.

"Where'd you get your permit?"

"Ranger got it for me."

"Ranger Mañoso? Christ, he probably made it in his cellar." He shook out the bullets and gave the gun back to me. "Find a new job. And stay away from Ramirez. He's nuts. He's been charged with rape on three separate occasions and been acquitted each time because the victim always disappears."

"I didn't know . . ."

"There's a lot you don't know."

His attitude was beginning to piss me off. I was only too well aware that I had a lot to learn about apprehension. I didn't need Morelli's sarcastic superiority. "So what's your point."

"Get off my case. You want a career in law enforcement? Fine. Go for it. Just don't learn on me. I have enough problems without worrying about saving your ass."

"No one asked you to save my ass. I would have saved my own ass if you hadn't interfered."

"Honey, you couldn't find your ass with both hands."

My palms were skinned and burned like the devil. My scalp was sore. My knees throbbed. I wanted to go back to my apartment and stand in a hot shower for five or six hours until I felt clean and strong. I wanted to get away from Morelli and regroup. "I'm going home."

"Good idea," he said. "Where's your car?"

"Stark Street and Tyler."

He flattened himself at the side of the door and took a quick look out. "It's okay."

My knees had stiffened up, and the blood had dried and caked on what was left of my pantyhose. Limping seemed like an indulgent weakness not to be witnessed by the likes of Morelli, so I forged ahead, thinking ouch, ouch, ouch but not saying a word. When we got to the corner I realized he was walking me all the way to Stark. "I don't need an escort," I said. "I'll be fine."

He had his hand at my elbow, steering me forward. "Don't flatter yourself. I'm not nearly so concerned about your welfare as I am about getting you the hell out of my life. I want to make sure you leave. I want to see your tailpipe fading off into the sunset."

Good luck, I thought. My tailpipe was somewhere on Route 1, along with my muffler.

We reached Stark, and I faltered at the sight of my car. It had been parked on the street for less than an hour, and in that time it had been spray-painted from one end to the other. Mostly Day-Glo pink and green, and the predominant word on both sides was "pussy." I checked the plate and looked in the backseat for the box of Fig Newtons. Yep, this was my car.

One more indignity in a day filled with indignities. Did I care? Not a whole lot. I was numb. I was becoming immune to indignity. I searched through my bag for my keys, found them, and plugged them into the door.

Morelli rocked back on his heels, hands in his pockets, a grin beginning to creep to his lips. "Most people are content with pinstriping and a vanity plate."

"Eat dirt and die."

Morelli tipped his head back and laughed out loud. His laughter was deep and rich and infectious, and if I hadn't been so distraught, I'd have laughed along with him. As it was, I jerked the car door open and rammed myself behind the wheel. I turned the key in the ignition, gave the dash a good hard smack, and left him choking in a cloud of exhaust and a blast of noise that had the potential to liquify his insides.

Officially, I lived at the eastern boundary of the city of Trenton, but in actuality my neighborhood felt more like Hamilton Township than Trenton proper. My apartment building was an ugly dark red brick cube built before central air and thermal pane windows. Eighteen apartments in all, evenly distributed over three floors. By modern-day standards it wasn't a terrific apartment. It didn't come with a pool membership or have tennis courts attached. The elevator was unreliable. The bathroom was vintage Partridge family with mustard yellow amenities and French Provincial trim on the vanity. The kitchen appliances were a notch below generic.

The good part about the apartment was that it had been built with sturdy stuff. Sound didn't carry from apartment to apartment. The rooms were large and sunny. Ceilings were high. I lived on the second floor, and my windows overlooked the small private parking lot. The building predated the balcony boom, but I was lucky enough to have an old-fashioned black metal fire escape skirt my bedroom window. Perfect for drying pantyhose, quarantining houseplants with aphids, and just big enough for sitting out on sultry summer nights.

Most important of all, the ugly brick building wasn't part of a sprawling complex of other ugly brick buildings. It sat all by itself on a busy street of small businesses, and it bordered a neighborhood of modest frame houses. Very much like living in the burg . . . but better. My mother had a hard time stretching the umbilical this far, and the bakery was only one block away.

I parked in the lot and slunk into the back entrance. Since Morelli wasn't around, I didn't have to be brave, so I bitched and complained and limped all the way to my apartment. I showered, did the first-aid thing, and dressed in T-shirt and shorts. My knees were missing the top layer of skin and were bruised, already turning shades of magenta and midnight blue. My elbows were in pretty much the same condition. I felt like a kid who'd fallen off her bike. I could hear myself singing out "I can do it; I can do it," and then next thing I know, I'm lying on the ground, looking the fool, with two scraped knees.

I flopped onto my bed, spread-eagle on my back. This was my thinking position when things appeared to be futile. It had obvious advantages: I could nap while I waited for something brilliant to pop into my mind. I lay there for what seemed like a long time. Nothing brilliant had popped into my mind, and I was too agitated to sleep.

I couldn't stop reliving my experience with Ramirez. I'd never before been attacked by a man. Never even come close. The afternoon's assault had been a degrading, frightening experience, and now that the dust had settled, and calmer emotions prevailed, I felt violated and vulnerable.

I considered filing a report with the police, but immediately shelved it. Whining to Big Brother wasn't going to win any points for me as a rough, tough bounty hunter. I couldn't see Ranger instituting an assault charge.

I'd been lucky, I told myself. I'd gotten away with superficial injuries. Thanks to Morelli.

The latter admission dragged a groan from me. Being rescued by Morelli had been damned embarrassing. And grossly unjust. All things considered, I didn't think I was doing all that badly. I'd been on the case for less than forty-eight hours, and I'd found my man twice. True, I hadn't been able to bring him in, but I was in a learning process. No one expected a first-year engineering student to build the perfect bridge. I figured I deserved to be cut the same kind of slack.

I doubted the gun would ever be of any use to me. I couldn't imagine myself shooting Morelli. Possibly in the foot. But what were my chances of hitting a small moving target? Not good at all. Clearly, I needed a less lethal way of subduing my quarry. Maybe a defense spray would be more my style. Tomorrow morning I'd go back to Sunny's Gun Shop and add to my bag of dirty tricks.

My clock radio blinked 5:50 P.M. I looked at it dully, not immediately responding to the significance of the time, then horror ripped through me. My mother was expecting me for dinner again!

I sprang out of bed and raced to the phone. The phone was dead. I hadn't paid my bill. I grabbed the car keys from the kitchen counter and hurtled out the door.

CHAPTER 4

My mother was standing on the porch steps when I parked at the curb. She was waving her arms and shouting. I couldn't hear her over the roar of the engine, but I could read her lips. "SHUT IT OFF!" she was yelling. "SHUT IT OFF!"

"Sorry," I yelled back. "Broken muffler."

"You've got to do something. I could hear you coming four blocks away. You'll give old Mrs. Ciak heart palpitations." She squinted at the car. "Did you have it decorated?"

"It happened on Stark Street. Vandals." I pushed her into the hallway before she could read the words.

"Wow, nice knees," Grandma Mazur said, bending down to take a closer look at my ooze. "I was watching some TV show last week, think it was Oprah, and they had a bunch of women on with knees like that. Said it was rug burn. Never figured out what that meant."

"Christ," my father said from behind his paper. He didn't need to say more. We all understood his plight.

"It's not rug burn," I told Grandma Mazur. "I fell on my roller blades." I wasn't worried about the lie. I had a long history of calamitous mishaps.

I glanced at the dining room table. It was set with the good lace tablecloth. Company. I counted the plates. Five. I rolled my eyes heavenward. "Ma, you didn't."

"I didn't what?"

The doorbell rang, and my worst fears were confirmed.

"It's company. It's no big deal," my mother said, going to the door. "I guess I can invite company into my own house if I want to."

"It's Bernie Kuntz," I said. "I can see him through the hall window."

My mother stopped, hands on hips. "So, what's wrong with Bernie Kuntz?"

"To begin with . . . he's a man."

"Okay, you had a bad experience. That don't mean you should give up. Look at your sister Valerie. She's happily married for twelve years. She has two beautiful girls."

"That's it. I'm leaving. I'm going out the back door."

"Pineapple upside-down cake," my mother said. "You'll miss dessert if you leave now. And don't think I'll save some for you."

My mother didn't mind playing dirty if she thought the cause was worthy. She knew she had me locked in with the pineapple cake. A Plum would suffer a lot of abuse for a good dessert.

Grandma Mazur glared out at Bernie. "Who are you?"

"I'm Bernie Kuntz."

"What do you want?"

I looked the length of the hall, and I could see Bernie shift uncomfortably on his feet.

"I've been invited for dinner," Bernie said.

Grandma Mazur still had the screen door shut. "Helen," she yelled over her shoulder, "there's a young man at the door. He says he's invited to dinner. Why didn't someone tell me about this? Look at this old dress I'm wearing. I can't entertain a man in this dress."

I'd known Bernie since he was five. I'd gone to grade school with Bernie. We ate lunch together in grades one through three, and I would forever associate him with peanut butter and jelly on Wonder bread. I'd lost touch with him in high school. I knew he'd gone to college, and that after college he'd gone to work selling appliances in his father's store.

He was medium height, with a medium build that had never lost its baby fat. He was all dressed up in shiny tassel loafers, dress slacks, and sports coat. So far as I could see, he hadn't changed much since sixth grade. He looked like he still couldn't add fractions, and the little metal pull on his zipper was sticking out, creating a tiny tent with his fly.

We took our seats at the table and concentrated on the business of eating.

"Bernie sells appliances," my mother said, passing the red cabbage. "He makes good money at it, too. He drives a Bonneville."

"A Bonneville. Imagine that," Grandma Mazur said.

My father kept his head bent over his chicken. He rooted for the Mets, he wore Fruit of the Loom underwear, and he drove a Buick. His loyalties were carved in stone, and he wasn't about to be impressed by some upstart of a toaster salesman who drove a Bonneville.

Bernie turned to me. "So what are you doing now?"

I fiddled with my fork. My day hadn't exactly been a success, and announcing to the world that I was a fugitive apprehension agent seemed presumptuous. "I sort of work for an insurance company," I told him.

"You mean like a claims adjuster?"

"More like collections."

"She's a bounty hunter!" Grandma Mazur announced. "She tracks down dirty rotten fugitives just like on television. She's got a gun and everything." She reached behind her to the sideboard, where I'd left my shoulder bag. "She's got a whole pocketbook full of paraphernalia," Grandma Mazur said, setting my bag on her lap. She pulled out the cuffs, the beeper, and a travel pack of tampons and set them on the table. "And here's her gun," she said proudly. "Isn't it a beauty?"

I have to admit it was a pretty cool gun. It had a stainless steel frame and carved wood grips. It was a Smith & Wesson 5-shot revolver, model 60. A .38 Special. Easy to use, easy to carry, Ranger had said. And it had been much more reasonable than a semiautomatic, if you can call $400 reasonable.

"My God," my mother shouted, "put it away! Someone take the gun from her before she kills herself!"

The cylinder was open and clearly empty of rounds. I didn't know much about guns, but I knew this one couldn't go bang without bullets. "It's empty," I said. "There are no bullets in it."

Grandma Mazur had both hands wrapped around the gun with her finger on the trigger. She scrinched an eye closed and sighted on the china closet. "Ka-pow," she said. "Ka-pow, ka-pow, ka-pow."

My father was busy with the sausage dressing, studiously ignoring all of us.

"I don't like guns at the table," my mother said. "And the dinner's getting cold. I'll have to reheat the gravy."

"This gun won't do you no good if you don't have bullets in it," Grandma Mazur said to me. "How're you gonna catch those killers without bullets in your gun?"

Bernie had been sitting open-mouthed through all of this. "Killers?"

"She's after Joe Morelli," Grandma Mazur told him. "He's a bona fide killer and a bail dodger. He plugged Ziggy Kulesza right in the head."

"I knew Ziggy Kulesza," Bernie said. "I sold him a big-screen TV about a year ago. We don't sell many big screens. Too expensive."

"He buy anything else from you?" I asked. "Anything recent?"

"Nope. But I'd see him sometimes across the street at Sal's Butcher Shop. Ziggy seemed okay. Just a regular sort of person, you know?"

No one had been paying attention to Grandma Mazur. She was still playing with the gun, aiming and sighting, getting used to the heft of it. I realized there was a box of ammo beside the tampons. A scary thought skittered into my mind. "Grandma, you didn't load the gun, did you?"

"Well of course I loaded the gun," she said. "And I left the one hole empty like I saw on television. That way you can't shoot nothing by mistake." She cocked the gun to demonstrate the safety of her action. There was a loud bang, a flash erupted from the gun barrel, and the chicken carcass jumped on its plate.

"Holy mother of God!" my mother shrieked, leaping to her feet, knocking her chair over.

"Dang," Grandma said, "guess I left the wrong hole empty." She leaned forward to examine her handiwork. "Not bad for my first time with a gun. I shot that sucker right in the gumpy."

My father had a white-knuckle grip on his fork, and his face was cranberry red.

I scurried around the table and carefully took the gun from Grandma Mazur. I shook out the bullets and shoveled all my stuff back into my shoulder bag.

"Look at that broken plate," my mother said. "It was part of the set. How will I ever replace it?" She moved the plate, and we all stared in silence at the neat round hole in the tablecloth and the bullet embedded in the mahogany table.

Grandma Mazur was the first to speak. "That shooting gave me an appetite," she said. "Somebody pass me the potatoes."

All in all, Bernie Kuntz had handled the evening pretty well. He hadn't wet his pants when Grandma Mazur shot off the chicken privates. He'd suffered through two helpings of my mother's dreaded brussels sprouts casserole. And he'd been tolerably nice to me, even though it was obvious we weren't destined to hit the sheets together and my family was nuts. His motives for geniality were clear. I was a woman lacking appliances. Romance is good for frittering away a few evening hours, but commissions will get you a vacation in Hawaii. Ours was a match made in heaven. He wanted to sell, and I wanted to buy, and I wasn't unhappy to accept his offer of a 10 percent discount. And, as a bonus for sitting through the evening, I'd learned something about Ziggy Kulesza. He bought his meat from Sal Bocha, a man better known for making book than slicing fillet.

I tucked this information away for future reference. It didn't seem significant now, but who knows what would turn out to be helpful.

I was at my table with a glass of iced tea and Morelli's file, and I was trying to put together a plan of action. I'd made a bowl of popcorn for Rex. The bowl was on the table by me, and Rex was in the bowl, his cheeks puffed out with popcorn, his eyes bright, his whiskers a blur of motion.

"Well Rex," I said, "what do you think? Do you think we'll be able to catch Morelli?"

Someone tapped on my front door, and both Rex and I sat perfectly still with our radar humming. I wasn't expecting anyone. Most of my neighbors were seniors. No one I was especially chummy with. No one I could imagine knocking on my door at nine-thirty at night. Mrs. Becker, maybe, on the third floor. Sometimes she forgot where she lived.

The tapping continued, and Rex and I swiveled our heads toward the door. It was a heavy metal fire door with a security peephole, a dead bolt, and a double-thick chain. When the weather was nice, I left my windows wide open all day and night, but I always kept my door locked. Hannibal and his elephants couldn't have gotten through my front door, but my windows were welcome to any idiot who could climb a fire escape.

I put the splatter screen to my fry pan over the popcorn bowl so Rex couldn't climb out and went to investigate. I had my hand on the doorknob when the tapping stopped. I looked through the peephole and saw nothing but blackness. Someone had a finger on my peephole. Not a good sign. "Who's there?" I called.

A whisper of laughter filtered through the door frame, and I jumped back. The laughter was followed by a single word. "Stephanie."

The voice was unmistakable. It was melodic and taunting. It was Ramirez.

"I've come to play with you, Stephanie," he sang. "You ready to play?"

I felt my knees go slack, felt irrational fear swell in my chest. "Go away or I'll call the police."

"You can't call *anyone,* bitch. You haven't got a phone. I know because I tried your number."

My parents have never been able to understand my need to be independent. They're convinced I live a frightened, lonely life, and no amount of talking can persuade them otherwise. In truth, I'm almost never frightened. Maybe sometimes by gross multifooted insects. In my opinion, the only good spider is a dead spider, and women's rights aren't worth dick if they mean I can't ask a man to do my bug squashing. I don't worry about serial skinheads bashing down my door or crawling through my open window. For the most part, they prefer to work the neighborhoods closer to the train station. Muggings and carjackings are also at a minimum in my neighborhood and almost never result in death.

Until this moment, my only truly worrisome times had been those infrequent occasions when I woke up in the middle of the night fearful of invasion by mystical horrors . . . ghosts, bogeymen, vampire bats, extraterrestrials. Held prisoner by my imagination gone berserk, I'd lay in bed, barely breathing, waiting to levitate. I must admit, it would be a comfort not to have to wait alone, although, aside from Bill Murray, what good would another mortal be in the face of a spook attack, anyway? Fortunately, I've never done a total head rotation, been beamed up, or had an Elvis visitation. And the closest I've come to an out-of-body experience was when Joe Morelli took his mouth to me fourteen years ago, behind the éclair case.

Ramirez's voice cut through the door. "Don't like having unfinished business with a woman, Stephanie Plum. Don't like when a woman run away from the champ."

He tried the doorknob, and for a gut-cramping moment my heart leapt to my throat. The door held, and my pulse dropped down to pre-stroke level.

I did some deep breathing and decided the best course of action was simply to ignore him. I didn't want to get into a shouting match. And I didn't want to make things worse than they already were. I shut and locked my living room windows and drew the drapes tight. I hurried to my bedroom and debated using the fire escape to go for help. It felt foolish, somehow, lending more weight to the threat than I was willing to concede. This is no big deal, I told myself. Nothing to worry about. I rolled my eyes. Nothing to worry about . . . only a criminally insane, two-hundred-and-fifty-pound man standing in my hall, calling me names.

I clapped a hand to my mouth to squelch a hysterical whine. Not to panic, I told myself. It wouldn't be long before my neighbors would begin to investigate, and Ramirez would be forced to leave.

I got my gun out of my pocketbook and went back to the door for another look. The peephole was uncovered, and the hallway seemed empty. I put my ear to the door and listened. Nothing. I slid the bolt and cracked the door, leaving my mega-chain firmly attached and my gun at the ready. No Ramirez in sight. I unhooked the chain and peeked out into the hall. Very peaceful. He was definitely gone.

A splot of some noxious substance sliding down the front of my door caught my eye. I was pretty sure it wasn't tapioca. I gagged, closed the door, and locked and chained it. Wonderful. Two days on the job and a world-class psycho had just jerked off on my door.

Things like this had never happened to me when I'd worked for E.E. Martin. Once a street person had urinated on my foot, and every now and then a man would drop his pants in the train station, but these were things you expected when you worked in Newark. I'd learned not to take them personally. This business with Ramirez was a whole other matter. This was very scary.

I yelped when a window opened and closed above me. Mrs. Delgado letting her cat out for the night, I told myself. Get a grip. I needed to get my mind off Ramirez, so I busied myself finding hockables. There wasn't much left. A Walkman, an iron, pearl earrings from my wedding, a kitchen clock that looked like a chicken, a framed Ansel Adams poster, and two bean-pot table lamps. I hoped it was enough to pay my phone bill and get myself reconnected. I didn't want a repeat performance of being trapped in my apartment, not able to call for help.

I returned Rex to his cage, brushed my teeth, changed into a nightshirt, and crawled into bed with every light in the apartment blazing away.

The first thing I did on waking the following morning was to check my peephole. Nothing seemed out of the ordinary, so I took a fast shower and dressed. Rex was sound asleep in his soup can after a tough night of running on his wheel. I gave him fresh water and filled his cup with the dreaded hamster nuggets. A cup of coffee would have tasted great. Unfortunately, there was no coffee in the house.

I went to my living room window and scoped out the parking lot for Ramirez, and returned to the door and doubled-checked the peephole. I slid the bolt and opened my door with the chain in place. I put my nose to the crack and sniffed. I didn't smell boxer, so I closed the door, unhooked the chain, and reopened the door. I looked out with my gun drawn. The hall was empty. I locked my door and crept down the hall. The elevator binged, the door droned open, and I almost shot old Mrs. Moyer. I apologized profusely, told her the gun wasn't real, and slunk off to the stairs, lugging the first load of junk out to the car.

By the time Emilio opened his pawnshop, I was in caffeine withdrawal. I haggled over the earrings, but my heart wasn't in it, and in the end I knew I'd gotten gypped. Not that I especially cared. I had what I needed. Money for a minor weapon, and the phone company, and enough change left over for a blueberry muffin and large coffee.

I took five minutes out to luxuriate over my breakfast, and then I hustled to the phone office. I stopped at a light and got hooted at by two guys in a pickup. From the hand gestures they were making I supposed they liked my paint job. I couldn't hear what they were saying because of the engine noise. Thank God for small favors.

I noticed a haze building around me and realized I was smoking.

Not the benign white exhaust of condensation on a cold day. This smoke was thick and black, and in the absence of a tailpipe was billowing out from my underbelly. I gave the dash a hard shot with my fist to see if any of the gauges would work, and sure enough, the red oil light blinked on. I pulled into a gas station on the next corner, bought a can of 10-W-30, dumped it in the car, and checked the dipstick. It was still low, so I added a second can.

Next stop, the phone company. Settling my account and arranging for service to be resumed were only slightly less complicated than getting a green card. Finally, I explained that my blind, senile grandmother was living with me between heart attacks and having a phone would possibly make the difference between life and death. I don't think the woman behind the counter believed me, but I think I got a few entertainment points, and I was promised someone would throw a switch later in the day. Good deal. If Ramirez came back, I'd be able to dial the cops. As a backup, I intended to get a quart of defense spray. I wasn't much good with a gun, but I was bitchin' with an aerosol can.

By the time I got to the gun store, the oil light was flickering again. I didn't see any smoke, so I concluded the gauge must be stuck. And who cared anyway, I wasn't squandering more money on oil. This car was just going to have to make do. When I collected my $10,000 bounty money, I'd buy it all the oil it wanted—then I'd push it off a bridge.

I'd always imagined gun store owners to be big and burly and to wear baseball caps that advertised motorcycle companies. I'd always imagined them with names like Bubba and Billy Bob. This gun store was run by a woman named Sunny. She was in her forties with skin tanned the color and texture of a good cigar, hair that had been bleached to canary yellow frizz, and a two-pack-a-day voice. She was wearing rhinestone earrings, skintight jeans, and she had little palm trees painted on her fingernails.

"Nice work," I said, alluding to her nails.

"Maura, at The Hair Palace, does them. She's a genius with nails, and she'll bikini wax you till you're bald as a billiard ball."

"I'll have to remember."

"Just ask for Maura. Tell her Sunny sent you. And what can I do for you today? Out of bullets already?"

"I need some defense spray."

"What kind of spray do you use?"

"There's more than one kind?"

"Goodness, yes. We carry a full line of self-defense sprays." She reached into the case next to her and pulled out several shrink-wrapped packages. "This is the original Mace. Then we have Peppergard, the environmentally safe alternative now used by many police departments. And, last but certainly not least, is Sure Guard, a genuine chemical weapon. This can drop a three-hundred-pound man in six seconds. Works on neurotransmitters. This stuff touches your skin and you're out cold. Doesn't matter if you're drunk or on drugs. One spray and it's all over."

"Sounds dangerous."

"You better believe it."

"Is it fatal? Does it leave permanent damage?"

"The only permanent damage to your victim is going to be the memory of a downright humiliating experience. Of course there'll be some initial paralysis, and when that wears off there's usually a lot of throwing up and a monster headache."

"I don't know. What if I accidentally spray myself?"

She grimaced. "Darlin', you should avoid spraying yourself."

"Sounds complicated."

"It's not complicated at all. It's as simple as putting your finger on the button. For goodness sakes, you're a professional now." She patted my hand. "Take the Sure Guard. You can't go wrong."

I didn't feel like a professional. I felt like an idiot. I'd criticized foreign governments for using chemical warfare, and here I was buying nerve gas from a woman who waxed off all her pubic hair.

"Sure Guard comes in several sizes," Sunny said. "I carry the seventeen-gram key-chain model. It has its own stainless steel quick-release loop, comes in an attractive leather case, and you get to choose from three decorator colors."

"Gee, three colors."

"You should try it out," Sunny told me. "Make sure you know how to use it."

I stepped outside, held my arm straight out, and sprayed. The wind shifted, and I ran inside and slammed the door.

"That wind can be sneaky," Sunny said. "Maybe you should go out the back way. You can exit through the gun range."

I did as she suggested, and when I reached the street, I rushed to my car and jumped inside lest any droplets of Sure Guard were hanging around, waiting to attack my neurotransmitters. I shoved my key into the ignition and tried hard not to panic over the fact that I had tear gas under 125 pounds of pressure per square inch, which in my mind spelled nerve bomb, dangling between my knees. The engine caught and the oil light came on again, looking very red and a little frantic. Fuck it. Take a number, I thought. On my list of problems to solve, oil wasn't even in the top ten.

I pulled into traffic and refused to check my rearview mirror for telltale clouds of smoke. Carmen lived several blocks east of Stark Street. Not a great neighborhood, but not the worst, either. Her building was yellow brick and looked like it could do with a good scrubbing. Four stories. No elevator. Chipped tile in the small ground-floor foyer. Her apartment was on the second floor. I was sweating by the time I got to her door. The yellow crime-scene tape had been removed, but a padlock was in place. There were two other apartments on the second floor. I knocked on each door. No one home at the first. A Hispanic woman, Mrs. Santiago, somewhere in her late forties, early fifties answered the second. She had a baby on her hip. Her black hair was pulled neatly back from her round face. She wore a blue cotton housecoat and terry-cloth bedroom slippers. A television droned from the dark interior of the apartment. I could see two small heads silhouetted against the screen. I introduced myself and gave her my card.

"I don't know what more I can tell you," she said. "This Carmen only lived here a short time. No one knew her. She was quiet. Kept to herself."

"Have you seen her since the shooting?"

"No."

"Do you know where she might be? Friends? Relatives?"

"I didn't know her. Nobody knew her. They tell me she worked in a bar . . . the Step In on Stark Street. Maybe somebody knew her there."

"Were you home the night of the shooting?"

"Yes. It was late, and Carmen had the television on real loud. I never heard her play it so loud. Then someone was banging on Carmen's door. A man. Turned out he was a cop. I guess he had to bang because no one could hear him over the television. Then there was a gunshot. That's when I called the police. I called the police, and when I got back to my front door I could hear there was a big commotion in the hall, so I looked out."

"And?"

"And John Kuzack was there, and some others from the building. We take care of our own here. We aren't like some of those people who pretend not to hear things. That's why we have no drugs here. We never have this kind of trouble. John was standing over the cop when I looked out. John didn't know the man was a cop. John saw someone shot dead in Carmen's doorway, and this other man had a gun, so John took matters into his own hands."

"Then what happened?"

"It was real confusing. There were so many people in the hall."

"Was Carmen there?"

"I didn't see her. There were just so many people. Everybody wanting to know what happened, you know? People trying to help the dead man, but it was no use. He was dead."

"Supposedly there were two men in Carmen's apartment. Did you see the second man?"

"I guess so. There was a man I didn't know. Never saw before. Skinny, dark hair, dark skin, about thirty, funny face. Like it'd been hit with a frying pan. Real flat nose. That's why I noticed him."

"What happened to him?"

She shrugged. "Don't know. I guess he just left. Like Carmen."

"Maybe I should talk to John Kuzack."

"He's in 4B. He should be home. He's between jobs right now."

I thanked her and walked up two more flights of stairs, wondering what sort of person would be willing and able to disarm Morelli. I knocked at 4B and waited. I knocked again, loud enough to bruise my knuckles. The door was thrown open and my "what kind of person" question was answered. John Kuzack was 6' 4" tall, weighed about two hundred and forty pounds, had his graying hair pulled into a ponytail, and had a rattler tattooed onto his forehead. He was holding a *TV Guide* in one hand and a can of beer in the other. The sweet aroma of pot drifted out of his hazy apartment. Vietnam vet, I thought. Airborne.

"John Kuzack?"

He squinted down at me. "What can I do for you?"

"I'm trying to get a lead on Joe Morelli. I was hoping you could tell me something about Carmen Sanchez."

"You a cop?"

"I work for Vincent Plum. He posted the bond on Morelli."

"I didn't know Carmen Sanchez real good," he said. "I'd seen her around. Said hello to her a couple times. She seemed nice enough. I was coming up the stairs when I heard the gunshot."

"Mrs. Santiago, on the second floor, said you subdued the gunman."

"Yeah. I didn't know he was a cop. All I knew was he'd shot someone, and he was still armed. There were a lot of people coming into the hall, and he was telling them all to stay away. I figured it wasn't a good situation, so I hit him with a six-pack. Knocked him out cold."

A six-pack? I almost laughed out loud. The police report had stated that Morelli had been hit with a blunt instrument. It hadn't said anything about a six-pack.

"That was very brave."

He grinned. "Hell, bravery didn't have anything to do with it. I was shitfaced."

"Do you know what happened to Carmen?"

"Nope. Guess she disappeared in the scuffle."

"And you haven't seen her since?"

"Nope."

"How about the missing male witness? Mrs. Santiago said there was a man with a flattened nose . . ."

"I remember seeing him, but that's about it."

"Would you recognize him if you saw him again?"

"Probably."

"Do you think there's anyone else in the building who might know more about the missing man?"

"Edleman was the only other person who got a good look at the guy."

"Is Edleman a tenant here?"

"Edleman *was* a tenant here. He got hit by a car last week. Right in front of the building. Hit and run."

My stomach gave a nervous flutter. "You don't suppose Edleman's death ties in to the Kulesza murder, do you?"

"No way of knowing."

I thanked Kuzack for his time and took the stairs slowly, enjoying the buzz from his secondary smoke.

It was close to noon, and the day was heating up. I'd gone with a suit and heels this morning, trying to look respectable and trust inspiring. I'd left the windows rolled down when I'd parked in front of Carmen's building, half hoping someone would steal my car. No one had, so I slouched behind the wheel and finished off the Fig Newtons I'd filched from my mom's pantry. I hadn't found out a whole lot from Carmen's neighbors, but at least I hadn't been attacked or fallen down a flight of stairs.

Morelli's apartment was next on my list.

CHAPTER 5

I'd called Ranger and asked for help, since I was too chicken to do breaking and entering on my own. When I pulled into the lot, Ranger was waiting. He was all in black. Sleeveless black T-shirt and black fatigue-type pants. He was leaning against a gleaming black Mercedes that had enough antennae on it to get to Mars. I parked several spaces away so my exhaust wouldn't tarnish his finish.

"Your car?" I asked. As if anyone else could possibly belong to this car.

"Life's been good to me." His eyes slid to my Nova. "Nice paint job," he said. "You been on Stark Street?"

"Yes, and they stole my radio."

"Heh, heh, heh. Good of you to make a contribution to the less fortunate."

"I'm willing to contribute the entire car, but no one wants it."

"Just 'cause the dudes be crazy don't mean they be stupid." He nodded toward Morelli's apartment. "Doesn't seem like anyone's home, so we'll have to do the unguided tour."

"Is this illegal?"

"Hell no. We got the law, babe. Bounty hunters can do anything. We don't even need a search warrant." He buckled a black nylon webbed gun belt around his waist and shoved his 9-mm Glock into it. He clipped cuffs onto the gun belt and shrugged into the same loose black jacket he'd worn when I'd met him at the coffee shop. "I don't expect

Morelli to be in there," he said, "but you never know. You always want to be prepared."

I supposed I should be taking similar precautions, but I couldn't see myself with a gun butt sticking out of my skirt waistband. It'd be an empty gesture anyway, since Morelli knew I didn't have the guts to shoot him.

Ranger and I crossed the lot and walked through the breezeway to Morelli's apartment. Ranger knocked on the door and waited a moment. "Anybody home?" he hollered. No one answered.

"Now what?" I asked. "You going to kick the door in?"

"No way. You could break your foot doing that macho shit."

"You're going to pick the lock, right? Use a credit card?"

Ranger shook his head. "You've been watching too much television." He took a key from his pocket and inserted it in the lock. "Got a key from the super while I was waiting for you."

Morelli's apartment consisted of living room, dining alcove, galley kitchen, bath, and bedroom. It was relatively clean and sparsely furnished. Small square oak table, four ladder-back chairs, comfortable overstuffed couch, coffee table, and one club chair. He had an expensive stereo system in the living room and a small TV in the bedroom.

Ranger and I searched through the kitchen, looking for an address book, riffling through bills carelessly heaped in front of the toaster oven.

It was easy to imagine Morelli at home in his apartment, tossing his keys onto the kitchen counter, kicking off his shoes, reading his mail. A wave of remorse washed over me when I realized Morelli would most likely never again be free to enjoy any of those simple rituals. He'd killed a man and in the process had effectively ended his own life as well. It was such a hideous waste. How could he have been so stupid? How could he have gotten himself into this godawful mess? How do these things happen to people?

"Nothing here," Ranger said. He punched the playback button on Morelli's answering machine. "Hi hotstuff," a female voice cooed. "This is Carlene. Give me a call back." Beep.

"Joseph Anthony Morelli, it's your mother. Are you there? Hello? Hello?" Beep.

Ranger turned the machine over and copied the security code and special message code. "You take these numbers and you can access his messages from an outside phone. Maybe something'll turn up."

We moved on to the bedroom, going through his drawers, leafing through books and magazines, studying the few photographs on his dresser. The photographs were family. Nothing useful. No pictures of Carmen. For the most part his drawers had been emptied. He'd taken all his socks and underwear. Too bad. I'd been sort of looking forward to seeing his underwear.

We ended up back in the kitchen.

"This place is clean," Ranger said. "You're not going to find anything to help you here. And I doubt he'll return. Looks to me like he took everything he needed." He lifted a set of keys from a small hook on the kitchen wall and dropped them into my hand. "Hang on to these. No sense bothering the super if you want to get in again."

We locked Morelli's apartment and slid the super's master key through a slot in his door. Ranger eased his body into the Mercedes, put on a pair of mirrored shades, powered back his sunroof, punched up a tape with a heavy bass, and rolled out of the parking lot like Batman.

I gave a resigned sigh and looked at my Nova. It was dripping oil onto the pavement. Two parking slots away Morelli's new red and gold Jeep Cherokee sat gleaming in the sunshine. I could feel the weight of his keys dangling from my finger. A house key and two car keys. I decided it wouldn't do any harm to take a closer look, so I opened the door to the Cherokee and peered inside. The car still smelled new. The instrument panel was dust-free, the rugs were freshly vacuumed and unstained, the red upholstery was smooth and perfect. The car had five on the floor, four-wheel drive, and enough horses to make a man proud. It was equipped with air-conditioning, an Alpine radio and tape deck, a two-way police radio, a cellular phone, and a CB scanner. It was a terrific car. And it belonged to Morelli. It didn't seem fair that a scofflaw like him should have such a great car and I should have such a piece of shit.

Probably as long as I had the car open, I should start it up for him, I thought. It wasn't good for a car to sit around and not get driven. Everybody knows that. I took a deep breath and cautiously maneuvered myself behind the wheel. I adjusted the seat and the rearview mirror. I put my hands to the wheel and tested the feel of it. I could catch Morelli if I had a car like this, I told myself. I was smart. I was tenacious. All I needed was a car. I wondered if I should drive it. Maybe simply running it wasn't enough. Maybe the car needed to go around the block. Better yet, maybe I should drive it for a day or two to really work the kinks out.

Okay, who was I trying to kid? I was contemplating stealing Morelli's car. Not steal, I reasoned. Commandeer. After all, I was a bounty hunter, and probably I could commandeer a car if an emergency situation arose. I glanced over at the Nova. Looked like an emergency to me.

There was an added advantage to snitching Morelli's car. I was pretty sure he wouldn't like it. And if he was pissed off enough, maybe he'd do something stupid and come after it.

I turned the key in the ignition and tried to ignore the fact that my heart was beating double-time. The secret to being a successful bounty hunter is being able to seize the moment, I told myself. Flexibility. Adaptation. Creative thought. All necessary attributes. And it didn't hurt to have balls.

I did some slow breathing so I wouldn't hyperventilate and crash my first stolen car. I had one more item on my day's itinerary. I needed to visit the Step In Bar and Grill, Carmen's last known place of employment. The Step In was located on lower Stark Street, two blocks from the gym. I debated going home to change into something more casual, but in the end decided to stick with the suit. No matter what I wore, I wasn't going to blend in with the bar regulars.

I found a parking space half a block away. I locked the car, and I walked the short distance to the bar only to discover the bar was closed. The door was padlocked. The windows were boarded. No explanation was given. I wasn't all that disappointed. After the incident in the gym, I hadn't been looking forward to breaking into another bastion of Stark Street manhood. I scurried back to the Cherokee and drove up and down Stark Street on the long shot that I might see Morelli. By the fifth pass it was getting old and my gas was low, so I gave it up. I checked the glove compartment for credit cards but found none. Swell. No gas. No money. No plastic.

If I was going to keep after Morelli I was going to need living expenses. I couldn't keep existing hand to mouth. Vinnie was the obvious answer to my problem. Vinnie was going to have to advance me some cash. I stopped for a light and took a moment to study Morelli's phone. I powered it up and his number blinked on. How convenient. I figured

I'd go whole hog. Why stop at stealing Morelli's car? Might as well run his phone bill up, too.

I called Vinnie's office, and Connie answered.

"Is Vinnie in?" I asked.

"Yeah," she said. "He'll be here all afternoon."

"I'll be around in about ten minutes. I need to talk to him."

"Did you catch Morelli?"

"No, but I've confiscated his car."

"Has it got a sunroof?"

I rolled my eyes skyward. "No sunroof."

"Bummer," she said.

I hung up and turned down Southard, trying to decide on a reasonable advance. I needed enough money to get me through two weeks, and if I was going to use the car to catch Morelli I might want to invest in an alarm system. I couldn't watch the car around the clock, and I didn't want Morelli sneaking it out from under me while I slept, or took a pee, or went to the market.

I was pondering an appropriate figure when the phone rang, the soft "brrrrp" almost causing me to run up onto the curb. It was a weird sensation. Like getting caught eavesdropping, or lying, or sitting on the toilet and having the bathroom walls suddenly drop away. I had an irrational urge to pull off the road and run shrieking from the car.

I gingerly put the handset to my ear. "Hello?"

There was a pause and a woman's voice came on the line. "I want to talk to Joseph Morelli."

Holy cow. It was Momma Morelli. As if I wasn't in deep enough do-do. "Joe isn't here right now."

"Who's this?"

"I'm a friend of Joe's. He asked me to run his car once in a while for him."

"That's a lie," she said. "I know who I'm talking to. I'm talking to Stephanie Plum. I know your voice when I hear it. What are you doing in my Joseph's car?"

No one can show disdain like Momma Morelli. If it had been an ordinary mother on the phone I might have explained or apologized, but Morelli's mother scared the hell out of me.

"What?" I shouted. "I can't hear you. What? What?"

I slammed the receiver down and flipped the off switch on the phone. "Good going," I said to myself. "Very adult. Very professional. Really quick thinking."

I parked on Hamilton and power walked half a block to Vinnie's. I was pumping myself up for the confrontation, getting my adrenaline going, raising my energy level. I barreled through the door like Wonder Woman, gave Connie a thumbs-up, and went straight to Vinnie's office. The door was open. Vinnie was behind his desk, hunched over a racing sheet.

"Hey," I said. "How's it going?"

"Oh shit," Vinnie said. "Now what?"

That's what I like about my family. We're so close, so warm, so polite to each other. "I want an advance on my fee. I have expenses associated with the job."

"An advance? Are you kidding me? You're joking, right?"

"I'm not joking. I'm going to get $10,000 when I bring Morelli in. I want a $2,000 advance."

"When hell freezes over. And don't think you can pull more of that blackmail crap on me. You blab to my wife, and I'll be as good as dead. See if you can squeeze a job out of a dead man, smartass."

He had a point. "Okay, so blackmail won't work. How about greed? You give me the $2,000 now, and I won't take my full 10 percent."

"What if you don't get Morelli? You ever think of that?"

Only every waking minute of my life. "I'll get Morelli."

"Un huh. Excuse me if I don't share your positive attitude. And remember I only agreed to this lunacy for a week. You've got four days left. If you haven't brought Morelli in by next Monday, I'm giving him to somebody else."

Connie came into the office. "What's the problem here? Stephanie needs money? Why don't you give her Clarence Sampson?"

"Who's Clarence Sampson?" I asked.

"He's one of our family of drunks. Usually, he's perfectly peaceful. Every now and then he does something stupid."

"Such as?"

"Such as try to drive with a 150-proof blood alcohol level. On this particular occasion he had the misfortune to total a police cruiser."

"He ran into a cruiser?"

"Not exactly," Connie said. "He was attempting to drive the cruiser. He ran into a liquor store on State Street."

"Do you have a picture of this guy?"

"I have a two-inch file with pictures spanning two decades. We've posted bail on Sampson so many times I know his social security number by heart."

I followed her to the outer office and waited while she sorted through a stack of manila folders.

"Most of our recovery agents work a bunch of cases simultaneously," Connie said. "It's more efficient that way." She handed me a dozen folders. "These are the FTAs Morty Beyers was handling for us. He's gonna be out for a while longer, so you might as well take a crack at them. Some are easier than others. Memorize the names and addresses and hook them up to the photographs. You never know when you'll get lucky. Last week Andy Zabotsky was standing in line for a bucket of fried chicken and recognized the guy in front of him as a skip. It was a good find, too. A dealer. We would have been out $30,000."

"I didn't know you posted bond for drug dealers," I said. "I always thought you did mostly low-key stuff."

"Drug dealers are good," Connie said. "They don't like to leave the area. They've got clients. They're making good money. If they skip you can usually count on them to resurface."

I tucked the files under my arm, promising to make copies and return the originals to Connie. The chicken story had been inspiring. If Andy Zabotsky could catch a crook in a chicken franchise, just think of my own personal potential. I ate that crappy food all the time. I even liked it. Maybe this bounty hunter business would work out. Once I became financially solvent, I could support myself by collecting people like Sampson and making an occasional fast-food bust.

I pushed through the front door and caught my breath at the sudden absence of air-conditioning. The day had gone from hot to blistering. The air was thick and muggy, the sky hazy. The sun prickled on exposed skin, and I looked up, shielding my eyes, half expecting to see the ozone hole gaping over me like a big cyclops eye shooting out lethal rays of radioactive whatever. I know the hole is supposedly hanging out over Antarctica, but it seemed logical to me that sooner or later it would slide on up to Jersey. Jersey produced urea formaldehyde and collected New York's garbage offshore. I thought it only fitting that it have the ozone hole as well.

I unlocked the Cherokee and swiveled behind the wheel. Sampson's recovery money wouldn't get me to Barbados, but it would put something in my refrigerator besides mold. Even more important, it would give me a chance to run through the motions of an apprehension. When Ranger had taken me to the police station to get my gun permit, he'd also explained the recovery procedure, but there was no substitute for hands-on experience.

I flipped the switch on the car phone and dialed Clarence Sampson's home number. No one answered. No work number had been given. The police report listed his address as 5077 Limeing Street. I wasn't familiar with Limeing Street, so I'd looked it up on a map and discovered Sampson lived two blocks over from Stark, down by the state buildings. I had Sampson's picture taped to the dash, and every few seconds I checked it against men on the street as I drove.

Connie had suggested I visit the bars on lower Stark. On my list of favorite things to do, spending happy hour at the Rainbow Room on the corner of Stark and Limeing fell just below cutting off both my thumbs with a dull knife. It seemed to me it would be just as effective and a lot less dangerous to sit locked up in the Cherokee and surveil the street. If Clarence Sampson was in one of the bars, sooner or later he'd have to come out.

It took several passes before I found a space I liked at the corner of Limeing and Stark. I had a good view of Stark, and I was also able to see half a block down Limeing. I was a little conspicuous in my suit, with all my whiteness and big shiny red car, but I wasn't nearly as conspicuous as I'd be sashaying into the Rainbow Room. I cracked the windows and slouched down in my seat, trying to get comfortable.

A kid with a lot of hair and $700 worth of gold around his neck stopped and looked in at me while his two friends stood nearby. "Hey babe," he said. "What you doin' here?"

"Waiting for someone," I said.

"Oh yeah? A fine babe like you shouldn't have to wait for no one."

One of his friends stepped up. He made sucking sounds and waggled his tongue at me. When he saw he had my attention he licked my window.

I rooted through my pocketbook until I found my gun and my neuro spray. I laid them both on the dash. People stopped and stared from time to time after that, but they didn't linger.

By five o'clock I was feeling antsy, and my rayon skirt had serious crotch wrinkles. I was looking for Clarence Sampson, but I was thinking about Joe Morelli. He was somewhere close by. I could feel it in the pit of my stomach. It was like a low-volt electric charge that hummed against the inside of my spine. In my mind I walked myself through the arrest. The easiest scenario would be for him not to see me at all, for me to come at him from behind and spray him. If that wasn't possible, I'd have to talk to him and wait for the right moment to go for the spray. Once he was on the ground and incapacitated, I could cuff him. After I got him cuffed I'd rest easier.

By six I'd done the mental arrest about forty-two times and was psyched. By six-thirty I was on the downside of the peak, and my left cheek had fallen asleep. I stretched as best I could and tried isometrics. I counted passing cars, mouthed the words to the national anthem, and slowly read the ingredients on a pack of gum I found in my pocketbook. At seven I called time to make sure Morelli's clock was right.

I was berating myself for being the wrong sex and the wrong color to operate effectively in over half the neighborhoods in Trenton when a man fitting Sampson's description reeled out of the Rainbow Room. I looked at the picture on the dash. I looked back at the man. I looked at the picture again. I was 90 percent sure it was Sampson. Big flabby body, mean little head, dark hair and beard, white Caucasian. Looked like Bluto. Had to be Sampson. Let's face it, how many bearded fat white men lived in this neighborhood?

I tucked the gun and the spray into my pocketbook, pulled away from the curb, and drove around two blocks so I could turn down Limeing and put myself between Sampson and his house. I double-parked and got out of the car. A group of teens stood talking on the corner, and two little girls sat on a nearby stoop with their Barbie dolls. Across the street a bedraggled couch, missing its cushions, had been set out on the sidewalk. The Limeing Street version of a porch swing. Two old men sat on the couch, wordlessly staring off into space, their lined faces inanimate.

Sampson was slowly weaving up the street, obviously in the glow. His smile was contagious. I smiled back at him. "Clarence Sampson?"

"Yep," he said. "That's me."

His words were thick, and he smelled stale, like clothes that had been forgotten for weeks in the hamper.

I extended my hand. "I'm Stephanie Plum. I represent your bonding company. You missed a court appearance, and we'd like you to reschedule."

Momentary confusion rippled across his brow, the information was processed, and he smiled again.

"I guess I forgot."

Not what you'd call a type A personality. I didn't think Sampson would ever have to worry about a stress-related heart attack. Sampson would most likely die from inertia.

More smiling on my part. "That's okay. Happens all the time. I have a car here. . . ." I waved in the direction of the Cherokee. "If it wouldn't be too much trouble I'll drive you to the station, and we can take care of the paperwork."

He looked beyond me to his house. "I don't know . . ."

I looped arms with him and nudged him over. Just a friendly ole cowpoke herding a dumber'n cat-shit steer. Git along little doggie. "This won't take long." Three weeks, maybe.

I was oozing well-being and charm, pushing my breast into the side of his fleshy arm as added incentive. I rolled him around the car and opened the passenger side door. "I really appreciate this," I said.

He balked at the door. "All I have to do is set a new court date, right?"

"Yeah. Right." And then hang around in a cell until that court date pops up on the calendar. I had no sympathy for him. He could have killed someone driving while intoxicated.

I coaxed him in and fastened the seat belt. I ran around, jumped in the car, and revved the engine, afraid the lightbulb would go on in his minuscule brain and he'd realize I was a recovery agent. I couldn't imagine what would happen when we got to the police station. One step at a time, I told myself. If he got violent I'd gas him . . . maybe.

My fears were premature. I hadn't driven a quarter mile before his eyes glazed over, and he fell asleep, slouched against the door like a giant slug. I said a fast prayer that he didn't wet himself, or throw up, or do any of the other gross involuntary bodily things drunks are prone to do.

Several blocks later I stopped for a light and glanced sideways at him. He was still asleep. So far so good.

A faded blue Econoline van caught my eye on the other side of the intersection. Three antennae. A lot of equipment for a junky old van, I thought. I squinted at the driver, shadowy behind tinted glass, and an eerie feeling crept along the nape of my neck. The light turned. Cars moved through the intersection. The van rolled by, and my heart jumped to my throat as I was treated to a view of Joe Morelli behind the wheel, gaping at me in astonishment. My first impulse was to shrink in size until I was no longer visible. In theory, I should have been pleased to have made contact, but the instant reality was hurling confusion. I was good at fantasizing Morelli's recovery. I wasn't so confident when it came to actually pulling it off. Brakes squealed behind me, and in my rearview mirror I saw the van jump the curb to complete a midblock U-turn.

I'd expected he'd come after me. I hadn't expected him to do it with such speed. The Jeep's doors were locked, but I pushed the lock button again anyway. The Sure Guard was nestled in my lap. The police station was less than a mile away. I debated giving Clarence the boot and going after Morelli. Morelli was, after all, my main objective.

I did a fast run-through of possible arrest attempts, and none of them turned out satisfactory. I didn't want Morelli to come at me while I was struggling with Clarence. And I didn't want to drop Morelli in the street. Not in this neighborhood. I wasn't sure I could control the outcome.

Morelli was five cars back when I stopped for a light. I saw the driver's door open, saw Morelli get out of the van, running toward me. I gripped the gas canister and prayed for the light to change. Morelli was almost on me when we all moved forward, and Morelli was forced to go back to the van.

Good old Clarence was still sound asleep, his head dropped forward, his mouth open and drooling, emitting soft snuffling sounds. I left-turned up North Clinton, and the phone chirped.

It was Morelli, and he didn't sound happy. "What the fuck do you think you're doing?" he yelled.

"I'm taking Mr. Sampson to the police station. You're more than welcome to follow us. It would make everything much easier for me."

A pretty ballsy reply, considering I was having an anxiety attack.

"THAT'S MY CAR YOU'RE DRIVING!"

"Mmmmm. Well, I've commandeered it."

"You've WHAT?"

I flipped the switch to shut the phone off before the conversation deteriorated to death threats. The van disappeared from sight two blocks from the station, and I continued on with my FTA still sleeping like a baby.

The Trenton police department houses itself in a cubelike three-story brick building representing the Practical Pig approach to municipal architecture. Clearly low on the funding food chain, Police Headquarters has been afforded few frills, which is just as well considering it is surrounded by ghetto, and the location almost certainly ensures annihilation should a riot of major proportions ever occur.

A chain-link-fenced lot adjoins the building and provides parking for squad cars and vans, employees, cops, and beleaguered citizens.

Gritty row houses and small businesses, typical of the area, face off with the headquarters' front entrance—Jumbos Seafood, a bar with no visible name and ominous metal grating on the windows, a corner grocery advertising RC Cola, Lydia's Hat Designs, a used-furniture store with a motley collection of washing machines displayed on the sidewalk, and the Tabernacle Church.

I pulled into the lot, tapped the phone back on, dialed dispatch, and requested aid with the transfer of custody. I was instructed to proceed to the rear security door, where a uniform would be waiting for me. I proceeded to the designated door and backed into the driveway, placing Clarence close to the building. I didn't see my uniform, so I made another call. I was promptly told not to get my shorts in a knot. Easy for them to say—*they* knew what they were doing.

A few minutes later Crazy Carl Costanza poked his head out the door. I'd made Communion with Crazy Carl, among other things.

He squinted past Clarence. "Stephanie Plum?"

"Hey, Carl."

His face cracked into a grin. "They told me there was a pain in the ass out here."

"That would be me," I said.

"What's with sleeping beauty?"

"He's FTA."

Carl came in for a closer look. "Is he dead?"

"I don't think so."

"He smells dead."

I agreed. "He could use to be hosed down." I gave Clarence a shake and yelled in his ear. "Let's go. Time to wake up."

Clarence choked on some spit and opened his eyes. "Where am I?"

"Police station," I said. "Everybody out."

He stared at me in unfocused drunken stupidity, and sat as still and unyielding as a sandbag.

"Do something," I said to Costanza. "Get him out of here."

Costanza grabbed Clarence's arms, and I put my foot to Clarence's butt. We pushed and pulled, and inch by inch, got Sampson's big ugly blob of putrid flesh off the seat and onto the pavement.

"This is why I became a cop," Costanza said. "I couldn't resist the glamour of it all."

We maneuvered Clarence through the security door, cuffed him to a wooden bench, and handed him over to the docket lieutenant. I ran back outside and moved the Cherokee into a regulation parking space where it would be less visible to cops who might mistake it for a stolen car.

When I returned, Clarence had been stripped of his belt and shoelaces and personal property and looked forlorn and pathetic. He was my first capture, and I'd expected to feel satisfaction for my success, but now found it was difficult to get elated over someone else's misfortune.

I collected my body receipt, spent a few minutes reminiscing with Crazy Carl, and headed for the lot. I'd hoped to leave before dark, but night had closed in early under a blanket of clouds. The sky was starless and moonless. Traffic was sporadic. Easier to spot a tail, I told myself, but I didn't believe it. I had minimal confidence in my ability to spot Morelli.

There was no sign of the van. That didn't mean much. Morelli could be driving whatever by now. I headed for Nottingham with one eye on the road and one on my rearview mirror. There was little doubt in my mind that Morelli was out there, but at least he was giving me the courtesy of not being obvious. That meant he took me moderately seriously. It was a cheery thought that prompted me to rise to the occasion with a plan. The plan was simple. Go home, park the Cherokee in the lot, wait in the bushes with my killer gas, and zap Morelli when he tried to reclaim his car.

CHAPTER 6

The front of my apartment building sat flush with the sidewalk. Parking was in the rear. The lot was minimally scenic, consisting of an asphalt rectangle subdivided into parking spaces. We weren't so sophisticated that we were assigned slots. Parking was dog-eat-dog, with all the really good places designated handicapped. Three Dumpsters hunkered at the entrance to the lot. One for general garbage. Two for recyclables. Good for the environment. Didn't do much for local aesthetics. The rear entrance had been improved by a strip of overgrown azaleas that hugged the building and ran almost the entire length of the lot. They were wonderful in the spring when they were filled with pink flowers, and they were magical in the winter when the super strung them with little blinking lights. The rest of the year they were better than nothing.

I chose a well-lighted slot in the middle of the lot. Better to see Morelli when he came to retrieve his property. Not to mention it was one of the few places left. Most of the people in my building were elderly and didn't like to drive after dark. By nine o'clock the lot was full and TVs were going full blast inside all the seniors' apartments.

I looked around to make sure there was no sign of Morelli. Then I popped the hood and removed the Cherokee's distributor cap. This was one of my many New Jersey survival skills. Anyone who has ever left their car in long-term parking at Newark Airport knows how to remove the distributor cap. It is virtually the only way of ensuring your car will be there upon your return.

I figured when the Cherokee didn't start, Morelli'd stick his head under the hood, and that's when I'd gas him. I scurried to the building and hid myself behind the azaleas, feeling fairly slick.

I sat on the ground on a newspaper in deference to my skirt. I'd have liked to change my clothes, but I was afraid of missing Morelli if I dashed upstairs. Cedar chips had been spread in front of the azaleas. Back where I sat the ground was hard-packed dirt. When I was a kid I might have thought this was cozy, but I wasn't a kid anymore, and I noticed things kids didn't notice. Mostly that azaleas don't look all that good from the rear.

A big Chrysler pulled into the lot, and a white-haired man got out. I recognized him, but I didn't know his name. He slowly walked to the building entrance. He didn't seem alarmed or yell out "Help, there's a crazy woman hiding in the bushes," so I felt secure that I was well hidden.

I squinted at my watch in the dark. Nine forty-five. Waiting wasn't among my favorite pastimes. I was hungry and bored and uncomfortable. There are probably people who put waiting time to good use organizing thoughts, composing chore lists, sinking into constructive introspection. Waiting, for me, was sensory deprivation. A black hole. Downtime.

I was still waiting at eleven o'clock. I was cranky, and I had to go to the bathroom. Somehow I managed to sit there for another hour and a half. I was reviewing my options, considering a new plan, when it started to rain. The drops were big and lazy, falling in slow motion, spattering on the azalea bushes, leaving their imprint on the hard-packed dirt where I sat, encouraging musty smells reminiscent of cobwebs and crawl spaces to rise up from the earth. I sat with my back pressed against the building and my legs drawn up to my chest. With the exception of an occasional renegade drop, I was untouched by the rain.

After a few minutes the tempo evened out, the drops grew small and consistent, and the wind picked up. Water pooled on the black macadam, catching clots of reflective light, and the rain beaded on the shiny red paint of the Cherokee.

It was a wonderful night to be in bed with a book, listening to the tic, tic, tic of drops on the window and fire escape. It was a lousy night to be crouched behind an azalea bush. The rain had taken to swirling with the wind, catching me in gusts, soaking into my shirt, plastering my hair to my face.

By one o'clock I was shivering and miserable, soaking wet, close to peeing in my pants. Not that it would matter. At five after one I abandoned the plan. Even if Morelli did show up, which I was beginning to doubt, I wasn't sure I was in good enough shape to make a capture. And, I definitely didn't want him to see me with my hair like this.

I was about to leave when a car swung into the lot, parked in a space at the far perimeter, and killed its lights. A man got out of the car and quickly walked, head down, to the Cherokee. It wasn't Joe. It was Mooch again. I rested my forehead on my knees and closed my eyes. I'd been naive to think Joe would fall into my trap. The entire police force was after his ass. He wasn't going to barge into a setup like this. I sulked for a few seconds and then pushed it aside, vowing to be smarter next time. I should have put myself in Joe's place. Would I have exposed myself by personally coming after the car? No. Okay, so I was learning. Rule number one: don't underestimate the enemy. Rule number two: think like a felon.

Mooch opened the driver's door with a key and slid behind the wheel. The starter churned but didn't catch. Mooch waited a few minutes and tried again. He got out and looked under the hood. I knew this wouldn't take long. It didn't take a genius to notice a missing distributor cap. Mooch pulled his head out from under the hood, slammed the hood down, kicked a tire, and said something colorful. He jogged back to his car and peeled out of the lot.

I slunk out of the shadows and trudged the short distance to the back entrance to my building. My skirt clung to my legs and water squished in my shoes. The night had been a bust, but it could have been worse. Joe could have sent his mother to get the car.

The lobby was empty, looking even bleaker than usual. I punched the elevator button and waited. Water dripped from the end of my nose and off the hem of my skirt, forming a small lake on the gray tile floor. Two side-by-side elevators serviced the building. No one, so far as I knew, had ever plummeted to their death or been skyrocketed out of the top of the elevator shaft in a runaway elevator, but chances of getting stuck between floors was excellent. Usually I used the stairs. Tonight, I decided to carry my masochistic stupidity to the max and take the elevator. The cage lurched into place, the doors gaped open, and I stepped in. I ascended to the second floor without incident and sloshed down the hall. I fumbled in my pocketbook for the key and was letting myself into my apartment when I remembered the distributor cap. I'd left it downstairs, behind the azaleas. I thought about retrieving it, but it was a short thought and of no consequence. No way was I going back downstairs.

I bolted the door behind me and peeled my clothes off while standing on the small patch of linoleum that served as my foyer. My shoes were ruined, and the seat of my skirt bore the imprint of yesterday's headlines. I left every stitch I'd worn in a sodden heap on the floor and went straight to the bathroom.

I adjusted the water, stepped into the tub, pulled the shower curtain closed, and let the hard spray beat down on me. The day hadn't been all bad, I told myself. I'd made a recovery. I was legitimate now. First thing in the morning I'd collect my money from Vinnie. I lathered up and rinsed off. I washed my hair. I turned the dial to shower massage and stood for a very long time, letting the tension ease from my body. Twice now Joe had used Mooch as his errand boy. Maybe I should be watching Mooch. Problem was I couldn't watch everyone at once.

I was distracted by a blur of color on the other side of the translucent, soap-slicked shower curtain. The blur moved and my heart momentarily stopped dead in my chest. Someone was in my bathroom. The shock was numbing. I stood statue still for a few beats without a thought in my head. Then I remembered Ramirez, and my stomach rolled. Ramirez could have come back. He could have talked the super into giving him a key, or he could have come in through a window. God only knows what Ramirez was capable of doing.

I'd brought my pocketbook into the bathroom, but it was out of reach on the vanity counter.

The intruder crossed the room in two strides and ripped the shower curtain off the rod with such force the plastic loops at the top popped off and scattered. I screamed and blindly threw the shampoo bottle, cowering back against the wall tiles.

It wasn't Ramirez. It was Joe Morelli. He had the curtain bunched in one hand; the other hand curled into a fist. A welt was forming on his forehead where the bottle had made contact. He was beyond angry, and

I wasn't so sure gender was going to keep me from getting a broken nose. Fine with me. I was spoiling for a fight. Who did this yodel think he was, first scaring me half to death and then wrecking my shower curtain.

"What the hell do you think you're doing?" I shrieked. "Haven't you ever heard of a goddamn doorbell? How did you get in here?"

"You left your bedroom window open."

"The screen was locked."

"Screens don't count."

"If you've ruined that screen I'll expect you to pay for it. And what about this shower curtain? Shower curtains don't grow on trees, you know." I'd lowered the volume on my voice, but the pitch was still a full octave higher than normal. In all honesty, I hadn't any idea what I was saying. My mind was racing down uncharted roads of fury and panic. I was furious that he'd violated my privacy, and I was panicked that I was naked.

Under the right circumstances naked is fine—taking showers, making love, being born. Standing naked and dripping wet in front of Joe Morelli, who was completely clothed, was the stuff nightmares are made of.

I shut the water off and grabbed at a towel, but Morelli slapped my hand away and threw the towel onto the floor behind him.

"Give me that towel," I demanded.

"Not until we've gotten a few things straightened out."

As a kid, Morelli'd been out of control. I'd reached the conclusion that as an adult Morelli had control in spades. The Italian temper was clear in his eyes, but the amount of violence displayed was tightly calculated. He was wearing a black rain-drenched T-shirt and jeans. When he twisted toward the towel rack I could see the gun stuck into his jeans at the small of his back.

It wasn't difficult to envision Morelli killing, but I found myself agreeing with Ranger and Eddie Gazarra—I couldn't see this grown-up Morelli being stupid and impulsive.

He had his hands on his hips. His hair was wet, curling on his forehead and over his ears. His mouth was hard and unsmiling. "Where's my distributor cap?"

When in doubt, always take the offensive. "If you don't get out of my bathroom this instant I'm going to start screaming."

"It's two o'clock in the morning, Stephanie. All your neighbors are sound asleep with their hearing aids on their nightstands. Scream away. No one's going to hear you."

I stood my ground and scowled at him. It was my best effort at defiance. I'd be damned if I was going to give him the satisfaction of looking vulnerable and embarrassed.

"I'm going to ask you one more time," he said. "Where's my distributor cap?"

"I don't know what you're talking about."

"Listen, Cupcake, I'll tear this place apart if I have to."

"I don't have the cap. The cap isn't here. And I'm not your cupcake."

"Why me?" he asked. "What did I do to deserve this?"

I raised an eyebrow.

Morelli sighed. "Yeah," he said. "I know." He took my pocketbook from the counter, turned it upside down, and let the contents fall to the floor. He picked the cuffs out of the mess and took a step forward. "Give me your wrist."

"Pervert."

"You wish." He flicked the cuff out and clicked it onto my right wrist.

I yanked my right arm back hard and kicked at him, but it was difficult to maneuver in the tub. He sidestepped my kick and locked the remaining steel bracelet onto the shower curtain rod. I gasped and froze, unable to believe what had just happened.

Morelli stepped back and looked at me, doing a slow whole-body scan. "You want to tell me where the cap is?"

I was incapable of speech, bereft of bravado. I could feel the flush of apprehension and embarrassment staining my cheeks, constricting my throat.

"Wonderful," Morelli said. "Do the silent thing. You can hang there forever for all I care."

He rummaged through the vanity drawers, emptied the wastebasket, and took the lid off the toilet tank. He stormed out of the bathroom without giving me so much as a backward glance. I could hear him methodically, professionally moving through my apartment, searching every square inch. Silverware clanked, drawers slammed, closet doors were wrenched open. There were sporadic patches of quiet, followed by mutterings.

I tried hanging my full weight on the bar, hoping to bend it, but the rod was industrial strength, built to endure.

At last Morelli appeared in the bathroom doorway.

"Well?" I snapped. "Now what?"

He indolently leaned against the frame. "Just came back to take another look." A grin surfaced at the corners of his mouth as his eyes locked halfway down my chest. "Cold?"

When I got loose I was going to track him down like a dog. I didn't care if he was innocent or guilty. And I didn't care if it took the rest of my life. I was going to get Morelli. "Go to hell."

The grin widened. "You're lucky I'm a gentleman. There are individuals out there who'd take advantage of a woman in your situation."

"Spare me."

He shifted off the doorjamb. "It's been a pleasure."

"Wait a minute! You're not leaving, are you?"

"Afraid so."

"What about me? What about the handcuffs?"

He debated his options for a moment. He stepped off into the kitchen and returned with the portable phone. "I'm going to lock the front door when I leave, so make sure whoever you call has a key."

"Nobody has a key!"

"I'm sure you'll think of something," Morelli said. "Call the police. Call the fire department. Call the fucking Marines."

"I'm naked!"

He smiled and winked and walked out the door.

I heard the front door to my apartment close and lock. I didn't expect an answer, but I felt compelled to call out to Morelli as a test. I waited a few moments, holding my breath, listening to the silence. Morelli seemed to be gone. My fingers curled tighter around the phone. God help the phone company if they'd reneged on their promise to resume my service. I climbed onto the edge of the tub to bring myself up to the height of my secured hand. I carefully extended the antenna, pushed the on button, and put my ear to the handset. The dial tone sang out loud and clear. I was so relieved I almost burst into tears.

Now I was faced with a new problem. Who to call? The police and the fire company were out. They'd roar into my parking lot with their lights flashing, and by the time they got to my door, forty senior citizens would be standing in my hall in their jammies, waiting to see what all the excitement was about, waiting for an explanation.

I'd come to realize there were certain peculiarities about the seniors in my building. They were vicious when it came to parking, and they had a fascination for emergencies that bordered on the ghoulish. At the first hint of a flashing light, every senior in my building had their nose pressed to the window glass.

I also could do without four or five of the city's finest leering at me chained naked to my shower curtain rod.

If I called my mother, I'd have to move out of state because she'd never let up. And besides, she'd send my father, and then my father would see me naked. Being naked and handcuffed in front of my father wasn't something I could visualize.

If I called my sister, she'd call my mother.

I'd hang here and rot before I'd call my ex-husband.

To make it even more complicated, whoever came to rescue me was either going to have to climb the fire escape or jimmy the front door. I could only come up with one name. I squeezed my eyes shut. "Shit." I was going to have to call Ranger. I took a deep breath and tapped out his number, praying I'd remembered it correctly.

It took only one ring for him to pick up. "Yo."

"Ranger?"

"Who wants to know?"

"Stephanie Plum. I have a problem."

There was a pause two beats long, and I could imagine him coming alert, sitting up in bed. "What's the problem?"

I rolled my eyes, only half believing I was making this phone call. "I'm handcuffed to my shower curtain rod, and I need someone to open the cuffs."

Another pause and he disconnected.

I redialed, punching the buttons so hard I almost broke a finger.

"Yo!" Ranger said, sounding good and pissed off.

"Don't hang up! This is serious, dammit. I'm trapped in my bathroom. My front door is locked and no one has a key."

"Why don't you call the cops? They love this rescue shit."

"Because I don't want to have to explain to the cops. And besides, I'm naked."

"Heh, heh, heh."

"It's not funny. Morelli broke into my apartment while I was in the shower, and the son of a bitch handcuffed me to the shower rod."

"You gotta like the guy."

"Are you going to help me, or what?"

"Where do you live?"

"The apartment building at the corner of St. James and Dunworth. Apartment 215. It's a rear apartment. Morelli got in by climbing the fire escape and going through the window. You can probably do the same."

I couldn't actually blame Morelli for cuffing me to the curtain rod. After all, I had sort of stolen his car. And I could understand that he needed to keep me out of the way while he searched my apartment. I might even be able to forgive him for destroying my shower curtain in a show of macho force, but he went too far when he left me hanging here naked. If he thought this would discourage me, he was wrong. This whole deal was now in the ballpark of double-dare, and childish as it might be, I was not going to walk away from the challenge. I'd get Morelli or die trying.

I'd been standing in the tub for what seemed like hours when I heard my front door open and close. The steam from the shower had long ago dissipated and the air had turned cool. My hand was numb from being held overhead. I was exhausted and hungry and had the beginnings of a headache.

Ranger appeared in the bathroom doorway, and I was too relieved to be embarrassed. "I appreciate your coming out in the middle of the night," I said.

Ranger smiled. "Didn't want to miss seeing you chained up naked."

"The keys are in the mess on the floor."

He found the keys, pried the phone loose from my fingers, and unlocked the cuffs. "You and Morelli got something kinky going on?"

"Remember when you gave me his keys this afternoon?"

"Un huh."

"I sort of borrowed his car."

"Borrowed?"

"Commandeered, actually. You know, about us having the law and all?"

"Un huh."

"Well, I commandeered his car, and he found out."

Ranger smiled and handed me a towel. "He understand about commandeering?"

"Let's just say he wasn't pleased. Anyway, I parked the car in the lot out here and removed the distributor cap as a safety precaution."

"Bet that went over big."

I got out of the tub and had to squelch a scream when I saw my reflection in the vanity mirror. My hair looked like it had taken 2,000 volts and been spray starched. "I need to install an alarm system in his car, but I haven't got the money."

Ranger laughed soft and low in his chest. "An alarm system. Morelli'll love that." He took a pen from the floor and wrote an address on a piece of toilet paper. "I know a garage that'll give you a price."

I padded past him into the bedroom and exchanged the towel for a long terry-cloth robe. "I heard you come in through the door."

"Picked the lock. Didn't think it prudent to wake up the super." He looked over at my window. Rain was spattering on the dark pane, and a piece of torn screening draped over the sill. "I only do the Spiderman shit in nice weather."

"Morelli wrecked my screen."

"Guess he in a hurry."

"I've noticed you only talk ghetto half of the time."

"I'm multilingual," Ranger said.

I followed him to the door, feeling jealous, wishing I knew a second language.

My sleep was deep and dreamless, and I might have slept until November if it weren't for the relentless pounding on my front door. I squinted at my bedside clock. The display read 8:35. Used to be I loved company. Now I cringed when someone knocked on my door. My first fear was of Ramirez. My second was that the police had come to haul me away for auto theft.

I picked the Sure Guard off my night table, stuffed my arms into my robe, and dragged myself to the door. I closed one eye and looked through the peephole with the other. Eddie Gazarra looked back at me. He was in uniform, holding two Dunkin' Donuts bags. I opened the door and sniffed the air like a hound on a scent. "Yum," I breathed.

"Hello to you, too," Gazarra said, squeezing past me in the little hallway, heading for the dining room table. "Where's your furniture?"

"I'm remodeling."

"Un huh."

We sat opposite each other, and I waited while he took two cardboard cups of coffee out of one of the bags. We uncapped the coffee, spread napkins, and dug into the donuts.

We were good enough friends that we didn't have to talk while we ate. We ate the Boston creams first. Then we divided up the remaining four jelly donuts. At two donuts down he still hadn't noticed my hair, and I was left to wonder what my hair usually looked like. He also hadn't said anything about the mess Morelli had created while searching my apartment, which gave me pause to consider my housekeeping habits.

He ate his third donut more slowly, sipping his coffee, savoring his donut, sipping his coffee, savoring his donut. "I hear you made a recovery yesterday," he said between savors.

He was left with just his coffee. He eyed my donut, and I protectively drew it closer to my edge of the table.

"Don't suppose you'd want to share that," Gazarra said.

"Don't suppose I would," I replied. "How did you find out about my recovery?"

"Locker room talk. You're prime conversation these days. The boys have a pool going on when you'll get boinked by Morelli."

My heart contracted so hard I was afraid my eyeballs might pop out of my head. I stared at Gazarra for a full minute, waiting for my blood pressure to ease out of the red zone, imagining capillaries bursting throughout my body.

"How will they know when I'm boinked?" I asked through clenched teeth. "Maybe he's boinked me already. Maybe we do it twice a day."

"They figure you'll quit the case when you get boinked. The winning time is actually when you quit the case."

"You in the pool?"

"Nope. Morelli nailed you when you were in high school. I don't think you'd let a second boinking go to your head."

"How do you know about high school?"

"Everybody knows about high school."

"Jesus." I swallowed the last piece of my last donut and washed it down with coffee.

Eddie sighed as he watched all hope for a part of the donut disappear into my mouth. "Your cousin, the queen of nags, has me on a diet," he said. "For breakfast I got decaf coffee, half a cup of cardboard cereal in skim milk, and a half grapefruit."

"I take it that's not cop food."

"Suppose I got shot," Eddie said, "and all I had in me was decaf and half a grapefruit. You think that'd get me to the trauma unit?"

"Not like real coffee and donuts."

"Damn straight."

"That overhang on your gun belt is probably good for stopping bullets, too."

Eddie drained his coffee cup, snapped the lid back on, and dumped it into the empty bag. "You wouldn't've said that if you weren't still pissed at the boinking stuff."

I agreed. "It was cruel."

He took a napkin and expertly flicked powdered sugar off his blue shirt. One of the many skills he'd learned at the academy, I thought. He sat back, arms folded across his chest. He was 5'10" and stocky. His features were eastern Slavic with flat pale blue eyes, white blond hair, and a stubby nose. When we were kids he lived two houses down from me. His parents still live there. All his life he'd wanted to be a cop. Now that he was a uniform he had no desire to go further. He enjoyed driving the car, responding to emergencies, being first on the scene. He was good at comforting people. Everyone liked him, with the possible exception of his wife.

"I've got some information for you," Eddie said. "I went to Pino's last night for a beer, and Gus Dembrowski was there. Gus is the PC working the Kulesza case."

"PC?"

"Plainclothesman."

This brought me up straight in my seat. "Did he tell you anything more about Morelli?"

"He confirmed that Sanchez was an informant. Dembrowski let it slip that Morelli had a card on her. Informants are kept secret. The controlling supervisor keeps all the cards in a locked file. I guess in this case it was released as necessary information to the investigation."

"So maybe this is more complicated than it would first appear. Maybe the killing tied in to something Morelli had been working on."

"Could be. Could also be that Morelli had romantic interests in Sanchez. I understand she was young and pretty. Very Latino."

"And she's still missing."

"Yeah. She's still missing. The department's traced back to relatives in Staten Island and nobody's seen her."

"I talked to her neighbors yesterday, and it turns out one of the tenants who remembered seeing Morelli's alleged witness has suffered sudden death."

"What kind of sudden death?"

"Hit and run in front of the building."

"Could have been an accident."

"I'd like to think so."

He glanced at his watch and stood. "I gotta go."

"One last thing, do you know Mooch Morelli?"

"I see him around."

"You know what he does or where he lives?"

"Works for public health. Some kind of inspector. Lives in Hamilton Township somewhere. Connie'll have cross–street reference books at the office. If he has a phone, you'll be able to get a street address."

"Thanks. And thanks for the donuts and coffee."

He paused in the hallway. "You need money?"

I shook my head. "I'm doing okay."

He gave me a hug and a kiss on the cheek, and he left.

I closed the door after him and felt tears pool behind my eyes. Sometimes friendship chokes me up. I padded back to the dining room, gathered together the bags and napkins, and carted them off to the kitchen wastebasket. This was the first opportunity I'd had to actually take stock of my apartment. Morelli'd obviously gone through it in a snit, venting his frustration by making the worst possible mess. Kitchen cupboards were open, contents partially strewn on the counter and floor, books had been knocked from the bookcase, the cushion had been removed from my one remaining chair, the bedroom was cluttered with clothes pulled from drawers. I replaced the cushion and put the kitchen in order, deciding the rest of the apartment could wait.

I showered and dressed in black spandex shorts and an oversized khaki T-shirt. My bounty hunter paraphernalia was still scattered over the bathroom floor. I stuffed it back into my black leather bag and slung the bag over my shoulder. I checked all the windows to make sure they were locked. This would become a morning and evening ritual. I hated living like a caged animal, but I didn't want any more surprise visitors. Locking my front door seemed more a matter of formality than security. Ranger had picked the lock with little difficulty. Of course, not everyone had Ranger's skills. Still, it wouldn't hurt to add another dead bolt to my collection of locking devices. First chance I got I'd talk to the super.

I said good-bye to Rex, dredged up some courage, and poked my head into the hall before venturing farther, making certain Ramirez hadn't suddenly appeared.

CHAPTER 7

The distributor cap was just where I'd left it, under a bush, tucked in close to the building. I put it back where it belonged and pulled out of the lot, heading for Hamilton. I found a spot in front of Vinnie's office and managed to wedge the Cherokee into it on the third try.

Connie was at her desk, peering into a hand mirror, picking clumps of dried goo off the tips of heavily mascaraed lashes.

She looked up when she saw me. "You ever use this lash lengthener stuff?" she asked. "Looks like it's laced with rat hairs."

I waved the police receipt at her. "I got Clarence."

She made a fist and jerked her elbow back hard. "Yes!"

"Vinnie here?"

"Had to go to the dentist. Having his incisors sharpened, I think." She pulled her master copy of the file and took my receipt. "We don't need Vinnie to do this. I can write you a check." She made a notation on the file cover, and placed the file in a bin on the far corner of her desk. She took a ledger-style checkbook from her middle drawer and wrote out a check. "How's it going with Morelli? You able to get a fix on him?"

"Not exactly a fix, but I know he's still in town."

"He's a serious babe," Connie said. "Saw him six months ago, before all this happened. He was ordering a quarter pound of provolone at the meat market, and I had all I could do to keep from sinking my teeth into his butt."

"Sounds carnivorous."

"Carnivorous ain't the half of it. That man is fine."

"He's also accused of murder."

Connie sighed. "Gonna be a lot of women in Trenton unhappy to see Morelli on ice."

I supposed that was true, but I didn't happen to be one of them. After last night, the thought of Morelli behind bars conjured only cozy feelings in my humiliated, vindictive heart. "You have a cross–street reference here?"

Connie swiveled to face the file cabinets. "It's the big book over the G drawer."

"You know anything about Mooch Morelli?" I asked while I looked up his name.

"Only that he married Shirley Gallo."

The only Morelli in Hamilton Township was listed at 617 Bergen Court. I checked it against the wall map behind Connie's desk. If I remembered the area correctly, it was a neighborhood of split-level houses that looked like they deserved my bathroom.

"You seen Shirley lately?" Connie asked. "She's big as a horse. Must have gained a hundred pounds since high school. I saw her at Margie Manusco's shower. She took up three folding chairs when she sat down, and she had her pocketbook filled with Ding Dongs. I guess they were for an emergency . . . like in case someone beat her to the potato salad."

"Shirley Gallo? Fat? She was a rail in high school."

"The Lord moves in mysterious ways," Connie said.

"Amen."

Burg Catholicism was a convenient religion. When the mind boggled, there was always God, waiting in the wings to take the rap.

Connie handed me the check and plucked at a clump of mascara hanging at the end of her left eyelash. "I'm telling you, it's fucking hard to be classy," she said.

The garage Ranger recommended was in a small light-industrial complex that had its backside rammed up against Route 1. The complex consisted of six concrete bunker-type buildings painted yellow, the color faded by time and highway exhaust. At the inception of the project, the complex architect had most likely envisioned grass and shrubs. The reality was hard-packed dirt littered with butts and Styrofoam cups and some spiky weeds. Each of the six buildings had its own paved drive and parking lot.

I slowly drove past Capital Printing and A. and J. Extrusions and stopped at the entrance to Al's Auto Body. Three bay doors had been set into the front of the building, but only one gaped open. Bashed-in, rusted cars in various stages of disassembly were crammed into the junkyard at the rear, and late-model fender-bended cars were parked adjacent to the third bay, in a chain-link-fenced compound topped with razor wire.

I rolled into the lot and parked next to a black Toyota 4×4 that had been jacked up on wheels that were sized for a backhoe. I'd stopped at the bank on the way and deposited my recovery check. I knew exactly how much money I was willing to spend on an alarm system, and I wasn't willing to pay a penny more. Most likely the job couldn't be done for my price, but it wouldn't hurt to inquire.

I opened the car door and stepped outside into oppressive heat, breathing shallowly so I didn't suck in any more heavy metals than was necessary. The sun looked squalid this close to the highway, the pollution diluting the light, compressing the image. The sound of an air wrench carried out of the open bay.

I crossed the lot and squinted into the dim hellhole of grease guns and oil filters and potentially rude men wearing Day-Glo orange jumpsuits. One of the men ambled over to me. He was wearing the cut off and knotted thigh portion of a pair of queen-size pantyhose on his head. Undoubtedly it was a time-saver in case he wanted to rob a 7-Eleven on the way home. I told him I was looking for Al, and he told me I'd found him.

"I need an alarm system installed in my car. Ranger said you'd give me a good price."

"How you come to know Ranger?"

"We work together."

"That covers a lot of territory."

I wasn't sure what he meant by that, and probably I didn't want to know. "I'm a recovery agent."

"So you need an alarm system because you gonna be in bad neighborhoods?"

"Actually, I sort of stole a car, and I'm afraid the owner will try to get it back."

Laughter flickered behind his eyes. "Even better."

He walked to a bench at the back of the building and returned with a black plastic gadget about three inches square. "This is state-of-the-art security," he said. "Works on air pressure. Anytime there's a change in air pressure, from a window getting broken or a door opening, this mother'll like to bust your eardrum." He turned it face up in his hand. "You push this button to set it. Then there's a twenty-second delay before it goes into effect. Gives you time to get out and close the door. There's another twenty-second delay after the door is opened, so you can punch in your code to disarm."

"How do I shut it off once the alarm is triggered?"

"A key." He dropped a small silver key in my hand. "I suggest you don't leave the key in the car. Defeats the purpose."

"It's smaller than I'd expected."

"Small but mighty. And the good news is it's cheap because it's easy to install. All you do is screw it onto your dash."

"How cheap?"

"Sixty dollars."

"Sold."

He pulled a screwdriver out of his back pocket. "Just show me where you want it."

"The red Jeep Cherokee, next to the monster truck. I'd like you to put the alarm some place inconspicuous. I don't want to deface the dash."

Minutes later I was on my way to Stark Street, feeling pretty pleased with myself. I had an alarm that was not only reasonably priced, but easily removed should I want to install it in the car I intended to buy when I cashed Morelli in. I'd stopped at a 7-Eleven on the way and gotten myself a vanilla yogurt and a carton of orange juice for lunch. I was drinking and driving and slurping, and I was very comfortable in my air-conditioned splendor. I had an alarm, I had nerve gas, I had a yogurt. What more could anyone want?

I parked directly across from the gym, guzzled the remaining orange juice, set the alarm, took my shoulder bag and file photos of Morelli, and locked up. I was waving the red flag at the bull. The only way I could possibly be more obvious was to plaster a sign to the windshield saying, "Here it is! Try and get it!"

Street activity was sluggish in the afternoon heat. Two hookers stood at the corner, looking like they were waiting for a bus, except buses didn't run down Stark Street. The women were standing there, obviously bored and disgusted, I suppose because nobody was buying at this time of day. They wore cheap plastic flip-flops, stretchy tank tops, and tight-fitting knit shorts. Their hair had been chopped short and cleverly straightened to boar-bristle quality. I wasn't sure exactly how prostitutes determined price, but if men bought hookers by the pound, these two would be doing okay.

They went into combat mode as I approached: Hands on hips, lower lips protruding, eyes opened so wide they bulged out like duck eggs.

"Hey girl," one of the lovelies called out. "What you think you doing here? This here's our corner, you dig?"

It would appear there was a fine line between being a babe from the burg and looking like a hooker.

"I'm looking for a friend. Joe Morelli." I showed them his picture. "Either of you see him around?"

"What you want with this Morelli?"

"It's personal."

"I bet."

"You know him?"

She shifted her weight. No small task. "Maybe."

"Actually, we were more than friends."

"How much more?"

"The son of a bitch got me pregnant."

"You don't look pregnant."

"Give me a month."

"There's things you can do."

"Yeah," I said, "and number one is find Morelli. You know where he is?"

"Nuh uh."

"You know someone named Carmen Sanchez? She worked at the Step In."

"She get you pregnant too?"

"Thought Morelli might be with her."

"Carmen's disappeared," one of the hookers said. "Happens to women on Stark Street. Environmental hazard."

"You want to elaborate on that?"

"She want to keep her mouth shut, is what she want to do," the other woman said. "We don't know about any of that shit. And we don't got time to stand here talking to you. We got work to do."

I looked up and down the street. Couldn't see any work in sight, so I assumed I was getting the old heave-ho. I asked their names and was told Lula and Jackie. I gave each of them my card and told them I'd appreciate a call if they saw Morelli or Sanchez. I'd have asked about the missing male witness, but what would I say? Excuse me, have you seen a man with a face like a frying pan?

I went door-to-door after that, talking to people sitting out on stoops, questioning storekeepers. By four I had a sunburned nose to show for my efforts and not much more. I'd started on the north side of Stark Street and had worked two blocks west. Then I'd crossed the street and inched my way back. I'd slunk past the garage and the gym. I also bypassed the bars. They might be my best source, but they felt dangerous to me and beyond my abilities. Probably I was being unnecessarily cautious, probably the bars were filled with perfectly nice people who could give a rat's ass about my existence. Truth is, I wasn't used to being a minority, and I felt like a black man looking up white women's skirts in a WASP suburb of Birmingham.

I covered the south side of the next two and a half blocks and recrossed to the north side. Most of the buildings on this side were residential, and as the day progressed more and more people had drifted outdoors, so that the going was slow now as I moved down the street back to my car.

Fortunately, the Cherokee was still at the curb, and unfortunately, Morelli was nowhere to be seen. I diligently avoided looking up at the gym windows. If Ramirez was watching me, I'd prefer not to acknowledge him. I'd pulled my hair up into a lopsided ponytail, and the back of my neck felt scratchy. I supposed I was burned there too. I wasn't very diligent with sunscreen. Mostly, I counted on the pollution to filter out the cancer rays.

A woman came hurrying across the street to me. She was solidly built and conservatively dressed, with her black hair pulled back into a bun at the nape of her neck.

"Excuse me," she said. "Are you Stephanie Plum?"

"Yes."

"Mr. Alpha would like to speak to you," she said. "His office is just across the street."

I didn't know anyone named Alpha, and I wasn't eager to hover in the shadow of Benito Ramirez, but the woman reeked of Catholic respectability, so I took a chance and followed after her. We entered the building next to the gym. It was an average Stark Street row house. Narrow, three stories, sooty exterior, dark, grimy windows. We hurried up a flight of stairs to a small landing. Three doors opened off the landing. One door was ajar, and I felt air-conditioning spilling out into the hallway.

"This way," the woman said, leading me into a cramped reception room dwarfed by a green leather couch and large scarred blond wood desk. A shopworn end table held dog-eared copies of boxing magazines, and pictures of boxers covered walls that cried out for fresh paint.

She ushered me into an inner office and shut the door behind me. The inner office was a lot like the reception room with the exception of two windows looking down at the street. The man behind the desk stood when I entered. He was wearing pleated dress slacks and a short-sleeved shirt open at the neck. His face was lined and had a good start on jowls. His stocky body still showed muscle, but age had added love handles to his waist and streaks of gunmetal gray to his slicked-back black hair. I placed him in his late fifties and decided his life hadn't been all roses.

He leaned forward and extended his hand. "Jimmy Alpha. I manage Benito Ramirez."

I nodded, not sure how to respond. My first reaction was to shriek, but that would probably be unprofessional.

He motioned me to a folding chair placed slightly to the side of his desk. "I heard you were back on the street, and I wanted to take this opportunity to apologize. I know what happened in the gym between you and Benito. I tried to call you, but your phone was disconnected."

His apology stirred fresh anger. "Ramirez's behavior was unprovoked and inexcusable."

Alpha looked genuinely embarrassed. "I never thought I'd have problems like this," he said. "All I ever wanted was to have a top boxer, and now I got one, and it's giving me ulcers." He took an economy-sized bottle of Mylanta from his top drawer. "See this? I buy this stuff by the case." He unscrewed the cap and chugged some. He put his fist to his sternum and sighed. "I'm sorry. I'm genuinely sorry for what happened to you in the gym."

"There's no reason for you to apologize. It's not your problem."

"I wish that was true. Unfortunately, it *is* my problem." He screwed the cap back on, returned the bottle to the drawer, and leaned forward, arms resting on his desk. "You work for Vinnie."

"Yes."

"I know Vinnie from way back. Vinnie's a character."

He smiled, and I figured somewhere in his travels he must have heard about the duck.

He sobered himself, fixed his eyes on his thumbs, and sagged a little in his seat. "Sometimes I don't know what to do with Benito. He's not a bad kid. He just doesn't know a lot of stuff. All he knows is boxing. All this success is hard on a man like Benito, who comes from nowhere."

He looked up to see if I was buying. I made a derisive sound, and he acknowledged my disgust.

"I'm not excusing him," he said, his face a study in bitterness. "Benito does things that are wrong. I don't have any influence on him these days. He's full of himself. And he's got himself surrounded by guys who only got brains in their boxing gloves."

"That gym was filled with able-bodied men who did nothing to help me."

"I talked to them about it. Was a time when women were respected, but now nothing's respected. Drive-by killings, drugs . . ." He went quiet and sunk into his own thoughts.

I remembered what Morelli had told me about Ramirez and previous rape charges. Alpha was either sticking his head in the sand or else he was actively engaged in cleaning up the mess made by the golden goose. I was putting money on the sand theory.

I stared at him in stony silence, feeling too isolated in his second-floor ghetto office to honestly vent my thoughts, feeling too angry to attempt polite murmurings.

"If Benito bothers you again, you let me know right away," Alpha said. "I don't like when this kind of stuff happens."

"He came to my apartment the night before last and tried to get in. He was abusive in the hall, and he made a mess on my door. If it happens again, I'm filing charges."

Alpha was visibly shaken. "Nobody told me. He didn't hurt anybody, did he?"

"No one was hurt."

Alpha took a card from the top of his desk and scribbled a number on it. "This is my home phone," he said, handing me the card. "You have any more trouble, you call me right away. If he damaged your door I'll make good on it."

"The door's okay. Just keep him away from me."

Alpha pressed his lips together and nodded.

"I don't suppose you know anything about Carmen Sanchez?"

"Only what I read in the papers."

I turned left at State Street and pushed my way into rush-hour traffic. The light changed, and we all inched forward. I had enough money left to buy a few groceries, so I bypassed my apartment and drove an extra quarter mile down the road to Super-Fresh.

It occurred to me while I was standing at the checkout that Morelli had to be getting food from somewhere or someone. Did he scuttle around Super-Fresh wearing a Groucho Marx mustache and glasses with a fake nose attached? And where was he living? Maybe he was living in the blue van. I'd assumed he'd dumped it after being spotted, but maybe not. Maybe it was too convenient. Maybe it was his command headquarters with a cache of canned goods. And, I thought it was possible he had monitoring equipment in the van. He'd been across the street, spying on Ramirez, so maybe he was listening as well.

I hadn't seen the van on Stark Street. I hadn't been actively looking for it, but I wouldn't have passed it by, either. I didn't know a whole lot about electronic surveillance, but I knew the surveillor had to be fairly close to the surveillee. Something to think about. Maybe I could find Morelli by looking for the van.

I was forced to park at the rear of my lot, and did so harboring a few testy thoughts about handicapped old people who took all the best parking slots. I gripped three plastic grocery bags in each hand, plus a six-pack. I eased the Cherokee's door closed with my knee. I could feel my arms stretching against the weight, the bags clumsily banging around my knees as I walked, reminding me of a joke I'd once heard having to do with elephant testicles.

I took the elevator, wobbled the short distance down the hall, and set my bags on the carpet while I felt around for my key. I opened the door, switched on the light, shuttled my groceries into the kitchen, and returned to lock my front door. I did the grocery unpacking bit, sorting out cupboard stuff from refrigerator stuff. It felt good to have a little cache of food again. It was my heritage to hoard. Housewives in the burg were always prepared for disaster, stockpiling toilet paper and cans of creamed corn in case the blizzard of aughty-aught should ever repeat itself.

Even Rex was excited by the activity, watching from his cage with his little pink hamster feet pressed against the glass.

"Better days are coming, Rex," I said, giving him an apple slice. "From here on in it's all apples and broccoli."

I'd gotten a city map at the supermarket, and I spread it out on my table while I picked at dinner. Tomorrow I'd be methodical about searching for the blue van. I'd check the area surrounding the gym, and I'd also check out Ramirez's home address. I hauled out my phone book and looked up Ramirez. Twenty-three were listed. Three had B as the first initial. There were two Benitos. I dialed the first Benito and a woman answered on the fourth ring. I could hear a baby crying in the background.

"Does Benito Ramirez, the boxer, live there?" I asked.

The reply came in Spanish and didn't sound friendly. I apologized for disturbing her and hung up. The second Benito answered his own phone and was definitely not the Ramirez I was looking for. The three Bs were also dead ends. It didn't seem worthwhile to call the remaining eighteen numbers. In a way I was relieved not to have found him. I don't know what I would have said. Nothing, I suppose. I was looking for an address, not a conversation. And the truth is the very thought of Ramirez sent a chill to my heart. I could stake out the gym and try to follow Ramirez when he left for the day, but the big red Cherokee wasn't exactly inconspicuous. Eddie might be able to help me. Cops had ways of getting addresses. Who else did I know who had access to addresses? Marilyn Truro worked for the DMV. If I had a license plate number, she could probably pull an address. Or I could call the gym. Nah, that'd be too easy.

Well, what the hell, I thought. Give it a shot. I'd torn the page advertising the gym out of my phone book, so I dialed information. I thanked the operator and dialed the number. I told the man who answered the phone that I was supposed to meet Benito, but I'd lost his address.

"Sure," he said. "It's 320 Polk. Don't know the apartment number, but it's on the second floor. It's at the rear of the hall. Got his name on the door. Can't miss it."

"Thanks," I told him. "Really appreciate it."

I pushed the phone to the far corner of the table and turned to the map to place Polk. The map showed it to be at the edge of the ghetto, running parallel to Stark. I circled the address with yellow marker. Now I had two sites to search for the van. I'd park and go on foot if I had to, prowling through alleys and investigating garages. I'd do this first thing in the morning, and if nothing developed, I'd go back to the stack of FTAs Connie had given me and try to make some rent money doing nickel-and-dime cases.

I double-checked all my windows to make sure they were locked, then I drew all the curtains. I wanted to take a shower and go to bed early, and I didn't want any surprise visitors.

I straightened my apartment, trying not to notice the empty spaces where appliances had been, trying to ignore the phantom furniture indentations persisting in the living room carpet. Morelli's $10,000 recovery fee would go a long way toward restoring some semblance of normalcy to my life, but it was a stopgap measure. Probably I should still be applying for jobs.

Who was I kidding. I'd covered all the bases in my field.

I could stay with skip tracing, but it seemed risky at best. And at worst . . . I didn't even want to think about worst. Besides getting used to being threatened, hated, and possibly molested, wounded, or God forbid killed, I'd have to establish a self-employed mind-set. And I'd have to invest in martial arts coaching and learn some police techniques for subduing felons. I didn't want to turn myself into the Terminator, but I didn't want to continue to operate at my present Elmer Fudd level, either. If I had a television I could watch reruns of *Cagney and Lacey.*

I remembered my plan to get another dead bolt installed and decided to visit Dillon Ruddick, the super. Dillon and I were buds, being that we were just about the only two people in the building who didn't think Metamusil was one of the four major food groups. Dillon moved his lips when he read the funnies, but put a tool in the man's hand and he was pure genius. He lived in the bowels of the building, in a carpeted efficiency that never saw the natural light of day. There was a constant background serenade as boilers and water heaters rumbled and water swished through pipes. Dillon said he liked it. Said he pretended it was the ocean.

"Hey Dillon," I said when he answered the door. "How's it going?"

"Going okay. Can't complain. What can I do for you?"

"I'm worried about crime, Dillon. I thought it would be a good idea to get another dead bolt put on my door."

"That's cool," he said. "A person can never be too careful. In fact, I just finished putting a dead bolt on Mrs. Luger's door. She said some big, huge guy was yelling in the halls, late at night, couple days ago. Said it scared the whatever out of her. Maybe you heard him, too. Mrs. Luger's just two doors down from you."

I resisted the urge to swallow and go "gulp." I knew the name of the big, huge guy.

"I'll try to get the lock on tomorrow," Dillon said. "In the meantime, how about a beer."

"A beer would be good."

Dillon handed me a bottle and a can of mixed nuts. He boosted the sound back up on the TV, and we both plopped down on the couch.

I'd set my alarm for eight, but I was up at seven, anxious to find the van. I took a shower and spent some time on my hair, doing the blow-drying thing, adding some gel and some spray. When I was done I looked like Cher on a bad day. Still, Cher on a bad day wasn't all that bad. I was down to my last clean pair of spandex shorts. I tugged on a matching sports bra that doubled as a halter top and slid a big, loose, purple T-shirt with a large, droopy neck over my head. I laced up my hightop Reeboks, crunched down my white socks, and felt pretty cool.

I ate Frosted Flakes for breakfast. If they were good enough for Tony the Tiger, they were good enough for me. I swallowed down a multivitamin, brushed my teeth, poked a couple of big gold hoops through my earlobes, applied glow-in-the-dark Cherry Red lipstick, and I was ready to go.

Cicadas droned their early warning of another scorcher day, and the blacktop steamed with what was left of morning dew. I pulled out of the lot into the steady stream of traffic on St. James. I had the map spread out on the seat next to me, plus a steno pad I'd begun to use for phone numbers, addresses, and miscellaneous bits of information relating to the job.

Ramirez's apartment building was set in the middle of the block, its identity lost in a crush of four-story walk-ups built cheek by jowl for the working poor. Most likely the building had originally held immigrant laborers—Irish, Italian, Polish hopefuls barged up the Delaware to work in Trenton's factories. It was difficult to tell who lived here now. There were no old men loitering on front stoops, no children playing on the sidewalk. Two middle-aged Asian women stood waiting at a bus stop, their purses held tight against their chests, their faces expressionless. There were no vans in sight, and no place to hide one. No garages or alleys. If Morelli was keeping tabs on Ramirez, it would have to be from the rear or from an adjacent apartment.

I drove around the corner and found the single-lane service road that cut the block. There were no garages back here, either. An asphalt slab had been laid tight to the rear of Ramirez's building. Diagonal parking for six cars had been lined off on the slab. Only four cars were parked. Three old clunkers and a Silver Porsche with a license plate holder that had "The Champ" printed on it in gold. None of the cars were occupied.

Across the service road were more tenement-type apartments. This would be a reasonable place for Morelli to watch or listen, I thought, but there was no sign of him.

I drove through the service road and circled the block, methodically enlarging the area until I'd covered all drivable streets for a nine-block square. The van didn't turn up.

I headed for Stark Street and repeated the procedure, looking for the van. There were garages and alleys here, so I parked the Cherokee and set out on foot. By twelve-thirty I'd snooped in enough broken-down, smelly garages to last me a lifetime. If I crossed my eyes I could see my nose peeling, my hair was sticking to the back of my sweaty neck, and I had bursitis from carrying my hulking shoulder bag.

By the time I got back to the Cherokee, my feet felt like they were on fire. I leaned against the car and checked to make sure my soles weren't melting. A block away I could see Lula and Jackie staking out their corner. I figured it wouldn't hurt to talk to them again.

"Still looking for Morelli?" Lula asked.

I shoved my dark glasses to the top of my head. "Have you seen him?"

"Nope. Haven't heard nothing about him, either. Man's keeping a low profile."

"How about his van?"

"Don't know nothing about a van. Lately, Morelli's been driving a red and gold Cherokee . . . like the one you're driving." Her eyes widened. "Sheee-it, that ain't Morelli's car, is it?"

"I sort of borrowed it."

Lula's face split in a grin. "Honey, you telling me you *stole* Morelli's car? Girl, he gonna kick your skinny white butt."

"Couple days ago I saw him driving a faded blue Econoline," I said. "It had antennae sticking out all over the place. You see anything like that cruise by?"

"We didn't see nothing," Jackie said.

I turned to Lula. "How about you, Lula? You see a blue van?"

"Tell me the truth now? You really pregnant?" Lula asked.

"No, but I could have been." Fourteen years ago.

"So what's going on here? What you really want with Morelli?"

"I work for his bondsman. Morelli is FTA."

"No shit? There any money in that?"

"Ten percent of the bond."

"I could do that," Lula said. "Maybe I should change my profession."

"Maybe you should stop talking and look like you want to give some before your old man beats the crap out of you," Jackie said.

I drove back to my apartment, ate some more Frosted Flakes, and called my mother.

"I made a nice big pot of stuffed cabbages," she said. "You should come for supper."

"Sounds good, but I have things to do."

"Like what? What's so important you can't take time to eat some stuffed cabbages?"

"Work."

"What kind of work? Are you still trying to find the Morelli boy?"

"Yeah."

"You should get a different job. I saw a sign at Clara's Beauty Salon, they need a shampoo girl."

I could hear my Grandma Mazur yelling something in the background.

"Oh yeah," my mother said. "You had a phone call this morning from that boxer you went to see, Benito Ramirez. Your father was so excited. Such a nice young man. So polite."

"What did Ramirez want?"

"He said he'd been trying to get in touch with you, but your phone had been disconnected. I told him it was okay now."

I mentally banged my head against the wall. "Benito Ramirez is a sleaze. If he calls up again, don't talk to him."

"He was polite to me on the phone."

Yeah, I thought, the most courteous homicidal rapist in Trenton. And now he knew he could call me.

CHAPTER 8

My apartment building was pre–laundry room vintage, and the present owner felt no compulsion to add amenities. The nearest coin-op, Super Suds, was about a half mile away on Hamilton. Not a journey of insurmountable proportions, but a pain in the ass all the same.

I tucked the stack of FTAs I'd received from Connie into my pocketbook and slung my pocketbook over my shoulder. I lugged my laundry basket into the hall, locked my door, and hauled myself out to the car.

As far as laundromats went, Super Suds wasn't bad. There was parking in a small lot to the side of the building and a luncheonette next door where a person could get a tasty chicken salad sandwich if a person had cash on hand. I happened to be low on cash on hand, so I dumped my laundry into a machine, added detergent and quarters, and settled down to review my FTAs.

Lonnie Dodd was at the top of the stack and seemed like the easiest apprehension. He was twenty-two and lived in Hamilton Township. He'd been charged with auto theft. A first-time offender. I used the laundromat pay phone to call Connie to verify that Dodd was still outstanding.

"He's probably in his garage, changing his oil," she said. "Happens all the time. It's one of those man things. Hell, they say to themselves, nobody's gonna push me around. All I did was steal a few cars. What's the big fuckin' deal? So they don't show up for their court date."

I thanked Connie for her insight and returned to my chair. As soon as my laundry was done, I'd mosey on over to Dodd's place and see if I could find him.

I slid the files back into my pocketbook and transferred my clothes to the dryer. I sat down, looked out the big plate glass front window, and the blue van rolled by. I was so startled I froze, mouth open, eyes glazed, mind blank. Not what you would call a quick draw. The van disappeared down the street, and in the distance I could see the brake lights go on. Morelli was stopped in traffic.

Now I moved. Actually, I think I flew, because I don't remember my feet touching pavement. I peeled out of the lot, smoking rubber. I got to the corner and the alarm went off. In my haste I'd forgotten to punch in the code.

I could barely think for the noise. The key was on my key ring, and the key ring was attached to the key in the ignition. I slammed my foot on the brake, fishtailing to a stop in the middle of the road. I looked in the rearview mirror after the fact, relieved to find there were no cars behind me. I deactivated the alarm and took off again.

Several cars were between me and Morelli. He turned right, and I gripped the wheel tighter, creeping along, inventing colorful new expletives as I made my way to the intersection. By the time I turned he was gone. I slowly worked my way up and down the streets. I was ready to quit when I spotted the van parked in the back lot to Manni's Deli.

I stopped at the entrance to the lot and stared at the van, wondering what to do next. I had no way of knowing if Morelli was behind the wheel. He could be stretched out in back, taking a snooze, or he could be in Manni's ordering tuna on a kaiser to go. Probably I should park and investigate. If it turned out he wasn't in the van, I'd hide behind one of the cars and gas him when he came into range.

I pulled into a slot at the back of the lot, four cars down from the van, and cut the engine. I was about to reach for my bag when suddenly the driver's side door was ripped open, and I was yanked from behind the wheel. I stumbled forward, slamming into the wall of Morelli's chest.

"Looking for me?" he asked.

"You might as well give up," I told him, "because I never will."

The line of his mouth tightened. "Tell me about it. Suppose I lay down on the pavement and you run over me a few times with my own car . . . just for old times. Would you like that? Do you get your money dead or alive?"

"No reason to get testy about it. I have a job to do. It's nothing personal."

"Nothing personal? You've harassed my mother, stolen my car, and now you're telling people I've gotten you pregnant! In my opinion, getting someone pregnant is pretty fucking personal! Jesus, isn't it enough I'm accused of murder? What are you, the bounty hunter from hell?"

"You're overwrought."

"I'm beyond overwrought. I'm resigned. Everyone has a cross to bear . . . you're mine. I give up. Take the car. I don't care anymore. All I ask is that you try not to get too many dings on the door and you change the oil when the red light goes on." His eyes flicked to the car interior. "You're not making phone calls, are you?"

"No. Of course not."

"Phone calls are expensive."

"Not to worry."

"Shit," he said. "My life is shit."

"Probably this is just a phase."

His expression softened. "I like this outfit you're wearing." He hooked a finger around the wide neck of my T-shirt and looked inside at the black spandex sports bra. "Very sexy."

A flash of heat shot through my stomach. I told myself it was anger, but I suspect carnal panic would be closer to the truth. I smacked his hand away. "Don't be rude."

"Well hell, I've made you pregnant, remember? One more little intimacy shouldn't bother you." He moved closer. "I like the lipstick, too. Cherry red. Very tempting."

He lowered his mouth and kissed me.

I know I should have kneed him in the groin, but the kiss was delicious. Joe Morelli still knew how to kiss. It had started out slow and tender in the beginning, and it had ended up hot and deep. He pulled back and smiled, and I knew I'd been had.

"Gotcha," he said.

"Dick breath."

He reached around me and removed the keys from the ignition. "I don't want you following."

"Furthest thought from my mind."

"Yeah, well I'm going to slow you down a little, anyway." He walked to the deli's Dumpster and pitched the keys inside. "Happy hunting," he said, heading for the van. "Make sure you wipe your feet before you get in my car."

"Wait a minute," I yelled after him. "I have some questions. I want to know about the murder. I want to know about Carmen Sanchez. And is it true there's a contract out on you?"

He hitched himself up into the van and drove out of the lot.

The Dumpster was industrial-sized. Five feet high, five feet wide, and six feet long. I stood on tiptoe and peered over the side. It was one-quarter full and smelled like dead dog. I couldn't see the keys.

A lesser woman would have burst into tears. A smarter woman would have had an extra set of keys. I dragged a wooden crate to the side of the Dumpster and stood on it for a better look. Most of the garbage was bagged. Some of the bags had split on impact, spewing out half-eaten subs, globs of potato salad, coffee grounds, grill grease, unrecognizable slop, and heads of lettuce turning to primordial ooze.

I was reminded of road kill. Ashes to ashes . . . mayo to its various components. Doesn't matter whether it's cats or cole slaw, death is not attractive.

I did a rundown of everyone I knew, but I couldn't think of anyone dumb enough to climb into the Dumpster for me. Okay, I told myself, now or never. I swung my leg up and over the side and hung there for a moment, gathering courage. I lowered myself slowly, upper lip curled. If I smelled even the *hint* of rat breath, I was out of there.

Cans rolled underfoot, giving way to soft, squishy gunk. I felt myself slide and hooked a hand onto the Dumpster rim, cracking my elbow against the side in the process. I swore and blinked back tears.

I found a plastic bread bag that was relatively clean and used it like a glove to carefully paw through the slop, moving cautiously, scared to death I'd fall face first into the artichoke and calf brains vinaigrette. The amount of discarded food was sobering, the wastefulness almost as revolting as the all-pervasive odor of rot that seared the inside of my nose and clung to the roof of my mouth.

After what seemed like an eternity I discovered the keys sunk into some yellow-brown glop. I didn't see any Pampers nearby, so I hoped the glop was mustard. I stuck my bagged hand in whatever-it-was and gagged.

I held my breath, tossed the keys over the edge onto the blacktop, and didn't waste any time following. I wiped off the keys as best I could with the bread bag. Most of the yellow stuff came off, rendering the keys good enough for emergency driving. I got out of my shoes by stepping on the heels, and I used the two-fingers sissy approach to peel my socks away. I inspected the rest of me. Aside from some Thousand Island dressing smeared on the front of my shirt, I seemed unscathed.

Newspapers had been stacked for recycling beside the Dumpster. I covered the driver's seat with the sports section, just in case I'd missed seeing some noxious substance stuck to my ass. I spread paper over the passenger-side floor mat and gingerly set my shoes and socks in the center.

I glanced at the remaining section of paper, and a headline jumped out at me. "Local Man Killed in Drive-by Shooting." Beneath the headline was a picture of John Kuzack. I'd seen him on Wednesday. Today was Friday. The paper in my hand was a day old. I read the story without breathing. Kuzack had been gunned down late Wednesday night in front of his apartment building. It went on to say how he'd been a hero in Nam, getting the purple heart, and how he was a colorful, well-liked neighborhood figure. As of press time, the police had no suspect and no motive.

I leaned against the Cherokee, trying to absorb the reality of John Kuzack's death. He'd been so big and alive when I'd spoken to him. And now he was dead. First Edleman, the hit and run, and now Kuzack. Of the three people who'd seen and remembered the missing witness, two were dead. I thought about Mrs. Santiago and her children and shivered.

I carefully folded the paper and slid it into the map pocket. When I got back to my apartment I'd call Gazarra and try to get some reassurance of Mrs. Santiago's safety.

I was beyond being able to smell myself, but I drove with the windows down as a precaution.

I parked in the laundromat lot and slipped in barefoot to get my clothes. Only one other person was in the room, an elderly woman at the folding table on the far wall.

"Oh my goodness," she said, looking bewildered. "What is that smell?"

I felt my cheeks heat up. "Must be outside," I said. "Must have followed me in when I opened the door."

"It's *awful!*"

I sniffed, but I couldn't smell anything. My nose had shut down in self-defense. I glanced at my shirt. "Does it smell like Thousand Island dressing?"

She had a pillowcase pressed to her face. "I think I'm going to be sick."

I rammed my laundry into the basket and made my exit. Halfway home I stopped for a light and noticed my eyes were watering. Ominous, I thought. Fortunately, no one was afoot when I swung into the parking lot to my apartment building. The foyer and the elevator were both empty. So far so good. The elevator doors opened to the second floor and no one was about there, either. I breathed a sigh of relief, dragged my laundry to my door, slunk into my apartment, stripped off my clothes, and tied them up in a big black plastic garbage bag.

I jumped into the shower and lathered and scrubbed and shampooed thrice. I dressed in clean clothes and went across the hall to Mr. Wolesky as a test.

He opened the door and instantly clamped a hand over his nose. "Whoa," he gasped. "What's that smell?"

"That's what I was wondering," I said. "It seems to be hanging in the hall here."

"Smells like dead dog."

I sighed. "Yeah. That was my first impression, too."

I retreated back to my apartment. I needed to rewash everything, and I'd run out of quarters. I was going to have to go home to do my laundry. I looked at my watch. It was almost six. I'd call my mother on the car phone and warn her I'd be there for dinner after all.

I parked in front of the house, and my mother appeared like magic, driven by some mysterious maternal instinct always to know when her daughter set foot on the curb.

"A new car," she said. "How nice. Where did you get it?"

I had the basket under one arm and the plastic trash bag under the other. "I borrowed it from a friend."

"Who?"

"You don't know him. Someone I went to school with."

"Well, you're lucky to have friends like that. You should bake him something. A cake."

I pushed past her, heading for the cellar stairs. "I brought my laundry. I hope you don't mind."

"Of course I don't mind. What's that smell? Is that you? You smell like a garbage can."

"I accidentally dropped my keys in a Dumpster, and I had to climb in and get them out."

"I don't understand how these things happen to you. They don't happen to anyone else. Who else do you know dropped their keys in a Dumpster? No one, that's who. Only you would do such a thing."

Grandma Mazur came out of the kitchen. "I smell throw-up."

"It's Stephanie," my mother said. "She was in a Dumpster."

"What was she doing in a Dumpster? Was she looking for bodies? I saw a movie on TV where the mob splattered some guy's brains all over the place and then left him for rat food in a Dumpster."

"She was looking for her keys," my mother told Grandma Mazur. "It was an accident."

"Well that's disappointing," Grandma Mazur said. "I expected something better from her."

When we were done eating, I called Eddie Gazarra, put the second load of laundry in the washer, and hosed down my shoes and my keys. I sprayed the inside of the Jeep with Lysol and opened the windows wide. The alarm wasn't usable with the windows open, but I didn't think I was running much risk of the car being reclaimed from in front of my parents' house. I took a shower and dressed in clean clothes fresh from the dryer.

I was spooked over John Kuzack's death and not anxious to walk into a dark apartment, so I made a point of getting home early. I'd just locked the door behind me when the phone rang. The voice was muffled, so that I had to strain to hear, squinting at the handset as if that would help.

Fear is not a logical emotion. No one can physically hurt me on the phone, but I flinched all the same when I realized it was Ramirez.

I immediately hung up, and when the phone rang again I snapped the plug from the wall jack. I needed an answering machine to monitor my calls, but I couldn't afford to buy one until I made a recovery. First thing in the morning I was going to have to go after Lonnie Dodd.

I awoke to the steady drumming of rain on my fire escape. Wonderful. Just what I needed to complicate my life further. I crawled out of bed and pulled the curtain aside, not pleased at the sight of an all-day soaker. The parking lot had slicked up, reflecting light from mysterious sources. The rest of the world was gunmetal gray, the cloud cover low and unending, the buildings robbed of color behind the rain.

I showered and dressed in jeans and a T-shirt, letting my hair dry on its own. No sense fussing when I was going to get drenched the instant I stepped out of the building. I did the breakfast thing, brushed my teeth, and applied a nice thick line of turquoise eyeliner to offset the gloom. I was wearing my Dumpster shoes in honor of the rain. I looked down and sniffed. Maybe I smelled a hint of boiled ham, but all things considered I didn't think that was so bad.

I did a pocketbook inventory, making sure I had all my goodies—cuffs, bludgeoning baton, flashlight, gun, extra ammo (not much good to me since I'd already forgotten how to load the gun—still, you never knew when you might need something heavy to throw at an escaping felon). I crammed Dodd's file in along with a collapsible umbrella and a package of peanut butter crackers for emergency snacking. I grabbed the ultracool black and purple Gore-Tex jacket I'd purchased when I was of the privileged working class, and I headed for the parking lot.

This was the sort of day to read comic books under a blanket tent and eat the icing from the middle of the Oreos. This was *not* the sort of day to chase down desperados. Unfortunately, I was hard up for money and couldn't be choosy about selecting desperado days.

Lonnie Dodd's address was listed as 2115 Barnes. I hauled my map out and looked up the coordinates. Hamilton Township is about three times the size of Trenton proper and roughly shaped like a wedge of pie that's suffered some nibbles. Barnes ran with its back pressed to the Conrail tracks just north of Yardville, the beginning of the lower third of the county.

I took Chambers to Broad and cut up on Apollo. Barnes struck off from Apollo. The sky had lightened marginally, and it was possible to read house numbers as I drove. The closer I got to 2115 the more depressed I became. Property value was dropping at a frightening rate. What had begun as a respectable blue-collar neighborhood with trim single-family bungalows on good-sized lots had deteriorated to neglected low-income to no-income housing.

Twenty-one fifteen was at the end of the street. The grass was overgrown and had gone to seed. A rusted bike and a washing machine with its top lid askew decorated the front yard. The house itself was a small cinder block rancher built on a slab. It looked to be more of an outbuilding than a home. Something intended for chickens or porkers. A sheet had been tacked haphazardly over the front picture window. Probably to afford the inhabitants privacy while they crushed cans of Bull's-Eye beer against their foreheads and plotted mayhem.

I told myself it was now or never. Rain pattered on the roof and sluiced down the windshield. I pumped myself up by applying fresh lipstick. There was no great surge of power, so I deepened the blue liner and added mascara and blush. I checked myself out in the rearview mirror. Wonder Woman, eat your heart out. Yeah, right. I studied Dodd's picture one last time. Didn't want to overwhelm the wrong man. I dropped my keys into my pocketbook, pulled my hood up, and got out of the car. I knocked on the door and caught myself secretly hoping no one was home. The rain and the neighborhood and the grim little house were giving me the creeps. If the second knock goes unanswered, I thought, I'll consider it the will of God that I'm not destined to catch Dodd, and I'll get the hell out of here.

No one answered on the second knock, but I'd heard a toilet flush, and I knew someone was in there. Damn. I gave the door a few good shots with my fist. "Open up," I yelled at the top of my voice. "Pizza delivery."

A skinny guy with dark, tangled shoulder-length hair answered the door. He was a couple inches taller than me. He was barefoot and shirtless, wearing a pair of filthy, low-slung jeans that were unsnapped and only half zipped. Beyond him I could see a trash-filled living room. The air drifting out was pungent with cat fumes.

"I didn't order no pizza," he said.

"Are you Lonnie Dodd?"

"Yeah. What's with the pizza delivery shit?"

"It was a ploy to get you to answer your door."

"A what?"

"I work for Vincent Plum, your bond agent. You missed your trial date, and Mr. Plum would like you to reschedule."

"Fuck that. I'm not rescheduling nothing."

The rain was running off my jacket in sheets, soaking my jeans and shoes. "It would only take a few minutes. I'd be happy to drive you."

"Plum doesn't have no limo service. Plum only hires two kinds of people . . . women with big pointy tits and scumbag bounty hunters. Nothing personal, and it's hard to see with that raincoat on, but you don't look like you got big pointy tits. That leaves scumbag bounty hunter."

Without warning he reached out into the rain, grabbed my pocketbook off my shoulder, and tossed the contents onto the tan shag carpet behind him. The gun landed with a thunk.

"You could get into a lot of crap carrying concealed in this state," he said.

I narrowed my eyes. "Are you going to cooperate here?"

"What do you think?"

"I think if you're smart you'll get a shirt and some shoes and come downtown with me."

"Guess I'm not that smart."

"Fine. Then just give me my stuff, and I'll be more than happy to leave." Truer words were never spoken.

"I'm not giving you nothing. This here stuff looks like *my* stuff now."

I was debating kicking him in the nuts when he gave me a shove to the chest, knocking me backward off the small cement pad. I came down hard on my ass in the mud.

"Take a hike," he said, "or I'll shoot you with your own fucking gun."

The door slammed shut and the bolt clicked into place. I got up and wiped my hands on my jacket. I couldn't believe I'd just stood there flat-footed and let him take my shoulder bag. What had I been thinking?

I'd been thinking about Clarence Sampson and not about Lonnie Dodd. Lonnie Dodd wasn't a fat drunk. I should have approached him with a much more defensive posture. I should have stood farther back, out of his reach. And I should have had my defense spray in my hand, not in my pocketbook.

I had a lot to learn as a bounty hunter. I lacked skills, but even more problematic, I lacked attitude. Ranger had tried to tell me, but it hadn't taken hold. Never let your guard down, he'd said. When you walk the street, you have to see everything, every second. You let your mind wander, and you could be dead. When you go after your FTA, always be prepared for the worst.

It had seemed overly dramatic at the time. Looking at it in retrospect, it had been good advice.

I stomped back to the Jeep and stood there fuming, swearing at myself and Dodd and E.E. Martin. I threw in a few choice thoughts about Ramirez and Morelli and kicked a tire.

"Now what?" I yelled in the rain. "Now what are you going to do, girl genius?"

Well, I sure as hell wasn't going to leave without Lonnie Dodd shackled and stuffed into my backseat. As I saw it, I needed help, and I had two choices. The police or Ranger. If I called the police I might be in trouble with the gun. It'd have to be Ranger.

I closed my eyes. I really didn't want to call Ranger. I'd wanted to do this myself. I'd wanted to show everyone I was capable.

"Pride goeth before the fall," I said. I wasn't sure exactly what that meant, but it felt right.

I took a deep groaning breath, shucked the muddy, dripping-wet raincoat, slid behind the wheel, and called Ranger.

"Yo," he said.

"I have a problem."

"Are you naked?"

"No, I'm not naked."

"Too bad."

"I have an FTA cornered in his house, but I'm not having any luck making an apprehension."

"You want to be more specific about the not having any luck part."

"He took my pocketbook and kicked me out of the house."

Pause. "I don't suppose you managed to keep your gun."

"Don't suppose I did. On the bright side, the gun wasn't loaded."

"You have ammo in your pocketbook?"

"I might have had a few loose bullets rolling around."

"Where are you now?"

"In front of the house, in the Jeep."

"And you want me to come over there and persuade your FTA to behave."

"Yeah."

"Good thing for you I'm into this Henry Higgins shit. What's the address?"

I gave him the address and hung up feeling disgusted with myself. I'd virtually armed my FTA, and now I was sending Ranger in to clean up the mess I'd made of things. I was going to have to get smarter faster. I was going to learn how to load the damn gun, and I was going to learn how to shoot it. I might not ever have the guts to shoot Joe Morelli, but I was pretty sure I could shoot Lonnie Dodd.

I watched the clock on the dash, waiting for Ranger, anxious to resolve this unfinished business. Ten minutes passed before his Mercedes appeared at the end of the street, gliding through the rain, sleek and sinister, water not daring to adhere to the paint finish.

We simultaneously got out of our cars. He wore a black baseball cap, tight black jeans, and a black T-shirt. He strapped on his black nylon gun belt and holster, the gun held tight to his leg by a black Velcro strap. At first glance he'd pass for a SWAT cop. He shrugged into a Kevlar vest. "What's the FTA's name?"

"Lonnie Dodd."

"You got a photo?"

I ran to the Jeep, pulled out Dodd's picture, and gave it to Ranger.

"What'd he do?" Ranger wanted to know.

"Auto theft. First-time offender."

"He alone?"

"As far as I know. I can't guarantee it."

"This house have a back door?"

"Don't know."

"Let's find out."

We took a direct route to the back, cutting through the tall grass, keeping our eyes on the front door, watching the windows for movement. I hadn't bothered with my jacket. It seemed like an unnecessary encumbrance at this point. My energies were directed at catching Dodd. I was soaked to the skin, and it was liberating to know I couldn't get any wetter. The backyard was similar to the front: tall grass, a rusted swing set, two garbage cans overflowing with garbage, their dented lids lying on the ground nearby. A back door opened to the yard.

Ranger pulled me close to the building, out of window sight. "You stay here and watch the back door. I'm going in the front. I don't want you to be a hero. You see anybody run for the train tracks, you keep out of their way. Got that?"

Water dripped from the tip of my nose. "Sorry to put you through this."

"This is partly my fault. I haven't been taking you serious enough. If you're really going to do this job, you're going to need somebody to help you with the takedown. And we need to spend some time talking about apprehension techniques."

"I need a partner."

"Yeah. You need a partner."

He moved off, rounding the house, his footsteps muffled by the rain. I held my breath, straining to hear, catching his knock on the door, hearing him identify himself.

There was obviously a reply from within, but it was lost to me. What followed after that was a blur of sound and action on fast-forward. Warnings from Ranger that he was coming in, the door crashing open, a lot of shouting. A single report from a gun.

The back door banged open and Lonnie Dodd charged out, heading not for the tracks, but for the next house down. He was still clad only in jeans. He was running blind in the rain, clearly panicked. I was partially hidden by a shed, and he ran right by me without a sideways glance. I could see the silver glint of a gun stuck in his waistband. Wouldn't you know it? On top of every other insult, now the creep was making off with my gun. Four hundred dollars shot to hell, and just when I'd decided to learn how to use the damn thing.

No way was I going to let this happen. I yelled for Ranger and took off after Dodd. Dodd wasn't that far in front of me, and I had the advantage of shoes. He was sliding in the rain-slicked grass, stepping on God-knows-what. He went down to one knee, and I body-slammed into the back of him, knocking us both to the ground. He hit with an "unh!" thanks to 125 pounds of angry female landing on top of him. Well okay, maybe 127, but not an ounce more, I swear.

He was laboring to breathe, and I grabbed the gun, not from any defensive instinct, but out of shear possessiveness. It was *my* gun, dammit. I scrambled to my feet and pointed the .38 in Dodd's direction, holding it with both hands to minimize the shaking. It never occurred to me to check for bullets. "Don't move!" I yelled. "Don't fucking move or I'll shoot."

Ranger appeared in my peripheral vision. He put his knee to the small of Dodd's back, snapped cuffs on him, and jerked him to his feet.

"The sonofabitch shot me," Ranger said. "Do you believe this shit? A lousy car thief shot me." He shoved Dodd ahead of him toward the road. "I'm wearing a fucking Kevlar vest. You think he could shoot me in the vest? No way. He's such a lousy shot, he's so chicken-shit scared, he shoots me in my fucking leg."

I looked down at Ranger's leg and almost keeled over.

"Run ahead and call the police," Ranger said. "And call Al at the body shop to come get my car."

"You sure you're going to be okay?"

"Flesh wound, babe. Nothing to worry about."

I made the calls, retrieved my pocketbook and assorted goods from Dodd's house, and waited with Ranger. We had Dodd trussed up like a Christmas goose, facedown in the mud. Ranger and I sat on the curb in the rain. He didn't seem concerned about the seriousness of his wound. He said he'd had worse, but I could see the pain wearing him down, pinching his face.

I wrapped my arms tight around myself and clamped my teeth together to keep them from chattering. Outwardly, I was keeping a stiff upper lip, trying to be as stoic as Ranger, trying to be confidently supportive. Inside, I was shaking so bad I could feel my heart shivering in my chest.

CHAPTER 9

The cops came first, then the paramedics, then Al. We gave preliminary statements, Ranger was trundled off to the hospital, and I followed the squad car to the station.

It was close to five by the time I reached Vinnie's office. I asked Connie to write out separate checks. Fifty dollars to me. The remainder to Ranger. I wouldn't have taken any money at all, but I really needed to screen my calls, and this was the only way I could buy an answering machine.

I dearly wanted to go home, take a shower, change into clean, dry clothes, and have a decent meal. I knew once I got settled in, I wasn't going to want to go out again, so I detoured to Kuntz Appliances before heading back to my apartment.

Bernie was using a small roller device to paste price stickers onto a carton of alarm clocks. He looked up when I walked in the door.

"I need an answering machine," I told him. "Something under fifty dollars."

My shirt and my jeans were relatively dry by now, but my shoes still leaked water when I walked. Everywhere I stood, amoeba-like puddles formed around me.

Bernie politely pretended not to notice. He shifted into salesman mode and showed me two models of answering machines, both in my price range. I asked which he recommended and followed his advice.

"MasterCard?" he asked.

"I just got a fifty-dollar check from Vinnie. Can I sign it over to you?"

"Sure," he said. "That'd be okay."

From where I was standing I could look out the front window, across the street, into Sal's Meat Market. There wasn't much to see—a shadowy display window with the name lettered in black and gold and the single glass door with the red and white OPEN sign affixed by a small suction cup halfway up. I imagined Bernie spending hours peering out his window, numbly staring at Sal's door.

"You said Ziggy Kulesza shopped at Sal's?"

"Yeah. Of course, there's all kinds of shopping you can do at Sal's."

"So I hear. What kind of shopping do you think Ziggy was doing?"

"Hard to say, but I didn't notice him coming out with bags of pork chops."

I tucked my answering machine under my shirt and ran to my car. I took a last wondering look at Sal's, and I pulled away.

Traffic was slow in the rain, and I found myself mesmerized by the beat and the swish of the wiper and the smear of red brake lights appearing in front of me. I was driving on autopilot, reviewing the day, worrying about Ranger. It's one thing to see someone shot on television. It's quite another to see the destruction firsthand. Ranger kept saying it wasn't a bad wound, but it was bad enough for me. I owned a gun, and I was going to learn how to use it correctly, but I'd lost some of my earlier enthusiasm for pumping lead into a body.

I turned into my lot and found a spot close to the building. I set the alarm and dragged myself out of the car and up the stairs. I left my shoes in the foyer and put the answering machine and my pocketbook on the kitchen counter. I cracked open a beer and called the hospital to check on Ranger. I was told he'd been treated and released. That was good news.

I stuffed myself full of Ritz crackers and peanut butter, washed them down with a second beer, and staggered into my bedroom. I peeled my damp clothes away, half expecting to see that I'd started to mildew. I didn't check everywhere, but the body parts I saw looked mold-free. Hot dog. What luck. I dropped a T-shirt–type nightgown over my head, hiked up a clean pair of undies, and crashed into bed.

I woke with my heart racing and not knowing why. The cobwebs parted, and I realized the phone was ringing. I fumbled for the receiver and stared stupidly at the bedside clock. Two o'clock. Someone must have died, I thought. My Grandma Mazur or my Aunt Sophie. Or maybe my father passed a kidney stone.

I answered breathless, expecting the worst. "Hello."

There was silence on the other end. I heard labored breathing, scuffling noises, and then someone moaned. A woman's voice carried from a distance. "No," she begged. "Oh God, no." A terrible scream split the air, jolting the phone from my ear, and I broke out in a cold sweat as I realized what I was hearing. I slammed the receiver down and switched on my bedside light.

I got out of bed on shaky legs and stumbled to the kitchen. I hooked up the answering machine and set it to answer on one ring. My recording said to leave a message. That was it. I didn't give my name. I went to the bathroom and brushed my teeth and returned to bed.

The phone rang, and I heard the machine snap on. I sat up and listened. The caller crooned to me, half song, half whisper. "Stephanie," he chanted. "Stephanie."

My hand instinctively went to my mouth. It was a reflex action designed to control a scream in primal man, but the scream had been bred out of me. What was left was a quick intake of air. Part gasp, part sob.

"You shouldn't have hung up, bitch," he said. "You missed the best part. You gotta know what the champ can do, so you can look forward to it."

I ran to the kitchen, but before I could disconnect the machine, the woman came on the line. She sounded young. Her words were barely audible, thick with tears and trembling with the effort of speech. "It was g-g-good," she said. Her voice broke. "Oh God help me, I'm hurt. I'm hurt something awful."

The connection was severed, and I immediately called the police. I explained the tape and told them it was originating with Ramirez. I gave them Ramirez's home address. I gave them my number if they wanted to institute a call trace. I hung up and padded around the apartment, triple-checking locked doors and windows, thankful that I'd had the dead bolt installed.

The phone rang, and the machine answered. No one came on the line, but I could feel the vibrations of evil and insanity pulsing in the silence. He was out there, listening, savoring the contact, trying to get a bead on my fear. Far off, almost too faint to discern, I heard a woman softly crying. I ripped the phone plug out of the wall jack, splintering the little plastic clip, and then I threw up in the sink. Thank God for garbage disposals.

I awoke at daybreak, relieved to have the night behind me. The rain had stopped. It was too early for bird chatter. There were no cars traveling St. James. It was as if the world was holding its breath, waiting for the sun to burst upon the horizon.

The phone call replayed in my mind. I didn't need the recorder to remember the message. The good, sensible Stephanie wanted to file for a restraining order. Stephanie the neophyte bounty hunter was still worried about credibility and respect. I could hardly go running to the police every time I was threatened and then expect them to accept me as an equal. I was on record for requesting help for the abused woman on my tape. I thought about it for a while, and I decided to leave it at that for now.

Later in the day I'd give Jimmy Alpha a call.

I'd intended to ask Ranger to take me to the firing range, but since he was recovering from the gunshot wound I would have to lay the burden on Eddie Gazarra. I glanced at the clock again. Gazarra should be at work. I dialed the station and left a message for a call back.

I dressed in T-shirt and shorts and laced up my running shoes. Running isn't one of my favorite activities, but it was time to get serious about the job, and keeping in shape seemed like part of it.

"Go for it," I said by way of a pep talk.

I trotted down the hall, the stairs, through the front door. I heaved a large sigh of resignation and pushed off on my three-mile route, mapped out with great care to avoid hills and bakeries.

I slogged through the first mile, and then it got really bad. I'm not one of those people who find their stride. My body was not designed to run. My body was designed to sit in an expensive car and drive. I was sweating and breathing hard when I turned the corner and saw my building half a block away. So near and yet so far. I sprinted the last piece as best I could. I came to a ragged stop at the door and bent at the waist, waiting for my vision to clear, feeling so fucking healthy I could hardly stand myself.

Eddie Gazarra pulled up to the curb in a patrol car. "I got your message," he said. "Jesus, you look like shit."

"I've been running."

"Maybe you should check with a doctor."

"It's my fair skin. It flushes easily. Did you hear about Ranger?"

"Only every detail. You're a real hot topic. I even know what you were wearing when you came in with Dodd. I take it your T-shirt was real wet. I mean *real* wet."

"When you first started out as a cop, were you afraid of your gun?"

"I've been around guns most of my life. I had an air rifle when I was a kid, and I used to go hunting with my dad and my Uncle Walt. I guess guns were always just another piece of hardware to me."

"If I decide to keep working for Vinnie, you think it's necessary for me to carry a gun?"

"It depends what kind of cases you take. If you're just doing skip tracing, no. If you're going after crazies, yes. Do you have a gun?"

"Smith and Wesson .38. Ranger gave me about ten minutes of instruction on it, but I don't feel comfortable. Would you be willing to baby-sit me while I do some target practice?"

"You're serious about this, aren't you?"

"There's no other way to be."

He nodded. "I heard about your phone call last night."

"Anything come of it?"

"Dispatch sent someone out, but by the time they got there Ramirez was alone. Said he didn't call you. Nothing came in from the woman, but you can register a harassment charge."

"I'll think about it."

I waved him off and huffed and puffed my way up the stairs. I let myself into my apartment, dug out an auxiliary phone cord, put a new tape in the answering machine, and took a shower. It was Sunday. Vinnie had given me a week, and the week was up. I didn't care. Vinnie could give the file to someone else, but he couldn't stop me from dogging Morelli. If someone else bagged him before I did, that was the breaks, but until that happened I intended to keep at it.

Gazarra had agreed to meet me at the pistol range behind Sunny's Gun Shop when he got off work at four o'clock. That left me with a whole day of snooping. I started out by driving past Morelli's mother's house, his cousin's house, and various other relatives' houses. I circled the parking lot to his apartment, noting that the Nova was still where

I'd left it. I cruised up and down Stark Street and Polk. I didn't see the van or anything else that might indicate Morelli's presence.

I drove by the front of Carmen's building, and then I went around back. The service road cutting the block was narrow and badly maintained, pocked with holes. There was no tenant parking back here. The single rear door opened onto the service road. Across the way, asphalt-shingled row houses also butted up to the road.

I parked as close to the apartment building as possible, leaving barely enough room for a car to squeeze by me. I got out and looked up, trying to place Carmen's second-floor apartment, surprised to see two boarded and fire-blackened windows. The windows belonged to the Santiago apartment.

The street-level back door was propped open, and the acrid odor of smoke and charred wood hung in the air. I heard the sweep of a broom and realized someone was working in the narrow corridor that led to the front foyer.

A trickle of sooty water tumbled over the sill, and a dark-skinned, mustached man looked out at me. He cut his eyes to my car, and jerked his head in the direction of the road. "No parking here."

I gave him my card. "I'm looking for Joe Morelli. He's in violation of his bond agreement."

"Last I saw him he was flat on his back, out cold."

"Did you see him get hit?"

"No. I didn't get there until after the police. My apartment's in the cellar. Sound doesn't carry good."

I looked up at the damaged windows. "What happened?"

"Fire in the Santiago apartment. Happened on Friday. I guess if you wanted to be picky you'd say it happened Saturday. Was about two in the morning. Thank God no one was home. Mrs. Santiago was at her daughter's. She was baby-sitting. Usually the kids come here, but on Friday she went to their place."

"Anybody know how it started?"

"Could have started a million ways. Not everything's up to code in a building like this. Not that this building's so bad compared to some others, but it's not new, you know what I mean?"

I shaded my eyes and took one last look and wondered how hard it'd be to lob a firebomb through Mrs. Santiago's bedroom window. Probably not hard, I decided. And, at two in the morning, in an apartment this size, a fire started in a bedroom would be a bitch. If Santiago had been home, she'd have been toast. There were no balconies and no fire escapes. All of these apartments had only one way out—through the front door. Although it didn't seem as though Carmen and the missing witness had left through the front door.

I turned and stared into the dark windows of the row houses across the way and decided it wouldn't hurt to question the residents. I got back into the Cherokee and drove around the block, finding a parking place one street over. I rapped on doors and asked questions and showed pictures. The responses were all similar. No, they didn't recognize Morelli's picture, and no, they hadn't seen anything unusual from their back windows on the night of the murder or the fire.

I tried the row house directly across from Carmen's apartment and found myself face-to-face with a stooped old man wielding a baseball bat. He was beady-eyed and hooked-nosed and had ears that probably kept him indoors when the wind was blowing.

"Batting practice?" I asked.

"Can't be too careful," he said.

I identified myself and asked if he'd seen Morelli.

"Nope. Never seen him. And I got better things to do than to look out my damn windows. Couldn't've seen anything anyway on the night of the murder. It was dark. How the hell was I supposed to see anything?"

"There are streetlights back there," I said. "It looks to me like it would be pretty well lit."

"The lights were out that night. I told this to the cops that come around. The damn lights are always out. Kids shoot them out. I know they were out because I looked to see what all the noise was about. I could hardly hear my TV what with all the noise from the cop cars and the trucks.

"The first time I looked out it was because of the motor running on one of them refrigerator trucks . . . like from a food store. Damn thing was parked right behind my house. I tell you the neighborhood's going to hell. People got no consideration. They park trucks and delivery cars here in the alley all the time while they do personal visits. Shouldn't be allowed."

I nodded in vague affirmation, thinking it was a good thing I owned a gun because if I ever got this crotchety I'd want to kill myself.

He took my nod as encouragement and kept going. "Then the next truck to come along was a police wagon about the same size as the refrigerator truck, and they left their motor running too. These guys must have gas to burn."

"So then you didn't really see anything suspicious?"

"Was too damn dark, I'm telling you. King Kong could have been climbing up that wall and nobody would've seen."

I thanked him for his help and walked back to the Jeep. It was close to noon, and the air was crackling hot. I drove to my Cousin Roonie's bar, snagged an ice-cold six-pack, and headed for Stark Street.

Lula and Jackie were hawking wares on the corner, just like always. They were sweating and swaying in the heat, yelling out intimate pet names and graphic suggestions to potential customers. I parked close by, set the six-pack on the hood, and popped one open.

Lula eyed the beer. "You tryin' to lure us away from our corner, girl?"

I grinned. I sort of liked them. "Thought you might be thirsty."

"Sheeit. Thirsty ain't the half of it." Lula sauntered over, took a beer, and chugged some. "Don't know why I'm wasting my time standing out. Nobody want to fuck in this weather."

Jackie followed. "You shouldn't be doing that," she warned Lula. "Your old man gonna get mad."

"Hunh," Lula said. "I suppose I care. Dumbass prick pimp. Don't see *him* standing out here in the sun, do you?"

"So what's the word on Morelli?" I asked. "Anything happening?"

"Haven't seen him," Lula said. "Haven't seen the van neither."

"You hear anything about Carmen?"

"Like what?"

"Like is she around somewhere?"

Lula was wearing a halter top with a lot of boob hanging out. She rolled the cold can of beer across her chest. I figured it was wasted effort. She'd need a keg to cool off a chest that size.

"Don't hear nothing about Carmen."

An ugly thought flashed through my mind. "Carmen ever spend time with Ramirez?"

"Sooner or later everybody spend time with Ramirez."

"You ever spend time with him?"

"Not me. He like to do his magic on skinny pussy."

"Suppose he wanted to do his magic on you? Would you go with him?"

"Honey, nobody refuses Ramirez nothing."

"I hear he abuses women."

"Lots of men abuse women," Jackie said. "Sometimes men get in a mood."

"Sometimes they're sick," I said. "Sometimes they're freaks. I hear Ramirez is a freak."

Lula looked down the street to the gym, her eyes locked on the second-story windows. "Yeah," she said softly. "He's a freak. He scares me. I had a friend go with Ramirez, and he cut her bad."

"Cut her? With a knife?"

"No," she said. "With a beer bottle. Broke the neck and then used it to . . . you know, do the deed."

I felt my head go light, and time stood still for a moment. "How do you know it was Ramirez?"

"People know."

"People don't know nothing," Jackie said. "People shouldn't be talking. Somebody gonna hear, and you be in for it. Be all your own fault, too, 'cause you know better'n to go shootin' your mouth. I'm not staying here and being party to this. Nuh unh. Not me. I'm going back to my corner. You know what's good for you, you'll come too."

"I know what's good for me I wouldn't be standing out here at all, would I?" Lula said, moving off.

"Be careful," I called after her.

"Big woman like me don't gotta be careful," she said. "I just stomp on them weird-ass motherfuckers. Nobody mess with Lula."

I stashed the rest of the beer in the car, slid behind the wheel, and locked the doors. I started the engine and turned the air on full blast, positioning all the vents so the cold hit me in the face. "Come on, Stephanie," I said. "Get a grip." But I couldn't get a grip. My heart was racing, and my throat was closed tight with grief for a woman I didn't even know, a woman who must have suffered terribly. I wanted to get as far away from Stark Street as was humanly possible and never come back. I didn't want to know about these things, didn't want the terror of it creeping into my consciousness at unguarded moments. I hung onto the wheel and looked down the street at the second-floor gym and was rocked with rage and horror that Ramirez hadn't been punished, and that he was free to mutilate and terrorize other women.

I lunged out of the car, slammed the door closed, and stalked across the street to Alpha's office building, taking the stairs two at a time. I barreled past his secretary and threw the door to Alpha's inner office open with enough force to make it crash against the wall.

Alpha jumped in his chair.

I leaned palms down on his desktop and got right in his face. "I got a phone call last night from your fighter. He was brutalizing some young woman, and he was trying to terrorize me with her suffering. I know all about his previous rape charges, and I know about his fondness for sexual mutilation. I don't know how he's managed to escape prosecution this far, but I'm here to tell you his luck has run out. Either you stop him, or else I'll stop him. I'll go to the police. I'll go to the press. I'll go to the fight commissioner."

"Don't do that. I'll take care of it. I swear, I'll take care of it. I'll get him into counseling."

"Today!"

"Yeah. Today. I promise, I'll get him some help."

I didn't believe it for a second, but I'd said my piece, so I left in the same whirlwind of bad temper that I'd entered. I forced myself to breathe deep on the stairs and cross the street with a calmness I didn't feel. I pulled out of the parking space and very slowly, very carefully drove away.

It was still early in the day, but I'd lost my energy for the hunt. My car headed home of its own volition, and next thing I knew I was in my parking lot. I locked up, climbed the stairs to my apartment, flopped down on the bed, and assumed my thinking position.

I woke up at three and felt better. While I was sleeping, my mind had obviously been hard at work finding secluded repositories for my latest collection of depressing thoughts. They were still with me, but they were no longer forcefully pressing against my forehead.

I made myself a peanut butter and jelly sandwich, gave a bite of it to Rex, and scarfed the rest down while I accessed Morelli's messages.

A photo studio had called with an offer of a free eight-by-ten if Morelli came in for a sitting. Someone wanted to sell him lightbulbs, and Carlene called with an indecent suggestion, did some heavy panting, and either had a hell of an orgasm or else stepped on her cat's tail. Unfortunately, she also ran the tape out, so there were no more messages. It was just as well. I couldn't have managed listening to much more.

I was straightening the kitchen when the phone rang and the machine picked it up.

"Are you listening, Stephanie? Are you home? I saw you talking to Lula and Jackie today. Saw you drinking beer with them. I didn't like that, Stephanie. Made me feel bad. Made me feel like you liked them better than me. Made me angry because you don't want what the champ want to give you.

"Maybe I'll give you a present, Stephanie. Maybe I'll deliver it to your door when you're sleeping. Would you like that? All women like presents. 'Specially the kind of presents the champ gives. Gonna be a surprise, Stephanie. Gonna be just for you."

With that promise ringing in my ears I made sure my gun and my bullets were in my pocketbook, and I took off for Sunny's. I got there at four and waited in the lot until Eddie showed up at four-fifteen.

He was out of uniform, and he had his off-duty .38 clipped to his waist.

"Where's your gun?" he asked.

I patted my pocketbook.

"That's considered carrying concealed. It's a serious offense in New Jersey."

"I have a permit."

"Let me see it."

I pulled the permit out of my wallet.

"This is a permit to own, not to carry," Eddie said.

"Ranger told me it was multipurpose."

"Ranger gonna come visit you when you're making license plates?"

"Sometimes I think he stretches the limits of the law a trifle. Are you going to arrest me?"

"No, but it's going to cost you."

"Dozen donuts?"

"Dozen donuts is what it takes to fix a parking ticket. This is worth a six-pack and a pizza."

It was necessary to go through the gun shop to get to the rifle range. Eddie paid the range fee and bought a box of shells. I did the same. The range was directly behind the gun shop and consisted of a room the size of a small bowling alley. Seven booths were partitioned off, each booth with a chest-high shelf. Beyond the booths was known as downrange. Standard targets of ungendered humans cut off at the knees, with bull's-eye rings radiating out from the heart, were hung on pulleys. Range etiquette was never to point the gun at the guy standing next to you.

"Okay," Gazarra said, "let's start at the beginning. You have a Smith and Wesson .38 Special. It's a 5-shot revolver, which puts it into the category of small gun. You're using hydroshock bullets to cause maximum pain and suffering. This little doohickey here gets pushed forward with your thumb, the cylinder releases, and you can load your gun. A bullet is a round. Load a round in each chamber and click the cylinder closed. Never leave your trigger finger resting on the trigger. It's a natural reflex to squeeze when surprised, and you could end up blowing a hole in your foot. Stretch your trigger finger straight toward the barrel until you're ready to shoot. We're going to use the most basic stance today. Feet shoulder-width apart, weight on the balls of your feet, hold the gun in both hands, left thumb over right thumb, arms straight. Look at the target, bring the gun up and sight. The front sight is a post. The rear sight is a notch. Line the sights up on the desired spot on the target and fire.

"This revolver is double action. You can fire by pulling the trigger or by cocking the hammer and then pulling the trigger." He'd been demonstrating while he talked, doing everything but fire the gun. He released the cylinder, spilled the bullets out onto the shelf, laid the gun on the shelf, and stepped back. "Any questions?"

"No. Not yet."

He handed me a pair of ear protectors. "Go for it."

My first shot was single action, and I hit the bull's-eye. I shot several more rounds single action, and then switched over to double action. This was more difficult to control, but I did pretty well.

After a half hour, I'd used up all my ammo, and I was shooting erratically from muscle fatigue. Usually when I go to the gym I spend most of my time working abdominals and legs because that's where my fat goes. If I was going to be any good at shooting, I was going to have to get more upper body strength.

Eddie pulled my target in. "Damn fair shooting, Tex."

"I'm better at single action."

"That's 'cause you're a girl."

"You don't want to say stuff like that when I've got a gun in my hand."

I bought a box of shells before I left. I dropped the shells into my pocketbook along with my gun. I was driving a stolen car. Worrying about carrying concealed at this point seemed like overkill.

"So do I get my pizza now?" Eddie wanted to know.

"What about Shirley?"

"Shirley's at a baby shower."

"The kids?"

"Mother-in-law."

"What about your diet?"

"You trying to get out of buying this pizza?"

"I've only got twelve dollars and thirty-three cents distinguishing me from the bag lady at the train station."

"Okay, I'll buy the pizza."

"Good. I need to talk. I have problems."

Ten minutes later, we met at Pino's Pizzeria. There were several Italian restaurants in the burg, but Pino's was the place to get pizza. I was told at night cockroaches as big as barn cats came out to raid the kitchen, but the pizza was first rate—crust that was crisp and puffy, homemade sauce, and enough grease from the pepperoni to run down your arm and drip off your elbow. There was a bar and a family room. Late at night the bar was filled with off-duty cops trying to wind down before they went home. At this time of the day the bar was filled with men waiting for take-out.

We got a table in the family room and asked for a pitcher while we waited for the pizza. There was a shaker of crushed hot pepper in the middle of the table, and another shaker of Parmesan. The tablecloth was red-and-white-checked plastic. The walls were paneled and lacquered to a shiny gloss and decorated with framed photos of famous Italians and a few non-Italian locals. Frank Sinatra and Benito Ramirez were the dominant celebs.

"So what's the problem?" Eddie wanted to know.

"Two problems. Number one. Joe Morelli. I've run into him four times since I've taken on this assignment, and I've never once come close to making an apprehension."

"Are you afraid of him?"

"No. But I am afraid to use my gun."

"Then do it the ladies' way. Spray him and cuff him."

Easier said than done, I thought. It's hard to spray a man when he has his tongue down your throat. "That was my plan, too, but he always moves faster than I do."

"You want my advice? Forget Morelli. You're a beginner, and he's a pro. He has years of experience behind him. He was a smart cop, and he's probably even better at being a felon."

"Forgetting Morelli isn't an option. I'd like you to run a couple car checks for me." I wrote the van's license number on a napkin and gave it to him. "See if you can find out who owns this. I'd also like to know if Carmen Sanchez owns a car. And if she does own a car, has it been impounded?"

I drank some beer and slouched back, enjoying the cold air and the buzz of conversation around me. Every table was filled now, and there was a knot of people waiting at the door. No one wanted to cook when it got this hot.

"So what's the second problem?" Eddie asked.

"If I tell you, you have to promise not to get overwrought."

"Christ, you're pregnant."

I stared at him, nonplussed. "Why would you think that?"

His expression was sheepish. "I don't know. It just popped out. It's what Shirley always says to me."

Gazarra had four kids. The oldest was nine. The youngest was a year. They were all boys, and they were all monsters.

"Well, I'm not pregnant. It's Ramirez." I gave him the full story on Ramirez.

"You should have filed a report on him," Gazarra said. "Why didn't you call the police when you got roughed up in the gym?"

"Would Ranger have filed a report if he got roughed up?"

"You're not Ranger."

"That's true, but you see my point?"

"Why are you telling me this?"

"I guess if I suddenly disappear, I want you to know where to start looking."

"Jesus. If you think he's that dangerous, you should get a restraining order."

"I don't have a lot of confidence in a restraining order. Besides, what am I going to tell the judge . . . that Ramirez threatened to send me a present? Look around you. What do you see?"

Eddie sighed. "Pictures of Ramirez, side by side with the Pope and Frank Sinatra."

"I'm sure I'll be fine," I said. "I just needed to tell someone."

"If you have any more problems I want you to call me right away."

I nodded.

"When you're home alone, make sure your gun is loaded and accessible. Could you use it on Ramirez if you had to?"

"I don't know. I think so."

"Scheduling got screwed up, and I'm working days again. I want you to meet me at Sunny's every day at four-thirty. I'll buy the ammo and pay the range fee. The only way to feel comfortable with a gun is to use it."

CHAPTER 10

I was home by nine, and for lack of something better to do, I decided to clean my apartment. There were no messages on my machine and no suspicious packages on my doorstep. I gave Rex new bedding, vacuumed the carpet, scrubbed the bathroom, and polished the few pieces of furniture I had left. This brought me up to ten. I checked one last time to make sure everything was locked, took a shower, and went to bed.

I awoke at seven feeling elated. I'd slept like a brick. My machine was still gloriously message free. Birds were warbling, the sun was shining, and I could see my reflection in my toaster. I pulled on shorts and shirt and started coffee brewing. I opened the living room curtains and gasped at the magnificence of the day. The sky was a brilliant blue, the air was still washed clean from the rain, and I had an overwhelming desire to belt out something from *The Sound of Music*. I sang, "The hills are aliiiiive with the sound of muuusic," but then I didn't know any more words.

I twirled myself into my bedroom and threw the curtain open with a flourish. I froze at the sight of Lula tied to my fire escape. She hung there like a big rag doll, her arms crooked over the railing at an unnatural angle, her head slumped forward onto her chest. Her legs were splayed so that she seemed to be sitting. She was naked and blood-smeared, the blood caked in her hair and clotted on her legs. A sheet had been draped behind her to hide her from view of the parking lot.

I shouted her name and clawed at the lock, my heart hammering so hard in my chest that my vision blurred. I heaved the window open and half fell onto the fire escape, reaching out for her, tugging ineffectually at her bindings.

Lula didn't move, didn't utter a sound, and I couldn't collect myself enough to tell if she was breathing. "You're going to be okay," I cried, my voice sounding hoarse, my throat closed tight, my lungs burning. "I'm going to get help." And under my breath I sobbed, "Don't be dead. God Lula, don't be dead."

I floundered back through the window to call for an ambulance, caught my foot on the sill, and crashed to the floor. There was no pain, only panic as I scrambled on hands and knees to the phone. I couldn't remember the emergency number. My mind had shut down in the face of hysteria, leaving me to cope helplessly with the confusion and denial accompanying sudden and unexpected tragedy.

I punched 0 and told the operator Lula was hurt on my fire escape. I had a flashback of Jackie Kennedy crawling over the car seat to get help for her dead husband, and I burst into tears, crying for Lula and Jackie and for myself, all victims of violence.

I clattered through the cutlery drawer, looking for my paring knife, finally finding it in the dish drainer. I had no idea how long Lula had been tied to the railing, but I couldn't bear her hanging there seconds longer.

I ran back with the knife and sawed at the ropes until they were severed, and Lula collapsed into my arms. She was almost twice my size, but somehow I dragged her inert, bloodied body through the window. My instincts were to hide and protect. Stephanie Plum, mother cat. I heard the sirens wailing from far away, getting closer and closer, and then the police were pounding on my door. I don't remember letting them in, but obviously I did. A uniformed cop took me aside, into the kitchen, and sat me down on a chair. A medic followed.

"What happened?" the cop asked.

"I found her on the fire escape," I said. "I opened the curtains and there she was." My teeth were chattering, and my heart was still racing in my chest. I gulped in air. "She was tied to keep her up, and I cut her down and dragged her through the window."

I could hear the medics shouting to bring the stretcher. There was the sound of my bed being shoved aside to make room. I was afraid to ask if Lula was alive. I sucked in more air and clenched my hands in my lap until my knuckles turned white and my nails dug into the fleshy part of my palm.

"Does Lula live here?" the cop wanted to know.

"No. I live here. I don't know where Lula lives. I don't even know her last name."

The phone rang and I automatically reached out to answer.

The caller's voice whispered from the handset. "Did you get my present, Stephanie?"

It was as if the earth suddenly stopped rotating. There was a moment of feeling off balance, and then everything snapped into focus. I pushed the record button on the machine and turned up the volume so everyone could hear.

"What present are you talking about?" I asked.

"You know what present. I saw you find her. Saw you drag her back through the window. I've been watching you. I could have come and got you last night when you were asleep, but I wanted you to see Lula. I wanted you to see what I can do to a woman, so you know what to expect. I want you to think about it, bitch. I want you to think about how it's going to hurt, and how you're going to beg."

"You like to hurt women?" I asked, control beginning to return.

"Sometimes women need to be hurt."

I decided to take a winger. "How about Carmen Sanchez? Did you hurt her?"

"Not as good as I'm going to hurt you. I have special things planned for you."

"No time like the present," I said, and I was shocked to realize that I meant it. There was no bravado in the statement. I was in the grip of cold, hard, sphincter-cramping fury.

"The cops are there now, bitch. I'm not coming when the cops are there. I'm going to get you when you're alone and you're not expecting me. I'm going to make sure we have lots of time together."

The connection was broken.

"Jesus Christ," the uniform said. "He's crazy."

"Do you know who that was?"

"I'm afraid to guess."

I popped the tape out of the machine, and wrote my name and the date on the label. My hand was shaking so badly the writing was barely readable.

A handheld radio crackled from the living room. I could hear the murmur of voices in my bedroom. The voices were less frantic, and the rhythm of activity had become more orderly. I looked at myself and realized I was covered with Lula's blood. It had soaked into my shirt and shorts, and it was coagulating on my hands and the bottoms of my bare feet. The phone was tacky with blood smears, as was the floor and the counter.

The cop and the medic exchanged glances. "Maybe you should get that blood washed off," the medic said. "How about we get you into the shower real fast."

I looked in at Lula on my way to the bathroom. They were getting ready to move her out. She was strapped to the stretcher, covered with a sheet and blanket. She was hooked up to an IV. "How is she?" I asked.

A squad member tugged the stretcher forward. "Alive," he said.

The medics were gone when I got out of the shower. Two uniformed cops had stayed, and the one who'd talked to me in the kitchen was conferring with a PC in the living room, the two of them going over notes. I dressed quickly and left my hair to dry on its own. I was anxious to make my statement and be done with it. I wanted to get to the hospital to see about Lula.

The PC's name was Dorsey. I'd seen him before. Probably at Pino's. He was medium height, medium build, and looked to be in his late forties. He was in shirtsleeves and slacks and penny loafers. I could see my recorder tape tucked into his shirt pocket. Exhibit A. I told him about the incident in the gym, omitting Morelli's name, leaving Dorsey to think the identity of my rescuer was unknown. If the police wanted to believe Morelli'd left town, that was fine with me. I still had hopes of bringing him in and collecting my money.

Dorsey took a lot of notes and looked knowingly at the patrolman. He didn't seem surprised. I suppose if you're a cop long enough, nothing surprises you.

When they left I shut off the coffeemaker, closed and locked the bedroom window, grabbed my pocketbook, and squared my shoulders to what I knew awaited me in the hall. I was going to have to make my way past Mrs. Orbach, Mr. Grossman, Mrs. Feinsmith, Mr. Wolesky, and who knows how many others. They would want to know the details, and I wasn't up to imparting details.

I put my head down, shouted apologies, and went straight for the stairs, knowing that would slow them. I bolted out of the building and ran to the Cherokee.

I took St. James to Olden and cut across Trenton to Stark. It would have been easier to go straight to St. Francis Hospital, but I wanted to get Jackie. I barreled down Stark and passed the gym without a sideways glance. As far as I was concerned, Ramirez was finished. If he slipped through the loopholes of the law on this one, I'd get him myself. I'd cut off his dick with a carving knife if I had to.

Jackie was just coming out of the Corner Bar, where I imagine she'd had breakfast. I screeched to a stop and half hung out the door. "Get in!" I yelled to Jackie.

"What's this about?"

"Lula's in the hospital. Ramirez got to her."

"Oh God," she wailed. "I was so afraid. I knew something was wrong. How bad is it?"

"I honestly don't know. I found her on my fire escape just now. Ramirez had left her tied there as a message to me. She's unconscious."

"I was there when he come for her. She didn't want to go, but you don't say no to Benito Ramirez. Her old man would've beat her bloody."

"Yeah. Well, she's been beaten bloody anyway."

I found a parking place on Hamilton one block from the emergency entrance. I set the alarm, and Jackie and I took off at a trot. She had about two hundred pounds on the hoof, and she wasn't even breathing hard when we pushed through the double glass doors. I guess humping all day keeps you in shape.

"A woman named Lula was just brought in by ambulance," I told the clerk.

The clerk looked at me, and then she looked at Jackie. Jackie was dressed in poison green shorts with half her ass hanging out, matching rubber sandals, and a hot pink tank top. "Are you family?" she asked Jackie.

"Lula don't got any family here."

"We need someone to fill out forms."

"I guess I could do that," she said.

When we were done with the forms, we were told to sit and wait. We did this in silence, aimlessly thumbing through torn magazines, watching with inhuman detachment as one tragedy after another rolled down the hall. After a half hour I asked about Lula and was told she was in X ray. How long would she be in X ray? I asked. The clerk didn't know. It would be a while, but then a doctor would come out to talk to us. I reported this to Jackie.

"Hunh," she said. "I bet."

I was a quart down on caffeine, so I left Jackie to wait and went in search of the cafeteria. I was told to follow the footprints on the floor, and darned if they didn't bring me to food. I loaded a take-out carton with pastries, two large coffees, and added two oranges just in case Jackie and I felt the need to be healthy. I thought it was unlikely, but I figured it was like wearing clean panties in case of a car crash. It never hurt to be prepared.

An hour later, we saw the doctor.

He looked at me, and he looked at Jackie. Jackie hiked up her top and tugged at her shorts. It was a futile gesture.

"Are you family?" he asked Jackie.

"I guess so," Jackie said. "What's the word?"

"The prognosis is guarded but hopeful. She's lost a lot of blood, and she's suffered some head trauma. She has multiple wounds that need suturing. She's being taken to surgery. It will probably be a while before she's brought to her room. You might want to go out and come back in an hour or two."

"I'm not going nowhere," Jackie said.

Two hours dragged by without further information. We'd eaten all the pastries and were forced to eat the oranges.

"Don't like this," Jackie said. "Don't like being cooped up in institutions. Whole fucking place smells like canned green beans."

"Spend much time in institutions, have you?"

"My share."

She didn't seem inclined to elaborate, and I didn't actually want to know anyway. I fidgeted in my chair, looked around the room, and spotted Dorsey talking to the clerk. He was nodding, getting answers to questions. The clerk pointed to Jackie and me, and Dorsey ambled over.

"How's Lula?" he asked. "Any news?"

"She's in surgery."

He settled himself into the seat next to me. "We haven't been able to pick up Ramirez yet. You have any idea where he might be? He say anything interesting before you started recording?"

"He said he was watching me pull Lula through the window. And he knew the police were in my apartment. He must have been close."

"Probably on a car phone."

I agreed.

"Here's my card." He wrote a number on the back. "This is my home phone. You see Ramirez, or you get another call, get in touch right away."

"It'll be hard for him to hide," I said. "He's a local celebrity. He's easy to recognize."

Dorsey returned his pen to an inside jacket pocket, and I got a glimpse of his hip holster. "There are a lot of people in this city who'll go out of their way to hide and protect Benito Ramirez. We've been this route with him before."

"Yes, but you've never had a tape."

"True. The tape might make a difference."

"Won't make no difference," Jackie said when Dorsey left. "Ramirez do what he want. Nobody cares about him beating on a whore."

"We care," I said to Jackie. "We can stop him. We can get Lula to testify against him."

"Hunh," Jackie said. "You don't know much."

It was three before we were allowed to see Lula. She hadn't regained consciousness and was in ICU. Our visit was restricted to ten minutes each. I squeezed her hand and promised her she'd be okay. When my time was up, I told Jackie I had an appointment I needed to keep. She said she was staying until Lula opened her eyes.

I got to Sunny's a half hour before Gazarra. I paid my fee, bought a box of shells, and went back to the range. I shot a few with the hammer pulled back, and then settled in for serious practice. I envisioned Ramirez in front of the target. I aimed for his heart, his balls, his nose.

Gazarra came on the range at four-thirty. He dropped a new box of shells on my loading table and took the booth next to me. By the time I was done with both boxes I was pleasantly relaxed and feeling comfortable with my gun. I loaded five rounds and slid the gun back into my bag. I tapped Gazarra on the shoulder and motioned that I was done.

He holstered his Glock and followed me out. We waited until we were in the parking lot to talk.

"I heard the call come in," he said. "Sorry I couldn't get to you. I was in the middle of something. I saw Dorsey at the station. He said you were cool. Said you switched on the recorder when Ramirez came on the line."

"You should have seen me five minutes before. I couldn't remember 911."

"I don't suppose you'd consider taking a vacation?"

"It's crossed my mind."

"You got your gun in your pocketbook?"

"Hell no, that would be breaking the law."

Gazarra sighed. "Just don't let anyone see it, okay? And call me if you get spooked. You're welcome to stay with Shirley and me for as long as you want."

"I appreciate it."

"I checked on the plate number you gave me. The plates belong to a vehicle seized for a parking violation, impounded, and never retrieved."

"I saw Morelli driving said vehicle."

"He probably borrowed it."

We both smiled at the thought of Morelli driving a vehicle stolen from the impound yard.

"What about Carmen Sanchez? Does she have a car?"

Gazarra dug a piece of paper out of his pocket. "This is the make and her license number. It hasn't been impounded.

"You want me to follow you home? Make sure your apartment's safe?"

"Not necessary. Half the building's population is probably still camped out in my hall."

What I really dreaded was facing the blood. I was going to have to walk into my apartment and face the grisly aftermath of Ramirez's handiwork. Lula's blood would still be on the phone, the walls, the countertops, and the floor. If the sight of that blood triggered a renewed rush of hysteria, I wanted to deal with it alone, in my own way.

I parked in the lot and slipped into the building unnoticed. Good timing, I thought. The halls were clear. Everyone was eating dinner. I had my defense spray in my hand and my gun wedged under my waistband.

I turned the key in the lock and felt my stomach lurch. Just get it over with, I told myself. Barge right in, check under the bed for rapists, pull on some rubber gloves, and clean up the mess.

I took a tentative step into my foyer, and realized someone was in my apartment. Someone was cooking in the kitchen, making cozy cooking sounds, clanking pots and running water. Under the clanking I could hear food sizzling in a frying pan.

"Hello," I called, gun now in hand, barely able to hear myself over the pounding of my heart. "Who's here?"

Morelli sauntered out of the kitchen. "Just me. Put the gun away. We need to talk."

"Jesus! You are so fucking arrogant. Did it ever occur to you I might shoot you with this gun?"

"No. It never occurred to me."

"I've been practicing. I'm a pretty good shot."

He moved behind me, closed and locked the door. "Yeah, I'll bet you're hell on wheels blasting the shit out of those paper men."

"What are you doing in my apartment?"

"I'm cooking dinner." He went back to his sautéing. "Rumor has it you've had a tough day."

My mind was spinning. I'd been wracking my brain, trying to find Morelli, and here he was in my apartment. He even had his back turned to me. I could shoot him in the butt.

"You don't want to shoot an unarmed man," he said, reading my thoughts. "The state of New Jersey frowns on that sort of thing. Take it from someone who knows."

All right, so I wouldn't shoot him. I'd zap him with the Sure Guard. His neurotransmitters wouldn't know what hit them.

Morelli added some fresh sliced mushrooms to the pan and continued to cook, sending heavenly food smells wafting my way. He was stirring red and green peppers, onions, and mushrooms, and my killer instincts were weakening in direct proportion to the amount of saliva pooling in my mouth.

I found myself rationalizing a decision to hold off on the spray, telling myself I needed to hear him out, but the ugly truth was my motives weren't nearly so worthy. I was hungry and depressed, and I was a lot more frightened of Ramirez than I was of Joe Morelli. In fact, I suppose in a bizarre way, I felt safe with Morelli in my apartment.

One crisis at a time, I decided. Have some dinner. Gas him for dessert.

He turned and looked at me. "You want to talk about it?"

"Ramirez almost killed Lula and hung her on my fire escape."

"Ramirez is like a fungus that feeds on fear. You ever see him in the ring? His fans love him because he goes the distance unless the referee calls the fight. He plays with his opponent. Loves to draw blood. Loves to punish. And all the time he's punishing, he's talking to his victim in that soothing voice of his, telling them how much worse it's going to get, telling them he'll only stop when they beg to get knocked out. He's like that with women. Likes to see them squirm in fear and pain. Likes to leave his mark."

I dumped my pocketbook on the counter. "I know. He's very large on mutilation and begging. In fact, you might say he's obsessed with it."

Morelli turned the heat down. "I'm trying to scare you, but I don't think it's working."

"I'm all scared out. I don't have any more scare left in me. Maybe tomorrow." I looked around and realized someone had cleaned up the blood. "Did you scrub the kitchen?"

"The kitchen and the bedroom. You're going to have to have your carpet professionally cleaned."

"Thank you. I wasn't looking forward to seeing more blood today."

"Was it bad?"

"Yeah. Her face is battered almost beyond recognition, and she was bleeding . . . everywhere." My voice broke and hitched in my throat. I looked down at the floor. "Shit."

"I have wine in the refrigerator. Why don't you trade in that gun for a couple glasses?"

"Why are you being nice to me?"

"I need you."

"Oh boy."

"Not that way."

"I wasn't thinking *'that way.'* All I said was oh boy. What are you making?"

"Steak. I put it in when you pulled into the parking lot." He poured the wine and gave me a glass. "You're living a little Spartan here."

"I lost my job and couldn't get another. I sold off my furniture to keep going."

"That's when you decided to work for Vinnie?"

"I didn't have a lot of options."

"So you're after me for the money. It's nothing personal."

"In the beginning it wasn't."

He was moving around my kitchen like he'd lived there all his life, setting plates on the counter, pulling a bowl of salad from the refrigerator. It should have seemed invasive and pushy, but it was actually very comfortable.

He flipped a rib steak onto each plate, covered them with the peppers and onions, and added a foil-wrapped baked potato. He set out salad dressing, sour cream, and steak sauce, shut the broiler off, and wiped his hands on a kitchen towel. "Why is it personal now?"

"You chained me to the shower rod! Then you made me go rooting around in a Dumpster to get my keys! Every time I catch up to you, you do everything possible to humiliate me."

"They weren't your keys. They were *my* keys." He took a sip of wine, and our eyes locked. "You stole my car."

"I had a plan."

"You were going to snag me when I came after my car?"

"Something like that."

He carried his plate to the table. "I hear Macy's has openings for makeover ladies."

"You sound like my mother."

Morelli grinned and dug into his steak.

The day had been exhausting, and the wine and good food were mellowing me out. We were eating at the table, sitting across from each other, absorbed in the meal like an old married couple. I cleaned my plate and pushed back in my chair. "What do you need from me?"

"Cooperation. And in return for that cooperation, I'll see to it that you collect your bounty money."

"You've got my attention."

"Carmen Sanchez was an informant. One night I'm sitting home watching television, and I get a call from her asking for help. She says she's been raped and beaten. She says she needs money, and she needs a safe place to stay, and in return she's going to give me something big.

"When I get to her apartment Ziggy Kulesza answers the door, and Carmen is nowhere in sight. Another guy, better known as the missing witness, comes out of the bedroom, recognizes me from who-knows-where, and panics. 'This guy's a cop,' he yells to Ziggy. 'I can't believe you opened the door to a goddamn cop.'

"Ziggy draws a gun on me. I return fire and shoot him almost point-blank. Next thing I know, I'm staring at the ceiling. The second guy is gone. Carmen's gone. Ziggy's gun is gone."

"How could he have missed you at such close range? And if he missed you, where'd the bullet go?"

"The only explanation I can come up with is that the gun misfired."

"And now you want to find Carmen so Carmen can back up your story."

"I don't think Carmen's going to be backing up anyone's story. My guess is she was beaten up by Ramirez, and Ziggy and his pal were sent to finish the job. Ziggy did all Ramirez's dirty work.

"When you're out on the street like I am, you hear things. Ramirez likes to punish women. Sometimes women last seen in his company are known to disappear. I think he gets carried away and kills them, or maybe he hurts them so bad he has to send someone to finish the job to keep things quiet. Then the body vanishes. No body. No crime. I think Carmen was dead in the bedroom when I arrived. That's why Ziggy freaked."

"There's only one door," I said, "and no one saw her leave . . . dead or alive."

"There's a window in the bedroom that overlooks the service road."

"You think Carmen was pitched out the window?"

Morelli took his plate into the kitchen and started coffee brewing. "I'm looking for the guy who recognized me. Ziggy dropped the gun when he hit the floor. I saw it skitter to the side. When I got hit from behind, Ziggy's partner must have taken the gun, slipped off into the bedroom, dumped Carmen out the window, and followed her."

"I've been back there. It's a long drop if you're not dead."

Morelli shrugged. "Maybe he was able to slide through the crowd hovering over Ziggy and me. Then he went out the back door, collected Carmen, and drove off."

"I want to hear the part about me getting the $10,000."

"You help me prove I shot Kulesza in self-defense, and I'll let you bring me in."

"I can hardly wait to hear how I'm going to do this."

"The only link I have to the missing witness is Ramirez. I've been watching him, but nothing's come of it. Unfortunately, my movements are getting restricted. I've called in just about every favor I had out there. Lately, I've been spending more hours hiding than looking. I feel like I'm running out of time and ideas.

"You're the one person no one would suspect of helping me," Morelli said.

"Why would I want to help you? Why don't I just use the opportunity to turn you in?"

"Because I'm innocent."

"That's your problem, not mine." It was a hardass answer and not entirely the truth. The truth was, I'd actually started to feel kind of soft on Morelli.

"Then let's up the ante for you. While you're helping me find my witness, I'll be protecting you from Ramirez."

I almost said I didn't need protection, but that was absurd. I needed all the protection I could get. "What happens when Dorsey picks up Ramirez and I no longer need your protection?"

"Ramirez will be out on bail and twice as hungry. He has some powerful friends."

"And how are you going to protect me?"

"I'm going to guard your body, Sweet Cakes."

"You're not sleeping in my apartment."

"I'll sleep in the van. Tomorrow I'll wire you up for sound."

"What about tonight?"

"It's your decision," he said. "Probably you'll be okay. My guess is Ramirez wants to play with you awhile. This is like a fight for him. He's going to want to go all ten rounds."

I agreed. Ramirez could have come crashing through my bedroom window any time he wanted, but he chose to wait.

"Even if I wanted to help you, I wouldn't know where to begin," I said. "What could I do that you haven't already done? Maybe the witness is in Argentina."

"The witness isn't in Argentina. He's out there killing people. He's killing everyone who can place him at the scene. He's killed two people from Carmen's apartment building and failed in his attempt to murder a third. I'm also on his list, but he can't find me while I'm in hiding, and if I go public to draw him out, the police will get me."

The lightbulb went on. "You're going to use me as bait. You're going to dangle me in front of Ramirez and expect me to extract information from him while he's coaching me on his torture techniques. Jesus, Morelli, I know you're pissed because I scored you with the Buick, but don't you think this is carrying revenge too far?"

"It's not revenge. The truth is . . . I like you." His mouth softened into a seductive smile. "If circumstances were different, I might even try to right some past wrongs."

"Oh boy."

"I can see when this is all over, we're going to have to do something about that streak of cynicism you've acquired."

"You're asking me to put my life on the line to help save your ass."

"Your life is already on the line. You're being stalked by a very large man who rapes and mutilates women. If we can find my witness, we can link him to Ramirez and hopefully put them both away for the rest of their unnatural lives."

He had a point.

"I'll put a bug in your foyer and bedroom," Morelli said, "and I'll be able to hear throughout your apartment, with the exception of the bathroom. If you close the bathroom door, I probably won't be able to hear. When you go out we'll hide a wire under your shirt, and I'll follow at a distance."

I took a deep breath. "And you'll let me collect the finder's fee on you when we get the missing witness?"

"Absolutely."

"You said Carmen was an informant. What sort of stuff was she informing about?"

"She sold whatever scraps came her way. Mostly low-level drug stuff and names of posse members. I don't know what she had for me when she called. I never got it."

"Posse members?"

"Jamaican gang members. Striker is the parent posse, based in Philly. It's got its finger in every drug deal in Trenton. Striker makes the mob look like a bunch of pussies. They're bringing in shit faster than they can sell it, and we can't figure out how they get it here. We had twelve deaths from heroin overdose this summer. The stuff is so available the dealers aren't bothering to cut it down to the standard."

"You think Carmen had information on Striker?"

Morelli stared at me for a few beats. "No," he finally said. "I think she had something to tell me about Ramirez. She probably picked something up while she was with him."

CHAPTER 11

My phone rang at seven A.M. The machine got it, and I recognized Morelli's voice. "Rise and shine, Badass," he said. "I'll be at your door in ten minutes to install equipment. Put the coffeepot on."

I started the coffee, brushed my teeth, and pulled on running shorts and a shirt. Morelli arrived five minutes early, carrying a toolbox. His short-sleeved shirt had an official-looking patch on the pocket that suggested he worked for Long's Service.

"What's Long's Service?" I asked.

"It's anything you want it to be."

"Ah hah," I said. "A disguise."

He tossed his shades onto my kitchen counter and headed for the coffee. "People don't notice repairmen. They remember the color of the uniform and that's it. And if you do it right, a uniform'll get you into almost any building."

I poured myself coffee and dialed the hospital for a progress report on Lula. I was told she was in stable condition and had been moved out of ICU.

"You need to talk to her," Morelli said. "Make sure she presses charges. They picked Ramirez up last night and questioned him for aggravated sexual assault. He's out already. Released on his own recognizance."

He put his coffee down, opened the toolbox, and took out a small screwdriver and two plates for covering electrical outlets. "These look like ordinary wall plugs," he said, "but they have listening devices built in. I like to use them because they don't require battery replacement. They run off your wires. They're very dependable."

He took the plate off my hall outlet and clamped off wires, working with rubber-tipped pliers. "I have the ability to listen and record from the van. If Ramirez breaks in, or if he shows up at your door, you're going to have to go with your instincts. If you think you can engage him in conversation and pull information out of him without endangering yourself, you should give it a shot."

He finished up in the foyer and moved on to the bedroom, repeating the procedure. "Two things you need to remember. If you play the radio, I can't hear what's going on up here. And if I have to break in, it's most likely going to be through your bedroom window. So leave your curtains closed to give me some cover."

"You think it'll come to that?"

"I hope not. Try to get Ramirez to talk on the phone. And remember to record." He put the screwdriver back in the box and took out a roll of surgical tape and a small plastic case about the size of a pack of gum. "This is a miniature body transmitter. It's got two nine-volt lithium batteries in it, which gives you fifteen hours of usable operating time. It has an external electret microphone, it weighs seven ounces, and it costs about $1200. Don't lose it and don't wear it in the shower."

"Maybe Ramirez will be on good behavior now that he's been charged with assault."

"I'm not sure Ramirez knows good from bad."

"What's the plan for the day?"

"I thought we'd put you back on Stark Street. Now that you don't have to worry about driving *me* crazy, you can concentrate on driving Ramirez crazy. Push him into making another move."

"Gosh, Stark Street. My favorite place. What am I supposed to do there?"

"Stroll around and look sexy, ask annoying questions, in general get on everyone's nerves. All those things that come naturally to you."

"You know Jimmy Alpha?"

"Everybody knows Jimmy Alpha."

"What do you think of him?"

"Mixed feelings. He's always been an okay guy in my dealings with him. And I used to think he was a great manager. He did all the right things for Ramirez. Got him the right fights. Got him good trainers." Morelli topped his coffee. "Guys like Jimmy Alpha spend their whole life hoping to get someone the caliber of Ramirez. Most of them never even come close. Managing Ramirez is like holding the winning ticket to the million-dollar lottery . . . only better because Ramirez will keep paying off. Ramirez is a gold mine. Unfortunately, Ramirez is also fucking nuts, and Alpha is caught between a rock and a hard spot."

"That was my opinion, too. I guess holding that winning ticket would tempt a person to turn a blind eye to some of Ramirez's personality faults."

"Especially now when they're just starting to make big money. Alpha supported Ramirez for years while he was just a punk kid. Now Ramirez has the title and has signed a contract for televised fights. He's literally worth millions to Alpha in future payoffs."

"So your opinion of Alpha is tarnished."

"I think Alpha is criminally irresponsible." He looked at his watch. "Ramirez does roadwork first thing in the morning, then he eats breakfast at the luncheonette across from the gym. After breakfast he works out and usually he stays at it until four."

"That's a lot of training."

"It's all half-assed. If he had to fight anybody decent he'd be in trouble. His last two opponents have been handpicked losers. He has a fight in three weeks with another bum. After that he'll start to get serious for his fight with Lionel Reesey."

"You know a lot about boxing."

"Boxing is the ultimate sport. Man against man. Primal combat. It's like sex . . . puts you in touch with the beast."

I made a strangled sound in the back of my throat.

He selected an orange from the bowl of fruit on the counter. "You're just pissed off because you can't remember the last time you saw the beast."

"I see the beast plenty, thank you."

"Honey, you don't see the beast at all. I've been asking around. You have no social life."

I gave him a stiff middle finger. "Oh yeah, well social life this."

Morelli grinned. "You're damn cute when you act stupid. Any time you want me to unleash the beast, you just let me know."

That did it. I was going to gas him. I might not turn him in, but I'd enjoy watching him pass out and throw up.

"I have to split," Morelli said. "One of your neighbors saw me come in. I wouldn't want to soil your reputation by staying too long. You should come onto Stark Street around noon and strut around for an hour or two. Wear your transmitter. I'll be watching and listening."

I had the morning to kill, so I went out for a run. It wasn't any easier, but at least Eddie Gazarra didn't show up and tell me I looked like death warmed over. I ate breakfast, took a long shower, and planned how I was going to spend my money after I bagged Morelli.

I dressed in strappy sandals, a tight black knit miniskirt, and a stretchy red top with a low scoop neck that showed as much cleavage as was possible, given my bra size. I did the mousse and the spray thing with my hair so that I had a lot of it. I lined my eyes in midnight blue, gunked them up with mascara, painted my mouth whore red, and hung the biggest, brassiest earrings I owned from my lobes. I lacquered my nails to match my lips and checked myself out in the mirror.

Damned if I didn't make a good slut.

It was eleven o'clock. A little early, but I wanted to get this strutting around over with so I could visit Lula. After Lula I figured I'd do some shooting and then go home and wait for my phone to ring.

I parked a block from the gym and started down the street with my pocketbook hung from my shoulder and my hand wrapped around the Sure Guard. I'd discovered that the transmitter showed under the stretchy top, so I had it snug inside my bikini underpants. Eat your heart out, Morelli.

The van was parked almost directly across from the gym. Jackie stood between me and the van. She looked even more sullen than usual.

"How's Lula?" I asked. "Have you seen her today?"

"They don't have no visiting hours in the morning. I don't got time to see her anyway. I gotta earn a living, you know."

"The hospital said her condition was stable."

"Yeah. They got her in a regular room. She gotta stay there awhile on account of she's still bleeding inside, but I think she'll be okay."

"She have a safe place to stay when she gets out?"

"Ain't no place gonna be safe for Lula to stay when she gets out unless she get smart. She gonna be telling the police some white motherfucker cut her."

I glanced down the street at the van and felt Morelli's telepathic grunt of exasperation. "Someone's got to stop Ramirez."

"Ain't gonna be Lula," Jackie said. "What kind of witness you think she gonna make, anyway? You think people gonna believe a whore? They gonna say she got what she deserved and probably her old man beat her and leave her for you to see. Maybe they say you been doing some whoring and not paying the price and this be a lesson to you."

"Have you seen Ramirez today? Is he in the gym?"

"Don't know. These eyes don't see Ramirez. He the invisible man far as I'm concerned."

I'd expected as much from Jackie. And she was probably right about Lula on the witness stand. Ramirez would hire the best defense lawyer in the state, and he wouldn't even have to work up a sweat to discredit Lula.

I moved on down the street. Has anyone seen Carmen Sanchez? I asked. Is it true she was seen with Benito Ramirez the night Ziggy Kulesza was shot?

No one had seen her. No one knew anything about her and Ramirez.

I paraded around for another hour and capped the effort with a trip across the street to lay some grief at Jimmy Alpha's feet. I didn't barge into his office this time. I waited patiently while his secretary announced me.

He didn't seem surprised. Probably he'd been watching from his window. He had dark circles under his eyes, the kind a person gets from sleepless nights and problems with no solutions. I stood in front of his desk, and we stared at each other for a full minute without talking.

"You know about Lula?" I asked him.

Alpha nodded.

"He almost killed her, Jimmy. He cut her and beat her and left her tied to my fire escape. Then he called and asked me if I'd received his present and told me I could look forward to an even worse fate."

Alpha's head was nodding again. This time it was nodding "no" in denial. "I talked to him," Alpha said. "Benito admits he spent some time with Lula, and maybe he got a little rough, but he said that was it. He said someone must have got to her after him. He says someone's trying to make him look bad."

"I talked to him on the phone. I know what I heard. I have it on tape."

"He swears it wasn't him."

"And you believe him?"

"I know he goes a little crazy with women. Got this tough-guy macho attitude. Got this thing about being disrespected. But I can't see him hanging a woman on a fire escape. I can't see him making that phone call. I know he's not Einstein, but I just can't see him being that dumb."

"He's not dumb, Jimmy. He's sick. He's done terrible things."

He ran his hand through his hair. "I don't know. Maybe you're right. Look, do me a favor and stay away from Stark Street for a while. The cops are going to investigate what happened to Lula. Whatever they find . . . I'm going to have to live with. In the meantime, I've got to get Benito ready to fight. He's going up against Tommy Clark in three weeks. Clark isn't much of a threat, but you have to take these things seriously all the same. The fans buy a ticket, they deserve a fight. I'm afraid Benito sees you, he gets all stirred up, you know? It's hard enough to get him to train . . ."

It was about forty degrees in his office, but Alpha had dark stains under his armpits. If I was in his place I'd be sweating, too. He was watching his dream turn into a nightmare, and he didn't have the guts to face up.

I told him I had a job to do and couldn't stay away from Stark Street. I let myself out and walked down the single flight of stairs. I sat on the bottom step and talked to my crotch. "Damn," I said. "That was fucking depressing."

Across the street, Morelli was listening in his van. I couldn't imagine what he was thinking.

Morelli knocked on my door at ten-thirty that night. He had a six-pack and a pizza and a portable TV tucked under his arm. He was out of uniform, back to wearing jeans and a navy T-shirt.

"Another day in that van, and I might be glad to go to jail," he said.

"Is that a Pino's pizza?"

"Is there any other kind?"

"How'd you get it?"

"Pino delivers to felons." He looked around. "Where's your cable hookup?"

"In the living room."

He plugged the TV in, set the pizza and the beer on the floor, and hit the remote. "You get any phone calls?"

"Nothing."

He opened a beer. "It's early yet. Ramirez does his best work at night."

"I talked to Lula. She's not going to testify."

"Big surprise."

I sat on the floor next to the pizza box. "Did you hear the conversation with Jimmy Alpha?"

"Yeah, I heard it. What the hell kind of outfit were you supposed to be wearing?"

"It was my slut outfit. I wanted to speed things up."

"Christ, you had guys running their cars up on the curb. And where did you hide the mike? It wasn't under that top. I'd have seen Scotch tape under that top."

"I stuck it in my underpants."

"Dang," Morelli said. "When I get it back I'm going to have it bronzed."

I popped open a beer and helped myself to a piece of pizza. "What do you make of Alpha? You think he could be pushed into testifying against Ramirez?"

Morelli flipped through the channels, clicked onto a ball-game, and watched it for a few seconds. "Depends how much he knows. If he's got his head deep in the sand, he's not going to have hard facts. Dorsey paid him a visit after you left, and he got less than you did."

"You have Alpha's office bugged?"

"No. Bar talk at Pino's."

There was one piece of pizza left. We both eyeballed it.

"It'll go straight to your hips," Morelli said.

He was right, but I took it anyway.

I kicked him out a little after one and dragged myself to bed. I slept through the night, and in the morning there were no messages on my machine. I was about to start coffee when the car alarm went off in the lot below. I grabbed my keys and ran from my apartment, taking the steps three at a time. The driver's door was open when I got to the Jeep. The alarm was wailing away. I deactivated and reset the alarm, locked the car, and returned to my apartment.

Morelli was in the kitchen, and I could tell the effort to stay calm was jacking his blood pressure into the red zone.

"I didn't want anyone to steal your car," I said. "So I had an alarm installed."

"It wasn't '*anyone*' you were worried about. It was *me*. You had a goddamn alarm installed in my goddamn car so I couldn't snatch it out from under you!"

"It worked, too. What were you doing in our car?"

"It's not *our* car. It's *my* car. I'm *allowing* you to drive it. I was going to get some breakfast."

"Why didn't you take the van?"

"Because I wanted to drive my car. I swear, when this mess gets cleared up, I'm moving to Alaska. I don't care what sort of sacrifice I have to make, I'm putting miles between us, because if I stay I'll strangle you, and they'll get me for murder one."

"Jesus, Morelli, you sound like you have PMS. You have to learn to lighten up a little. It's just a car alarm. You should be thanking me. I had it installed with my own money."

"Well shit, what was I thinking of?"

"You're under a lot of strain lately."

There was a knock on the door, and we both jumped.

Morelli beat me to the peephole. He stepped back several paces and pulled me with him. "It's Morty Beyers," he said.

There was another knock on the door.

"He can't have you," I said. "You're mine, and I'm not sharing."

Morelli grimaced. "I'll be under the bed if you need me."

I went to the door and took a look for myself. I'd never seen Morty Beyers before, but this guy looked like he'd just had an appendectomy. He was close to forty, overweight, ashen-faced, and he was stooped over, holding his stomach. His sandy hair was thin, combed over the top of his balding dome, and slick with sweat.

I opened the door to him.

"Morty Beyers," he said, extending his hand. "You must be Stephanie Plum."

"Aren't you supposed to be in the hospital?"

"An exploded appendix only gets you a couple hours' stay. I'm back to work. They tell me I'm good as new."

He didn't look good as new. He looked like he had met Vampira on the stairs. "Your stomach still hurt?"

"Only when I straighten up."

"What can I do for you?"

"Vinnie said you had my FTAs. I thought now that I was feeling okay . . ."

"You want the paperwork back."

"Yeah. Listen, I'm sorry it didn't work out for you."

"It wasn't a complete bust. I brought two of them in."

He nodded. "Didn't have any luck with Morelli?"

"None at all."

"I know this sounds weird, but I could've sworn I saw his car in your parking lot."

"I stole it. I thought maybe I could flush him out by making him come after his car."

"You stole it? No shit? Jesus, that's great." He was leaning against the wall with his hand pressed to his groin.

"You want to sit down for a minute? You want some water?"

"Nah, I'm fine. I gotta get to work. I just wanted the pictures and stuff."

I ran to the kitchen, gathered up the files, and rushed back to the door. "This is it."

"Great." He tucked the folders under an arm. "So are you gonna keep the car awhile?"

"I'm not sure."

"If you spotted Morelli walking down the street, would you bring him in?"

"Yeah."

He smiled. "If I was you, I'd do the same thing. I wouldn't pack it in just because my week was up. Just between you and me, Vinnie would pay out to anyone brought Morelli back. Well, I'll be on my way. Thanks."

"Take care of yourself."

"Yeah. I'm gonna use the elevator."

I closed the door, slid the bolt home, and latched the security chain. When I turned around, Morelli was standing in the bedroom doorway. "Do you think he knew you were here?" I asked.

"If he knew I was here, he'd have his gun aimed at my forehead by now. Don't underestimate Beyers. He's not as stupid as he looks. And he's not nearly as nice as he'd like you to believe. He was a cop. Got kicked off the force for demanding favors from prostitutes of both genders. We used to call him Morty the Mole because he'd bury his doodah in whatever hole was available."

"I bet he and Vinnie get along just great."

I went to the window and stared down at the parking lot. Beyers was examining Morelli's car, peering into the windows. He tried the door handle and the trunk latch. He wrote something on the outside of a folder. He straightened slightly and looked around the lot. His attention caught on the van. He slowly walked over and pressed his nose against the windows in an attempt to see the interior; then he laboriously climbed on the front bumper and tried to see through the windshield. He stepped back and stared at the antennae. He stood to the rear and copied the tag. He turned and looked up at my building, and I jumped back from the window.

Five minutes later, there was another knock on my door.

"I was wondering about that van in your lot," Beyers said. "Have you noticed it?"

"The blue one with the antennae?"

"Yeah. Do you know the owner?"

"No, but it's been here for a while."

I closed and locked the door and watched Beyers through the peephole. He stood thinking for a moment, and then he knocked on Mr. Wolesky's door. He showed Morelli's picture and asked a few questions. He thanked Mr. Wolesky, gave him his card, and backed away.

I returned to the window, but Beyers didn't appear in the lot. "He's going door-to-door," I said.

We continued to watch from the window, and eventually Beyers limped to his car. He drove a late-model dark blue Ford Escort equipped with a car phone. He left the lot and turned toward St. James.

Morelli was in the kitchen with his head in my refrigerator. "Beyers is going to be a real pain in the ass. He's going to check on the van plates and put it together."

"What's this going to do for you?"

"It's going to knock me out of Trenton until I get a different vehicle." He took a carton of orange juice and a loaf of raisin bread. "Put this on my tab. I've got to get out of here." He stopped at the door. "I'm afraid you're going to be on your own for a while. Stay locked up in the apartment here, don't let *anyone* in, and you should be okay. The alternative is to come with me, but if we get caught together, you'll be an accessory."

"I'll stay here. I'll be fine."

"Promise me you won't go out."

"I promise! I promise!"

Some promises are meant to be broken. This was one of them. I had no intention of sitting on my hands, waiting for Ramirez. I wanted to hear from him yesterday. I wanted the whole ugly affair to be done. I wanted Ramirez behind bars. I wanted my apprehension money. I wanted to get on with my life.

I looked out the window to make sure Morelli was gone. I got my pocketbook and locked up after myself. I drove to Stark Street and parked across from the gym. I didn't have the nerve to move freely on the street without Morelli backing me up, so I stayed in the car with the windows closed and the doors locked. I was sure by this time Ramirez knew my car. I figured it was better than no reminder at all.

Every half hour I ran the air-conditioning to get the temperature down and break the monotony. Several times I'd looked up at Jimmy Alpha's office and seen a face at a window. The gym windows showed less activity.

At twelve-thirty Alpha trotted across the street and knocked on my window.

I powered it down. "Sorry to have to park here, Jimmy, but I need to continue my surveillance for Morelli. I'm sure you understand."

A wrinkle creased his brow. "I don't get it. If I was looking for Morelli, I'd watch his relatives and his friends. What's this thing with Stark Street and Carmen Sanchez?"

"I have a theory about what happened. I think Benito abused Carmen just like he abused Lula. Then I think he panicked and sent Ziggy and some other guy over to Carmen's to make sure she didn't make noise. I think Morelli walked in on it and probably shot Ziggy in self-defense just like he said. Somehow Carmen and the other guy and Ziggy's gun managed to disappear. I think Morelli's trying to find them. And I think Stark Street is the logical place to look."

"That's crazy. How'd you come up with such a crazy idea?"

"From Morelli's arrest statement."

Alpha looked disgusted. "Well what'd you expect Morelli to say? That he shot Ziggy for the hell of it? Benito's an easy target. He has a reputation for being a little too aggressive with the ladies, and Ziggy worked for him, so Morelli took it from there."

"How about the missing witness? He must have worked for Benito, too."

"I don't know anything about the missing witness."

"People tell me he had a nose that looked like it had been smashed with a frying pan. That's pretty distinctive."

Alpha smiled. "Not in a third-rate gym. Half the bums who work out here have noses like that." He looked at his watch. "I'm late for a lunch. You look hot in there. You want me to bring something back for you? A cold soda? A sandwich, maybe?"

"I'm okay. I think I'm going to break for lunch soon, too. Have to use the little girl's room."

"There's a john on the second floor. Just get the key from Lorna. Tell her I said it was okay."

I thought it was decent of Alpha to offer the use of his facilities, but I didn't want to take a chance on Ramirez cornering me while I was on the toilet.

I took one last look up and down the street and drove off in search of fast food. A half hour later I was back in the very same parking space, feeling much more comfortable and twice as bored. I'd brought a book back with me, but it was hard to read and sweat at the same time, and sweating took precedence.

By three my hair was wet against my neck and face and had frizzed out to maximum volume. My shirt was plastered to my back, and perspiration stained over my chest. My legs were cramped, and I'd developed a nervous twitch to my left eye.

I still hadn't seen a sign of Ramirez. Pedestrian traffic was restricted to pockets of shade and had disappeared into smoky air-conditioned bars. I was the only fool sitting baking in a car. Even the hookers had disappeared for a midafternoon crack break.

I palmed my defense spray and got out of the Cherokee, whimpering as all my little spine bones decompressed and realigned themselves. I stretched and jogged in place. I walked around the car and bent to touch my toes. A breeze trickled down Stark Street, and I felt inordinately blessed. True, the air index was lethal and the temperature hovered at blast-furnace range, but it was a breeze all the same.

I leaned against the car and pulled the front of my shirt away from my sweaty body.

Jackie emerged from the Grand Hotel and lumbered down the street toward me, en route to her corner. "You look like heatstroke," she said, handing me a cold Coke.

I popped the tab, drank some soda, and held the cold can against my forehead. "Thanks. This is great."

"Don't think I'm getting soft on your skinny white ass," she said. "It's just you're gonna die sitting in that car, and you're gonna give Stark Street a bad name. People gonna say it a race murder, and my white trash pervert business'll get ruined."

"I'll try not to die. God forbid I should ruin your pervert business."

"Fucking A," she said. "Them little white perverts pay fine money for my big nasty ass."

"How's Lula?"

Jackie shrugged. "She's doing as good as she can. She appreciated that you sent flowers."

"Not much activity here today."

Jackie slid her eyes up to the gym windows. "Thank sweet Jesus for that," she said softly.

I followed her gaze to the second floor. "You better not be seen talking to me."

"Yeah," she said. "I gotta get back to work, anyway."

I stood there for a few minutes longer, enjoying the soda and the luxury of being fully vertical. I turned to get back in the car and gasped at the sight of Ramirez standing next to me.

"Been waiting all day for you to get out of this car," he said. "Bet you're surprised at how quiet I move. Didn't even hear me come up on you, did you? That's how it's always gonna be. You're never gonna hear me until I pounce. And then it's gonna be too late."

I took a slow breath to quiet my heart. I waited a moment longer to steady my voice. When I felt some control, I asked him about Carmen. "I want to know about Carmen," I said. "I want to know if she saw you coming."

"Carmen and me, we had a date. Carmen asked for what she got."

"Where is she now?"

He shrugged. "Don't know. She split after Ziggy got offed."

"What about the guy that was with Ziggy that night? Who was he? What happened to him?"

"Don't know nothing about that either."

"I thought they worked for you."

"Why don't we go upstairs and talk about this? Or we could go for a ride. I got a Porsche. I could take you for a ride in my Porsche."

"I don't think so."

"See, there you go again. Refusing the champ. You're always refusing the champ. He don't like that."

"Tell me about Ziggy and his friend . . . the guy with the smashed nose."

"Be more interesting to tell you about the champ. How he gonna teach you some respect. How he gonna punish you so you learn not to refuse him." He stepped closer, and the heat coming off his body made the air feel cool by comparison. "Think maybe I'll make you bleed before I fuck you. You like that? You want to get cut, bitch?"

That's it. I'm out of here. "You're not going to do anything to me," I said. "You don't scare me, and you don't excite me."

"You lie." He wrapped his hand around my upper arm and squeezed hard enough to make me cry out.

I kicked him hard in the shin, and he hit me. I never saw his hand move. The crack rang in my ears and my head snapped back. I tasted blood and blinked hard several times to clear the cobwebs. When most of the stars faded, I shot him square in the face with the Sure Guard.

He howled in pain and rage and reeled into the street with his hands to his eyes. The howling metamorphosed to choking and gasping, and he went down on all fours like some monstrous animal—a big, pissed-off, wounded buffalo.

Jimmy Alpha came running from across the street, followed by his secretary and a man I'd never seen before.

The man went down on the ground with Ramirez, trying to calm him, telling him he'd be okay in a minute, to take deep breaths.

Alpha and the secretary rushed over to me.

"Jesus," Jimmy Alpha said, pressing a clean handkerchief into my hand. "Are you okay? He didn't break anything, did he?"

I put the handkerchief to my mouth and held it there while I ran my tongue over my teeth to see if any were missing or loose. "I think I'm okay."

"I'm really sorry," Jimmy said. "I don't know what's the matter with him, the way he treats women. I apologize for him. I don't know what to do."

I wasn't in the mood to accept an apology. "There are lots of things you can do," I said. "Get him psychiatric help. Lock him up. Take him to the vet and get him neutered."

"I'll pay for a doctor," Jimmy Alpha said. "Do you want to go to a doctor?"

"The only place I'm going is to the police station. I'm pressing charges, and nothing you can say is going to stop me."

"Think about it for a day," Jimmy pleaded. "At least wait until you're not so upset. He can't take another assault charge now."

CHAPTER 12

I wrenched the driver's door open and jammed myself behind the wheel. I eased away from the curb, being careful not to run over anyone. I drove at a moderate speed, and I didn't look back. I stopped for a light and assessed the damage in the rearview mirror. My upper lip was split on the inside and still bleeding. I had a purple bruise forming on my left cheek. My cheek and my lip were beginning to swell.

I was holding tight to the wheel, and I was using every strength I possessed to stay calm. I drove south on Stark to State Street and followed State to Hamilton. When I reached Hamilton I felt as if I was safe in my own neighborhood and could allow myself to stop and think. I pulled into a convenience store lot and sat there for a while. I needed to go to the police station to report the assault, but I didn't want to leave the security and comfort of home turf, and I wasn't sure how the police would regard this latest incident with Ramirez. He'd threatened me, and then I'd deliberately provoked him by parking across from the gym. Not smart.

I'd been on adrenaline overdose ever since Ramirez appeared at my side, and now that the adrenaline was slacking out, exhaustion and pain were creeping in. My arm and my jaw ached and my pulse rate felt like it had dropped to twelve.

Face up, I said to myself, you're not going to make it to the police station today. I shuffled through my shoulder bag until I found Dorsey's card. Might as well keep some continuity and whine to Dorsey. I dialed his number and left a message to call back. I didn't specify the problem. I didn't think I could go through it twice.

I hauled myself into the store and got myself a grape popsicle. "Hadda akthident," I said to the clerk. "My lip ith thwollen."

"Maybe you should see a doctor."

I ripped the paper off the popsicle and put the ice to my lip. "Ahhh." I sighed. "Thas bedda."

I returned to the car, put it into gear, and backed into a pickup truck. My whole life flashed in front of me. I was drowning. Please God, I prayed, don't let there be a dent.

We both got out and examined our cars. The pickup didn't have a scratch. No dent, no paint chipped, not even a smudge in the wax. The Cherokee looked like someone had taken a can opener to its right rear fender.

The guy driving the pickup stared at my lip. "Domestic quarrel?"

"A akthident."

"Guess this just isn't your day."

"No day ith my day," I said.

Since the accident had been my fault, and there'd been no damage to his car, we didn't do the ritual of trading insurance information. I took one last look at the damage, shuddered violently, and slunk away, debating the value of suicide as opposed to facing Morelli.

The phone was ringing as I came through my front door. It was Dorsey.

"I haf an assault charge againth Ramireth," I said. "He hit me in the mouff."

"Where'd this happen?"

"Thark Threet." I gave him the details and refused his offer to come to my apartment to get my statement. I didn't want to chance his running into Morelli. I promised I'd stop in tomorrow to complete the paperwork.

I took a shower and had ice cream for supper. Every ten minutes I'd look out the window to see if there was any sign of Morelli in the lot. I'd parked in a far corner where the lighting was poor. If I could just get through the night, tomorrow I'd take the Cherokee to Al at the body shop and see if he could do an instant repair. I had no idea how I'd pay for it.

I watched television until eleven and went to bed, lugging Rex's cage into the bedroom to keep me company. There'd been no phone calls from Ramirez and no sign of Morelli. I wasn't sure if I was relieved or disappointed. I had no idea if Morelli was listening, protecting me as agreed, so I slept with my defense spray, my portable phone, and my gun on the nightstand.

My phone rang at six-thirty. It was Morelli.

"Time to get up," he said.

I checked my bedside clock. "It's practically the middle of the night."

"You'd have been up hours ago if you had to sleep in a Nissan Sentra."

"What are you doing in a Sentra?"

"I'm having the van painted a different color and the antennae removed. I've managed to 'find' a new set of plates. In the meantime, the body shop gave me a loaner. I waited until dark and then parked on Maple, just behind the lot."

"So you could guard my body?"

"Mostly I didn't want to miss hearing you get undressed. What was that weird squeaking sound all night?"

"Rex on his wheel."

"I thought he lived in the kitchen."

I didn't want Morelli to know I'd been scared and lonely, so I lied. "I cleaned the sink, and he didn't like the smell of the cleanser, so I brought him into the bedroom."

The silence stretched for a couple beats.

"Translation," Morelli said. "You were scared and lonely, and you brought Rex in for company."

"These are difficult times."

"Tell me about it."

"I suppose you need to get out of Trenton before Beyers returns."

"I suppose I do. I'm too visible in this car. I can get the van at six tonight, and then I'll be back."

"Catch you later."

"Ten-four, Captain Video."

I went back to bed, and two hours later I was jolted awake by the car alarm blaring away in the lot below me. I flew out of bed, rushed to the window, and threw the curtains open in time to see Morty Beyers smash the alarm to smithereens with his gun butt.

"Beyers!" I bellowed from my open window. "What the hell do you think you're doing?"

"My wife left me, and she took the Escort."

"So?"

"So I need a car. I was gonna rent one, and then I thought of Morelli's Jeep sitting here, and I figured it'd save me some money to use it until I tracked Mona down."

"Christ, Beyers, you can't just come into a lot and take someone's car! That's stealing. You're a goddamn car thief."

"So?"

"Where'd you get the keys?"

"Same place you did. Morelli's apartment. He had an extra set in his dresser."

"You won't get away with this."

"What are you gonna do, call the police?"

"God will get you for this."

"Fuck God," Beyers said, sliding behind the wheel, taking time to adjust the seat and fiddle with the radio.

Arrogant bastard, I thought. Not only is he stealing the damn car, but he's sitting there flaunting his ability to take it. I grabbed my defense spray and bolted out the door and down the stairs. I was barefoot, wearing a Mickey Mouse nightshirt and a pair of Jockey string bikinis, and I could have cared less.

I was through the back door with my foot on the pavement when I saw Beyers turn the key and step on the accelerator. A split second later the car exploded with a deafening blast, sending doors flying off into space like Frisbees. Flames licked up from the undercarriage and instantly consumed the Cherokee, turning it into a brilliant yellow fireball.

I was too astonished to move. I stood open-mouthed and speechless while parts of roof and fender reversed their trajectory and clanked down to earth.

Sirens sounded in the distance, and tenants poured from the building to stand beside me and stare at the burning Jeep. Clouds of black smoke boiled into the morning sky, and searing heat rippled across my face.

There'd never been any possibility of saving Morty Beyers. Even if

I'd immediately responded, I couldn't have gotten him out of the car. And probably he was dead from the blast, not the fire. It occurred to me that chances of this being an accident were slim. And that chances of this being meant for me were large.

On the positive side, I didn't have to sweat Morelli finding out about yesterday's accident damage.

I backed away from the fire and eased my way through the small crowd that had formed. I took the stairs two at a time and locked myself in my apartment. I'd carelessly left the front door wide open when I'd dashed out after Beyers, so I did a thorough search with my gun drawn. If I came on the guy who roasted Morty Beyers, I wasn't going to fool around with his neurotransmitters—I was going to go for a bullet in the gut. The gut made a nice big target.

When I was sure my apartment was secure, I got dressed in shorts and shirt. I took a fast bathroom break and checked my appearance in the bathroom mirror. I had a purple bruise on my cheekbone and a small gash in my upper lip. Most of the swelling had gone down. As a result of the morning's fire, my complexion looked like it had been sunburned and sandblasted. My eyebrows and the hair around my face had gotten singed and stuck out in spikes about an eighth of an inch long. Very attractive. Not that I was complaining. I could have been dead and missing a few body parts that had landed in the azaleas. I laced up my Reeboks and went downstairs to take another look.

The parking lot and adjoining streets were filled with fire trucks and police cars and ambulances. Barricades had been set up, holding the curious away from the smoldering remains of Morelli's Jeep. Oily, sooty water slicked the blacktop, and the air smelled like charred pot roast. I didn't want to pursue that train of thought. I saw Dorsey standing on the perimeter, talking to a uniform. He looked up and caught my eye and headed over.

"I'm getting a bad feeling about this," he said.

"You know Morty Beyers?"

"Yeah."

"He was in the Jeep."

"No shit. Are you sure?"

"I was talking to him when it blew."

"I guess that explains your missing eyebrows. What were you talking about?"

"Vinnie had only given me a week to bring Morelli in. My week was up, and Morty took up the hunt. We were sort of talking about Morelli."

"You couldn't have been talking too close or you'd be hamburger."

"Actually I was right about where we're standing now, and we were yelling at each other. We were sort of . . . disagreeing."

A uniform came over with a twisted license plate. "We found this over by the Dumpster," he said. "You want me to run an ID?"

I took the plate. "Don't bother. The car belongs to Morelli."

"Oh boy," Dorsey said. "I can hardly wait to hear this."

I figured I'd embellish the truth a little, since the police might not be up on the finer points of bounty hunterism and might not understand about commandeering. "It's like this," I said. "I went to see Morelli's mother, and she was very upset that no one was running Joe's car. You know how bad it is for the battery to let a car sit. Well one thing led to another and next thing I'd agreed to drive the car around for her."

"So you've been driving Morelli's car as a favor to his mother?"

"Yes. He'd asked her to take care of it, but she didn't have time."

"Very noble of you."

"I'm a noble person."

"Go on."

So I did. I explained about Beyers's wife leaving him, and about how he tried to steal the car, and how he made the mistake of saying "Fuck God," and then the car blew up.

"You think God got pissed off and fried Beyers?"

"That would be one theory."

"When you come to the station to complete the report on Ramirez, we might want to talk further on this."

I watched for a few more minutes and then went back to my apartment. I didn't especially want to be around when they scooped up the ashes that had been Morty Beyers.

I sat in front of the television until noon, keeping my windows closed and my curtains drawn to the crime scene below. Every once in a while I'd wander into the bathroom and stare at myself in the mirror to see if my eyebrows had grown back yet.

At twelve o'clock I parted my curtains and braved a peek at the lot. The Cherokee had been removed, and only two patrolmen remained.

From my window it appeared they were filling out property damage forms for the handful of cars that had been pelted with debris from the explosion.

A morning of television had anesthetized me sufficiently that I felt ready to cope, so I took a shower and got dressed, being careful not to dwell on thoughts of death and bombings.

I needed to go down to the police station, but I didn't have a car. I had a few dollars in my pocket. Nothing in my checking account. My credit cards were in collection. I had to make another apprehension.

I called Connie and told her about Morty Beyers.

"This is going to make a serious hole in Vinnie's dike," Connie said. "Ranger's recovering from gunshot and now Morty Beyers is out of the picture. They were our two best agents."

"Yeah. It sure is a shame. I guess Vinnie's left with me."

There was a pause at the other end of the phone. "You didn't do Morty, did you?"

"Morty sort of did himself. You have anything easy come in? I could use some fast money."

"I have an exhibitionist gone FTA on a $2,000 bond. He's been kicked out of three retirement homes. He's currently living in an apartment somewhere." I could hear her shuffling through papers. "Here it is," she said. "Ommigod, he's living in your building."

"What's his name?"

"William Earling. He's in apartment 3E."

I grabbed my pocketbook and locked up. I took the stairs to the third floor, counted off apartments, and knocked on Earling's door. A man answered, and right off I suspected I had the right person because he was old and he was naked. "Mr. Earling?"

"Yup. That's me. I'm in pretty good shape, huh chickie? You think I've got some fearful equipment?"

I gave myself a mental command not to look, but my eyes strayed south of their own volition. Not only wasn't he fearful, but his doodles were wrinkled. "Yeah. You're pretty fearful," I said. I handed him my card. "I work for Vincent Plum, your bond agent. You failed to appear for a court hearing, Mr. Earling. I need to take you downtown so you can reschedule."

"Damn court hearings are a waste of time," Earling said. "I'm seventy-six years old. You think they're gonna send some seventy-six-year-old guy to prison because he flashed his stuff around?"

I sincerely hoped so. Seeing Earling naked was enough to make me turn celibate. "I need to take you downtown. How about you go put some clothes on."

"I don't wear clothes. God brought me into the world naked, and that's the way I'm going out."

"Okay by me, but in the meantime I wish you'd get dressed."

"The only way I'm going with you is naked."

I took out my cuffs and snapped them on his wrists.

"Police brutality. Police brutality," he yelled.

"Sorry to disappoint you," I said. "I'm not a cop."

"Well what are you?"

"I'm a bounty hunter."

"Bounty hunter brutality. Bounty hunter brutality."

I went to the hall closet, found a full-length raincoat, and buttoned him into it.

"I'm not going with you," he said, standing rigid, his hands cuffed under the coat. "You can't make me go."

"Listen, Grandpa," I said, "either you go peaceably or I'll gas you and drag you out by your heels."

I couldn't believe I was saying this to some poor senior citizen with a snail dick. I was appalled at myself, but what the hell, it was worth $200.

"Don't forget to lock up," he said. "This neighborhood's going to heck in a handbasket. The keys are in the kitchen."

I got the keys, and one of them had a little Buick insignia on it. What a break. "One more thing," I said. "Would you mind if I borrowed your car to take you downtown?"

"I guess that'd be okay as long as we don't use too much gas. I'm on a fixed income, you know."

I buzzed Mr. Earling through in record time and took care not to run into Dorsey. I stopped at the office on the way home to pick up my check and stopped at the bank to cash it. I parked Mr. Earling's car as close to the door as possible to cut down on his streaking distance when he got out of jail. I didn't want to see any more of Mr. Earling than was absolutely unavoidable.

I jogged upstairs and called home, cringing at the thought of what I was about to do.

"Is Daddy out with the cab?" I asked. "I need a ride."

"He's off today. He's right here. Where do you need to go?"

"An apartment complex on Route 1." Another cringe.

"Now?"

"Yeah." Very large sigh. "Now."

"I'm having stuffed shells tonight. Would you like some stuffed shells?"

Hard to believe how much I wanted those stuffed shells. More than good sex, a fast car, a cool night, or eyebrows. I wanted temporary respite from adulthood. I wanted to feel unconditionally safe. I wanted my mom to cluck around me, filling my milk glass, relieving me of the most mundane responsibilities. I wanted to spend a few hours in a house cluttered with awful overstuffed furniture and oppressive cooking smells. "Stuffed shells would be good."

My father was at the back door in fifteen minutes. He gave a start at the sight of me.

"We had an accident in the parking lot," I said. "A car caught fire, and I was standing too close." I gave him the address and asked him to stop at K-Mart on the way. Thirty minutes later he dropped me off in Morelli's parking lot.

"Tell Mom I'll be there by six," I said to him.

He looked at the Nova and the case of motor oil I'd just purchased. "Maybe I should stay to make sure it runs."

I fed the car three cans and checked the dipstick. I gave my father an A-okay sign. He didn't seem impressed. I got behind the wheel, gave the dash a hard shot with my fist, and cranked her over. "Starts every time," I yelled.

My father was still impassive, and I knew he was thinking I should have bought a Buick. These indignities never befell Buicks. We pulled out of the lot together, and I waved him off on Route 1, pointing the Nova in the direction of Ye Olde Muffler Shoppe. Past the orange-peaked roof of the Howard Johnson Motel, past the Shady Grove Trailer Park, past Happy Days Kennels. Other drivers were giving me a wide berth, not daring to enter into my thundering wake. Seven miles down the road I cheered at the sight of the yellow and black muffler shop sign.

I wore my Oakleys to hide my eyebrows, but the counterman still did a double take. I filled out the forms and gave him the keys and took a seat in the small room reserved for the parents of sick cars. Forty-five minutes later I was on my way. I only noticed the smoke when I stopped at an intersection, and the red light only blinked on occasionally. I figured that was as good as I could expect.

My mother started as soon as I hit the front porch. "Every time I see you, you look worse and worse. Bruises and cuts and now what happened to your hair, and ommigod you haven't got eyebrows. What happened to your eyebrows? Your father said you were in a fire."

"A car caught fire in my parking lot. It wasn't anything."

"I saw it on the TV," Grandma Mazur said, elbowing her way past my mother. "They said it was a bombing. Blew the car sky high. And some guy was in the car. Some sleazoid named Beyers. Except there wasn't much left of him."

Grandma Mazur was wearing a pink and orange print cotton blouse with a tissue waded up in the sleeve, bright blue spandex shorts, white tennies, and stockings rolled just above her knee.

"I like your shorts," I said to her. "Great color."

"She went like that to the funeral home this afternoon," my father yelled from the kitchen. "Tony Mancuso's viewing."

"I tell you it was something," Grandma Mazur said. "The VFW was there. Best viewing I've been to all month. And Tony looked real good. They gave him one of those ties with the little horse heads on."

"We got seven phone calls so far," my mother said. "I told everyone she forgot to take her medicine this morning."

Grandma Mazur clacked her teeth. "Nobody knows fashion around here. You can't hardly ever wear anything different." She looked down at her shorts. "What do you think?" she asked me. "You think these are okay for an afternoon viewing?"

"Sure," I said, "but if it was at night I'd wear black."

"Just exactly what I was thinking. I gotta get me some black ones next."

By eight o'clock I was sated with good food and overstuffed furniture and ready to once again take up the mantle of independent living. I staggered out of my parents' house, arms loaded with leftovers, and motored back to my apartment.

For the better part of the day I'd avoided thinking about the explosion, but it was time to face facts. Someone had tried to kill me, and it wasn't Ramirez. Ramirez wanted to inflict pain and hear me beg. Ramirez was frightening and abhorrent, but he was also predictable. I knew where Ramirez was coming from. Ramirez was criminally insane.

Planting a bomb was a different kind of insanity. A bombing was calculated and purposeful. A bombing was meant to rid the world of a particular, annoying person.

Why me? I thought. Why would someone want me dead? Even articulating the question sent a chill through my heart.

I parked the Nova in the middle of my lot and wondered if I'd have the courage to step on the accelerator tomorrow morning. Morelli's car had been shoveled away and there was little evidence of the fire. The macadam was pocked and cracked where the Jeep had burned, but there was no crime scene tape or charred debris to further mark the spot.

I let myself into my apartment and found my answering machine light furiously blinking. Dorsey had called three times requesting a call back. He didn't sound friendly. Bernie had called to say they were having a storewide sale and I should drop by. Twenty percent off blenders and a complimentary bottle of daiquiri mix to the first twenty customers. My eyes glazed over at the thought of a daiquiri. I still had a few dollars left, and blenders had to be pretty cheap in the overall scheme of things, right? The last call was from Jimmy Alpha with another apology and his hopes that I hadn't been badly hurt by Ramirez.

I looked at my watch. It was almost nine. I couldn't get to Bernie before closing. Too bad. I was pretty sure if I had a daiquiri I could think much more clearly and probably figure out who tried to send me into orbit.

I turned the television on and sat in front of it, but my mind was elsewhere. It was scanning for potential assassins. Of my captures only Lonnie Dodd was a possibility, and he was in jail. More likely this had to do with the Kulesza murder. Someone was worried about me poking around. I couldn't imagine anyone being worried enough to want to kill me. Death was very serious shit.

There had to be something I was missing here. Something about Carmen or Kulesza or Morelli . . . or maybe the mystery witness.

An ugly little thought wriggled around in a back corner of my brain. So far as I could see, I was a genuine, mortal threat to only one person. That person was Morelli.

The phone rang at eleven, and I caught it before the machine picked up.

"Are you alone?" Morelli asked.

I hesitated. "Yes."

"Why the hesitation?"

"How do you feel on the subject of murder?"

"Whose murder are we talking about?"

"Mine."

"I feel warm all over."

"Just wondering."

"I'm coming up. Watch for me at the door."

I tucked the defense spray into the waistband of my shorts and covered it with my T-shirt. I glued my eye to the peephole and opened the door when Morelli strolled down the hall. Every day he looked a little bit worse. He needed a haircut, and he had a week's worth of beard that probably had only taken him two days to grow. His jeans and T-shirt were street-person quality.

He closed and locked the door behind himself. He took in my scorched, bruised face and the bruises on my arm. His expression was grim. "You want to tell me about it?"

"The cut lip and the bruises are from Ramirez. We had a tussle, but I think I won. I gassed him and left him throwing up in the road."

"And the singed eyebrows?"

"Mmmm. Well, that's a little complicated."

His face darkened. "What happened?"

"Your car blew up."

There was no reaction for several beats. "You want to run that by me again?" he finally said.

"The good news is . . . you don't have to worry about Morty Beyers anymore."

"And the bad news?"

I took his license plate from the kitchen counter and handed it to him. "This is all that's left of your car."

He stared down at the plate in shocked silence.

I told him about Morty Beyers's wife leaving him, and the bomb, and the three phone calls from Dorsey.

He drew the same conclusion I'd drawn. "It wasn't Ramirez."

"I made a mental list of people who might want me dead, and your name was at the top."

"Only in my dreams," he said. "Who else was on the list?"

"Lonnie Dodd, but I think he's still in prison."

"You ever get death threats? How about ex-husbands or ex-boyfriends? You run over anyone recently?"

I had no intention of dignifying that question with a reaction.

"Okay," he said. "So you think this is associated with the Kulesza murder?"

"Yes."

"Are you scared?"

"Yes."

"Good. Then you'll be careful." He opened my refrigerator door, pulled out the leftovers my mom had sent home with me, and ate them cold. "You need to be careful when you talk to Dorsey. If he finds out you've been working with me, he could charge you with aiding and abetting."

"I have this very disturbing suspicion that I've been talked into an alliance that's not in my best interest."

He cracked a beer open. "The only way you're going to collect that $10,000 is if I allow you to bring me in. And I'm not going to allow you to bring me in if I can't prove myself innocent. Any time you want to call the deal off, just let me know, but you can kiss your money good-bye."

"That's a rotten attitude."

He shook his head. "Realistic."

"I could have gassed you any number of times."

"I don't think so."

I whipped the spray out, but before I could aim he'd knocked the canister from my hand and sent it flying across the room.

"Doesn't count," I said. "You were expecting it."

He finished his sandwich and slid his dish into the dishwasher. "I'm always expecting it."

"Where do we go from here?"

"We keep doing more of the same. Obviously we're hitting a nerve."

"I don't like being a target."

"You aren't going to whine about this, are you?" He settled himself in front of the television and starting working the channel changer. He looked tired, sitting with his back against the wall, one leg bent at the knee. He locked in a late night show and closed his eyes. His breathing grew deep and even and his head slumped to his chest.

"I could gas you now," I whispered.

He raised his head, but he didn't open his eyes. A smile played at the corners of his mouth. "It's not your style, Cupcake."

He was still sleeping on the floor in front of the television when I got up at eight. I tiptoed past him and went out to run. He was reading the paper and drinking coffee when I returned.

"Anything in there about the bombing?" I asked.

"Story and pictures on page three. They're calling it an unexplained explosion. Nothing especially interesting." He looked over the top of the paper at me. "Dorsey left another message on your machine. Maybe you should see what he wants."

I took a fast shower, dressed in clean clothes, slathered some aloe cream on my blistered face, and followed my scaly nose to the coffeepot. I drank half a cup while I read the funnies, and then I called Dorsey.

"We've got the analysis back from the lab," he said. "It was definitely a bomb. Professional job. Of course, you can get a book out of any library will tell you how to do a professional bombing. You could build a fucking nuke if you wanted to. Anyway, I thought you'd want to know."

"I suspected as much."

"You have any ideas who would do such a thing?"

"No names."

"How about Morelli?"

"That's a possibility."

"I missed you at the station yesterday."

He was fishing. He knew there was something screwy about all of this. He just hadn't figured it out yet. Welcome to the club, Dorsey. "I'll try to get there today."

"Try real hard."

I hung up and topped off my coffee. "Dorsey wants me to come in."

"Are you going?"

"No. He's going to ask questions I can't answer."

"You should put in some time on Stark Street this morning."

"Not this morning. I have things to do."

"What things?"

"Personal things."

He raised an eyebrow.

"I have some loose ends to tie up . . . just in case," I said.

"Just in case what?"

I made an exasperated gesture. "Just in case something happens to me. For the past ten days I've been stalked by a professional sadist, and now I'm on the happy bomber's hit list. I feel a little insecure, okay? Give me a break, Morelli. I need to see some people. I have a few personal errands to run."

He gently peeled a strip of loose skin off my nose. "You're going to be okay," he said softly. "I understand that you're scared. I get scared too. But we're the good guys, and the good guys always win."

I really felt like a jerk, because here was Morelli being nice to me, and what I actually wanted to do was hop on over to Bernie's to buy a blender and get my free daiquiri mix.

"How were you planning on running these errands without the Jeep?" he asked.

"I retrieved the Nova."

He winced. "You didn't park it in the lot, did you?"

"I was hoping the bomber wouldn't know it was my car."

"Oh boy."

"I'm sure I have nothing to worry about," I said.

"Yeah. I'm sure, too. I'll go down with you just to make double sure."

I collected my gear, checked the windows, and reset the answering machine. Morelli was waiting for me at the door. We walked downstairs together, and we both paused when we reached the Nova.

"Even if the bomber knew this was your car, he'd have to be stupid to try the same thing twice," Morelli said. "Statistically the second hit comes from a different direction."

Made perfect sense to me, but my feet were stuck to the pavement and my heart was rocketing around in my chest. "All right. Here I go," I said. "Now or never."

Morelli had dropped to his belly and was looking under the Nova.

"What do you see?" I asked him.

"A hell of an oil leak." He crawled out and got to his feet.

I raised the hood and checked the dipstick. Wonder of wonders, the car needed oil. I fed it two cans and slammed the hood down.

Morelli had taken the keys from the door handle and angled himself behind the wheel. "Stand back," he said to me.

"No way. This is my car. I'll start it up."

"If one of us is going to get blown apart it might as well be me. I'm as good as dead if I don't find that missing witness, anyway. Move away from the car."

He turned the key. Nothing happened. He looked at me.

"Sometimes you have to smack it around," I said.

He turned the key again and brought his fist down hard on the dash. The car coughed and caught. It idled rough and then settled in.

Morelli slumped against the wheel, eyes closed. "Shit."

I looked in the window at him. "Is my seat wet?"

"Very funny." He got out of the car and held the door for me. "Do you want me to follow?"

"No. I'll be fine. Thanks."

"I'll be on Stark Street if you need me. Who knows . . . maybe the witness will show up at the gym."

When I got to Bernie's store I noticed people weren't standing in line to go through the door, so I assumed I was in good shape for the daiquiri mix.

"Hey," Bernie said, "look who's here."

"I got your message about the blender."

"It's this little baby," he said, patting a display blender. "It chops nuts, crushes ice, mashes bananas, and makes a hell of a daiquiri."

I looked at the price affixed to the blender. I could afford it. "Sold. Do I get my free daiquiri mix?"

"You bet." He took a boxed blender to the register, bagged it, and rang it up. "How's it going?" he asked cautiously, his eyes fixed on the singed stumps of hair that had once been eyebrows.

"It's been better."

"A daiquiri will help."

"Without a shadow of a doubt."

On the other side of the street, Sal was Windexing his front door. He was a pleasant-looking man, thick-bodied and balding, wrapped in his white butcher's apron. So far as I knew, he was a small-time bookie.

Nothing special. I doubted he was connected. So why would a guy like Kulesza, whose entire life centered on Stark Street, drive all the way across town to see Sal? I knew a few of Kulesza's vital statistics, but I didn't know anything of his personal life. Shopping at Sal's was the only moderately interesting piece of information I had about Kulesza. Maybe Ziggy was a betting man. Maybe he and Sal were old friends. Maybe they were related. Now that I thought about it, maybe Sal would know about Carmen or the guy with the flat nose.

I chatted with Bernie for a few more minutes while I settled into the idea of interviewing Sal. I watched a woman enter the shop and make a purchase. This seemed like a good approach to me. It would give me an opportunity to look around.

I promised Bernie I'd be back for bigger and better appliances and walked across the street to Sal's.

CHAPTER 13

I pushed through Sal's front door and went to the long case filled with steaks and ground meat patties and twine-bound roasts.

Sal gave me a welcoming smile. "What can I do for you?"

"I was at Kuntz's, buying a blender . . ." I held the bag up for him to see. "And I thought I'd get something for supper while I was here."

"Sausage? Fresh fish? Nice piece of chicken?"

"Fish."

"I got some flounder just caught off the Jersey shore."

Probably it glowed in the dark. "That'll be fine. Enough for two people."

Somewhere in the back a door opened, and I could hear the drone of a truck motor. The door clanged shut, and the motor noise disappeared.

A man entered from the hallway beside the walk-in, and my heart jumped into triple time. Not only was the man's nose smashed, but his entire face looked as if it had been pressed flat . . . as if it had been hit with a frying pan. I couldn't know for sure until Morelli took a look, but I suspected I'd found the missing witness.

I was torn between wanting to jump up and down and make sounds of excitement and wanting to bolt and run before I was hacked up into chops and roasts.

"Got a delivery for you," the man said to Sal. "You want it in the lockup?"

"Yeah," Sal said. "And take the two barrels set by the door. One of them's heavy. You'll need the dolly."

Sal's attention turned back to the fish. "How you gonna cook these fillets?" he asked me. "You know you can pan fry them, or bake them, or stuff them. Personally, I like them fried. Heavy batter, deep fat."

I heard the back door close after the guy with the flat face. "Who was that?" I asked.

"Louis. Works for the distributor in Philly. He brings up meat."

"And then what does he take back in the barrels?"

"Sometimes I save up trim. They use it for dog food."

I had to grit my teeth to keep from flying out the door. I'd found the witness! I was sure of it. By the time I got to the Nova I was dizzy with the effort of restraint. I was saved! I was going to be able to pay my rent. I'd succeeded at something. And now that the missing witness was found, I'd be safe. I'd turn Morelli in and have nothing more to do with Ziggy Kulesza. I'd be out of the picture. There'd be no reason for anyone to want to kill me . . . except, of course, Ramirez. And, hopefully, Ramirez would be implicated sufficiently to put him away for a long, long time.

The old man across from Carmen's apartment had said he'd been bothered by the noise from a refrigerator truck. Dollars to donuts it had been a meat truck. I couldn't know for sure until I did another check on the back of Carmen's apartment building, but if Louis had parked close enough he might have been able to ease himself down onto the roof of the refrigerator truck. Then he put Carmen on ice and drove away.

I couldn't figure the connection with Sal. Maybe there was no connection. Maybe it was just Ziggy and Louis working as cleanup for Ramirez.

I had a decent view of Sal's from where I sat. I shoved the key into the ignition and took one last look. Sal and Louis were talking. Louis was cool. Sal was agitated, throwing his hands into the air. I decided to watch awhile. Sal turned his back on Louis and made a phone call. Even from this distance I could see he wasn't happy. He slammed the receiver down, and both men went into the walk-in freezer and reappeared moments later rolling out the trim drum. They shunted the drum down the hallway leading to the back exit. Louis reappeared a short while later with what appeared to be a side of beef slung over his shoulder. He deposited the meat in the freezer and rolled out the second drum. He paused at the back hallway and stared toward the front of the store. My heart skipped in my chest, and I wondered if he could see me snooping. He walked forward, and I reached for my Sure Guard. He stopped at the door and turned the little OPEN sign to CLOSED.

I hadn't expected this. What did this mean? Sal was nowhere in sight, the store was closed, and so far as I knew it wasn't a holiday. Louis left through the back hallway, and the lights went out. I got a bad feeling in the pit of my stomach. The bad feeling escalated to panic, and the panic told me not to lose Louis.

I put the Nova in gear and drove to the end of the block. A white refrigerator truck with Pennsylvania plates eased into traffic ahead of me, and two blocks later we turned onto Chambers. I would have liked nothing better than to drop the whole thing in Morelli's lap, but I hadn't a clue how to get in touch with him. He was north of me on Stark Street, and I was heading south. He probably had a phone in the van, but I didn't know the number, and besides, I couldn't call him until we stopped somewhere.

The refrigerator truck picked up Route 206 at Whitehorse. Traffic was moderately heavy. I was two car lengths back, and I found it fairly easy to stay hidden and at the same time keep sight of Louis. Just past the junction of Route 70 my oil light went on and stayed on. I did some vigorous swearing, screeched to a stop on the shoulder, poured two cans of oil with breakneck precision, slammed the hood, and took off.

I pushed the Nova up to eighty, ignoring the shimmy in the front end and the startled looks of other drivers as I rattled past them in my pussymobile. After an agonizing couple of miles I caught sight of the truck. Louis was one of the slower drivers on the road, holding his speed down to only ten miles an hour over the limit. I breathed a sigh of relief and fell into place. I prayed he wasn't going far. I only had a case and a half of oil in the backseat.

At Hammonton, Louis left turned onto a secondary road and drove east. There were fewer cars on this road, and I had to drop farther back. The countryside was rolling farmland and patches of woods. After about fifteen miles, the truck slowed and pulled into a gravel drive that led to a corrugated metal warehouse-type building. The sign on the front of the building said this was the Pachetco Inlet Marina and Cold Storage. Beyond the building I could see boats and beyond the boats the glare of sun on open water.

I sailed by the lot and made a U-turn a quarter mile up the road where it dead-ended at the Mullico River. I returned and did a slow drive-by. The truck was parked at the board walkway that led to the boat slips. Louis and Sal were out of the truck, leaning against the back step bumper, looking like they were waiting for something or someone. They were alone in the lot. It was a small marina, and it seemed that even though it was summer, most of the activity was still weekend-based.

I'd passed a gas station a few miles back. I decided it would be an inconspicuous place to wait. If Sal or Louis left the marina they'd go in this direction, back to civilization, and I could follow. There was the added advantage of a public phone and the possibility of getting in touch with Morelli.

The station was pre-computer age with two old-fashioned gas pumps on a stained cement pad. A sign propped on one of the pumps advertised live bait and cheap gas. The single-level shack behind the pumps was brown shingle patched with flattened jerry cans and assorted pieces of plywood. A public phone had been installed next to the screen door.

I parked, partially hidden, behind the station, and walked the short distance to the phone, happy for the opportunity to stretch my legs. I called my own number. It was the only thing I could think to do. The phone rang once, the machine answered, and I listened to my own voice tell me I wasn't home. "Anybody there?" I asked. No reply. I gave the public phone number and suggested if anyone needed to get in touch with me I'd be at that number for an indeterminate number of minutes.

I was about to get back into my car when Ramirez's Porsche sped by. This is curiouser and curiouser, I thought. Here we have a butcher, a shooter, and a boxer, meeting at the Pachetco Inlet Marina. It seemed unlikely that they were just three guys going fishing. If it had been anyone other than Ramirez who had driven down the road, I might have ventured closer to take a peek. I told myself I was holding back because Ramirez might recognize the Nova. This was only part of the truth. Ramirez had succeeded in his goal. The mere sight of his car sent me into a cold sweat of terror that left serious doubts about my ability to function through another confrontation.

A short time later, the Porsche hummed past me, en route to the highway. The windows were tinted, obscuring vision, but at best it could only seat two men, so that left at least one man at the marina. Hopefully, that one man was Louis. I made another call to my answering machine. This message was more urgent. "CALL ME!" I said.

It was close to dark before the phone finally rang.

"Where are you?" Morelli asked.

"I'm at the shore. At a gas station on the outskirts of Atlantic City. I've found the witness. His name is Louis."

"Is he with you?"

"He's down the road." I briefed Morelli on the day's events and gave him directions to the marina. I bought a soda from an outside machine and went back to do more waiting.

It was deep twilight when Morelli finally pulled up next to me in the van. There'd been no traffic on the road since Ramirez, and I was sure the truck hadn't slipped by. It had occurred to me that Louis might be on a boat, possibly spending the night. I couldn't see any other reason for the truck to still be in the marina lot.

"Is our man at the marina?" Morelli asked.

"So far as I know."

"Has Ramirez come back?"

I shook my head no.

"Think I'll take a look around. You wait here."

No way was I doing any more waiting anywhere. I was fed up with waiting. And I didn't entirely trust Morelli. He had an annoying habit of making beguiling promises and then waltzing out of my life.

I followed the van to the water's edge and parked beside it. The white refrigerator truck hadn't been moved. Louis wasn't out and about. The boats tied up to the wharf were dark. The Pachetco Inlet Marina was not exactly a bustling hub of activity.

I got out of the Nova and walked around to Morelli.

"I thought I told you to wait at the gas station," Morelli said. "We look like a fucking parade."

"I thought you might need help with Louis."

Morelli was out of the van and standing beside me, looking disreputable and dangerous in the dark. He smiled, and his teeth were startlingly white against his black beard. "Liar. You're worried about your $10,000."

"That too."

We stared at each other for a while, making silent assessments.

Morelli finally reached through the open window, snatched a jacket off the front seat, pulled a semiautomatic from the jacket pocket, and shoved it into the waistband of his jeans. "I suppose we might as well look for my witness."

We walked to the truck and peered inside the cab. The cab was empty and locked. No other cars were parked in the lot.

Nearby, water lapped at pilings, and boats groaned against their moorings. There were four board docks with fourteen slips each, seven to a side. Not all of the slips were in use.

We quietly walked the length of each dock, reading boat names, looking for signs of habitation. Halfway down the third dock we stopped at a big Hatteras Convertible with a flying bridge, and we both mouthed the boat's name. "Sal's Gal."

Morelli boarded and crept aft. I followed several feet behind. The deck was littered with fishing gear, long-handled nets and gaffs. The door to the salon was padlocked on the outside, telling us Louis was probably not on the inside. Morelli pulled a penlight from his pocket and shone it into the cabin window. The largest portion of the boat interior appeared to have been stripped down for serious fishing, similar to a head boat, with utilitarian benches in place of more luxurious accommodations. The small galley was cluttered with crushed beer cans and stacks of soiled paper plates. The residue from some sort of powder spill glittered under the penlight.

"Sal's a slob," I said.

"You sure Louis wasn't in the car with Ramirez?" Morelli asked.

"I have no way of knowing. The car has tinted glass. But it only seats two, so at least one person is left here."

"And there were no other cars on the road?"

"No."

"He could have gone in the other direction," Morelli said.

"He wouldn't have gone far. It dead-ends in a quarter mile."

The moon was low in the sky, spilling silver dollars of light onto the water. We looked back at the white refrigerator truck. The cooler motor hummed quietly in the darkness.

"Maybe we should take another look at the truck," Morelli said.

His tone gave me an uneasy feeling, and I didn't want to voice the question that had popped into my head. We'd already determined Louis wasn't in the cab. What was left?

We returned to the truck, and Morelli scanned the outside thermostat controls for the refrigeration unit.

"What's it set at?" I asked.

"Twenty."

"Why so cold?"

Morelli stepped down and moved to the back door. "Why do you think?"

"Somebody's trying to freeze something?"

"That would be my guess, too." The back door to the truck was held closed by a heavy-duty bolt and padlock. Morelli weighed the padlock in the palm of his hand. "Could be worse," he said. He jogged to the van and returned with a small hacksaw.

I nervously looked around the lot. I didn't especially want to get caught hijacking a meat truck. "Isn't there a better way to do this?" I stage-whispered over the rasp of the saw. "Can't you just pick the lock?"

"This is faster," Morelli said. "Just keep your eyes peeled for a night watchman."

The saw blade lunged through the metal, and the lock swung open. Morelli threw the bolt back and pulled on the thick, insulated door. The interior of the truck was stygian black. Morelli hauled himself up onto the single-step bumper, and I scrambled after him, wrestling my flashlight out of my shoulder bag. The frigid air pressed against me and took my breath away. We both trained our lights on the frost-shrouded walls. Huge, empty meathooks hung from the ceiling. Nearest the door was the large trim barrel I'd seen them roll out earlier in the afternoon. The empty barrel stood nearby, its lid slanted between the barrel and the truck wall.

I slid my spot of light farther to the rear and dropped it lower. My eyes focused, and I sucked in cold air when I realized what I was seeing. Louis was sprawled spread-eagle on his back, his eyes impossibly wide and unblinking, his feet splayed. Snot had run out of his nose and frozen to his cheek. A large urine stain had crystallized on the front of his work pants. He had a large, dark dot in the middle of his forehead. Sal lay next to him with an identical dot and the same dumbstruck expression on his frozen face.

"Shit," Morelli said. "I'm not having any luck at all."

The only dead people I'd ever seen had been embalmed and dressed up for church. Their hair had been styled, their cheeks had been rouged, and their eyes had been closed to suggest eternal slumber. None of them had been shot in the forehead. I felt bile rise in my throat and clapped a hand over my mouth.

Morelli yanked me out the door and onto the gravel. "Don't throw up in the truck," he said. "You'll screw up the crime scene."

I did some deep breathing and willed my stomach to settle.

Morelli had his hand at the back of my neck. "You going to be okay?"

I nodded violently. "I'm fine. Just t-t-took me b-b-by surprise."

"I need some stuff from the van. Stay here. Don't go back in the truck and don't touch anything."

He didn't have to worry about me going back into the truck. Wild horses couldn't drag me back into the truck.

He returned with a crowbar and two pairs of disposable gloves. He gave one pair to me. We snapped the gloves on, and Morelli climbed up the step bumper. "Shine the light on Louis," he ordered, bending over the body.

"What are you doing?"

"I'm looking for the missing gun."

He stood and tossed a set of keys at me. "No gun on him, but he had these keys in his pocket. See if one of them opens the cab door."

I opened the passenger side door and searched the map pockets, the glove compartment, and under the seat, but I didn't come up with a gun. When I went back to Morelli he was working at the sealed drum with a crowbar.

"No gun up front," I said.

The lid popped off, and Morelli flicked his flashlight on and looked inside.

"Well?" I asked.

His voice was tight when he answered. "It's Carmen."

I was hit with another wave of nausea. "You think Carmen's been in Sal's freezer all this time?"

"Looks like it."

"Why would he keep her around? Wouldn't he be afraid someone would discover her?"

Morelli shrugged. "I suppose he felt safe. Maybe he's done this sort of thing before. You do something often enough, and you become complacent."

"You're thinking about those other women who've disappeared from Stark Street."

"Yeah. Sal was probably just waiting for a convenient time to take Carmen out and dump her at sea."

"I don't understand Sal's connection."

Morelli hammered the lid back on. "Me either, but I feel pretty confident Ramirez can be persuaded to explain it to us."

He wiped his hands on his pants and left smudges of white.

"What's with all this white stuff?" I asked. "Sal got a thing with baby powder or cleanser or something?"

Morelli looked down at his hands and his pants. "I hadn't noticed."

"There was powder on the floor of the boat. And now you picked some up from the drum and wiped it on your pants."

"Jesus," Morelli said, staring at his hand. "Holy shit." He flipped the lid off the drum and ran his finger around the inside rim. He put the finger to his mouth and tasted it. "This is dope."

"Sal doesn't strike me as a crackhead."

"It's not crack. It's heroin."

"Are you sure?"

"I've seen a lot of it."

I could see him smiling in the dark.

"Sweet Pea, I think we've just found ourselves a drop boat," he said. "All along I've been thinking this was about protecting Ramirez, but now I'm not so sure. I think this might be about drugs."

"What's a drop boat?"

"It's a small boat that goes out to sea to rendezvous with a larger ship engaged in drug smuggling.

"Most of the world's heroin comes from Afghanistan, Pakistan, Burma. It's usually routed through northern Africa, then up to Amsterdam or some other European city. In the past, the favored method of entry for the northeast has been to body-pack it through Kennedy. For a year now, we've been getting tips that the stuff is traveling big time on ships coming into Port Newark. The DEA and Customs have been working overtime and coming up empty." He held his finger in the air for inspection. "I think this could be the reason. By the time the ship sails into Newark, the heroin's already been offloaded."

"Onto a drop boat," I said.

"Yeah. The drop boat snags the dope from the mother ship and brings it back to a small marina like this where there are no customs inspectors.

"My guess is they load the stuff into these barrels after it's handed down, and one of the bags broke last time out."

"Hard to believe someone would be that sloppy about leaving incriminating evidence."

Morelli grunted. "You work with drugs all the time and they become commonplace. You wouldn't believe what people leave in full view in apartments and garages. Besides, the boat belongs to Sal, and chances are Sal wasn't along for the ride. That way if the boat gets busted, Sal says he loaned it to a friend. He didn't know it was being used for illegal activities."

"You think this is why there's so much heroin in Trenton?"

"Could be. When you have a drop boat like this you can bring in large quantities and eliminate the couriers, so you have good availability at low overhead. The cost on the street goes down and the purity goes up."

"And addicts start dying."

"Yeah."

"Why do you think Ramirez shot Sal and Louis?"

"Maybe Ramirez had to burn some bridges."

Morelli played his light over the back corners of the truck. I could barely see him in the dark, but I could hear the scrape of his feet as he moved.

"What are you doing?" I asked.

"I'm looking for a gun. In case you haven't noticed I'm shit out of luck. My witness is dead. If I can't find Ziggy's missing gun with an intact latent, I'm as good as dead, too."

"There's always Ramirez."

"Who may or may not be feeling talkative."

"I think you're overreacting. I can place Ramirez at the scene of two execution-type killings, and we've uncovered a major drug operation."

"Possibly this casts some doubt about Ziggy's character, but it doesn't alter the fact that I appeared to have shot an unarmed man."

"Ranger says you've got to trust in the system."

"Ranger *ignores* the system."

I didn't want to see Morelli in jail for a crime he didn't commit, but I also didn't want him living the life of a fugitive. He was actually a pretty good guy, and as much as I hated to admit it, I'd become fond of him. When the manhunt was over I'd miss the teasing and the late-night companionship. It was true that Morelli still touched a nerve every now and then, but there was a new feeling of partnership that transcended most of my earlier anger. I found it hard to believe he would be sent to jail in light of all the new evidence. Possibly he would lose his job on the force. This seemed like a minor disgrace to me when compared to spending long years in hiding.

"I think we should call the police and let them sort through this," I said to Morelli. "You can't stay in hiding for the rest of your life. What about your mother? What about your phone bill?"

"My phone bill? Oh shit, Stephanie, you haven't been running up my phone bill, have you?"

"We had an agreement. You were going to let me bring you in when we found the missing witness."

"I hadn't counted on him being dead."

"I'll be evicted."

"Listen, Stephanie, your apartment isn't all that great. Besides, this is wasted talk. We both know you aren't capable of bringing me in by force. The only way you're going to collect your money is by my permission. You're just going to have to sit tight."

"I don't like your attitude, Morelli."

The light whirled, and he lunged toward the door. "I don't much care what you think of my attitude. I'm not in a good mood. My witness is dead, and I can't find the damn murder weapon. Probably Ramirez will squeal like a pig, and I'll be exonerated, but until that happens I'm staying hidden."

"The hell you are. I can't believe it's in your best interest. Suppose some cop sees you and shoots you? Besides, I have a job to do, and I'm going to do it. I should never have made this deal with you."

"It was a good deal," he said.

"Would you have made it?"

"No. But I'm not you. I have skills you could only dream about. And I'm a hell of a lot meaner than you'll ever be."

"You underestimate me. I'm pretty fucking mean."

Morelli grinned. "You're a marshmallow. Soft and sweet and when you get heated up you go all gooey and delicious."

I was rendered speechless. I couldn't believe just seconds before I'd been thinking friendly, protective thoughts about this oaf.

"I'm a fast learner, Morelli. I made a few mistakes in the beginning, but I'm capable of bringing you in now."

"Yeah, right. What are you going to do, shoot me?"

I wasn't soothed by his sarcasm. "The thought isn't without appeal, but shooting isn't necessary. All I have to do is close the door on you, you arrogant jerk."

In the dim light I saw his eyes widen as understanding dawned a nanosecond before I swung the heavy, insulated door shut. I heard the muffled thud of his body slam against the interior, but he was too late. The bolt was already in place.

I adjusted the refrigeration temperature to forty. I figured that would be cold enough to keep the corpses from defrosting, but not so cold I'd turn Morelli into a popsicle on the ride back to Trenton. I climbed into the cab and cranked the motor over—compliments of Louis's keys. I lumbered out of the lot and onto the road and headed for the highway.

Halfway home I found a pay phone and called Dorsey. I told him I was bringing Morelli in, but I didn't provide any details. I told him I'd be rolling into the station's back lot in about forty-five minutes and it'd be nice if he was waiting for me.

I swung the truck into the driveway on North Clinton right on time and caught Dorsey and two uniforms in my headlights. I cut the engine, did some deep breathing to still my nervous stomach, and levered myself out of the cab.

"Maybe you should have more than two uniforms," I said. "I think Morelli might be mad."

Dorsey's eyebrows were up around his hairline. "You've got him in the back of the truck?"

"Yeah. And he isn't alone."

One of the uniforms slid the bolt, the door flew open, and Morelli catapulted himself out at me. He caught me midbody, and we both went down onto the asphalt, thrashing and rolling and swearing at each other.

Dorsey and the uniforms hauled Morelli off me, but he was still swearing and flailing his arms. "I'm gonna get you!" he was yelling at me. "When I get outta here I'm gonna get your ass. You're a goddamn lunatic. You're a menace!"

Two more patrolmen appeared, and the four uniforms wrestled Morelli through the back door. Dorsey lagged behind with me. "Maybe you should wait out here until he calms down," he said.

I picked some cinders out of my knee. "That might take a while."

I gave Dorsey the keys to the truck and explained about the drugs and Ramirez. By the time I was done explaining, Morelli had been moved upstairs, and the coast was clear for me to get my body receipt from the docket lieutenant.

It was close to twelve when I finally let myself into my apartment, and my one real regret for the evening was that I'd left my blender at the marina. I truly needed a daiquiri. I locked my front door and tossed my shoulder bag onto the kitchen counter.

I had mixed feelings about Morelli . . . not sure if I'd done the right thing. In the end, it hadn't been the retrieval money that had mattered. I'd acted on a combination of righteous indignation and my own conviction that Morelli should surrender himself.

My apartment was dark and restful, lit only by the light in the hall. Shadows were deep in the living room, but they didn't generate fear. The chase was over.

Some thought needed to be given to my future. Being a bounty hunter was much more complicated than I'd originally assumed. Still, it had its high points, and I'd learned a lot in the past two weeks.

The heat wave had broken late in the afternoon and the temperature had dropped to a lovely seventy degrees. My curtains were closed, and a breeze played in the lightweight chintz. A perfect night for sleeping, I thought.

I kicked my shoes off and sat on the edge of my bed, suddenly feeling mildly uneasy. I couldn't pinpoint the source of the problem. Something seemed off. I thought about my pocketbook far away on the kitchen counter, and my apprehension increased. Paranoia, I told myself. I was locked in my apartment, and if someone tried to come through the window, which was highly unlikely, I'd have time to stop them.

Still, the ripple of anxiety nagged at me.

I looked over at the window, at the gently billowing curtains, and cold understanding struck like a knife slice. When I'd left my apartment the window had been closed and locked. The window was open now. Jesus, the window was *open*. Fear skittered through me, snatching my breath away.

Someone was in my apartment . . . or possibly waiting on my fire escape. I bit down hard on my lower lip to keep from wailing. Dear God, don't let it be Ramirez. Anyone but Ramirez. My heart beat with a ragged thud, and my stomach sickened.

As I saw it, I had two choices. I could run for the front door or dive down the fire escape. That was assuming my feet would move. I decided chances were greater that Ramirez was in the apartment than on the fire escape, so I went to the window. On a sharp intake of breath I ripped the curtains open and stared at the latch. It was secure. A circle of glass had been removed from the top window, allowing Whoever to slip an arm through and open the lock. The cool night air whistled softly through the neatly cut circle.

Professional, I thought. Maybe not Ramirez. Maybe just your garden variety second-story man. Maybe he'd gotten discouraged by my poverty, decided to move on to fatter pickings, and locked up after himself. I looked through the opening at the fire escape. It was empty and felt benign.

Call the police and report the break-in, I told myself. The phone was at bedside. I punched it on and nothing happened. Shit. Someone must have disconnected it in the kitchen. A little voice in my head whispered to get out of the apartment. Use the fire escape, it said. Move fast.

I turned back to the window and fumbled with the latch. I heard movement behind me, felt the intruder's presence. In the window's reflection I could see him standing in the open bedroom door, framed by the weak light from the hall.

He called my name, and I felt my hair stand on end like the cartoon version of an electrocuted cat.

"Close the curtains," he said, "and turn around nice and slow so I can see you."

I did as I was told, squinting in the dark in blind confusion, recognizing the voice but not understanding the purpose. "What are you doing here?" I asked.

"Good question." He flipped the light switch. It was Jimmy Alpha, and he was holding a gun. "I ask myself that question all the time," he said. "How did it come to this? I'm a decent man, you know? I try to do what's right."

"Doing what's right is good," I told him.

"What happened to all your furniture?"

"I had some hard times."

He nodded. "Then you know what it's like." He grinned. "That why you started working for Vinnie?"

"Yeah."

"Vinnie and me, we're sort of alike. We do what we have to do to hang in there. I guess you're like that too."

I didn't like being lumped in with Vinnie, but I wasn't about to argue with a guy who was holding a gun. "I guess I am."

"You follow the fights?"

"No."

He sighed. "A manager like me waits a whole lifetime for a decent fighter to come along. Most managers die without ever getting one."

"But you got one. You have Ramirez."

"I took Benito in when he was just a kid. Fourteen years old. I knew right away he was gonna be different from the others. There was something about him. Drive. Power. Talent."

Insanity, I thought. Don't forget insanity.

"Taught him everything he knows about boxing. Gave him all my time. Made sure he ate right. Bought him clothes when he had no money. Let him sleep in the office when his mother was crazy on crack."

"And now he's champ," I said.

His smile was tight. "It's my dream. All my life I've worked for this."

I was beginning to see the direction of the conversation. "And he's out of control," I said.

Jimmy sagged against the doorjamb. "Yeah. He's out of control. He's gonna ruin everything . . . all the good times, all the money. I can't tell him anything, anymore. He don't listen."

"What are you going to do about it?"

"Ahh," Alpha sighed. "That's the big question. And the answer to the question is diversify. I diversify, I make a shitload of money, excuse my language, and I get out.

"You know what it means to diversify? It means I take the money I make on Ramirez, and I invest it in other businesses. A chicken franchise, a laundromat, maybe even a butcher shop. Maybe I can get a butcher shop real cheap because the guy who owns it can't make good on some bad bets he took."

"Sal."

"Yeah. Sal. You got Sal real upset today. Bad timing, the way you walked in just when Louis got there, but I guess in the end it's gonna work out okay."

"I didn't realize Sal knew me."

"Honey, you're not hard to recognize. You don't got no eyebrows."

"Sal was worried that I spotted Louis."

"Yeah. So, he called me, and I said we should all meet at the marina. Louis was going to the marina anyway. There's a drop coming in tomorrow, and I'm thinking maybe I'm going to have to do Louis because he's such a fuck-up. The guy can't do anything right. He lets people see him at Carmen's, then he has to take care of them. He only gets two out of three. He can't score Morelli. The dumb shit found Morelli's car in your parking lot and didn't stop to think maybe Morelli wasn't driving it, so he ends up roasting Morty Beyers. Now you've got Louis fingered. I figure his time is up.

"So I borrow Benito's car, and I go to the marina, and on the way I see you at the gas station, and I get a brilliant idea. Jimmy, I say to myself, this is your way out."

I was having a hard time following. I still didn't completely understand Jimmy's involvement. "Out of what?" I asked.

"Out of the whole fucking mess. See, there's something you got to understand about me. I gave up a lot for the fight game. I never got around to getting married or to having a family. All my life I never had anything but boxing. When you're young, you don't mind. You keep thinking there's time. But then one day you wake up, and you find out there's no more time.

"I've got a fighter who likes to hurt people. It's a sickness. There's something messed up in his head, and I can't make it better. I know he's not gonna go the count on his career, so I take the money we make, and I buy a couple properties. Next thing I know I meet this Jamaican guy says he's got a better way to make money. Drugs. I make the buy, his organization does the distribution, I wash the money through my businesses and Ramirez. We do this for a while and it works real good. All we have to do is keep Ramirez out of jail so we can launder.

"Problem is, I've got a lot of money now, and I can't get out. The organization's got me by my gonads, you know what I mean?"

"Striker."

"Yeah. Big motherfucking Jamaican posse. Greedy, nasty beggars.

"So I'm going down the road to whack Louis, I see you sitting there, and I get a plan. The plan is that I execute Sal and Louis Striker style. Then I leave some high-quality H spilled in the boat and on the barrel so the cops figure out the operation and shut it down. Now no one's left to talk about me behind my back, and I'm too risky for Striker to use for a while. And the beauty of it is that Sal and Louis get pinned on Ramirez, thanks to you. I'm sure when you made your statement to the cops you told them all about Ramirez buzzing by you at the gas station."

"I still don't understand why you're here, holding me at gunpoint."

"I can't take a chance on Ramirez talking to the cops and maybe they come to the conclusion he's really as dumb as he looks. Or maybe he tells them I borrowed his car, and they believe him. So I'm going to have you put a bullet in him. Then there's no Benito, no Sal, no Louis."

"What about Stephanie?"

"There's not going to be any Stephanie, either." He had the phone base shoved into his slacks. He plugged it into my bedroom wall jack and dialed. "My man," he said when the connection was made. "I've got a girl here wants attention."

Something was said at the other end.

"Stephanie Plum," Jimmy answered. "She's at home, waiting for you. And Benito, make sure no one sees you. Maybe you better come up the fire escape."

The conversation was severed and the phone discarded.

"Is this what happened to Carmen?" I asked.

"Christ, Carmen was a mercy killing. I don't know how she ever made it home. By the time we heard about it she'd already called Morelli."

"Now what?"

He leaned back against the wall. "Now we wait."

"What happens when Ramirez gets here?"

"I turn my back while he does his thing, then I shoot him with your gun. By the time the police show up, you'll both have bled to death, and there'll be no more loose ends."

He was deadly serious. He was going to watch while Ramirez raped and tortured me, and then he was going to make sure I was mortally injured.

The room swam in front of me. My legs wobbled, and I found myself sitting on the edge of the bed. I dropped my head between my knees and waited for the fog to clear. A vision of Lula's battered body flashed into my mind, feeding my terror.

The dizziness faded, but my heart pounded hard enough to rock my body. Take a chance, I thought. Do something! Don't just sit here and wait for Ramirez.

"You okay?" Alpha said to me. "You don't look good."

I kept my head down. "I'm going to be sick."

"You need to go to the can?"

My head was still between my knees. I shook it, no. "Just give me a minute to catch my breath."

Nearby, Rex ran in his cage. I couldn't bear to look over, knowing it might be the last time I'd see him. Funny how a person can get so attached to a little creature like that. A lump formed in my throat at the thought of Rex being orphaned, and the message came back to me. Do something! *Do something!*

I said a short prayer, gritted my teeth, and bucked forward, lunging at Alpha, catching him off guard, nailing him in the gut with a head butt.

Alpha let out a *woof!* of air, and the gun discharged over my head, shattering my window. If I'd had any cool at all I would have followed up with a good hard kick to the crotch, but I was operating on thoughtless energy, with adrenaline pumping into my system at warp speed. I was in fight-or-flight mode, and flight was the hands-down choice.

I scrambled away from him, through the open bedroom door, into the living room. I was almost to the front hall when I heard another crack from his gun, and an electric stab of heat shot down my left leg. I yelped in pain and surprise, whirling off balance, into the kitchen. I grabbed my shoulder bag off the counter with two hands and searched for my .38. Alpha moved into the kitchen doorway. He aimed his gun and steadied it. "Sorry," he said. "There's no other way."

My leg was on fire and my heart was banging in my chest. My nose was running and tears blurred my vision. I had both hands on the little Smith & Wesson, still in my pocketbook. I blinked the tears away and fired.

CHAPTER 14

Rain pattered gently on my living room window, competing with the sound of Rex running in his wheel. It had been four days since I'd been shot, and the pain was down to an annoying but manageable ache.

The mental healing would be slower. I still had night terrors, still found it difficult to be alone in my apartment. After shooting Jimmy Alpha, I'd crawled to the phone and called the police before I'd passed out. They'd arrived in time to catch Ramirez halfway up my fire escape. Then they'd trundled him off to jail and me off to the hospital. Fortunately, I'd fared better than Alpha. He was dead. I was alive.

Ten thousand dollars had been deposited in my bank account. Not a cent of it had been spent yet. I was slowed down by seventeen stitches in my butt. When the stitches came out I figured I'd do something irresponsible like fly to Martinique for the weekend. Or maybe I'd get a tattoo or dye my hair red.

I jumped at the sound of someone knocking on my door. It was almost seven P.M., and I wasn't expecting company. I cautiously made my way to the foyer and looked out the peephole. I gasped at the sight of Joe Morelli in sports coat and jeans, clean shaven, hair freshly trimmed. He stared directly at the peephole. His smile was smug. He knew I was looking at him, wondering if it would be wise to open the door. He waved, and I was reminded of a time two weeks earlier when our positions had been reversed.

I unlocked the two dead bolts but left the chain in place. I cracked the door. "Yes?"

"Take the chain off," Morelli said.

"Why?"

"Because I brought you a pizza, and if I tip it on end to give it to you the cheese will slide off."

"Is it a Pino's pizza?"

"Of course it's a Pino's pizza."

I shifted my weight to ease my left leg. "Why are you bringing me pizza?"

"I don't know. I just felt like it. Are you going to open the door or what?"

"I haven't decided."

This brought a slow, evil smile. "Are you afraid of me?"

"Uh . . . yes."

The smile stayed fixed in place. "You should be. You locked me in a refrigerator truck with three dead people. Sooner or later, I'm going to get you for it."

"But not tonight?"

"No," he said. "Not tonight."

I closed the door, slid the chain free, and opened the door to him.

He put the white pizza box and a six-pack on the kitchen counter and turned to me. "Looks like you're walking a little slow. How are you feeling?"

"Okay. Fortunately, Alpha's bullet tore through some fat and did most of its damage to the wall in the hallway."

His smile had faded. "How are you really feeling?"

I'm not sure what it is about Morelli, but he never fails to strip my defenses. Even when I'm on guard, being watchful, Morelli can piss me off, turn me on, make me question my judgment, and, in general, provoke inconvenient emotions. Concern pinched the corners of his eyes, and there was a seriousness to his mouth that belied the casual tone of his question.

I bit down hard on my lip, but the tears came anyway, silently spilling down my cheeks.

Morelli gathered me into his arms and held me close. He rested his cheek against the top of my head and pressed a kiss into my hair.

We stood like that for a long time, and if it hadn't been for the pain in my butt I might have fallen asleep, finally comforted and at peace, feeling safe in Morelli's arms.

"If I ask you a serious question," Morelli murmured against my ear, "will you give me an honest answer?"

"Maybe."

"Do you remember that time in my father's garage?"

"Vividly."

"And when we went at it in the bakery . . ."

"Un huh."

"Why did you do it? Are my powers of persuasion really that strong?"

I tipped my head back to look at him. "I suspect it had more to do with curiosity and rebellion on my part." Not to mention hormones on the rampage.

"So you're willing to share some of the responsibility?"

"Of course."

The smile had returned to his mouth. "And, if I made love to you here in the kitchen . . . how much of the blame would you be willing to assume?"

"Jesus, Morelli, I've got seventeen stitches in my ass!"

He sighed. "Do you think we could be friends after all these years?"

This from the person who had tossed my keys into a Dumpster. "I suppose it's possible. We wouldn't have to sign a pact and seal it in blood, would we?"

"No, but we could belch over beer."

"My kind of contract."

"Good. Now that we have that settled, there's a ball game I'd like to see, and you have my television."

"Men always have ulterior motives," I said, carting the pizza into the living room.

Morelli followed with the beer. "How do you manage this sitting business?"

"I have a rubber donut. If you make any cracks about it, I'll gas you."

He shrugged out of his jacket and shoulder holster, hung them on the doorknob to my bedroom door, buzzed the TV on, and searched for his channel. "I got some reports for you," he said. "Are you up to it?"

"A half hour ago I might have said no, but now that I have this pizza I'm up to anything."

"It's not the pizza, darlin'. It's my masculine presence."

I raised an eyebrow.

Morelli ignored the eyebrow. "First of all, the medical examiner said you were due for the Robin Hood sharpshooter award. You got Alpha with five rounds to the heart, all within an inch of each other. Pretty amazing, considering you also shot the shit out of your pocketbook."

We both chugged some beer, since neither of us was sure yet how we felt about me killing a man. Pride seemed out of place. Sorrow didn't quite fit. There was definitely regret.

"Do you think it could have ended any other way?" I asked.

"No." Morelli said. "He would have killed you if you hadn't killed him first."

This was true. Jimmy Alpha would have killed me. There was no doubt in my mind.

Morelli leaned forward to see the pitch. Howard Barker struck out. "Shit," Morelli said. He turned his attention back to me. "Now for the good part. I had a recorder attached to the utility pole on the far side of your parking lot. I was using it for backup when I wasn't around. I could check it at the end of the day and catch up if I'd missed anything. The damn thing was still working when Jimmy dropped in on you. Recorded the whole conversation, the shooting and everything, clear as a bell."

"Dang!"

"Sometimes I'm so slick I scare myself," Morelli said.

"Slick enough not to be locked up in jail."

He selected a piece of pizza, losing some green pepper and onion slices in the process, scooping them back on with his fingers. "I've been cleared of all charges and reinstated in the department, pay retroactive. The gun was in the barrel with Carmen. It had been refrigerated all this time, so the prints were clear, and forensics found traces of blood on it. DNA hasn't come back yet, but preliminary lab tests suggest the blood is Ziggy's, proving Ziggy was armed when I shot him. Apparently, the gun jammed when Ziggy fired at me, just as I'd suspected. When Ziggy hit the floor, the gun fell out of his hand, and Louis picked it up and took it with him. Then Louis must have decided to get rid of it."

I took a deep breath and asked the question that had been uppermost in my mind for the last three days. "What about Ramirez?"

"Ramirez is being held without bail pending psychiatric evaluation. Now that Alpha is out of the picture, several very creditable women have come forward to testify against Ramirez."

The sense of relief was almost painful.

"What are your plans?" Morelli asked. "You going to keep working for Vinnie?"

"I'm not sure." I ate some pizza. "Probably," I said. "Almost definitely probably."

"Just to clear the air," Morelli said. "I'm sorry I wrote that poem about you on the stadium wall when we were in high school."

I felt my heart stutter. "On the stadium wall?"

Silence.

Color rose to Morelli's cheekbones. "I thought you knew."

"I knew about Mario's Sub Shop!"

"Oh."

"Are you telling me you wrote a poem about me on the *stadium wall*? A poem detailing what transpired behind the éclair case?"

"Would it help any if I told you the poem was flattering?"

I wanted to smack him, but he was on his feet and moving before I could get out of my rubber tube.

"It was years ago," he said, dancing away from me. "Shit, Stephanie, it's unattractive to hold a grudge."

"You are scum, Morelli. *Scum.*"

"Probably," Morelli said, "but I give good . . . pizza."

TWO FOR THE DOUGH

To Alex and Peter

Because they've always had more faith than common sense—and are careful not to step on a dream

CHAPTER 1

I knew Ranger was beside me because I could see his earring gleaming in the moonlight. Everything else about him—his T-shirt, his flack vest, his slicked-back hair, and 9-mm Glock—was as black as the night. Even his skin tone seemed to darken in shade. Ricardo Carlos Mañoso, the Cuban-American chameleon.

I, on the other hand, was the blue-eyed, fair-skinned product of a Hungarian-Italian union and was not nearly so cleverly camouflaged for clandestine evening activities.

It was late October, and Trenton was enjoying the death throes of Indian summer. Ranger and I were squatting behind a hydrangea bush at the corner of Paterson and Wycliff, and we weren't enjoying Indian summer, each other's company, or much of anything else. We'd been squatting there for three hours, and squatting was taking its toll on our good humor.

We were watching the small clapboard Cape Cod at 5023 Paterson, following a tip that Kenny Mancuso was scheduled to visit his girlfriend, Julia Cenetta. Kenny Mancuso had recently been charged with shooting a gas station attendant (who also happened to be his former best friend) in the knee.

Mancuso had posted a bail bond via the Vincent Plum Bail Bonding Company, insuring his release from jail and returning him to the bosom of polite society. After his release he'd promptly disappeared and three days later failed to show face at a preliminary hearing. This did not make Vincent Plum happy.

Since Vincent Plum's losses were my windfalls, I saw Mancuso's disappearance from a more opportunistic perspective. Vincent Plum is my cousin and my employer. I work for Vinnie as a bounty hunter, dragging felons who are beyond the long arm of the law back into the system. Dragging Kenny back was going to net me 10 percent of his $50,000 bond. A portion of that would go to Ranger for assisting with the takedown, and the rest would pay off my car loan.

Ranger and I had a sort of loose partnership. Ranger was a genuine, cool-ass, numero-uno bounty hunter. I asked him to help me because I was still learning the trade and needed all the help I could get. His participation was in the ballpark of a pity fuck.

"Don't think this is gonna happen," Ranger said.

I'd done the intel and was feeling defensive that maybe I'd had my chain yanked. "I spoke to Julia this morning. Explained to her that she could be considered an accessory."

"And that made her decide to cooperate?"

"Not exactly. She decided to cooperate when I told her how before the shooting Kenny had been sometimes seeing Denise Barkolowski."

Ranger was smiling in the dark. "You lie about Denise?"

"Yeah."

"Proud of you, babe."

I didn't feel bad about the lie since Kenny was a scumbag felon, and Julia should be setting her sights higher anyway.

"Looks like maybe she thought twice about reaping the rewards of revenge and waved Kenny away. You find out where he's living?"

"He's moving around. Julia doesn't have a phone number for him. She says he's being careful."

"He a first-time offender?"

"Yeah."

"Probably nervous about checking into the big house. Heard all those stories about date rape."

We turned silent as a pickup approached. It was a new Toyota 4×4 fresh off the showroom floor. Dark color. Temporary plates. Extra antennae for a car phone. The Toyota eased up at the Cape Cod and pulled into the driveway. The driver got out and walked to the front door. His back was to us and the lighting was poor.

"What do you think?" Ranger asked. "Is that Mancuso?"

I couldn't tell from this distance. The man was the right height and weight. Mancuso was twenty-one years old, six feet tall, 175 pounds, dark brown hair. He'd been discharged from the army four months ago, and he was in good shape. I had several pictures that were obtained when the bond had been posted, but they didn't do me any good from this angle.

"Could be him, but I can't swear to it without seeing his face," I said.

The front door of the house opened and the man disappeared inside. The door closed shut.

"We could go knock on the door nice and polite and ask if he's the man," Ranger said.

I nodded in agreement. "That might work."

We stood and adjusted our gun belts.

I was dressed in dark jeans, long-sleeved black turtleneck, navy Kevlar vest, and red Keds. I had my curly, shoulder-length brown hair tied in a ponytail, tucked under a navy ball cap. I wore my five-shot .38 Smith & Wesson Chief's Special in a black nylon webbed hip holster with cuffs and a defense spray wedged into the back of the belt.

We walked across the lawn and Ranger rapped on the front door to the house with a flashlight that was eighteen inches long and eight inches round at the reflector. It gave good light, and Ranger said it was excellent for making serious head dents. Fortunately, I've never had to witness any bludgeoning. I'd fainted flat out watching *Reservoir Dogs* and had no illusions about my blood-and-guts comfort level. If Ranger ever had to use the flashlight to crack skulls while I was around, I intended to close my eyes . . . and then maybe I'd take up another profession.

When no one answered I stepped to the side and unholstered my revolver. Standard procedure for the backup partner. In my case, it was more or less an empty gesture. I religiously went to the range to practice, but truth is I'm hopelessly unmechanical. I harbor an irrational fear of guns, and most of the time keep my little S & W empty of bullets so I won't accidentally blast the toes off my foot. On the one occasion I'd had to shoot somebody I'd been so flustered I'd forgotten to take my gun out of my pocketbook before pulling the trigger. I wasn't eager to repeat the performance.

Ranger rapped again, with more force. "Fugitive apprehension agent," he called out. "Open the door."

This drew a response, and the door was opened, not by Julia Cenetta or Kenny Mancuso, but by Joe Morelli, a Trenton Police Department plainclothesman.

We all stood silent for a moment, everyone surprised to see everyone else.

"That your truck in the driveway?" Ranger finally asked Morelli.

"Yeah," Morelli said. "Just got it."

Ranger nodded. "Good-looking vehicle."

Morelli and I were both from the burg, a blue-collar chunk of Trenton where dysfunctional drunks were still called bums and only pansies went to Jiffy Lube for an oil change. Morelli had a long history of taking advantage of my naiveté. I'd recently had the opportunity to even the score, and now we were in a period of reevaluation, both of us jockeying around for position.

Julia peeked at us from behind Morelli.

"So what happened?" I said to Julia. "I thought Kenny was supposed to stop around tonight?"

"Yeah, right," she said. "Like he ever does anything he says."

"Did he call?"

"Nothing. No call. Nothing. He's probably with Denise Barkolowski. Why don't you go knock on her stupid door?"

Ranger stayed stoic, but I knew he was smiling inside. "I'm out of here," he said. "Don't like to get involved in these domestic unpleasantries."

Morelli had been watching me. "What happened to your hair?" he asked.

"It's under my hat."

He had his hands shoved into his jeans pockets. "Very sexy."

Morelli thought everything was sexy.

"It's late," Julia said. "I gotta go to work tomorrow."

I looked at my watch. It was ten-thirty. "You'll let me know if you hear from Kenny?"

"Yeah, sure."

Morelli followed me out. We walked to his truck and stared at it in silence for a while, thinking our own thoughts. His last car had been a

Jeep Cherokee. It had been bombed and blown to smithereens. Fortunately for Morelli, he hadn't been in the car at the time.

"What are you doing here?" I finally asked.

"Same as you. Looking for Kenny."

"I didn't think you were in the bond enforcement business."

"Mancuso's mother was a Morelli, and the family asked if I'd look for Kenny and talk to him before he got himself into any more trouble."

"Jesus. Are you telling me you're related to Kenny Mancuso?"

"I'm related to everyone."

"You're not related to me."

"You have any leads besides Julia?"

"Nothing exciting."

He gave that some thought. "We could work together on this."

I raised an eyebrow. Last time I worked with Morelli I'd gotten shot in the ass. "What would you contribute to the cause?"

"Family."

Kenny might be dumb enough to turn to family. "How do I know you won't cut me out at the end?" As he was sometimes prone to do.

His face was all hard planes. The sort of face that started off handsome and gained character as it aged. A paper-thin scar sliced through his left eyebrow. Mute testimony to a life lived outside the normal range of caution. He was thirty-two. Two years older than me. He was single. And he was a good cop. The jury was still out on its assessment of him as a human being.

"Guess you'll just have to trust me," he said, grinning, rocking back on his heels.

"Oh boy."

He opened the door to the Toyota and new-car aroma washed over us. He hitched himself up behind the wheel and cranked the engine over. "Don't suppose Kenny will show up this late," he said.

"Not likely. Julia lives with her mother. Her mother's a nurse on the night shift at St. Francis. She'll be home in half an hour, and I can't picture Kenny waltzing in when Momma's here."

Morelli nodded agreement and drove off. When his taillights disappeared in the distance I walked to the far corner of the block where I'd parked my Jeep Wrangler. I'd gotten the Wrangler secondhand from

Skoogie Krienski. Skoogie had used it to deliver pizza from Pino's Pizzeria, and when the car got warm it smelled like baking bread and marinara sauce. It was the Sahara model, painted camouflage beige. Very handy in case I wanted to join an army convoy.

Probably I was right about it being too late for Kenny to show, but I figured it wouldn't hurt to hang out a little longer and make sure. I snapped the top on the Jeep so I wouldn't be so visible, and slouched back to wait. It wasn't nearly as good a vantage point as the hydrangea bush, but it was okay for my purposes. If Kenny appeared, I'd call Ranger on my cellular phone. I wasn't anxious to do a single-handed capture of a guy going down for grievous wounding.

After ten minutes a small hatchback passed by the Cenetta house. I slunk down in my seat and the car continued on. A few minutes later, it reappeared. It stopped in front of the Cape Cod. The driver beeped the horn. Julia Cenetta ran out and jumped into the passenger seat.

I rolled my engine over when they were half a block away, but waited for them to turn the corner before I hit the lights. We were on the edge of the burg, in a residential pocket of moderately priced single-family houses. There was no traffic, making it easier to spot a tail, so I stayed far behind. The hatchback connected with Hamilton and headed east. I hung tight, closing the gap now that the road was more traveled. I held this position until Julia and friend pulled into a mall lot and parked on the dark fringe.

The lot was empty at this time of night. No place for a nosy bounty hunter to hide. I cut my lights and eased into a parking place at the opposite end. I retrieved binoculars from the backseat and trained them on the car.

I almost jumped out of my shoes when someone rapped on my driver-side door.

It was Joe Morelli, enjoying the fact that he'd been able to catch me by surprise and scare the heck out of me.

"You need a night scope," he said affably. "You're not going to see anything at this distance in the dark."

"I haven't got a night scope, and what are you doing here anyway?"

"I followed you. Figured you'd watch for Kenny a while longer. You're not very good at this law enforcement stuff, but you're freaking lucky, and you've got the temperament of a pit bull with a soup bone when you're on a case."

Not a flattering assessment, but dead accurate. "You on good terms with Kenny?"

Morelli shrugged. "Don't know him all that well."

"So you wouldn't want to drive over there and say hello."

"Hate to ruin Julia's good time if it isn't Kenny."

We were both staring at the truck, and even without a night scope we could see it had begun to rock. Rhythmic grunting sounds and whimpers carried across the empty lot.

I resisted the urge to squirm in my seat.

"Damn," Morelli said. "If they don't pace themselves they're going to kill the shocks on that little car."

The car stopped rocking, the motor caught, and the lights flashed on.

"Jeez," I said. "That didn't take long."

Morelli hustled around to the passenger seat. "Must have gotten a head start on the way over. Wait until he hits the road before you use your lights."

"That's a great idea, but I can't see without my lights."

"You're in a parking lot. What's to see besides three acres of unobstructed macadam?"

I crept forward a little.

"You're losing him," Morelli said. "Step on it."

I pushed it up to 20, squinting into the darkness, swearing at Morelli that I couldn't see jackshit.

He made chicken sounds, and I mashed the gas pedal to the floor.

There was a loud *wump,* and the Wrangler bucked out of control. I slammed my foot to the brake and the car came to a sudden stop with the left side tilted at a 30-degree angle.

Morelli got out to take a look. "You're hung up on a safety island," he said. "Back up, and you should be okay."

I eased off the island and rolled several feet. The car pulled hard to the left. Morelli did the take-a-look thing again while I thrashed around in the driver's seat, sputtering and fuming and berating myself for listening to Morelli.

"Tough break," Morelli said, leaning into the open window. "You bent your rim when you hit the curb. You got road service?"

"You did this on purpose. You didn't want me to catch your rotten cousin."

"Hey, cupcake, don't blame me just because you made some bad driving decisions."

"You're scum, Morelli. Scum."

He grinned. "Better be nice. I could give you a ticket for reckless driving."

I yanked the phone out of my pocketbook and called Al's Auto Body. Al and Ranger were good friends. During the day Al ran a legitimate business. I suspected that at night he ran a chop shop, hacking up stolen cars. It didn't matter to me. I just wanted to get my tire fixed.

An hour later I was on my way. No sense trying to track down Kenny Mancuso. He'd be long gone. I stopped at a convenience store, bought a pint of artery-clogging coffee ice cream, and headed for home.

I live in a blocky three-story brick apartment building located a couple miles from my parents' house. The front door to the building opens to a busy street filled with little businesses, and a tidy neighborhood of single-family bungalows sprawls to the rear.

My apartment is in the back of the building, on the second floor, overlooking the parking lot. I have one bedroom, one bath, a small kitchen, and a living room that combines with the dining area. My bathroom looks like it came off the set from *The Partridge Family*, and due to temporarily strained finances my furniture could be described as eclectic—which is a snooty way of saying nothing matches.

Mrs. Bestler from the third floor was in my hall when I got off the elevator. Mrs. Bestler was eighty-three and didn't sleep well at night, so she walked the halls to get exercise.

"Hey, Mrs. Bestler," I said. "How's it going?"

"Don't do no good to complain. Looks like you've been out working tonight. You catch any criminals?"

"Nope. Not tonight."

"That's a pity."

"There's always tomorrow," I said, unlocking my door, slipping inside.

My hamster, Rex, was running on his wheel, his feet a blur of pink. I tapped on the glass cage by way of greeting, causing him to momentarily pause, his whiskers twitching, his shiny black eyes large and alert.

"Howdy, Rex," I said.

Rex didn't say anything. He's the small, silent type.

I dumped my black shoulder bag on the kitchen counter and got a spoon from the cutlery drawer. I popped the top on the ice cream container and listened to my phone messages while I ate.

All of the messages were from my mother. She was making a nice roast chicken tomorrow, and I should come for dinner. I should be sure not to be late because Betty Szajack's brother-in-law died and Grandma Mazur wanted to make the seven o'clock viewing.

Grandma Mazur reads the obituary columns like they're part of the paper's entertainment section. Other communities have country clubs and fraternal orders. The burg has funeral parlors. If people stopped dying the social life of the burg would come to a grinding halt.

I finished off the ice cream and put the spoon in the dishwasher. I gave Rex a few hamster nuggets and a grape and went to bed.

I woke up to rain slapping against my bedroom window, drumming on the old-fashioned black wrought-iron fire escape that serves as my balcony. I liked the way rain sounded at night when I was snug in bed. I couldn't get excited about rain in the morning.

I needed to harass Julia Cenetta some more. And I needed to run a check on the car that had picked her up. The phone rang, and I automatically reached for the portable at bedside, thinking it was early to be getting a phone call. The digital readout on my clock said 7:15.

It was my cop friend, Eddie Gazarra.

" 'Morning," he said. "Time to go to work."

"Is this a social call?" Gazarra and I had grown up together, and now he's married to my cousin Shirley.

"This is an information call, and I didn't make it. Are you still looking for Kenny Mancuso?"

"Yes."

"The gas station attendant he nailed in the knee got dead this morning."

This put me on my feet. "What happened?"

"A second shooting. I heard from Schmidty. He was working the desk when the call came in. A customer found the attendant, Moogey Bues, in the gas station office with a big hole in his head."

"Jesus."

"I thought you might be interested. Maybe there's a tie-in, maybe not. Could be Mancuso decided shooting his pal in the knee wasn't enough, and he came back to blow the guy's brains out."

"I owe you."

"We could use a baby-sitter next Friday."

"I don't owe you that much."

Eddie grunted and disconnected.

I took a fast shower, blasted my hair with the hair dryer, and squashed it under a New York Rangers hat, turning the brim to the back. I was wearing button-fly Levi's, a red plaid flannel shirt over a black T-shirt, and Doc Martens in honor of the rain.

Rex was asleep in his soup can after a hard night on the wheel, so I tiptoed past him. I switched the answering machine on, grabbed my pocketbook and my black-and-purple Gore-Tex jacket, and locked up behind myself.

The gas station, Delio's Exxon, was on Hamilton, not far from my apartment. I stopped at a convenience store on the way and got a large coffee to go and a box of chocolate-covered doughnuts. I figured if you had to breathe New Jersey air there wasn't much point in getting carried away with always eating healthy food.

There were a lot of cops and cop cars at the gas station, and an emergency rescue truck had backed itself up close to the office door. The rain had tapered off to a fine drizzle. I parked half a block away and made my way through the crowd, taking my coffee and doughnuts with me, looking to spot a familiar face.

The only familiar face I saw belonged to Joe Morelli.

I sidled up to him and opened the doughnut box.

Morelli took a doughnut and shoved half in his mouth.

"No breakfast?" I asked.

"Got yanked out of bed for this."

"I thought you were working vice."

"I am. Walt Becker is the primary here. He knew I was looking for Kenny, and thought I'd want to be included."

We both chewed some doughnut.

"So what happened?" I asked.

There was a crime photographer working in the office. Two paramedics stood by, waiting to zip the body into a bag and take off.

Morelli watched the action through the plate-glass window. "The M.E. estimates time of death at six-thirty. That's right about when the victim would have been opening up. Apparently someone just walked in and blew him away. Three shots to the face, close range. No indication of theft. The cash drawer was intact. No witnesses so far."

"A hit?"

"Looks like it."

"This garage selling numbers? Dealing dope?"

"Nothing I know about."

"Maybe it's personal. Maybe he was screwing someone's wife. Maybe he owed money."

"Maybe."

"Maybe Kenny came back to shut him up."

Morelli didn't move a muscle. "Maybe."

"You think Kenny'd do that?"

He shrugged. "Hard to say what Kenny'd do."

"You run the plate on that car last night?"

"Yeah. It belongs to my cousin Leo."

I raised an eyebrow.

"It's a big family," he said. "I'm not that close anymore."

"You going to talk to Leo?"

"Soon as I'm out of here."

I sipped some of the steaming coffee and watched his eyes lock onto the Styrofoam cup. "Bet you'd like to have some nice hot coffee," I said.

"I'd kill for coffee."

"I'll let you have some if you'll let me tag along when you talk to Leo."

"Deal."

I took one last sip and passed him the cup. "You check on Julia?"

"Did a drive-by. The lights were out. Didn't see the car. We can talk to her after we talk to Leo."

The photographer was finished and the paramedics went to work, trundling the body into a bag, hefting it onto a stretcher. The stretcher clattered as it rolled over the doorstep, the bag jiggling with its dead weight.

The doughnut say heavy in my stomach. I didn't know the victim, but I felt his loss all the same. Vicarious grief.

There were two homicide detectives on the scene, looking professional in trench coats. Under the trench coats they wore suits and ties. Morelli was wearing a navy T-shirt, Levi's, a tweed sport coat, and running shoes. A fine mist had settled on his hair.

"You don't look like the other guys," I said. "Where's your suit?"

"You ever see me in a suit? I look like a casino pit boss. I have special dispensation never to wear a suit." He took his keys from his pocket and gestured to one of the detectives that he was leaving. The detective nodded acknowledgment.

Morelli was driving a city car. It was an old tan Fairlane sedan with an antenna wired from the trunk and a hula doll stuck in the back window. It looked like it couldn't do 30 going uphill. It was dented and rusted and grime-coated.

"You ever wash this thing?" I asked.

"Never. I'm afraid to see what's under the dirt."

"Trenton likes to make law enforcement a challenge."

"Yeah," he said. "Wouldn't want it to be too easy. Take all the fun out of it."

Leo Morelli lived with his parents in the burg. He was the same age as Kenny, and he worked for the Turnpike Authority, like his father.

A blue-and-white was parked in their driveway, and the whole family was outside talking to a uniform when we pulled up.

"Someone stole Leo's car," Mrs. Morelli said. "Can you imagine? What's this world coming to? These things never used to happen in the burg. Now look."

These things never happened in the burg because it was like a retirement village for the mob. Years ago when Trenton rioted no one even considered sending a squad car in to protect the burg. Every old soldier and capo was up in his attic getting out his tommy gun.

"When did you notice it gone?" Morelli asked.

"This morning," Leo said. "When I came out to go to work. It wasn't here."

"When did you see it last?"

"Last night. When I came home from work at six o'clock."

"When was the last time you saw Kenny?"

Everybody blinked.

"Kenny?" Leo's mother said. "What's Kenny got to do with this?"

Morelli was back on his heels with his hands in his pockets. "Maybe Kenny needed a car."

No one said anything.

Morelli repeated it. "So, when was the last time anybody talked to Kenny?"

"Christ," Leo's father said to Leo. "Tell me you didn't let that asshole idiot have your car."

"He promised me he'd bring it right back," Leo said. "How was I to know?"

"Shit for brains," Leo's father said. "That's what you got . . . shit for brains."

We explained to Leo how he'd been aiding and abetting a felon, and how a judge might look askance at such an activity. And then we explained how if he ever saw or heard from Kenny again he should right away rat on him to his cousin Joe or Joe's good friend Stephanie Plum.

"Do you think he'll call us if he hears from Kenny?" I asked when we were alone in the car.

Morelli stopped for a light. "No. I think Leo will beat the crap out of Kenny with a tire iron."

"It's the Morelli way."

"Something like that."

"A man thing."

"Yeah. A man thing."

"How about after he beats the crap out of him? Do you think he'll call us then?"

Morelli shook his head. "You don't know much, do you?"

"I know a lot."

This brought a smile to Morelli's lips.

"Now what?" I asked.

"Julia Cenetta."

Julia Cenetta worked in the bookstore at Trenton State College. We checked her house first. When no one answered we headed off for the college. Traffic was steady, with everyone around us rigidly obeying the speed limit. Nothing like an unmarked cop car to slow things down to a crawl.

Morelli entered through the main gate and looped around toward the single-level brick-and-cement bookstore complex. We passed by a duck pond and a few trees and expanses of lawn that hadn't yet succumbed to winter blight. The rain had picked up again and was coming down with the boring relentlessness of an all-day soaker. Students walked head down, with the hoods pulled up on raincoats and sweatshirts.

Morelli took a look at the bookstore lot, filled to capacity with the exception of a few slots on the outermost rim, and without hesitation parked in a no-parking zone at the curb.

"Police emergency?" I asked.

"You bet your sweet ass," Morelli said.

Julia was working the register, but no one was buying, so she was standing hip against the cash drawer, picking at her fingernail polish. Little frown lines appeared between her eyebrows when she saw us.

"Looks like a slow day," Morelli said to her.

Julia nodded. "It's the rain."

"Hear anything from Kenny?"

Color crept into Julia's cheeks. "Actually, I sort of saw him last night. He called right after you left, and then he came over. I told him you wanted to talk to him. I told him he should call you. I gave him your card with your beeper numbers and everything."

"Do you think he'll come back tonight?"

"No." She shook her head for emphasis. "He said he wasn't coming back. He said he had to keep a real low profile because there were people after him."

"The police?"

"I think he meant someone else, but I don't know who."

Morelli gave her another card with instructions to call him anytime, day or night, if she heard from Kenny.

She looked noncommittal, and I didn't think we should count on much help from Julia.

We went back out into the rain and hustled to the car. Aside from

Morelli, the only piece of cop equipment in the Fairlane was a recycled two-way radio. It was tuned to the police tactical channel and the dispatcher relayed calls between bursts of static. I had a similar radio in my Jeep, and I was struggling to learn the police codes. Like all other cops I knew, Morelli listened unconsciously, miraculously processing the garbled information.

He turned out of the campus, and I asked the inevitable question. "Now what?"

"You're the one with the instincts. You tell me."

"My instincts aren't doing a lot for me this morning."

"Okay, then let's run down what we have. What do we know about Kenny?"

After last night we knew he was a premature ejaculator, but that probably wasn't what Morelli wanted to hear. "Local boy, high school graduate, enlisted in the army, got out four months ago. Still unemployed, but obviously not hurting for money. For unknown reasons he decided to shoot his friend Moogey Bues in the knee. He got caught in the process by an off-duty cop. He had no priors and was released on bond. He violated his bond contract and stole a car."

"Wrong. He borrowed a car. He just hasn't gotten around to returning it yet."

"You think that's significant?"

Morelli stopped for a light. "Maybe something happened to change his plans."

"Like acing ol' Moogey."

"Julia said Kenny was afraid someone was after him."

"Leo's father?"

"You're not taking this seriously," Morelli said.

"I'm taking it very seriously. I'm just not coming up with much, and I don't notice you sharing a lot of your thoughts with me. For instance, who do you think is after Kenny?"

"When Kenny and Moogey were questioned about the shooting they both said it was over a personal issue and wouldn't discuss it. Maybe they had some bad business going on."

"And?"

"And that's it. That's what I think."

I stared at him for a moment, trying to decide if he was holding out on me. Probably he was, but there was no way to tell for sure. "Okay," I finally said on a sigh, "I have a list of Kenny's friends. I'm going to run through it."

"Where'd you get this list?"

"Privileged information."

Morelli looked pained. "You broke into his apartment and stole his little black book."

"I didn't steal it. I copied it."

"I don't want to hear any of this." He glanced down at my pocketbook. "You're not carrying concealed, are you?"

"Who, me?"

"Shit," Morelli said. "I must be crazy to team up with you."

"It was your idea!"

"Want me to help with the list?"

"No." I figured that might be like giving a lottery ticket to your neighbor and having him win the jackpot on it.

Morelli parked behind my Jeep. "There's something I need to tell you before you leave."

"Yes?"

"I hate those shoes you're wearing."

"Anything else?"

"I'm sorry about your tire last night."

Yeah, right.

By five o'clock I was cold and wet, but had gotten through the list. I'd done a combination of phone calls and face-to-faces, and had netted very little. Most of the people were from the burg and had known Kenny all of his life. No one admitted to having contact with him after his arrest, and I had no reason to suspect they were lying. No one knew of any business deals or personal problems between Kenny and Moogey. Several people testified to Kenny's volatile personality and wheeler-dealer mentality. These comments were interesting, but too general to be really helpful. A few conversations had long, pregnant pauses that made me uncomfortable, wondering what was left unsaid.

As my last effort of the day I'd decided to check Kenny's apartment again. The super had let me in two days before when he'd been temporarily confused as to my law enforcement affiliation. I'd surreptitiously lifted a spare key while admiring the kitchen, and now I could tippy-toe around whenever I wanted. The legality of this was a tad gray, but it would only be bothersome if I got caught.

Kenny lived just off Route 1 in a large apartment complex named Oak Hill. Since there were no hills or oaks in sight I can only guess they were leveled to make way for the three-story brick bunkers advertised as affordable luxury housing.

I parked in one of the slots and squinted through the dark and the rain to the lighted front entrance. I waited a moment while a couple sprinted from their car and hurried into the building. I transferred Kenny's keys and my defense spray from my big black leather purse to my jacket pocket, pulled my jacket hood over my damp hair, and lurched out of the Jeep. The temperature had dropped during the course of the day, and the chill seeped through my wet jeans. So much for Indian summer.

I walked through the lobby with my head down and hood still up and had the good fortune to get an empty elevator. I rode to the third floor and hurried down the corridor to 302. I listened at the door for a moment, and heard nothing. I knocked. I knocked again. No answer. I inserted the key and with hammering heart quickly stepped inside, immediately flicking the lights on. The apartment appeared to be empty. I went room to room in a cursory search and decided Kenny hadn't returned since my last visit. I checked his answering machine. No messages.

Once again, I listened at the door. All was silent on the other side. I turned the lights out, took a deep breath, and propelled myself out into the hall, gasping with relief that the whole thing was over and I hadn't been seen.

When I got back to the lobby I went straight to the mailboxes and checked Kenny's. It was crammed full of stuff. Stuff that might help me find Kenny. Unfortunately, tampering with the mail is a federal offense. Stealing mail is an especially big no-no. It would be wrong, I told myself. Mail is sacred. Yes, but wait a minute. I had a *key!* Didn't that give me some rights? Again, this was a gray issue since I'd sort of stolen the key. I put my nose to the grate and looked inside. A phone bill. This might give me clues. My fingers itched with the need to get at the phone bill. I was dizzy with temptation. Temporary insanity, I thought. I was in the grip of temporary insanity. All right!

I took a deep breath, rammed the key into the tiny keyhole, opened the mailbox, and shoveled the mail into my big black bag. I clicked the little mailbox door closed and left in a sweat, trying to get to the safety of my car before sanity returned and my defense was screwed.

CHAPTER 2

I crammed myself behind the wheel, locked the doors, and furtively looked around to see if I'd been spotted committing a federal offense. I had my pocketbook pressed to my chest, and there were little black dots dancing in front of my eyes. Okay, so I wasn't the coolest, baddest bounty hunter ever. What mattered was that I was going to get my man, right?

I stuck the key into the ignition, cranked the engine over, and pulled out of the lot. I slapped Aerosmith into the tape deck and punched up the volume when I hit Route 1. It was dark and raining, with bad visibility, but this was Jersey, and we don't slow down for anything. Brake lights flashed in front of me, and I fishtailed to a stop. The traffic light turned green, and we all took off with our foot to the floor. I cut over two lanes to line up for the turnoff, beating out a Beemer. The driver flipped me the bird and blew his horn.

I responded with some derisive Italian hand gestures and commented on his mother. Being born in Trenton carries a certain responsibility in these situations.

Traffic dragged along city streets, and I was relieved to finally cross over the train tracks and feel the burg growing closer, sucking me forward. I reached Hamilton, and the tractor beam of familial guilt locked onto my car.

My mother was peering out the storm door when I parked at the curb. "You're late," she said.

"Two minutes!"

"I heard sirens. You weren't in an accident, were you?"

"No. I wasn't in an accident. I was working."

"You should get a real job. Something steady with normal hours. Your cousin Marjorie got a nice secretarial job with J and J. I hear she makes big money."

Grandma Mazur was standing in the hall. She lived with my parents now that Grandpa Mazur was scarfing down his normal two-eggs-and-a-half-pound-of-bacon breakfast in the hereafter.

"We better get a move on with this dinner if we're gonna make the viewing," Grandma Mazur said. "You know how I like to get there early, so I can get a good seat. And the Knights of Columbus will be there tonight. There'll be a big crowd." She smoothed the front of her dress. "What do you think of this dress?" she asked me. "You think it's too flashy?"

Grandma Mazur was seventy-two and didn't look a day over ninety. I loved her dearly, but when you got her down to her skivvies, she resembled a soup chicken. Tonight's dress was a fire-engine-red shirtwaist with shiny gold buttons. "It's perfect," I told her. Especially for the funeral home, which would be cataract central.

My mother brought the mashed potatoes to the table. "Come and eat," she said, "before the mashed potatoes get cold."

"So what did you do today?" Grandma Mazur asked. "You have to rough anyone up?"

"I spent the day looking for Kenny Mancuso, but I didn't have much luck."

"Kenny Mancuso is a bum," my mother said. "All those Morelli and Mancuso men are trash. You can't trust a one of them."

I looked over at my mother. "Have you heard any news about Kenny? Anything going through the gossip mill?"

"Just that he's a bum," my mother said. "Isn't that enough?"

In the burg it is possible to be born into bumhood. The Morelli and Mancuso women are above reproach, but the men are jerks. They drink, they cuss, they slap their kids around and cheat on their wives and girlfriends.

"Sergie Morelli will be at the viewing," Grandma Mazur said. "He'll be there with the K of C. I could grill him for you. I'd be real sneaky about it too. He's always been kind of sweet on me, you know."

Sergie Morelli was eighty-one years old and had a lot of bristly gray hair coming out of ears that were half the size of his withered head. I didn't expect Sergie knew where Kenny was hiding, but sometimes bits and pieces of seemingly benign information turned out to be useful. "How about if I come to the viewing with you," I said, "and we can grill Sergie together?"

"I guess that would be okay. Just don't cramp my style."

My father rolled his eyes and forked into his chicken.

"Do you think I should carry?" Grandma Mazur asked. "Just in case?"

"Jesus," my father said.

We had warm homemade apple pie for dessert. The apples were tart and cinnamony. The crust was flaky and crisp with a sprinkling of sugar. I ate two pieces and almost had an orgasm. "You should open a bakery," I said to my mother. "You could make a fortune selling pies."

She was busy stacking pie plates and gathering up silverware. "I have enough to do to take care of the house and your father. Besides, if I was to go to work, I'd want to be a nurse. I've always thought I'd make a good nurse."

Everyone stared at her openmouthed. No one had ever heard her voice this aspiration. In fact, no one had ever heard her voice *any* aspiration that didn't pertain to new slipcovers or draperies.

"Maybe you should think about going back to school," I told my mother. "You could enroll in the community college. They have a nursing program."

"I wouldn't want to be a nurse," Grandma Mazur said. "They gotta wear them ugly white shoes with the rubber soles, and they empty bedpans all day. If I was going to get a job, I'd want to be a movie star."

There are five funeral homes in the burg. Betty Szajack's brother-in-law, Danny Gunzer, was laid out at Stiva's Mortuary.

"When I die you make sure I'm taken to Stiva," Grandma Mazur said on the way over. "I don't want that no-talent Mosel laying me out. He don't know nothing about makeup. He uses too much rouge. Nobody looks natural. And I don't want Sokolowsky seeing me naked. I heard some funny things about Sokolowsky. Stiva is the best. If you're anybody at all, you go to Stiva."

Stiva's was on Hamilton, not far from St. Francis Hospital, in a large converted Victorian sporting a wraparound porch. The house was painted white with black shutters, and in deference to the wobbly old folks, Stiva had installed green indoor-outdoor carpeting from the front door, down the stairs to the sidewalk. A driveway ranto the back, where a four-car garage housed the essential vehicles. A brick addition had been added to the side opposite the driveway. There were two viewing rooms in the addition. I had never been given the full tour, but I assumed the embalming equipment was there as well.

I parked on the street and ran around the Jeep to help Grandma Mazur get out. She'd decided she couldn't do a good job of worming information out of Sergie Morelli in her standard-fare tennis shoes and was now precariously teetering on black patent leather heels, which she said all babes wore.

I took a firm grip on her elbow and ushered her up the stairs to the lobby, where the K of C were massing in their fancy hats and sashes. Voices were hushed, and footsteps muffled by new carpet. The aroma of cut flowers was overbearing, mingling with the pervasive odor of breath mints that didn't do much in the way of hiding the fact that the K of C had shored themselves up with large quantities of Seagram's.

Constantine Stiva had set up business thirty years ago and had presided over mourners every day since. Stiva was the consummate undertaker, his mouth forever fixed in Muzak mode, his high forehead pale and soothing as cold custard, his movements always unobtrusive and silent. Constantine Stiva . . . the stealth embalmer.

Lately Constantine's stepson, Spiro, had begun making undertaker noises, hovering at Constantine's side during evening viewings and assisting in morning burials. Death was clearly Constantine Stiva's life. It seemed more a spectator sport to Spiro. His smiles of condolence were all lips and teeth and no eyes. If I had to venture a guess as to his industry pleasures I'd go with the chemistry—the tilt-top tables and the pancreatic harpoons. Mary Lou Molnar's little sister went to grade school with Spiro and reported to Mary Lou that Spiro had saved his fingernail clippings in a glass jar.

Spiro was small and dark with hairy knuckles and a face that was dominated by nose and sloping forehead. The uncharitable truth was that he looked like a rat on steroids, and this rumor about the fingernail-saving did nothing to enhance his image in my eyes.

He'd been friends with Moogey Bues, but he hadn't seemed especially disturbed by the shooting. I'd spoken to him briefly while working my way through Kenny's little black book. Spiro's response had been politely guarded. Yes, he'd hung with Moogey and Kenny in high school. And yes, they'd stayed friends. No, he couldn't think of a motive for either shooting. No, he hadn't seen Kenny since his arrest and hadn't a clue as to his whereabouts.

Constantine was nowhere to be seen in the lobby, but Spiro stood directing traffic in a conservative dark suit and crisp white shirt.

Grandma looked him over as one would a cheap imitation of good jewelry. "Where's Con?" she asked.

"In the hospital. Herniated disk. Happened last week."

"No!" Grandma said on a sharp intake of air. "Who's taking care of the business?"

"Me. I pretty much run the place, anyway. And then Louie's here, of course."

"Who's Louie?"

"Louie Moon," Spiro told her. "You probably don't know him because he mostly works mornings, and sometimes he drives. He's been with us for about six months."

A young woman pushed through the front door and stood halfway into the foyer. She searched the room while she unbuttoned her coat. She caught Spiro's eye, and Spiro did his official undertaker nod of greeting. The young woman nodded back.

"Looks like she's interested in you," Grandma said to Spiro.

Spiro smiled, showing prominent incisors and lowers crooked enough to give an orthodontist wet dreams. "A lot of women are interested in me. I'm a pretty good catch." He spread his arms wide. "This will all be mine someday."

"I guess I never looked at you in that light," Grandma said. "I suppose you could support a woman in fine style."

"I'm thinking of expanding," he said. "Maybe franchising the name."

"Did you hear that?" Grandma said to me. "Isn't it nice to find a young man with ambition."

If this went on much longer I was going to ralph on Spiro's suit.

"We're here to see Danny Gunzer," I told Spiro. "Nice talking to you, but we should be running along before the K of C takes up all the good seats."

"I understand perfectly. Mr. Gunzer is in the green room."

The green room used to be the parlor. It should have been one of the better rooms, but Stiva had painted it a bilious green and had installed overhead lighting bright enough to illuminate a football field.

"I hate that green room," Grandma Mazur said, hustling after me. "Every wrinkle shows in that room what with all those overhead lights. This is what it comes to when you let Walter Dumbowski do the electric. Them Dumbowski brothers don't know nothing. I tell you, if Stiva tries to lay me out in the green room you just take me home. I'd just as leave be put out on the curb for Thursday trash pickup. If you're anybody at all, you get one of the new rooms in the back with the wood paneling. Everybody knows that."

Betty Szajack and her sister were standing at the open casket. Mrs. Goodman, Mrs. Gennaro, old Mrs. Ciak, and her daughter were already seated. Grandma Mazur rushed forward and put her purse on a folding chair in the second row. Her place secured, she wobbled up to Betty Szajack and made her condolences while I worked the back of the room. I learned that Gail Lazar was pregnant, that Barkalowski's deli was cited by the health department, and that Biggy Zaremba was arrested for indecent exposure. But I didn't learn anything about Kenny Mancuso.

I meandered through the crowd, sweating under my flannel shirt and turtleneck, with visions of my damp hair steaming as it frizzed out to maximum volume. By the time I got to Grandma Mazur I was panting like a dog.

"Just look at this tie," she said, standing over the casket, eyes glued to Gunzer. "It's got little horse heads on it. If this don't beat all. Almost makes me wish I was a man so I could be laid out with a tie like this."

Bodies shuffled at the back of the room and conversation ceased as the K of C made its appearance. The men moved forward two by two, and Grandma Mazur went up on tiptoe, pivoting on her patent-leather spikes to get a good look. Her heel caught in the carpet and Grandma Mazur pitched back, her body board stiff.

She smacked into the casket before I could get to her, flailing with her arms for support, finally finding purchase on a wire stand supporting a large milk-glass vase of gladioli. The stand held, but the vase tipped out, crashing down onto Danny Gunzer, clonking him square in the forehead. Water sloshed into Gunzer's ears and dripped off his chin, and gladioli settled onto Gunzer's charcoal gray suit in colorful confusion. Everyone stared in speechless horror, half expecting Gunzer to jump up and shriek, but Gunzer didn't do anything.

Grandma Mazur was the only one not frozen to the floor. She righted herself and adjusted her dress. "Well, I guess it's a good thing he's dead," she said. "This way no harm's done."

"No harm? *No harm?*" Gunzer's widow yelled, wild-eyed. "Look at his tie. His tie is ruined. I paid extra for that tie."

I mumbled apologies to Mrs. Gunzer and offered to make good on the tie, but Mrs. Gunzer was in the middle of a fit and wasn't hearing any of it.

She shook her fist at Grandma Mazur. "You ought to be locked up. You and your crazy granddaughter. A bounty hunter! Who ever heard of such a thing?"

"Excuse me?" I said, slitty-eyed with fists on hips.

Mrs. Gunzer took a step back (probably afraid I was going to shoot her), and I used the space to retreat. I snagged Grandma Mazur by the elbow, gathered her belongings together, and steered her toward the door, almost knocking Spiro over in my haste.

"It was an accident," Grandma said to Spiro. "I caught my heel on the carpet. Could have happened to anybody."

"Of course," Spiro said. "I'm sure Mrs. Gunzer realizes this."

"I don't realize nothing," Mrs. Gunzer bellowed. "She's a threat to normal people."

Spiro guided us into the foyer. "Hope this incident won't keep you from returning to Stiva's," he said. "We always like to see pretty women come to visit." He leaned closer, his lips hovering at my ear in a conspiratorial whisper. "I'd like to speak to you in private about some business I need conducted."

"What sort of business?"

"I need something found, and I hear you're very good at finding. I asked around after you inquired about Kenny."

"Actually I'm pretty busy right now. And I'm not a private investigator. I'm not licensed."

"A thousand dollars," Spiro said. "Flat finder's fee."

Time stood still for several heartbeats while I went on a mental spending binge. "Of course if we kept it quiet, I don't see any harm in helping a friend." I lowered my voice. "What are we looking for?"

"Caskets," Spiro whispered. "Twenty-four caskets."

Morelli was waiting for me when I got home. He was slouched against the wall, hands stuffed into pockets, ankles crossed. He looked up expectantly when I stepped out of the elevator and smiled at the brown grocery bag I carried.

"Let me guess," he said. "Leftovers."

"Gee, now I know why you made detective."

"I can do better." He sniffed the air. "Chicken."

"Keep it up and you might make the K-9 Corps."

He held the bag while I opened the door. "Have a tough day?"

"My day passed tough at five o'clock. If I don't get these clothes off soon I'm going to mildew."

He sidestepped into the kitchen and pulled a foil-wrapped packet of chicken out of the bag, along with a container of stuffing, a container of gravy, and a container of mashed potatoes. He put the gravy and potatoes in the microwave and set it for three minutes. "How'd the list go? Anything interesting turn up?"

I gave him a plate and silverware and took a beer from the refrigerator. "Big zero. No one's seen him."

"You have any clever ideas about where we go from here?"

"No." Yes! The mail! I'd forgotten about the mail in my pocketbook. I hauled it out and spread it on the kitchen counter—phone bill, MasterCard bill, a bunch of junk mail, and a postcard reminder that Kenny was due for a dental checkup.

Morelli glanced over while he ladled gravy on the dressing, potatoes, and cold chicken. "Is that your mail?"

"Don't look."

"Shit," Morelli said. "Isn't anything sacred to you?"

"Mom's apple pie. So what should I do here? Should I steam the envelopes or something?"

Morelli dropped the envelopes on the floor and smushed them with his shoe. I picked them up and examined them. They were torn and dirty.

"Received in damaged condition," Morelli said. "Do the phone bill first."

I paged through the statement and was surprised to find four overseas calls.

"What do you make of this?" I asked Morelli. "You know any of these codes?"

"The top two are Mexico."

"Can you put names to the numbers?"

Morelli set his plate on the counter, slid the antennae up on my portable phone, and dialed. "Hey, Murphy," he said, "I need you to get me names and addresses for numbers." He read the numbers off and ate while he waited. Minutes later, Murphy came back on the line, and Morelli acknowledged information given. His face was impassive when he hung up. I'd come to know this as his cop face.

"The second two numbers are El Salvador. Murphy couldn't get more specific."

I snitched a piece of chicken from his plate and nibbled on it. "Why is Kenny calling Mexico and El Salvador?"

"Maybe he's planning a vacation."

I didn't trust Morelli when he went bland like this. Morelli's emotions were usually clear on his face.

He opened the MasterCard bill. "Kenny's been busy. He charged almost two thousand dollars' worth of stuff last month."

"Any airline tickets?"

"No airline tickets." He handed the bill over to me. "Look for yourself."

"Mostly clothes. All local stores." I laid the bills out on the kitchen counter. "About those phone numbers . . ."

He had his head back in the grocery bag. "Is that apple pie I see?"

"You touch that pie and you're a dead man."

Morelli chucked me under the chin. "I love it when you talk tough like that. I'd like to stay and hear more, but I have to get moving."

He let himself out, walked the short distance down the hall, and disappeared into the elevator. When the elevator doors clicked closed I realized he'd walked off with Kenny's phone bill. I smacked the heel of my hand to my forehead. "Unh!"

I retreated back into my apartment, locked my front door, shucked my clothes en route to the bathroom, and plunged into a steaming shower. After the shower I dug out a flannel nightie. I towel-dried my hair and padded barefoot into the kitchen.

I ate two pieces of apple pie, gave a couple chunks of leftover apple and a wedge of crust to Rex, and went to bed, wondering about Spiro's caskets. He hadn't given me any further information. Just that the caskets were missing and had to be found. I wasn't sure how one went about losing twenty-four caskets, but I suppose anything is possible. I'd promised to return without Grandma Mazur so we could discuss case details.

I dragged my body out of bed at seven and peered out the window. The rain had stopped, but the sky was still overcast and dark enough to look like the end of the world. I dressed in shorts and a sweatshirt and laced up my running shoes. I did this with the same amount of enthusiasm I could muster for self-immolation. I tried to run at least three times a week. It never ever occurred to me I might enjoy it. I ran to burn off the occasional bottle of beer, and because it was good to be able to outrun the bad guys.

I ran three miles, staggered into the lobby, and took the elevator back to my apartment. No point to overdoing this exercise junk.

I started coffee brewing and ripped through a fast shower. I dressed in jeans and denim shirt, downed a cup of coffee, and made arrangements with Ranger to meet him for breakfast in half an hour. I had access to the burg underground, but Ranger had access to the underground underground. He knew the dealers and pimps and gun runners. This business with Kenny Mancuso was beginning to feel uncomfortable, and I wanted to know why. Not that it affected my job. My job was very straightforward. Find Kenny, bring him in. The problem was with Morelli. I didn't trust Morelli, and I hated the possibility that he knew more than I did.

Ranger was already seated when I got to the coffee shop. He was wearing black jeans, hand-tooled, high-shine, black snakeskin cowboy boots, and a black T-shirt that spanned tight across his chest and biceps. A black leather jacket was draped across the back of his chair, one side hanging lower than the other, weighted by an ominous pocket bulge.

I ordered hot chocolate and blueberry pancakes with extra syrup.

Ranger ordered coffee and half a grapefruit. "What's up?" he asked.

"You hear about the shooting at Delio's Exxon on Hamilton?"

He nodded. "Somebody buzzed Moogey Bues."

"You know who hit him?"

"Don't have a name."

The hot chocolate and coffee arrived. I waited until the waitress left before asking my next question.

"What do you have?"

"A real bad feeling."

I sipped my hot chocolate. "I got one of those, too. Morelli says he's looking for Kenny Mancuso as a favor to Kenny's mother. I think there's more to it."

"Uh-oh," Ranger said. "You been reading those Nancy Drew books again?"

"So what do you think? You hear anything weird about Kenny Mancuso? You think he did Moogey Bues?"

"I think it don't matter to you. All you've got to do is find Kenny and bring him in."

"Unfortunately, I'm all out of bread crumbs to follow."

The waitress brought my pancakes and Ranger's grapefruit.

"Boy, that looks yummy," I said about Ranger's grapefruit as I poured syrup. "Maybe next time I'll get one of those."

"Better be careful," Ranger said. "Nothing uglier than a fat old white woman."

"You're not being much help here."

"What do you know about Moogey Bues?"

"I know he's dead."

He ate a section of grapefruit. "You might check Moogey out."

"And while I'm checking out Moogey, you could put your ear to the ground."

"Kenny Mancuso and Moogey don't necessarily move in my neighborhood."

"Wouldn't hurt, though."

"True," Ranger said. "Wouldn't hurt."

I finished my hot chocolate and pancakes and wished I'd worn a sweater so I could open the top snap to my jeans. I burped discreetly and paid the bill.

I went back to the scene of the crime and identified myself to Cubby Delio, the station owner.

"Can't understand it," Delio said. "I've owned this station for twenty-two years and never had any trouble."

"How long had Moogey worked for you?"

"Six years. Started working here when he was in high school. I'm going to miss him. He was a likable person, and he was real reliable. He always opened up in the morning for me. I never had to worry about a thing."

"He ever say anything about Kenny Mancuso? Do you know why they were arguing?"

He shook his head, no.

"How about his personal life?"

"I don't know much about his personal life. He wasn't married. So far as I know he was between girlfriends. Lived alone." He sifted through some papers on his desk, coming up with a dog-eared, black-smudged list of employees. "Here's the address," he said. "Mercerville. Over by the high school. Just moved there. Rented himself a house."

I copied the information, thanked him for his time, and got back to my Jeep. I took Hamilton to Klockner, passed Stienert High School, and hung a left into a subdivision of single-family homes. Yards were well tended and fenced for small children and dogs. Houses were mostly white sided with conservative trim colors. There were few cars parked in driveways. This was a neighborhood of double-income families. Everyone was out working, earning enough money to maintain the lawn service, pay off Ms. Maid, and warehouse their offspring at day care centers.

I ticked off numbers until I came to Moogey's house. It was indistinguishable from the others, with no sign that a tragedy had just occurred.

I parked, crossed the lawn to the front door, and knocked. No one answered. I hadn't expected anyone would. I peeked into a narrow window bordering the door but saw very little: a foyer with a wood floor, carpeted stairs leading up, a hall extending from the foyer to the kitchen. Everything seemed to be in order.

I walked down the sidewalk to the driveway and peeked into the garage. There was a car in there, and I assumed it was Moogey's. It was a red BMW. I thought it looked a little pricey for a guy who worked in a gas station, but what did I know. I took down the plate number and returned to my Jeep.

I was sitting there, thinking "Now what?" when my cellular phone rang.

It was Connie, the secretary from the bond office. "I've got an easy recovery for you," she said. "Stop by the office when you get the chance, and I'll give you the paperwork."

"How easy is easy?"

"This one's a bag lady. The old babe at the train station. She lifts undies and then forgets her court date. All you have to do is pick her up and get her to the judge."

"Who posts her bond if she's homeless?"

"Some church group has adopted her."

"I'll be right over."

Vinnie had a storefront office on Hamilton. Vincent Plum Bail Bonding Company. Aside from his penchant for kinky sex, Vinnie was a reputable person. For the most part he kept black-sheep miscreants from hardworking blue-collar Trenton families out of the holding pens at police headquarters. Once in a while he got a genuine slimebag, but that sort of case rarely fell into my hands.

Grandma Mazur had a Wild West image of bounty hunters breaking down doors with six-shooters blazing. The reality of my job was that most of my days were spent coercing dummies into my car and then chauffeuring them to the police station, where they were rescheduled and rereleased. I picked up a lot of DWIs and disorderlies and occasionally I got a shoplifter or recreational car thief. Vinnie had given me Kenny Mancuso because in the beginning it had looked very straightforward. Kenny was a first-time offender from a good burg family. And besides, Vinnie knew I'd do the takedown with Ranger.

I parked the Jeep in front of Fiorello's Deli. I had Fiorello make me a tuna on a kaiser and then went next door to Vinnie.

Connie looked up from her desk that sat like a guardhouse blocking the way to Vinnie's inner office. Her hair had been teased out a good six inches, framing her face in a rat's nest of black curls. She was a couple years older than me, three inches shorter, thirty pounds heavier, and, like me, she'd gone back to using her maiden name after a discouraging divorce. In her case, the name was Rosolli, a name given a wide berth in the burg since her Uncle Jimmy had been made. Jimmy was ninety-two now and couldn't find his dick if it glowed in the dark, but still he was made all the same.

"Hey," Connie said. "How's it going?"

"That's a pretty complicated question right now. Do you have the paperwork ready for the bag lady?"

Connie handed me several forms stapled together. "Eula Rothridge. You can find her at the train station."

I leafed through the file. "No picture?"

"You don't need one. She'll be sitting on the bench closest to the parking lot, soaking up rays."

"Any suggestions?"

"Try not to get downwind."

I grimaced and left.

Trenton's placement on the banks of the Delaware River made it ripe for industry and commerce. Over the years, as the Delaware's navigability and importance dwindled, so did Trenton's, bringing the city to its present-day status of being just one more big pothole in the state highway system. Recently, though, we'd gotten minor league baseball, so could fame and fortune be far behind?

The ghetto had crept in around the train station, making it virtually impossible to get to the station without passing through streets of small, yardless, depressed row houses filled with chronically depressed people. During summer months the neighborhoods steeped in sweat and open aggression. When the temperature dropped the tone turned bleak, and animosity sat behind insulating walls.

I drove along these streets with my doors locked and my windows shut tight. It was more out of habit than conscious protection, since anyone with a paring knife could slash through my canvas roof.

The Trenton train station is small and not especially memorable. There's a curved drop-off driveway at the front entrance where a few taxis wait and a uniformed cop keeps his eye on things. Several municipal-style benches line the driveway.

Eula was sitting on the farthermost bench, dressed in several winter coats, a purple wool cap, and running shoes. Her face was lined and doughy, her steel gray hair was chopped short and stuck out in ragged clumps from the cap. Her legs were ankleless, feeding into her shoes like giant knockwursts, her knees comfortably spread for the world to see sights better left unseen.

I parked in front of her, in a no-parking zone, and received a warning glare from the cop.

I waved my bond papers at him. "I'll only be a minute," I yelled. "I'm here to take Eula to court."

He gave me an *oh yeah, well, good luck* look and went back to staring off into space.

Eula harrumphed at me. "I ain't goin' to court."

"Why not?"

"The sun's out. I gotta get my vitamin D."

"I'll buy you a carton of milk. It's got vitamin D in it."

"What else you gonna buy me? You gonna buy me a sandwich?"

I took the tuna sandwich out of my pocketbook. "I was going to eat this for lunch, but you can have it."

"What kind is it?"

"Tuna on a kaiser. I got it at Fiorello's."

"Fiorello makes good sandwiches. Did you get extra pickles?"

"Yeah. I got extra pickles."

"I don't know. What about my stuff here?"

She had a supermarket cart behind her, and she'd rammed two big black plastic garbage bags filled with God knows what into the cart.

"We'll put your stuff in lockers in the train station."

"Who's gonna pay for the locker? I'm on a fixed income, you know."

"I'll spring for the locker."

"You're gonna hafta carry my stuff. I got a gimpy leg."

I looked over at the cop, who was staring down at his shoes and smiling.

"You want anything out of those bags before I lock them up?" I asked Eula.

"Nope," she said. "I got all I need."

"And when I lock away all your worldly possessions, and get your milk, and give you the sandwich, you're going to come with me, right?"

"Right."

I hauled the bags up the steps, dragged them down the corridor, and tipped a porter a buck to help me wedge the damn things into the lockers. One bag to one locker. I dropped a fistful of quarters into the lockers, took the keys, and leaned against the wall to catch my breath, thinking I should try to make time for the gym and some upper body work. I trotted back to the front of the building, pushed my way through the doors to the McDonald's franchise, and bought Eula a container of lowfat milk. I swung back out the main entrance and looked for Eula. She was gone. The cop was gone too. And, I had a parking ticket on my windshield.

I walked over to the first cab in line and rapped on his window. "Where'd Eula go?" I asked.

"I dunno," he said. "She took a cab."

"She had money for a cab?"

"Sure. She makes out pretty good here."

"Do you know where she lives?"

"She lives on that bench. The last one on the right."

Wonderful. I got into my car and made a U-turn into the small, metered parking lot. I waited until someone pulled out, then I parked in their slot, ate my sandwich, drank the milk, and waited with my arms crossed over my chest.

Two hours later a cab pulled up and Eula got out. She waddled to her bench and sat down with an obvious sense of possession. I pulled out of my parking spot and eased to the curb in front of her. I smiled.

She smiled back.

I got out of the car and walked over to her. "Remember me?"

"Yeah," she said. "You went off with my stuff."

"I put it in a locker for you."

"Took you long enough."

I was born a month premature, and I never did learn the value of patience. "You see these two keys? Your stuff's locked up in lockers that can only be opened with these two keys. Either you get in my car, or I'm flushing these keys."

"That'd be a mean thing to do to a poor old lady."

It was all I could do to keep from growling.

"Okay," she said, heaving herself up. "I guess I may as well go. It ain't so sunny anymore anyway."

The Trenton Police Department houses itself in a three-story red-brick block-type building. A sister block, attached at street level, provides space for the courts and related offices. On every side of the municipal complex is the ghetto. This is very convenient, as the police never have to go far to find crime.

I parked in the lot attached to the station and squired Eula through the front hall to the cop at the front desk. If it had been after business hours, or if I'd had an unruly fugitive on my hands, I'd have gotten myself buzzed through the back door directly to the docket lieutenant. None of that was necessary for Eula, so I sat her down while I tried to determine if the judge who'd originally set her bond was working cases. It turned out he wasn't, and I had no recourse but to take her to the docket lieutenant anyway and have them hold her.

I gave her the locker keys, picked up my body receipt, and left through the back door.

Morelli was waiting for me in the parking lot, leaning against my car, hands shoved into his pockets, doing his imitation of a street tough, which probably wasn't an imitation.

"What's new?" Morelli said.

"Not much. What's new with you?"

He shrugged. "Slow day."

"Un-huh."

"Got any leads on Kenny?" he asked.

"Nothing I'd share with you. You swiped the phone bill last night."

"I didn't swipe it. I forgot I had it in my hand."

"Un-huh. So why don't you tell me about the Mexican numbers?"

"Nothing to tell."

"I don't believe that for a second. And I don't believe you're putting all this effort into finding Kenny because you're a good family person."

"You have a reason for your doubts?"

"I have a queasy feeling in the pit of my stomach."

Morelli grinned. "You can take that to the bank."

Okay. Different approach. "I thought we were a team."

"There's all kinds of teams. Some teams work more independent of each other."

I felt my eyes roll back in my head. "Let me get this straight," I said. "What this comes down to is that I share all my information, but you don't. Then when we find Kenny you spirit him off for reasons as yet unknown to me and cut me out of my recovery."

"It's not like that. I wouldn't cut you out of your recovery."

Give me a break. It was exactly like that, and we both knew it.

CHAPTER 3

Morelli and I had done battle before with only short-lived victories on both sides. I suspected this would be another war, of sorts. And I figured I'd have to learn how to live with it. If I went head-on with Morelli, he could make my life as a bounty hunter difficult to impossible.

Not to say that I should be a total doormat. What was important was that I *look* like a doormat at appropriate moments. I decided this wasn't one of those moments and that my demeanor now should be angry and offended. This was an easy act to pull off, since it was true. I peeled out of the police lot, pretending to know where I was going when in fact I didn't. It was close to four, and I had no more stones to turn in the hunt for Mancuso, so I headed home, driving on autopilot, reviewing my progress.

I knew I should go see Spiro, but I couldn't muster a lot of joy over the project. I didn't share Grandma's enthusiasm for mortuaries. Actually, I thought death was just a bit creepy, and I though Spiro was downright subterranean. Since I wasn't in all that good of a mood anyway, procrastination seemed like the way to go.

I parked behind my building and skipped the elevator in favor of the stairs since the morning's blueberry pancakes were still oozing over the top of my Levi's. I let myself into my apartment and almost stepped on an envelope that had been shoved under the door. It was a plain white business-size envelope with my name printed in silver paste-on letters. I opened the envelope, removed the single piece of white paper, and read the two-sentence message, which had also been formed from paste-ons.

"Take a vacation. It will be good for your health."

I didn't see any travel agency brochures stuck in the envelope, so I assumed this wasn't a cruise advertisement.

I considered the other option. Threat. Of course, if the threat was from Kenny, that meant he was still in Trenton. Even better, it meant I'd done something to get him worried. Beyond Kenny I couldn't imagine who would be threatening me. Maybe one of Kenny's friends. Maybe Morelli. Maybe my mother.

I said howdy to Rex, dumped my pocketbook and the envelope on the kitchen counter, and accessed my phone messages.

My cousin Kitty, who worked at the bank, called to say she was keeping her eye on Mancuso's account just like I'd asked, but there was no new activity.

My best friend since the day I was born, Mary Lou Molnar, who was now Mary Lou Stankovic, called to ask if I'd dropped off the face of the earth since she hadn't heard from me since God knows when.

And the last message was from Grandma Mazur.

"I hate these stupid machines," she said. "Always feel like a dang fool talking to nobody. I saw in the paper where there's gonna be a viewing for that gas station fellow tonight, and I could use a ride. Elsie Farnsworth said she'd take me, but I hate to go with her because she's got arthritis in her knees and sometimes her foot gets stuck on the gas pedal."

A viewing for Moogey Bues. That seemed worthwhile. I went across the hall to borrow the paper from Mr. Wolesky. Mr. Wolesky kept his TV going day and night, so it was always necessary to pound real loud on his door. Then he'd open it and tell you not to knock his door down. When he had a heart attack four years ago, he called the ambulance but refused to get wheeled out until after *Jeopardy!* was over.

Mr. Wolesky opened the door and glared out at me. "You don't have to knock the door down," he said. "I'm not deaf, you know."

"I was wondering if I could borrow your paper."

"As long as you bring it right back. I need the TV section."

"I just wanted to check the viewings." I opened the paper to the obits and read down. Moogey Bues was at Stiva. Seven o'clock.

I thanked Mr. Wolesky and returned his paper.

I called Grandma and told her I'd pick her up at seven. I declined my mother's dinner invitation, promised her I wouldn't wear jeans to the viewing, disconnected, and, doing pancake damage control, searched my refrigerator for fat-free food.

I was plowing through a salad when the phone rang.

"Yo," Ranger said. "Bet you're eating salad for supper."

I stuck my tongue out and crossed my eyes at the handset. "You have anything to tell me about Mancuso?"

"Mancuso don't live here. He don't visit here. He don't do business here."

"Just out of morbid curiosity, if you were going to look for twenty-four missing caskets, where would you start?"

"Are these caskets empty or full?"

Oh shit, I'd forgotten to ask. I squeezed my eyes closed. Please God, let them be empty.

I hung up and dialed Eddie Gazarra.

"It's your nickel," Gazarra said.

"I want to know what Joe Morelli's working on."

"Good luck. Half the time Morelli's captain doesn't know what Morelli's working on."

"I know, but you hear things."

Heavy sigh. "I'll see what I can dig up."

Morelli was vice, which meant he was in a different building, in a different part of Trenton than Eddie. Vice did a lot of work with DEA and Customs and kept pretty closemouthed about their projects. Still, there was bar talk and clerical gossip and talk among spouses.

I shucked my Levi's and did the panty hose–business suit bit. I slid my feet into heels, fluffed my hair up with some gel and hairspray, and swiped at my lashes with mascara. I stepped back and took a look. Not bad, but I didn't think Sharon Stone would drive off a bridge in a jealous rage.

"Look at that skirt," my mother said when she opened the door to me. "It's no wonder we have so much crime today what with these short skirts. How can you sit in a skirt like that? Everyone can see everything."

"It's two inches above my knee. It's not *that* short."

"I haven't got all day to stand here talking about skirts," Grandma

Mazur said. "I got to get to the funeral parlor. I gotta see how they laid this guy out. I hope they didn't smooth over those bullet holes too good."

"Don't get your hopes up," I told Grandma Mazur. "I think this will be closed coffin." Not only was Moogey shot, but he was also autopsied. I figured it would take all the king's horses and all the king's men to put Moogey Bues back together again.

"Closed coffin! Well, that would be darn disappointing. Word gets out that Stiva is having closed coffins and his attendance'll drop like a rock." She buttoned a cardigan sweater over her dress and tucked her pocketbook under her arm. "Didn't say anything in the paper about closed coffins."

"Come back after," my mother said. "I made chocolate pudding."

"You sure you don't want to go?" Grandma Mazur asked my mother.

"I didn't know Moogey Bues," my mother told her. "I've got better things to do than to go to a viewing of some perfect stranger."

"I wouldn't go either," Grandma Mazur said, "but I'm helping Stephanie with this here manhunt. Maybe Kenny Mancuso will show up, and Stephanie will need some extra muscle. I was watching television, and I saw how you stick your fingers in a person's eyes to slow them down."

"She's your responsibility," my mother said to me. "She sticks her finger in anybody's eye I'm holding you accountable."

The double-wide viewing room door was propped open to better accommodate the crush of people who'd come to see Moogey Bues. Grandma Mazur immediately began elbowing her way to the front with me in tow.

"Well, don't that beat all," she said when she reached the end of the chairs. "You were right. They got the lid down." Her eyes narrowed. "How are we supposed to know if Moogey's really in there?"

"I'm sure someone has checked."

"But we don't know for certain."

I gave her the silent stare.

"Maybe we should peek inside and see for ourselves," she said.

"NO!"

Conversation paused as heads swiveled in our direction. I smiled apologetically and put a restraining arm around Grandma.

I lowered my voice and added some stern to my whisper. "It's not polite to peek into a closed casket. And besides, it's none of our business, and it doesn't really matter to us if Moogey Bues is here or there. If Moogey Bues is missing, it's police business."

"It could be important to the case," she said. "It could have to do with Kenny Mancuso."

"You're just nosy. You want to see the bullet holes."

"There's that," she said.

I noticed Ranger had also come to the viewing. As far as I knew, Ranger wore only two colors: army green and bad-ass black. Tonight he was bad-ass black, the monotony broken only by double-stud earrings, sparkling under the lights. As always, his hair was pulled back into a ponytail. As always, he wore a jacket. This time the jacket was black leather. One could only guess what was hidden under the jacket. Probably enough firepower to wipe out a small European country. He'd positioned himself against a back wall, standing with arms crossed, body relaxed, eyes watchful.

Joe Morelli stood opposite him in a similar pose.

I watched a man slide past a knot of people congregated at the door. The man took a fast survey of the room, then acknowledged Ranger with a nod.

Only if you knew Ranger would you know he replied.

I looked at Ranger, and he mouthed "Sandman" to me. Sandman. The name didn't mean anything.

Sandman approached the casket and studied the polished wood in silence. There was no expression to his face. He looked like he'd seen it all and didn't think much of it. His eyes were dark, deep-set, and lined. I guessed the lines were from dissipation more than sun and laughter. His hair was black, oiled back from his face.

He caught me staring and our eyes locked for a moment before he turned away.

"I need to talk to Ranger," I said to Grandma Mazur. "If I leave you alone will you promise not to get into trouble?"

Grandma sniffed. "Well, that's plain insulting. I guess after all these years I know how to behave myself."

"No fooling around, trying to see in the casket."

"Hmmph."

"Who was the guy that just paid his respects?" I asked Ranger. "Sandman?"

"His name is Perry Sandeman. Got the name of Sandman on account of if you irritate him he'll put you to sleep for a real long time."

"How do you know him?"

"He gets around. Buys a little dope from the brothers."

"What's he doing here?"

"Works at the garage."

"Moogey's garage?"

"Yeah. I hear he was there when Moogey got shot in the knee."

Someone screamed in the front of the room, and there was the sound of a heavy object being slammed shut. A heavy object like a coffin lid. I felt my eyes involuntarily roll skyward.

Spiro appeared in the doorway not far from me. Two small frown lines had fixed themselves between his eyebrows. He strode forward, cutting a swath through the crowd. I had a clear view in his wake, and the view was of Grandma Mazur.

"It was my sleeve," Grandma said to Spiro. "It got caught by accident on the lid and the dang thing just opened up. It could of happened to anyone."

Grandma looked back at me and gave a thumbs-up.

"Is that your granny?" Ranger wanted to know.

"Yup. She was checking to make sure Moogey was here."

"You've got a helluva gene pool, babe."

Spiro tested the lid to make sure it was securely closed and replaced the flower spray that had fallen to the floor.

I hustled up, ready to lend support to the lid-caught-on-the-sleeve theory, but support wasn't necessary. Spiro clearly wanted to minimize the incident. He made some sounds of comfort to the closest mourners and was busy wiping Grandma's fingerprints off the glossy wood.

"I couldn't help but notice while the lid was up that you did a nice job," Grandma said, hovering over Spiro. "Couldn't hardly see those holes at all, except for where your mortician's putty'd sunk in a little."

Spiro nodded solemnly, and with the touch of a fingertip to

Grandma's back, deftly turned her away from the casket. "We have tea in the lobby," he said. "Perhaps you would like a cup of tea after this unfortunate experience?"

"I guess a cup of tea wouldn't hurt," Grandma said. "I was pretty much done here anyway."

I accompanied Grandma to the lobby and made sure she was actually going to drink tea. When she settled into a chair with her cup and some cookies, I went on my own in search of Spiro. I found him loitering just outside the side door, standing in a halo of artificial light, sneaking a smoke.

The air had grown cool, but Spiro seemed oblivious to the chill. He dragged the smoke deep into his lungs and exhaled slowly. I figured he was trying to absorb as much tar as possible, the sooner to end his wretched life.

I knocked lightly on the glass door to get his attention. "Would you like to discuss the, um, you know . . . now?"

He nodded to me, took one last long drag, and pitched his cigarette onto the driveway. "I would have called you this afternoon, but I figured you'd come to see Bues tonight. I need these things found yesterday." He shifted his eyes over the lot to make sure we were alone.

"Caskets are like anything else. Manufacturers have surplus, they have seconds, they have sales. Sometimes it's possible to buy bulk and get a good price. About six months ago I put in a bulk bid and got twenty-four caskets below cost. We're short on storage space here, so I stowed the caskets in a rental locker."

Spiro took an envelope from his jacket pocket. He removed a key from the envelope and held it up for my inspection. "This is the key to the locker. The address is inside the envelope. The caskets were wrapped in protective plastic for shipment and crated so they could be stacked. I've also included a photograph of one of the caskets. They were all the same. Very plain."

"Have you reported this to the police?"

"I haven't reported the theft to anyone. I want to get the caskets back and generate as little publicity as possible."

"This is out of my league."

"A thousand dollars."

"Jesus, Spiro, these are caskets we're talking about! What kind of a person would steal caskets? And where would I begin to look? You have clues or something?"

"I have a key and an empty locker."

"Maybe you should cut your losses and collect the insurance."

"I can't file for insurance without a police report, and I don't want to bring in the police."

The thousand dollars was tempting, but the job was beyond bizarre. I honestly didn't know where to start looking for twenty-four lost caskets. "Suppose I actually find the caskets . . . what then? How do you expect to get them back? Seems to me if a person's low enough to steal a casket, he's going to be mean enough to fight to keep it."

"Let's just go one step at a time," Spiro said. "Your finder's fee doesn't involve retrieving. Retrieving will be my problem."

"I suppose I could ask around."

"We need to keep this confidential."

No sweat. As if I'd want people to know I was looking for caskets. Get real. "My lips are sealed." I took the envelope and stuffed it into my pocketbook. "One other thing," I said. "These caskets are empty, right?"

"Right."

I went back to look for Grandma, and I was thinking maybe this wouldn't be so bad. Spiro had lost a shitload of caskets. They wouldn't be that easy to hide. It wasn't as if you could pack them into the trunk of your car and drive away. Someone had come in with a flatbed or a semi and taken those caskets. Maybe it was an internal job. Maybe someone from the locker company had ripped Spiro off. Then what? The market for caskets is pretty limited. You could hardly use them as planters or lamp stands. The caskets would have to be sold to other mortuaries. These thieves had to be on the cutting edge of crime. Black-market caskets.

I found Grandma sipping tea with Joe Morelli. I'd never seen Morelli with a teacup in his hand, and the sight was unnerving. As a teenager Morelli had been feral. Two years in the navy and twelve more on the police force had taught him control, but I was convinced nothing short of removing his gonads would ever completely domesticate him. There was always a barbarous part of Morelli that hummed beneath the surface. I found myself helplessly sucked in by it, and at the same time it scared the hell out of me.

"Well, here she is," Grandma said when she saw me. "Speak of the devil."

Morelli grinned. "We've been talking about you."

"Oh, goody."

"I hear you had a secretive meeting with Spiro."

"Business," I said.

"This business have anything to do with the fact that Spiro and Kenny and Moogey were friends in high school?"

I gave him an eyebrow raise to signify surprise. "They were friends in high school?"

He held three fingers up. "Like this."

"Hmmm," I said.

His grin widened. "I guess you're still in war mode."

"Are you laughing at me?"

"Not exactly laughing."

"Well then, what?"

He rocked back on his heels, hands rammed into his pockets. "I think you're cute."

"Jesus."

"Too bad we're not working together," Morelli said. "If we were working together I could tell you about my cousin's car."

"What about his car?"

"They found it late this afternoon. Abandoned. No bodies in the trunk. No bloodstains. No Kenny."

"Where?"

"The parking lot at the mall."

"Maybe Kenny was shopping."

"Unlikely. Mall security remembers seeing the car parked overnight."

"Were the doors locked?"

"All but the driver's door."

I considered that for a moment. "If I was abandoning my cousin's car, I'd make sure all the doors were locked."

Morelli and I stared into each other's eyes and let the next thought go unsaid. Maybe Kenny was dead. There was no real basis in fact to draw such a conclusion, but the premonition skittered through my mind, and I wondered how this related to the letter I'd just received.

Morelli acknowledged the possibility with a grim set to his mouth. "Yeah," he said.

Stiva had formed a lobby by removing the walls between what had originally been the foyer and the dining room of the large Victorian. Wall-to-wall carpet unified the room and silenced footsteps. Tea was served on a maple library table just outside the kitchen door. Lights were subdued, Queen Anne period chairs and end tables were grouped for conversation, and small floral arrangements were scattered throughout. It would have been a pleasant room if it wasn't for the certain knowledge that Uncle Harry or Aunt Minnie or Morty the mailman was naked in another part of the house, dead as a doorknob, getting pumped full of formaldehyde.

"You want some tea?" Grandma asked me.

I shook my head no. Tea held no appeal. I wanted fresh air and chocolate pudding. And I wanted to get out of my panty hose. "I'm ready to leave," I said to Grandma. "How about you?"

Grandma looked around. "It's still kind of early, but I guess I haven't got anybody left to see." She set her teacup on the table and settled her pocketbook into the crook of her arm. "I could use some chocolate pudding anyway."

She turned to Morelli. "We had chocolate pudding for dessert tonight, and there's still some left. We always make a double batch."

"Been a long time since I've had homemade chocolate pudding," Morelli said.

Grandma snapped to attention. "Is that so? Well, you're welcome to join us. We've got plenty."

A small strangled sound escaped from the back of my throat, and I glared *no, no, no* at Morelli.

Morelli gave me one of those ultranaive *what?* looks. "Chocolate pudding sounds great," he said. "I'd love some chocolate pudding."

"Then it's settled," Grandma announced. "You know where we live?"

Morelli assured us he could find the house with his eyes closed, but just to make sure we'd be safe in the night, he'd follow us home.

"Don't that beat all," Grandma said when we were alone in the car. "Imagine him worrying about our safety. And have you ever met a more polite young man? He's a real looker too. And he's a cop. I bet he has a gun under that jacket."

He was going to need a gun when my mother saw him standing on her doorstep. My mother would look out the storm door, and she wouldn't see Joe Morelli, a man in search of pudding. She wouldn't see Joe Morelli who had graduated from high school and joined the navy. She wouldn't see Morelli the cop. My mother would see Joe Morelli the fast-fingered, horny little eight-year-old who had taken me to his father's garage to play choo-choo when I was six.

"This here's a good opportunity for you," Grandma said as we pulled up to the curb. "You could use a man."

"Not this one."

"What's wrong with this one?"

"He's not my type."

"You've got no taste when it comes to men," Grandma said. "Your ex-husband is a cow's tail. We all knew he was a cow's tail when you married him, but you wouldn't listen."

Morelli pulled up behind me and got out of his truck. My mother opened the storm door and even from a distance I could see the stern set to her mouth and a stiffening of her spine.

"We all came back for pudding," Grandma said to my mother when we reached the porch. "We brought Officer Morelli with us on account of he hasn't had any homemade pudding in an awful long time."

My mother's lips pinched tight.

"I hope I'm not intruding," Morelli said. "I know you weren't expecting company."

This is the opening statement that will get you into any burg house. No housewife worth her salt will ever admit to having her house not up to company twenty-four hours a day. Jack the Ripper would have easy access if he used this line.

My mother gave a curt nod and grudgingly stepped aside while the three of us slid past.

For fear of mayhem, my father had never been informed of the choo-choo incident. This meant he regarded Morelli with no more and no less contempt and apprehension than any of the other potential suitors my mother and grandmother dragged in off the street. He gave Joe a cursory inspection, engaged in the minimum necessary small talk, and returned his attention to the TV, studiously ignoring my grandmother as she passed out pudding.

"They had a closed casket all right for Moogey Bues," my grandmother said to my mother. "I got to see him anyway on account of the accident."

My mother's eyes opened wide in alarm. "Accident?"

I shrugged out of my jacket. "Grandma caught her sleeve on the lid, and the lid accidentally flew open."

My mother raised her arms in appalled supplication. "All day I've had people calling and telling me about the gladioli. Now tomorrow I'll have to hear about the lid."

"He didn't look so hot," Grandma Mazur said. "I told Spiro that he did a good job, but it was pretty much a fib."

Morelli was wearing a blazer over a black knit shirt. He took a seat, and his jacket swung wide, exposing the gun at his hip.

"Nice piece!" Grandma said. "What is it? Is that a forty-five?"

"It's a nine-millimeter."

"Don't suppose you'd let me see it," Grandma said. "I'd sure like to get the feel of a gun like that."

"NO!" everyone shouted in unison.

"I shot a chicken once," Grandma explained to Morelli. "It was an accident."

I could see Morelli searching for a reply. "Where did you shoot it?" he finally asked.

"In the gumpy," Grandma said. "Shot it clear off."

Two puddings and three beers later, Morelli peeled himself away from the TV. We left together and lingered to talk privately at the curb. The sky was starless and moonless and most of the houses were dark. The street was empty of traffic. In other parts of Trenton the night might feel dangerous. In the burg the night felt soft and secure.

Morelli turned my suit collar up against the chill air. His knuckles brushed my neck, and his gaze lingered on my mouth. "You have a nice family," he said.

I narrowed my eyes. "If you kiss me I'll scream, and then my father will come out and punch you in the nose." And before any of those things happened, I'd probably wet my pants.

"I could take your father."

"But you wouldn't."

Morelli still had his hands on my collar. "No, I wouldn't."

"Tell me about the car again. There was no sign of struggle?"

"No sign of struggle. The keys were in the ignition and the driver's door was closed but unlocked."

"Any blood on the pavement?"

"I haven't been out to the scene, but the crime lab checked around and didn't come up with any physical evidence."

"Prints?"

"They're in the system."

"Personal possessions?"

"None found."

"Then he wasn't living out of the car," I reasoned.

"You're getting better at this apprehension agent stuff," Morelli said. "You're asking all the right questions."

"I watch a lot of television."

"Let's talk about Spiro."

"Spiro hired me to look into a mortuarial problem."

Morelli's face creased in laughter. "Mortuarial problem?"

"I don't want to talk about it."

"Doesn't have anything to do with Kenny?"

"Cross my heart and hope to die."

The upstairs window opened and my mother stuck her head out. "Stephanie," she stage-whispered, "what are you doing out there? What will the neighbors think?"

"Nothing to worry about, Mrs. Plum," Morelli called. "I was just leaving."

Rex was running in his wheel when I got home. I switched the light on, and he stopped dead in his tracks, black eyes wide, whiskers twitching in indignation that night had suddenly disappeared.

I kicked my shoes off en route to the kitchen, dropped my pocketbook onto the counter, and punched PLAY on my answering machine.

There was only one message. Gazarra had called at the end of his shift to tell me no one knew much about Morelli. Only that he was working on something big, and that it tied in to the Mancuso-Bues investigation.

I hit the off button and dialed Morelli.

He answered slightly out of breath on the sixth ring. Probably had just gotten into his apartment.

There didn't seem to be much need for small talk. "Creep," I said, cutting to the heart of the matter.

"Gosh, I wonder who this could be."

"You lied to me. I knew it, too. I knew it right from the beginning, you jerk."

Silence stretched taut between us, and I realized my accusation covered a lot of territory, so I narrowed the field. "I want to know about this big secret case you're working on, and I want to know how it ties in to Kenny Mancuso and Moogey Bues."

"Oh," Morelli said. "*That* lie."

"Well?"

"I can't tell you anything about that lie."

CHAPTER 4

Thoughts of Kenny Mancuso and Joe Morelli had kept me thrashing around most of the night. At seven I rolled myself out of bed, feeling cranky and bedraggled. I showered, dressed in jeans and T-shirt, and made a pot of coffee.

My basic problem was that I had plenty of ideas about Joe Morelli and hardly any about Kenny Mancuso.

I poured out a bowl of cereal, filled my Daffy Duck mug with coffee, and picked through the contents of the envelope Spiro had given me. The storage facility was just off Route 1 in an area of strip-mall-type light-industrial complexes. The photo of the missing casket had been cut from some sort of flyer or brochure and showed a casket that was clearly at the bottom of the funeral food chain. It was little more than a plain pine box, devoid of the carvings and beveled edges usually found on burg caskets. Why Spiro would buy twenty-four of these crates was beyond my comprehension. People spent money on funerals and weddings in the burg. Being buried in one of these caskets would be lower than ring around the collar. Even Mrs. Ciak next door, who was on Social Security and turned her lights off each night at nine to save money, had thousands set aside for her burial.

I finished my cereal, rinsed the bowl and spoon, poured a second cup of coffee, and filled Rex's little ceramic food dish with Cheerios and blueberries. Rex popped out of his soup can with his nose twitching in excitement. He rushed to the dish, crammed everything into his cheeks, and rushed back to his soup can, where he hunkered in butt side out, vibrating with happiness and good fortune. That's the neat part about a hamster. It doesn't take much to make a hamster happy.

I grabbed my jacket and the large black leather pocketbook that held all my bounty-hunter paraphernalia and headed for the stairs. Mr. Wolesky's TV droned through his closed door and the aroma of bacon frying hung in the hallway just in front of Mrs. Karwatt's apartment. I exited the building in solitude and paused for a moment to enjoy the crisp morning air. A few leaves still tenaciously clung to trees, but for the most part limbs were bare and spidery against the bright sky. A dog barked in the neighborhood behind my apartment building and a car door slammed. Mr. Suburbia was going to work. And Stephanie Plum, bounty hunter extraordinaire, was off to find twenty-four cheap coffins.

Trenton traffic looked insignificant compared to the Holland Tunnel outbound on a Friday afternoon, but it was a pain in the ass all the same. I decided to preserve what little sanity had surfaced this morning and forgo safe, scenic, car-clogged Hamilton. I turned onto Linnert after two blocks of stop-and-go tedium and threaded my way through the blighted neighborhoods that surround center city. I skirted the area around the train station, cut through town, and picked up Route 1 for a quarter mile, getting off at Oatland Avenue.

R and J Storage occupied about a half acre of land on Oatland Avenue. Ten years ago, Oatland Avenue had been a hardscrabble patch of throwaway property. Its spiky grass had been littered with broken bottles and bottle caps, filter tips, condoms, and tumbleweed trash. Industry had recently found Oatland, and now the hardscrabble land supported Gant Printing, Knoblock Plumbing Supply House, and R and J Storage. The spiky grass had given way to blacktop parking lots, but the shards of glass, bottle caps, and assorted urban flotsam had endured, collecting in unattended corners and gutters.

Sturdy chain-link fencing surrounded the self-storage facility, and two drives, designated IN and OUT, led to the honeycomb of garage-sized warehouses. A small sign fixed to the fence stated business hours as 7:00 to 10:00 daily. The gates to the entrance and exit were open, and a small OPEN sign had been hung in the glass-paned office door. The buildings were all painted white with bright blue trim. Very crisp and efficient looking. Just the place to snug away hot caskets.

I pulled into the entrance and crept along, counting off numbers until I reached 16. I parked on the apron in front of the unit, inserted the key in the lock, and pressed the button that triggered the hydraulic door. The door rolled up along the ceiling and, sure enough, the warehouse was empty. Not a coffin or clue in sight.

I stood there for a moment, visualizing the pine boxes stacked chockablock. Here one day, gone the next. I turned to leave and almost crashed into Morelli.

"Jesus," I exclaimed, hand on heart, after squelching a yelp of surprise. "I hate when you creep up behind me like that. What are you doing here, anyway?"

"Following you."

"I don't want to be followed. Isn't that some sort of an infringement of my rights? Police harassment?"

"Most women would be happy to have me follow them."

"I'm not most women."

"Tell me about it." He gestured at the empty bay. "What's the deal?"

"If you must know . . . I'm looking for caskets."

This drew a smile.

"I'm serious! Spiro had twenty-four caskets stored here, and they've disappeared."

"Disappeared? As in stolen? Has he reported the theft to the police?"

I shook my head. "He didn't want to bring the police in. Didn't want word to get out that he'd bulk-bought a bunch of caskets and then lost them."

"I hate to rain on your parade, but I think this smells bad. People who lose things worth lots of money file police reports so they can collect their insurance."

I closed the door and dropped the key into my pocketbook. "I'm getting paid one thousand dollars to find lost caskets. I'm not going to try to identify the odor. I have no reason to believe there's anything bogus going on."

"What about Kenny? I thought you were looking for Kenny."

"Kenny's a dead end right now."

"Giving up?"

"Dropping back."

I opened the door to the Jeep, slid behind the wheel, and shoved the key into the ignition. By the time the engine cranked over, Morelli had seated himself next to me.

"Where are we going?" Morelli asked.

"*I'm* going to the office to talk to the manager."

Morelli was smiling again. "This could be the start of a whole new career. You do good on this one and maybe you can advance to catching grave robbers and headstone vandals."

"Very funny. Get out of my car."

"I thought we were partners."

Yeah, right. I put the Jeep into reverse and K-turned. I parked at the office and swung out of the Jeep, with Morelli following close on my heels.

I stopped and turned, facing him, hand to his chest to keep him at arm's length. "Halt. This is not a group project."

"I could be helpful," Morelli said. "I could lend authority and credibility to your questions."

"Why would you want to do that?"

"I'm a nice guy."

I felt my fingers begin to clutch at his shirt and made an effort to relax. "Try again."

"Kenny, Moogey, and Spiro were practically joined at the hip in high school. Moogey's dead. I've got a feeling Julia, the girlfriend, is out of the picture. Maybe Kenny's turned to Spiro."

"And I'm working for Spiro, and you're not sure you believe the coffin story."

"I don't know what to think of the coffin story. You have any more information on these coffins? Where they were originally purchased? What they look like?"

"They're made of wood. About six foot long . . ."

"If there's one thing I hate, it's a wise-ass bounty hunter."

I showed him the picture.

"You're right," he said. "They're made of wood, and they're about six foot long."

"And they're ugly."

"Yeah."

"And very plain," I added.

"Grandma Mazur wouldn't be caught dead in one of these," Morelli said.

"Not everyone is as discerning as Grandma Mazur. I'm sure Stiva keeps a wide range of caskets on hand."

"You should let me question the manager," Morelli said. "I'm better at this than you are."

"That does it. Go sit in the car."

In spite of all the sparring that went on between us, I sort of liked Morelli. Good judgment told me to stand clear of him, but then I've never been a slave to good judgment. I liked his dedication to the job, and the way he'd risen above his wild teen years. He'd been a street-smart kid, and now he was a street-smart cop. True, he was sort of a chauvinist, but it wasn't entirely his fault. After all, he was from New Jersey, and on top of that he was a Morelli. All things considered, I thought he was coping pretty well.

The office consisted of a small room divided in half by a service counter. A woman wearing a white T-shirt sporting a blue R and J Storage logo stood behind the counter. She was in her late forties–early fifties, with a pleasant face and a body that had comfortably gone to plump. She gave me a perfunctory nod before focusing on Morelli, who had paid no attention to my order and was standing close behind me.

Morelli was wearing washed-out jeans that had suggestively molded to an impressive package in front and the state's best buns in back. His brown leather jacket hid only his gun. The R and J lady swallowed visibly and dragged her eyes upward from Morelli's crotch.

I told her I was checking on some stored items for a friend of mine and that I was concerned with security.

"Who was this friend?" she asked.

"Spiro Stiva."

"No offense," she said, fighting back a grimace, "but he's got that locker filled with coffins. He said they were empty, but I don't care. I wouldn't come within fifty feet of that place. And I don't think you have to worry about security. Who on earth would steal a coffin?"

"How do you know he has coffins in there?"

"Saw them come in. He had so many they had to come in a semi and get off loaded with a forklift."

"Do you work here full-time?" I asked.

"I work here *all* the time," she said. "My husband and I own it. I'm the R in the R and J. Roberta."

"You have any other big trucks come in here in the last couple of months?"

"A few real big U-Hauls. Is there a problem?"

Spiro had sworn me to secrecy, but I didn't see any way I could get the information I needed without bringing Roberta into the investigation. Besides, she undoubtedly had a master key, and coffins or not, she'd probably check on Spiro's locker when we left and discover it was empty.

"Stiva's coffins are missing," I said. "The locker is empty."

"That's impossible! A person can't just make off with a locker full of caskets. That's a lot of caskets. They filled the locker from one end to the other!

"We have trucks coming and going all the time, but I would have known if they were loading caskets!"

"Locker sixteen is in the back," I said. "You can't see it from here. And maybe they didn't take them all at once."

"How did they get in?" she wanted to know. "Was the lock broken?"

I didn't know how they got in. The lock wasn't broken, and Spiro had been emphatic that the key had never left his possession. Of course, that could be a lie.

"I'd like to see a list of your other renters," I said. "And it would be helpful if you could think back to trucks in the vicinity of Spiro's locker. Trucks big enough to haul those caskets."

"He's insured," she said. "We make everybody take insurance."

"He can't collect on insurance without filing a police report, and at this preliminary stage Mr. Stiva would prefer to keep things quiet."

"Tell you the truth I'm not anxious for this to get around, either. Don't want people thinking our lockers aren't safe." She punched up her computer and produced a printout of renters. "These are renters that are on the books right now. When someone vacates we keep them in file for three months and then the computer drops them."

Morelli and I scanned the list, but we didn't recognize any of the names.

"Do you require identification?" Morelli asked.

"Driver's license," she said. "The insurance company makes us get a photo ID."

I folded the printout, tucked it into my pocketbook, and gave Roberta one of my cards with instructions to call should something turn up. As an afterthought I asked her to use her set of master keys and check each locker on the odd possibility that the caskets weren't taken off the premises.

When we got back to the Jeep, Morelli and I looked the list over one more time and drew a big zero.

Roberta hustled out of her office with keys in hand and the portable phone stuffed into her pocket.

"The great coffin search," Morelli said, watching her disappear around the end of the first row of lockers. He slouched in his seat. "Doesn't compute to me. Why would someone choose to steal caskets? They're big and heavy, and the resale market is limited to nonexistent. People probably have all kinds of things stored here that would be easier to fence. Why steal caskets?"

"Maybe that's what they needed. Maybe some down-on-his-luck undertaker took them. Like Mosel. Ever since Stiva opened up his new addition, Mosel has been on a downslide. Maybe Mosel knew Spiro had caskets stashed here, and he tippy-toed in one dark night and swiped them."

Morelli looked at me like I was from Mars.

"Hey, it's possible," I said. "Stranger things have happened. I think we should go around to a bunch of viewings and see if anyone's laid out in one of Spiro's caskets."

"Oh, boy."

I shifted my bag higher onto my shoulder. "There was a guy at the viewing last night named Sandeman. Do you know him?"

"I busted him for possession about two years ago. He got caught in a sweep."

"Ranger tells me Sandeman worked with Moogey at the garage. Said he heard Sandeman was there the day Moogey got shot in the knee. I was wondering if you'd talked to him."

"No. Not yet. Scully was the investigating officer that day. Sandeman gave him a statement, but it didn't say much. The shooting took place in the office, and Sandeman was in the garage working on a car at the time. Had an air wrench going and didn't hear the shot."

"Thought maybe I'd see if he had any ideas on Kenny."

"Don't get too close. Sandeman's a real jerk. Bad temper. Bad attitude." Morelli pulled car keys out of his pocket. "Terrific mechanic."

"I'll be careful."

Morelli gave me a look of total no-confidence. "You sure you don't want me to go with?" he asked. "I'm good at thumbscrews."

"I'm not really into thumbscrews, but thanks for the offer."

His Fairlane was parked next to my Jeep.

"I like the hula girl in the back window," I said. "Nice touch."

"It was Costanza's idea. It covers an antenna."

I looked at the top of her head and, sure enough, there was the tip of an antenna poking through. I squinted at Morelli. "You're not going to follow me, are you?"

"Only if you say please."

"Not in this lifetime."

Morelli looked like he knew better.

I cut across town and left turned onto Hamilton. Seven blocks later I nosed into a parking slot to the side of the garage. Early morning and evening the pumps were in constant use. At this hour they didn't see much action. The office door was open, but the office was empty. Beyond the office the doors to the bays were up. The third bay had a car on a rack.

Sandeman worked nearby, balancing a tire. He was wearing a faded black Harley tank top that stopped two inches short of low-rider, grease-stained jeans. His arms and shoulders were covered with tattoos of snakes, fangs bared, forked tongues sticking out. Stuck between snakes was a red heart with the inscription I LOVE JEAN. Lucky girl. I decided Sandeman could only be enhanced by a mouthful of rotting teeth and possibly a few festering facial sores.

He straightened when he saw me and wiped his hands on his jeans. "Yeah?"

"You're Perry Sandeman?"

"You got it."

"Stephanie Plum," I said, forgoing the usual formality of an introductory handshake. "I work for Kenny Mancuso's bondsman. I'm trying to locate Kenny."

"Haven't seen him," Sandeman said.

"I understand he and Moogey were friends."

"That's what I hear."

"Did Kenny come around the garage a lot?"

"No."

"Did Moogey ever talk about Kenny?"

"No."

Was I wasting my time? Yes.

"You were here the day Moogey was shot in the knee," I said. "Do you think the shooting was accidental?"

"I was in the garage. I don't know anything about it. End of quiz. I got work to do."

I gave him my card and told him to get in touch if he should think of anything useful.

He tore the card in half and let the pieces float to the cement floor.

Any intelligent woman would have made a dignified retreat, but this was New Jersey, where dignity always runs a poor second to the pleasure of getting in someone's face.

I leaned forward, hands on hips. "You got a problem?"

"I don't like cops. That includes pussy cops."

"I'm not a cop. I'm a bond enforcement agent."

"You're a fucking pussy bounty hunter. I don't talk to fucking pussy bounty hunters."

"You call me pussy one more time, and I'm going to get mad."

"Is that supposed to worry me?"

I had a canister of pepper spray in my pocketbook, and I was itching to give him a blast. I also had a stun gun. The lady who owned the local gun shop had talked me into buying it, and so far it was untested. I wondered if 45,000 volts square in his Harley logo would worry him.

"Just make sure you're not withholding information, Sandeman. Your parole officer might find it annoying."

He gave me a shot to the shoulder that knocked me back a foot. "Somebody yanks my parole officer's chain, and somebody might find out why they call me the Sandman. Maybe you want to think about that."

Not anytime soon.

CHAPTER 5

It was still early afternoon when I left the garage. About the only thing I'd learned from Sandeman was that I thoroughly disliked him. Under ordinary circumstances I couldn't see Sandeman and Kenny being buddies, but these weren't ordinary circumstances, and there was something about Sandeman that had my radar humming.

Poking around in Sandeman's life wasn't high on my list of favored activities, but I thought I should probably spare him some time. At the very least I needed to take a look at his home sweet home and make sure Kenny wasn't sharing the rent.

I drove down Hamilton and found a parking place two doors from Vinnie's office. Connie was stomping around the office, slamming file drawers and cussing when I walked in.

"Your cousin is dog shit," Connie yelled at me. "*Stronzo!*"

"What did he do now?"

"You know that new file clerk we just hired?"

"Sally Something."

"Yeah. Sally Who Knew the Alphabet."

I looked around the office. "She seems to be missing."

"You bet she's missing. Your cousin Vinnie caught her at a forty-five-degree angle in front of the D drawer and tried to play hide the salami."

"I take it Sally wasn't receptive."

"Ran out of here screaming. Said we could give her paycheck to charity. Now there's no one to do the filing, so guess who gets the extra work?" Connie kicked a drawer shut. "This is the third file clerk in two months!"

"Maybe we should chip in and get Vinnie neutered."

Connie opened her middle desk drawer and extracted a stiletto. She pressed the button and the blade flashed out with a lethal click. "Maybe we should do it ourselves."

The phone rang and Connie flipped the knife back into her drawer. While she was talking I thumbed through the file cabinet looking for Sandeman. He wasn't in the file, so either he hadn't bothered making bail on his arrest, or else he'd used another bondsman. I tried the Trenton area phone book. No luck there. I called Loretta Heinz at the DMV. Loretta and I went way back. We'd been Girl Scouts together and had bitched our way through the worst two weeks of my life at Camp Sacajawea. Loretta punched up her handy-dandy computer and, *voilà*, I had Sandeman's address.

I copied the address and mouthed " 'bye" to Connie.

Sandeman lived on Morton Street in an area of large stone houses that had gone to trash. Lawns were neglected, torn shades hung limp in dirty windows, cornerstones bore spray-painted gang slogans, and paint blistered from window trim. Most of the houses had been converted to multiple occupancy. A few of the houses had been torched or abandoned and were boarded. A few of the houses had been restored and struggled to recapture some of their original grandeur and dignity.

Sandeman lived in one of the multifamily houses. Not the nicest on the street, but not the worst either. An old man sat on the front stoop. The whites of his eyes had yellowed with age, gray stubble clung to cadaverous cheeks, and his skin was the color of road tar. A cigarette hung from the side of his mouth. He sucked in some smoke and squinted at me.

"Guess I know a cop when I see one," he said.

"I'm not a cop." What was it with this cop stuff? I looked down at my Doc Martens, wondering if it was the shoes. Maybe Morelli was right. Maybe I should get rid of the shoes. "I'm looking for Perry Sandeman," I said, presenting my card. "I'm interested in finding a friend of his."

"Sandeman isn't home. Works at the garage during the day. Not home much at night either. Only comes here when he's drunk or doped up. And then he's mean. You want to stay away from him when he's drunk. Gets extra mean when he's drunk. Good mechanic, though. Everybody says so."

"You know his apartment number?"

"Three C."

"Anybody there now?"

"Haven't seen anybody go in."

I moved past the man, into the foyer, and stood for a moment letting my eyes adjust to the darkness. The air was stagnant, thick with the smell of bad plumbing. Stained wallpaper peeled back at the edges. The wood floor was gritty underfoot.

I transferred the canister of pepper spray from my pocketbook to my jacket pocket and ascended the stairs. There were three doors on the third floor. All were closed and locked. A television droned on behind one of the doors. The other two apartments were silent. I rapped on 3C and waited for a reply. I rapped again. Nothing.

On the one hand, the thought of confronting a felon scared the hell out of me, and I wanted nothing more than to leave pronto. On the other hand, I wanted to catch Kenny and felt obligated to see this through.

There was a window to the back of the hall, and through the window I could see black rusty bars that looked like a fire escape. I moved to the window and looked out. Yep, it was a fire escape all right, and it bordered part of Sandeman's apartment. If I got out onto the fire escape I could probably look in Sandeman's window. No one seemed to be on the ground below. The house to the rear had all the shades drawn.

I closed my eyes and took a deep breath. What was the worst that could happen? I could get arrested, shot, pitched overboard, or beaten to a pulp. Okay, what was the best that could happen? No one would be home, and I'd be off the hook.

I opened the window and crawled out feet first. I was an old hand at fire escapes, since I'd spent many hours on my own. I quickly scuttled to Sandeman's window and looked in. There was an unmade cot that served as his bed, a small Formica kitchen table and chair, a TV on a metal stand, and a dorm-sized refrigerator. Two hooks on the wall held several wire clothes hangers. A hot plate rested on the table, along with crushed beer cans, soiled paper plates, and crumpled food wrappers. There were no doors other than the front door, so I assumed

Sandeman had to use the john on the second floor. I bet that was a treat.

Most important, there was no Kenny.

I had one foot through the hall window when I looked down between the bars and saw the old man standing directly below me, looking up, shading his eyes from the sun, my card still pressed between his fingers.

"Anybody home?" he asked.

"Nope."

"That's what I thought," he said. "Won't be home for a while yet."

"Nice fire escape."

"Could use some repair, what with the bolts being all rusted out. Don't know if I'd trust it. Course if there was a fire a body might not care about rust."

I sent him a tight smile and crawled the rest of the way through the window. I wasted little time getting down the stairs and out of the building. I hopped into my Jeep, locked the doors, and took off.

Half an hour later I was back in my apartment, deciding what to wear for an evening of sleuthing. I settled on boots, a long denim skirt, and a white knit shirt. I spiffed up my makeup and put a few hot rollers in my hair. When the rollers came out I was several inches taller. I still wasn't tall enough to make it in pro ball, but I bet I could intimidate the hell out of the average Pakistani.

I was debating Burger King versus Pizza Hut when the phone rang.

"Stephanie," my mother said, "I have a big potful of stuffed cabbages. And spice cake for dessert."

"Sounds good," I said, "but I've made plans for this evening."

"What plans?"

"Dinner plans."

"Do you have a date?"

"No."

"Then you don't have any plans."

"There's more to life than dates."

"Like what?"

"Like work."

"Stephanie, Stephanie, Stephanie, you work for your no-good cousin Vinnie catching hoodlums. This is no kind of work."

I mentally bashed my head against the wall.

"I've got vanilla ice cream, too, for the spice cake," she said.

"Is it low-fat ice cream?"

"No, it's the expensive kind that comes in the little cardboard tub."

"Okay," I said. "I'll be there."

Rex popped out of his soup can and stretched, front feet out, hindquarters raised. He yawned and I could see down his throat all the way to the insides of his toes. He sniffed at his food cup, found it lacking, and moved on to his wheel.

I gave him a rundown on my night, so he wouldn't worry if I came home late. I left the light burning in the kitchen, turned my answering machine on, grabbed my pocketbook and brown leather bomber jacket, and locked up after myself. I'd be a little early, but that was okay. It'd give me time to read through the obits and decide where to go after supper.

Streetlights were blinking on when I pulled up to the house. A harvest moon hung low and swollen in the dusky evening sky. The temperature had dropped since the afternoon.

Grandma Mazur met me in the foyer. Her steel gray hair was tightly curled in little sausage rolls all over her head. Pink scalp gleamed between the rolls.

"Went to the beauty parlor today," she said. "Thought I might pick up some information for you on the Mancuso case."

"How'd it go?"

"Pretty good. I got a nice set. Norma Szajack, Betty's second cousin, was there getting her hair dyed, and everyone said that's what I should do. I would have tried it out, but I saw on a show that some of them hair dyes give you cancer. I think it might have been Kathy Lee. Had on this woman with a tumor the size of a basketball, and she said it came from hair dye.

"Anyway, Norma and me got to talking. You know Norma's boy Billie went to school with Kenny Mancuso and now Billie works at one of them casinos in Atlantic City. Norma said when Kenny got out of the army he started going down to Atlantic City. She said Billie told her Kenny was one of them high rollers."

"Did she say if Kenny had been to Atlantic City lately?"

"Didn't say. Only other thing was that Kenny called Billie three days ago and asked to borrow some money. Billie said yeah, he could do that, but then Kenny never showed up."

"Billie told all this to his mother?"

"Billie told it to his wife, and she went and told Norma. I guess she wasn't too happy that Billie was gonna loan money to Kenny.

"You know what I think?" Grandma Mazur said. "I think someone whacked Kenny. I bet he's fish food. I saw a show about how real professionals get rid of people. It was on one of them educational channels. What they do is they slit their throats, and then they hang them upside down in the shower to drain all the blood so they don't ruin the carpet what with the bleeding and all. Then the trick is to gut the dead guy and puncture his lungs. If you don't puncture the lungs they float when you dump them in the river."

My mother made a strangled sound from the kitchen, and I could hear my father choking behind his paper in the living room.

The doorbell rang and Grandma Mazur jumped to attention. "Company!"

"Company," my mother said. "What company? I wasn't expecting company."

"I invited a man for Stephanie," Grandma said. "This one's a real catch. Not much to look at, but he's got a good job with money."

Grandma opened the front door and Spiro Stiva walked in.

My father peered over the top of his paper. "Christ," he said, "it's a fucking undertaker."

"I don't need stuffed cabbage this bad," I said to my mother.

She patted my arm. "It might not be so awful, and it wouldn't hurt to be a little friendly with Stiva. Your grandmother's not getting any younger, you know."

"I invited Spiro over, being his mother's spending all that time with Con in the hospital, and Spiro isn't getting any good home-cooked meals." Grandma winked at me and whispered in my direction. "Got you a live one this time!"

Just barely.

My mother slid an extra plate on the table. "It's certainly nice to have company," she said to Spiro. "We're always telling Stephanie she should bring her friends home for dinner."

"Yeah, except lately she's gotten so picky with her men friends she don't see much action," Grandma told Spiro. "Just wait until you taste the spice cake for dessert. Stephanie made it."

"No, I didn't."

"She made the cabbages too," Grandma said. "She's gonna make someone a good wife some day."

Spiro glanced at the lace tablecloth and the plates decorated with pink flowers. "I've been shopping around for a wife. A man in my position needs to think about his future."

Shopping around for a wife? Excuse me?

Spiro took the seat next to me at the table, and I discreetly inched my chair away with the hope that distance would get the little hairs on my arm to lie flat.

Grandma passed the cabbages to Spiro. "I hope you don't mind talking about business," she said. "I've got a lot of questions. For instance, I've always wondered about whether you dress the deceased in underwear. It don't seem really necessary, but on the other hand . . ."

My father paused with the tub of margarine in one hand and the butter knife in the other, and for an irrational moment I thought he might stab Grandma Mazur.

"I don't think Spiro wants to talk about underwear," my mother said.

Spiro nodded and smiled at Grandma Mazur. "Trade secret."

At ten minutes to seven Spiro finished off his second piece of cake and announced he would have to leave for the evening viewing.

Grandma Mazur waved to him as he pulled away. "That went pretty good," she said. "I think he likes you."

"Do you want more ice cream?" my mother asked. "Another cup of coffee?"

"No thanks. I'm stuffed. And besides, I have things to do tonight."

"What things?"

"There are some funeral homes I need to visit."

"What funeral homes?" Grandma yelled from the foyer.

"I'm starting with Sokolowsky's."

"Who's at Sokolowsky's?"

"Helen Martin."

"Don't know her, but maybe I should pay my respects all the same if you're such good friends," Grandma said.

"After Sokolowsky's I'm going to Mosel's and then to The House of Eternal Slumber."

"The House of Eternal Slumber? Never been to that one," Grandma said. "Is it new? Is it in the burg?"

"It's over on Stark Street."

My mother crossed herself. "Give me strength," she said.

"Stark Street isn't that bad," I told her.

"It's full of drug dealers and murderers. You don't belong on Stark Street. Frank, are you going to let her go to Stark Street at night?"

My father looked up from his plate at the mention of his name. "What?"

"Stephanie's going to Stark Street."

My father had been engrossed in his cake and was clearly lost. "Does she need a ride?"

My mother rolled her eyes. "You see what I live with."

Grandma was on her feet. "Won't take me a minute. Just let me get my pocketbook, and I'll be ready to go."

Grandma applied fresh lipstick in front of the hall mirror, buttoned herself into her "good wool" coat, and hooked her black patent leather purse over her arm. Her "good wool" coat was a brilliant royal blue with a mink collar. Over the years the coat had seemed to grow in volume in direct proportion to the rate at which Grandma was shrinking, so that the coat was now almost ankle length. I took her elbow and steered her to my Jeep half expecting her knees to buckle under the weight of the wool. I had visions of her lying helpless on the sidewalk in a pool of royal blue, looking like the Wicked Witch of the West with nothing showing but shoes.

We went to Sokolowsky's first as planned. Helen Martin looked fetching in a pale blue lace dress, her hair tinted to match. Grandma studied Helen's makeup with the critical eye of a professional.

"Should have used the green-toned concealer under the eyes," she said. "You got to use a lot of concealer when you got lighting like this. Now Stiva's got recessed lighting in his new rooms and that makes all the difference."

I left Grandma to her own devices and went in search of Melvin Sokolowsky, locating him in his office just off the front entrance. The door to the office was open, and Sokolowsky was seated behind a handsome mahogany desk, tapping who knows what into a laptop. I rapped lightly to get his attention.

He was a nice-looking man in his mid-forties, dressed in the standard conservative dark suit, white dress shirt, and sober striped tie.

He raised eyebrows at the sight of me standing in his doorway. "Yes?"

"I want to speak to you about funeral arrangements," I said. "My grandmother is getting on in years, and I thought it wouldn't hurt to get some ballpark figures on caskets."

He hauled a large leather-bound catalog up from the bowels of the desk and flipped it open. "We have several plans and a good selection of caskets."

He turned to the casket called the Montgomery.

"This is nice," I said, "but it looks a little pricey."

He thumbed back a couple pages to the pine section. "This is our economy line. As you can see, they're still quite attractive, with a nice mahogany stain and brass handles."

I checked out the economy line but didn't see anything nearly as cheap-looking as Stiva's missing caskets. "Is this as cheap as you get?" I asked. "You have anything without the stain?"

Sokolowsky looked pained. "Who did you say this was for?"

"My grandmother."

"She cut you out of the will?"

Just what the world needs . . . one more sarcastic undertaker. "Do you have any plain boxes or what?"

"Nobody buys plain boxes in the burg. Listen, how about if we put you on a payment plan? Or maybe we could skimp on the makeup . . . you know, only set your grandmother's hair in the front."

I was on my feet and halfway to the door. "I'll think about it."

He was on his feet equally as fast, shoving brochures into my hand. "I'm sure we can work something out. I could get you a real good buy on a plot. . . ."

I ran into Grandma Mazur in the foyer.

"What was he saying about a plot?" she asked. "We already got a plot. It's a good one too. Real close to the water spigot. The whole family's buried there. Of course, when they put your aunt Marion in the ground they had to lower Uncle Fred and put her in on top on account of there wasn't much space left. I'll probably end up on top of your grandfather. Isn't that always the way? Can't even get no privacy when you're dead."

From the corner of my eye I could see Sokolowsky lurking in his doorway, sizing up Grandma Mazur.

Grandma Mazur noticed too.

"Look at that Sokolowsky," she said. "Can't keep his eyes off me. Must be this new dress I'm wearing."

We went to Mosel's next. Then we visited Dorfman's and Majestic Mortuary. By the time we were on the road to The House of Eternal Slumber I was punchy with death. The smell of cut flowers clung to my clothes, and my voice had locked into hushed funereal tones.

Grandma Mazur had enjoyed herself through Mosel but had started to fade toward the end of Dorfman's, and had sat out Majestic Mort, waiting for me in the Jeep while I ran inside and priced burial arrangements.

The House of Eternal Slumber was the only home left on my list. I cut through city center, past the state buildings and turnoffs to Pennsylvania. It was after nine, and the downtown streets were left to the night people—hookers, dealers, buyers, and the kiddie crews.

I turned right onto Stark, instantly plunging us into a despairing neighborhood of dingy brick-fronted row houses and small businesses. Doors to Stark Street bars stood open, spilling rectangles of smoking light onto dark cement sidewalks. Men loitered in front of the bars, passing time, transacting business, looking cool. The colder weather had driven most of the residents inside, leaving the stoops to the even less fortunate.

Grandma Mazur was on the edge of her seat, nose pressed to the window. "So this is Stark Street," she said. "I hear this part of town is filled with hookers and drug dealers. I sure would like to see some of them. I saw a couple hookers on TV once, and they turned out to be men. This one hooker was wearing spandex tights, and he said he had to tape his penis up tight between his legs so it wouldn't show. Can you imagine that?"

I double-parked just short of the mortuary and studied The House of Eternal Slumber. It was one of the few buildings on the street not covered with graffiti. Its white masonry looked freshly scrubbed and an overhead fixture threw a wide arc of light. A small knot of suited men stood talking and smoking in the light. The door opened and two women, dressed in Sunday clothes, exited the building, joined two of the men, and walked to a car. The car left, and the remaining men went into the funeral home, leaving the street deserted.

I zipped into the vacated parking space and did a quick review of my cover story. I was here to see Fred "Ducky" Wilson. Dead at the age of sixty-eight. If anyone asked, I would claim he was my grandfather's friend.

Grandma Mazur and I quietly entered the funeral parlor and scoped the place out. It was small. Three viewing rooms and a chapel. Only one viewing room was being used. The lighting was subdued and the furnishings were inexpensive but tasteful.

Grandma sucked on her dentures and surveyed the crush of people spilling out of Ducky's room. "This isn't gonna float," she said. "We're the wrong color. We're gonna look like hogs in the henhouse."

I'd been thinking the same thing. I'd hoped for a mix of races. This end of Stark Street was pretty much a melting pot, with hard luck being the common denominator more than skin color.

"What's the deal here, anyway?" Grandma asked. "What's with all these funeral homes? I bet you're looking for someone. I bet we're on one of them manhunts."

"Sort of. I can't tell you the details."

"Don't worry about me. My mouth is zipped and locked."

I had a fleeting view of Ducky's casket and even from this distance I knew his family had spared no expense. I knew I should look into it further, but I was tired of doing the bogus pricing out a funeral routine. "I've seen enough," I told Grandma. "I think it's time to go home."

"Fine by me. I could use to get these shoes off. This man-hunting stuff takes it out of a body."

We swung through the front door and stood squinting under the overhead light.

"That's funny," Grandma said. "I could have swore we parked the car here."

I heaved a sigh. "We did park the car here."

"It isn't here anymore."

It sure as hell wasn't. The car was gone, gone, gone. I pulled my phone out of my pocketbook and called Morelli. There was no answer at his home number, so I tried his car phone.

There was a short crackle of static and Morelli came on.

"It's Stephanie," I said. "I'm at The House of Eternal Slumber on Stark Street and my car's been stolen."

There was no immediate response, but I thought I heard some muffled laughter. "Have you called it in?" he finally asked.

"I'm calling it in to you."

"I'm honored."

"Grandma Mazur is with me, and her feet hurt."

"Ten-four, Keemo Sabe."

I dropped my phone back into my pocketbook. "Morelli's on his way."

"Nice of him to come get us."

At the risk of sounding cynical, I suspected Morelli had been camped out in my parking lot, waiting for me to come home so he could get briefed on Perry Sandeman.

Grandma Mazur and I huddled close to the door, ever on the alert should my car cruise by. It was an uneventful, tedious wait, and Grandma seemed disappointed not to have been approached by drug dealers or pimps looking for fresh blood.

"Don't know what all the to-do is about," she said. "Here it is a perfectly good night, and we haven't seen any crime. Stark Street isn't what it's cracked up to be."

"Some slimeball stole my car!"

"That's true. I guess this evening wasn't a complete bust. Still, I didn't see it happen. It just isn't the same if you don't see it happen."

Morelli's truck turned at the corner and made its way up Stark Street. He double-parked, set his flasher, and sauntered around to us. "What happened?"

"The Jeep was parked and locked in this empty space here. We were in the funeral home for less than ten minutes. When we came out, the Jeep was gone."

"Any witnesses?"

"None that I know of. I didn't canvass the neighborhood." If there was one thing I'd learned in my short career as a bounty hunter, it was that no one saw anything on Stark Street. Asking questions was an exercise in futility.

"I had the dispatcher notify all cars as soon as I got your call," Morelli said. "You should come down to the station tomorrow and fill out a report."

"Any chance I'll get my car back?"

"There's always a chance."

"I saw a TV show about stolen cars," Grandma Mazur said. "It was on these chop shops that take cars apart. Probably by now there's nothing left of that Jeep but a grease spot on some garage floor."

Morelli opened the passenger-side door to his pickup and hoisted Grandma onto the seat. I scootched up beside her and told myself to think positive. Not all stolen cars ended up as spare parts, right? My car was so cute that probably someone couldn't resist taking it for a short joyride. Think positive, Stephanie. Think positive.

Morelli made a U-turn and retraced back to the burg. We made a perfunctory stop at my parents' house, only staying long enough to deposit Grandma Mazur in the La-Z-Boy rocker and reassure my mother that nothing terrible had happened to us on Stark Street . . . aside from having my car grand-thefted.

On the way out my mother handed me the traditional bag of food. "A little something for a snack," she said. "Some spice cake."

"I love spice cake," Morelli told me when we were back in his truck, heading for my apartment.

"Forget it. You're not getting any."

"Of course I am," Morelli said. "I went out of my way to help you tonight. The least you can do is give me some spice cake."

"You don't really want spice cake, anyway. You just want to come up to my apartment so you can find out about Perry Sandeman."

"That's not the only reason."

"Sandeman wasn't in a talky mood."

Morelli stopped for a light. "Learn anything at all?"

"He hates cops. He hates me. I hate him. He lives in a walkup on Morton Street, and he's a mean drunk."

"How do you know about him being a mean drunk?"

"Went to his home address and talked to one of his neighbors."

Morelli slid a glance at me. "That was pretty ballsy."

"It was nothing," I said, making the most of the lie. "All in a day's work."

"I hope you had the sense not to give out your name. Sandeman won't be happy to find you snooping around his crib."

"I think I might have left my card." No need to tell him about getting caught on the fire escape. Wouldn't want to weigh him down with unnecessary details.

Morelli gave me a *boy, are you stupid or what* look. "I understand they have positions available for makeover ladies at Macy's."

"Don't start with that makeover stuff again. So I made a mistake."

"Cookie, you're making a career out of making mistakes."

"It's my style. And don't call me Cookie."

Some people learn from books, some listen to the advice of others, some learn from mistakes. I fit into the last category. So sue me. At least I rarely made the same mistake twice . . . with the possible exception of Morelli. Morelli had this habit of periodically screwing up my life. And I had a habit of letting him do it.

"Have any luck on the funeral circuit?"

"None."

He cut the engine and leaned close to me. "You smell like carnations."

"Watch it. You'll crush the cake."

He looked down at the bag. "That's a lot of cake."

"Un-huh."

"You eat all that cake, and it'll go straight to your hips."

I heaved a sigh. "Okay, you can have some of the cake. Just don't try anything funny."

"What's that supposed to mean?' "

"You know what that means!"

Morelli grinned.

I thought about looking haughty, but decided it was too late, and I probably couldn't pull it off anyway, so I settled for a grunt of exasperation and levered myself out of the pickup. I stalked off with Morelli following close on my heels. We rode the elevator in silence, exited at the second floor, and stopped short at the sight of my door slightly ajar. There were gouge marks where a tool had been inserted between jamb and door and used to pry the door open.

I heard Morelli unholster his gun, and I slid a glance in his direction. He motioned for me to step aside, his eyes locked on the door.

I pulled the .38 out of my pocketbook and muscled my way in front of him. "My apartment, my problem," I said, not actually anxious to be a hero, but not wanting to relinquish control.

Morelli grabbed me by the back of my jacket and yanked. "Don't be an idiot."

Mr. Wolesky opened his door with a bag of garbage in his arms and caught us scuffling. "What's going on?" he asked. "You want me to call the cops?"

"I am the cops," Morelli said.

Mr. Wolesky gave him a long, considering look, and then turned to me. "He give you any trouble, you let me know. I'm just going down the hall with my garbage."

Morelli stared after him. "I don't think he trusts me."

Smart man.

We both peeked cautiously inside my apartment, entering the foyer glued at the hip like Siamese twins. The kitchen and the living room area were empty of intruders. We immediately went to the bedroom and bath, checking out closets, looking under the bed, peering out at the fire escape beyond the window.

"It's clear," Morelli said. "You assess the damage and see if anything's been stolen. I'll try to secure the front door."

At first glance damage seemed to consist exclusively of spray-painted slogans having to do with female organs and anatomically impossible suggestions. Nothing seemed to be missing from my jewelry box. Sort of insulting since I had a very nice pair of cubic zirconias that I thought looked every bit as good as diamonds. Well, what did this guy know? This was a person who'd misspelled *vagina.*

"The door won't lock, but I was able to attach the security chain," Morelli called from the foyer. I heard him walk to the living room and stop. Silence followed.

"Joe?"

"Un-huh."

"What are you doing?"

"Watching your cat."

"I don't have a cat."

"What do you have?"

"A hamster."

"Are you sure?"

A little ripple of alarm raced through my chest. *Rex!* I rushed from the bedroom into the living room, where Rexy's glass aquarium rested on an end table beside the couch. I halted dead center in the room and clapped a hand to my mouth at the sight of a huge black cat stuffed into the hamster cage, the mesh lid held tight with duct tape.

My heart beat with sickening clarity and my throat closed over. It was Mrs. Delgado's cat, and the cat sat hunkered down, slitty-eyed and as pissed off as any cat could get. It didn't look especially hungry, and Rex was nowhere in sight.

"Shit," Morelli said.

I made a sound that was half gurgle, half sob and bit into my hand to keep from wailing.

Morelli had his arm around me. "I'll buy you a new hamster. I know this guy who owns a pet store. He's probably still up. I'll get him to open the store—"

"I don't want a new h-h-hamster," I cried. "I want Rex. I loved him."

Morelli held me tighter. "It's okay, honey. He had a good life. I bet he was pretty old too. How old was he?"

"Two years."

"Hmmm."

The cat squirmed in the cage and growled low in its throat.

"It's Mrs. Delgado's cat," I said. "She lives directly above me, and the cat lives on the fire escape."

Morelli went into the kitchen and returned with scissors. He cut the duct tape, lifted the mesh lid, and the cat jumped out and bolted for the bedroom. Morelli followed after the cat, opened the window, and the cat scurried on home.

I looked into the cage, but I didn't see any hamster remains. No fur. No little bones. No yellow fangs. Nothing.

Morelli looked too. "Pretty thorough job," he said.

This drew another sob.

We stayed like that for a minute, squatting in front of the cage, numbly staring at pine shavings and the back of Rex's soup can.

"What's the soup can for?" Morelli wanted to know.

"He slept in the soup can."

Morelli tapped on the can, and Rex rushed out.

I almost fainted with relief, caught midway between laughing and crying, too choked to speak.

Rex was clearly in the same state of emotional overload. He rushed from one end of his cage to the other, nose twitching, beady black eyes bugging out of his head.

"Poor guy," I said, reaching into the aquarium, taking Rex in my hand, raising him up to my face for a closer look.

"Maybe you should let him relax awhile," Morelli said. "He seems pretty agitated."

I stroked his back. "Hear that, Rex . . . are you agitated?"

Rex responded by sinking his fangs into the tip of my thumb. I let out a shriek and jerked my hand away, flipping Rex off into space like a Frisbee. He sailed halfway across the room, landed with a soft thunk, lay stunned for five seconds, and then scrambled behind a bookcase.

Morelli looked at the two puncture wounds in my thumb, then he looked at the bookcase. "You want me to shoot him?"

"No, I don't want you to shoot him. I want you to go into the kitchen, get the big strainer, and trap Rex in it while I wash my hands and get a Band-Aid."

When I came out of the bathroom five minutes later, Rex was crouched still as stone under the strainer, and Morelli was at the dining room table eating the spice cake. He'd set out a wedge for me and poured glasses of milk.

"I think we can hazard a pretty good guess at the identity of the villain here," Morelli said, glancing at my business card impaled on my carving knife, which was sunk into the middle of my square wood table. "Nice centerpiece," he offered. "Did you say you left your calling card with one of Sandeman's neighbors?"

"Seemed like a good idea at the time."

Morelli finished his milk and cake and rocked back in his chair. "How spooked are you about all of this?"

"On a scale of one to ten, I guess I'm at six."

"Do you want me to stay until you can get your door fixed?"

I took a minute to consider. I'd been in worrisome situations before, and I knew it was no fun being alone and scared. Problem was, I didn't want to admit any of this to Morelli. "You think he'll be back?"

"Not tonight. Probably not ever unless you push him again."

I nodded. "I'll be okay. But thanks for the offer."

He stood. "You've got my number if you need me."

I wasn't about to touch that one.

He looked at Rex. "You need any help getting Dracula settled in?"

I knelt down, lifted the strainer, scooped Rex up, and gently set him back in his cage. "He doesn't usually bite," I said. "He was just excited."

Morelli gave me a chuck under the chin. "Happens to me sometimes, too."

I slid the chain home after Morelli left and jury-rigged an alarm system for myself by stacking glasses in front of the door. If the door opened, it'd knock the pyramid over, and the glasses smashing on the linoleum floor would wake me up. There was the added advantage that if the intruder was barefoot, he'd cut himself on the broken glass. Of course, this was unlikely since it was November and forty degrees.

I brushed my teeth, got into my jammies, put my gun on the table beside my bed, and crawled into bed, trying not to be disturbed by the writing on my wall. First thing in the morning I'd call the super to get my door fixed, and while I was at it, I'd mooch some paint.

I lay awake for a long time, unable to sleep. My muscles were twitchy with nerves and my brain was uneasy. I hadn't shared my opinion with Morelli, but I was pretty sure Sandeman hadn't vandalized my apartment. One of the messages on my wall had mentioned conspiracy, and a silver letter *K* had been pasted below the message. Probably I should have shown Morelli the *K*, and probably I should have shown him the silver-lettered note suggesting I take a vacation. I wasn't sure why I'd held back. I suspected the reason was childish. Sort of like . . . you won't tell me your secret, then I won't tell you mine. Nah, nah, nah, nah, nah.

My mind wandered in the dark. I wondered why Moogey was killed, and why I couldn't find Kenny, and if I had any cavities.

I awoke with a start, finding myself sitting bolt upright in bed. The sun was streaming in through the crack in my bedroom curtains, and my heart was pounding. There was a scraping sound from far away. My mind cleared, and I realized it had been the glasses crashing to the floor that had jolted me awake.

CHAPTER 6

I was on my feet with my gun in my hand, but I couldn't make a decision on direction. I could call the cops, jump out my window, or rush out and attempt to shoot the son of a bitch at my door. Fortunately, I didn't have to choose because I recognized the voice cussing in the hall. Morelli's.

I looked at the bedside clock. Eight. I'd overslept. Happens when you don't close your eyes until daybreak. I slipped my feet into my Doc Martens and shuffled to the foyer, where glass shards were scattered over a four-foot area. Morelli had managed to work the chain off the latch and was standing in the open doorway, surveying the mess.

He raised his eyes and gave me the once-over. "You sleep in those shoes?"

I sent him a nasty look and went to the kitchen for a broom and dustpan. I handed him the broom, dropped the dustpan on the floor, and crunched my way over glass, back to the bedroom. I exchanged my flannel nightgown for sweatpants and sweatshirt and almost screamed out loud when I caught sight of myself in the oval mirror above my dresser. No makeup, bags under my eyes, hair out to here. I wasn't sure brushing would make much of a difference, so I slapped on my Rangers hat.

When I got back to the foyer the glass was gone, and Morelli was in the kitchen making coffee.

"You ever think of knocking?" I asked him.

"I did knock. You didn't answer."

"You should have knocked louder."

"And disturb Mr. Wolesky?"

I stuck my head in the refrigerator and pulled out the remains of the leftover cake, then divided it up. Half for me. Half for Morelli. We stood at the kitchen counter and ate our cake while we waited on the coffee.

"You're not doing too good here, babe," Morelli said. "You've had your car stolen, your apartment vandalized, and someone tried to snuff your hamster. Maybe you should drop back and punt."

"You're worried about me."

"Yeah."

We both shuffled our feet some at this.

"Awkward," I said.

"Tell me about it."

"Hear anything about my Jeep?"

"No." He pulled some folded papers from his inside jacket pocket. "This is the report of theft. Look it over and sign it."

I did a fast read-through, added my name to the bottom, and returned it to Morelli. "Thanks. I appreciate the help."

Morelli stuffed the papers in his pocket. "I need to get back downtown. Do you have a plan for the day?"

"Fix my door."

"Are you going to report the break-in and vandalism?

"I'm going to make repairs and pretend it didn't happen."

Morelli acknowledged this and stared down at his shoes, making no move to leave.

"Something wrong?" I asked.

"Lots of things." He blew out a long breath. "About this case I'm working on . . ."

"The big top-secret one?"

"Yeah."

"If you tell me about it, I won't tell a soul. I swear!"

"Right," Morelli said. "Only Mary Lou."

"Why would I tell Mary Lou?"

"Mary Lou is your best friend. Women always blab everything to their best friend."

I slapped my forehead. "Unh. That is stupid and sexist."

"So sue me," Morelli said.

"Are you going to tell me, or what?"

"This is to be kept quiet."

"Sure."

Morelli hesitated. Clearly a cop between a rock and a hard place. Another exhale. "If this gets around . . ."

"It won't!"

"Three months ago a cop was killed in Philadelphia. He was wearing a Kevlar vest but he caught a couple high-penetration rounds square in the chest. One tore into his left lung; the other hit the heart."

"Cop killers."

"Exactly. Illegal armor-piercing bullets. Two months ago Newark had a real effective drive-by where the weapon of choice was a LAW—Light Anti-Tank Weapon. Army issue. Significantly decreased the population of the Sherman Street Big Dogs and turned Big Dog Lionel Simms's new Ford Bronco into pixie dust. The casing from the rocket was recovered and traced to Fort Braddock. Braddock ran an inventory and discovered some munitions missing.

"When we got Kenny into custody we put his gun through NCRC, and what do you think?"

"It came from Braddock."

"Yeah."

This was an excellent secret. This made life much more interesting. "What'd Kenny say about the hot gun?"

"Said he bought it on the street. Said he didn't know the vendor by name, but he'd work with us to try to make an ID."

"And then he disappeared."

"This is an interagency operation," Morelli said. "CID wants it kept confidential."

"Why did you decide to tell me?"

"You're in the middle of it. You need to know."

"You could have told me sooner."

"In the beginning it looked like we had good leads. I was hoping we'd have Kenny in custody by now and wouldn't have to involve you."

My mind was moving at warp speed, generating all sorts of wonderful possibilities.

"You could have bagged him in the parking lot when he was doing his thing with Julia," I said to Morelli.

He agreed. "I could have."

"That might not have told you what you really wanted to know."

"Which is?"

"I think you wanted to follow him to see where he was hiding out. I think you aren't just looking for Kenny. I think you're looking for more guns."

"Keep going."

I was feeling really pleased with myself, now, trying hard not to smile too wide. "Kenny was stationed at Braddock. He got out four months ago and started spending money. He bought a car. Paid cash. Then he rented a relatively expensive apartment and furnished it. He filled the closets with new clothes."

"And?"

"And Moogey was doing pretty good, too, considering he was living on a gas station attendant's wages. He had a megabucks car in his garage."

"Your conclusion?"

"Kenny didn't buy that gun on the street. He and Moogey were involved in the Braddock ammo rip-off. What was Kenny doing at Braddock? Where did he work?"

"He was a shipping clerk. He worked in the warehouse."

"And the missing munitions were stored in the warehouse?"

"Actually they were stored in a compound adjacent to the warehouse, but Kenny had access to it."

"Ah-ha!"

Morelli grinned. "Don't get all wired over this. Kenny's working in the warehouse is hardly conclusive proof of guilt. Hundreds of soldiers have access to that warehouse. And as far as Kenny's affluence goes . . . he could be dealing drugs, betting on horses, or blackmailing Uncle Mario."

"I think he was running guns."

"I think so, too," Morelli said.

"Do you know how he got the stuff out?"

"No. CID doesn't know either. It could all have gone out at once, or it could have trickled out over a period of time. No one checks inventory unless something is needed or, in this case, unless something turns up stolen. CID is conducting a background search on Kenny's army friends and coworkers in the warehouse. So far none of those people have been labeled suspects."

"So where do we go from here?"

"Thought it might be helpful to talk to Ranger."

I grabbed the phone off the kitchen counter and tapped out Ranger's number.

"Yo," Ranger answered. "This better be good."

"It has potential," I said. "You free for lunch?"

"Big Jim's at twelve."

"Going to be a threesome," I told him. "You and me and Morelli."

"He there now?" Ranger wanted to know.

"Yeah."

"You naked?"

"No."

"Still early," Ranger said.

I heard the disconnect, and I hung up.

When Morelli left I called Dillon Ruddick, the building superintendent, who was also an all-around good guy and friend. I explained my problem and about half an hour later, Dillon showed up with his trusty box of tools, a half gallon of paint, and assorted paint paraphernalia.

He went to work on the door, and I tackled the walls. It took three coats to cover the spray paint, but by eleven my apartment was threat free and had all new locks installed.

I took a shower, scrubbed my teeth, dried my hair, and got dressed in jeans and black turtleneck.

I placed a call to my insurance company and reported the theft of my car. I was told my policy did not cover car rental and that payment would be made in thirty days if my car didn't turn up by then. I was doing some heavy sighing when my phone rang. Even before I touched the receiver the urge to scream told me it was my mother.

"Have you gotten your car back?" she asked.

"No."

"Not to worry. We have it all figured out. You can use your uncle Sandor's car."

Uncle Sandor had gone into a nursing home last month, at the age of eighty-four, and had given his car to his only living sister, Grandma Mazur. Grandma Mazur had never learned to drive. My parents and the rest of the free world weren't anxious for her to start now.

While I hated to look a gift horse in the mouth, I really didn't want

Uncle Sandor's car. It was a 1953 powder blue Buick with a shiny white top, whitewall tires big enough to fit a backhoe, and gleaming chrome portholes. It was the same size and shape as a beluga whale and probably got six miles to the gallon on a good day.

"Wouldn't think of it," I said to my mother. "Nice of you to offer, but that's Grandma Mazur's car."

"Grandma Mazur wants you to have it. Your father's on his way over. Drive it in health."

Damn. I declined her offer of dinner and disconnected. I peeked in at Rex to make sure he wasn't suffering any delayed reactions to last night's ordeal. He seemed in good spirits, so I gave him a broccoli floret and a walnut, grabbed my jacket and pocketbook, and locked the apartment behind me. I slogged down the stairs and stood outside, waiting for my father to appear.

The far-off sound of a mammoth engine arrogantly sucking gas carried to the parking lot, and I shrank back against the building, hoping for a reprieve, praying this wasn't the Buick approaching.

A bulbous-nosed behemoth of a car turned the corner, and I felt my heart beat in time to the pounding of pistons. It was the Buick, all right, in all its glory, not a speck of rust anywhere. Uncle Sandor had bought the car new in 1953 and had kept it in showroom condition.

"I don't think this is a good idea," I said to my father. "What if I scratch it?"

"It won't get scratched," my father said, putting the car in park, sliding over on the big bench seat. "It's a Buick."

"But I like little cars," I explained.

"That's what's wrong with this country," my father said, "little cars. Soon as they started bringing those little cars over from Japan everything went to pot." He thumped on the dash. "Now, this is a car. This baby is made to last. This is the kind of car a man can be proud to drive. This is a car with *cojones*."

I got in next to my father and peered over the wheel, staring open-mouthed at the amount of hood. Okay, so it was big and ugly, but hell, it had *cojones*.

I took a firm grip on the wheel and thumped my left foot to the floor before my brain registered "no clutch."

"Automatic," my father said. "That's what America is all about."

I dropped my father at the house and forced a smile. "Thanks."

My mother was at the front stoop. "Be careful," she yelled. "Keep your doors locked."

Morelli and I walked into Big Jim's together. Ranger was already there, sitting with his back to the wall at a table that afforded a good view of the room. Always the bounty hunter, and most likely feeling naked since he'd probably left most of his personal arsenal in the car in honor of Morelli.

There was no need to look at a menu. If you knew anything at all, you ate ribs and greens at Jim's. We ordered and sat in silence until drinks were served. Ranger kicked back in his chair, arms crossed over his chest. Morelli in a less aggressive, more indolent slouch. Me on the edge of my seat, elbows on the table, ready to jump and run should they decide to have a shootout just for the hell of it.

"So," Ranger finally said, "what's going on here?"

Morelli leaned forward slightly. The pitch of his voice was casual and low. "The army's lost some toys. So far they've turned up in Newark and Philadelphia and Trenton. You hear anything about this stuff being out on the street?"

"There's always stuff out on the street."

"This is different stuff," Morelli said. "Cop killers, LAWs, M-16s, new 9-mm Berettas stamped 'Property of U.S. Government.' "

Ranger nodded. "I know about the car in Newark and the cop in Philly. What have we got in Trenton?"

"We've got the gun Kenny used to shoot Moogey in the knee."

"No shit?" Ranger tipped his head back and laughed. "This gets better all the time. Kenny Mancuso accidentally shoots his best friend in the knee, is apprehended by a cop who by chance stops in to get gas even as the gun is smoking, and it turns out he's got a funny gun."

"What's the word?" Morelli asked. "You know anything?"

"Nada," Ranger said. "What's Kenny give you?"

"Nada," Morelli said.

Conversation stopped while we shuffled silver and glasses to make room for the plates of ribs and bowls of greens.

Ranger continued to stare at Morelli. "I get the feeling there's more."

Morelli selected a rib and did his lion-on-the-Serengeti imitation. "The stuff was stolen from Braddock."

"While Kenny was stationed there?"

"Possibly."

"I bet the little devil had access too."

"So far all we have is coincidence," Morelli said. "It'd be nice if we could get a line on the distribution."

Ranger did a scan on the room and focused his attention back to Morelli. "Been quiet here. I can ask in Philly."

My pager beeped deep in my pocketbook. I stuck my head in and rummaged around, finally resorting to extracting the contents one by one—cuffs, flashlight, Mace, stun gun, hairspray, hairbrush, wallet, sports Walkman, Swiss army knife, pager.

Ranger and Morelli watched in grim fascination.

I glanced at the digital readout. "Roberta."

Morelli brought his head up from his ribs. "Are you a betting person?"

"Not with you."

Jim had a public phone in the narrow hallway leading to the restrooms. I dialed Roberta's number and leaned a hip against the wall while I waited. Roberta picked up after several rings. I was hoping she'd found the caskets, but no such luck. She'd checked every locker and found nothing unusual, but she'd remembered a truck that had made several trips to a locker in the vicinity of number 16.

"At the end of the month," she said. "I remember because I was doing the monthly billing, and this truck went in and out a couple times."

"Can you describe it?"

"It was fairly large. Like a small moving van. Not an eighteen-wheeler or anything. More that it could hold a couple rooms of furniture. And it wasn't a rental. It was white with black lettering on the door, but it was too far to read from the office."

"Did you see the driver?"

"Sorry, I didn't pay that close attention. I was doing the billing."

I thanked her and hung up. Hard to say if the truck information was worth anything. There had to be a hundred trucks in the Trenton area to fit that description.

Morelli looked at me expectantly when I got back to the table. "Well?"

"She didn't find anything, but she remembered seeing a white truck with black lettering on the door make several passes at the end of the month."

"That narrows it down."

Ranger'd picked his ribs clean. He looked at his watch and pushed back. "Gotta see a man."

He and Morelli did some ritualistic hand thing, and Ranger left.

Morelli and I ate in silence for a while. Eating was one of the few body functions we felt comfortable sharing. When the last of the greens had been consumed we gave a collective sigh of satisfaction and signaled for the check.

Big Jim's didn't have five-star prices, but there wasn't much left in my wallet after I anted up my share. Probably it would be wise to visit Connie and see if she had any more easy pickups for me.

Morelli had parked on the street, and I'd opted to leave the blimp in a public lot two blocks down on Maple. I left Morelli at the door and marched off, telling myself a car was a car. And what did it matter if people saw me driving a 1953 Buick? It was transportation, right? Sure. That's why I'd parked a quarter mile away in an underground garage.

I retrieved the car and motored down Hamilton, past Delio's Exxon and Perry Sandeman, and found an empty parking space in front of the bond office. I squinted at the slope of the baby blue hood and wondered exactly where the car came to an end. I eased forward, rolled up on the curb, and nudged the parking meter. I decided this was close enough, cut the engine, and locked up behind myself.

Connie was at her desk, looking even meaner than usual, with her thick black eyebrows drawn low and menacing, and her mouth held in a tight slash of bloodred lipstick. Unfiled files were stacked on the tops of the cabinets, and her desk was a jumble of loose papers and empty coffee cups.

"So," I said, "how's it going?"

"Don't ask."

"Hire anyone yet?"

"She starts tomorrow. In the meantime I can't find a goddamn thing because nothing's in order."

"You should make Vinnie help."

"Vinnie isn't here. Vinnie went to North Carolina with Mo Barnes to pick up a Failure to Appear."

I took a wad of folders and started alphabetizing. "I'm at a temporary impasse with Kenny Mancuso. Anything new come in that looks like a fast bust?"

She handed me several forms stapled together. "Eugene Petras missed his court appearance yesterday. Probably at home, drunk as a skunk, and doesn't know what day it is."

I glanced at the bond agreement. Eugene Petras showed a burg address. The charge was spousal batterment. "Should I know this guy?"

"You might know his wife, Kitty. Maiden name was Lukach. I think she was a couple years behind you in school."

"Is this his first arrest?"

Connie shook her head. "Got a long history. A real asshole. Everytime he gets a couple beers in him he knocks Kitty around. Sometimes he goes too far and puts her in the hospital. Sometimes she files charges, but eventually she always backs off. Scared, I guess."

"Lovely. What's his bond worth?"

"He's out on two thousand dollars. Domestic violence doesn't count for much of a threat."

I tucked the paperwork under my arm. "I'll be back."

Kitty and Eugene lived in a narrow row house at the corner of Baker and Rose, across from the old Milped Button Factory. The front door sat flush to the sidewalk without benefit of yard or porch. The exterior was maroon asphalt shingle with weathered white trim. Curtains were drawn in the front room. Upstairs windows were dark.

I had the pepper spray easily accessible in my jacket pocket, and my cuffs and stun gun stuck into my Levi's. I knocked on the door and heard scrambling going on inside. I knocked again, and a man's voice shouted something incoherent. Again, more shuffling sounds, and then the door opened.

A young woman peered out at me from behind a security chain. "Yes?"

"Are you Kitty Petras?"

"What do you want?"

"I'm looking for your husband, Eugene. Is he at home?"

"No."

"I heard a man's voice in there. I thought it sounded like Eugene."

Kitty Petras was rail thin with a pinched face and large brown eyes.

She wore no makeup. Her brown hair was pulled back in a ponytail at the nape of her neck. She wasn't pretty, but she wasn't unattractive, either. Mostly, she was nothing. She had the forgettable features that abused women get after years of trying to make themselves invisible.

She gave me a wary look. "You know Eugene?"

"I work for his bonding agent. Eugene missed his court date yesterday, and we'd like him to reschedule." Not so much a lie as a half-truth. First we'd reschedule him, and then we'd lock him up in a dingy, smelly cell until his new date came around.

"I don't know . . ."

Eugene reeled into my line of sight through the crack in the door. "What's going on?"

Kitty stepped away. "This woman would like you to reschedule your court date."

Eugene shoved his face up close. All nose and chin and squinty red eyes and 100-proof breath. "What?"

I repeated the baloney about rescheduling and moved to the side so he would be forced to open the door if he wanted to see me.

The chain slid free and clanked against the jamb. "You're shitting me, right?" Eugene said.

I positioned myself halfway into the door, adjusted my pocketbook on my shoulder, and lied my little heart out. "This will only take a few minutes. We need you to stop in at the courthouse and register for a new date."

"Yeah, well, you know what I have to say to that?" He turned his back to me, dropped his pants, and bent over. "Kiss my hairy white ass."

He was facing in the wrong direction to give him a snootful of pepper spray, so I reached into my Levi's and pulled out the stun gun. I'd never used it, but it didn't seem complicated. I leaned forward, firmly pressed the gadget against Eugene's butt, and hit the go button. Eugene gave a short squeak and crumpled to the floor like a sack of flour.

"My God," Kitty cried, "what have you done?"

I looked down at Eugene, who was lying motionless, eyes glazed, drawers at his knees. He was breathing a little shallowly, but I thought that was to be expected from a man who'd just taken enough juice to light up a small room. His color was pasty white, so nothing had changed there. "Stun gun," I said. "According to the brochure it leaves no lasting damage."

"Too bad. I was hoping you'd killed him."

"Maybe you should fix his pants," I said to Kitty. There was already too much ugliness in this world without my having to look at Eugene's Mr. Droopy.

When she had him zipped up I prodded him with the toe of my shoe and got minimal response. "Probably it'd be best if we get him out to my car before he comes around."

"How're we gonna do that?" she asked.

"Guess we'll have to drag him."

"No way. I don't want no part of this. Lordy, this is terrible. He'll beat the daylights out of me for this."

"He can't beat you if he's in jail."

"He'll beat me when he gets out."

"If you're still here."

Eugene made a feeble attempt to move his mouth, and Kitty yelped. "He's gonna get up! Do something!"

I didn't really want to give him any more volts. Didn't think it would look good if I hauled him into court with his hair curled. So I grabbed him by the ankles and tugged toward the door.

Kitty raced upstairs and I assumed, from the sounds of drawers being wrenched open, she was packing.

I managed to get Eugene out of the house and onto the sidewalk next to the Buick, but there was no way I was going to get Eugene into the car without some help.

I could see Kitty assembling suitcases and tote bags in the front room. "Hey, Kitty," I yelled, "I need a hand here."

She peeked out the open door. "What's the problem?"

"Can't get him into the car."

She chewed on her lower lip. "Is he awake?"

"There are all kinds of awake. This kind of awake isn't nearly so awake as some other kinds."

She inched forward. "His eyes are open."

"True, but the pupils are mostly rolled up behind his lids. I don't imagine he can see much like that."

In response to our conversation, Eugene had begun ineffectually flailing his legs.

Kitty and I each took an arm and hoisted him to shoulder level.

"This would be easier if you'd parked closer," Kitty said, breathing heavily. "You practically parked in the middle of the street."

I steadied myself under the burden. "I can only park on the curb when there's a parking meter to aim for."

We gave a joint heave and slammed up against the rear quarter panel with rubber-limbed Eugene. We shoved him into the backseat and cuffed him to the sissy bar, where he hung like a sandbag.

"What will you do?" I asked Kitty. "Do you have someplace to go?"

"I have a girlfriend in New Brunswick. I can stay with her for a while."

"Make sure you keep the court informed of your address."

She nodded her head and scuttled back into her house. I hopped behind the wheel and threaded my way through the burg to Hamilton. Eugene's head snapped around some on the curves, but aside from that the trip to the police station was uneventful.

I drove to the rear of the building, climbed out of the Buick, hit the attention button on the locked door, which led to the docket desk, and stepped away to wave at the security camera.

Almost instantly the door opened and Crazy Carl Costanza poked his head out at me. "Yeah?"

"Pizza delivery."

"It's against the law to lie to a cop."

"Help me get this guy out of my car."

Carl rocked back on his heels and smiled. "This is your car?"

I narrowed my eyes. "You want to make something of it?"

"Hell no. I'm fucking politically correct. I don't make cracks about women's big cars."

"She electrocuted me," Eugene said. "I want to talk to a lawyer."

Carl and I exchanged looks.

"It's terrible what drink can do to a man," I said, unlocking the cuffs. "The craziest things come out of their mouths."

"You didn't really electrocute him, did you?"

"Of course not!"

"Scrambled his neurons?"

"Buzzed him on the ass."

By the time I got my body receipt it was after six. Too late to stop by the office and get paid. I idled in the parking lot for a few moments, staring beyond the wire fence at the odd assortment of businesses across the street. The Tabernacle Church, Lydia's Hat Designs, a used-furniture store, and a corner grocery. I'd never seen any customers in any of the stores, and I wondered how the owners survived. I imagined it was marginal, although the businesses seemed stable, their facades never changing. Of course, petrified wood looks the same year after year, too.

I was worried my cholesterol level had dropped during the day, so I opted for Popeye's spicy fried chicken and biscuits for dinner. I got it to go, and I drove me and my food to Paterson Street and parked across from Julia Cenetta's house. I figured it was as good a place as any to eat, and who knows, maybe I'd get lucky and Kenny would show up.

I finished my chicken and biscuits with a side of slaw, slurped down a Dr Pepper, and told myself it didn't get much better than this. No Spiro, no dishes, no aggravation.

Lights were on in Julia's house but curtains were drawn, so I couldn't snoop. There were two cars in the driveway. I knew one was Julia's, and I assumed the other belonged to her mother.

A late-model car pulled up to the curb and parked. A hulking blond guy got out of the car and went to the door. Julia answered, wearing jeans and a jacket. She called something over her shoulder to someone in the house and left. The blond guy and Julia sat kissing in the car for a few minutes. The blond guy cranked the engine over and the two of them drove away. So much for Kenny.

I rumbled off to Vic's Video and rented *Ghostbusters*, my all-time favorite inspirational movie. I picked up some microwave popcorn, a KitKat, a bag of bite-sized Reese's peanut butter cups, and a box of instant hot chocolate with marshmallows. Do I know how to have a good time, or what?

The red light was blinking on my answering machine when I got home.

Spiro wondered if I'd made any progress finding his caskets, and did I want to go to dinner with him tomorrow after the Kingsmith viewing? The answer to both questions was an emphatic *NO!* I procrastinated relaying this to him, as even the sound of his voice on my machine gave me bowel problems.

The other message was from Ranger. "Call me."

I tried his home phone. No answer. I tried his car phone.

"Yo," Ranger said.

"It's Stephanie. What's happening?"

"Gonna be a party. Think you should get dressed for it."

"You mean like heels and stockings?"

"I mean like a thirty-eight S and W."

"I suppose you want me to meet you somewhere."

"I'm in an alley at the corner of West Lincoln and Jackson."

Jackson ran for about two miles, skirting junkyards, the old abandoned Jackson Pipe factory, and a ragged assortment of bars and rooming houses. It was an area of town so intensely depressed, it was deemed unworthy even of gang graffiti. Few cars traveled the second mile, beyond the pipe factory. Streetlights had been shot out and never replaced, fires were a common occurrence, leaving more and more buildings blackened and boarded, and discarded drug paraphernalia clogged garbage-filled gutters.

I gingerly took my gun out of the brown bear cookie jar and checked to make sure it was loaded. I slid it into my pocketbook, along with the KitKat, tucked my hair under my Rangers hat so I'd look androgynous, and crammed myself back into my jacket.

At least I was giving up a date with Bill Murray for a good cause. Most likely Ranger had a line on either Kenny or the caskets. If Ranger needed help with the takedown on someone he was personally tracking he wouldn't call me. If you gave Ranger fifteen minutes he could assemble a team that would make the invasion of Kuwait look like a kindergarten exercise. Needless to say, I wasn't at the head of his commando-for-hire list. I wasn't even on the bottom of it.

I felt fairly safe driving down Jackson in the Buick. Anyone desperate enough to carjack Big Blue would probably be too stupid to pull it off. I figured I didn't even have to worry about a drive-by shooting. It's hard for a person to aim a gun when he's laughing.

Ranger drove a black Mercedes sports car when he wasn't expecting to transport felons. When it was hunting season, he came loaded for bear in a black Ford Bronco. I spotted the Bronco in the alley, and I feared the contents of my intestines would liquefy at the possibility of snagging someone on Jackson Street. I parked directly in front of Ranger and cut my lights, watching him come forward from the shadows.

"Something happen to the Jeep?" he asked.

"Stolen."

"Word is there's going to be a gun deal going down tonight. Military weapons with hard-to-get ammo. The guy with the goods is supposed to be white."

"Kenny!"

"Maybe. Thought we should take a look. My source tells me there's gonna be a yard sale at two-seventy Jackson. That's the house facing us with the broken front window."

I squinted at the street. A rusted Bonneville sat up on blocks two houses down from 270. The rest of the world was empty of life. All houses were dark.

"We're not interested in busting up this business deal," Ranger said. "We're going to stay here and be nice and quiet and try to get a look at the white guy. If it's Kenny, we'll follow him."

"It's pretty dark to make an identification."

Ranger handed me a pair of binoculars. "Night scope."

Of course.

We were heading into the second hour of waiting when a panel van cruised down Jackson. Seconds later the van reappeared and parked.

I trained the scope on the driver. "He seems to be white," I told Ranger, "but he's wearing a ski mask. I can't see him."

A BMW sedan slid into place behind the van. Four brothers got out of the BMW and walked to the van. Ranger had his window down, and the sound of the side door to the van swinging open carried across the street to the alley. Voices were muffled. Someone laughed. Minutes passed. One of the brothers shuffled between the van and the Beemer carrying a large wooden box. He popped the trunk, stored the box, returned to the van, and repeated the procedure with a second wooden box.

Suddenly the door to the house with the car on blocks crashed open and cops bolted out, yelling instructions, guns drawn, running for the Beemer. A police car barreled down the street and swerved to a stop. The four brothers scattered. Shots were fired. The van revved up and jumped away from the curb.

"Don't lose sight of the van," Ranger shouted, sprinting back to the Bronco. "I'll be right behind you."

I slammed the Buick into drive and pressed my foot to the floor. I shot out of the alley as the van roared past, and realized too late that the van was being pursued by another car. There was a lot of screeching tires and cussing on my part, and the car in pursuit bounced off the Buick with a good solid *whump.* A little red flasher popped off the roof of the car and sailed away into the night like a shooting star. I'd hardly felt the impact, but the other car, which I assumed was a cop car, had been propelled a good fifteen feet.

I saw the van's taillights disappearing down the street and debated following. Probably not a good idea, I decided. Might not look good to leave the scene after trashing one of Trenton's finest unmarked.

I was fishing in my pocketbook, looking for my driver's license, when the door was opened and I was yanked out and onto my feet by none other than Joe Morelli. We stared at each other in openmouthed astonishment for a beat, barely able to believe our eyes.

"I don't believe this," Morelli yelled. "I don't fucking believe this. What do you do, sit in bed at night and think about ways to fuck up my life?"

"Don't flatter yourself."

"You almost killed me!"

"You're overreacting. And it wasn't personal. I didn't even know that was your car." If I'd known I wouldn't have hung around. "Besides, you don't hear me whining and complaining because *you* got in my way. I would have caught him if it hadn't been for you."

Morelli passed a hand over his eyes. "I should have moved out of state when I had the chance. I should have stayed in the navy."

I looked over at his car. Part of the rear quarter panel had been ripped away, and the back bumper lay on the ground. "It's not so bad," I said. "Probably you can still drive it."

We both turned our attention to Big Blue. There wasn't so much as a scratch on it.

"It's a Buick," I said, by way of apology. "It's a loaner."

Morelli looked off into space. "Shit."

A patrol car pulled up behind Morelli. "You okay?"

"Yeah. Wonderful," Morelli said. "I'm fucking fine."

The patrol car left.

"A Buick," Morelli said. "Just like old times."

When I was eighteen I'd sort of run over Morelli with a similar car.

Morelli looked beyond me. "I suppose that's Ranger in the black Bronco."

I cut my eyes to the alley. Ranger was still there, doubled over the steering wheel, shaking with laughter.

"You want me to file an accident report?" I asked Morelli.

"I wouldn't dignify this with an accident report."

"Did you get a look at the guy in the van? Do you think it was Kenny?"

"Same height as Kenny, but he seemed slimmer."

"Kenny could have lost weight."

"I don't know," Morelli said. "It didn't feel like Kenny to me."

Ranger's lights flashed on, and the Bronco eased around the back of the Buick.

"Guess I'll be leaving now," Ranger said. "I know how three's a crowd."

I helped Morelli load his bumper into his backseat and kick the rest of the debris to the side of the road. Around the corner, I could hear the police packing up.

"I have to go back to the station," Morelli said. "I want to be there when they talk to these guys."

"And you're going to run the plates on the van."

"The van was probably stolen."

I returned to the Buick and backed down the alley to avoid the broken glass in the road. I took the first driveway to Jackson and headed for home. After several blocks I swung around and drove to the police station. I parked deep in shadow, a car length back from the corner, across from the bar with the RC Cola sign. I'd been there for less than five minutes when two blue-and-whites rolled into the station parking lot, followed by Morelli in his bumperless Fairlane, followed by one of the big blue-and-white Suburbans. The Fairlane fit right in with the blue-and-whites. Trenton doesn't waste money on cosmetic surgery. If a cop car gets a dent, it's there for life. There wasn't a car in the lot that didn't look like it'd been used for demolition derby.

At this time of night the side lot was relatively empty. Morelli parked the Fairlane next to his truck and walked into the building. The blue-and-whites lined up at the cage to unload prisoners. I put the Buick into drive, slid into the lot, and parked next to Morelli's truck.

After an hour the chill had begun to creep into the Buick, so I ran the heater until everything was toasty. I ate half the KitKat and stretched out on the bench seat. A second hour passed, and I repeated the procedure. I'd just finished the last morsel of chocolate when the side door to the station opened and the silhouette of a man appeared backlit through the door frame. Even in silhouette I knew it was Morelli. The door closed behind him, and Morelli headed for his truck. Halfway across the lot he spotted me in the Buick. I saw his lips move, and it didn't take a genius to figure out the single word.

I got out of the car so it'd be more difficult to ignore me. "Well," I said, all little Miss Cheerful. "How'd it go?"

"The stuff was from Braddock. That's about it." He took a step closer and sniffed. "I smell chocolate."

"I had half a KitKat."

"I don't suppose you still have the other half?"

"I ate it earlier."

"Too bad. I might have been able to remember some crucial piece of information if I had a KitKat."

"Are you telling me I'm going to have to feed you?"

"You have anything else in your pocketbook?"

"No."

"Any more apple pie at home?"

"I have popcorn and candy. I was going to watch a movie tonight."

"Is it buttered popcorn?"

"Yeah."

"Okay," Morelli said. "I guess I could settle for buttered popcorn."

"You're going to have to give me something pretty damn good if you expect to get half of my popcorn."

Morelli did the slow smile.

"I was talking about information!"

"Sure," Morelli said.

CHAPTER 7

Morelli followed me from the station, hanging back in his new 4×4, no doubt worried about turbulence caused by the Buick as it plowed through the night.

We pulled into the lot behind my apartment building and parked side by side. Mickey Boyd was lighting up under the back door overhang. Mickey's wife, Francine, got a nicotine patch the week before, and now Mickey wasn't allowed to consume tar in their apartment.

"Whoa," Mickey said, cigarette magically stuck to his lower lip, eye squinting against the smoke, "check out the Buick. Sweet car. I tell you, they don't make cars like that anymore."

I looked sideways at Morelli. "I guess this big car with portholes stuff is another one of those man things."

"It's the size," Morelli said. "A man has to be able to haul."

We took the stairs, and halfway up I felt my heart contract. Eventually the fright of having my apartment violated would dissipate, and the old casual security would return. Eventually. Not today. Today I struggled to hide my anxiety. Didn't want Morelli to think I was a wimp. Fortunately, my door was locked and intact, and when we entered the apartment, I could hear the hamster wheel spinning in the dark.

I flipped the light switch and dropped my jacket and pocketbook onto the little hall table.

Morelli followed me into the kitchen and watched while I slid the popcorn into the microwave. "I bet you rented a movie to go with this popcorn."

I opened the bag of peanut butter cups, and held the bag out to Morelli. "*Ghostbusters*."

Morelli took a peanut butter cup, unwrapped it, and lobbed it into his mouth. "You don't know much about movies either."

"It's my favorite!"

"It's a sissy movie. Hasn't even got DeNiro in it."

"Tell me about the bust."

"We got all four of the guys in the BMW," Morelli said, "but no one knows anything. The deal was set up by phone."

"What about the van?"

"Stolen. Just like I said. Local."

The timer pinged, and I removed the popcorn. "Hard to believe anyone would bop out to Jackson Street in the middle of the night to buy hot GI guns from someone they'd only dealt with on the phone."

"The seller knew names. Guess that was enough for these guys. They're not big players."

"Nothing to implicate Kenny?"

"Nothing."

I dumped the popcorn into a bowl and handed the bowl to Morelli. "So what names did the seller use? Anyone I know?"

Morelli stuck his head into the refrigerator and came out with beer. "You want one?"

I took a can and snapped it open. "About those names . . ."

"Forget about the names. They aren't going to help you find Kenny."

"What about a description? What'd the seller's voice sound like? What color were his eyes?"

"He was an average white guy with an average voice and no outstanding characteristics. No one noticed eye color. The interrogation went in the general direction that the brothers were looking for guns, not a fuckin' date."

"We wouldn't have lost him if we'd been working together. You should have called me," I said. "As an apprehension agent I have the right to be in on combined operations."

"Wrong. Being invited to participate in combined operations is a professional courtesy we can extend to you."

"Fine. Why wasn't it extended?"

Morelli took a handful of popcorn. "There was no real indicator that Kenny would be driving the van."

"But there was a possibility."

"Yeah. There was a possibility."

"And you chose not to include me. I knew it right from the beginning. I knew you'd cut me out."

Morelli moved to the living room. "So what are you trying to tell me, that we're back to war?"

"I'm trying to tell you that you're slime. And what's more, I want my popcorn back and I want you out of my apartment."

"No."

"What do you mean, no?"

"We made a deal. Information for popcorn. You got your information, and now I'm entitled to my popcorn."

My first thought was of my pocketbook, lying on the hall table. I could give Morelli the Eugene Petras treatment.

"Don't even think about it," Morelli said. "You get anywhere near the hall table, and I'll write you up for carrying concealed."

"That's disgusting. That's an abuse of your power as a police officer."

Morelli took the *Ghostbusters* cartridge from the top of the TV and slid it into the VCR. "Are you going to watch this movie with me, or what?"

I woke up feeling grumpy and not sure why. I suspected it had something to do with Morelli and the fact that I hadn't gotten to gas him or zap him or shoot him. He'd left when the movie had run its course and the popcorn bowl was empty. His parting words were that I should have faith in him.

"Sure," I'd said. When pigs fly.

I got the coffee going, dialed Eddie Gazarra, and left a message for a call back. I painted my toenails while I waited, drank some coffee, and made a pan of Rice Krispies marshmallow treats. I sliced the pan into bars, ate two, and the phone rang.

"Now what?" Gazarra asked.

"I need the names of the four brothers that got busted on Jackson Street last night. And I want the names the van driver gave as reference."

"Shit. I don't have access to that stuff."

"You still need a baby-sitter?"

"I always need a baby-sitter. I'll see what I can do."

I took a fast shower, ran my fingers through my hair, and dressed in Levi's and a flannel shirt. I removed the gun from my pocketbook and cautiously returned it to the cookie jar. I turned on the answering machine and locked up after myself.

The air was crisp and the sky was almost blue. Frost sparkled on the Buick's windows like pixie dust. I slid behind the wheel, powered up, and turned the defroster on full blast.

Going with the philosophy that doing *anything* (no matter how tedious and insignificant) is better than doing nothing, I dedicated the morning to drive-bys on Kenny's friends and relatives. While I drove I kept an eye out for my Jeep and for white trucks with black lettering. I wasn't finding anything, but the list of items to look for was getting longer, so maybe I was making progress. If the list got long enough, sooner or later I was bound to find something.

After the third pass I gave up and headed for the office. I needed to pick up my check for bringing Petras in, and I wanted to access my answering machine. I found a space available two doors down from Vinnie, and I took a stab at parallel-parking Big Blue. In slightly less than ten minutes, I got the car pretty well angled in, with only one rear tire on the sidewalk.

"Nice parking job," Connie said. "I was afraid you were going to run out of gas before you berthed the *QE Two*."

I dumped my pocketbook onto the Naugahyde couch. "I'm getting better. I only hit the car behind me twice, and I missed the parking meter totally."

A familiar face popped up from behind Connie. "Sheee-it, that better not a been my car you hit."

"Lula!"

Lula posed her 230 pounds with hand on outthrust hip. She was wearing white sweats and white sneakers. Her hair had been dyed orange and looked like it had been cut by a bush hog and straightened with wallpaper paste.

"Hey, girl," Lula said. "What you doing dragging your sad ass in here?"

"Came to pick up a paycheck. What are you doing here? Trying to make bail?"

"Hell no. I just been hired to whip this office into shape. I'm gonna file my ass off."

"What about your previous profession?"

"I'm retired. I gave the corner over to Jackie. I couldn't go back to bein' a ho after I was cut so bad last summer."

Connie was smiling ear to ear. "I figure she can handle Vinnie."

"Yeah," Lula said. "He try anything with me, and I'll stomp on the little motherfucker. He mess with a big woman like me, and he be nothin' more than a smelly spot on the carpet."

I liked Lula a lot. We'd met a few months ago, when I was just starting out on my bounty hunter career, and I'd found myself looking for answers on her corner on Stark Street.

"So, do you still get around? You still hear things on the street?" I asked Lula.

"What kinda things?"

"Four brothers tried to buy some guns last night and got busted."

"Hah. Everybody knows about that. That's the two Long boys, and Booger Brown and his dumber'n-cat-shit cousin, Freddie Johnson."

"You know who they were buying the guns from?"

"Some white dude. Don't know more'n that."

"I'm trying to get a line on the white dude."

"Sure does feel funny being on this side of the law," Lula said. "Think this is gonna take some getting used to."

I dialed my number and accessed my messages. There was another invitation from Spiro and a list of names from Eddie Gazarra. The first four were the same names Lula had given me. The last three were the gangster references given by the gun seller. I wrote them down and turned to Lula.

"Tell me about Lionel Boone, Stinky Sanders, and Jamal Alou."

"Boone and Sanders deal. They go in and out of lockup like it was a vacation condo. Life expectancy don't look good, if you know what I mean. Don't know Alou."

"How about you?" I asked Connie. "You know any of these losers?"

"Not offhand, but you can check the files."

"Whoa," Lula said. "That's my job. You just stand back and watch me do this."

While she was checking the files I called Ranger.

"Talked to Morelli last night," I said to Ranger. "They didn't get a lot out of the brothers in the BMW. Mostly all they got was that the driver of the van used Lionel Boone, Stinky Sanders, and Jamal Alou as references."

"Bunch of bad people," Ranger said. "Alou is a craftsman. Can customize anything that goes bang."

"Maybe we should talk to them."

"Don't think you'd want to hear what they'd have to say to you, babe. Be better if I look the boys up by myself."

"Okay by me. I have other things to do anyway."

"Ain't got none of those assholes on file," Lula called. "Guess we too high-class."

I got my check from Connie and moseyed out to Big Blue. Sal Fiorello had come out of the deli and was peering into Blue's side window. "Will you look at the condition of this honey," he said to no one in particular.

I rolled my eyes and stuck the key in the door lock. "Morning Mr. Fiorello."

"That's some car you got here," he said.

"Yep," I replied. "Not everyone can drive a car like this."

"My uncle Manni had a fifty-three Buick. They found him dead in it. Found him at the landfill."

"Gee, I'm really sorry."

"Ruined the upholstery," Sal said. "Was a damn shame."

I drove to Stiva's and parked across the street from the mortuary. A florist's truck pulled into the service driveway and disappeared around the side of the building. There was no other activity. The building seemed eerily still. I wondered about Constantine Stiva in traction in St. Francis. I'd never known Constantine to take a vacation, and now here he was flat on his back with his business turned over to his ratty stepson. It had to be killing him. I wondered if he knew about the caskets. My guess was no. My guess was that Spiro had screwed up and was trying to keep it from Con.

I needed to give Spiro a no-progress report and decline his dinner invitation, but I was having a hard time motivating myself to cross the street. I could manage a mortuary at seven at night when it was filled with the K of C. I wasn't crazy about tippy-toeing around at eleven in the morning, just me and Spiro and the dead people.

I sat there awhile longer, and I got to thinking how Spiro, Kenny, and Moogey had been best friends all through school. Kenny, the wise guy. Spiro, the not-too-bright kid with bad teeth and an undertaker for a stepfather. And Moogey, who as far as I could tell was a good guy. It's funny how people form alliances around the common denominator of simply needing a friend.

Now Moogey was dead. Kenny was missing in action. And Spiro was out twenty-four cheap caskets. Life can get pretty strange. One minute you're in high school, shooting baskets and stealing little kids' lunch money, and then next thing you know you're using mortician's putty to fill in the holes in your best friend's head.

A weird thought steamed from my brain like the Phoenix rising. What if this was all tied together? What if Kenny stole the guns and hid them in Spiro's caskets? Then what? I didn't know then what.

Feathery clouds had stolen into the sky, and the wind had picked up since I left my apartment this morning. Leaves rattled across the street and whipped against the windshield. I thought if I sat there long enough I'd probably see Piglet soar by.

By twelve it was clear that my feet weren't going to bypass my chicken heart. No problem. I'd go with plan number two. I'd go home to my parents, mooch lunch, and drag Grandma Mazur back with me.

It was almost two o'clock when I pulled into Stiva's small side lot with Grandma perched beside me on the big bench seat, straining to see over the dashboard.

"Ordinarily I don't go to afternoon viewings," Grandma said, gathering her purse and gloves together. "Sometimes in the summer when I feel like taking a walk I might stop in, but usually I like the crowd that comes in the evening. Of course things are all different when you're bounty hunters . . . like us."

I helped Grandma out of the car. "I'm not here as a bounty hunter. I'm here to talk to Spiro. I'm helping him with a small problem."

"I bet. What's he lost? I bet he lost a body."

"He didn't lose a body."

"Too bad. I wouldn't mind looking for a body."

We made our way up the stairs and through the door. We stopped for a moment to study the viewing schedule.

"Who're we supposed to be here to see?" Grandma wanted to know. "We gonna see Feinstein or Mayer?"

"Do you have a preference?"

"I guess I could go see Mayer. Haven't seen him in years. Not since he quit working at the A and P."

I left Grandma to herself and went looking for Spiro. I found him in Con's office, sitting behind the big walnut desk, phone in hand. He broke the connection and motioned me into a chair.

"That was Con," he said. "He calls all the time. I can't get off the phone with him. He's getting to be a real pain in the ass."

I thought it would be nice if Spiro made a move on me, so I could give him some volts. Maybe I could give the little jerk some anyway. If I could get him to turn around I could give it to him in the back of the neck and claim it was someone else. I could say some crazed mourner ran into the office and stuck it to Spiro and then ran off.

"So, what's the word?" Spiro asked.

"You're right about the caskets. They're gone." I put the locker key on his desk. "Let's think about the key again. You only got one, right?"

"Right."

"Did you ever make a duplicate?"

"No."

"Did you ever pass it on to someone else?"

"No."

"How about valet parking? Was it on your key chain?"

"No one had access to the key. I kept the key at home, in the top drawer of my dresser."

"What about Con?"

"What about him."

"Did he ever have access to the key?"

"Con doesn't know about the caskets. I did this on my own."

I wasn't surprised. "Just out of morbid curiosity, what did you expect to do with these caskets? You're not going to sell them to anyone in the burg."

"I was sort of a middleman. I had a buyer."

A buyer. Unh! Mental head slap. "Does this buyer know his coffins are history?"

"Not yet."

"And you'd prefer not to ruin your credibility."

"Something like that."

I didn't think I wanted to know any more. I wasn't even sure I wanted to continue to look for the caskets.

"Okay," I said. "New subject. Kenny Mancuso."

Spiro sunk deeper into Con's chair. "We used to be friends," Spiro said. "Me and Kenny and Moogey."

"I'm surprised Kenny didn't ask you for help. Maybe ask you to hide him out."

"I should be so lucky."

"You want to enlarge on that?"

"He's out to get me."

"Kenny?"

"He was here."

This brought me out of my chair. "When? Did you see him?"

Spiro slid the middle drawer open and extracted a sheet of paper. He flipped the paper over to me. "I found this on my desk when I came in this morning."

The message was cryptic. "You have something that's mine, now I have something that's yours." The message was formed from silver paste-on letters. It was signed with a silver *K*. I stared at the paste on the letters and swallowed audibly. Spiro and I had a common pen pal.

"What does this mean?" I asked Spiro.

Spiro was still sunk into the chair. "I don't know what it means. It means he's crazy. You're going to keep looking for the caskets, aren't you?" Spiro asked. "We made a deal."

Here Spiro is, totally stressed over this bizarre note from Kenny, and in the next breath he's quizzing me about the caskets. Very suspicious, Dr. Watson.

"I suppose I'll keep looking," I told him, "but in all honesty, I'm stumped."

I found Grandma still in the Mayer room, manning the command post at the head of the casket with Marjorie Boyer and Mrs. Mayer. Mrs. Mayer was nicely snockered on 100-proof tea, entertaining Grandma and Marjorie with a slightly slurred version of the story of her life, concentrating on the seamier moments. She was swaying and gesturing, and every now and then a splot of whatever would slurp out of her teacup and splatter onto her shoe.

"You have to see this," Grandma said to me. "They gave George a dark blue satin liner on account of his lodge colors are blue and gold. Isn't that something?"

"All the lodge brothers'll be here tonight," Mrs. Mayer said. "They're gonna have a ceremony. And they sent a spray . . . THIS BIG!"

"That's a pip of a ring George is wearing," Grandma said to Mrs. Mayer.

Mrs. Mayer chugged the rest of her tea. "It's his lodge ring, the Lord rest his soul, George wanted to be buried with his lodge ring."

Grandma bent down for a better look. She leaned into the casket and touched the ring. "Uh-oh."

We were all afraid to ask.

Grandma straightened and turned to face us. "Well, will you look at this," she said, holding an object the size of a Tootsie Roll in her hand. "His finger came off."

Mrs. Mayer fainted crash onto the floor, and Marjorie Boyer ran screaming out of the room.

I inched forward for a better look. "Are you sure?" I asked Grandma Mazur. "How could that happen?"

"I was just admiring his ring, feeling the smooth glass stone, and next thing I knew his finger came off in my hand," she said.

Spiro charged into the room with Marjorie Boyer close on his heels. "What's this about a finger?"

Grandma held it out for him to see. "I was just taking a close look, and next thing I knew here was the finger."

Spiro snatched at the finger. "This isn't a real finger. This is wax."

"It came off his hand," Grandma said. "See for yourself."

We all peered into the casket, staring at the little stump where George's middle finger used to be.

"There was a man on TV the other night said aliens were snatching up people and doing scientific experiments on them," Grandma said. "Maybe that's what happened here. Maybe aliens got George's finger. Maybe they got some other parts too. You want me to check out the rest of George's parts?"

Spiro flipped the lid closed. "Sometimes accidents happen during the preparation process," he said. "Sometimes it's necessary to do a little artificial enhancement."

A creepy thought skittered into my mind regarding George's finger loss. Nah, I told myself. Kenny Mancuso wouldn't do something like that. That would be too gross even for Mancuso.

Spiro stepped over Mrs. Mayer and moved to the intercom just outside the door. I followed after him and waited while he instructed Louie Moon to call the ERT and then to bring some putty to room number four.

"About that finger," I said to Spiro.

"If you were doing your job he'd be locked up by now," Spiro said. "I don't know why I ever hired you to find the caskets when you can't find Mancuso. How hard can it be? The guy's freaking nuts, leaving me notes, hacking up stiffs."

"Hacking up stiffs as in cutting off fingers?"

"Only one finger," Spiro said.

"Have you called the police?"

"What, are you serious? I can't call the police. They'll go right to Con. Con finds out about any of this he'll go ape-shit."

"I'm still sort of shaky on the finer points of the law, but it seems to me you have an obligation to report this stuff."

"I'm reporting it to you."

"Oh no, I'm not taking responsibility for this."

"It's my business if I want to report a crime," Spiro said. "There's no law says you have to tell the cops everything."

Spiro's gaze settled on a spot over my left shoulder. I turned to see what had caught his attention and was unnerved to see Louie Moon standing just inches from me. He was easy to identify because his name was written in red thread just over the breast pocket of his white cotton jumpsuit. He was average height and average weight and probably in his thirties. His skin was very pale, and his eyes were flat and faded blue. His blond hair had started to recede. He gave me a fast glance, just enough to acknowledge my presence, and handed Spiro the putty.

"We have a fainter in here," Spiro told him. "How about if you direct the ERT to the back door and then send them up here?"

Moon left without saying a word. Very mellow. Maybe working with dead people does that for you. I suppose it could be peaceful once you get over the body fluids stuff. Not much conversation going on, but probably good for the blood pressure.

"How about Moon?" I said to Spiro. "Did he ever have access to the locker key? Does he know about the caskets?"

"Moon doesn't know about anything. Moon has the IQ of a lizard."

I didn't exactly know how to reply to this, since Spiro was so lizardlike himself.

"Let's go through this from the beginning," I said. "When did you get the note?"

"I came in to make some phone calls and found the note on my desk. It must have been a few minutes before twelve."

"How about the finger? When did you find out about the finger?"

"I always do a walk-through before viewings. I noticed old George was short a finger and gave him a patch-up job."

"You should have told me."

"It wasn't something I wanted to share. I didn't think anybody'd find out. I didn't count on Granny Disaster showing up."

"You have any idea how Kenny got in?"

"Must have just walked in. When I leave at night I set the alarm. I shut it off when I open up in the morning. During the day the back door is always open for deliveries. Usually the front door's open too."

I'd watched the front door for a good part of the morning and no one had used it. A florist had pulled around back. That was about it. Of course, Kenny could have waltzed in before I got there.

"You didn't hear anything?"

"Louie and I were working in the addition most of the morning. People know to use the intercom if they need us."

"So who was in and out?"

"Clara does hair for us. She got here around nine-thirty to work on Mrs. Grasso. She left about an hour later. I guess you could talk to her. Just don't tell her anything. Sal Munoz delivered some flowers. I was up here when he came and left, so I know he won't be any help."

"Maybe you should check around. Make sure you're not missing anything else."

"I don't want to know what else I'm missing."

"So what is it that you have and Kenny wants?"

Spiro grabbed his crotch and gave a hoist. "He was small. You know what I mean?"

I felt my upper lip curl back. "You're kidding, right?"

"You never know what motivates people. Sometimes these things eat at them."

"Yeah, well, if you come up with anything else let me know."

I went back to the room and collected Grandma Mazur. Mrs. Mayer was on her feet, looking okay. Marjorie Boyer seemed a little green, but maybe it was just the lighting.

When we got to the lot I noticed an odd tilt to the Buick. Louie Moon was standing beside it, his expression serene, his eyes locked onto a large screwdriver sticking out of the whitewall. He could just as well have been watching grass grow.

Grandma squatted down to get a better look. "Don't seem right that someone should do this to a Buick," she said.

I hated to give in to paranoia, but I didn't for a minute think this was an act of random vandalism.

"Did you see who did this?" I asked Louie.

He shook his head no. When he spoke his voice was soft and as flat as his eyes. "I just came out here to wait for the ERT."

"And no one was in the lot? You didn't see any cars driving away?"

"No."

I allowed myself the luxury of a sigh and went back inside to call for road service. I used the pay phone in the hall, unhappy to find that my hand was shaking as I fumbled to find a quarter in the bottom of my pocketbook. It's just a punctured tire, I told myself. It's no big deal. It's a car, for chrissake . . . an old car.

I had my father come to rescue Grandma Mazur, and while I waited for the tire to be replaced, I tried to imagine Kenny sneaking into the funeral home and leaving the note. It would have been fairly easy for Kenny to come in the back door and not be seen. Slicing off a finger would have been more difficult. It would have taken time.

CHAPTER 8

The back door to the funeral home opened to a short hall, which led to the lobby. The door to the basement, the side door to the kitchen, and Con's office all opened from the hall. A small vestibule and double glass door, located between Con's office and the basement door, gave access to the macadam driveway running back to the garages. It was through this door that the deceased rolled on his last journey.

Two years ago Con had hired a decorator to spiff the place up. The decorator's colors of choice, mauve and lime, dotted the walls with pastoral landscapes. The floors were heavily padded and carpeted. Nothing squeaked. The entire house was designed to keep noise to a minimum, and now Kenny was sneaking about and not being heard.

I ran into Spiro in the hall. "I want to know more about Kenny," I said to him. "Where would Kenny go to hide out? Someone must be helping him. Who would he turn to?"

"Morellis and Mancusos always go back to the family. Someone dies, it's like they all died. They come in here in their ugly black dresses and coats and cry buckets for each other. My guess is he's living in a Mancuso attic."

I wasn't so sure. Seemed to me Joe would know by now if Kenny was hiding in a Mancuso attic. The Mancusos and Morellis weren't known for their ability to keep secrets from each other.

"If he wasn't in a Mancuso attic?"

Spiro shrugged. "He went to Atlantic City a lot."

"He seeing any girls besides Julia Cenetta?"

"You want to go through the phone book?"

"That many, huh?"

I left through the side door and waited impatiently while Al from Al's Auto Body unjacked my car. Al stood and wiped his hands on his coveralls before handing me the bill.

"Weren't you driving a Jeep last time I gave you a new tire?"

"The Jeep got stolen."

"You ever think about using public transportation?"

"What happened to the screwdriver?"

"I put it in your trunk. Never know when you need a screwdriver."

Clara's Beauty Parlor was three blocks down Hamilton, next to Buckets of Donuts. I found a parking space, gritted my teeth, held my breath, and backed the Buick in at warp speed. Better to get it over with. I knew I was close when I heard glass breaking.

I slunk out of the Buick and assessed the damage. None to the Buick. Broken headlight on the other guy's car. I left a note with insurance information and made for Clara's.

Bars, funeral homes, bakeries, and beauty parlors form the hub of the wheel that spins the burg. Beauty parlors are especially important because the burg is an equal-opportunity neighborhood caught in a 1950s time warp. The translation of this is that girls in the burg become obsessed with hair at a very early age. The hell with coed peewee football. If you're a little girl in the burg you spend your time combing out Barbie's hair. Barbie sets the standard. Big gunky black eyelashes, electric-blue eye shadow, pointy outthrust breasts, and a lot of platinum-blond phony-looking hair. This is what we all aspire to. Barbie even teaches us how to dress. Tight glittery dresses, skimpy shorts, an occasional feather boa, and, of course, spike heels with everything. Not that Barbie doesn't have more to offer, but little girls in the burg know better than to get sucked in by yuppie Barbie. They don't buy into any of that tasteful sportswear, professional business suit stuff. Little girls in the burg go for the glamour.

The way I see it is, we're so far behind we're actually ahead of the rest of the country. We never had to go through any of that messy readjustment with roles stuff. You are who you want to be in the burg. It's never been men against women. In the burg it's always been weak against strong.

When I was a little girl I got my bangs cut at Clara's. She set my hair for my first communion and for my high school graduation. Now I go to the mall to get my hair trimmed by Mr. Alexander, but I still go to Clara sometimes to get my nails done.

The beauty parlor is in a converted house that was gutted to form one large room with a bathroom at the rear. There are a few chrome-and-upholstered chairs in the front where you can wait your turn and read dog-eared magazines or flip through hairdressing books showing styles no one can duplicate. Beyond the waiting area the washing bowls face off with the comb-out chairs. Just in front of the bathroom is a small manicure station. Posters showing more exotic, unobtainable hairstyles line the walls and reflect in the bank of mirrors.

Heads swiveled under dryers when I walked in.

Under the third dryer from the rear was my archenemy, Joyce Barnhardt. When I was in the second grade Joyce Barnhardt spilled a paper cup filled with water onto the back of my chair and told everyone I'd wet my pants. Twenty years later I'd caught her flagrante delicto on my dining room table, riding my husband like he was Dickie the Wonder Horse.

"Hello, Joyce," I said. "Long time no see."

"Stephanie. How's it going?"

"Pretty good."

"I understand you lost your job selling undies."

"I didn't sell undies." Bitch. "I was the lingerie buyer for E.E. Martin, and I lost my job when they consolidated with Baldicott."

"You always did have a problem with undies. Remember when you wet your pants in the second grade?"

If I'd been wearing a blood pressure cuff it would have popped off my arm. I punched the hood back on the dryer and got so far in her face our noses were touching. "You know what I do for a living now, Joyce? I'm a bounty hunter, and I carry a gun, so don't piss me off."

"Everybody in New Jersey carries a gun," Joyce said. She reached into her pocketbook and pulled out a 9-mm Beretta.

This was embarrassing because not only didn't I have my gun with me, but my gun was smaller.

Bertie Greenstein was under the dryer next to Joyce. "I like a forty-five," Bertie Greenstein said, hauling a Colt government model out of her tote bag.

"Too much kick," Betty Kuchta told Bertie from across the room. "And it takes up too much room in your pocketbook. You're better off with a thirty-eight. That's what I carry now. A thirty-eight."

"I carry a thirty-eight," Clara said. "I used to carry a forty-five but I got bursitis from the weight, so my doctor said to switch to a lighter gun. I carry pepper spray, too."

Everyone but old Mrs. Rizzoli, who was getting a perm, had pepper spray.

Betty Kuchta waved a stun gun in the air. "I've got one of these, too."

"Kiddie toy," Joyce said, brandishing a taser.

Nobody could one-up the taser.

"So, what'll it be?" Clara asked me. "Manicure? I just got in some new polish. Luscious Mango."

I looked at the bottle of Luscious Mango. I hadn't actually intended to get my nails done, but the Luscious Mango was pretty awesome. "Luscious Mango will be good," I said. I dropped my jacket and pocketbook over the back of the chair, sat down at the little manicure stand, and plunged my fingers into the soaking bowl.

"Who are you after now?" old Mrs. Rizzoli wanted to know. "I heard it was Kenny Mancuso."

"Have you seen him?"

"Not me," Mrs. Rizzoli said. "But I heard Kathryn Freeman saw him coming out of that Zaremba girl's house at two in the morning."

"That wasn't Kenny Mancuso," Clara said. "That was Mooch Morelli. I heard it right from Kathryn herself. She lives across the street, and she was up letting her dog out. He had diarrhea from eating chicken bones. I told her not to give that dog chicken bones, but she never listens."

"Mooch Morelli!" Mrs. Rizzo said. "Can you imagine? Does his wife know?"

Joyce pulled the dryer back over her head. "I hear she's filing for divorce."

They all went back under the dryers and buried their faces in magazines since this was getting kind of close to home for Joyce and me. It was common knowledge who'd been caught with whom on my dining room table, and no one wanted to risk being present at a shootout with her hair in curlers.

"How about you?" I asked Clara while she filed a nail into a perfect oval. "Have you seen Kenny?"

She shook her head. "Not in a long time."

"I heard someone saw him sneaking into Stiva's this morning."

Clara stopped filing, and her head came up. "Holy mother. I was at Stiva's this morning."

"You see or hear anything?"

"No. It must have been after I left. I guess it doesn't surprise me. Kenny and Spiro were real good friends."

Betty Kuchta leaned forward from the dryer hood. "He was never all there, you know," she said, pointing a finger to her head. "He was in my Gail's class in the second grade. The teachers all knew never to turn their back."

Mrs. Rizzoli nodded in agreement. "A bad seed. Too much violence in the blood. Like his uncle Guido. *Pazzo*."

"You want to be careful of that one," Mrs. Kuchta said to me. "You ever notice his pinky finger? When Kenny was ten he chopped off the end of his pinky finger with his father's ax. Wanted to see if it would hurt."

"Adele Baggionne told me all about it," Mrs. Rizzoli said. "Told me about the finger and lots of other things, too. Adele said she was watching out her back window, wondering what Kenny was going to do with the ax. Said she saw him put his hand on the wood stump next to the garage and chop his finger off. Said he never cried. Said he just stood there looking at it, smiling. Adele said he would have bled to death if she hadn't called the rescue squad."

It was close to five when I left Clara's. The more I heard about Kenny and Spiro the creepier I felt. I'd started the search thinking Kenny was a wise-ass, and now I was worried he was crazy. And Spiro didn't sound any better.

I drove straight home with my mood darkening by the minute. I was so spooked by the time I reached my apartment I had my pepper spray in my hand when I unlocked my front door. I flashed the lights on and relaxed a little when everything seemed in order. The red light was blinking on my answering machine.

It was Mary Lou. "So what's the deal here? You shacked up with Kevin Costner or something and don't have time to call?"

I shrugged out of my jacket and dialed her number. "I've been busy," I told her. "Not with Kevin Costner."

"Then with who?" she asked.

"With Joe Morelli, for one."

"Even better."

"Not that way. I've been looking for Kenny Mancuso and not having any luck."

"You sound depressed. You should get a manicure."

"I got a manicure, and it didn't help."

"Then there's only one thing left."

"Shopping."

"Fuckin' A," Mary Lou said. "I'll meet you at Quaker Bridge at seven. Macy's shoes."

Mary Lou was already deep into shoes when I showed up.

"What do you think of these shoes?" she asked, pirouetting in black ankle-high boots with stiletto heels.

Mary Lou is five foot three and built like a brick shithouse. She had a lot of hair, which happened to be red this week, and she favored huge hoop earrings and the wet look in lipstick. She'd been happily married for six years and had two kids. I liked her kids, but for right now I was content with a hamster. A person doesn't need a diaper pail with a hamster.

"They look familiar," I said about the shoes. "I think Witch Hazel was wearing shoes like that when she found Little Lulu picking beebleberries in her front yard."

"You don't like them?"

"Are these special occasion shoes?"

"New Year's Eve."

"What, no sequins?"

"You should get shoes," she said. "Something sexy."

"I don't need shoes. I need a night scope. You think they sell night scopes someplace here?"

"Omigod," Mary Lou said, holding up a pair of purple suede platform pumps. "Look at these shoes. These shoes were made for you."

"I don't have the money. I'm between paychecks."

"We could steal them."

"I don't do that anymore."

"Since when?"

"Since a long time. Anyway, I never stole anything big. There was just that once we took some gum from Sal's because we hated Sal."

"What about the jacket from Salvation Army?"

"It was MY jacket!" When I was fourteen my mother gave my favorite denim jacket to Salvation Army, and Mary Lou and I retrieved it. I told my mother I'd bought it back, but really we'd shoplifted it.

"You should at least try them on," Mary Lou said. She snagged a salesman. "We want these shoes in a size seven and a half."

"I don't want new shoes," I said. "I need too many other things. I need a new gun. Joyce Barnhardt has a bigger gun than me."

"Ah-ha! Now we're getting somewhere."

I sat down and unlaced my Doc Martens. "I saw her in Clara's today. It was all I could do to keep from choking her."

"She did you a favor. Your ex-husband was a jerk."

"She's evil."

"She works here, you know. Cosmetics. I saw her doing a makeover when I came in. Had some old lady looking like Lily Munster."

I took the shoes from the salesman and slid them on.

"Are they wonderful, or what?" Mary Lou said.

"They're pretty nice, but I can't shoot anyone with them."

"You never shoot anyone anyway. Well, okay, maybe once."

"You think Joyce Barnhardt has purple shoes?"

"I happen to know Joyce Barnhardt has size ten feet and would look like a cow in these shoes."

I walked over to the mirror at the end of the shoe department and admired the shoes. Eat your heart out, Joyce Barnhardt.

I turned to look at them from the back and slammed into Kenny Mancuso.

He had my arms in an iron grip, and he yanked me flat to his chest. "Surprised to see me?"

I was speechless.

"You're a real pain in the ass," he said. "You think I didn't see you sneaking around in the bushes at Julia's house? You think I don't know about you telling her I fucked Denise Barkolowsky?" He gave me a shake that made my teeth clack together. "And now you've got this cozy deal going with Spiro, don't you? The two of you think you're both so smart."

"You should let me take you back to court. If Vinnie assigns another bounty hunter he might not be gentle about bringing you in."

"Haven't you heard? I'm special. I don't feel pain. Probably I'm freaking immortal."

Oh boy.

He flicked his hand, and a knife appeared. "I keep sending you messages, but you aren't listening," he said. "Maybe I should cut off your ear. Would that get your attention?"

"You don't scare me. You're a coward. You can't even face up to a judge." I'd tried this tack before on belligerent FTAs and found it helpful.

"Of course I scare you," Kenny said. "I'm a scary guy." The knife flashed out and slashed into my sleeve. "Now your ear," Kenny said, hanging tight to my jacket.

My pocketbook, with my bounty hunter paraphernalia, was on the seat beside Mary Lou, so I did what any intelligent, unarmed woman would do. I opened my mouth and screamed at the top of my lungs, startling Kenny enough to screw up his aim, so that I lost some hair but kept my ear.

"Jesus," Kenny said. "You're freaking embarrassing me." He shoved me into a shoe display, gave a backward skip, and took off.

I scrambled to my feet and charged after him, blasting through handbags and junior wear, operating on a surplus of adrenaline and a shortage of common sense. I could hear Mary Lou and the shoe clerk running hard behind me. I was swearing at Kenny and bitching about being in pursuit in goddamn platform heels when I slammed into an old lady at the cosmetics counter and almost knocked her on her ass.

"Jeez," I yelled at her. "I'm sorry!"

"Go!" Mary Lou shouted at me from junior wear. "Catch that sonovabitch!"

I reeled off the old lady and barreled into two other women. One of the women was Joyce Barnhardt in her makeover smock. We all went down in a heap on the floor, grunting and thrashing.

Mary Lou and the shoe clerk waded in to separate us, and somehow in the confusion of the moment, Mary Lou gave Joyce a good hard kick in the back of her knee. Joyce rolled away, howling in pain, and the shoe clerk quickly hoisted me to my feet.

I looked for Kenny, but he was long gone.

"Holy crap," Mary Lou said. "Was that Kenny Mancuso?"

I nodded my head yes while I struggled for air.

"What'd he say to you?"

"Asked me for a date. Said he liked the shoes."

Mary Lou snorted.

The shoe clerk was smiling. "You'd have caught him if you'd been trying on sneakers."

In all honesty I wasn't sure what I would have done if I'd caught him. He had a knife, and all I had were sexy shoes.

"I'm calling my lawyer," Joyce said, pulling herself up. "You attacked me! I'm going to sue the shit out of you."

"It was an accident," I told her. "I was chasing after Kenny, and you got in my way."

"This is the cosmetics department," Joyce shouted. "You can't just go around being a lunatic, chasing people through the cosmetics department."

"I was not being a lunatic. I was doing my job."

"Of course you were being a lunatic," Joyce said. "You're a dented can. You and your grandmother are screwy tunes."

"Well, at least I'm not a slut."

Joyce's eyes got as big as golf balls. "Who are you calling a slut?"

"You." I leaned forward in my purple pumps. "I'm calling you a slut."

"If I'm a slut, then you're a tramp."

"You're a liar and a sneak."

"Bitch."

"Whore."

"So what do you think?" Mary Lou said to me. "Are you going to get these shoes, or what?"

By the time I got home I wasn't so sure I'd done the right thing with the shoes. I shifted the box under my arm while I unlocked my door. True, they were gorgeous shoes, but they were purple. What was I going to do with purple shoes? I'd have to buy a purple dress. And what about makeup? A person couldn't wear just any old makeup with a purple dress. I'd have to buy new lipstick and eyeliner.

I flipped the light switch and closed the door behind me. I dumped my pocketbook and new shoes on the kitchen counter and jumped back with a yelp when the phone rang. Too much excitement for one day, I told myself. I was on overload.

"How about now?" the caller said. "Are you scared now? Have I got you thinking?"

My heart missed a beat. "Kenny?"

"Did you get my message?"

"What message are you talking about?"

"I left a message for you in your jacket pocket. It's for you and your new buddy, Spiro."

"Where are you?"

The disconnect clicked in my ear.

Shit.

I plunged my hand into my jacket pocket and started pulling stuff out . . . used Kleenex, lipstick, a quarter, a Snickers wrapper, a dead finger. "YOW!"

I dropped everything on the floor and ran out of the room. "Shit, damn, shit!" I stumbled into the bathroom and stuck my head into the toilet to throw up. After a few minutes I decided I wasn't going to throw up (which was kind of too bad since it'd be good to get rid of the hot fudge sundae I'd had with Mary Lou).

I washed my hands with a lot of soap and hot water and crept back to the kitchen. The finger was lying in the middle of the floor. It looked very embalmed. I snatched at the phone, staying as far away from the finger as was humanly possible, and dialed Morelli.

"Get over here," I said.

"Something wrong?"

"JUST GET OVER HERE!"

Ten minutes later the elevator doors opened and Morelli stepped out.

"Uh-oh," he said, "the fact that you're waiting for me in the hall is probably not a good sign." He looked at my apartment door. "You don't have a dead body in there, do you?"

"Not entirely."

"You want to enlarge on that?"

"I have a dead finger on my kitchen floor."

"Is the finger attached to anything? Like a hand or an arm?"

"It's just a finger. I think it belongs to George Mayer."

"You recognized it?"

"No. It's just that I know George is missing one. You see, Mrs. Mayer was going on about George's lodge, and how he wanted to be buried with his ring, and so Grandma had to check the ring out, and in the process broke off one of George's fingers. Turns out the finger was wax. Somehow Kenny got into the mortuary this morning, left Spiro a note, and chopped off George's finger. And then while I was at the mall tonight with Mary Lou, Kenny threatened me in the shoe department. That must have been when he put the finger in my pocket."

"Have you been drinking?"

I gave him a don't-be-stupid look and pointed to my kitchen.

Morelli moved past me and stood hands on hips, staring down at the finger on the floor. "You're right. It's a finger."

"When I came in tonight the phone was ringing. It was Kenny, telling me he left a message in my jacket pocket."

"And the message was the finger."

"Yeah."

"How did it get on the floor?"

"It sort of dropped there when I went to the bathroom to throw up."

Morelli helped himself to a paper towel and used it to pick up the finger. I gave him a plastic bag, he dropped the finger in, sealed the bag, and slipped the bag into his jacket pocket. He leaned against the kitchen counter and crossed his arms over his chest. "Let's start from the beginning."

I gave him all the details except for the part about Joyce Barnhardt. I told him about the silver-lettered note I'd received, and about the silver *K* on my bedroom wall, and about the screwdriver, and about how it would seem they'd come from Kenny.

He was quiet when I finished. After several seconds he asked me if I bought the shoes.

"Yeah," I said.

"Let's see."

I showed him the shoes.

"Very sexy," he said. "I think I'm getting excited."

I quickly put the shoes back in the box. "You have any idea what Kenny meant when he said Spiro had something of his?"

"No. Do you?"

"No."

"Would you tell me if you did?"

"I might."

Morelli opened the refrigerator and stared at the shelves. "You're out of beer."

"I had to choose between food and the shoes."

"You made the right choice."

"I bet this all has to do with the stolen guns. I bet Spiro was in on it. Maybe that's why Moogey got killed. Maybe Moogey found out about Spiro and Kenny stealing guns from the army. Or maybe all three of them did the job, and Moogey got cold feet."

"You should encourage Spiro," Morelli said. "You know, go to the movies with him. Let him hold your hand."

"Oh, ugh! Gross. Yuk!"

"I wouldn't let him see you in the shoes, though. He might go berserk. I think you should save the shoes for me. Wear something slinky with them. And a garter belt. They're definitely garter belt shoes."

Next time I find a finger in my pocket I'll flush it down the toilet. "It bothers me that we haven't been able to spot Kenny, but he doesn't seem to be having any trouble tailing me."

"How did he look? He grow a beard? Dye his hair?"

"He looked just like himself. Didn't look like he was living in dark alleys. He was clean, fresh shaven. Didn't look hungry. Had on clean clothes. Seemed to be alone. Was a little, um, upset. Said I was a pain in the ass."

"No! You? A pain in the ass? I can't imagine why anyone would think that."

"Anyway, he's not living hand to mouth. If he's selling guns, maybe he has money. Maybe he's staying in motels out of the area. Maybe in New Brunswick or down by Burlington or Atlantic City."

"His picture's been circulated in Atlantic City. Nothing's turned up. To tell you the truth, his trail has been dead cold. Having him pissed off at you is the best news I've had all week. All I have to do now is follow you around and wait for him to make another move."

"Oh good. I love being bait for a homicidal mutilator."

"Don't worry. I'll take care of you."

I didn't bother to hold back the grimace.

"Right," Morelli said, cop face in place. "Time out on the flirting and bullshit. We need some serious conversation here. I know what people say about the Morelli and Mancuso men . . . that we're bums and drunks and womanizers. And I'll be the first to admit that it's pretty much true. The problem with this kind of blanket judgment is that it makes it hard for the occasional good guy, like me . . ."

I rolled my eyes.

"And it tags a guy like Kenny a congenital wise-ass when anyplace else on the planet he'd be labeled a sociopath. When Kenny was eight years old he set fire to his dog and never showed a flicker of remorse. He's a manipulative user. He's totally self-centered. He's fearless because he feels no pain. And he's not stupid."

"Is it true he cut off his finger?"

"Yeah. It's true. If I'd known he was threatening you, I'd have done things differently."

"Like what?"

Morelli stared at me for a few moments before answering. "I'd have given you the sociopath lecture sooner, for one thing. And I wouldn't have left you alone in an unlocked apartment protected by juice glasses."

"I wasn't actually sure it was Kenny until I saw him tonight."

"From now on carry your pepper gas on your belt, not in your pocketbook."

"At least we know Kenny's still in the area. My guess is that whatever Spiro has is keeping Kenny here. Kenny isn't going to take off without it."

"Did Spiro seem rattled about the finger?"

"Spiro seemed . . . annoyed. Inconvenienced. He was worried Con would find out things weren't running smoothly. Spiro has plans. He expects to take over and franchise."

Morelli's face creased into a broad smile. "Plans to franchise the funeral parlor?"

"Yeah. Like McDonald's."

"Maybe we should just let Kenny and Spiro go at each other and scrape the remains off the floor when they're done."

"Speaking of remains, what are you going to do with the finger?"

"See if it matches up to what's left of George Mayer's stump. And while I'm doing that I thought I'd subtly ask Spiro what the hell is going on."

"I don't think that's a good idea. He doesn't want the police involved. Wouldn't report the mutilation or the note. If you go barging in there he's going to kick me out of the loop."

"What do you suggest?"

"Give me the finger. I'll take it back to Spiro tomorrow. See if I can learn anything interesting."

"I can't let you do that."

"The hell you can't! It's my finger, dammit. It was in my coat."

"Give me a break. I'm a cop. I have a job to do."

"I'm a bounty hunter. I have a job to do too."

"Okay, I'll give you the finger, but you have to promise to keep me informed. The first hint I get that you're holding out on me I'll pull the plug."

"Good. Now give me the finger, and go home before you change your mind."

He took the plastic bag out of his jacket pocket and plunked it into my freezer. "Just in case," he said.

When Morelli left I locked the door and checked on the windows. I looked under the bed and in all the closets. When I was confident my apartment was secure I went to bed and slept like a rock, with all the lights blazing.

The phone rang at seven. I squinted at the clock and then at the phone. There is no such thing as a good call at 7 A.M. It's been my experience that all calls between the hours of 11 P.M. and 9 A.M. are disaster calls.

" 'Lo," I said into the phone. "What's wrong?"

Morelli's voice came back at me. "Nothing's wrong. Not yet anyway."

"It's seven o'clock. Why are you calling me at seven o'clock?"

"Your curtains are closed. I wanted to make sure you were okay."

"My curtains are closed because I'm still in bed. How do you know my curtains are closed?"

"I'm in your parking lot."

CHAPTER 9

I dragged myself out of bed, pulled the curtain aside, and looked down into the lot. Sure enough, the tan Fairlane was parked next to Uncle Sandor's Buick. I could see the bumper still in Morelli's backseat, and someone had spray-painted PIG on his driver's-side door. I opened my bedroom window and stuck my head out. "Go away."

"I have a staff meeting in fifteen minutes," Morelli yelled up. "Shouldn't take more than an hour, and then I'll be free for the rest of the day. I want you to wait for me to get back before you go to Stiva's."

"No problem."

By the time Morelli got back to me it was nine-thirty, and I was feeling restless. I was watching at the window when he pulled into the lot, and I was out of the building like a flash with the finger rolling around in my pocketbook. I was wearing my Doc Martens in case I had to kick someone, and I'd attached the pepper spray to my belt for instant access. I had my stun gun fully charged and stuffed into my jacket pocket.

"In a hurry?" Morelli asked.

"George Mayer's finger is making me nervous. I'll feel a lot better when it's back home with George."

"If you need to talk to me just give me a call," Morelli said. "You have my car phone number?"

"Committed to memory."

"My pager?"

"Yes."

I powered up the Buick and rumbled out of the lot. I could see Morelli keeping a respectable distance behind me. Half a block from Stiva's I caught sight of the flashing lights of a motorcycle escort. Great. A funeral. I pulled to the side and watched the hearse roll by, followed by the flower car, followed by the limo with the immediate family. I glanced in the limo window and recognized Mrs. Mayer.

I checked my rearview mirror and saw Morelli parked directly behind me, shaking his head as if to say *don't even think about it.*

I punched his number into my phone. "They're burying George without his finger!"

"Trust me. George doesn't care about his finger. You can give it back to me. I'll save it for evidence."

"Evidence of what?"

"Tampering with a dead body."

"I don't believe you. You'll probably toss it into a Dumpster."

"Actually, I was thinking of putting it in Goldstein's locker."

The cemetery was a mile and a half from Stiva's. There were maybe seven or eight cars in front of me, crawling along in the somber procession. Outside, the air was mid-thirties and the sky was a wintery blue, and it felt more like I was in traffic to go to a football game than a funeral. We pulled through the cemetery gates and wound our way to the middle of the cemetery where the grave had been prepared and chairs set up. By the time I parked, Spiro had the widow Mayer already seated.

I sidled up to Spiro and leaned close. "I have George's finger."

No response.

"George's finger," I repeated in my mommy-to-three-year-old voice. "The real one. The one he's missing. I've got it in my pocketbook."

"What the hell is George's finger doing in your pocketbook?"

"It's sort of a long story. What we have to do now is get George put back together again."

"What, are you crazy? I'm not going to open that casket to give George his finger back! No one gives a shit about George's finger."

"I do!"

"Why don't you do something useful like find my damn caskets?

Why are you wasting your time finding things I don't want? You don't expect to get paid for finding the finger, do you?"

"Jesus, Spiro, you're such a slime sucker."

"Yeah, so what's your point?"

"My point is that you better figure out how to get old George his finger, or I'm going to make a scene."

Spiro didn't look convinced.

"I'll tell Grandma Mazur," I added.

"Shit, don't do that."

"What about the finger?"

"We don't drop the casket until everyone's in the cars with motors running. We can pitch the finger in then. Will that work for you?"

"Pitch the finger?"

"I'm not opening the casket. You're gonna have to settle for having it buried in the same hole."

"I feel a scream coming on."

"Christ." He pressed his lips together, but his lips weren't ever able to entirely close over his overbite. "All right. I'll open the casket. Anyone ever tell you you're a pain in the ass?"

I moved away from Spiro to the edge of the gathering, where Morelli stood watching. "Everyone tells me I'm a pain in the ass."

"Then it must be true," Morelli said, throwing an arm around my shoulders. "Have any luck getting rid of the finger?"

"Spiro's going to give it back to George after the ceremony, after the cars have cleared out."

"Are you going to stay?"

"Yes. It'll give me a chance to talk to Spiro."

"I'm going to leave with the rest of the warm bodies. I'll be in the area if you need me."

I tilted my face to the sun and let my mind float through the short prayer. When the temperature dropped below fifty Stiva didn't waste time at graveside. No widow in the burg ever wore sensible shoes to a funeral, and it was the funeral director's responsibility to keep old feet warm. The entire service took less than ten minutes, not even enough time to turn Mrs. Mayer's nose red. I watched the old folks beating their retreat over the blighted grass and hard ground. In a half hour they'd all be at the Mayer house, eating pencil points and drinking highballs. And by one o'clock Mrs. Mayer would be alone, wondering what she was going to do rattling around in the family house all by herself for the rest of her life.

Car doors slammed closed and engines revved. The cars drove away.

Spiro stood hands on hips, a study of the long-suffering undertaker. "Well?" he said to me.

I pulled the bag out of my pocketbook and handed it over.

Two cemetery employees stood on either side of the casket. Spiro gave the baggie to one of them with instructions to open the casket and lay the bag inside.

Neither man blinked an eye. I guess when you make a living dropping lead-lined boxes into the ground you aren't necessarily the inquisitive type.

"So," Spiro said, turning to me. "How'd you get the finger?"

I gave him the rundown on Kenny in the shoe department and how I found the finger when I got home.

"You see," Spiro said, "this is the difference between Kenny and me. Kenny always has to grandstand. Likes to set things up and then see how they play. Everything's a game to Kenny. When we were kids, I'd step on a bug and squash it dead, and Kenny'd stick it with a pin to see how long it'd take the bug to die. Guess Kenny likes to see things squirm, and I like to get the job done. If it was me I'd have gotten you in a dark, empty parking lot, and I'd have shoved the finger up your butt."

I felt my head go light.

"Just talking theoretically, of course," Spiro said. "I wouldn't ever do that to you on account of you're such a fox. Not unless you wanted me to."

"I have to go now."

"Maybe we could see each other later. Like for dinner or something. Just because you're a pain in the ass, and I'm a slime sucker, doesn't mean we can't get together."

"I'd rather stick a needle in my eye."

"You'll come around," Spiro said. "I got what you want."

I was afraid to ask. "Apparently you've got what Kenny wants, too."

"Kenny's a jerk."

"He used to be your friend."

"Things happen."

"Like what?" I asked.

"Like nothing."

"I got the impression Kenny thought we were partners in some sort of plot against him."

"Kenny's nuts. Next time you see him you should shoot him. You can do that, can't you? You got a gun?"

"I really do have to go."

"Later," Spiro said, making a gun with his hand and pulling the trigger.

I practically ran back to the Buick. I slid behind the wheel, locked the door, and called Morelli.

"Maybe you're right about my going into cosmetology."

"You'd love it," Morelli said. "You'd get to draw eyebrows on a bunch of old babes."

"Spiro wouldn't tell me anything. At least not anything I wanted to hear."

"I picked up something interesting on the radio while I was waiting for you. There was a fire on Low Street last night. It was in one of the buildings belonging to the old pipe factory. Clearly arson. The pipe factory's been boarded up for years, but it seems someone was using the building to store caskets."

"Are you telling me someone torched my caskets?"

"Did Spiro put any contingencies on casket condition, or do you get paid dead or alive?"

"I'll meet you over there."

The pipe factory was on a mean piece of land caught between Low Street and the train tracks. It had been shut down in the seventies and left to decay. On either side were flat fields of no value. Beyond the fields were surviving industries: an auto graveyard, a plumbing supply house, Jackson Moving and Storage.

The gate leading to the pipe factory lot was rusted open, the blacktop cracked and pocked, littered with glass and weathered refuse. A leaden sky reflected in pools of sooty water. A fire truck idled in the lot. An official-type car had been parked next to the truck. A blue-and-white and a fire marshal's car were angled closer to the loading dock, where the fire had obviously taken place.

Morelli and I parked side by side and walked toward a group of men who were talking and writing on clipboards.

They looked up when we approached and nodded acknowledgment to Morelli.

"What's the story?" Morelli said.

I recognized the man who answered. John Petrucci. When my father worked in the post office Petrucci was his supervisor. Now Petrucci was the fire marshal. Go figure.

"Arson," Petrucci said. "Pretty much confined to the one bay. Somebody soaked a bunch of caskets in gasoline and set a fuse. The fire trail is clear."

"Any suspects?" Morelli asked.

They looked at him like he was crazy.

Morelli grinned. "Just thought I'd ask. Mind if we look around?"

"Help yourself. We're done here. The insurance investigator's already gone through. There wasn't much structural damage. Everything's cement. Someone's coming over to board things up."

Morelli and I scrambled up to the loading dock. I pulled my flashlight out of my pocketbook and flicked it on a heap of charred, waterlogged trash sitting in the middle of the bay. Only at the far perimeter of the sodden mess were remains that could be recognized as a casket. An outer wood box and an inner wood box. Nothing fancy. Both blackened from fire. I reached out to touch a corner, and the casket and packaging collapsed in on itself, settling with a sigh.

"If you wanted to be real diligent about this, you could tell how many caskets were here by collecting the hardware," Morelli said. "Then you could take the hardware back to Spiro and see if he could identify it."

"How many caskets do you think were here?"

"A bunch."

"Good enough for me." I selected a clasp, wrapped it in Kleenex, and slid it into my jacket pocket. "Why would someone steal caskets and then burn them?"

"A lark? A grudge? Maybe ripping off caskets seemed like a good idea at the time, but whoever took them couldn't get rid of them."

"Spiro isn't going to be happy."

"Yeah," Morelli said. "Kind of warms your heart, doesn't it?"

"I needed that money."

"What were you going to do with it?"

"Pay off my Jeep."

"Honey, you don't have a Jeep."

The casket clasp felt heavy in my pocket. Not in terms of ounces and pounds, but in measurements of dread. I didn't want to go knocking on Spiro's door. When in dread, my rule was always to procrastinate.

"I thought maybe I'd go home for lunch," I said to Morelli. "And then I could bring Grandma Mazur back to Stiva's with me. There'll be someone new in George Mayer's room, and Grandma really likes to get out to afternoon viewings."

"Very thoughtful of you," Morelli said. "Am I invited for lunch?"

"No. You already had pudding. If I bring you home for a meal they'll never let up. Two meals are as good as engaged."

I stopped for gas on the way to my parents' and was relieved not to see Morelli anywhere. Maybe this wouldn't be so bad, I thought. I probably wouldn't get the finder's fee, but at least I'd be done with Spiro. I turned at Hamilton and drove past Delio's Exxon.

My heart dropped when I hit High Street and saw Morelli's Fairlane parked in front of my parents' house. I attempted to park behind him, misjudged, and took out his right taillight.

Morelli got out of his car and examined the damage. "You did that on purpose," he said.

"I didn't! It's this Buick. You can't tell where it ends." I gave him the evil eye. "What are you doing here? I told you no lunch."

"I'm protecting you. I'll wait in the car."

"Fine."

"Fine," Morelli said.

"Stephanie," my mother called from the door. "What are you doing standing out there with your boyfriend?"

"You see?" I said to Morelli. "What did I tell you? Now you're my boyfriend."

"Lucky you."

My mother was waving us forward. "Come in. What a nice surprise. Good thing I have extra soup. And we have some fresh bread your father just got from the bakery."

"I like soup," Morelli said.

"No. No soup," I told him.

Grandma Mazur appeared at the door. "What are you doing with him?" she asked. "I thought you said he wasn't your type."

"He followed me home."

"If I'd known I'd have put on some lipstick."

"He's not coming in."

"Of course he's coming in," my mother said. "I have plenty of soup. What would people think if he didn't come in?"

"Yeah," Morelli said to me. "What would people think?"

My father was in the kitchen putting a new washer in the kitchen faucet. He looked relieved to see Morelli standing in the hallway. He'd probably prefer I bring home someone useful, like a butcher or a car mechanic, but I guess cops are a step up from undertakers.

"Sit at the table," my mother said. "Have some bread with cheese. Have some cold cuts. I got the cold cuts at Giovichinni's. He's always got the best cold cuts."

While everyone was ladling out soup and scarfing up cold cuts I pulled the paper with the casket photo out of my pocketbook. The detail in the photo wasn't especially good, but the hardware looked similar to what I'd seen at the fire site.

"What's that?" Grandma Mazur wanted to know. "Looks like a picture of a casket." She took a closer look. "You aren't thinking of buying that for me, are you? I want one with some carving. I don't want one of them military caskets."

Morelli's head came up. "Military?"

"Only place they got caskets this ugly is the military. I saw on TV about how they got all these caskets left over from Desert Storm. Not enough Americans died over there and now they have acres of caskets to get rid of, so the army's been auctioning them off. They're—what do you call it—surplus."

Morelli and I looked at each other. Duh.

Morelli put his napkin on the table and slid his chair back. "I need to make a phone call," he said to my mother. "Is it okay if I use your phone?"

It seemed pretty far-fetched to think Kenny had smuggled the guns and ammo off the base in caskets. Still, crazier things have been known to happen. And it would explain Spiro's casket anxiety.

"How'd it go?" I asked when Morelli returned to the table.

"Marie's checking for me."

Grandma Mazur paused with a spoonful of soup halfway to her mouth. "Is this police business? Are we working on a case?"

"Trying to get a dental appointment," Morelli said. "I've got a loose filling."

"You need teeth like mine," Grandma told him. "I can mail them to the dentist."

I was having second thoughts about dragging Grandma off to Stiva's. I figured she could hold her own with a disgusting undertaker. I didn't want her involved with a dangerous one.

I finished my soup and bread and helped myself to a handful of cookies from the cookie jar, glancing at Morelli, wondering at his lean body. He'd eaten two bowls of soup, half a loaf of bread slathered in butter, and seven cookies. I'd counted.

He saw me staring and raised his eyebrows in silent question.

"I suppose you work out," I said, more statement than question.

"I run when I can. Do some weights." He grinned. "Morelli men have good metabolism."

Life was a bitch.

Morelli's beeper went off, and he returned the call from the kitchen phone. When he came back to the table he looked like the cat that swallowed the canary. "My dentist," he said. "Good news."

I stacked all the soup bowls and plates and hustled them into the kitchen. "Got to go," I said to my mother. "Got work to do."

"Work," my mother said. "Hah! Some work."

"It was wonderful," Morelli said to my mother. "The soup was terrific."

"You should come again," she told him. "We're having pot roast tomorrow. Stephanie, why don't you bring him back tomorrow?"

"No."

"That's not polite," my mother said. "How is that to treat a boyfriend?"

When my mother was willing to accept a Morelli as a boyfriend, this only went to show how desperate my mother was to get me married, or at least for me to have a social life. "He's not my boyfriend."

My mother gave me a bag of cookies. "I'll make cream puffs tomorrow. I haven't made cream puffs in a long time."

When we got outside I stood straight and tall and looked Morelli square in the eye. "You are *not* coming to dinner."

"Sure," Morelli said.

"What about the phone call?"

"Braddock had a shitload of surplus caskets. The DRMO conducted a sale six months ago. That was two months before Kenny was discharged. Stiva's Mortuary bought twenty-four. The caskets were stored in the same general area as the munitions, but we're talking about a lot of ground. A couple warehouses and an acre or two of open yard, all behind fence."

"Of course the fence was no problem for Kenny, because he worked in the compound."

"Yep. And when bids were accepted the caskets were marked for pickup. So Kenny knew which caskets were assigned to Spiro." Morelli snitched a cookie from my bag. "My uncle Vito would have been proud."

"Vito stole a few caskets in his day?"

"Mostly Vito filled caskets. Hijacking was a sideline."

"So you think it's possible Kenny used the caskets to smuggle the guns off the base?"

"Seems risky and unnecessarily melodramatic, but yeah, I think it's possible."

"Okay, so Spiro, Kenny, and probably Moogey maybe stole all this stuff from Braddock, and stored it at R and J. Then all of a sudden the stuff is missing. Someone pulled a double cross, and we know it wasn't Spiro because Spiro hired me to find the caskets."

"Doesn't seem like it was Kenny either," Morelli said. "When he said Spiro had something that belonged to him, my guess is he was talking about the stolen guns."

"So who does that leave? Moogey?"

"Dead men don't set up late-night sales meetings with the Long brothers."

I didn't want to run over the jagged remnants of Morelli's taillight, so I picked the major pieces out of the gutter, and for lack of something better to do with them, handed the chunks of plastic to Morelli. "Probably you're insured for this," I said.

Morelli looked pained.

"Are you still following me?" I asked.

"Yeah."

"Then watch out for my tires when I go into Stiva's."

Stiva's little side lot was totally filled with the matinee crowd, forcing me to park on the street. I got out of the Buick and tried to be cool about looking for Morelli. I couldn't find him, but I knew he was close because my stomach felt hot and squishy.

Spiro was in the lobby doing his best impersonation of God directing traffic.

"How's it going?" I said.

"Busy. Joe Loosey came in last night. Aneurysm. And Stan Radiewski is here. He was an Elk. The Elks always get a big turnout."

"I have some good news and some bad news," I said. "The good news is . . . I think I found your caskets."

"And the bad news?"

I took the blackened clasp out of my pocket. "The bad news is . . . this is all that's left."

Spiro looked at the clasp. "I don't get it."

"Someone barbecued a bunch of caskets last night. Had them all stacked up in one of the loading bays at the pipe factory, soaked the caskets in gasoline, and lit a fuse. They were pretty badly burned, but there was enough of one to identify as a casket in a crate."

"And you saw this? What else got burned? Was there anything else?"

Like a few LAWs? "From what I could see there were just caskets. You might want to check for yourself."

"Christ," Spiro said. "I can't go now. Who's gonna baby-sit all these fucking Elks?"

"Louie?"

"Jesus. Not Louie. It's going to have to be you."

"Oh no. Not me."

"All you have to do is make sure there's hot tea and say a lot of crapola like . . . the Lord moves in mysterious ways. I'll only be gone a half hour." He dug his keys out of his pocket. "Who was there when you got to the pipe factory?"

"The fire marshal, a uniform, some guy I didn't know, Joe Morelli, a bunch of firemen packing up."

"They say anything worth remembering?"

"Nope."

"You tell them the caskets belonged to me?"

"No. And I'm not staying. I want my finder's fee, and then I'm out of here."

"I'm not handing over any money until I see this for myself. For all I know they could be someone else's caskets. Or maybe you're making all this up."

"Half hour," I yelled to his back. "That's all you get!"

I checked the tea table. Nothing to do there. Lots of hot water and cookies set out. I sat down in a side chair and contemplated some nearby cut flowers. The Elks were all in the new addition with Radiewski, and the lobby was uncomfortably quiet. No magazines to read. No television. Music to die by softly filtered over the sound system.

After what seemed like four days, Eddie Ragucci ambled in. Eddie was a CPA and a big magoo in the Elks.

"Where's the weasel?" Eddie asked.

"Had to go out. He said he wouldn't be long."

"It's too hot in Stan's room. The thermostat must be broken. We can't get it to cut off. Stan's makeup is starting to run. Things like this never happened when Con was here. It's a damn shame Stan had to go when Con was in the hospital. Talk about the lousy breaks."

"The Lord moves in mysterious ways."

"Ain't that the truth."

"I'll see if I can find Spiro's assistant."

I pushed a few buttons on the intercom, yelling Louie's name into the thing, telling him to come to the lobby.

Louie appeared just as I got to the last button. "I was in the workrooms," he said.

"Anybody else in there?"

"Mr. Loosey."

"I mean, are there any other employees? Like Clara from the beauty parlor?"

"No. Just me."

I told him about the thermostat and sent him to take a look.

Five minutes later he trundled back. "The little thing was bent," he said. "It happens all the time. People lean on it, and the little thing gets bent."

"You like working in a funeral home?"

"I used to work in a nursing home. This is a lot easier on account of you can just hose people down here. And once you get them on the table they don't move around."

"Did you know Moogey Bues?"

"Not until after he was shot. Took about a pound of putty to fill in his head."

"How about Kenny Mancuso?"

"Spiro said it was Kenny Mancuso that shot Moogey Bues."

"You know what Kenny looks like? He ever come around here?"

"I know what he looks like, but I haven't seen him in a while. I hear people say how you're a bounty hunter, and that you're looking for Kenny."

"He failed to appear in court."

"If I see him I'll tell you."

I gave him a card. "Here are some numbers where I can be reached."

The back door banged open and was slammed closed. A moment later Spiro stalked into the room. His black dress shoes and the cuffs of his slacks were powdered with ash. His cheeks were an unhealthy red, and his little rodent eyes were dilated black.

"Well?" I asked.

His eyes fixed over my shoulder. I turned and saw Morelli cross the lobby.

"You looking for someone?" Spiro said to Morelli. "Radiewski's in the addition."

Morelli flashed his badge.

"I know who you are," Spiro said. "There a problem here? I leave for a half hour, and I come back to a problem."

"Not a problem," Morelli told him. "Just trying to find the owner of some caskets that burned."

"You found him. And I didn't set the fire. The caskets were stolen from me."

"Did you report the theft to the police?"

"I didn't want the publicity. I hired Ms. Marvel here to find the damn things."

"The one casket that was left looked a little plain for a burg casket," Morelli said.

"I got them on sale from the army. Surplus. I was thinking maybe I'd franchise out into other neighborhoods. Maybe take them down to Philly. Lot of poor people in Philly."

"I'm curious about this army surplus stuff," Morelli said. "How does this work?"

"You submit a bid to the DRMO. If the bid gets picked up, you've got a week to haul your shit off the base."

"Which base are we talking about?"

"Braddock."

Morelli was a study of calm. "Wasn't Kenny Mancuso stationed at Braddock?"

"Yeah. A lot of people are stationed at Braddock."

"Okay," Morelli said, "so they accept your bid. How do you get the caskets back here?"

"Me and Moogey went down with a U-Haul."

"One last question," Morelli said. "You have any idea why someone would steal your caskets and then set a match to them?"

"Yeah. They were stolen by a nut. I've got things to do," Spiro said. "You're done here, right?"

"For now."

They locked eyes, a muscle worked in Spiro's jaw, and he wheeled off to his office.

"See you back at the ranch," Morelli said to me, and he was off, too.

The door to Spiro's office was closed. I knocked and waited. No answer. I knocked louder. "Spiro," I yelled, "I know you're in there!"

Spiro ripped the door open. "Now what?"

"My money."

"Christ, I have more things to think about than your chickenshit money."

"Like what?"

"Like crazy Kenny Mancuso setting fire to my goddamn caskets."

"How do you know it was Kenny?"

"Who else could it be? He's looney tunes, and he's threatening me."

"You should have told Morelli."

"Yeah, right. That's all I need. Like I haven't got enough problems, I should have the cops looking up my butt."

"I've noticed you're not fond of cops."

"Cops stuck."

I felt breath on the back of my neck and turned to find Louie Moon standing almost on top of me.

"Excuse me," he said, "I've got to talk to Spiro."

"Talk," Spiro said.

"It's about Mr. Loosey. There's been an accident."

Spiro didn't say a word, but his eyes bore like drill bits into Louie's forehead.

"I had Mr. Loosey on the table," Louie said, "and I was gonna get him dressed, and then I had to go fix the thermostat, and when I got back to Mr. Loosey I noticed he was missing his . . . um, private part. I don't know how this could happen. One minute it was there, and then the next minute it was gone."

Spiro knocked Louie aside with a sweep of his hand and charged out, yelling, "Jesus H. Christ and motherfucker."

Minutes later, Spiro was back in his office, his face mottled, his hands clenched. "I don't fucking believe this," he roared through clenched teeth. "I leave for half an hour, and someone comes in and hacks off Loosey's dick. You know who that someone was? Kenny, that's who. I leave you in charge, and you let Kenny come in and hack off a dick."

The phone rang and Spiro snatched at it. "Stiva."

His lips narrowed, and I knew it was Kenny.

"You're nuts," Spiro said. "Too much nose candy. Too many of those little tattoos."

Kenny did some talking, and Spiro cut in.

"Shut up," Spiro said. "You don't know what the fuck you're talking about. And you don't know what the fuck you're doing when you mess with me. I see you around here, and I'll kill you. And if I don't kill you I'll have Cookie here kill you."

Cookie? Was he talking about me? "Excuse me," I said to Spiro, "what was that last part?"

Spiro slammed the phone down. "Fucking jerk."

I put palms flat on his desk and leaned forward. "I am *not* a cookie. And I am *not* a hired gun. And if I was in the protection business I would *not* protect *your* slimy body. You are a mold spore, a boil, a dog turd. If you ever tell anyone I will kill them on your behalf again, I'll make sure you sing soprano for the rest of your life."

Stephanie Plum, master of the empty threat.

"Let me guess . . . you're on the rag, right?"

Good thing I didn't have my gun with me, because I might have shot him.

"There are a lot of people who wouldn't pay you anything for finding burned-up stuff," Spiro said, "but because I'm such a good guy I'm going to write you a check. We could consider it like a retainer. I could see where it'd be handy to have a chick like you around."

I took the check and left. I didn't see the value in talking any further since there clearly wasn't anyone home. I stopped to get gas and Morelli pulled in behind me.

"This is getting strange," I said to Morelli. "I think Kenny's gone over the edge."

"Now what?"

I told him about Mr. Loosey and his mishap, and about the phone call.

"You should be giving this car high-test," Morelli said. "You're going to get engine knock."

"God forbid I'd get engine knock."

Morelli looked disgusted. "Shit," he said.

I thought this seemed like a strong reaction to my lack of automotive maintenance. "Is engine knock that bad?"

He leaned against the fender. "A cop was killed in New Brunswick last night. Took two hits through his vest."

"Army ammo?"

"Yeah." He raised his eyes to me. "I have to find this stuff. It's right under my nose."

"You think Kenny could be right about Spiro? You think Spiro could have emptied the caskets and hired me to cover his ass?"

"I don't know. Doesn't feel right. My gut instinct is that this started off with Kenny, Moogey, and Spiro, and somehow a fourth player came in and screwed everything up. I think someone snatched the stuff out from under Kenny, Moogey, and Spiro and started them fighting among themselves. And it's probably not someone from Braddock, because it's being sold piecemeal in Jersey and Philly."

"It would have to be someone close to one of those three. A confidant . . . like a girlfriend."

"It could be someone who found out by accident," Morelli said. "Someone who overheard a conversation."

"Like Louie Moon."

"Yeah. Like Louie Moon," Morelli said.

"And it would have to be someone who had access to the locker key. Like Louie Moon."

"There are probably lots of people Spiro could have talked to and who would have had access to his key. Everyone from his cleaning lady to Clara. Same with Moogey. Just because Spiro told you no one but him had a key doesn't mean it's true. Probably all three of them had keys."

"If that's the case, then what about Moogey's key? Has that been accounted for? Was it on his key chain when he was killed?"

"His key chain was never found. It was assumed that he left his keys somewhere in the garage and sooner or later they'd turn up. It didn't seem like an important issue at the time. His parents came with an extra key and drove his car home.

"Now that the caskets have surfaced I have some cause to harass Spiro. I think I'll go back and lean on him. And I want to talk to Louie Moon. Can you keep out of trouble for a while?"

"Don't worry about me. I'm fine. I thought maybe I'd go shopping. See if I could find a dress to go with the purple shoes."

The line of Morelli's mouth tightened. "You're lying. You're going to do something stupid, aren't you?"

"Boy, that really hurts. I thought you'd be excited about a purple dress with the purple shoes. I was going to look for spandex, too. A short spandex dress with bugle beads and sequins."

"I know you, and I know you're not going shopping."

"Cross my heart and hope to die. I'm going shopping. I swear to you."

One corner of Morelli's mouth hitched up a fraction of an inch. "You'd lie to the Pope."

I caught myself halfway through the sign of the cross. "I almost never lie." Only when it's absolutely necessary. And on those occasions when the truth doesn't seem appropriate.

I watched Morelli drive away, and then I headed over to Vinnie's office to get some addresses.

CHAPTER 10

Connie and Lula were yelling at each other when I walked into the office.

"Dominick Russo makes his own sauce," Connie shouted. "With plum tomatoes. Fresh basil. Fresh garlic."

"I don't know about any of that plum tomato shit. All I know is the best pizza in Trenton comes from Tiny's on First Street," Lula shouted back. "Ain't nobody makes pizza like Tiny. That man makes soul pizza."

"Soul pizza? What the hell is soul pizza?" Connie wanted to know.

They both turned and glared at me.

"You settle it," Connie said. "Tell know-it-all here about Dominic's pizza."

"Dom makes good pizza," I said. "But I like the pizza at Pino's."

"Pino's!" Connie curled her upper lip. "They use marinara sauce that comes in five-gallon cans."

"Yeah," I said. "I love that canned marinara sauce." I dropped my pocketbook on Connie's desk. "Glad to see you two getting along so well."

"Hunh," Lula said.

I plopped onto the couch. "I need some addresses. I want to do some snooping."

Connie got a directory from the bookcase behind her. "Who you need?"

"Spiro Stiva and Louie Moon."

"Wouldn't want to look under the cushions in Spiro's house," Connie said. "Wouldn't look in his refrigerator, either."

Lula grimaced. "He the undertaker guy? Shoot, you aren't gonna do breaking and entering on an undertaker, are you?"

Connie wrote an address on a piece of paper and searched for the second name.

I looked at the address she'd gotten for Spiro. "You know where this is?"

"Century Court Apartments. You take Klockner to Demby." Connie gave me the second address. "I haven't a clue on this one. Somewhere in Hamilton Township."

"What are you looking for?" Lula asked.

I stuffed the addresses into my pocket. "I don't know. A key, maybe." Or a couple crates of guns in the living room.

"Maybe I should come with you," Lula said. "Skinny ass like you shouldn't be sneaking around all by yourself."

"I appreciate your offer," I told her, "but riding shotgun isn't part of your job description."

"Don't think I got much of a job description," Lula said. "Seems to me I do whatever got to be done, and right now I've done it all unless I want to sweep the floor and scrub the toilet."

"She's a filing maniac," Connie said. "She was born to file."

"You haven't seen anything yet," Lula said. "Wait'll you see me be an assistant bounty hunter."

"Go for it," Connie said.

Lula packed herself into her jacket and grabbed her pocketbook. "This is gonna be good," she said. "This is gonna be like Cagney and Lacey."

I searched the big wall map for Moon's address. "Okay by me if it's okay with Connie, but I want to be Cagney."

"No way! I want to be Cagney," Lula said.

"I said it first."

Lula stuck her lower lip out and narrowed her eyes. "Was my idea, and I'm not doing it if I can't be Cagney."

I looked at her. "We aren't serious about this, are we?"

"Hunh," Lula said. "Speak for yourself."

I told Connie not to wait up, and held the front door for Lula. "We're going to check out Louie Moon first," I said to her.

Lula stopped in the middle of the sidewalk and looked at Big Blue. "We going in this big motherfucker Buick?"

"Yep."

"I knew a pimp once had a car like this."

"It belonged to my uncle Sandor."

"He a businessman?"

"Not that I know of."

Louie Moon lived on the far perimeter of Hamilton Township. It was almost four when we turned onto Orchid Street. I counted off homes, searching for 216, amused that such an exotically named street had been blessed with a lineup of unimaginative crackerbox houses. It was a neighborhood built in the sixties when land was available, so the plots were large, making the two-bedroom ranches seem even smaller. Over the years homeowners had personalized their carbon-copy houses, adding a garage here, a porch there. The houses had been modernized with vinyl siding of various muted shades. Bay windows had been inserted. Azalea bushes had been planted. And still the sameness prevailed.

Louie Moon's house was set apart by a bright turquoise paint job, a full array of Christmas lights, and a five-foot-tall plastic Santa strapped to a rusted TV antenna.

"Guess he gets into the spirit early," Lula said.

From the droop of the lights haphazardly stapled to his house and the faded look to Santa, I'd guess he was in the spirit all year long.

The house didn't have a garage, and there were no cars in the driveway or parked at the curb. The house looked dark and undisturbed. I left Lula in the car and went to the front door. I knocked twice. No answer. The house was one floor built on a slab. The curtains were all open. Louie had nothing to hide. I circled the house, peeking into windows. The inside was neat and furnished with what I guessed to be an accumulation of discards. There was no sign of recent wealth. No boxes of ammo stacked on the kitchen table. Not a single assault rifle in sight. It looked to me like he lived alone. One cup and one bowl in the dish drain. One side of the double bed had been slept in.

I could easily see Louie Moon living here, content with his life because he had a little blue house. I toyed with the idea of illegal entry, but I couldn't produce enough motivation to warrant the intrusion.

The air was damp and cold and the ground felt hard underfoot. I pulled my jacket collar up and returned to the car.

"That didn't take long," Lula said.

"Not much to see."

"We going to the undertaker next?"

"Yeah."

"Good thing he don't live where he do his thing. I don't want to see what they collect in those buckets at the end of those tables."

It was heavy twilight by the time we got to Century Court. The two-story buildings were red brick with white window trim. Doors were set in four-door clusters. There were five clusters to a building, which meant there were twenty apartments. Ten up and ten down. All of the buildings were set on pipestems coming off Demby. Four buildings per pipestem.

Spiro had an end unit on the ground floor. His windows were dark, and his car wasn't in the lot. With Con in the hospital, Spiro was forced to keep long hours. The Buick was easily recognizable, and I didn't want to get caught if Spiro should decided to bop in for a fast change of socks, so I drove one pipestem over and parked.

"I bet we find some serious shit here," Lula said, getting out of the car. "I got a feeling about this one."

"We're just going to scope things out," I said. "We're not going to do anything illegal . . . like breaking and entering."

"Sure," Lula said. "I know that."

We cut across the grassy area to the side of the buildings, walking casually, as if we were out for a stroll. Curtains were drawn on the windows in the front of Spiro's apartment, so we went to the back. Again, curtains were drawn. Lula tested the sliding patio door and the two windows and found them both to be locked.

"Ain't this a bitch?" she said. "How we supposed to find anything out this way? And just when I had a feeling, too."

"Yeah," I said. "I'd love to get into this apartment."

Lula swung her pocketbook in a wide arc and crashed it into Spiro's window, shattering the glass. "Where there's a will, there's a way," she said.

My mouth dropped open, and when words finally came out they were in a whispered screech. "I don't believe you did that! You just broke his window!"

"The Lord provides," Lula said.

"I told you we weren't doing anything illegal. People can't just go around breaking windows."

"Cagney would of done it."

"Cagney would *never* have done that."

"Would of."

"Would not!"

She slid the window open and poked her head inside. "Don't look like nobody home. Guess we should go in and make sure this broken glass didn't do any damage." She had the entire upper half of her body shoved into the window. "Could of made this window bigger," she said. "Can't hardly fit a full-bodied woman like me in this sucker."

I gnawed on my lower lip and held my breath, not sure whether I should push her through or pull her out. She looked like Pooh when he was stuck in the rabbit hole.

She gave a grunt and suddenly the back half of her disappeared behind Spiro's curtain. A moment later the patio door clicked open and Lula poked her head out. "You gonna stand out there all day, or what?"

"We could get arrested for this!"

"Hah, like you never did any illegal entry shit?"

"I never broke anything."

"You didn't this time neither. I did the breaking. You just gonna do the entering."

I supposed it was okay since she put it that way.

I slipped behind the patio curtain and let my eyes adjust to the darkness. "Do you know what Spiro looks like?"

"Ratty-faced little guy?"

"Yeah. You do lookout on the front porch. Knock three times if you see Spiro drive up."

Lula opened the front door and peeked out. "Everything clear," she said. Then she let herself out and closed the door.

I locked both doors and flipped the dining room light on, turning the dimmer until the light was low. I started in the kitchen, methodically going through cabinets. I checked the refrigerator for phony jars and did a cursory search of the kitchen trash.

I made my way through the dining room and living room without discovering anything worthwhile. Breakfast dishes were still in the sink, the morning paper was strewn across the table. A pair of black dress shoes had been kicked off and left in front of the TV. Other than that the apartment was clean. No guns, no keys, no threatening notes. No addresses hastily scribbled on a pad beside the kitchen wall phone.

I flicked on the light in the bathroom. Dirty clothes lay in a heap on the bathroom floor. There wasn't enough money in the world to get me to touch Spiro's dirty clothes. If there was a clue in his pocket, it was safe from me. I went through the medicine chest and glanced at the wastebasket. Nothing.

His bedroom door was closed. I held my breath, opened the door, and almost fainted with the relief of finding the room empty. The furniture was Danish modern, the bedspread was black satin. The ceiling over the bed had been covered with paste-on mirror tiles. Porn magazines were stacked on a chair beside the bed. A used condom was stuck to one of the covers.

Soon as I got home I was going to take a shower in boiling water.

A desk hugged the wall in front of his window. I thought this looked promising. I sat in the black leather chair and carefully rifled through the junk mail, bills, and personal correspondence that lay scattered across the polished desktop. The bills all seemed within reason, and most of the correspondence related to the funeral home. Thank-you notes from the recently bereaved. "Dear Spiro, thank you for overcharging me in my time of sorrow." Phone messages had been recorded on whatever was handy . . . backs of envelopes and letter margins. None of the messages were labeled "death threats from Kenny." I made a list of unexplained phone numbers and stuffed it into my pocketbook for future investigation.

I opened the drawers and poked through paper clips, rubber bands, and other assorted stationery flotsam. There were no messages on his answering machine. Nothing under his bed.

I found it hard to believe there were no guns in the apartment. Spiro seemed like the kind of person to take trophies.

I pawed through his clothes in the dresser and turned to his closet. The closet was filled with undertaker suits and shirts and shoes. Six pairs of black shoes lined up on the floor, and six shoe boxes. Hmmm. I opened a shoe box. Bingo. A gun. A Colt .45. I opened the other five boxes and ended up with a tally of three handguns and three shoe boxes filled with ammo. I copied the serial numbers off the guns and took down the information on the boxes of ammo.

I pulled the bedroom window aside and peeked out at Lula. She was sitting on the stoop, filing her nails. I rapped on the windowpane, and the file flew from her fingers. Guess she wasn't as calm as she looked. I motioned to her that I was leaving and would meet her out back.

I made sure everything was as I'd found it, shut off all lights, and exited through the patio door. It would be obvious to Spiro that someone had broken into his apartment, but chances were good he'd blame it on Kenny.

"Give me the shit," Lula said. "You found something, didn't you?"

"I found a couple guns."

"That don't float my boat. Everybody got guns."

"Do you have a gun?"

"Yo, momma. Damn right I got a gun." She pulled a big black gun out of her pocketbook. "Blue steel," she said. "Got it off Harry the Horse back when I was a ho. You want to know why we call him Harry the Horse?"

"Don't tell me."

"That mother was fearful. He just wouldn't fit in anywhere. Hell, I had to use two hands to give him the poor man's special."

I dropped Lula back at the office and went on home. By the time I pulled into my lot, the sky had blackened under the cloud cover and a light rain had begun to fall. I slung my pocketbook over my shoulder and hurried into the building, happy to be home.

Mrs. Bestler was doing hall laps with her walker. Step, step, clomp. Step, step, clomp.

"Another day, another dollar," she said.

"True enough," I replied.

I could hear the rise and fall of audience participation as Mr. Wolesky's TV droned on behind his closed door.

I plugged my key into my lock and did a quick, suspicious look around my apartment. All was secure. There were no messages on the machine, and there'd been no mail downstairs.

I made hot chocolate and a peanut butter and honey sandwich. I stacked the plate on top of the mug, tucked the phone under my arm, grabbed the list of numbers I'd retrieved from Spiro's apartment, and carted everything off to the dining room table.

I dialed the first number and a woman answered.

"I'd like to speak to Kenny," I said.

"You must have the wrong number. There's no Kenny here."

"Is this the Colonial Grill?"

"No, this is a private number."

"Sorry," I said.

I had seven numbers to check out. The first four were exactly alike. All private residences. Probably clients. The fifth was pizza delivery. The sixth was St. Francis Hospital. The seventh was a motel in Bordentown. I thought this last one had some potential.

I gave Rex a corner of my sandwich, heaved a sigh at having to leave the warmth and comfort of my apartment, and shrugged back into my jacket. The motel was on Route 206, not far from the turnpike entrance. It was a cut-rate motel, built before the motel chains moved in. There were forty units, all ground floor, opening to a narrow porch. Lights shone from two. The neon sign at roadside advertised efficiencies available. The exterior was neat, but it was a foregone conclusion that the inside would be dated, the wallpaper faded, the chenille spread threadbare, the bathroom sink rust-stained.

I parked close to the office and hustled inside. An elderly man sat behind the desk, watching a small TV.

"Evening," he said.

"Are you the manager?"

"Yep. The manager, the owner, the handyman."

I took Kenny's picture out of my pocketbook. "I'm looking for this man. Have you seen him?"

"Mind telling me why you're looking for him?"

"He's in violation of a bond agreement."

"What's that mean?"

"It means he's a felon."

"Are you a cop?"

"I'm an apprehension agent. I work for his bonding company."

The man looked at the picture and nodded. "He's in unit seventeen. Been there for a couple days." He thumbed through a ledger on the counter. "Here he is. John Sherman. Checked in on Tuesday."

I could hardly believe it! Damned if I wasn't good. "Is he alone?"

"So far as I know."

"Do you have vehicle information?"

"We don't bother with that. We got lots of parking space here."

I thanked him and told him I'd hang around for a while. I gave him my card and asked that he didn't give me away should he see Sherman.

I drove to a dark corner of the lot, shut the engine off, locked the windows, and hunkered down for the duration. If Kenny showed up I'd call Ranger. If I couldn't reach Ranger, I'd go to Joe Morelli.

By nine o'clock I was thinking I might have chosen the wrong profession. My toes were frozen, and I had to pee. Kenny hadn't materialized, and there was no activity at the motel to break the monotony of waiting. I ran the engine to warm things up and did some isometrics. I fantasized about going to bed with Batman. He was a little dark, but I liked the look of the codpiece on his rubber suit.

At eleven I begged the manager to let me use his bathroom. I mooched a cup of coffee from him and returned to Big Blue. I had to admit, while the wait was uncomfortable, it was immeasurably better than it would have been in my little Jeep. There was a feeling of encapsulation in the Buick. Sort of like being in a rolling bomb shelter with windows and overstuffed furniture. I was able to stretch my legs across the front bench seat. Behind me, the backseat had real boudoir potential.

I dozed off somewhere around twelve-thirty and woke up at one-fifteen. Kenny's unit was still dark, and there were no new cars in the lot.

I had several choices available to me. I could try to stick it out myself, I could ask Ranger to rotate shifts with me, or I could pack it in for the night and return before daybreak. If I asked Ranger to rotate shifts I'd have to give him a bigger piece of the pie than I'd originally intended. On the other hand, if I tried to stick it out by myself I was afraid I'd nod off and freeze to death like the little match girl. I chose door number three. If Kenny returned tonight it would be to sleep, and he'd still be here at six in the morning.

I sang "Row, row, row your boat" all the way home to keep awake. I dragged myself into my apartment building, up the stairs, and down the hall. I let myself into my foyer, locked the door behind me, and crawled into bed fully clothed, shoes and all. I slept flat out until six, when an inner alarm clock prodded me awake.

I stumbled out of bed, relieved to find I was already dressed and could forgo that chore. I did the bare minimum in the bathroom, grabbed my jacket and my pocketbook, and trudged out to the parking lot. It was pitch black above the lot lights, still drizzly, and ice had formed on car windows. Lovely. I started the car, turned the heater on full blast, took the scraper out of the map pocket and chipped the windows free. By the time I was done chipping I was pretty much awake. I stopped at a 7-Eleven en route to Bordentown and stocked up on coffee and doughnuts.

It was still dark when I reached the motel. There were no lights on in any of the units, and there were no new cars in the lot. I parked to the dark side of the office and cracked the lid on my coffee. I was feeling less optimistic today and considered the possibility that the old man in the office had been having some fun at my expense. If Kenny didn't show by midafternoon I'd ask to be let into his room.

If I'd been clever, I'd have changed my socks and brought a blanket. If I'd been *really* clever, I'd have given the guy in the office a twenty and asked him to call me if Kenny showed up.

At ten minutes to seven a woman drove up in a Ford truck and parked in front of the office. She gave me a curious look and went inside. Ten minutes later the old man came out and ambled across the lot to a beat-up Chevy. He waved and smiled and drove off.

There was no way I could be sure the old guy had told the woman about me, and I didn't want her calling the police to report a strange person loitering on the premises, so I hauled myself over to the office and went through the same drill as the night before.

The answers were the same. Yes, she recognized the picture. Yes, he was registered as John Sherman.

"Good-looking guy," she said. "But not real friendly."

"Did you notice the car he was driving?"

"Honey, I noticed everything about him. He was driving a blue van. Wasn't one of those fancy conversion vans. Was more of a work van. The kind without all the windows."

"Did you get a plate number?" I asked.

"Hell no. I wasn't interested in his plates."

I thanked her and retreated to my car to drink cold coffee. Every now and then I got out and stretched and stomped my feet. I took a half-hour break for lunch, and nothing had changed when I got back.

Morelli pulled his cop car beside me at three. He got out and slid onto the seat next to me.

"Christ," he said. "It's freezing in this car."

"Is this a chance meeting?"

"Kelly drives by here on his way to work. He saw the Buick and started a pool on who you were shacked up with."

I gritted my teeth. "Unh."

"So what *are* you doing here?"

"Through some superb detective work, I discovered that Kenny is staying here, registered as John Sherman."

A spark of excitement flickered across Morelli's face. "You have an ID?"

"Both the night clerk and the day clerk recognized Kenny from his picture. He's driving a blue panel van and was last seen yesterday morning. I got here early last night and sat until one. I was back here at six-thirty this morning."

"No sign of Kenny."

"None."

"Have you been through his room?"

"Not yet."

"The maid been through?"

"Nope."

Morelli opened his door. "Let's take a look."

Morelli identified himself to the day clerk and got a key to number 17. He rapped on the unit's door twice. No answer. He unlocked the door, and we both entered.

The bed was unmade. A navy duffel bag sat open on the floor. The bag contained socks and shorts and two black T-shirts. A flannel shirt and a pair of jeans had been tossed across the back of a chair. A shaving kit sat open in the bathroom.

"Looks to me like he's been scared off," Morelli said. "My guess is he spotted you."

"Impossible. I parked in the darkest part of the lot. And how did he know it was me?"

"Sweet thing, everyone knows it's you."

"It's this awful car! It's ruining my life. It's sabotaging my career."

Morelli grinned. "That's a lot to ask of a car."

I tried to look contemptuous, but it was hard with my teeth chattering from the cold. "Now what?" I asked.

"Now I talk to the clerk and ask her to call me if Kenny returns." He gave me a fast head-to-foot appraisal. "You look like you slept in those clothes."

"How'd it go with Spiro and Louie Moon yesterday?"

"I don't think Louie Moon is involved. He doesn't have what it takes."

"Intelligence?"

"Contacts," Morelli said. "Whoever has the guns is selling them off. I did some checking. Moon doesn't move in the right circles. Moon wouldn't even know how to go about finding the right circles."

"What about Spiro?"

"Wasn't ready to give me a confession." He flipped the light off. "You should go home and take a shower and get dressed for dinner."

"Dinner?"

"Pot roast at six."

"You aren't serious."

The grin was back. "I'll pick you up at quarter to six."

"No! I'll drive myself."

Morelli was wearing a brown leather bomber jacket and a red wool scarf. He took the scarf off and wrapped it around my neck. "You look frozen," he said. "Go home and warm up." Then he sauntered off to the motel office.

It was still drizzling. The sky was gunmetal gray, and my mood was equally grim. I'd had a good line on Kenny Mancuso, and I'd blown it. I smacked the heel of my hand against my forehead. Stupid, stupid, stupid. I'd sat out there in this big dumb Buick. What was I thinking?

The motel was twelve miles from my apartment building, and I berated myself all the way home. I made a quick stop at the supermarket, fed Big Blue more gas, and by the time I pulled into my lot, I was thoroughly disgusted and demoralized. I'd had three chances to nail Kenny: at Julia's house, at the mall, and now at the motel, and I'd screwed up every time.

Probably at this stage in my career I should stick to the low-level criminals, like shoplifters and drunk drivers. Unfortunately, the payout on those criminals wasn't sufficient to keep me afloat.

I did more self-flagellation while I rode the elevator and made my way down the hall. A sticky note from Dillon was taped to my door. Got a package for you, the note said.

I went back to the elevator and hit the button for basement. The elevator opened to a small vestibule with four closed, locked doors freshly painted battleship gray. One door led to storage cages for the use of the residents, the second door opened into the boiler room with its ominous rumblings and gurglings, the third door gave way to a long corridor and rooms dedicated to building maintenance, and Dillon lived in rent-free contentment behind the fourth door.

I always felt claustrophobic when I came down here, but Dillon said that it suited him fine and that he found the boiler noises soothing. He'd stuck a note to his door, saying that he'd be home at five.

I returned to my apartment, gave Rex some raisins and a corn chip, and took a long, hot shower. I staggered out red as a boiled lobster and foggy-brained from the chlorine gas. I flopped on the bed and contemplated my future. It was a short contemplation. When I woke up it was quarter to six, and someone was pounding on my door.

I wrapped myself in a robe and padded into the foyer. I put my eye to the peephole. It was Joe Morelli. I cracked the door and looked at him over the security chain. "I just got out of the shower."

"I'd appreciate it if you'd let me in before Mr. Wolesky comes out and gives me the third degree."

I slipped the chain and opened the door.

Morelli stepped into the foyer. His mouth curved at the edges. "Scary hair."

"I sort of slept on it."

"No wonder you have no sex life. It'd take a lot out of a man to wake up to hair like that."

"Go sit in a chair in the living room, and don't get up until I tell you. Don't eat my food, and don't scare my hamster, and don't make any long-distance calls."

He was watching television when I came out of my bedroom ten minutes later. I was wearing a granny dress over a white T-shirt, with ankle-high brown lace-up boots, and an oversized, loose-weave cardigan sweater. It was my Annie Hall look, and it made me feel feminine, but it always had the opposite effect on the opposite sex. Annie Hall was guaranteed to wilt the most determined dick. It was better than Mace on a blind date.

I wrapped Morelli's red scarf around my neck and buttoned myself into my jacket. I grabbed my pocketbook and shut the lights off. "There's going to be hell to pay if we're late."

Morelli followed me out the door. "I wouldn't worry about it. Once your mother sees you in that get-up, she'll forget about the time."

"It's my Annie Hall look."

"Looks to me like you've put a jelly doughnut in a bag labeled bran muffin."

I rushed down the hall and took the stairs. I got to the ground floor and remembered the package Dillon was holding. "Wait a minute," I yelled to Morelli. "I'll be right back."

I scrambled down the stairs to the cellar and pounded on Dillon's door.

Dillon peered out.

"I'm late, and I need my package," I said.

He handed me a bulky overnight mail envelope, and I ran back up the stairs.

"Three minutes one way or the other can make or break a pot roast," I told Morelli, grabbing him by the hand, dragging him across the lot to his truck. I hadn't intended to go with him, but I figured if we hit traffic he could use his rooftop flasher. "You have a flasher on this truck?" I asked, climbing on board.

Morelli buckled himself in. "Yeah, I have a flasher. You don't expect me to use it for pot roast, do you?"

I swiveled in my seat and stared out the back window.

Morelli cut his eyes to the rearview mirror. "Are you looking for Kenny?"

"I can feel him out there."

"I don't see anyone."

"That doesn't mean he isn't there. He's good at this sneaking around stuff. He walks into Stiva's and chops off body parts, and nobody sees him. He came out of nowhere at the mall. He spotted me at Julia Cenetta's house and in the motel parking lot, and I never had a clue. Now I have this creepy feeling he's watching me, following me around."

"Why would he be doing that?"

"For starters, Spiro told Kenny I'd kill him if he continued to harass him."

"Oh boy."

"Probably I'm just being paranoid."

"Sometimes paranoia is justified."

Morelli stopped for a light. The digital readout on his dashboard clock blinked to 5:58. I cracked my knuckles, and Morelli glanced over at me, eyebrows raised.

"Okay," I said, "so my mother makes me nervous."

"It's part of her job," Morelli said. "You shouldn't take it personally."

We turned off Hamilton, into the burg, and traffic disappeared. There were no car lights behind us, but I couldn't shake the feeling that Kenny had me in his sights.

My mother and Grandma Mazur were at the door when we parked. Usually it was the differences between my mother and grandmother that caught my attention. Today it was the similarities that seemed obvious. They stood tall, with their shoulders back. It was a defiant posture, and I knew it was my posture, too. Their hands were clasped in front of them, their gaze was unwavering, fixed on Morelli and me. Their faces were round; their eyes were hooded. Mongol eyes. My Hungarian relatives had come from the steppes. Not a city dweller among them. My mother and grandma were small women and had grown even smaller with age. They were dainty-boned and petite, with baby-fine hair. Probably they were descended from pampered, caravan-cosseted Gypsy women.

I, on the other hand, was a throwback to some plow-pulling, raw-boned wife of a barbarian farmer.

I hiked up my skirt to jump from the truck, and saw my mother and grandmother flinch at the sight.

"What's this outfit?" my mother demanded. "Can't you afford clothes? Are you wearing other people's? Frank, give Stephanie some money. She needs to buy clothes."

"I don't need to buy clothes," I said. "This is new. I just bought it. It's the style."

"How will you ever get a man when you're dressed like this?" My mother turned to Morelli. "Am I right?"

Morelli grinned. "I think she's kind of cute. It's the Monty Hall look."

I still had the package in my hand. I set it on the foyer table and took my jacket off. "Annie Hall!"

Grandma Mazur picked the envelope up and studied it. "Overnight mail. Must be something important. Feels like there's a box in here. Return address says R. Klein from Fifth Avenue in New York. Too bad it isn't for me. I wouldn't mind getting some overnight mail."

I hadn't thought much about the package until now. I didn't know anyone named R. Klein, and I hadn't ordered anything from New York. I took the envelope from Grandma and peeled the flap back. There was a little cardboard box inside. It was taped closed. I took the box out, and held it in my hand. It wasn't especially heavy.

"Smells funny," Grandma said. "Like insecticide. Or maybe it's one of them new perfumes."

I ripped the tape away, opened the box, and sucked in my breath. There was a penis inside the box. The penis was neatly sliced off at the root, perfectly embalmed, and secured to a square of Styrofoam with a hat pin.

Everyone stared at the penis in dumbfounded horror.

Grandma Mazur spoke first, and when she did it was with a touch of wistfulness. "Been a long time since I've seen one of those," she said.

My mother started screaming, hands in air, eyes bugging out of her head. "Get it out of my house! What's the world coming to? What will people think?"

My father left his chair in the living room and padded out to the hall to see what the fuss was all about. "What's going on?" he asked, sticking his head into the huddle.

"It's a penis," Grandma said. "Stephanie got it in the mail. It's a pretty good one too."

My father recoiled. "Jesus and Joseph!"

"Who would do such a thing?" my mother shouted. "What is it? Is it rubber? Is it one of those rubber penises?"

"Don't look rubber to me," Grandma Mazur said. "Looks to me like a real penis, except it's kind of discolored. I don't remember them being this color."

"That's crazy!" my mother said. "What person would mail his penis?"

Grandma Mazur looked at the envelope. "Says Klein on the return address. I always thought that was a Jewish name, but this doesn't look to me like a Jewish penis."

Everyone turned their attention to Grandma Mazur.

"Not that I'd know much about it," Grandma said. "It's just that I might have seen one of them Jewish ones in *National Geographic*."

Morelli took the box from me and replaced the lid. We both knew the name to attach to the penis. Joseph Loosey.

"I'm going to take a raincheck on dinner," Morelli said. "I'm afraid this is a police matter." He snagged my pocketbook off the hall table and draped it over my shoulder. "Stephanie needs to come too, so she can make a statement."

"It's that bounty hunter job," my mother said to me. "You meet all the wrong kinds of people. Why can't you get a good job like your cousin Christine? No one ever sends Christine these things in the mail."

"Christine works in a vitamin factory. She spends her whole day watching the cotton stuffer to make sure it doesn't malfunction."

"She makes good money."

I zipped my jacket. "I make good money . . . sometimes."

CHAPTER 11

Morelli yanked the door to the truck open, tossed the overnight envelope onto the seat, and made an impatient gesture for me to follow. His face was composed, but I could feel the vibrations of anger radiating in waves from his body.

"Goddamn him," Morelli said, slamming the truck into gear. "He thinks this is fucking funny. Him and his damn games. When he was a kid he used to tell me stories about the things he'd done. I never knew what was real and what was made up. I'm not sure Kenny knew. Maybe it was all real."

"Were you serious about this being a police matter?"

"The post office frowns on the mailing of human body parts for sport purposes."

"That was why you rushed us out of my parents' house?"

"I rushed us out of your parents' house because I didn't think I could manage two hours at the dinner table with everyone focused on Joe Loosey's joystick sitting in the refrigerator next to the applesauce."

"I'd appreciate it if you could keep this quiet. I wouldn't want people to get the wrong idea about me and Mr. Loosey."

"Your secret is safe."

"Do you think we should tell Spiro?"

"I think *you* should tell Spiro. Let him think the two of you are in this together. Maybe you can learn something."

Morelli eased the truck into the Burger King drive-through and got a couple bags of food. He rolled the window up, pulled out into traffic, and the truck immediately filled with the smell of America.

"It's not pot roast," Morelli said.

That was true, but with the exception of dessert, food is food. I stuck the straw into my milk shake and dug around in the bag for the french fries. "These stories Kenny used to tell you . . . what were they about?"

"Nothing you want to hear. Nothing I even want to remember. Very sick shit."

He took a handful of fries. "You never told me how you happened to locate Kenny in the motel."

"Probably I shouldn't divulge my professional secrets."

"Probably you should."

Okay, public relations time. Time to appease Morelli by giving him some worthless information. With the added advantage of implicating him in an illegal activity. "I broke into Spiro's apartment and went through his trash. I found some phone numbers, ran them down, and came up with the motel."

Morelli stopped for a light and turned his face to me. His expression was unreadable in the dark. "You broke into Spiro's apartment? Was this by way of an accidentally unlocked door?"

"It was by way of a window that managed to get broken by a pocketbook."

"Shit, Stephanie, that's breaking and entering. People get arrested for that kind of stuff. They go to jail."

"I was careful."

"That makes me feel a lot better."

"I figure Spiro will think it was Kenny and not report it."

"So Spiro knew where Kenny was staying. I'm surprised Kenny wasn't more cautious."

"Spiro has a caller ID device on his phone at the funeral parlor. Maybe Kenny didn't realize he could be picked up like that."

The light changed, Morelli moved forward, and we rode in silence for the rest of the trip. He swung into the lot, parked, and cut his lights.

"Do you want to come in, or would you prefer to be left out of the loop?" he wanted to know.

"I'd rather be left out of the loop. I'll wait here."

He took the envelope with the penis, and he took a bag of food. "I'll do this as fast as I can."

I gave him the paper with the guns and ammo information from Spiro's apartment. "I found some hardware in Spiro's bedroom. You might want to check to see if it came from Braddock." I wasn't enamored with the idea of helping Morelli when he was still holding back on me, but I had no way of tracing the guns on my own, and besides, if the stuff was stolen, Morelli'd owe me.

I watched him jog to the side door. The door opened, showing a fleeting rectangle of light in the otherwise dark brick facade. The door closed, and I unwrapped my cheeseburger, wondering if Morelli would have to bring someone in to identify the evidence. Louie Moon or Mrs. Loosey. I hoped he had the sense to remove the hat pin before lifting the lid for Mrs. Loosey.

I scarfed down my cheeseburger and fries and worked at the milk shake. There was no activity in the lot or on the street, and the silence in the truck was deafening. I listened to myself breathe for a while. I snooped in the glove compartment and map pockets. I found nothing interesting. According to Morelli's dashboard clock he'd been gone for ten minutes. I finished the milk shake and crammed all the wrappers back in the bag. Now what?

It was almost seven. Visiting hours for Spiro. The perfect time to tell him about Loosey's dick. Unfortunately, I was stuck twiddling my thumbs in Morelli's truck. The glint of keys dangling from the ignition caught my eye. Maybe I should borrow the truck and slip over to the funeral parlor. Take care of business. After all, who knows how long it would take Morelli to do the paperwork? I could be stuck here for hours! Morelli would probably be grateful to me for getting the job done. On the other hand, if he came out and found his truck missing it could get ugly.

I dug around in my pocketbook and came up with a black Magic Marker. I couldn't find paper, so I wrote a note on the side of the food bag. I backed the truck up a few feet, deposited the bag in the empty space, jumped back in the truck, and took off.

Lights were blazing from Stiva's, and a crowd of people milled about on the front porch. Stiva always got a big draw on Saturdays. The lot was full and there were no parking places for two blocks down on the street, so I zoomed into the driveway reserved for "funeral cars only." I would only be a few minutes, and besides, nobody was going to tow away a truck with a PBA shield in the back window.

Spiro did a double take when he saw me. The first reaction was relief; the second was reserved for my dress.

"Nice outfit," he said. "You look like you just got off the bus from Appalachia."

"I've got news for you."

"Yeah, well, I've got news for you, too." He jerked his head in the direction of the office. "In here."

He hotfooted it across the lobby, wrenched the door to the office open, and closed it behind us with a slam.

"You're not going to believe this," he said. "That asshole Kenny is such a prick. You know what he did now? He broke into my apartment."

My eyes rounded in surprise. "No!"

"Yeah. Can you believe it? Broke a goddamn window."

"Why would he break into your apartment?"

"Because he's fucking crazy."

"Are you sure it was Kenny? Was anything missing?"

"Of course it was Kenny. Who the hell else could it be? Nothing was stolen. The VCR is still there. My camera, my money, my jewelry weren't touched. It was Kenny, all right. The dumb crazy fucker."

"Did you report this to the police?"

"What's between me and Kenny is private. No police."

"You might have to change that game plan."

Spiro's eyes contracted and dulled and focused on mine. "Oh?"

"You remember the little incident yesterday concerning Mr. Loosey's penis?"

"Yeah?"

"Kenny mailed it to me."

"No shit?"

"It came Express Mail."

"Where is it now?"

"The police have it. Morelli was there when I opened the package."

"*Fuck!*" He kicked his wastebasket across the room. "Fuck, fuck, fuck, fuck, fuck."

"I don't know why you're so upset about all this," I cooed. "Seems to me this is crazy Kenny's problem. I mean, after all, you didn't do anything wrong." Humor the jerk, I thought. See where he runs with it.

Spiro stopped raving and looked at me, and I imagined I heard the sound of little bitty gears meshing in his head. "That's true," he said. "I didn't do anything wrong. I'm the victim here. Does Morelli know the package came from Kenny? Was there a note? A return address?"

"No note. No return address. Hard to say what Morelli knows."

"You didn't tell him it came from Kenny?"

"I have no real proof that it came from Kenny, but the thing clearly had been embalmed, so the police will be checking funeral parlors. I imagine they'll want to know why you didn't report the . . . um, theft."

"Maybe I should just come clean. Tell the cops about how crazy Kenny is. Tell them about the finger and about my apartment."

"What about Con? You coming clean to him too? Is he still in the hospital?"

"Came home today. Got a week of rehab, and then he'll be back at work part-time."

"He's not going to be happy when he finds out his clients have been getting parts whacked off."

"Tell me about it. I've heard enough of his 'the body is holy' crap to last me three lifetimes. I mean, what's the big deal? It isn't like Loosey was gonna use his dick."

Spiro dropped into the padded executive chair behind the desk and slid into a slouch. The mask of civility dropped from his face, and his sallow skin tightened over slanted cheekbones and pinched across spiky teeth as he morphed into Rodent Man. Furtive, foul-breathed, evil-spirited. Impossible to tell if he'd been born the rodent, or if years of schoolyard taunts had shaped his soul to suit his face.

Spiro leaned forward. "You know how old Con is? Sixty-two. Anyone else would be thinking retirement, but not Constantine Stiva. I'll be dead from natural causes, and Stiva'll still be kissing ass. He's like a snake with a heart rate of twelve. Pacing himself. Sucking formaldehyde like the elixir of life. Hanging on just to piss me off.

"Should have been cancer instead of a back injury. What the hell good is a back injury? You don't die from a damn back injury."

"I thought you and Con got along."

"He drives me nuts. Him and his rules and goody-goody attitude. You should see him in the embalming room. Everything just so. You'd think it was a fucking shrine down there. Constantine Stiva at the altar of the fucking dead. You know what I think of the dead? I think they stink."

"Why do you work here?"

"There's money to be made, chicky. And I like money."

I held myself tight in check to keep from physically recoiling. Here was the muck and slime of Spiro's brain, spilling out of every orifice, dribbling down his corded neck onto his pristine white undertaker's shirt. Butthead, all dressed up with no place to go. "Have you heard from Kenny since he broke into your apartment?"

"No." Spiro turned broody. "Used to be we were friends. Him and Moogey and me used to do everything together. Then Kenny went into the army, and he got different. Thought he was smarter than the rest of us. Had all these big ideas."

"Like what?"

"I can't tell you, but they were big. Not that I couldn't come up with ideas like that, but I'm busy with other stuff."

"He include you in these big ideas? You make any money from them?"

"Sometimes he included me. You never knew with Kenny. He was slick. He'd hold out, and you never knew. He was like that with women. They all thought he was this cool guy." Spiro's lips pulled back in a smile. "Used to crack us up how he'd play the faithful-till-death-do-us-part-boyfriend role and all the while he'd be porking everyone in sight. He could really sucker women in. Even when he smacked them around they kept coming back for more. You had to admire the guy, you know. He had something. I've seen him burn women with cigarettes and stick them with pins, and they'd still suck up to him."

The cheeseburger slid in my stomach. I didn't know who was more disgusting . . . Kenny for sticking pins in women, or Spiro for admiring him. "I should be moving along," I said. "Got things to do." Like maybe fumigating my mind after talking to Spiro.

"Wait a minute. I wanted to talk to you about security. You're an expert in this kind of stuff, right?"

I wasn't an expert at anything. "Right."

"So, what should I do about Kenny? I was thinking about a bodyguard again. Just for at night. Someone to close up with me here, and make sure I got into my apartment okay. I figure I was lucky Kenny wasn't waiting for me in my apartment."

"You're afraid of Kenny?"

"He's like smoke. You can't put your finger on him. He's always in a shadow somewhere. He watches people. He plans things." Our eyes locked. "You don't know Kenny," Spiro said. "Sometimes he's a real fun guy, and sometimes the things he thinks are pure evil. Believe me, I've seen him in action, you don't want to be on the receiving side of the evil."

"I told you before . . . I'm not interested in guarding your body."

He took a pack of twenties from his top desk drawer and counted them out. "Hundred dollars a night. All you have to do is get me into my apartment safe and sound. I'll take it from there."

Suddenly I saw the value of guarding Spiro. I'd be right there on the spot if Kenny actually did show up. I'd be in a position to wheedle information. And I could legally search through Spiro's house every night. Okay, so along with all that I was selling out for the money, but hell, it could be worse. I could have sold out for fifty. "When do I start?"

"Tonight. I close up at ten. Get here five or ten minutes ahead."

"Why me? Why don't you get some big tough guy?"

Spiro put the money back in the drawer. "I'd look like a fag. This way people think you're after my ass. Better for my image. Unless you keep wearing dresses like that. Then I might reconsider."

Wonderful.

I left his office and caught sight of Morelli slouched against the wall next to the front door, hands shoved in pants pockets, clearly pissed off. He spotted me, and his expression didn't change, but the rise and fall of his chest picked up. I plastered a phony smile on my face and breezed across the lobby to him, whisking out the door before Spiro had a chance to see us together.

"I see you got my message," I said when we reached the truck, turning up the wattage on the smile.

"Not only did you steal my truck, but you parked it illegally."

"You park illegally all the time."

"Only when it's official police business, and I have no other choice . . . or when it's raining."

"I don't know why you're upset. You wanted me to talk to Spiro. So that's what I did. I came here and talked to Spiro."

"For starters, I had to flag down a blue-and-white to get a ride over here. And more important, I don't like you running around on your own. I want you in eyesight until we nail Mancuso."

"I'm touched you're worried about my safety."

"Safety hasn't got much to do with it, Skippy. You have an uncanny knack for running into people you're looking for, and you're completely inept at taking them down. I don't want you screwing up another encounter with Kenny. I want to make sure I'm around next time you stumble across him."

I settled onto the seat with a sigh. When you're right, you're right. And Morelli was right. I wasn't totally up to speed as a bounty hunter.

We were silent for the ride back to my apartment. I knew these streets like I knew my own hand. Half the time, I drove them unconsciously, suddenly realizing I was in my parking lot, wondering how the devil I'd gotten there. Tonight I paid closer attention. If Kenny was out there, I didn't want to miss him. Spiro had said Kenny was like smoke, that he lived in the shadows. I told myself this was a romanticized vision. Kenny was your everyday sociopath who went sneaking around thinking he was God's second cousin.

The wind had picked up, and clouds scudded overhead, periodically obliterating the sliver of moon. Morelli parked next to the Buick and cut the engine. He reached over and toyed with the collar on my jacket. "Do you have any plans for tonight?"

I told him about the bodyguard deal.

Morelli just stared at me. "How do you do it?" he asked. "How do you walk into this stuff? If you knew what you were doing, you'd be a real threat."

"Guess I lead a charmed life." I looked at my watch. It was 7:30, and Morelli was still working. "You put in long hours," I said. "I thought cops clocked on in eight-hour shifts."

"Vice is flexible. I work when I need to."

"You have no life."

He shrugged. "I like my job. When I need a break I take off for a weekend at the shore or a week in the Islands."

This was pretty interesting. I'd never thought of Morelli as being an "Islands" person. "What do you do when you go to the Islands? What's the appeal?"

"I like to dive."

"And what about the shore? What do you do at the Jersey shore?"

Morelli grinned. "I hide under the boardwalk and abuse myself. Old habits die hard."

I had a tough time visualizing Morelli diving off the coast of Martinique, but the thought of him abusing himself under the boardwalk was crystal clear. I could see him as a horny little eleven-year-old, hanging outside the Seaside bars, listening to the bands, eyeballing the women in their elastic tank tops and skimpy shorts. And later, crawling under the boardwalk with his cousin Mooch, the two of them whacking off together before they had to meet up with Uncle Manny and Aunt Florence for the ride back to the bungalow in Seaside Heights. Two years later he would have substituted his cousin Sue Ann Beale for his cousin Mooch, but the basic routine would be the same.

I pushed the truck door open and lurched out into the parking lot. The wind whistled around Morelli's antennae and whipped at my skirt. My hair flew about my face in a frenzied explosion of tangled frizz.

I made an attempt to tame it in the elevator while Morelli looked on, calmly curious about my efforts to shove the mess into an elastic band I'd found in my jacket pocket. He stepped into the hall when the doors opened. Waited while I fumbled for the key.

"How scared is Spiro?" Morelli wanted to know.

"Scared enough to hire me to protect him."

"Maybe it's just a ploy to get you into his apartment."

I stepped into the entrance hall, flipped the light switch, and shrugged out of my jacket. "It's an expensive ploy."

Morelli went straight to the TV and buzzed in ESPN. The Rangers' blue jerseys blinked onto the screen. The Caps were at home in white. I watched a face-off before bobbing into the kitchen to check my answering machine.

There were two messages. The first from my mother, calling to say she heard First National had openings for tellers and that I should be sure to wash my hands if I touched Mr. Loosey. The second call was from Connie. Vinnie had gotten back from North Carolina and wanted me to stop in the office tomorrow. Pass on that one. Vinnie was worried about the Mancuso money. If I stopped in to see him, he'd yank Mancuso out from under me, and give it to someone with more experience.

I pushed the off button, grabbed a bag of blue corn chips from the cupboard, and snagged a couple beers from the refrigerator. I slouched next to Morelli on the couch, setting the corn chips between us. Ma and Pa on a Saturday night.

Halfway through the first period the phone rang.

"How's it going?" the caller asked. "You and Joe doing it doggy style? I hear he likes that. You really are something. Doing both Spiro and Joe-boy."

"Mancuso?"

"Just thought I'd call to see if you enjoyed your surprise package."

"It was a real kick. What's the point?"

"No point. Just having fun. I was watching when you opened it in the hall. Nice touch bringing the old lady into it. I like old ladies. You might say they're my specialty. You'll have to ask Joe about the things I do to old ladies. No wait, better yet, why don't I show you first-hand?"

"You're sick, Mancuso. You need help."

"It's your granny who's gonna need help. Maybe you, too. Wouldn't want you to feel left out. In the beginning I was pissed off. You kept bungling around in my business. Now I'm seeing this from a new angle. Now I think I could have a good time with you and Granny Halfwit. It's always best when you have someone watching, waiting their turn.

"Maybe I could even get you to tell me about Spiro, and how he steals from his friends."

"How do you know it wasn't Moogey who stole from his friends?"

"Moogey didn't know enough to steal from his friends."

The disconnect clicked in my ear.

Morelli was standing beside me in the kitchen, beer bottle dangling from one hand, looking casual, but his eyes were still and hard.

"That was your cousin," I said. "He was calling to see if I enjoyed my surprise package, and then he suggested he might have some fun with me and Grandma Mazur."

I thought I was doing a pretty good imitation of the tough-as-nails bounty hunter, but the truth is I was shaking inside. I wasn't going to ask Morelli what Kenny Mancuso did to old women. I didn't want to know. And whatever it was, I didn't want it done to Grandma Mazur.

I called my parents' house to make sure Grandma Mazur was safe at home. Yes, she was watching television, my mother said. I assured her I'd washed my hands, and begged off on coming back for dessert.

I changed out of the dress into jeans and sneakers and a flannel shirt. I retrieved my .38 from the cookie jar, made sure it was loaded, and slipped it into my pocketbook.

When I came back to the living room Morelli was hand-feeding a corn chip to Rex.

"Looks to me like you're dressed for action," Morelli said. "I heard you lifting the lid on the cookie jar."

"Mancuso made threatening sounds about my grandmother."

Morelli pulled the power on the Rangers. "He's getting restless and frustrated, and he's getting stupid. It was stupid to come after you in the mall. It was stupid of him to sneak into Stiva's. And it was stupid to call you. Every time he does something like that he risks exposure. Kenny can be cunning when he's on top of himself. When he loses it, he's all ego and impulse.

"He's feeling desperate because his gun deal got screwed up. He's looking for a scapegoat, looking for someone to punish. Either he had a buyer who paid him some front money, or else he sold off a batch of shit before the bulk of it was stolen. My money's on the buyer theory. I think he's in a sweat because he can't meet his contract and the front money's been spent."

"He thinks Spiro has the stuff."

"These two would eat their young if you gave them the chance."

I had my jacket in my hand when the phone rang again. It was Louie Moon.

"He was here," Moon said. "Kenny Mancuso. He came back, and he cut Spiro."

"Where's Spiro now?"

"He's at St. Francis. I took him there, and then I came back to see to things. You know, close up and all."

Fifteen minutes later we were at St. Francis. Two uniforms, Vince Roman and a new guy I didn't know, stood flatfooted, weighted to the earth by their gun belts, at the emergency room desk.

"What's the deal?" Morelli asked.

"Took a statement from Stiva's kid. Got slashed by your cousin." Vince cut his eyes to the door behind the desk. "Got Spiro back there, stitching him up."

"How bad?"

"Could have been worse. Guess Kenny tried to cut Spiro's hand off, but the blade glanced off the rodent's big gold ID bracelet. Wait'll you see the bracelet. Right out of the Liberace collection."

This got a chuckle out of Vince and his partner.

"Don't suppose anyone tagged Kenny?"

"Kenny's the wind."

Spiro was sitting up on a hospital bed in the ER when we found him. There were two other people in the ER, and Spiro was separated from them by a privacy curtain partially pulled closed. His right arm was heavily bandaged from hand to forearm. His white shirt was blood-splattered, open at the neck. A blood-soaked necktie and kitchen towel had been tossed onto the floor beside the bed.

Spiro came out of his stupor when he saw me. "You were supposed to protect me!" he yelled. "Where the hell were you when I needed you?"

"I don't go on duty until ten of ten, remember?"

His eyes swiveled to Morelli. "He's nuts. Your cousin is fucking nuts. He tried to chop my goddamn hand off. He should be locked up. He should be in a looney bin. I was in my office, minding my own business, working on Mrs. Mayer's bill, when I look up and there's Kenny. He's raving about me stealing from him. I don't know what the hell he's talking about. He's a fucking fruitcake. Then next thing he says he's gonna chop me up piece by piece until I tell him what he wants to know. Lucky for me I was wearing that bracelet, or I would have been learning how to write left-handed. I started yelling, and Louie came in, and Kenny took off.

"I want some police protection," Spiro said. "Ms. Marvel here doesn't perform."

"I can have a blue-and-white drive you home tonight," Morelli said. "After that you're on your own." He passed his card to Spiro. "If there's a problem you can give me a call. If you need someone fast go to nine-one-one."

Spiro made a derisive sound and glared at me.

I smiled nicely and rocked back on my heels. "See you tomorrow?"

"Yeah," he said. "Tomorrow."

The wind had slacked off, and it was drizzling when we came out of the hospital.

"Warm front coming in," Morelli said. "Supposed to be nice weather behind the rain."

We climbed into Morelli's truck and sat, watching the hospital. Roman's squad car was parking in the driveway reserved for emergency vehicles. After about ten minutes Roman and his partner escorted Spiro into the squad car. We followed them to Demby and waited while they made sure Spiro's apartment was secure.

The cruiser rolled out of the lot, and we sat for a few minutes longer. Lights were on in Spiro's apartment, and I suspected they'd be burning all night.

"We should watch him," Morelli said. "Kenny's not thinking good. He's going to keep after Spiro until he gets what he wants."

"Wasted effort. Spiro doesn't have what Kenny wants."

Morelli was motionless, staring irresolutely through the rain-streaked windshield. "I need a different car. Kenny knows my truck."

It went unsaid that he knew my Buick. The whole world knew my Buick. "What about the tan cop car?"

"He's probably got that spotted, too. Besides, I need something that'll give me more cover. A van or a Bronco with tinted windows." He cranked the engine over and put the truck into gear. "You have any idea when Spiro opens in the morning?"

"He usually gets to work by nine."

Morelli knocked on my door at six-thirty, and I was way ahead of him. I'd already showered and dressed in what I'd come to think of as my work uniform. Jeans, warm shirt, shoes of the day. I'd cleaned Rex's cage and had Mr. Coffee cooking.

"This is the plan," Morelli said. "You follow Spiro, and I follow you."

I didn't think that sounded like much of a plan, but I didn't have anything better, so I didn't complain. I filled my thermos with coffee, packed two sandwiches and an apple into my little cooler, and turned my answering machine on.

It was still dark when I walked to my car. Sunday morning. No traffic. Neither of us was in a talkative mood. I didn't see Morelli's truck in the lot.

"What are you driving?" I asked.

"A black Explorer parked on the street, to the side of the building."

I unlocked the Buick and threw everything into the backseat, including a blanket, which it looked like I wouldn't need. It had stopped raining and the air felt much warmer. In the fifties, I guessed.

I wasn't sure if Spiro kept the same schedule on Sundays. The funeral home was open seven days a week, but I suspected weekend hours depended on bodies received. Spiro didn't seem like the sort to go to church. I crossed myself. I couldn't remember the last time I'd attended Mass.

"What was that all about?" Morelli asked. "What's with the sign of the cross?"

"It's Sunday, and I'm not in church . . . again."

Morelli put his hand on the top of my head. It felt steady and reassuring, and heat seeped into my scalp.

"God loves you anyway," he said.

His hand slid to the back of my head, he pulled me to him, and kissed me on the forehead. He gave me a hug, and then he was suddenly gone, striding across the lot, disappearing into the shadows.

I stuffed myself into the Buick, feeling warm and fuzzy, wondering if something was going on with Morelli and me. What did a kiss on the forehead mean, anyway? Nothing, I told myself. It didn't mean anything at all. It meant that sometimes Morelli could be a nice guy. Okay, so why was I smiling like an idiot? Because I was deprived. My love life was nonexistent. I shared an apartment with a hamster. Well, I thought, it could be worse. I could still be married to Dickie Orr, the horse's patoot.

The drive to Century Court was quiet. The sky had begun to lighten. Black layers of clouds and blue strips of sky. Spiro's apartment complex was dark, with the exception of Spiro's apartment. I parked and watched the rearview mirror for Morelli's headlights. No headlights appeared. I swiveled in my seat and scanned the lot. No Explorer.

No matter, I told myself. Morelli was out there, somewhere. Probably.

I had few illusions about my place in the scheme of things. I was the decoy, making myself clearly visible in the Buick, so Kenny wouldn't look too hard for a second man.

I poured coffee and settled in for the long wait. A band of orange appeared on the horizon. A light blinked on in the apartment next to Spiro. Another light appeared a few apartments down. The charcoal sky turned azure. Ta daaa! It was morning.

Spiro's shades were still drawn. There was no sign of life in his apartment. I was beginning to worry when his door opened and Spiro walked out. He tried his door to make sure it was locked and quickly walked to his car. He drove a navy blue Lincoln Town Car. The car of choice for all young undertakers. Undoubtedly leased and charged off to the business.

He was dressed more casually than usual. Stone-washed black jeans and running shoes. Bulky dark green sweater. A white bandage was wrapped around his thumb and peeked out from under his sweater sleeve.

He gunned the Lincoln out of the lot and turned onto Klockner. I'd expected some sort of acknowledgment, but Spiro barreled past without a sideways glance. Most likely he was concentrating on not messing his pants.

I followed at a leisurely pace. There weren't a lot of cars on the road, and I knew where Spiro was heading. I parked half a block from the funeral home, at an angle where I could see the front entrance, the side entrance, and also the small parking lot on the side with the walkway leading to the back door.

Spiro parked in the drive-through and entered through the side. The door stayed open while he punched in the security code. The door closed and a light flicked on in Spiro's office.

Ten minutes later Louie Moon showed up.

I poured more coffee and ate half a sandwich. No one else went in or out. At nine-thirty Louie Moon left in the hearse. He returned an hour later, and someone was rolled into the back of the house. I guessed this was why Louie and Spiro had to come in on a Sunday morning.

At eleven I used my cellular phone to call my mother and make sure Grandma Mazur was okay.

"She's out," my mother said. "I leave the house for ten minutes, and what happens? Your father lets your grandmother go off with Betty Greenburg."

Betty Greenburg was eighty-nine and was hell on wheels.

"Ever since that stroke in August Betty Greenburg can't remember anything," my mother said. "Last week she drove to Asbury Park. Said she meant to go to Kmart and made a wrong turn."

"How long has Grandma Mazur been gone?"

"Almost two hours. They were supposed to be going to the bakery. Maybe I should call the police."

There was the sound of a door slamming and a lot of shouting in the background.

"It's your grandmother," my mother said. "And she's got her hand all wrapped up."

"Let me talk to her."

Grandma Mazur came on the phone. "You won't believe this," she said, her voice trembling with anger and indignation. "The most terrible thing just happened. Betty and me were coming out of the bakery with a box full of fresh-made Italian cookies when none other than Kenny Mancuso himself walked out from behind a car, just as brazen as could be, and came right up to me.

" 'Well, looky here,' he says, 'it's Grandma Mazur.'

" 'Yeah, and I know who you are, too,' I said to him. 'You're that no-good Kenny Mancuso.'

" 'That's right,' he says. 'And I'm gonna be your worst nightmare.' "

There was a pause, and I could hear her breathing, collecting herself.

"Mom said your hand was bandaged?" I asked, not wanting to push her but needing to know.

"Kenny stuck me. He took hold of my hand, and he stuck an ice pick into it," Grandma said, her voice unnaturally shrill, her words thick with the pain of the experience.

I pushed the big bench seat all the way back and put my head between my knees.

"Hello," Grandma said. "Are you still there?"

I took a deep breath. "So how are you now? Are you okay?"

"Sure I'm okay. They fixed me up good at the hospital. Gave me some of that Tylenol with codeine. You take some of that, and you could get run over by a truck and never feel a thing. And then on account of I was in a state, they gave me some relaxer pills.

"Doctors said I was lucky that the pick missed everything important. Just kind of slid between the bones and such. Went in real clean."

More deep breathing. "What happened to Kenny?"

"Took off like the yellow-bellied dog that he is. Said he'd be coming back. That this was just the beginning." Her voice broke. "Can you imagine?"

"Maybe it'd be best if you stay in the house for a while."

"That's what I think, too. I'm plain tired. I could use a cup of hot tea."

My mother came back on the line. "What's this world coming to?" she asked. "An old woman gets attacked in broad daylight, in her own neighborhood, coming out of a bakery!"

"I'm going to leave my cellular phone on. Keep Grandma in the house, and call me if anything else happens."

"What else could happen? Isn't this enough?"

I disconnected and plugged my cellular phone into the cigarette lighter. My heart was beating triple time, and my palms were slick with sweat. I told myself I had to think clearly, but my mind was clouded with emotion. I got out of the Buick and stood on the sidewalk, looking for Morelli. I waved my arms over my head in a here-I-am signal.

The cell phone chirped inside the Buick. It was Morelli, his voice laced with impatience or anxiety. Hard to tell which.

"What?" Morelli said.

I told him about Grandma Mazur and waited while the silence stretched taut between us. Finally there was an oath and a disgusted sigh. It had to be hard for him. Mancuso was family.

"I'm sorry," he said. "Is there anything I can do?"

"You can help me catch Mancuso."

"We'll catch him."

What was left unsaid was the mutual fear that we wouldn't catch him soon enough.

"You okay to follow the game plan?" Morelli asked.

"Until six. I'm going home for dinner tonight. I want to see Grandma Mazur."

There was no further activity until one o'clock, when the funeral home opened for afternoon viewings. I trained my binoculars on the front-room windows and caught a glimpse of Spiro in suit and tie. Obviously he kept a change of clothes on the premises. Cars were constantly coming and going in the parking lot, and I realized how easily Kenny could get lost in the traffic. He could paste on a beard or a mustache, wear a hat or a wig, and no one would notice one more pedestrian coming into the front door, side door, or back door.

I strolled across the street at two o'clock.

Spiro sucked in some air when he saw me, and instinctively brought his injured arm closer to his body. His movements were unnaturally abrupt, his expression dark, and I had a sense of a disorganized mind.

He was the rat dropped into a maze, scrabbling over obstacles, scurrying down dead-end corridors, looking for the way out.

A man stood alone at the tea table. Fortyish, medium height, medium weight, upper body on the beefy side. He was wearing a sport coat and slacks. I'd seen him before. It took me a moment to figure it out. He'd been at the garage when they'd hauled Moogey out in a body bag. I'd assumed he was homicide, but maybe he was vice, or maybe he was a fed.

I approached the tea table and introduced myself.

He extended his hand. "Andy Roche."

"You work with Morelli."

He went immobile for a heartbeat while his regrouping reflex jerked into fast forward. "Sometimes."

I took a winger. "Fed."

"Treasury."

"You going to stay inside?"

"As much as possible. We brought in a bogus body today. I'm the long-lost grieving brother."

"Very clever."

"This guy, Spiro, always piss in short jerks?"

"He had a bad day yesterday. Didn't get a lot of sleep last night."

CHAPTER 12

All right, so Morelli didn't tell me about Andy Roche. What's new. Morelli played his cards close to his vest. That was his style. He didn't show his whole hand to anyone. Not to his boss, not to his partners, and certainly not to me. Nothing personal. After all, the goal was to catch Kenny. I no longer cared how it was accomplished.

I backed off from Roche and had a few words with Spiro. Yes, Spiro wanted me to tuck him in. And no, he hadn't heard from Kenny.

I used the ladies' room and returned to the Buick. At five o'clock I packed it in, not able to shake the visions of Grandma Mazur getting stuck with an ice pick. I drove back to my apartment, threw some clothes in a laundry basket, added makeup, hair gel, and hair dryer, and dragged the basket out to the car. I went back and fetched Rex, set the answering machine, left the kitchen light burning, and locked the door behind me. The only way I knew to protect Grandma Mazur was to move back home.

"What's this?" my mother said when she saw the glass hamster cage.

"I'm moving in for a few days."

"You quit that job. Thank God! I always thought you could do better."

"I didn't quit my job. I just need a change."

"I have the sewing machine and the ironing board in your room. You said you'd never come home."

I had both arms wrapped around the hamster cage. “I was wrong. I’m home. I’ll make do.”

“Frank,” my mother yelled. “Come help Stephanie, she’s moving in with us again.”

I nudged my way past her and started up the stairs. “Only for a few days. It’s temporary.”

“Stella Lombardi’s daughter said that same thing, and three years later she’s still living with them.”

I felt a scream starting somewhere deep inside.

“If you’d given me some notice, I’d have cleaned,” my mother said. “I’d have gotten a new bedspread.”

I pushed the door open with my knee. “I don’t need a new bedspread. This one is fine.” I maneuvered around the clutter in the small room and set Rex on the bed while I cleaned off the top of the single dresser. “How’s Grandma?”

“She’s taking a nap.”

“Not no more I’m not,” Grandma said from inside her room. “There’s enough noise out there to wake the dead. What’s going on?”

“Stephanie’s moving back home.”

“Why’d she want to do a thing like that? It’s damn boring here.” Grandma peeked into my room. “You aren’t pregnant, are you?”

Grandma Mazur got her hair curled once a week. In between sets she must have slept with her head hanging over the side of the bed because the tight little rolls lost some precision as the week marched on, but never seemed totally disturbed. Today she looked like she’d spray-starched her hair and been put through a wind tunnel. Her dress was rumpled from sleep, she was wearing pink velour bedroom slippers, and her left hand was encased in bandage.

“How’s your hand?” I asked.

“Starting to throb. Think I must need some more of them pills.”

Even with the ironing board and sewing machine occupying space, my room hadn’t changed much in the past ten years. It was a small room with one window. The curtains were white with a rubberized backing. The first week in May they were exchanged for sheers. The walls were painted dusty rose. The trim was white. The double bed was covered with a quilted, pink-flowered bedspread, softened in texture and color by age and the spin cycle. I had a small closet, which was filled with seasonal clothes, a single maple dresser, and a maple nightstand with a milk-glass lamp. My high school graduation picture still hung on the wall. And a picture of me in my majorette uniform. I had never completely mastered the art of baton twirling, but I'd been perfection in boots when I'd strutted onto a football field. Once during a half-time show I'd lost control of my baton and flipped it into the trombone section. A shudder ripped through me at the memory.

I hauled the laundry basket up and stashed it in a corner, clothes and all. The house was filled with food smells and the clank of flatware being set. My father channel-surfed in the living room, raising the volume to compete with the kitchen activity.

"Shut it down," my mother shouted at my father. "You'll make us all deaf."

My father concentrated on the screen, pretending oblivion.

By the time I sat down to dinner my fillings were vibrating, and I'd developed a twitch in my left eye.

"Isn't this nice?" my mother said. "Everyone sitting down to dinner together. Too bad Valerie isn't here."

My sister, Valerie, had been married to the same man for a hundred years and had two children. Valerie was the normal daughter.

Grandma Mazur was directly across from me and was downright frightening, with her hair still uncombed and her eyes focused inward. As my father would put it, her lights were on, but there was no one home.

"How much of that codeine has Grandma taken so far?" I asked my mother.

"Just one pill that I know of," my mother said.

I felt my eye jump and put my finger to it. "She seems to be . . . disconnected."

My father stopped buttering his bread and looked up. His mouth opened to say something, but he thought better of it and went back to buttering his bread.

"Mom," my mother called out, "how many pills have you taken?"

Grandma's head rotated in my mother's direction. "Pills?"

"It's a terrible thing that an old lady can't be safe on the streets," my mother said. "You'd think we lived in Washington, D.C. Next thing we'll have drive-by shootings. The burg was never like this in the old days."

I didn't want to burst her bubble about the old days, but in the old days the burg had a Mafia staff car parked in every third driveway.

Men were walked out of their homes, still in pajamas, and taken at gunpoint to the Meadowlands or the Camden landfill for ceremonial dispatch. Usually families and neighbors weren't at risk, but there'd always been the possibility that a stray bullet would embed itself in the wrong body.

And the burg was never safe from the Mancuso and Morelli men. Kenny was crazier and more brazen than most, but I suspected he wasn't the first of the Mancusos to leave a scar on a woman's body. To my knowledge none of them had ever ice-picked an old woman, but the Mancusos and Morellis were notorious for their violent, alcohol-fueled tempers and for their ability to sweet-talk a woman into an abusive relationship.

I knew some of this firsthand. When Morelli had charmed the pants off me fourteen years ago, he hadn't been abusive, but he hadn't been kind, either.

Grandma was sound asleep by seven o'clock, snoring like a drunken lumberjack.

I slipped into my jacket and grabbed my pocketbook.

"Where are you going?" my mother wanted to know.

"To Stiva's. He's hired me to help him close."

"Now that's a job," my mother said. "You could do a lot worse than to work for Stiva."

I closed the front door behind me, and took a deep, cleansing breath. The air felt cool on my face. My eye relaxed under the dark night sky.

I drove to Stiva's and parked in the lot. Inside, Andy Roche had reclaimed his position at the tea table.

"How's it going?" I asked.

"Some old lady just told me I looked like Harrison Ford."

I selected a cookie from the plate behind him. "Shouldn't you be with your brother?"

"We weren't all that close."

"Where's Morelli?"

Roche casually scanned the room. "No one ever knows the answer to that question."

I returned to my car and had just settled in when the phone rang.

"How's Grandma Mazur?" Morelli asked.

"She's sleeping."

"I hope this move to your parents' house is temporary. I had plans for those purple shoes."

This caught me by surprise. I'd expected Morelli to keep watching Spiro, but he'd followed me instead. And I hadn't spotted him. I pressed my lips together. I was a dismal bounty hunter. "I didn't see any other good alternatives. I'm worried about Grandma Mazur."

"You have a terrific family, but they'll have you on Valium in forty-eight hours."

"Plums don't do Valium. We mainline cheesecake."

"Whatever works," Morelli said, and hung up.

At ten of ten I pulled into the mortuary driveway and parked to one side, leaving room for Spiro to squeeze past. I locked the Buick and entered the funeral home through the side door.

Spiro was looking nervous, saying good-byes. Louie Moon was nowhere to be seen. And Andy had disappeared. I slipped into the kitchen and clipped a holster to my belt. I loaded the fifth round into my .38 and shoved the gun into the holster. I clipped on a second holster for my pepper spray, and a third for a flashlight. I figured at $100 a shot, Spiro deserved the full treatment. I'd have heart palpitations if I had to use the gun, but that was my little secret.

I was wearing a hip-length jacket that for the most part hid my paraphernalia. Technically this meant I was carrying concealed, which was a legal no-no. Unfortunately, the alternative would generate instant phone calls all over the burg that I was packing at Stiva's. The threat of arrest seemed pale by comparison.

When the last of the mourners cleared the front porch I walked Spiro through the public areas on the top two floors of the house, securing windows and doors. Only two rooms were occupied. One by the bogus brother.

The silence was eerie, and my discomfort with death was enhanced by Spiro's presence. Spiro Stiva, Demonic Mortician. I had my hand on the butt of the little S & W, thinking it wouldn't have hurt to load up with silver bullets.

We paced through the kitchen, into the back hall. Spiro opened the door to the cellar.

"Hold it," I said. "Where are you going?"

"We need to check the cellar door."

"We?"

"Yeah, we. Like in me and my fucking bodyguard."

"I don't think so."

"You want to get paid?"

Not that bad. "Are there bodies down there?"

"Sorry, we're fresh out of bodies."

"So what's down there?"

"The furnace, for Chrissake!"

I unholstered my gun. "I'll be right behind you."

Spiro looked at the five-shot Smith & Wesson. "Cripes, that's a goddamn sissy gun."

"I bet you wouldn't say that if I shot you in the foot with it."

His obsidian eyes locked with mine. "I hear you killed a man with that gun."

Not something I wanted to rap about with Spiro. "Are we going downstairs, or what?"

The basement was basically one large room, and pretty much what you'd expect from a basement. With the possible exception of caskets stacked in one of the corners.

The outside door was just to the right at the foot of the stairs. I checked the door to make sure the bolt was thrown. "Nobody here," I said to Spiro, holstering my gun. I'm not sure whom I'd expected to shoot. Kenny, I suppose. Maybe Spiro. Maybe ghosts.

We returned to the first floor, and I waited in the hall while Spiro bumbled around in his office, finally emerging wearing a top coat, carrying a gym bag.

I followed him to the back door and held the door open, watching him activate the alarm and hit the light switch. The lights inside dimmed. The exterior lights remained on.

Spiro shut the door and pulled car keys from his coat pocket. "We'll take my car. You ride shotgun."

"How about you take your car, I take my car."

"No way. I pay a hundred bucks, I want my gunny sitting next to me. You can take the car home with you and pick me up in the morning."

"That wasn't part of the deal."

"You were out there anyway. I saw you in the lot this morning, waiting for Kenny to make a move, so you could haul his ass back to jail. What's the big deal, so you drive me to work."

Spiro's Lincoln was parked close to the door. He aimed his remote at the car, and the alarm chirped off. He lit up when we were safely inside.

We were sitting in a pool of light on a deserted patch of driveway. Not a good spot to linger. Especially if Morelli wasn't in a position to see this part of the property.

"Put it in gear," I said to Spiro. "It's too easy for Kenny to get to us here."

He rolled the engine over, but he didn't move forward. "What would you do if all of a sudden Kenny jumped up alongside the car and pointed a gun at you?"

"I don't know. You never really know what you'll do in a situation like that until you do it."

Spiro thought about that for a moment. He took another drag on his cigarette and shifted to drive.

We stopped for a light at Hamilton and Gross. Spiro's head didn't move, but his eyes cut to Delio's Exxon. The pumps were lit, and there was a light on in the office. The bays were dark and closed. Several cars and a truck had been parked in front of the end bay. Drop-offs to be serviced first thing in the morning.

Spiro stared in silence, his face devoid of emotion, and I couldn't guess at his thoughts.

The light changed, and we motored through the intersection. We were halfway down the block when my brain kicked in. "Oh my God," I said. "Go back to the gas station."

Spiro braked and pulled to the side. "You didn't see Kenny, did you?"

"No. I saw a truck! A big white truck with black lettering on the side!"

"You're gonna have to do better than that."

"When I talked to the woman who managed the storage lockers she said she remembered seeing a white truck with black lettering make several passes in the area of your locker. It was too vague to mean anything at the time."

Spiro waited for a break in traffic and wheeled a U-turn. He parked at the edge of the macadam apron, behind the drop-offs. Chances of Sandeman still being at the station were slim, but I strained to see in the office all the same. I didn't want a confrontation with Sandeman if I could avoid it.

We got out and took a look at the truck. It belonged to Macko Furniture. I knew the store. It was a small family-owned business that had steadfastly stayed with a downtown location when others were moving to highway strip malls.

"This mean anything to you?" I asked.

He shook his head. "No. Don't know anybody at Macko Furniture."

"It's the right size for caskets."

"There must be fifty trucks in Trenton that fit this description."

"Yes, but this one is at the garage where Moogey worked. And Moogey knew about the caskets. He went down to Braddock and drove them back for you."

Dumb chick feeds information to slimy guy. Come on, slimy guy, I thought. Get careless. Give me some information in return.

"So you think Moogey was tight with someone from Macko Furniture, and they decided to steal my caskets," Spiro said.

"It's possible. Or maybe while the truck was being serviced, Moogey borrowed it."

"What would Moogey want with twenty-four caskets?"

"You tell me."

"Even with the hydraulic tailgate, you'd need at least two guys to move those caskets."

"Doesn't seem like a problem to me. You find some big oaf, pay him minimum wage. He helps you move caskets."

Spiro had his hands in his pockets. "I don't know," he said. "It's just hard to believe Moogey'd do something like that. There were two things you could always count on from Moogey. He was loyal, and he was dumb. Moogey was a big, dumb shit. Kenny and me let him hang out with us because he was good for laughs. He'd do anything we told him. We'd say, hey, Moogey, how about you run over your dick with a lawn mower. And he'd say, sure, you want me to get a hard-on first?"

"Maybe he wasn't as dumb as you thought."

Spiro didn't say anything for a couple beats, then he turned on his heel and walked back to the Lincoln. We kept quiet for the rest of the trip. When we reached Spiro's parking lot I couldn't resist another shot with the caskets.

"Kind of funny about you and Kenny and Moogey. Kenny thinks you've got something that belongs to him. And now we think maybe Moogey had something that belonged to you."

Spiro slid into a space, put the car in park, and swiveled his body in my direction. He draped his left arm over the wheel, his top coat gaped, and I caught a glimpse of a gun butt and shoulder holster.

"What are you getting at?" Spiro asked.

"Nothing. Just thinking out loud. Thinking that you and Kenny have a lot in common."

Our eyes held, and cold fear ran the length of my spine and crawled through my stomach. Morelli was right about Spiro. He'd eat his young, and he wouldn't think twice about putting a bullet in my worthless brain. I hoped I hadn't pushed too hard.

"Maybe you should stop thinking out loud. Maybe you should stop thinking altogether," Spiro said.

"I'm going to raise my rates if you're going to get cranky."

"Christ," Spiro said, "you're already fucking overpaid. For a hundred dollars a night, the least you could do is throw in a blow job."

What I was going to throw in was a nice long time behind bars. It was a comforting thought, and it kept me going while I did my bodyguard thing in his apartment, flipping on lights, scoping out closets, counting dustballs under his bed, and gagging at the soap scum behind his shower curtain.

I gave his place a green light, drove the Lincoln back to the funeral home, and exchanged it for my Buick.

I caught Morelli in my rearview mirror half a block from my parents' house. He idled in front of the Smullenses' until I parked the Buick. When I stepped out of the car, he crept forward and parked behind me. I suppose I couldn't blame him for being cautious.

"What were you doing at Delio's?" Morelli wanted to know. "I assume you were baiting Spiro about the truck."

"You assume right."

"Anything come of it?"

"He said he didn't know anyone from Macko Furniture. And he discounted the possibility that Moogey might have taken the caskets. Apparently Moogey was the group idiot. I'm not even sure Moogey was involved."

"Moogey drove the caskets to New Jersey."

I leaned back against the Buick. "Maybe Kenny and Spiro didn't include Moogey in the master plan, but somewhere along the line Moogey found out and decided to cut himself in."

"And you think he borrowed the furniture truck to move the caskets."

"It would be one theory." I pushed off from the Buick and hitched my bag higher onto my shoulder. "I'm picking Spiro up at eight tomorrow to take him to work."

"I'll catch up with you in his lot."

I let myself into the darkened house and paused for a moment in the front hall. The house was always at its best when it was asleep. There was an air of satisfaction to the house at the end of the day. Maybe the day hadn't gone exactly right, but the day had been lived and the house had been there for its family.

I hung my jacket in the hall closet and tiptoed into the kitchen. Finding food in my kitchen was always hit or miss. Finding food in my mother's kitchen was a sure thing. I heard the stairs creak and knew from the tread that it was my mother.

"How did it go at Stiva's?" she asked.

"It went okay. I helped him lock up, and then I drove him home."

"I guess it's hard for him to drive with his wrist. I hear he got twenty-three stitches."

I pulled out some ham and provolone cheese.

"Here, let me," my mother said, taking the ham and cheese, reaching for the loaf of rye bread on the counter.

"I can do it," I said.

My mother took her good carving knife from the knife drawer. "You don't slice the ham thin enough."

When she'd made each of us a sandwich, she poured two glasses of milk and set it all on the kitchen table. "You could have invited him in for a sandwich," she said.

"Spiro?"

"Joe Morelli."

My mother never ceased to amaze me. "There was a time when you would have chased him out of the house with that carving knife."

"He's changed."

I tore into the sandwich. "So he tells me."

"I hear he's a good cop."

"A good cop is different from a good person."

I woke up disoriented, staring at a ceiling from a previous life. Grandma Mazur's voice snapped me back to the present.

"If I don't get into that bathroom there's gonna be a big mess in the hall," she yelled. "Last night's supper's going through me like goose grease."

I heard the door open. Heard my father mumble something indiscernible. My eye started to twitch, and I squinched it closed. I focused my other eye on the bedside clock. Seven-thirty. Damn. I'd wanted to get to Spiro's early. I jumped out of bed and rummaged through the laundry basket for clean jeans and a shirt. I ran a brush through my hair, grabbed my pocketbook, and rushed into the hall.

"Grandma," I hollered through the door. "Are you going to be long?"

"Is the Pope Catholic?" she yelled back.

All right, I could postpone the bathroom for half an hour. After all, if I'd gotten up at nine I wouldn't have used the bathroom for another hour and a half.

My mother caught me with my jacket in hand. "Where are you going?" she asked. "You haven't had breakfast."

"I told Spiro I'd pick him up."

"Spiro can wait. The dead people won't mind if he's fifteen minutes late. Come eat your breakfast."

"I don't have time for breakfast."

"I made some nice oatmeal. It's on the table. I poured your juice." She looked down at my shoes. "What kind of shoes are they?"

"They're Doc Martens."

"Your father wore shoes like that when he was in the army."

"These are great shoes," I said. "I love these shoes. Everyone wears shoes like this."

"Women interested in getting married to a nice man do not wear shoes like that. Women who like other women wear shoes like that. You don't have any funny ideas about women, do you?"

I clapped my hand over my eye.

"What's wrong with your eye?" my mother asked.

"It's twitching."

"You're too nervous. It's that job. Look at you rushing out of the house. And what's that on your belt?"

"Pepper spray."

"Your sister, Valerie, doesn't wear such things on her belt."

I looked at my watch. If I ate real fast, I could still get to Spiro by eight.

My father was at the table, reading his paper, drinking coffee. "How's the Buick?" he asked. "You giving it high-test?"

"The Buick's fine. No problems."

I chugged the juice and tried the oatmeal. It needed something. Chocolate, maybe. Or ice cream. I added three spoons of sugar and some milk.

Grandma Mazur took her seat at the table. "My hand feels better," she said, "but I got the devil of a headache."

"You should stay at home today," I said. "Take it easy."

"I'm going to take it easy at Clara's. I look a fright. Don't know how my hair got like this."

"No one will see you if you don't go out of the house," I argued.

"Suppose someone comes over? Suppose that good-looking Morelli boy comes to visit again? You think I want him seeing me like this? Besides, I got to go while I still got the bandage on and I'm big news. Not every day a person gets attacked at the bakery."

"I have things to do first thing this morning, but then I'll be back, and I'll take you to Clara's," I told Grandma. "Don't go without me!"

I wolfed down the rest of the oatmeal and had a fast half cup of coffee. I grabbed my jacket and pocketbook and took off. I had my hand on the door when the phone rang.

"It's for you," my mother said. "It's Vinnie."

"I don't want to talk to him. Tell him I've already left."

The cell phone rang just as I hit Hamilton.

"You should have talked to me at home," Vinnie said. "It would have been cheaper."

"You're breaking up . . . lousy connection."

"Don't give me that lousy connection crap."

I made some static sounds.

"And I'm not going to fall for that phony static, either. Make sure you get your keester in here this morning."

I didn't see Morelli lurking in Spiro's parking lot, but I assumed he was there. There were two vans and a truck with a cap. Both good possibilities.

I collected Spiro and headed for the funeral home. When I stopped for the light at Hamilton and Gross, we both turned our attention to the Exxon station.

"Maybe we should stop in and ask a few questions," Spiro said.

"What kind of questions?"

"Questions about the furniture truck. Just for the hell of it. I guess it would be interesting to see if Moogey was the one who took the caskets."

I figured I had a couple choices. I could torture him by saying, what's the point? Let's just get on with our lives. And then I'd drive right on by. Or I could play along to see how it goes. There was definitely some merit to torturing Spiro, but my best instincts told me to let him run with the ball and tag along.

The bays were open. Most likely Sandeman was there. Big deal. Compared to Kenny, Sandeman was starting to look small-time. Cubby Delio was working the office. Spiro and I ambled in together.

Cubby snapped to attention at the sight of Spiro. Little prick that he was, Spiro still represented Stiva's mortuary, and Stiva threw a lot of business to the station. All of Stiva's cars were serviced and gassed here.

"I heard about your arm," Cubby said to Spiro. "Damn shame. I know you and Kenny used to be friends. I guess he just went crazy. That's what everyone says."

Spiro passed it off with a wave of his hand that implied it was nothing more than an annoyance. He pivoted on his heel and looked out the office window at the truck, still parked in front of the bay. "I wanted to ask you about the Macko truck. Do you always service that truck? Does it come in regularly?"

"Yep. Macko has an account, just like you. They've got two trucks, and we do both of them."

"Who usually brings them in? Usually the same guy?"

"Usually it's Bucky or Biggy. They've been driving for Macko for a lot of years. Is there a problem? You looking to get some furniture?"

"Thinking about it," Spiro said.

"It's a good company. Family run. Keep their trucks in real good condition."

Spiro stuck his injured arm in his jacket. Small man imitates Napoleon. "Looks like you haven't found a replacement for Moogey."

"Thought I had a guy, but he didn't work out. Hard to replace Moogey. When Moogey was running the station I hardly had to be here. Could take a day off once a week to go to the track. Even after he got shot in the knee, he was still reliable. Still came to work."

I suspected Spiro and I had parallel thoughts, and I was thinking that maybe Moogey borrowed the truck on one of those track days. Of course, if he borrowed the truck, someone else would have to be minding the store. Or someone else would have to be driving the truck.

"It's hard to get good help," Spiro said. "I have the same problem."

"I've got a good mechanic," Cubby said. "Sandeman's got his own ways, but he's a damn good mechanic. The rest of the people come and go. Don't need a rocket scientist to pump gas or change a tire. If I could find someone to work full-time in the office, I'd be set."

Spiro did some oily chitchat and oozed himself out of the office.

"You know any of the guys who work here?" he asked me.

"I've spoken to Sandeman. He has an attitude. Does a little recreational drug use."

"You tight with him?"

"I'm not his favorite person."

Spiro's gaze dropped to my feet. "Maybe it's the shoes."

I wrenched the car door open. "Anything else you want to comment on? Maybe you have a few words to say about my car?"

Spiro angled onto the seat. "Hell, the car is awesome. At least you know how to pick out a car."

I squired Spiro into the funeral parlor, where all security systems seemed intact. We did a superficial examination of his two customers and felt fairly certain no one had relieved them of any obvious body parts. I told Spiro I'd return for the night run and that he should beep me if he needed me sooner.

I would have liked to keep Spiro under surveillance. I figured he'd keep picking at the lead I'd given him, and who knows what he'd find? And even more important, if Spiro started moving around, maybe Kenny would move with him. Unfortunately, I couldn't conduct any meaningful surveillance in Big Blue. I'd have to find a different car if I wanted to tail Spiro.

The half cup of coffee I'd gulped at breakfast was working its way through my system, so I decided to go back to my parents' house, where I could use the bathroom. I could take a shower and give some thought to my car problem. At ten I'd chauffeur Grandma Mazur over to Clara's for an overhaul.

When I got home my father was in the bathroom, and my mother was in the kitchen, cutting vegetables for minestrone.

"I have to use the bathroom," I said. "Do you think Daddy will be long?"

My mother rolled her eyes. "I don't know what he does in there. Takes the paper in with him, and we don't see him for hours."

I snitched a chunk of carrot and a chunk of celery for Rex and hustled up the stairs.

I knocked on the bathroom door. "How much longer?" I yelled.

There was no answer.

I knocked louder. "Are you okay in there?"

"Christ," was the muttered reply. "A man can't even take a crap in this house . . ."

I went back to my room. My mother had made my bed and folded all my clothes. I told myself it was nice to be back home and have someone doing little favors for me. I should be grateful. I should enjoy the luxury.

"Isn't this fun?" I said to a sleeping Rex. "It's not every day we get to visit Grandmom and Grandpop." I lifted the lid to give him his breakfast, but my eye was twitching so badly I missed the cage entirely and dropped his carrot chunk on the floor.

By ten o'clock my father still hadn't come out of the bathroom, and I was dancing in the hall. "Hurry up," I said to Grandma Mazur. "I'm going to explode if I don't get to a bathroom soon."

"Clara has a nice bathroom. She keeps potpourri in it, and she's got a crocheted doll that sits on the extra roll of toilet paper. She'll let you use her bathroom."

"I know, I know. Get a move on, will you?"

She was wearing her blue wool coat and had a gray wool scarf wrapped around her head.

"You're going to be hot in that coat," I told her. "It's not very cold out."

"Haven't got anything else," she said. "Everything's gone to rags. I thought maybe after Clara's we could go shopping. I got my Social Security check."

"You sure your hand feels okay to go shopping?"

She held her hand in front of her face and stared at the bandage. "Feels okay so far. The hole wasn't real big. Tell you the truth, I didn't even know how deep it was until I got to the hospital. It happened so fast.

"I always thought I was pretty good at taking care of myself, but I don't know anymore. I don't move like I used to. I just stood there like a damn fool and let him stick me in the hand."

"I'm sure there wasn't anything you could do, Grandma. Kenny's a lot bigger than you, and you were unarmed."

Her eyes clouded behind a film of tears. "He made me feel like a silly old woman."

Morelli was slouched against the Buick when I came out of Clara's. "Whose idea was it to talk to Cubby Delio?"

"Spiro's. And I don't think he's going to stop with Delio. He needs to find those guns so he can get Kenny off his back."

"You learn anything interesting?"

I repeated the conversation for Morelli.

"I know Bucky and Biggy," he said. "They wouldn't get mixed up in something like this."

"Maybe we've jumped to the wrong conclusion about the furniture truck."

"I don't think so. I stopped by the Exxon station first thing this morning and took some pictures. Roberta says she thinks it's the same truck."

"I thought you were supposed to be following me! What if I was attacked? What if Kenny came after me with the ice pick?"

"I followed you part of the time. Anyway, Kenny likes to sleep in."

"That's no excuse! The least you could have done was let me know I was on my own!"

"What's the plan here?" Morelli wanted to know.

"Grandma will be done in an hour. I promised I'd take her shopping. And sometime today I have to stop in to see Vinnie."

"He going to yank you off the case?"

"No. I'll take Grandma Mazur with me. She'll straighten him out."

"I've been thinking about Sandeman . . ."

"Yeah," I said. "I've been thinking about Sandeman, too. Initially I thought he might be hiding Kenny. Maybe it's just the opposite. Maybe he screwed Kenny over."

"You think Moogey threw in with Sandeman?"

I shrugged. "It makes some sense. Whoever stole the guns had street contacts."

"You said Sandeman didn't show any signs of sudden wealth."

"I think Sandeman's wealth goes up his nose."

CHAPTER 13

"I feel much better now that my hair's back in shape," Grandma said, hoisting herself up onto the front seat of the Buick. "I even had her put a rinse in it. Can you tell the difference?"

She'd gone from gunmetal gray to apricot.

"It's more of a strawberry blond now," I said.

"Yeah, that's it. Strawberry blond. I always wanted to be one of those."

Vinnie's office was just down the street. I parked at the curb and pulled Grandma in after me.

"I've never been here before," Grandma said, taking it all in. "Isn't this something?"

"Vinnie's on the phone," Connie said. "He'll be with you in a minute."

Lula came over to get a closer look at Grandma. "So you're Stephanie's grandma," Lula said. "I've heard a lot about you."

Grandma's eyes brightened. "Oh yeah? What'd you hear?"

"For starters I heard you got stuck with an ice pick."

Grandma held her bandaged hand out for Lula to see. "It was this here hand, and it got stuck just about clean through."

Lula and Connie looked at the hand.

"And that isn't all that's happened," Grandma said. "The other night Stephanie got a man's part in Express Mail. Opened it up right in front of me. I saw the whole thing. It was stuck to a piece of foam with a hatpin."

"Get out," Lula said.

"That's just the way it came through the mail," Grandma said. "Sliced off like a chicken neck and stuck with a hatpin. Reminded me of my husband."

Lula leaned forward so she could whisper. "You talking about size? Was your man's part that big?"

"Heck no," Grandma said. "His part was that dead."

Vinnie stuck his head out of his office door, and swallowed hard when he saw Grandma. "Oh jeez," he said.

"I just picked Grandma up at the beauty parlor," I told him "And now we're going shopping. Thought I'd stop by to see what you wanted, since I was just down the street."

Vinnie's five-foot-nine frame hunched. His thinning black hair was slicked back and had the same level of shine as his pointy-toed black shoes. "I want to know what's happening with Mancuso. This was supposed to be a simple pickup, and now I'm hanging out for a lot of money."

"I'm closing in," I said. "Sometimes these things take time."

"Time is money," Vinnie said. "My money."

Connie rolled her eyes.

And Lula said, "Say what?"

We all knew Vinnie's bond business was financed by an insurance company.

Vinnie balanced on his toes, hands loose at his sides. City boy. Slack-jointed. Tight-assed. "This case is out of your league. I'm giving it over to Mo Barnes."

"I don't know Mo Barnes from Adam's donkey," Grandma said to Vinnie. "But I know he can't hold a candle to my granddaughter. She's the best there is when it comes to bounty huntering, and you'd be a darn fool to take her off this Mancuso case. Especially now that I'm working with her. We're about to crack his case wide open."

"No offense," Vinnie said, "but you and your granddaughter couldn't crack a walnut with both hands, much less bring Mancuso in."

Grandma pulled herself up and edged her chin out a half inch.

"Uh-oh," Lula said.

"Bad things happen to people who take away from family," Grandma told Vinnie.

"What kinds of bad things?" Vinnie asked. "What's my hair gonna fall out? My teeth gonna rot in my head?"

"Maybe," Grandma said. "Maybe I'll put the evil eye on you. Or maybe I'll talk to your grandma Bella. Maybe I'll tell your grandma Bella how you talk fresh to an old woman."

Vinnie swayed foot to foot like a caged cat. He knew better than to displease Grandma Bella. Grandma Bella was even scarier than Grandma Mazur. Grandma Bella had on more than one occasion taken a grown man by the ear and brought him to his knees. Vinnie made a low sound behind clenched teeth and narrowed his eyes. He muttered something through tight lips, tipped backward into his office, and slammed his door shut.

"Well," Grandma said. "That's the Plum side of the family for you."

It was late afternoon when we finished shopping. My mother opened the door for us with a grim set to her mouth.

"I had nothing to do with the hair," I told her. "Grandma did that all by herself."

"This is my cross to bear," my mother said. She looked down at Grandma's shoes and genuflected.

Grandma Mazur was wearing Doc Martens. She was also wearing a new hip-length, downfilled ski jacket, jeans that she'd rolled and pegged, and a flannel shirt to match mine. We looked like *Tales from the Crypt* does the Bobbsey Twins.

"I'm going to take a nap before dinner," Grandma said. "Shopping wore me out."

"I could use help in the kitchen," my mother said to me.

This was bad news. My mother never needed help in the kitchen. The only time my mother requested help was when she had something on her mind and intended to browbeat some unfortunate soul into submission. Or when she wanted information. Have some chocolate pudding, she'd say to me. By the way, Mrs. Herrel saw you going into the Morellis' garage with Joseph Morelli. And why are your panties on inside out?

I dragged after her, into her lair, where potatoes boiled on the stove, steaming the air and fogging the window over the sink. My mother opened the oven door to check on the roast, and the smell of leg of lamb washed over me. I felt my eyes glaze and my mouth fall open in a stupor of expectation.

She moved from the oven to the refrigerator. "Some carrots would be nice with the lamb. You can peel the carrots," she said, handing me the bag and the paring knife. "By the way, why did someone send you a penis?"

I almost sliced off the tip of my finger. "Um . . ."

"The return address was New York, but the postmark was local," she said.

"I can't tell you about the penis. It's under police investigation."

"Thelma Biglo's son, Richie, told Thelma that the penis belonged to Joe Loosey. And that Kenny Mancuso cut it off while Loosey was getting dressed at Stiva's."

"Where did Richie Biglo hear this?"

"Richie tends bar at Pino's. Richie knows everything."

"I don't want to talk about the penis."

My mother took the paring knife out of my hand. "Look at these carrots you peeled. I can't serve these carrots. Some of the skins are left on."

"You shouldn't cut the skins off anyway. You should scrub them with a brush. All the vitamins are in the skin."

"Your father won't eat them with the skins on. You know how particular he is."

My father would eat cat shit if it was salted, fried, or frosted, but it took an act of Congress to get him to eat a vegetable.

"Seems to me Kenny Mancuso has it in for you," my mother said. "It's not a nice thing to send a penis to a woman. It's disrespectful."

I searched the kitchen for a new task, but I couldn't come up with anything.

"And I know what's going on with your grandmother, too," she said. "Kenny Mancuso is getting to you through your grandmother. That's why he attacked her at the bakery. That's why you're living here . . . so you can be close by if he attacks her again."

"He's crazy."

"Of course he's crazy. Everybody knows he's crazy. All the Mancuso men are crazy. His uncle Rocco hung himself. He liked little girls. Mrs. Ligatti caught him with her Tina. And then the next day Rocco hung himself. Good thing, too. If Al Ligatti had gotten hold of Rocco . . ." My mother shook her head. "I don't even want to think about it." She shut the heat off under the potatoes and turned to me. "How good are you at this bounty hunter business?"

"I'm learning."

"Are you good enough to catch Kenny Mancuso?"

"Yes." Maybe.

She lowered her voice. "I want you to catch that son of a bitch. I want you to get him off the streets. It's not right that a man like that is free to hurt old women."

"I'll do the best I can."

"Good." She took a can of cranberries from the pantry. "Now that we have things straight, you can set the table."

Morelli showed up at one minute to six.

I answered his knock and stood blocking the doorway, preventing him from slipping into the front hall. "What is it?"

Morelli leaned into me, forcing me to take a step back.

"I was driving by, doing a security check," Morelli said, "and I smelled leg of lamb."

"Who is it?" my mother called.

"It's Morelli. He was driving by, and he smelled the lamb. And he's leaving. RIGHT NOW!"

"She has no manners," my mother said to Morelli. "I don't know what happened. I didn't raise her like that. Stephanie, lay out an extra plate."

Morelli and I left the house at seven-thirty. He trailed after me in a tan panel van and parked in Stiva's lot when I pulled into the driveway.

I locked the Buick and walked over to Morelli. "You have anything to tell me?"

"I went through invoices from the garage. The truck was in for an oil change at the end of the month. Bucky brought it in around seven in the morning and picked it up the next day."

"Let me guess. Cubby Delio was gone that day. Moogey and Sandeman were working."

"Yeah. Sandeman signed off on the job. His name was on the invoice."

"Have you talked to Sandeman?"

"No. I got to the garage right after he left for the night. I checked his room and some bars, but I couldn't find him. Thought I'd make the rounds again later."

"Did you find anything interesting in his room?"

"His door was locked."

"You didn't look in through the window?"

"Thought I'd save that little adventure for you. I know how much you like to do that sort of thing."

In other words, Morelli didn't want to get caught on the fire escape. "You going to be here when I close up with Spiro?"

"Wild horses couldn't drag me away."

I crossed the lot and entered the funeral home through the side door. Word of Kenny Mancuso's bizarre behavior was obviously spreading because Joe Loosey, minus his penis, was laid out in the V.I.P. room and the crowd packed into the room rivaled the record-breaking viewing held for Silvestor Bergen, who died in the middle of his term as grand poo-bah of the VFW.

Spiro was holding court on the far side of the lobby, cradling the arm injured in the line of duty, making the most of his role as undertaker célèbre. People were clustered around him, listening intently as he told them God knows what.

A few people looked in my direction and whispered behind their memorial programs.

Spiro bowed out on his audience and signaled me to follow him into the kitchen. He grabbed the big silver cookie plate on his way, ignoring Roche, who was once again positioned at the tea table.

"Do you believe this bunch of losers?" Spiro said, emptying a bag of bulk-bought supermarket cookies onto the plate. "They're eating me out of house and home. I should be charging after-hours admission to see Loosey's stump."

"Anything new from Kenny?"

"Nothing. I think he's shot his wad. Which brings me to business at hand. I don't need you anymore."

"Why the sudden change of heart?"

"Things have quieted down."

"That's it?"

"Yeah. That's it." He swung out the kitchen door with the cookies and slapped them down on the table. "How're you doing?" he asked Roche. "I see your brother's getting some overflow from Loosey.

Probably a bunch of people going in there wondering about your brother's state of affairs, if you know what I mean. You notice I gave him a half-casket viewing tonight so no one could try copping a feel."

Roche looked like he might choke. "Thanks," he said. "Glad you're thinking ahead."

I went back to Morelli and gave him the news.

Morelli was lost in the shadows of the dark van. "Sudden."

"I think Kenny's got the guns. I think we gave Spiro a place to start looking, he passed it on to Kenny, and Kenny lucked out. And now the heat's off Spiro."

"It's possible."

I had my car keys in hand. "I'm going to check on Sandeman. See if he's come home yet."

I parked half a block from Sandeman's rooming house, on the opposite side of the street. Morelli parked directly behind me. We stood for a moment on the sidewalk, taking in the bulky house, black against blue night sky. Harsh light poured from a shadeless downstairs window. Upstairs two orange rectangles gave muted testimony to life within the front rooms.

"What kind of car does he drive?" I asked Morelli.

"He's got a hog and a Ford pickup."

We didn't see either on the street. We followed the driveway to the back of the house and found the Harley. No windows were lit in any of the rear rooms. No light in Sandeman's upstairs window. No one sat on the stoop. The back door was unlocked. The hall leading from the back door was dim, lit by a bare 40-watt bulb hanging from an overhead fixture in the front foyer. Television sounds escaped from one of the upstairs rooms.

Morelli stopped in the foyer for a moment, listening to the house, before continuing on to the second floor and then the third floor. The third floor was dark and quiet. Morelli listened at Sandeman's door. He shook his head no. No noise coming from Sandeman's room.

He went to the window, opened it, and looked out. "It would be unethical for me to break into his apartment," Morelli said.

As opposed to downright illegal for me.

Morelli glanced at the heavy-duty flashlight I held in my hand. "Of course a bounty hunter would have the authority to go in after her man."

"Only if she was convinced her man was in there."

Morelli looked at me expectantly.

I peeked out at the fire escape. "It's really rickety," I told him.

"Yeah," he said. "I noticed that. It might not hold me." He put a finger under my chin and gazed into my eyes. "I bet it would hold a dainty little thing like you."

I am many things. Dainty isn't one of them. I took a deep breath and angled myself out onto the fire escape. Iron joints groaned, and rusted metal shards flaked off underfoot and fell to the ground. I whispered an oath and inched toward Sandeman's window.

I cupped my hands to the glass and looked inside. The interior was blacker than black. I tried the window. It was unlocked. I gave the bottom window a shove, and it rose halfway and stuck.

"Can you get in?" Morelli whispered.

"No. The window's stuck." I squatted down, peered through the opening and worked the flashlight around the room. So far as I could see, nothing had changed. There was the same clutter, the same squalor, the stink of unwashed clothes and overflowing ashtrays. I saw no signs of struggle, flight, or affluence.

I thought I'd give one more try with the window. I braced my feet and pushed hard against the old wood frame. Masonry bolts tore loose from crumbling brick, and the slatted floor of the fire escape tipped to a 45-degree angle. Stairs slid out of place, railings ripped from their moorings, angle irons wrenched free, and I skidded feet first, ass second off into space. My hand connected with a crossbar, and in an act of blind panic and reflexive action, I held fast . . . for ten seconds. At the end of those ten seconds, the entire third-floor gridwork crashed onto the second-floor fire escape. There was a momentary pause. Long enough for me to whisper, "Oh shit."

Above me, Morelli leaned out the window. "Don't move!"

CHAAANG! The second-floor fire escape separated from the building and crumbled to the ground, carrying me with it. I landed flat on my back with a solid *whump* that knocked the air out of my lungs.

I lay there stunned until Morelli's face once again loomed over me, just inches away.

"Fuck," he whispered. "Jesus, Stephanie, say something!"

I stared straight ahead, unable to talk, not yet able to breathe.

He felt for the pulse in my neck. Then his hands were on my feet, moving up my legs. "Can you move your toes?"

Not when his hand was feeling up the inside of my thigh like this. My skin felt scorched under his palm, and my toes were curled into a cramp. I heard myself make a sucking sound. "Your fingers go any higher up my leg, and I'm filing for sexual harassment."

Morelli rocked back on his heels and passed a hand over his eyes. "You just scared the hell out of me."

"What's going on out there?" A loud voice from one of the windows. "I'm calling the police. I'm not putting up with this shit. We got noise ordinances in this neighborhood."

I propped myself up on my elbow. "Get me out of here."

Morelli gently hoisted me to my feet. "You sure you're okay?"

"Nothing seems broken." I wrinkled my nose. "What is that smell? Oh God, I didn't mess myself, did I?"

Morelli turned me around. "Whoa!" he said. "Someone in this building has a big dog. A big, *sick* dog. And it looks like you hit ground zero."

I shrugged out of the jacket and held it at arm's length. "Am I okay now?"

"Some of it's splattered down the back of your jeans."

"Anyplace else?"

"Your hair."

This sent me into instant hysteria. "GET IT OUT! GET IT OUT!"

Morelli clapped a hand over my mouth. "Quiet!"

"Get it out of my hair!"

"I can't get it out of your hair. You're going to have to wash it out." He pulled me toward the street. "Can you walk?"

I staggered forward.

"That's good," Morelli said. "Keep doing that. Before you know it you'll be to the van. And then we'll get you to a shower. After an hour or two of scrubbing you'll be good as new."

"Good as new." My ears were ringing, and my voice sounded far away . . . like a voice in a jar. "Good as new," I repeated.

When we got to the van Morelli opened the rear door. "You don't mind riding in back, do you?"

I stared at him blank-minded.

Morelli shone my flashlight in my eyes. "You sure you're okay?"

"What kind of dog do you think it was?"

"A big dog."

"What kind?"

"Rottweiler. Male. Old and overweight. Bad teeth. Ate a lot of tuna fish."

I started to cry.

"Oh jeez," Morelli said. "Don't cry. I hate when you cry."

"I've got rottweiler shit in my hair."

He used his thumb to wipe the tears from my cheeks. "It's okay, honey. It's really not so bad. I was kidding about the tuna." He gave me a boost into the van. "Hold tight back here. I'll have you home before you know it."

He brought me to my apartment.

"I thought this was best," he said. "Didn't think you'd want your mother to see you in this condition." He searched through my pocketbook for the key and opened the door.

The apartment felt cool and neglected. Too quiet. No Rex spinning in his wheel. No light left burning to welcome me home.

The kitchen beckoned to my left. "I need a beer," I said to Morelli. I was in no rush for the shower. I'd lost my ability to smell. I'd accepted the condition of my hair.

I shuffled into the kitchen and tugged at the refrigerator door. The door swung wide, the fridge light went on, and I stared in dumb silence at a foot . . . a large, filthy, bloody foot, separated from the leg just above the ankle, placed next to a tub of margarine and a three-quarters-filled bottle of cranberry cocktail.

"There's a foot in my refrigerator," I said to Morelli. Bells clanged, lights flashed, my mouth went numb, and I crashed to the floor.

I struggled up from unconscious muck and opened my eyes. "Mom?"

"Not exactly," Morelli said.

"What happened?" I asked.

"You fainted."

"It was just too much," I said to Morelli. "The dog shit, the foot . . ."

"I understand," Morelli said.

I pushed myself up onto shaky legs.

"Why don't you go stand in the shower while I take care of things here?" Morelli said. He handed me a beer. "You can take your beer with you."

I looked at the beer. "Did this come from my refrigerator?"

"No," Morelli said. "It came from someplace else."

"Good. I couldn't drink it if it came from the refrigerator."

"I know," Morelli said, maneuvering me toward the bathroom. "Just go take a shower and drink your beer."

Two uniforms, a crime lab guy, and two guys in suits were in my kitchen when I got out of the shower.

"I've got an idea on the identity of that foot," I said to Morelli.

He was writing on a clipboard. "I've got the same idea." He turned the clipboard over to me. "Sign at the dotted line."

"What am I signing?"

"Preliminary report."

"How did Kenny get the foot into my refrigerator?"

"Broken bedroom window. You need an alarm system."

One of the uniforms left, carrying a large Styrofoam cooler.

I swallowed down a wave of revulsion. "Is that it?" I asked.

Morelli nodded. "I did a fast cleanup of your refrigerator. You'll probably want to do a more thorough job when you have time."

"Thanks. I appreciate the help."

"We went through the rest of the apartment," he said. "Didn't find anything."

The second uniform left, followed by the suits and the crime scene men.

"Now what?" I asked Morelli. "Not much point in staking out Sandeman's place."

"Now we watch Spiro."

"What about Roche?"

"Roche will stay with the funeral home. We'll tag after Spiro."

We taped a big plastic garbage bag over the broken window, shut the lights off, and locked the apartment. There was a small crowd in the hall.

"Well?" Mr. Wolesky asked. "What was this about? Nobody'll tell us nothing."

"It was just a broken window," I said. "I thought it might have been something more serious, so I called the police."

"Were you robbed?"

I shook my head no. "Nothing was taken." So far as I knew, that was the truth.

Mrs. Boyd didn't look like she was buying any of it. "What about the ice chest? I saw a policeman carry an ice chest out to his car."

"Beer," Morelli said. "They were friends of mine. We're going to a party later."

We ducked down the stairs and trotted to the van. Morelli opened the driver's side door, and sick-dog odor poured out, forcing us to retreat.

"Should have left the windows open," I said to Morelli.

"We'll let it sit for a minute," he said. "It'll be fine."

After a few minutes we crept closer.

"It still smells bad," I said.

Morelli stood fists on hips. "I don't have time to scrub it down. We'll try riding around with the windows open. Maybe we can blow it out."

Five minutes later, the smell hadn't faded.

"That's it for me," Morelli said. "I can't take this smell anymore. I'm trading up."

"You going home for your truck?"

He made a left onto Skinner Street. "Can't. The guy I borrowed the van from has my truck."

"The undercover pig car?"

"Being fixed." He hooked onto Greenwood. "We'll use the Buick."

Suddenly I had a new appreciation for the Buick.

Morelli pulled up behind Big Blue, and I had the door open and my foot to the pavement while the van was still rolling. I stood outside in the crisp air, breathing deep, flapping my arms and shaking my head to rid myself of any residual stench.

We got into the Buick together and sat there for a moment appreciating the lack of odor.

I rolled the engine over. "It's eleven o'clock. You want to go straight to Spiro's apartment, or do you want to try the funeral home?"

"Funeral home. I spoke to Roche just before you got out of the shower, and Spiro was still in his office."

The lot was empty when I got to Stiva's. There were several cars on the street. None looked occupied. "Where's Roche?"

"Apartment across the street. Over the deli."

"He can't see the back entrance from there."

"True, but the exterior lights work on motion sensors. If someone approaches the back door the lights will go on."

"I imagine Spiro can disengage that."

Morelli slouched in his seat. "There's no good vantage point for watching the back door. If Roche was sitting in the parking lot, he still couldn't see the back door."

Spiro's Lincoln was parked in the drive-through. The light was on in Spiro's office.

I eased the Buick to the curb and cut the engine. "He's working late. Usually he's out of here by now."

"You have your cell phone with you?"

I gave him the phone, and he tapped in a number.

Someone responded on the other end, and Morelli asked if anyone was home. I didn't hear the response. Morelli ended the call and returned the phone.

"Spiro's still there. Roche hasn't seen anyone go in since the doors closed at ten."

We were parked on a side street, beyond the reach of the streetlight. The side street was lined with modest row houses. Most were dark. The burg was an early-to-bed, early-to-rise community.

Morelli and I sat there in comfortable silence for half an hour, watching the funeral home. Just a couple of old law enforcement partners doing their job.

Twelve o'clock rolled around. Nothing had changed, and I was feeling antsy. "There's something wrong with this," I said. "Spiro never stays this late. He likes money when it comes easy. He's not the conscientious type."

"Maybe he's waiting for someone."

I had my hand on the door handle. "I'm going to snoop around."

"NO!"

"I want to see if the back sensors are working."

"You'll screw everything up. You'll spook Kenny if he's out there."

"Maybe Spiro shut the sensors off, and Kenny's already in the house."

"He's not."

"How can you be so sure?"

Morelli shrugged. "Gut instinct."

I cracked my knuckles.

"You're lacking some critical attributes of a good bounty hunter," Morelli said.

"Like what?"

"Patience. Look at you. You're all tied up in knots."

He applied pressure at the base of my neck with his thumb and inched his way up to my hairline. My eyes drooped closed, and my breathing slowed.

"Feel good?" Morelli asked.

"Mmmmm."

He worked my shoulders with both hands. "You need to relax."

"If I relax any more I'll melt and slide off the seat."

His hands stilled. "I like the melting part."

I turned my face toward him, and our eyes held.

"No," I said.

"Why not?"

"Because I've already seen the movie, and I hate the ending."

"Maybe it'll have a different ending this time."

"Maybe it won't."

His thumb traced over the pulse in my neck, and when he spoke his voice was low and cat's-tongue rough. "How about the middle of the movie? Did you like the middle?"

The middle of the movie had smoked. "I've seen better middles."

Morelli's face creased into a wide grin. "Liar."

"Besides, we're supposed to be watching for Spiro and Kenny."

"Don't worry about it. Roche is watching. If he sees anything he'll call my pager."

Was this what I wanted? Sex in a Buick with Joe Morelli? No! Maybe.

"I think I might be getting a cold," I said. "This might not be a good time."

Morelli made chicken sounds.

My eyes rolled to the top of my head. "That is so juvenile. That is just the response I'd expect from you."

"No it's not," Morelli said. You expected action." He leaned forward and kissed me. "How's this? Is this a better response?"

"Umm . . ."

He kissed me again, and I thought, well, what the hell—if he wants to get a cold, that's his problem, right? And maybe I wasn't getting a cold, anyway. Maybe I had been mistaken.

Morelli pushed my shirt aside and slipped the straps of my bra over my shoulders.

I felt a shiver ripple through me and chose to believe the shiver was from the cool air . . . as opposed to a premonition of doom. "So you're sure Roche will page you if he sees Kenny?" I asked.

"Yeah," Morelli said, lowering his mouth to my breast. "Nothing to worry about."

Nothing to worry about! He had his hand in my pants, and he was telling me I had nothing to worry about!

My eyes rolled to the top of my head again. What was my problem? I was an adult. I had needs. What was so wrong about satisfying those needs once in a while? Here I had a chance for a real quality orgasm. And it wasn't as if I had false expectations. I wasn't some dumb sixteen-year-old expecting a marriage proposal. All I expected was a goddamn orgasm. And I sure as hell deserved one. I hadn't had a social orgasm since Reagan was president.

I did a fast check of the windows. Totally fogged. That was good. Okay, I said to myself. Go for it. I kicked my shoes off, and stripped of everything but my black string bikinis.

"Now you," I said to Morelli. "I want to see you."

It took less than ten seconds for him to get undressed, five seconds of which he used up on guns and cuffs.

I snapped my mouth closed and surreptitiously checked for drool. Morelli was even more amazing than I'd remembered. And I'd remembered him as being freaking outstanding.

He hooked a finger under my bikini string, and in one fluid movement removed my panties. He tried to mount me, and hit his head on the steering wheel. "Been a long time since I've done this in a car," he said.

We scrambled to the back and fell together, Morelli in an unbuttoned washed denim shirt and white sweat socks, and me in a fresh rush of uncertainty.

"Spiro could kill the lights, and Kenny could sneak in the back door," I said.

Morelli kissed my shoulder. "Roche would know if Kenny was in the house."

"How would Roche know?"

Morelli sighed. "Roche would know because he's wired the house."

I pushed away. "You didn't tell me! How long has the house been wired?"

"You aren't going to make a big deal of this, are you?"

"What else haven't you told me?"

"That's it. I swear."

I didn't believe it for a second. He was wearing his cop face. I thought back to dinner, and how he'd miraculously appeared. "How did you know my mother was cooking lamb?"

"I smelled it when you opened the door."

"Bullshit!" I grabbed my purse from the front seat and dumped the contents between us. Hairbrush, hair spray, lipstick, pepper spray, travel pack of tissues, stun gun, gum, sunglasses . . . black plastic transformer. Fuck.

I snatched at the bug. "You son of a bitch! You wired my pocketbook!"

"It was for your own good. I was worried about you."

"That's despicable! That's an invasion of privacy! How dare you do this without asking me first!" And it was also a lie. He was afraid I'd get a bead on Kenny and not cut him in. I rolled the window down and threw the transformer out into the street.

"Shit," Morelli said. "That thing's worth four hundred dollars." He opened the door and went out to retrieve it.

I pulled the door closed and locked it. Damn him anyway. I should have known better than to try to work with a Morelli. I climbed over the seat and slid behind the wheel.

Morelli tried the passenger side door, but it was locked. All the doors were locked, and they were going to stay that way. He could freeze his stupid dick off for all I cared. Serve him right. I revved the engine and took off, leaving him standing in the middle of the street in his shirt and socks, with his woody hanging half-mast.

I got a block down Hamilton and reconsidered. Probably it wasn't a good idea to leave a cop standing naked in the middle of the street.

What would happen if a bad guy came along? Morelli probably couldn't even run in his condition. Okay, I thought, I'll help him out. I made a U-turn and retraced to the side street. Morelli was right where I'd left him. Hands on hips, looking disgusted.

I slowed, rolled my window down, and tossed him his gun. "Just in case," I said. Then I floored it and roared away.

CHAPTER 14

I quietly crept up the stairs and breathed a long sigh of relief when I was safely locked in my bedroom. I didn't want to explain my I've-been-making-out-in-a-Buick-rat's-nest hair to my mother. Nor did I want her to glean through X-ray vision that my panties were stuffed into my jacket pocket. I undressed with the lights off, slunk into bed, and pulled the covers up to my chin.

I awoke with two regrets. The first was that I'd left the stakeout and had no idea if Kenny had been caught. The second was that I'd missed my window of opportunity to use the bathroom, and once again, I was last in line.

I lay in bed, listening to people shuffle in and out of the bathroom . . . first my mother, then my father, then my grandmother. When Grandma Mazur creaked down the stairs, I wrapped myself in the pink quilted robe I'd gotten for my sixteenth birthday and padded to the bathroom. The window over the tub was closed against the cold, and the air inside was thick with the scent of shaving cream and Listerine.

I took a fast shower, towel-dried my hair, and dressed in jeans and a Rutgers sweatshirt. I had no special plans for the day, other than to keep an eye on Grandma Mazur and to keep tabs on Spiro. Of course, that was working on the assumption that Kenny hadn't gotten himself caught last night.

I followed my nose to coffee brewing in the kitchen and found Morelli eating breakfast at the kitchen table. From the look of his plate he'd just finished bacon and eggs and toast. He slouched back at the sight of me, coffee cup in hand. His expression was speculative.

"Morning," he said, voice even, eyes not giving up any secrets.

I poured coffee into a mug. "Morning." Noncommittal. "What's new?"

"Nothing. Your paycheck is still out there."

"You come by to tell me that?"

"I came by to get my wallet. I think I left it in your car last night."

"Right." Along with various articles of clothing.

I took a slurp of coffee and set the cup on the counter. "I'll get your wallet."

Morelli stood. "Thank you for breakfast," he said to my mother. "It was wonderful."

My mother beamed. "Any time. Always nice to have Stephanie's friends here."

He followed me out and waited while I unlocked the car and scooped his clothes together.

"Were you telling the truth about Kenny?" I asked. "He didn't show up last night?"

"Spiro stayed until a little after two. Sounded like he was playing computer games. That was all Roche picked up on the bug. No phone calls. No Kenny."

"Spiro was waiting for something that never happened."

"Looks like it."

The tan wreck of a cop car was parked behind my Buick. "I see you got your car back," I said to Morelli. It had all the same dents and scrapes, and the bumper was still in the backseat. "I thought you said it was being fixed."

"It was," Morelli said. "They fixed the lights." He glanced over at the house and then back at me. "Your mother is standing at the door, watching us."

"Yep."

"If she wasn't standing there, I'd grab you and shake you until the fillings fell out of your teeth."

"Police brutality."

"It has nothing to do with being a cop. It has to do with being Italian."

I handed him his shoes. "I'd really like to be in on the takedown."

"I'll do the best I can to include you."

We locked eyes. Did I believe him? No.

Morelli fished car keys out of his pocket. "You'd better think of a good story to tell your mother. She's going to want to know why my clothes were in your car."

"She won't think anything of it. I've got men's clothes in my car all the time."

Morelli grinned.

"What were those clothes?" my mother asked when I came into the house. "Pants and shoes?"

"You don't want to know."

"I want to know," Grandma Mazur said. "I bet it's a pip of a story."

"How's your hand?" I asked her. "Does it hurt?"

"Only hurts if I make a fist, and I can't do that with this big bandage on. I'd be in a pickle if it had been my right hand."

"Got any plans for today?"

"Not until tonight. Joe Loosey is still laid out. I only got to see his penis, you know, so I thought I'd like to go see the rest of him at the seven o'clock viewing."

My father was in the living room, reading his paper. "When I go, I want to be cremated," he said. "No viewing."

My mother turned from the stove. "Since when?"

"Since Loosey lost his Johnson. I don't want to take any chances. I want to go right from wherever I fall to the crematorium."

My mother set a plateful of scrambled eggs in front of me. She added a side of bacon, toast, and juice.

I ate my eggs and considered my options. I could sequester myself in the house and do my protective granddaughter thing, I could drag Grandma around with me while I did my protective granddaughter thing, or I could go about my business and hope Grandma wasn't on Kenny's agenda today.

"More eggs?" my mother asked. "Another piece of toast?"

"I'm fine."

"You're all bones. You should eat more."

"I'm not all bones. I'm fat. I can't button the top snap on my jeans."

"You're thirty years old. You have to expect to spread when you hit thirty. What are you doing still wearing jeans, anyway? A person your age shouldn't be dressing like a kid." She leaned forward and studied my face. "What's wrong with your eye? It looks like it's twitching again."

All right, eliminate option number one.

"I need to keep some people under surveillance," I said to Grandma Mazur. "You want to tag along?"

"I guess I could do that. You think it'll get rough?"

"No. I think it'll be boring."

"Well, if I wanted to be bored I could sit home. Who are we looking for, anyway? Are we looking for that miserable Kenny Mancuso?"

Actually, I'd intended to hang tight to Morelli. In a roundabout way I suppose it amounted to the same thing. "Yeah, we're looking for Kenny Mancuso."

"Then I'm all for it. I have a score to settle with him."

Half an hour later she was ready to go, wearing her jeans and ski jacket and Doc Martens.

I spotted Morelli's car a block down from Stiva's on Hamilton. Didn't look like Morelli was in the car. Probably Morelli was with Roche, swapping war stories. I parked behind Morelli, being careful not to creep too close and knock out his lights, again. I could see the front and side door to the funeral home, and the front door to Roche's building.

"I know all about how to do this stakeout stuff," Grandma said. "They had some private eyes on television the other night, and they didn't leave out a thing." She stuck her head into the canvas tote bag she'd hauled along. "I got everything we need in here. I got magazines to pass the time. I got sandwiches and sodas. I even got a bottle."

"What kind of bottle?"

"Used to have olives in it." She showed me the bottle. "It's so we can pee on the job. All the private eyes said they did this."

"I can't pee in that bottle. Only men can pee in bottles."

"Darn," Grandma said. "Why didn't I think of that? I went and threw away all the olives, too."

We read the magazine and tore out a few recipes. We ate the sandwiches and drank the sodas.

After drinking the sodas we both needed to go to the bathroom, so we went back to my parents' house for a potty break. We returned to

Hamilton, slid into the same parking place behind Morelli, and continued to wait.

"You're right," Grandma said after an hour. "This is boring."

We played hangman and counted cars and verbally trashed Joyce Barnhardt. We'd just started twenty questions when I glanced out the window at oncoming traffic and recognized Kenny Mancuso. He was driving a two-tone Chevy Suburban that looked to be as big as a bus. We exchanged surprised stares for the longest heartbeat in history.

"Shit!" I shouted, fumbling with the ignition key, swiveling in my seat to keep him in sight.

"Get this car moving," Grandma yelled. "Don't let that son of a skunk get away!"

I wrenched the gearshift into drive and was about to pull out when I realized Kenny had U-turned at the intersection and was closing ground between us. There were no cars parked behind me. I saw the Suburban swerve to the curb and told Grandma to brace herself.

The Suburban crashed into the back of the Buick, bouncing us forward into Morelli's car, which crashed into the car in front of him. Kenny backed the Suburban up, stepped on the gas, and rammed us again.

"Well, that takes it," Grandma said. "I'm too old for this kind of bouncing around. I got delicate bones at my age." She pulled a .45 long-barrel out of her tote bag, wrenched her door open, and scrambled out onto the sidewalk. "Guess this will show you something," she said, aiming the gun at the Suburban. She pulled the trigger, fire flashed from the barrel, and the kick knocked her on her ass.

Kenny floored the Suburban in reverse all the way to the intersection and took off.

"Did I get him?" Grandma wanted to know.

"No," I said, helping her to her feet.

"Did I come close?"

"Hard to say."

She had her hand to her forehead. "Hit myself in the head with the dang gun. Didn't expect that much of a kick."

We walked around the cars, surveying the damage. The Buick was virtually unscathed. A scratch in the chrome on the big back bumper. No damage that I could find in the front.

Morelli's car looked like an accordion. The hood and the trunk lid were crumpled, and all the lights were broken. The first car in line had been shoved a couple feet forward, but didn't look bashed. A small dent in the back bumper, which may or may not have been the result of this accident.

I looked up the street, expecting Morelli to come running, but Morelli didn't appear.

"Are you okay?" I asked Grandma Mazur.

"Sure," Grandma said. "I would have got that slimeball too if it wasn't for my injury. Had to shoot with one hand."

"Where'd you get the forty-five?"

"My friend Elsie loaned it to me," Grandma said. "She got it at a yard sale when she lived in Washington, D.C." She rolled her eyes up in her head. "Am I bleeding?"

"No, but you've got a notch in your forehead. Maybe we should take you home to rest."

"That might be a good idea," she said. "My knees feel sort of rubbery. Guess I'm not so tough as them television people. Shooting off guns never seems to take anything out of them."

I got Grandma in the car and clicked the seat belt across her chest. I took one last look at the damage and wondered about liability for the first car in line. The damage was minimal to none, but I left my business card under the windshield wiper in case he discovered the dent and wanted an explanation.

I assumed I didn't have to do this for Morelli, since I'd be the first person who came to mind.

"Probably it'd be best if we don't mention anything about the gun when we get home," I told Grandma. "You know how Mom is about guns."

"That's okay by me," Grandma said. "I'd just as leave forget the whole thing. Can't believe I missed that car. Didn't even blow out a tire."

My mother raised her eyebrows when she saw the two of us straggle in. "Now what?" my mother asked. She squinted at Grandma. "What happened to your head?"

"Hit myself with a soda can," Grandma said. "Freak accident."

Half an hour later Morelli came knocking at the door. "I want to see you . . . outside," he said, hooking his hand around my arm, jerking me forward.

"It wasn't my fault," I told him. "Grandma and I were sitting in the

Buick, minding our own business, when Kenny came up behind us and knocked us into your car."

"You want to run that by me again?"

"He was driving a two-tone Suburban. He saw Grandma and me parked on Hamilton. He made a U-turn and rammed us from behind. Twice. Then Grandma jumped out of the car and shot at him, and he drove away."

"That's the lamest story I've ever heard."

"It's true!"

Grandma stuck her head out the door. "What's going on out here?"

"He thinks I made up the story about Kenny hitting us with the Suburban."

Grandma snagged the tote bag from the hall table. She rummaged through it, came up with the .45-long barrel, and aimed it at Morelli.

"Jesus!" Morelli said, ducking out of the way, taking the gun from Grandma. "Where the hell did you get this cannon?"

"Borrowed it," Grandma said. "And I used it on your no-good cousin, but he got away."

Morelli studied his shoes for a beat before speaking. "I don't suppose this gun is registered?"

"What do you mean?" Grandma asked. "Registered where?"

"Get rid of it," Morelli said to me. "Get it out of my sight."

I shoved Grandma back inside with the gun and closed the door. "I'll take care of it," I said to Morelli. "I'll make sure it's returned to its owner."

"So this ridiculous story is true?"

"Where were you? Why didn't you see any of this?"

"I was relieving Roche. I was watching the funeral home. I wasn't watching my car." He glanced over at the Buick. "No damage?"

"Scratched the rear bumper."

"Does the army know about this car?"

I thought it was time to remind Morelli of my usefulness. "Did you run a check on Spiro's guns?"

"They all checked out. Registered nice and legal."

So much for usefulness.

"Stephanie," my mother called from inside. "Are you out there without a coat? You're going to catch your death."

"Speaking of death," Morelli said. "They found a body to go with your foot. It floated into one of the bridge supports this morning."

"Sandeman?"

"Yeah."

"You think Kenny is self-destructing, looking to get caught?"

"I think it's not that complicated. He's a squirrel. This started out as a clever way to make a lot of money. Something went wrong, the operation got fucked up, and Kenny couldn't handle it. Now he's wound up so tight his eyes are crossed, and he's looking for people to blame . . . Moogey, Spiro, you."

"He's lost it, hasn't he?"

"Big time."

"You think Spiro is as crazy as Kenny?"

"Spiro isn't crazy. Spiro is small."

It was true. Spiro was a pimple on the burg's butt. I glanced over at Morelli's car. It didn't look drivable. "You need a ride somewhere?"

"I can manage."

Stiva's lot was already filled at seven o'clock, and cars lined the curb for two blocks down Hamilton. I double-parked just short of the service driveway and told Grandma she should go in without me.

She'd changed into a dress and the big blue coat and looked very colorful marching up Stiva's front steps with her apricot hair. She had her black patent leather purse tucked into the crook of her arm, and her bandaged hand stood out like a white flag, proclaiming her as one of the walking wounded in the war against Kenny Mancuso.

I circled the block twice before finding a spot. I hustled to the funeral parlor, entered through the side door, and steeled myself against the claustrophobic hothouse heat and crowd murmur. When this was over I was never again going into a funeral parlor. I didn't care who died. I wasn't having any part of it. Could be my mother or my grandmother. They were going to have to manage on their own.

I sidled up to Roche at the tea table. "I see your brother's being buried tomorrow morning."

"Yeah. Boy, I sure am going to miss this place. I'm going to miss these cheapskate, sawdust cookies. And I'm going to miss the tea. Yum, I sure do love tea." He looked around. "Hell, I don't know what

I'm complaining about. I've had worse assignments. Last year I was on a stakeout, dressed up like a bag lady, and I got mugged. Got two broken ribs."

"Have you seen my grandmother?"

"Yeah. I saw her come in, but then I lost her in the crowd. I imagine she's trying to get a look at the guy that had his . . . um, thing, whacked off."

I put my head down and muscled my way into the room where Joe Loosey was laid out. I elbowed to the front until I reached the casket and the widow Loosey. I'd expected Grandma to have insinuated herself into the space reserved for the immediate family, her reasoning being that she'd seen Joe's penis and was now on intimate terms.

"I'm sorry for your loss," I said to Mrs. Loosey. "Have you seen Grandmother Mazur?"

She looked alarmed. "Edna is here?"

"I dropped her off about ten minutes ago. I expected she'd have come to pay her respects."

Mrs. Loosey put a protective hand on the casket. "I haven't seen her."

I pushed through the crowd and dropped in on Roche's fake brother. A handful of people were in the back of the room. From the level of animation I'd guess they were talking about the great penis scandal. I asked if anyone had seen Grandma Mazur. The answers were negative. I returned to the lobby. I checked the kitchen, the ladies' room, the porch to the side door. I questioned everyone in my path.

No one had seen a little old lady in a big blue coat.

Prickles of alarm had begun to dance along my spine. This was uncharacteristic of Grandma. She liked to be in the thick of things. I'd seen her walk through Stiva's front door, so I knew she was in the house . . . at least for a short time. I didn't think it likely she'd gone back outside. I hadn't seen her on the street while I was searching for a parking space. And I couldn't imagine her leaving without taking a peek at Loosey.

I walked upstairs and prowled through the second story rooms where caskets and files were stored. I cracked the door to the business office and flipped the light switch. The office was empty. The upstairs bathroom was empty. The walk-in linen closet that was filled with office supplies was empty.

I returned to the lobby and noticed Roche was no longer at the tea table. Spiro was alone at the front door, looking sour.

"I can't find Grandma Mazur," I said to him.

"Congratulations."

"Not funny. I'm worried about her."

"You should be. She's nuts."

"Have you seen her?"

"No. And it's the only decent thing that's happened to me in two days."

"I thought maybe I should check the back rooms."

"She's not in the back. I keep the doors locked during public hours."

"She can be sort of ingenious when she has her mind set on something."

"If she managed to get back there she wouldn't stay long. Fred Dagusto is on table number one, and he's not a pretty sight. Three hundred and ten pounds of ugly flesh. Fat as far as the eye can see. Gonna have to grease him up to shoehorn him into a casket."

"I want to look at those rooms."

Spiro glanced at his watch. "You're going to have to wait until hours are over. I can't leave these ghouls unsupervised. You get a big crowd like this, and people start walking off with souvenirs. You don't watch the door, and you could lose the shirt off your back."

"I don't need a guide. Just give me the key."

"Forget it. I'm liable when there's a stiff on the table. I'm not taking any chances after Loosey."

"Where's Louie?"

"Has the day off."

I went out onto the front porch and stared across the street. The windows in the surveillance apartment were dark. Roche was probably there, listening and looking. Maybe Morelli was there, too. I was worried about Grandma Mazur, but I wasn't ready to drag Morelli into it. Better to let him watch the exterior of the building, for now.

I stepped off the porch and made my way to the side entrance. I scanned the parking lot and continued on to the garages at the rear, cupping my hands to see through the tinted hearse windows, examining the bed of the open-backed flower car, knocking on the trunk lid to Spiro's Lincoln.

The door to the cellar was locked, but the service door to the kitchen was open. I let myself in and did another run-through of the house, trying the door to the workrooms and finding it sealed tight, as promised.

I slipped into Spiro's office and used his phone to call home.

"Is Grandma Mazur there?" I asked my mother.

"Oh my God," my mother said. "You've lost your grandmother. Where are you?"

"I'm at the funeral parlor. I'm sure Grandma is here somewhere. It's just that there's a crush of people, and I'm having a hard time finding her."

"She isn't here."

"If she shows up, call me at Stiva's."

I dialed Ranger next and told him my problem, and that I might need help.

I went back to Spiro and told him if he didn't give me a tour of the embalming room I'd zing some electricity into his worthless hide. He thought about it for a moment, whirled on his heel, and stalked past the viewing rooms. He threw the hall door open with a crash and snapped back at me to make it fast.

As if I'd want to dawdle over Fred Dagusto.

"She isn't here," I said, returning to Spiro, who was straddling the doorjamb, keeping an eagle eye out for unusual bulges in overcoats that might indicate a mourner was absconding with a stolen roll of toilet paper.

"Yeah, right," he said. "Big surprise."

"The only place I haven't looked is the basement."

"She isn't in the basement. The door is locked. Just like this one was locked."

"I want to see."

"Listen," Spiro said. "She's probably gone off with some other old broad. She's probably at some diner, driving some poor waitress nuts."

"Let me into the cellar, and I swear I won't bother you anymore."

"That's a cheery thought."

An old man clapped a hand on Spiro's shoulder. "How's Con doing? He outta the hospital yet?"

"Yeah," Spiro said, brushing past. "He's out of the hospital. He'll be back to work next week. Monday."

"Bet you'll be happy to see him come back."

"Yeah, I'm jumping for joy just thinking about it."

Spiro crossed to the other side of the lobby, slithering between knots of people, ignoring some, toadying up to others. I followed him to the cellar door and waited impatiently while he fumbled with keys. My heart was skittering in my chest, fearful of what I might find at the foot of the stairs.

I wanted Spiro to be right. I wanted Grandma to be at a diner somewhere with one of her cronies, but I didn't think it was likely.

If she'd been forcibly removed from the house, Morelli or Roche would have acted. Unless she'd been taken out the back door. The back door was their blind spot. Still, they'd compensated for that by planting a bug. And if the bugs were working, Morelli and Roche would have heard me looking for Grandma and would be doing their thing . . . whatever that was.

I flipped the stairwell light switch and called out. "Grandma?"

The furnace roared in some far-off place, and there was the murmur of voices in the rooms behind me. A small circle of light brightened the cellar floor at the bottom of the stairs. I squinted to see beyond the light, strained to hear whatever small sound the cellar might offer up.

My stomach clenched at the silence. Someone was down there. I could feel it, just as surely as I could feel Spiro's breath on my neck.

The truth is, I'm not the heroic type. I'm afraid of spiders and extraterrestrials and sometimes feel the need to check under my bed for drooly guys with claws. If I ever found one I'd run screaming out of my apartment and never come back.

"The meter's running," Spiro said. "You going down there, or what?"

I rummaged through my pocketbook for my .38 and descended the stairs with gun drawn. Stephanie Plum, chickenshit bounty hunter, takes stairs one at a time, practically blinded because her heart is beating in her throat so hard it's knocking her head back and forth, blurring her vision.

I steadied myself on the last step, reached left, and flipped the light switch. Nothing happened.

"Hey, Spiro," I called. "The lights won't go on."

He hunkered down at the top of the stairs. "Must be the circuit breaker."

"Where's the box?"

"To your right, behind the furnace."

Damn. Everything was black to my right. I reached for my flashlight, and before I could withdraw my hand from my pocketbook, Kenny sprang out of the shadows. He hit me from the side, and we both crashed to the floor, the impact knocking me breathless, the jolt sending my .38 skittering off into the dark, beyond my grasp. I scrambled to my feet and was slammed flat onto my chest. A knee jammed between my shoulder blades, and there was the prick of something very sharp pressed against the side of my neck.

"Don't fucking move," Kenny said. "You move an inch, and I'll shove this knife into your throat."

I heard the door close at the top of the stairs, heard Spiro hurry down. "Kenny? What the hell are you doing down here? How'd you get in?"

"I got in through the cellar door. I used the key you gave me. How the hell else would I get in."

"I didn't know you were coming back. I thought you got all the stuff stashed last night."

"Came back to check on things. Wanted to make sure everything was still here."

"What the hell's that supposed to mean?"

"It means you make me nervous," Kenny said.

"I make *you* nervous? That's good. You're the one who's fucking squirrelly, and I make *you* nervous."

"Better watch who you're calling fucking squirrelly."

"Let me tell you the difference between you and me," Spiro said. "This is all business for me. I act like a professional. Somebody stole the caskets, so I hired an expert to find them. I didn't go around shooting my partner in the knee because I was pissed. And I wasn't so stupid that I used a fucking stolen gun to shoot him with and then got myself caught by an off-duty cop. I wasn't so fucking nuts that I thought my partners were plotting against me. I didn't think this was some fucking coup.

"And I didn't go wacko over sweetie pie here. You know what your problem is, Kenny? You get on an idea, and you can't get off. You get obsessed with shit, and then you can't see anything else. And you always have to be the fucking show-off. You could have gotten rid of

Sandeman nice and quiet, but no, you had to hack off his fucking foot."

Kenny chuckled. "And I'll tell you what *your* problem is, Spiro. You don't know how to have fun. Always the serious undertaker. You should try sticking that big-bore needle into something alive for a change."

"You're sick."

"Yeah, you're not so healthy yourself. You've spent enough time watching me work my magic."

I could hear Spiro shift behind me. "You're talking too much."

"Doesn't matter. Sweetie pie isn't going to tell anyone. She and her granny are going to disappear."

"Fine by me. Just don't do it here. I don't want to be involved." Spiro crossed the room, flipped the circuit breaker, and the lights flashed on.

Five crated caskets lined one wall, the furnace and water heater sat in the middle of the room, and a jumble of crates and boxes had been stacked next to the back door. It didn't take a genius to guess the contents of the crates and boxes.

"I don't get it," I said. "Why did you bring the stuff here? Con is coming back to work on Monday. How will you keep this from him?"

"It'll be gone by Monday," Spiro said. "We brought everything in yesterday, so we could take inventory. Sandeman was carrying the whole shitload around in his pickup, doing fucking tailgate sales. Lucky for us you saw the furniture truck in Delio's. Another couple of weeks with Sandeman running loose and nothing would have been left."

"I don't know how you got it in, but you'll never get it out," I said. "Morelli is watching the house."

Kenny snorted. "It goes out the same way it came in. In the meat wagon."

"For Christ's sake," Spiro said. "It's not a meat wagon."

"Oh yeah, I forgot. It's a slumber coach." Kenny stood up and yanked me to my feet. "The cops watch Spiro, and they watch the house. They don't watch the slumber coach and Louie Moon. Or at least who they think is Louie Moon. You could put a hat on Bonzo the chimp and put him behind those tinted windows, and the cops would think it was Louie Moon. And good old Louie is real cooperative. You just give Louie a hose and tell him to clean things up, and Louie is busy for hours. He don't know who's driving around in his goddamn slumber coach."

Not bad. They dressed Kenny up to look like Louie Moon, brought the guns and ammo to the funeral home in the hearse, parked the hearse in the garage, and then all they had to do was run the boxes between the garage and the back door to the cellar. And Morelli and Roche couldn't see the back door to the cellar. They probably couldn't hear anything in the cellar either. I didn't think it likely Roche would have bugged the cellar.

"So what's with the old lady?" Spiro asked Kenny.

"She was in the kitchen looking for a teabag, and she saw me cutting across the lawn."

Spiro's face tightened. "Did she tell anybody?"

"No. She came barreling out of the house, yelling at me for stabbing her in the hand. Telling me I needed to learn respect for old people."

So far as I could see, Grandma wasn't in the cellar. I hoped it meant Kenny had her locked in the garage. If she was in the garage she might still be alive, and she might be unhurt. If she was tucked away somewhere in the cellar, beyond my view, she was much too quiet.

I didn't want to consider the reasons for too quiet, preferring to squash the panic clawing at my stomach and replace it with some more constructive emotion. How about cool reasoning? Nope. I didn't have any of that available. How about cunning? Sorry, low on cunning. How about anger? Did I have any anger? Fucking A. I had so much anger my skin could hardly contain it all. Anger for Grandma, anger for all the women Mancuso'd abused, anger for the cops who were killed with the stolen ammo. I pulled the anger in until it was hard and razor sharp.

"Now what?" I said to Kenny. "Where do we go from here?"

"Now we put you on ice for a while. Until the house empties out. Then I'll see what kind of a mood I'm in. We have a bunch of options being that we're in a funeral parlor. Hell, we could strap you to the table and embalm you while you're still alive. That would be fun." He pressed the tip of the knife blade to the back of my neck. "Walk."

"Where?"

He jerked his head. "Over to the corner."

The crated caskets were stacked in the corner. "To the caskets?"

He smiled and prodded me forward. "The caskets come later."

I squinted into the corner shadows and realized the caskets weren't flush to the wall. Tucked behind the caskets was a refrigeration unit with two body drawers. The drawers were closed, the metal trays locked behind heavy metal doors.

"Gonna be nice and dark in there," Kenny said. "Give you time to think."

Fear slid down my spine and sickened my stomach. "Grandma Mazur . . ."

"Turning into a Popsicle, even as we speak."

"NO! Let her out! Open the drawer, I'll do whatever you want!"

"You'll do whatever I want anyway," Kenny said. "You're not going to be moving too fast after an hour in there."

Tears were pouring down my cheeks and sweat prickled under my arms. "She's old. She's no threat to you. Let her go."

"No threat? Are you kidding? That old lady is criminally insane. You know what it took to get her in that drawer?"

"She's probably dead by now, anyway," Spiro said.

Kenny looked at him. "You think so?"

"How long she been in there?"

Kenny checked his watch. "Maybe ten minutes."

Spiro stuffed his hands into his pockets. "You lower the temperature?"

"No," Kenny said. "I just shoved her in."

"We don't keep the drawers cold if they're unoccupied," Spiro explained. "Saves on electricity. Probably it's only around room temperature."

"Yeah, but she could have died from fright. What do you think?" Kenny asked me. "You think she's dead?"

A sob stuck in my chest.

"Sweetie pie is speechless," Kenny said. "Maybe we should open the drawer and see if the old bag's breathing?"

Spiro released the latch and yanked the door open. He grabbed the end of the stainless steel tray and slowly rolled it toward him, so that the first thing I saw was Grandma Mazur's shoes pointing toes up, then Grandma's bony shin, her big blue coat, arms rigidly at her sides, hands hidden under the folds of the coat.

I felt myself sway under a wave of grief. I forced air into my lungs and blinked to clear my vision.

The tray reached its full extension and clicked into place. Grandma stared unflinching at the ceiling, eyes open, mouth set, still as stone.

We all gaped at her in silence for several moments.

Kenny was the first to speak. "She looks dead all right," he said. "Roll her back in."

The whisper of a sound stuck in the corner. A hiss. We all pricked our ears and concentrated. I saw the very slightest tightening around Grandma's eye. The hiss again. Louder this time. Grandma sucking air through her dentures!

"Hmmm," Kenny said. "Maybe she's not dead yet."

"You should have cranked the unit down," Spiro offered. "This baby'll go down to zero. She wouldn't have lasted ten minutes if you'd had it at zero."

Grandma made some feeble movements on the tray.

"What's she doing?" Spiro asked.

"She's trying to sit up," Kenny said. "But she's too old. Can't get those old bones to cooperate, huh, Granny?"

"Old," she whispered. "I'll show you old."

"Shove the drawer back in," Kenny said to Spiro. "And fix the freezer setting."

Spiro started to roll the tray in, but Grandma kicked out with her feet, stopping the slide. She had her knees bent, and she was pounding against the steel with her feet, clawing and knocking inside the drawer.

Spiro grunted and rammed the tray home, but the tray was inches short of clicking into place, and the door wouldn't close.

"Something's stuck," Spiro said. "This won't go in all the way."

"Open it up," Kenny said, "and see what's wrong."

Spiro eased the tray back.

Grandma's chin appeared, her nose, her eyes. Her arms were extended over her head.

"You making problems, Granny?" Kenny asked. "You jamming the drawer with something?"

Grandma didn't say anything, but I could see her mouth working, her dentures grinding against each other.

"Get your arms down at your sides," Kenny told her. "Stop fucking with me. I'm gonna lose my patience."

Grandma struggled to get her arms out, and finally her bandaged hand popped free. The other hand followed, and in that hand was the .45 long-barrel. She swung her arm straight from the shoulder and squeezed off a round.

We all hit the floor, and she fired again.

Silence followed the second shot. No one moved but Grandma. She elbowed herself to a sitting position, and took a moment to settle.

"I know what you're thinking," Grandma said into the silence. "Do I have any more bullets in this here gun? Well, with all the confusion, what with being locked up in a refrigerator, I plum forgot what was in here to start with. But being that this is a forty-five Magnum, the most powerful handgun in existence, and it could blow your head clean off, you just got to ask yourself one question. Do you feel lucky today? Well, do you, punk?"

"Christ," Spiro whispered. "She thinks she's fucking Clint Eastwood."

BAM! Grandma fired and knocked out a light.

"Dang," she said, "must be something wrong with this sight."

Kenny scrambled to the ammo cases to get a gun, Spiro ran for the stairs, and I inched toward Grandma on my belly.

BAM! She got another shot off. It missed Kenny, but it tore into one of the cases. There was an instant explosion, and a fireball rose to the basement ceiling.

I jumped to my feet and dragged Grandma off the tray.

Another case exploded. Fire crackled across the floor and traced along the wooden casket casings. I didn't know what was exploding, but I thought we were lucky not to have been hit by flying fragments. Smoke roiled from the burning boxes, cutting into the light, stinging my eyes.

I yanked Grandma to the back door and shoved her out into the yard.

"Are you okay?" I yelled at her.

"He was going to kill me," she said. "He was going to kill you too."

"Yes."

"It's terrible what happens to people. That they lose respect for life."

"Yes."

Grandma looked back at the house. "Good thing not everyone's like Kenny. Good thing some human beings are decent."

"Like us," I said.

"Well, I suppose, but I was thinking more of Dirty Harry."

"That was some speech you gave."

"Always wanted to give that speech. Guess there's a silver lining to everything."

"Can you walk around to the front of the building? Can you find Morelli and tell him I'm back here?"

Grandma lurched toward the driveway. "If he's there, I'll find him."

Kenny had been on the opposite side of the cellar when we rushed to get out. Either he'd gone up the stairs, or he was still inside, making his way close to the floor, trying to get to the back door. I was putting my money on the latter. Too many people at the top of the stairs.

I was standing about twenty feet from the door, and I wasn't sure what I'd do if Kenny appeared. I didn't have a gun or a defense spray. I didn't even have a flashlight. Probably I should get the hell out of there and forget about Kenny. The money's not worth it, I said to myself.

Who was I kidding? This wasn't about money. This was about Grandma.

There was another small explosion, and flames flared through the kitchen windows. People shouted from the street, and I could hear sirens in the distance. Smoke poured through the cellar door and swirled around a human form. A hellish creature, backlit by fire. Kenny.

He bent at the waist and coughed and took in some air. His hands hung loose at his sides. Didn't look like he'd been able to find a gun. That was a break. I saw him glance side to side and then come straight toward me. My heart almost jumped out of my chest, until I realized he didn't see me. I was standing, lost in shadow, in his line of escape. He was going to skirt the garage and disappear into the back alleys of the burg.

He moved stealthily forward, silent against the roar of the fire. He was less than five feet away when he saw me. He stopped short, startled, and our eyes locked. My first thought was that he would bolt and run, but he lunged at me on an oath, and we both went down, kicking and clawing. I gave him a good shot with my knee and stuck my thumb in his eye.

Kenny howled and pushed off, rising to a crouch. I grabbed for his foot, and he went down again, hard on his knees. We did more rolling on the ground. More kicking and clawing and swearing.

He was bigger and stronger than me, and probably crazier. Although some might argue that last point. What I had on my side was anger. Kenny was desperate, but I was freaked-out enraged.

I didn't just want to stop him . . . I wanted to hurt him. Not a nice thing to have to admit. I'd never thought of myself as a mean and vengeful person, but there it was.

I squeezed my hand tight in a fist and swung into him backhand, landing a blow that sent shock waves up my arm. There'd been a crunch and a gasp, and I saw him flail out in the darkness, arms wide open.

I grabbed hold of his shirt and shouted for help.

His hands clamped onto my neck, his breath hot on my face. His voice was thick. "Die."

Maybe, but he'd go down with me. I had his shirt in a death grip. The only way he was going to get away was to take the damn thing off. If he strangled me unconscious, I'd still have my fingers dug into his shirt.

I was so focused on the shirt it took me a while to realize the pack had enlarged to three.

"Jesus," Morelli was yelling in my ear. "Let go of his shirt!"

"He'll get away!"

"He won't get away," Morelli shouted. "I've got him."

I looked beyond Morelli and saw Ranger and Roche round the corner of the house with two uniforms.

"Get her off me," Kenny screeched. "Jesus! These Plum bitches are goddamn animals!"

There was another crunch in the darkness, and I suspected Morelli had accidentally broken something belonging to Kenny. Like his nose, maybe.

CHAPTER 15

I had Rex's cage wrapped in a big blue blanket so he wouldn't get a chill while I transported him. I eased him off the Buick's front seat and pushed the door closed with my butt. It was nice to be moving back to my apartment. And it was nice to feel safe. Kenny was locked up without bail, and I expected he'd be locked up for a good long time. Hopefully for life.

Rex and I took the elevator. The doors slid open on the second floor, and I stepped out feeling good inside. I loved my hallway, and I loved Mr. Wolesky, and I loved Mrs. Bestler. It was nine o'clock in the morning, and I was going to take a shower in my very own bathroom. I loved my bathroom.

I balanced Rex on my hip while I unlocked my door. Later today I'd stop by the office and pick up my recovery fee. Then I'd go shopping. Maybe I'd buy a new refrigerator.

I set Rex on the table by the couch and opened the curtains. I loved my curtains. I stood there for a while, admiring my view of the parking lot, thinking that I also loved the parking lot.

"Home," I said. Nice and quiet. Private.

There was a knock at the door.

I squinted through the peephole. It was Morelli.

"Thought you'd want to get filled in on some details," Morelli said.

I opened the door to him and stepped back. "Kenny talked?"

Morelli moved into the foyer. His posture was relaxed, but his eyes ticked off the details of his surroundings. Always the cop. "Enough to piece things together," he said. "Turns out there were three conspirators, just as we thought . . . Kenny, Moogey, and Spiro. And they each had a key to the storage locker."

"One for all, and all for one."

"More like nobody trusted anybody else. Kenny was the brains behind it all. He planned the theft, and he had an overseas buyer for the stolen ammo."

"The phone numbers to Mexico and El Salvador."

"Yeah. He also got a nice advance . . ."

"Which he spent ahead of time."

"Yep. Then he went to the locker to get the stuff ready for shipment, and guess what?"

"No stuff."

"Yep again," Morelli said. "Why are you wearing your jacket?"

"I just got in." I looked wistfully toward the bathroom. "I was about to take a shower."

"Hmmm," Morelli said.

"No hmmm. Tell me about Sandeman. Where does Sandeman figure in?"

"Sandeman heard some conversations between Moogey and Spiro and got curious. So he tapped into one of the many skills he acquired during a life of petty crime, duped the locker key off Moogey's key ring, and by process of lengthy elimination, found the locker."

"Who killed Moogey?"

"Sandeman. He got nervous. Thought Moogey might have eventually figured out about the borrowed furniture truck."

"And Sandeman told all of this to Kenny?"

"Kenny can be very persuasive."

There was no doubt in my mind.

Morelli played with the zipper on my jacket. "About that shower . . ."

I pointed with straight arm and extended finger to my door. "Out."

"Don't you want to know about Spiro?"

"What about Spiro?"

"We haven't caught him yet."

"He's probably gone underground."

Morelli winced.

"That's undertaker humor," I told him.

"One more thing. Kenny had an interesting spin on how the fire got started."

"Lies. All lies."

"You could have avoided a lot of terror if you'd just left that bug in your pocketbook."

I narrowed my eyes and crossed my arms over my chest. "This is a subject best forgotten."

"You left me standing bare-assed in the middle of the street!"

"I gave you your gun, didn't I?"

Morelli grinned. "You're going to give me more than that, cupcake."

"Forget it."

"Not likely," Morelli said. "You owe me."

"I owe you nothing! If anyone is owed, it's me! I caught your cousin for you!"

"And in the process burned down Stiva's Mortuary and destroyed thousands of dollars' worth of government property."

"Well, if you're going to be picky about it . . ."

"Picky? Sweetie pie, you are the worst bounty hunter in the history of the world."

"That does it. I have better things to do than to stand here and take your insults."

I pushed him out of my foyer, into the hall, slammed the door closed, and threw the bolt. I pressed my nose to the door and looked through the peephole.

Morelli grinned at me.

"This is war," I yelled through the door.

"Lucky for me," Morelli said. "I give good war."

THREE TO GET DEADLY

CHAPTER 1

It was January in Trenton. The sky was gunmetal gray, and the air sat dead cold on cars and sidewalks. Inside the offices of Vincent Plum, bail bond agent, the atmosphere was no less grim, and I was sweating not from heat but from panic.

"I can't do this," I said to my cousin, Vinnie. "I've never refused a case before, but I can't pick this guy up. Give the paperwork to Ranger. Give it to Barnes."

"I'm not giving this two-bit Failure to Appear to Ranger," Vinnie said. "It's the kind of penny-ante stuff you do. For chrissake, be a professional. You're a bounty hunter. You've been a bounty hunter for five fucking months. What's the big deal?"

"This is Uncle Mo!" I said. "I can't apprehend Uncle Mo. Everyone will hate me. My mother will hate me. My best friend will hate me."

Vinnie slumped his slim, boneless body into the chair behind his desk and rested his head on the padded leather back. "Mo jumped bail. That makes him a slimeball. That's all that counts."

I rolled my eyes so far into the top of my head I almost fell over backward.

Moses Bedemier, better known as Uncle Mo, started selling ice cream and penny candy on June 5, 1958, and has been at it ever since. His store is set on the edge of the burg, a comfy residential chunk of Trenton where houses and minds are proud to be narrow and hearts are generously wide open. I was born and raised in the burg and while my current apartment is approximately a mile outside the burg boundary I'm still tethered by an invisible umbilical. I've been hacking away at the damn thing for years but have never been able to completely sever it.

Moses Bedemier is a solid burg citizen. Over time, Mo and his linoleum have aged, so that both have some pieces chipped at the corners now, and the original colors have blurred from thirty-odd years under fluorescent lights. The yellow brick facade and overhead sheet metal sign advertising the store are dated and weatherbeaten. The chrome and Formica on the stools and countertop have lost their luster. And none of this matters, because in the burg Uncle Mo's is as close as we come to a historic treasure.

And I, Stephanie Plum, 125 pounds, five feet, seven inches, brown-haired, blue-eyed bounty hunter at large, have just been assigned the task of hauling Uncle Mo's revered ass off to jail.

"So what did he do?" I asked Vinnie. "Why was he arrested in the first place?"

"Got caught doing thirty-five in a twenty-five-mile-per-hour zone by Officer Picky . . . better known as Officer Benny Gaspick, fresh out of police academy and so wet behind the ears he doesn't know enough to take Mo's get-out-of-jail-free PBA card and forget the whole thing."

"Bond isn't required on a traffic ticket."

Vinnie planted a pointy-toed patent leather shoe on the corner of his desk. Vinnie was a sexual lunatic, especially enamored with dark-skinned young men wearing nipple rings and pointy-breasted women who owned fourteenth-century torture tools. He was a bail bondsman, which meant he loaned people money to post the bond set by the court. The bond's purpose was to make it economically unpleasant for the suspect to skip town. Once the bond was posted the incarcerated suspect was set free, enabling him to sleep in his own bed while awaiting trial. The price for using Vinnie's service was fifteen percent of the bond and was nonrefundable no matter what the outcome of the charges. If the bailee failed to appear for his court appearance, the court kept Vinnie's money. Not just the fifteen percent profit. The court kept the whole ball of wax, the entire bail bond amount. This never made Vinnie happy.

And that's where I came in. I found the bailee, who was at that point officially a felon, and brought him back into the system. If I found the Failure to Appear, better known as an FTA, in a timely fashion, the court gave Vinnie his cash back. For this fugitive apprehension I received ten percent of the bond amount, and Vinnie was left with a five percent profit.

I'd originally taken the job out of desperation when I'd been laid off (through no fault of my own) as lingerie buyer for E. E. Martin. The alternative to unemployment had been overseeing the boxing machine at the tampon factory. A worthy task, but not something that got me orgasmic.

I wasn't sure why I was still working for Vinnie. I suspected it had something to do with the title. Bounty hunter. It held a certain cachet. Even better, the job didn't require panty hose.

Vinnie smiled his oily smile, enjoying the story he was telling me. "In his misplaced zeal to be Most Hated Cop of the Year, Gaspick delivers a little lecture to Mo on road safety, and while Gaspick is lecturing, Mo squirms in his seat, and Gaspick catches a glimpse of a forty-five stuck in Mo's jacket pocket."

"And Mo got busted for carrying concealed," I said.

"Bingo."

Carrying concealed was frowned upon in Trenton. Permits were issued sparingly to a few jewelers, and judges and couriers. Getting caught carrying concealed illegally was considered unlawful possession of a firearm and was an indictable offense. The weapon was confiscated, bail was set and the bearer of the weapon was shit out of luck.

Of course, this didn't stop a sizable percentage of the population of Jersey from carrying concealed. Guns were bought at Bubba's Gun Shop, inherited from relatives, passed off among neighbors and friends and purchased second-, third- and fourthhand from and by citizens who were fuzzy on the details of gun control. Logic dictated that if the government issued a license to own a gun then it must be okay to put it in your purse. I mean, why else would a person want a gun if not to carry it in her purse. And if it wasn't okay to carry a gun in your purse, then the law was stupid. And no one in Jersey was going to put up with a stupid law.

I was even known, on occasion, to carry concealed. At this very moment I could see Vinnie's ankle holster causing a bulge at the cuff line of his polyester slacks. Not only was he carrying concealed but I'd lay odds his gun wasn't registered.

"This is not a big-time offense," I said to Vinnie. "Not something worth going Failure to Appear."

"Probably Mo forgot he had a court date," Vinnie said. "Probably all you have to do is go remind him."

Hold that thought, I told myself. This might not be such a disaster after all. It was ten o'clock. I could mosey on over to the candy store and talk to Mo. In fact, the more I thought about it, the more I realized my panic had been ungrounded. Mo had no reason to go FTA.

I closed the door on my way out of Vinnie's office, and sidestepped around Connie Rosolli. Connie was the office manager and Vinnie's guard dog. She held Vinnie in the same high esteem one would reserve for slug slime, but she'd worked for Vinnie for a lot of years, and had come to accept that even slug slime was part of God's great scheme.

Connie was wearing fuchsia lipstick, matching nail enamel and a white blouse with big black polka dots. The nail enamel was very cool, but the blouse wasn't a good choice for someone who carried sixty percent of her body weight on her chest. Good thing the fashion police didn't do too many tours of Trenton.

"You aren't going to do it, are you?" she asked. The tone implying that only a dog turd would cause Uncle Mo a moment of grief.

No offense taken. I knew where she lived. We had the same mental zip code. "You mean am I going to talk to Mo? Yeah, I'm going to talk to Mo."

Connie's black eyebrows fused into a straight line of righteous indignation. "That cop had no business arresting Uncle Mo. Everyone knows Uncle Mo would never do anything wrong."

"He was carrying concealed."

"As if that was a crime," Connie said.

"That *is* a crime!"

Lula's head came up from her filing. "What's all the deal about this Uncle Mo, anyway?"

Lula was a former hooker turned file clerk. She'd just recently embarked on a makeover program that included dyeing her hair blond and then straightening it and recurling it into ringlets. The transformation had her looking like a 230-pound black kick-ass Shirley Temple.

"Moses Bedemier," I said. "He runs a candy store on Ferris Street. Very popular person."

"Uh-oh," she said. "I think I know him. He about in his early sixties? Going bald on top? Lotta liver spots? Got a nose looks like a penis?"

"Um, I never really noticed his nose."

Vinnie had given me Uncle Mo's file, which consisted of stapled-together copies of his arrest sheet, his signed bond agreement and a photo. I turned to the photo and stared at Uncle Mo.

Lula stared over my shoulder. "Yup," she said. "That's him all right. That's Old Penis Nose."

Connie was out of her chair. "Are you telling me Uncle Mo was a client? I don't believe that for a second!"

Lula narrowed her eyes and stuck her lip out. "Yo momma."

"Nothing personal," Connie said.

"Hunh," Lula replied, hand on hip.

I zipped my jacket and wrapped my scarf around my neck. "You sure about knowing Uncle Mo?" I asked Lula.

She took one last look at the picture. "Hard to say. You know how all them old white men look alike. Maybe I should come with you to check this dude out in person."

"No!" I shook my head. "Not a good idea."

"You think I can't do this bounty hunter shit?"

Lula hadn't yet embarked on the language makeover.

"Well, of course you can do it," I said. "It's just that this situation is sort of . . . delicate."

"Hell," she said, stuffing herself into her jacket. "I can delicate your ass off."

"Yes, but . . ."

"Anyway, you might need some help here. Suppose he don't want to come peaceful. You might need a big, full-figure woman like me to do some persuading."

Lula and I had crossed paths while I was on my first felon hunt. She'd been a streetwalker, and I'd been street-stupid. I'd unwittingly involved her in the case I was working on, and as a result, one morning I found her battered and bloody on my fire escape.

Lula credited me with saving her life, and I blamed myself for endangering it. I was in favor of wiping the slate clean, but Lula formed a sort of attachment to me. I wouldn't go so far as to say it was hero worship. It was more like one of those Chinese things where if you save a person's life they belong to you . . . even if you don't want them.

"We're not doing any persuading," I said. "This is Uncle Mo. He sells candy to kids."

Lula had her pocketbook looped over her arm. "I can dig it," she said, following me out the door. "You still driving that old Buick?"

"Yeah. My Lotus is in the shop."

Actually, my Lotus was in my dreams. A couple months ago my Jeep got stolen, and my mother, in a burst of misguided good intentions, strong-armed me into the driver's seat of my uncle Sandor's '53 Buick. Strained finances and lack of backbone had me still peering over the mile-long powder-blue hood, wondering at the terrible acts I must have committed to deserve such a car.

A gust of wind rattled the Fiorello's Deli sign next to Vinnie's office. I pulled my collar up and searched in my pocket for gloves.

"At least the Buick's in good shape," I told Lula. "That's what counts, right?"

"Hunh," Lula said. "Only people who don't have a cool car say things like that. How about the radio. It got a bad radio? It got Dolby?"

"No Dolby."

"Hold on," she said. "You don't expect me to ride around with no Dolby. I need some hot music to get me in the mood to bust ass."

I unlocked the doors to the Buick. "*We are not busting ass.* We're going to *talk* to Uncle Mo."

"Sure," Lula said, settling herself in, giving a disgusted glare to the radio. "I know that."

I drove one block down Hamilton and turned left onto Rose into the burg. There was little to brighten the neighborhood in January. The blinking twinkle lights and red plastic Santas of Christmas were packed away, and spring was still far in the future. Hydrangea bushes were nothing more than mean brown sticks, lawns were frost-robbed of color and streets were empty of kids, cats, car washers and blaring radios. Windows and doors were shut tight against the cold and gloom.

Even Uncle Mo's felt sterile and unwelcoming as I slowed to a stop in front of the store.

Lula squinted through my side window. "I don't want to rain on your parade," she said, "but I think this sucker's closed."

I parked at the curb. "That's impossible. Uncle Mo never closes. Uncle Mo hasn't been closed a day since he opened in nineteen fifty-eight."

"Well guess what? I'm telling you he's closed now."

I hopped out of Big Blue and walked to Mo's door and looked inside. No lights were on, and Uncle Mo was nowhere to be seen. I tried the door. Locked. I knocked on the door good and loud. Nothing. Damn.

"He must be sick," I said to Lula.

The candy store sat on a corner, facing Ferris Street, with the side of the store running down King. A long line of neat duplexes stretched the length of Ferris, pushing their way to the heart of the burg. King, on the other hand, had fallen on hard times, with most of its duplexes converted to multiple families. The tidy white sheers and starched Martha Washington curtains of the burg weren't in evidence on King. Privacy on King came by way of tacked-up sheets and tattered shades, and from an unpleasant sense that this was no longer a desired community.

"Some scary old lady's looking at us out of the window of that house next door," Lula said.

I looked one house down on Ferris and shivered. "That's Mrs. Steeger. She was my teacher when I was in the third grade."

"Bet that was fun."

"Longest year of my life."

To this day I got cramps when I had to do long division.

"We should talk to her," I said to Lula.

"Yeah," Lula said. "Nosy old woman like that probably knows lots of stuff."

I hiked my pocketbook higher on my shoulder, and Lula and I marched over and knocked on Mrs. Steeger's door.

The door was opened just far enough for me to see that Mrs. Steeger hadn't changed much over the years. She was still rail thin, with a pinched face and snappy little eyes lying in wait under eyebrows that appeared to have been drawn on with brown marker. She'd been widowed last year. Retired the year before that. She was dressed in a brown dress with little white flowers, stockings and sensible shoes. Her glasses hung from a chain around her neck. Her hair was curled tight, dyed brown. She didn't look like she was adapting to a life of leisure.

I handed her my business card and introduced myself as a fugitive apprehension agent.

"What's that mean?" she wanted to know. "Are you a police officer?"

"Not exactly. I work for Vincent Plum."

"So," she said, considering the information. "You're a bounty hunter."

This was said with the same affection one would have for a drug pusher or child abuser. The tilt of her chin warned of possible disciplinary action, and her attitude implied if I'd mastered long division I might have made something of myself.

"What's this have to do with Moses?" she asked.

"He was arrested on a minor charge and then missed a court appearance. The Plum agency arranged bail, so I need to find Mo and help him set a new date."

"Mo would never do anything wrong," Mrs. Steeger said.

God's word.

"Do you know where he is?" I asked.

She drew herself up an extra half inch. "No. And I think it's a shame you can't find anything better to do than to go out harassing good men like Moses Bedemier."

"I'm not harassing him. I'm simply going to help him arrange a new court date."

"Liar, liar, pants on fire," Mrs. Steeger said. "You were a little fibber in the third grade, and you're a little fibber now. Always trying to sneak gum into my classroom."

"Well, thanks anyway," I said to Mrs. Steeger. "Nice seeing you after all these years."

SLAM. Mrs. Steeger closed her door.

"Should of lied," Lula said. "You never learn anything telling the truth like that. Should of told her you worked for the lottery commission, and Mo won a shitload of money."

"Maybe next time."

"Maybe next time we just open the door and start out with some bitch slapping."

I gave Lula a horrified glare.

"Just a suggestion," Lula said.

I stepped over to the next porch and was about to knock when Mrs. Steeger stuck her head out her door again.

"Don't bother," she said. "The Whiteheads are in Florida. Harry always takes his vacation this time of the year. Won't be back for two weeks."

SLAM. She vanished behind the closed door.

"No problem," I said to Lula. "We'll try door number three."

Dorothy Rostowski opened door number three.

"Dorothy?"

"Stephanie?"

"I didn't realize you were living here."

"Almost a year now."

She had a baby on her hip and another in front of the television. She smelled like she'd been knocking back mashed bananas and Chablis.

"I'm looking for Uncle Mo," I said. "I expected he'd be working in the store."

Dorothy shifted the baby. "He hasn't been here for two days. You aren't looking for him for Vinnie, are you?"

"Actually . . ."

"Mo would never do anything wrong."

"Well, sure, but . . ."

"We're just trying to find him on account of he won the lottery," Lula said. "We're gonna lay a whole load of money on his ass."

Dorothy made a disgusted sound and slammed the door closed.

We tried the house next to Dorothy and received the same information. Mo hadn't been at the store for two days. Nothing else was forthcoming, with the exception of some unsolicited advice that I might consider seeking new employment.

Lula and I piled into the Buick and took another look at the bond agreement. Mo listed his address as 605 Ferris. That meant he lived over his store.

Lula and I craned our necks to see into the four second-story windows.

"I think Mo took a hike," Lula said.

Only one way to find out. We got out of the car and walked to the back of the brick building where outdoor stairs led to a second-story porch. We climbed the stairs and knocked on the door. Nothing. We tried the doorknob. Locked. We looked in the windows. Everything was tidy. No sign of Mo. No lights left burning.

"Mo might be dead in there," Lula said. "Or maybe he's sick. Could of had a stroke and be laying on the bathroom floor."

"We are *not* going to break in."

"Would be a humanitarian effort," Lula said.

"And against the law."

"Sometimes these humanitarian efforts go into the gray zone."

I heard footsteps and looked down to see a cop standing at the bottom of the stairs. Steve Olmney. I'd gone to school with him.

"What's going on?" he asked. "We got a complaint from old lady Steeger that someone suspicious was snooping around Uncle Mo's."

"That would be me," I said.

"Where's Mo?"

"We think he might be dead," Lula said. "We think someone better go look to see if he's had a stroke on the bathroom floor."

Olmney came up the stairs and rapped on the door. "Mo?" he yelled. He put his nose to the door. "Doesn't smell dead." He looked in the windows. "Don't see any bodies."

"He's Failure to Appear," I said. "Got picked up on carrying concealed and didn't show in court."

"Mo would never do anything wrong," Olmney said.

I stifled a scream. "Not showing up for a court appearance is wrong."

"Probably he forgot. Maybe he's on vacation. Or maybe his sister in Staten Island got sick. You should check with his sister."

Actually, that sounded like a decent idea.

Lula and I went back to the Buick, and I read through the bond agreement one more time. Sure enough, Mo had listed his sister and given her address.

"We should split up," I said to Lula. "I'll go see the sister, and you can stake out the store."

"I'll stake it out good," Lula said. "I won't miss a thing."

I turned the key in the ignition and pulled away from the curb. "What will you do if you see Mo?"

"I'll snatch the little fucker up by his gonads and squash him into the trunk of my car."

"*No!* You're not authorized to apprehend. If you see Mo, you should get in touch with me right away. Either call me on my cellular phone or else call my pager." I gave her a card with my numbers listed.

"Remember, *no squashing anyone into the trunk of your car!*"

"Sure," Lula said. "I know that."

I dropped Lula at the office and headed for Route 1. It was the middle of the day and traffic was light. I got to Perth Amboy and lined up for the bridge to Staten Island. The roadside leading to the toll booth was littered with mufflers, eaten away from winter salt and rattled loose by the inescapable craters, sinkholes and multilevel strips of macadam patch that composed the bridge.

I slipped into bridge traffic and sat nose to tail with Petrucci's Vegetable Wholesalers and a truck labeled DANGEROUS EXPLOSIVES. I checked a map while I waited. Mo's sister lived toward the middle of the island in a residential area I knew to be similar to the burg.

I paid my toll and inched forward, sucking in a stew of diesel exhaust and other secret ingredients that caught me in the back of the throat. I adjusted to the pollution in less than a quarter of a mile and felt just fine when I reached Mo's sister's house on Crane Street. Adaptation is one of the great advantages to being born and bred in Jersey. We're simply not bested by bad air or tainted water. We're like that catfish with lungs. Take us out of our environment and we can grow whatever body parts we need to survive. After Jersey the rest of the country's a piece of cake. You want to send someone into a fallout zone? Get him from Jersey. He'll be fine.

Mo's sister lived in a pale green duplex with jalousied windows and white-and-yellow aluminum awnings. I parked at the curb and made my way up two flights of cement stairs to the cement stoop. I rang the bell and found myself facing a woman who looked a lot like my relatives on the Mazur side of my family. Good sturdy Hungarian stock. Black hair, black eyebrows and no-nonsense blue eyes. She looked to be in her fifties and didn't seem thrilled to find me on her doorstep.

I gave her my card, introduced myself and told her I was looking for Mo.

Her initial reaction was surprise, then distrust.

"Fugitive apprehension agent," she said. "What's that supposed to mean? What's that got to do with Mo?"

I gave the condensed version by way of explanation. "I'm sure it was just an oversight that Mo didn't appear for his court session, but I need to remind him to reschedule," I told her.

"I don't know anything about this," she said. "I don't see Mo a whole lot. He's always at the store. Why don't you just go to the store."

"He hasn't been at the store for the last two days."

"That doesn't sound like Mo."

None of this sounded like Mo.

I asked if there were other relatives. She said no, not close ones. I asked about a second apartment or vacation house. She said none that she knew of.

I thanked her for her time and returned to my Buick. I looked out at the neighborhood. Not much happening. Mo's sister was locked up in her house. Probably wondering what the devil was going on with Mo. Of course there was the possibility that she was protecting her brother, but my gut instinct said otherwise. She'd seemed genuinely surprised when I'd told her Mo wasn't behind the counter handing out Gummi Bears.

I could watch the house, but that sort of surveillance was tedious and time-consuming, and in this case, I wasn't sure it would be worth the effort.

Besides, I was getting a weird feeling about Mo. Responsible people like Mo didn't forget court dates. Responsible people like Mo worried about that kind of stuff. They lost sleep over it. They consulted attorneys. And responsible people like Mo didn't just up and leave their businesses without so much as a sign in the window.

Maybe Lula was right. Maybe Mo was dead in bed or lying unconscious on his bathroom floor.

I got out of the car and retraced my steps back to the sister's front door.

The door was opened before I had a chance to knock. Two little frown lines had etched themselves into Mo's sister's forehead. "Was there something else?" she asked.

"I'm concerned about Mo. I don't mean to alarm you, but I suppose there's the possibility that he might be sick at home and unable to get to the door."

"I've been standing here thinking the same thing," she said.

"Do you have a key to his apartment?"

"No, and as far as I know no one else does, either. Mo likes his privacy."

"Do you know any of his friends? Did he have a girlfriend?"

"Sorry. We aren't real close like that. Mo is a good brother, but like I said, he's private."

An hour later I was back in the burg. I motored down Ferris and parked behind Lula.

"How's it going?" I asked.

Lula was slouched at the wheel of her red Firebird. "Isn't going at all. Most boring bullshit job I ever had. A person could do this in a coma."

"Anyone stop around to buy candy?"

"A momma and her baby. That's all."

"Did they walk around back?"

"Nope. They just looked in the front door and left."

I glanced at my watch. School would be out soon. There'd be a lot of kids coming by then, but I wasn't interested in kids. I was interested in an adult who might show up to water Mo's plants or retrieve his mail.

"Hang tight here," I said. "I'm going to speak to more neighbors."

"Hang tight, hunh. I'm gonna like freeze to death sitting in this car. This isn't Florida, you know."

"I thought you wanted to be a bounty hunter. This is what bounty hunters do."

"Wouldn't mind doing this if I thought at the end of it all I'd get to shoot someone, but there isn't even any guarantee of that. All I hear's don't do this and don't do that. Can't even stuff the sonovabitch in my trunk if I find him."

I crossed the street and spoke to three more neighbors. Their replies were standard. They had no idea where Mo could be, and they thought I had a lot of nerve implying he was a felon.

A teenager answered in the fourth house. We were dressed almost identically. Doc Martens, jeans, flannel shirt over T-shirt, too much eye makeup, lots of brown curly hair. She was fifteen pounds slimmer and fifteen years younger. I didn't envy her youth, but I did have second thoughts about the dozen doughnuts I'd picked up on my way through the burg, which even as we spoke were calling to me from the backseat of my car.

I gave her my card, and her eyes widened.

"A bounty hunter!" she said. "*Cool!*"

"Do you know Uncle Mo?"

"Sure I know Uncle Mo. Everybody knows Uncle Mo." She leaned forward and lowered her voice. "He do something wrong? Are you after Uncle Mo?"

"He missed a court date on a minor charge. I want to remind him to reschedule."

"That is like amazing. When you find him are you going to rough him up and lock him in the trunk of your car?"

"*No!*" What was with this trunk business? "I just want to talk to him."

"I bet he did something really terrible. I bet you want him for cannibalism."

Cannibalism? The man sold candy. What would he want with fingers and toes? This kid had great taste in shoes, but her mind was a little scary. "Do you know anything about Mo that might be helpful? He have any close friends in the neighborhood? Have you seen him recently?"

"I saw him a couple days ago in the store."

"Maybe you could keep a lookout for me. My numbers are on the card. You see Mo or anyone suspicious you give me a call."

"Like I'd almost be a bounty hunter?"

"Almost."

I jogged back to Lula. "Okay," I told her, "you can return to the office. I found a replacement. The kid across the street is going to spy for us."

"Good thing too. This was getting old."

I followed Lula to the office and called my friend Norma, who worked at the DMV. "Got a name," I told her. "Need a plate and a car."

"What's the name?"

"Moses Bedemier."

"Uncle Mo?"

"That's the one."

"I'm not giving you information on Uncle Mo!"

I gave her the bull about rescheduling, which was sounding very tired.

Computer keys clicked in the background. "If I find out you harmed a single hair on Uncle Mo's head I'll never give you another plate."

"I'm not going to hurt him," I said. "I never hurt anyone."

"What about that guy you killed last August? And what about when you blew up the funeral home?"

"Are you going to give me this information, or what?"

"He owns a ninety-two Honda Civic. Blue. You got a pencil? I'll read off the plate."

"Oh boy," Lula said, peering over my shoulder. "Looks like we got more clues. We gonna look for this car?"

"Yes." And then we'd look for a key to the apartment. Everyone worries about getting locked out. If you don't have someone in the neighborhood you can trust with your key, you hide it nearby. You carefully place it over the doorjamb, put it in a fake rock next to your foundation or slide it under the doormat.

I wasn't about to do forced entry, but if I found a key . . .

"I haven't had any lunch," Lula said. "I can't keep working if I don't have lunch."

I pulled the bag of doughnuts out of my big black leather shoulder bag, and we dug in.

"Things to do. Places to go," I said minutes later, shaking powdered sugar off my shirt, wishing I'd stopped at two doughnuts.

"I'm going with you," Lula said. "Only this time I drive. I got a big motherfucker stereo in my car."

"Just don't drive too fast. I don't want to get picked up by Officer Gaspick."

"Uh-oh," Lula said. "You carrying concealed like Uncle Mo?"

Not at the moment. My .38 Smith & Wesson was at home, sitting on my kitchen counter, in the brown bear cookie jar. Guns scared the hell out of me.

We piled into Lula's red Firebird and headed for Ferris with rap rattling windows in our wake.

"Maybe you should turn it down," I yelled to Lula after a couple blocks. "I'm getting arrhythmia."

Lula punched the air. "Un ha, ha, ha, haa."

"Lula!"

She cut her eyes to me. "You say something?"

I edged the volume back. "You're going to go deaf."

"Hunh," Lula said.

We cruised down Ferris and looked for blue Civics, but there were none parked near the store. We scoped out the cross streets and parallel streets on either side. No blue Civics. We parked at the corner of Ferris and King and walked the alley behind the store, looking into all the garages. No blue Civics. The single-car garage that sat at the edge of the small yard backing off from the candy store was empty.

"He's flown the coop," Lula said. "I bet he's in Mexico laughing his ass off, figuring we're out here doing the two-step through a bunch of bullshit garages."

"What about the dead on the bathroom floor theory?"

Lula was wearing a hot-pink down ski jacket and white fake-fur knee-high boots. She pulled the jacket collar up around her neck and glanced up at Mo's second-story back porch. "We would of found his car. And if he was dead he would of started to smell by now."

That's what I thought, too.

"Course, he could have locked himself in the ice cream freezer," Lula said. "Then he wouldn't smell on account of he'd be frozen. Probably that didn't happen though because Mo would have had to take the ice cream out before he could fit himself in, and we already looked in the store window, and we didn't see a lot of ice cream cartons sitting around melting themselves into next year. Of course, Mo could have eaten all the ice cream first."

Mo's garage was wood and shingle with an old-fashioned double wood door that swung open on hinges and had been left ajar. The garage accessed from the alley, but it had a side door toward the rear that led to a short cement sidewalk running to the back of the store.

The interior of the garage was dark and musty, the walls lined with boxes of Tastee Straws, napkins, cleanser, Drygas, Del Monte fruit cup, Hershey's syrup and 10W40 motor oil. Newspapers were stacked in the corner, awaiting recycling.

Mo was a popular person and presumably a trusting soul, but leaving his garage doors open when his garage was filled with store supplies seemed like an excessive burden on human nature. Possibilities were that he left in a hurry and was too distracted to think about the door. Or perhaps he wasn't planning to return. Or maybe he'd been forced to leave, and his abductors had other things on their minds besides garage doors.

Of all the possibilities I liked the last one the least.

I pulled a flashlight out of my pocketbook and gave it to Lula with instructions to search the garage for a house key.

"I'm like a bloodhound on a scent when it comes to house keys," Lula said. "Don't you worry about that house key. It's as good as found."

Mrs. Steeger glared at us from the window next door. I smiled and waved, and she stepped back. Most likely en route to the telephone to call the cops on me again.

There was a small yard stuck between the store and the garage, and there were no signs of recreational use of the yard. No swing sets, grills, rusting lawn chairs. Only the sidewalk broke the scrubby grass and hard-packed dirt. I followed the sidewalk to the store's back entry and looked in the trash cans lining the brick wall. All cans were full, garbage neatly bagged in plastic sacks. Some empty cardboard cartons had been stacked beside the garbage cans. I toed through the area around the cans and the boxes, looking for some sign of a hidden key. I found nothing. I felt over the doorjamb on the back door that led to the candy store. I walked up the stairs and ran my hand under the railing on the small back porch. I knocked on the door one more time and looked in the window.

Lula emerged from the garage and crossed the yard. She climbed the stairs and proudly handed me a key.

"Am I good, or what?" she said.

CHAPTER 2

I plunged the key into the Yale lock on Mo's door, and the door opened.

"Mo?" I yelled.

No answer.

Lula and I looked around. No cops. No kids. No nosy neighbors. Our eyes met, and we silently slid into the apartment. I did a fast walk-through, noting that Mo wasn't dead in the bedroom, bathroom, kitchen or living room. There was food in the refrigerator and clothes in his bedroom closet.

The apartment was clean and tidy. He didn't have an answering machine, so I couldn't snoop on his messages. I riffled through drawers but didn't find an address book. There were no hastily scribbled notes left lying around, detailing plane reservations or hotel accommodations. No brochures advertising Disney World.

I was about to trip downstairs and search the store when Carl Costanza appeared on the back porch. Carl was one of my favorite cops. We'd done Communion together, among other things.

"I should have known," Carl said, standing flat-footed, gravity pulling hard on his gun and utility belt. "I should have known when the call came in that it would be you."

"I gotta go," Lula said, easing past Carl, tiptoeing down the stairs. "I can see you two want to have a conversation. Wouldn't want to be an interference."

"Lula," I shouted, "don't you dare leave without me!"

Lula was already rounding the corner of the building. "I might even be coming down with a cold, and I wouldn't want to pass that on to you-all."

"Well," Carl said, "want to tell me about this?"

"You mean about Lula and me being in Uncle Mo's apartment?"

Carl grimaced. "You're going to make up some ridiculous story, aren't you?"

"Mo's FTA. I came here looking for him, and his door was wide open. Must have been the wind."

"Uh-huh."

"And then Lula and I got worried. What if Mo was injured? Like maybe he'd fallen in the bathroom and hit his head and was unconscious."

Carl held his hands up. "Stop. I don't want to hear any more. Are you finished with your search?"

"Yes."

"Did you find Mo unconscious on the bathroom floor?"

"No."

"You're going home now, right?"

"Right." Carl was a good guy, but I thought breaking into Mo's store while Carl was looking over my shoulder might be pressing my luck, so I closed Mo's door and made sure the lock clicked.

When I got out to the street, Lula and the Firebird were nowhere to be seen. I put my head down and walked to my parents' house, where I was pretty sure I could mooch a ride.

My parents lived deep in the burg in a narrow duplex that on a cold day like this would smell like chocolate pudding cooking on the stove. The effect was similar to Lorelei, singing to all those sailors, sucking them in so they'd crash on the rocks.

I walked three blocks down Ferris, and turned onto Green. The raw cold ate through my shoes and gloves and made my ears ache. I was wearing a Gore-Tex shell with a heavy fleece liner, a black turtleneck and a sweatshirt advertising my alma mater, Douglass College. I pulled the jacket hood over my head and tightened the drawstring. Very dorky, but at least my ears wouldn't crack off like icicles.

"What a nice surprise," my mother said when she opened the door to me. "And we're having roast chicken for dinner. Lots of gravy. Just like you like it."

"I can't stay. I have plans."

"What plans? A date?"

"Not a date. These are work plans."

Grandma Mazur peeked around the kitchen door. "Oh boy, you're on a case. Who is it this time?"

"No one you know," I said. "It's something small. Really, I'm doing it as a favor to Vinnie."

"I heard old Tom Gates got arrested for spitting in line at Social Security. Is it Tom Gates you're after?" Grandma asked.

"No. It's not Tom Gates."

"How about that guy they were talking about in the paper today? The one who pulled that motorist through his car window by his necktie."

"That was just a misunderstanding," I said. "They were in dispute over a parking space."

"Well, who then?" Grandma wanted to know.

"Moses Bedemier."

My mother made the sign of the cross. "Holy mother of God, you're hunting down Uncle Mo." She threw her hands into the air. "The man is a saint!"

"He's not a saint. He got arrested for carrying concealed, and then he didn't show up for a court appearance. So now I have to find him and get him rescheduled."

"Carrying concealed," my mother said, rolling her eyes. "What moron would arrest a good man like Mo Bedemier for carrying concealed?"

"Officer Gaspick."

"I don't know any Officer Gaspick," my mother said.

"He's new."

"That's what comes of getting new cops," Grandma said. "No telling what they might do. I bet that gun was planted on Mo. I saw a TV show the other night about how when cops want a promotion they plant drugs on people so they can arrest them. I bet that's what happened here. I bet that Officer Gaspick planted a gun on Mo. Everybody knows Mo would never do anything wrong."

I was getting tired of hearing how Mo would never do anything wrong. In fact, I was beginning to wonder what sort of person this wonderful Uncle Mo really was. It seemed to me everyone knew him, but no one knew him.

My mother had her hands up in supplication. "How will I ever explain this? What will people say?"

"They'll say I'm doing my job," I told my mother.

"Your job! You work for your no-good cousin. If it isn't bad enough you go around shooting people, now you're hunting down Uncle Mo as if he was a common criminal."

"I only shot *one* person! And Uncle Mo *is* a common criminal. He broke the law."

"Course it wasn't one of those laws we care much about," Grandma said, weighing the crime.

"Has Mo ever been married?" I asked. "Does he have a girlfriend?"

"Of course not," my grandmother said.

"What do you mean, of course not? What's wrong with him?"

My mother and my grandmother looked at each other. Obviously they'd never thought of it in those terms before.

"I guess he's sort of like a priest," Grandma Mazur finally said. "Like he's married to the store."

Oh boy. Saint Mo, the celibate candyman . . . better known as Old Penis Nose.

"Not that he doesn't know how to have a good time," Grandma said. "I heard him tell one of those lightbulb jokes, once. Nothing blue, though. He would never say anything off-color. He's a real gentleman."

"Do you know anything about him?" I asked. "Does he go to church? Does he belong to the VFW?"

"Well, I don't know," Grandma said. "I just know him from the candy store."

"When was the last time you talked to him?"

"Must have been a couple months ago. We stopped to buy ice cream on the way home from shopping. Remember that, Ellen?"

"It was before Christmas," my mother said.

I made hand gestures for her to elaborate. "And?"

"There's no more," she said. "We went in. We talked about weather. We got ice cream and left."

"Mo looked okay?"

"He looked like he always looks," my mother said. "Maybe a little less hair, a little more of a roll around his middle. He was wearing a white shirt that said UNCLE MO over the pocket, just like always."

"So about the chicken?" my mother wanted to know.

"Rain check," I said. "I need a ride to Vinnie's. Can someone give me a ride?"

"Where's your car?" Grandma asked. "Was your car stolen again?"

"It's parked at Vinnie's. It's sort of a long story."

My mother took her coat out of the hall closet. "I guess I can give you a ride. I need to go to the store anyway."

The phone rang, and Grandma Mazur answered.

"Yep," she said. "Yep. Yep. Yep." Her face wrinkled into a frown. "I hear you," she answered.

"Well, if that isn't something," she said when she got off. "That was Myra Biablocki. She said she was talking to Emma Rodgers and Emma told her she heard Stephanie was on a manhunt to bring down Uncle Mo. Myra said she thought it was a sad day when a person hasn't anything better to do than to make trouble for a good man like Moses Bedemier."

"Your cousin Maureen just got a job at the button factory," my mother said to me. "They're probably still hiring."

"I don't want to work at the button factory. I like my job just fine."

The phone rang again, and we all looked at each other.

"Maybe it's a wrong number," Grandma Mazur offered.

My mother brushed past Grandma and snatched at the phone. "Yes?" Her mouth pinched into a thin line. "Moses Bedemier is *not* above the law," she said. "I suggest you get the facts right before spreading gossip. And for that matter, if I were you, I'd clean my front windows before I took the time to talk on the phone."

"Must be Eleanor, down the street," Grandma said. "I noticed her windows, too."

Life was simple in the burg. Sins were absolved by the Catholic Church, dirty windows were an abomination to the neighborhood, gossip greased the wheel of life and you'd better be damned careful what you said face-to-face to a woman about her daughter. No matter if it was true.

My mother got off the phone, wrapped a scarf around her head and took her pocketbook and keys off the hall table. "Are you coming with us?" she asked Grandma Mazur.

"I got some TV shows I've gotta watch," Grandma said. "And besides, someone's got to take care of the phone calls."

My mother shuddered. "Give me strength."

Five minutes later she dropped me off in front of Vinnie's.

"Think about the button factory," she said. "I hear they pay good. And you'd get benefits. Health insurance."

"I'll think about it," I said. But neither of us was paying much attention to what I said. We were both staring at the man leaning against my car.

"Isn't that Joe Morelli?" my mother asked. "I didn't know things were still friendly between you."

"It isn't, and it never was," I said, which was sort of a fib. Morelli and I had a history that ranged from almost friendly, to frighteningly friendly, to borderline murderous. He'd taken my virginity when I was sixteen, and at eighteen I'd tried to run him down with my father's Buick. Those two incidents pretty much reflected the tone of our ongoing relationship.

"Looks like he's waiting for you."

I blew out some air. "Lucky me."

Morelli was a cop now. Plainclothes. A misnomer for Morelli, because he's lean-hipped and hard-muscled, and there's nothing plain about the way he fits a pair of Levi's. He's two years older than me, five inches taller, has a paper-thin scar slicing through his right eyebrow and an eagle tattooed onto his chest. The eagle is left over from a hitch in the navy. The scar is more recent.

I got out of the car and pasted a big phony smile on my mouth. "Gosh, what a terrific surprise."

Morelli grinned. "Nice lie."

"I can't imagine what you mean by that."

"You've been avoiding me."

The avoiding had been mutual. Morelli had given me the big rush back in November and then all of a sudden . . . nothing.

"I've been busy," I said.

"So I hear."

I gave him a raised eyebrow.

"Two suspicious conduct complaints in one day, plus breaking and entering. You must be going for some sort of personal record," Morelli said.

"Costanza has a big mouth."

"You were lucky it was Costanza. If it had been Gaspick you'd be calling Vinnie for bail right now."

We were caught in a gust of wind, and we hunkered down into our jackets.

"Can I talk to you off the record?" I asked Morelli.

"Shit," Morelli said. "I hate when you start a conversation like this."

"There's something strange about Uncle Mo."

"Oh boy."

"I'm serious!"

"Okay," Morelli said. "So what have you got?"

"A feeling."

"If anyone else said that to me I'd walk away."

"Mo's gone FTA on a carrying charge. It would have gotten him a fine and a slap on the hand. It doesn't make sense."

"Life never makes sense."

"I've been out looking for him. He's nowhere. His car is gone, but his garage door was left open. There are dry goods in the garage. Things he wouldn't want stolen. It doesn't feel right. His store has been closed up for two days. No one knows where he is. His sister doesn't know. His neighbors don't know."

"What did you find in his apartment?"

"Clothes in the closet. Food in the fridge."

"Any sign of struggle?"

"None."

"Maybe he needed to go off to think," Morelli said. "Did he have an attorney?"

"Waived an attorney."

"I think you're jumping to conclusions."

I shrugged. "Maybe, but it still feels strange."

"Out of character for Mo."

"Yeah."

Mrs. Turkevich came out of Fiorello's Deli carrying a grocery bag.

I nodded to her. "Pretty cold today."

"Hmmmph," she said.

"Listen, it's not my fault!" I told her. "I'm just doing my job."

The grin widened on Morelli's face. "Us crime stoppers have a tough life, huh?"

"Are you still working vice?"

"I'm working homicide. Temporarily."

"Is that a promotion?"

"It's more like lateral movement."

I wasn't sure I could see Morelli as a homicide cop. Morelli liked to get out there and make things happen. Homicide was a more cerebral, reactive position.

"Was there a reason for this visit?" I asked.

"I was in the area. Thought I'd see how things were going."

"You mean things like Moses Bedemier?"

"You need to be more careful. Mo has some very protective, very noisy neighbors."

I held my coat collar tight to my neck. "I don't get it. What's so great about this guy?"

Morelli did a palms up. "I guess he's just one of those lovable types. Friends with everyone."

"What I'm finding is that he's friends with no one. He's a very private person. Doesn't even confide in his sister. My grandmother says it's like he's married to the store. Like a priest."

"A lot of people let their work take over their life. It's the American way," Morelli said.

Morelli's pager beeped.

"Christ," Morelli said. "I hope this is something horrible. A decapitation or maybe a bullet-riddled body found in a Dumpster. Homicide in Trenton is like watching grass grow. We just don't have enough good ones to go around."

I opened the door to my car and slid behind the wheel. "Let me know if it turns out to be Mo."

Morelli had his own keys in hand. His black Toyota 4×4 was parked directly behind me. "Try to stay out of trouble."

I drove off wondering what to do next. I'd covered all of the information given on Mo's bond agreement. I'd canvassed the neighborhood, searched his apartment, spoken to his only sister.

After ten minutes of cruising I found myself in the parking lot of my apartment building. The building and the lot were sterile in January. Brick and macadam unsoftened by summer shrubbery. Leaden Jersey sky, dark enough for the streetlights to blink on.

I got out of the car and walked head down to the building's back entrance, pushed through the double glass doors and was grateful for the sudden warmth.

I stepped into the elevator and punched the button for the second floor, wondering what I'd missed in my search for Bedemier. Usually something popped up in the initial investigation . . . a girlfriend, a hobby, a favorite bakery or liquor store. Nothing had popped up today.

The elevator doors opened, and I walked the short distance down the hall, planning out phone calls. I could check on Mo's bank account to see if there were any recent withdrawals. I could check his credit rating. Sometimes a credit check turned up hidden problems. I could run down utilities accounts on a possible second home. I could call Sue Ann Grebek, who knew everything about everyone.

I unlocked my apartment door, stepped into the quiet foyer and took stock of my apartment. My hamster, Rex, was sleeping in the soup can in his glass cage. There were no lights blinking on my answering machine. There were no sounds of big, hairy, snaggle-toothed guys scrambling to hide under my bed.

I dumped my pocketbook on the kitchen counter and draped my jacket over a chair. I poured some milk into a mug, nuked it for two minutes and dumped a couple spoons of instant hot chocolate mix into the hot milk. I added two marshmallows, and while they were getting gooey I made myself a peanut butter sandwich on mushy, worthless white bread.

I took all this, plus my cordless phone, to the dining room table and dialed Sue Ann.

"Stephanie, Stephanie, Stephanie," Sue Ann said. "My phone's been ringing off the hook. Everybody's talking about how you're out to get Uncle Mo."

"I'm not out to *get* Uncle Mo. He needs to reschedule a court date. It's no big deal."

"So why is everybody in such a snit?"

"You tell me."

"I don't know," Sue Ann said. "Not much to tell. Everybody likes him. He minds his own business. He's nice to the kids."

"There must be something. Haven't you ever heard any rumors?"

"Do you care if they're true?"

"Not at all."

"So, in other words, you're looking for unsubstantiated dirt."

"Exactly."

Silence.

"Well?" I asked.

"My niece says sometimes Mo's store smells like dookey."

"Yuk."

"That's about it," Sue Ann said.

"That's not much."

"He's a saint. What can I say?"

"Saints don't smell like dookey," I told her.

"Maybe old ones do."

After I talked to Sue Ann I ate my sandwich and drank my cocoa and thought about Moses Bedemier. His apartment had been neat, and his furniture had been worn but comfortable. Sort of like mine. The television set was the focal point of the living room. The *TV Guide* on the coffee table had been a week old. The food in the fridge had been simple. Lunch meat, bread, juice, milk.

Mo had been living alone for a lot of years, and I suspected his life relied heavily on routine. No real surprises in his apartment. The one note of whimsy had been the movie magazines. A stack of them in the bedroom. Moses Bedemier must have read himself to sleep with soap opera gossip.

I put in a call to my cousin Bunnie at the credit bureau, and drew another blank. There'd been nothing derogatory or recent under either personal or business files.

I tipped back in my chair and stared aimlessly across the room. The window glass was black and reflective. Occasionally headlights flashed into the parking lot below. Car doors slammed. My neighbors were returning from a hard day at whatever.

Mo was missing, and I hadn't a clue and I didn't know how to go about getting one. I'd run all the usual drills. What was left was to wait. And waiting wasn't my strong suit.

I carted my dishes back to the kitchen and thought some more about Uncle Mo. The problem with finding a missing person is that they could be missing very far away. Here I am looking all around Trenton for Moses Bedemier, and he could be in Guadeloupe wearing thick glasses and a fake nose. Truth is, if he was in Guadeloupe I was out of luck, so best not to think about it. Better to assume Mo is close to home, and then I can feel hopeful.

Most of the time people stay close to home anyway. They'd be much better off if they ran far away, but far away doesn't feel safe.

Home feels safe. Sooner or later most FTAs touch base with their relatives, girlfriends, neighborhood cronies. And usually it's sooner rather than later.

I exchanged my flannel shirt for a Rangers jersey and zapped the television on. Probably I should make more phone calls, but the Rangers were playing and priorities were priorities.

My alarm rang at 7 A.M. I slammed my hand on the off button and peered at the clock, wondering why I had set the thing for such an ungodly hour. There was no sign of the sun anywhere, and rain pinged against my windowpane. Even at the best of times, morning is not my favorite part of day, and this wasn't nearly the best of times.

The next time I awoke it was eight-thirty. Rain still slashed at my window, but at least the sky had lightened from black to gray. I dragged myself out of bed and into the bathroom and stood under the shower for a while. I thought about Mel Gibson and Joe Morelli and tried to decide who had the best butt. Then I thought about Mike Richter, the goalie for the Rangers, because he was no slouch either.

By the time I was towel-drying my hair I'd gone from Richter to Uncle Mo. The conclusion I reached about Uncle Mo was that I'd dead-ended. Intuition told me Uncle Mo hadn't gone far and would eventually surface. Unfortunately, the word "eventually" was not favored in the bounty hunter vocabulary. Eventually did not pay this month's rent.

I gassed my hair with some maximum-hold hair spray, dressed in my usual uniform of jeans and flannel shirt and snapped my bedroom curtains open.

I chanted Rain, rain, go away, come again some other day. But the rain didn't go away, so I revisited my dresser and added thick socks and a sweatshirt to my outfit.

For lack of something better to do, I took myself down to the office. On the way, I cruised past Blue Ribbon Used Cars and wistfully glanced over the lot. Every morning I got up and hoped the car fairy had visited me overnight. Every morning I was disappointed. Maybe it was time to take matters into my own hands.

I parked at the curb and squinted through the rain at the lineup of cars. All very boring . . . except for a little blue Nissan pickup at the end of the lot. The little blue pickup was CUTE. I got out to take a closer look. New paint. Bench seat, slightly worn but not torn. Standard transmission.

A man in a yellow slicker ran over to me. "Want to buy this car?"

"How much?"

"For you? We can make a deal. It's an eighty-four. Runs like a top."

I looked in my checkbook. "I probably can't afford it."

"Hey," he said. "Your credit's good here. We can finance it for you. You'll hardly notice the payments."

"I'd have to take it on a test drive."

"Hold on a minute, and I'll pop some plates on for you."

I did a four-block test drive and I was sold. So I'd give up eating oranges. And I'd cut back on movie rentals. The sacrificing would be worth it. I'd have a truck!

Lula glanced up from the files when I slogged through the door, dripping water on the utility-grade carpet. "Hope you didn't spend a lot of time on your hair this morning," she said.

I took a swipe at the wet mess with my hand. "Beauty is in the eye of the beholder."

"Hah," Lula replied. "If that isn't some load of cocky doody."

"Is the man in?" I asked Connie.

"Not yet."

I slouched back on the brown Naugahyde couch. "I'm not having any luck with Uncle Mo, and I need money. Don't suppose you'd have any quickies?"

"Only got one Failure to Appear yesterday, and it's strictly chump change. Stuart Baggett." She took a manila folder from her "in" box and flipped the file open. "Age twenty-two. White male Caucasian. Five feet six. Went on a drunken late-night joyride three weeks ago with two of his buddies and shot up fourteen parked cars. Did it with an air rifle. Missed his court date and is now a fugitive . . . not to mention an idiot. Two of the cars he shot up were unoccupied police cars."

I was surprised anyone noticed the damage on the cop cars. Trenton's blue-and-whites had not gone gently into the night. Trenton's blue-and-whites all looked like they'd survived Bosnia.

I took the folder from Connie.

"He lives on Applegate with his parents," she said. "Works at the hot dog place at the mall. Looks like his mother put up the bond."

I dialed his home phone and got his mother. I asked if Stuart was working today and was told he was working until four.

"I could use to go to the mall," Lula said. "I could use to take a break, and then I could watch your bounty huntering technique when you make this apprehension."

"There won't be any technique to watch," I said. "This is just some stupid guy who got drunk and did a stupid stunt. Either he forgot his date, or else he was too embarrassed to show up at court."

"Yeah, but you're gonna finesse him, right? You're gonna pull some bogus shit on him and lure him out to the parking lot where we cuff him and kick his ass into the car."

"I'm going to very nicely inform him of his error and request that he accompany me to the station to reschedule his court date."

"They never gonna make a TV series out of this job," Lula said.

"If you're going near Macy's get me some nail polish. Something real red," Connie said.

I dropped the file into my big black shoulder bag and zipped my jacket. Lula buttoned herself into an ankle-length dark brown oiled canvas duster and settled a matching brown leather cowboy hat on her head.

"Do I look like a bounty hunter or what?" she said.

I just hoped poor Stuart Baggett didn't fall over dead at the sight of her.

The door opened and Ranger stepped in from the rain.

Ranger had been my mentor when I'd started in the business and was one very bad bounty hunter. In this case, bad meaning ultracool. He'd been one of those army guys who went around disguised as the night, eating tree bark and beetles, scaring the bejeezus out of emerging third-world insurgents. He was a civilian now, of sorts, sometimes working for Vinnie as an apprehension agent. He supposedly lived in the 'hood among his Cuban relatives, and he knew things I'd never, ever know.

He wore his black hair slicked back into a ponytail, dressed in black and khaki, had a washboard belly, cast-iron biceps and the reflexes of a rattler.

His mouth twitched into a smile at the sight of Lula in her Wild West garb. He acknowledged my presence with eye contact and an almost imperceptible nod, which was the Ranger equivalent to a double-cheek kiss.

"Congratulations," I said to him. "I heard you captured Jesus Rodrigues." Jesus Rodrigues skipped out on a $500,000 bond and was howling-dog crazy. Ranger always got the biggies. Fine by me. I don't have a death wish.

"Had some luck," Ranger said, pulling a police body receipt from his jacket pocket—the body receipt certifying that Ranger had delivered a wanted body to the authorities.

He brushed past us on his way to Connie's desk, and I thought Lula would keel over on the spot. She clapped a hand to her heart and staggered out the door after me.

"Gives me a fit every time he comes in," she confided. "You get close to that man, and it's like being close to a lightning strike. Like all the little hairs are standing on end all over your body."

"Sounds like you've been watching *X-Files*."

"Hmm," Lula said, eyeing the key chain. "Maybe we should take my car again. That Buick you drive don't say 'Law Enforcement,' you know what I'm saying? It ain't no Starsky and Hutch car. What you need is to work on your image. You need one of these bad-ass coats. You need a car with real wheels. You need to be a blonde. I'm telling you honey, blonde is where it's at."

"I have a truck," I said, gesturing to the Nissan. "Bought it this morning." After signing the papers I'd gotten my father to drive back with me, so he could take the Buick home, and I could go with my new pickup. You're making a mistake, he said. Japs don't know how to make cars for Americans. This truck isn't half the car the Buick is.

And that was exactly why I preferred the truck . . . it was half the car the Buick was.

"Isn't this cute as a bug," Lula said. "A baby truck!" She looked in the window. "I don't suppose you'd let me drive. I always wanted to drive one of these itty-bitty trucks."

"Well, sure," I said, handing her the keys. "I guess that'd be okay."

Lula cranked the engine over and pulled away from the curb. The rain had turned sleety and shavings of ice slapped against the windshield. Chunks of slush stuck to the wipers and tracked across the arc of cleared glass.

I looked at the snapshot attached to the bond papers and memorized the face. Didn't want to nab the wrong person. I rooted through my pocketbook and did a fast paraphernalia inventory. I was carrying defense spray, which was a big no-no in a crowded mall. And I carried a stun gun, which on close examination turned out to need a new battery. My two pairs of cuffs were in working order, and I had an almost full can of hair spray. Okay, probably I wasn't the world's best-equipped bounty hunter. But then what did I really need to bring in an old guy with a nose that looked like a penis and a loser hot dog vendor?

"We gotta be professional about this," Lula said, aiming us toward Route 1. "We need a plan."

"How about we get the nail polish first, then we get the guy?"

"Yeah, but how are we going to do this? We can't just stand in line, and when it's our turn we say, 'Two chili dogs to go, and you're under arrest.' "

"It's not that complicated. I simply take him aside, show him my identification and explain the procedure to him."

"You think he's gonna stand still for that? This here's a fugitive we're talking about."

Lula gunned the little truck and hopped over a lane. We spun slush at a few cautious drivers and skipped back into line. The heater was going full blast, and I could feel my eyebrows starting to smoke.

"So what do you think?" I asked Lula. "Drives good, huh? And it's got a great heater."

Brake lights flashed in front of us, red smears beyond the beat of the wipers, and Lula silently stared ahead.

"Lula?"

No response.

"Uh, those cars are stopped ahead," I said, not wanting to offend, but suspecting Lula might be having an out-of-body experience.

She bobbed her head. "Not that I'm afraid of no fugitive . . ."

"CARS!" I yelled. "STOPPED CARS!"

Lula's eyes popped open, and she stomped on the brakes. "Holy shit!"

The Nissan skidded forty feet and careened onto the shoulder, missing a van by half an inch. We did a one-eighty and sat facing traffic.

"Light in the back," Lula said. "You might want to put some weight over the wheels."

My first choice of ballast would be a 230-pound file clerk. "Maybe I should drive."

"I'm okay now," Lula said, easing back into traffic. "It's just I've never been along when you actually apprehended someone."

"It's like picking up laundry. You go to the dry cleaner. You show him your ticket. You take your stuff home. Only in this case, we take the stuff to the police station."

"I know my way around the police station," Lula said.

CHAPTER 3

Lula and I parked at the mall entrance nearest the hot dog stand and hustled, under low gray skies, through the rain and sleet and slush. We marched straight across the mall to Macy's, with people walking into walls, mouths agape at Lula in her duster.

"Uh-oh, look at this," Lula said. "They got pocketbooks on sale here. I'd be fine carrying that little red one with the gold chain."

We paused to look at the red pocketbook and to test-drive it on Lula's shoulder.

"Hard to tell with this big coat on," Lula said.

A salesperson had been hovering. "If you care to take the coat off I'd be happy to hold it for you."

"I sure would like to," Lula said, "but it might not be a good idea. We're bounty hunters after a man, and I got a gun on under this coat."

"Bounty hunters?" the woman said on a gasp. The term synonymous with "lunatic vermin."

I slipped the pocketbook off Lula's shoulder and put it back on the counter. I grabbed Lula by the elbow and yanked her after me. "You don't really have a gun under that coat, do you?"

"A woman's got to protect herself."

I was afraid to ask what sort of gun she was carrying. Probably an assault rifle or a military-issue rocket launcher.

"We need to get nail polish for Connie," I told her. "Something red."

Lula stopped at the fragrance counter and squirted herself with a tester. "What do you think?"

"If it doesn't wear off by the time we get back to the truck, you're taking a bus home."

She tried another one. "This any better?"

"No more perfume! They're making my nose clog up."

"Boy, no pocketbooks, no perfume. You don't know much about shopping, do you?"

"What do you like in nail polish?" I held two colors out for her opinion.

"The one on the left is serious red. Looks like someone opened a vein and bottled it. Dracula'd go ape shit for that red."

I supposed if it was good enough for Dracula, it was good enough for Connie.

I bought the nail enamel, and then we dallied in lipsticks, testing a few on the backs of our hands, not finding any worthy of purchase.

We crossed the mall and took a moment to scope out the hot dog place. Thanks to the weather and the time of day, the mall was relatively empty. That was good. We'd make less of a spectacle of ourselves and Stuart. There were no customers buying hot dogs. One person worked the counter. That one person was Stuart Baggett, right down to his little plastic name tag.

What I needed here was a pimpled skinhead. Or a big nasty ogre-type guy. I needed an arrest where the lines were clearly drawn. I didn't want another Mo fiasco. I wanted bad man against the good bounty hunter.

What I had was Stuart Baggett, five feet, six inches tall, with freshly cut sandy blond hair and eyes like a cocker spaniel. I did a mental grimace. I was going to look like an idiot arresting this guy.

"Remember," I said to Lula, "I do the talking. And most of all, don't shoot him."

"Not unless he starts something."

"He isn't going to start something, and even if he does there will be *no shooting!*"

"Hunh," Lula said. "No pocketbooks, no perfume, no shooting. You got an awful lot of rules, you know that?"

I put my hands on the counter. "Stuart Baggett?"

"Yes ma'am," he said. "What can I get for you? Chili dog? Frank-n-kraut? Cheese dog?"

I showed him my identification and told him I represented his bond agent.

He blinked. "Bond agent?"

"Yeah," Lula said. "The Italian pervert who sprung your white ass from the tank."

Stuart still looked confused.

"You missed your court date," I said to Stuart.

His face brightened as the lightbulb suddenly snapped on. "Right! My court date. I'm sorry about that, but I had to work. My boss, Eddie Rosenberg, couldn't find anybody to sub for me."

"Did you inform the court of this fact and ask to have your date rescheduled?"

His face returned to nobody home. "Should I have done that?"

"Oh boy," Lula said. "Stupid alert."

"You need to check in with the court," I told Stuart. "I'll give you a ride downtown."

"I can't just walk off," he said. "I'm the only one working today. I have to work until nine."

"Maybe if you called your boss he could find someone to fill in for you."

"Tomorrow's my day off," Stuart said. "I could go tomorrow."

On the surface that sounded like a reasonable idea. My bounty hunting experience, limited as it was, told me otherwise. When tomorrow arrived Stuart would have pressing plans that didn't include a trip to the pokey.

"It would be best if we took care of this today," I said.

"It would be irresponsible," Stuart said, starting to look panicky. "I can't do it now."

Lula grunted. "It isn't like you're doing big business here. We're in the middle of a slush storm, Stuart. Get real."

"Does she work for my bond agent too?" Stuart asked.

"You bet your ass I do," Lula said.

I looked out at the mall, and then I looked at Stuart and his hot dog concession. "She's right, Stuart," I said. "This mall is empty."

"Yeah, but look, I've got all these hot dogs on the grill."

I scrounged in the bottom of my pocketbook and came up with a twenty. "Here's enough money to cover them. Throw the hot dogs in the trash and close up."

"I don't know," Stuart said. "They're really good hot dogs. It doesn't seem right to throw them away."

I did some mental screaming. "Okay, then wrap them up. We'll take them with us."

"I want two chili dogs," Lula said. "And then I want two with sauerkraut and mustard. And do you have any of them curly fries?"

Stuart looked at me. "How about you? How do you want the rest of the hot dogs?"

"Plain."

"Hunh-uh," Lula said. "You better get some chili dogs for Connie. She's gonna be real disappointed she sees my chili dogs, and she's left with some plain-ass dog."

"Okay, okay! Two more chili dogs," I told Stuart, "and then just put the rest in a bag."

"How about soda?" Lula asked. "I can't eat all these hot dogs without soda."

I ordered three medium fries and three large root beers, and forked over another twenty.

Stuart called his boss and lied his heart out about how he was sick and throwing up all over the place, and that he'd sold all his hot dogs, and no one was in the mall anyway on account of the weather and he was going home.

We pulled the front grate, locked up the concession and left with our bags of food and soda.

The parking lot had some remnants of slush, but the sleet had turned to driving rain. We wedged Stuart and the bags between us and rode in silence back to Trenton. From time to time I checked Stuart's expression. His face was pale, and I suspected he hadn't tried very hard to make his trial date. He looked like a person who'd given his best shot to denial and had lost. I guess being short and cute didn't help all that much when it was time to grow up.

If he hadn't shot up police cars he probably wouldn't even have needed bail. And if he'd played by the rules he probably would have gotten away with probation and fine. New Jersey was up to its armpits in criminals. It didn't have a lot of room in the prison system for amateurs like Stuart.

Lula took a turnoff into center city, stopped for a light and the Nissan stalled out. She started it up again; it ran rough for a few seconds and went into another stall.

"Maybe you're not doing the clutch right," I suggested.

"I guess I know how to do a clutch," Lula said. "Looks to me like you got a lemon car."

"Let me try it," I said, opening my door, running to the driver's side.

Lula stood at roadside and watched. "This car is busted," she said. "You know what I'm telling you?"

I started it up. The car bucked forward a few feet and died.

"Maybe we should look under the hood," Lula said. "Maybe you got a cat in your engine. My neighbor, Midgie, once got a cat in his engine. Cat looked like it had been put through a food processor by the time Midgie figured out to check under the hood."

Stuart made a face that said, *Yuk!*

"Happens all the time," Lula said. "They get cold and they go to the warm engine. Then they fall asleep and when you go to start the car . . . cat stew."

I popped the hood and Lula and I checked for cats.

"Guess that wasn't it," Lula said. "I don't see any cat guts."

We slammed the hood down, and Lula got back behind the wheel. "I can do this," she said. "All I gotta do is race the engine, so it don't stall."

We drove two more blocks and cringed when the light turned red ahead. Lula eased up to the last car in line. "No sweat," she said. "Got this made." She raced the engine. The truck idled rough and started to stall. Lula raced the engine some more and somehow the truck lurched forward and smashed into the car in front.

"Oops," Lula said.

We got out to take a look. The car in front had a nasty crumple in its left rear quarter panel. The Nissan had a chunk torn out of its snoot and a deep gash in its bumper.

The man driving the car in front of us wasn't happy. "Why don't you watch where you're going?" he yelled at Lula. "Why don't you learn how to drive?"

"Don't you yell at me," Lula told him. "I don't take no yelling at. And on top of that I can drive just fine. It happens that my vehicle wasn't working properly."

"You got insurance?" the man wanted to know.

"Damn skippy I got insurance," Lula said. "Not only do I have insurance, but I'm filling out a police report. And on that police report I'm telling them about your brake lights all covered with dirt and ice, which were a contributing factor."

I exchanged information with the man, and Lula and I turned back to the Nissan.

"Uh-oh," Lula said, opening the driver's side door. "I don't see Stuart Baggett in here. Stuart Baggett's done the good-bye thing."

Cars were lined up behind us, straggling around the accident one at a time. I climbed into the truck bed to get some height and looked in all directions, up and down the road, but Stuart was nowhere to be seen. I thunked my head with the heel of my hand. Stupid, stupid, stupid. I hadn't even cuffed him.

"He didn't look smart enough to run off," Lula said.

"Deceptively cute."

"Yeah, that was it. Deceptively cute."

"I suppose we should go to the police station and file an accident report," I said.

"Yeah, and we don't want to forget about the dirty taillights. Insurance companies love that shit."

I piled in next to Lula, and we kept our eyes open for Stuart as we drove, but Stuart was long gone.

Lula looked nervous when we finally chugged into the lot for the municipal building that housed the courts and the police station. "I'd appreciate it if you'd run in and fill out the form," Lula said. "Wouldn't want anybody to get the wrong idea about me being at the police station. Think they see me sitting on the bench they might take away my shoelaces."

I had my hand on the door handle. "You aren't going to leave me stranded again, are you?"

"Who me?"

It took me a half hour to complete the paperwork. When I exited the building there was no blue Nissan parked in the lot and no blue Nissan parked on the street. I wasn't surprised. I went back into the station and called the office.

"I'm stranded again," I said to Connie.

I could hear wrappers rustling, and I could hear Connie swallow.

"What is that?" I demanded. "Are you eating hot dogs? Let me talk to Lula."

" 'Lo," Lula said. "What's up?"

"I'm wet and cold and stranded . . . that's what's up. And I'm hungry. You better not have eaten all those hot dogs."

"We would have waited for you, but didn't seem right to let the food set around."

There was a pause, and I could hear her sipping soda.

"You want a ride?" she finally said. "I could come get you."

"That would be nice."

A half hour later we were back at the office. Lula's hooker friend Jackie was there, and she was eating a hot dog.

"Hey, girlfriend," Lula shouted to Jackie. "You come to see me?"

"Nope," Jackie said, "Came to see Stephanie."

Connie handed me a cold hot dog. "Jackie's got man problems."

"Yeah," Jackie said. "Missing man problems."

Lula leaned forward. "You telling me your old man took off?"

"That's what I'm telling you," Jackie said. "I've been standing out on that corner in the freezing cold, doing my thing, supporting that loser in fine style, and this is the thanks I get. No note. No good-bye. No nothin'. And that isn't even the worst of it. That no good jerk-off took my car."

Lula looked appalled. "He took the Chrysler?"

"That's it, woman. He took the Chrysler. I still have ten payments on that car."

I finished my hot dog and handed the little nail polish bag to Connie. "Vinnie ever show?"

"No. He hasn't come in yet."

"Bet he be doing a nooner somewhere," Lula said. "That man got a 'tosterone problem. He's one of those do it with barnyard animals."

"Anyway, I came to you for help on account of you're good at finding missing shit," Jackie said to me. "I got money. I can pay you."

"She's the best," Lula said. "Stephanie here can find any shit you want. You want her to find your old man, it's a done deal."

"Hell, I don't give a flip about that worthless piece of trash. I want her to find my car," Jackie said. "How am I supposed to get around without a car? I had to take a cab over here today. And how am I supposed to ply my trade in weather like this without no backseat? You think all johns got their own backseat? No way. My business is hurting because of this."

"Have you reported the theft to the police?" I asked.

Jackie shifted her weight, one hand on hip. "Say what?"

"Maybe your car's been impounded," I suggested.

"I already checked impound," Connie said. "They don't have it."

"Was a ninety-two Chrysler LeBaron. Dark blue. Got it used six months ago," Jackie said. She handed me a file card. "Here's the license number. Last I saw it was two days ago."

"Anything else missing? Money? Clothes? This guy pack a bag when he leave?" I asked.

"Only thing missing is his worthless body and my car."

"Maybe he just out drunk somewhere," Lula said. "Maybe he just ho'in' around."

"Nuh-uh. I would of known. He's gone, I'm telling you."

Lula and I exchanged glances, and I suspected Jackie was right about the worthless body part.

"Why don't we take Jackie home," Lula said to me. "And then we could kind of cruise around and see what we can see."

The tone surprised me. Soft and serious. Not the Lula who played bounty hunter at the mall.

"We could do that," I said. "We might find something."

All of us watching Jackie. Jackie not showing much but anger at losing her car. That was Jackie's way.

Lula had her hat on her head and her duster buckled up. "I'll be back later to do the filing," she told Connie.

"Just don't go into any banks in that getup," Connie said.

Jackie rented a two-room apartment three blocks from Uncle Mo's. Since we were in the neighborhood, we made a short detour to Ferris Street and looked things over.

"Nothing new here," Lula said, letting her Firebird idle in the middle of the empty street. "No lights, no nothing."

We drove down King and turned into the alley behind Mo's store. I hopped out and peeked into the garage. No car. No lights on in the back of the upstairs apartment.

"There's something going on here," I said. "It doesn't make sense."

Lula slowly made her way to Jackie's rooming house, taking a street for four blocks and then doubling back one street over, the three of us on the lookout for Jackie's car. We'd covered a sizable chunk of neighborhood by the time we reached Jackie's house, but nothing turned up.

"Don't you worry," Lula said to Jackie. "We'll find your car. You go on in and watch some TV. Only thing good to do on a day like this is watch TV. Go check out the bitches on them daytime shows."

Jackie disappeared behind a screen of rain, into the maroonshingled two-story row house. The street was lined with cars. None of them Jackie's Chrysler.

"What's he like?" I asked Lula.

"Jackie's old man? Nothing special. Comes and goes. Sells some."

"What's his name?"

"Cameron Brown. Street name is Maggot. Guess that tell you something."

"Would he take off with Jackie's car?"

"In a heartbeat." Lula pulled away from the curb. "You're the expert finder here. What we do next?"

"Let's do more of the same," I said. "Let's keep driving. Canvass the places Brown would ordinarily hang at."

Two hours later Lula missed a street in the rain, and before we could make a correction we were down by the river, weaving our way through a complex of high-rises.

"This is getting old," Lula said, "Bad enough straining my eyeballs looking for some dumb car, but now I'm lost."

"We're not lost," I told her. "We're in Trenton."

"Yeah, but I've never been in this part of Trenton before. I don't feel comfortable driving around buildings that haven't got gang slogans sprayed on them. Look at this place. No boarded-up windows. No garbage in the gutter. No brothers selling goods on the street. Don't know how people can live like this." She squinted into the gray rain and eased the car into a parking lot. "I'm turning around," she said. "I'm taking us back to the office, and I'm gonna nuke up some of them left-over hot dogs and then I'm gonna do my filing."

It was okay by me because riding around in the pouring rain in slum neighborhoods wasn't my favorite thing to do anyway.

Lula swung down a line of cars and there in front of us was the Chrysler.

We both sat dumbstruck, barely believing our eyes. We'd painstakingly covered every likely street and alley, and here was the car, parked in a most unlikely place.

"Sonovabitch," Lula said.

I studied the building at the edge of the lot. Eight stories high. A big cube of uninspired brick and low-energy window glass. "Looks like apartments."

Lula nodded, and we returned our attention to the Chrysler. Not especially anxious to investigate.

"I guess we should take a look," Lula finally said.

We both heaved a sigh and got out of the Firebird. The rain had tapered to a drizzle, and the temperature was dropping. The cold seeped through my skin, straight to my bones, and the possibility of finding Cameron Brown dead in the trunk of Jackie's car did nothing to warm me from the inside out.

We gingerly looked in the windows and tried the doors. The doors were locked. The interior of the car was empty. No Cameron Brown. No obvious clues . . . like notes detailing Brown's recent life history or maps with a bright orange X to mark the spot. We stood side by side, looking at the trunk.

"Don't see no blood dripping out," Lula said. "That's a good sign." She went to her own trunk and returned with a crowbar. She slipped it under the Chrysler's trunk lid and popped the lid open.

Spare tire, dirty yellow blanket, a couple grimy towels. No Cameron Brown.

Lula and I expelled air in a simultaneous whoosh.

"How long has Jackie been seeing this guy?" I asked.

"About six months. Jackie doesn't have good luck with men. Doesn't want to see what's real."

Lula tossed the crowbar onto her backseat and we both got back into the Firebird.

"So what's real this time around?" I asked.

"This Maggot's a user from the word go. He pimping Jackie and then using her car to deal. He could of got a car of his own, but he uses Jackie's because everybody knows she a ho, and if the cops stop him and there's stuff in the trunk he just say he don't know how it got there. He say he just borrowed the car from his ho girlfriend. And everybody knows Jackie do some drugs. Only reason anybody be a ho is 'cause they do drugs."

"Think Brown was selling drugs here?"

Lula shook her head, no. "He don't sell drugs to this kind of folks. He pushes to the kiddies."

"Then maybe he has a girlfriend upstairs."

Lula rolled the engine over and pulled out of the lot. "Maybe, but it looks kind of high-class for Cameron Brown."

By the time I dragged into my apartment at five o'clock I was thoroughly depressed. I was back to driving the Buick. My pickup was at a Nissan service center awaiting repairs after Blue Ribbon Used Cars refused responsibility, citing a clause on my sales receipt that said I'd bought the car "as is." No returns. No guarantees.

My shoes were soaked through, my nose was running and I couldn't stop thinking about Jackie. Finding her car seemed totally inadequate. I wanted to improve her life. I wanted to get her off drugs, and I wanted to change her profession. Hell, she wasn't so dumb. She could probably be a brain surgeon if she just had a decent haircut.

I left my shoes in the hall and dropped the rest of my clothes on the bathroom floor. I stood in the shower until I was defrosted. I toweled my hair dry and ran my fingers through it by way of styling. I dressed in thick white socks, sweatpants and sweatshirt.

I took a soda from the fridge, snatched a pad and pen from the kitchen counter and settled myself at the dining table. I wanted to review my ideas on Mo Bedemier, and I wanted to figure out what I was missing.

I awoke at nine o'clock with the spiral binding of the steno pad imprinted on the left side of my face and my notebook pages as blank as my mind. I shoved the hair out of my eyes, punched 4 on my speed dial and ordered a pizza to be delivered—extra cheese, black olives, peppers and onions.

I took hold of the pen and drew a line on the empty page. I drew a happy face. I drew a grumpy face. I drew a heart with my initials in it, but then I didn't have anyone else's initials to write next to mine, so I went back to thinking about Mo.

Where would Mo go? He left most of his clothes behind. His drawers were filled with socks and underwear. His toiletries were intact. Toothbrush, razor, deodorant in the medicine chest over the bathroom sink. That had to mean something, right? The logical conclusion was that he had another apartment where he kept a spare toothbrush. Trouble was . . . life wasn't always logical. The utilities check hadn't turned up anything. Of course that only meant that if Mo had a second house or apartment, it wasn't registered under his name.

The other possibility, that Mo was snatched and most likely was dead somewhere, waiting to be found, was too depressing to ponder. Best to set that one aside for now, I decided.

And what about Mo's mail? I couldn't remember seeing a mailbox. Probably the mailman brought the mail into the store and gave it to Mo. So what was happening to the mail now?

Check the post office, I wrote on the pad.

I smelled pizza get off the elevator, and I hustled to the foyer, flipped the chain, threw the bolts back on the two Yale locks, opened the door and stared out at Joe Morelli.

"Pizza delivery," he said.

I narrowed my eyes.

"I was at Pino's when the order came in."

"So this really is my pizza?"

Morelli pushed past me and set the pizza on the kitchen counter. "Cross my heart and hope to die." He got two beers out of the refrigerator, balanced the pizza box on one hand and carted everything into the living room and set it all on the coffee table. He picked the channel changer off the sofa and punched the Knicks game on.

"Make yourself at home," I said.

Morelli smiled.

I set two plates, a roll of paper towels and a pizza cutter next to the pizza box. Truth is, I wasn't completely unhappy to see Morelli. He radiated body heat, which I seemed to be lacking today, and as a cop he had resources that were useful to a bounty hunter. There might be other reasons as well, having to do with ego and lust, but I didn't feel like admitting to those reasons.

I recut the pizza and slid pieces onto plates. I handed one plate to Morelli. "You know a guy named Cameron Brown?"

"Pimp," Morelli said. "Very oily. Deals some dope." He looked at me over the edge of his pizza. "Why?"

"You remember Jackie? Lula's friend?"

"Jackie the hooker."

"Yeah. Well she came to Vinnie's office today to see if I could find her car. Seems her boyfriend, Cameron Brown, took off with it."

"And?"

"And, Lula and I cruised around awhile and finally found the car parked in the RiverEdge Apartments parking lot."

Morelli stopped eating. "Keep going."

"That's about it. Jackie said she didn't care about finding Cameron. She just wanted her car."

"So what's your problem?"

I chewed some pizza. "I don't know. The whole thing feels . . . nasty. Unfinished."

"Stay out of it."

"Excuse me?"

"It's Jackie's problem," Morelli said. "Mind your own business. You got her car back. Let it rest."

"She's sort of my friend."

"She's a doper. She's nobody's friend."

I knew he was right, but I was still surprised at the harsh comment and at the emphatic tone. A little alarm sounded in my brain. Usually when Morelli felt this strongly about my not getting involved in something it was because he didn't want me muddying waters he'd staked out for himself.

Morelli sank back into the couch with his bottle of beer. "Whatever happened to the all-out search for Mo?"

"I'm all out of ideas." I had wolfed down two pieces of pizza and was eyeing a third. "So tell me," I said to Morelli. "What's going on with Jackie and her old man? Why don't you want me getting involved?"

"Like I said, it's none of your business." Morelli leaned forward, raised the lid on Rex's hamster cage and chucked a chunk of pizza crust into Rex's little ceramic food dish.

"Tell me anyway," I said.

"There's not much to tell. I just think there's a funny climate on the streets. The dealers are pulling back, getting cautious. Rumor has it some have disappeared."

His attention was diverted to the television. "Watch this," he said. "Watch the replay of this layup."

"The guys in vice must be ecstatic."

"Yeah," Morelli said. "They're sitting around playing cards and eating jelly doughnuts for lack of crime."

I was still debating the third piece of pizza. My thighs really didn't need it, but life was so short, and physical gratification was hard to come by these days. The hell with it. Eat the damn thing and get it over with, I thought.

I saw a smile twitch at the corners of Morelli's mouth.

"What?" I yelled at him.

He held two hands in the air. "Hey, don't yell at me just because you have no willpower."

"I have plenty of willpower." Man, I *hated* when Morelli was right. "Why are you here anyway?"

"Just being sociable."

"And you want to see if I have anything new on Mo."

"Yeah."

I'd expected him to deny it, and now I was left with nothing accusatory to say.

"Why are you so interested in Mo?" I asked.

Morelli shrugged. "Everyone in the burg is interested in Mo. I spent a lot of time in that store as a kid."

Morning dawned late under a tedious cloud cover that was the color and texture of cement curbing. I finished up the pizza for breakfast and was feeding Rex Cheerios and raisins when the phone rang.

"Man, this is one ugly morning," Lula said. "And it's getting uglier by the minute."

"Are you referring to the weather?" I asked.

"That too. Mostly I'm referring to human nature. We got a situation on our hands. Jackie's got herself staked out in the FancyAss parking lot, looking to catch her old man doin' the deed. I told her to go home, but she don't listen to me. I told her he probably isn't even there. What would he be doing with a woman could afford to live in a place like that? I told her that motherfucker got capped. I told her she be better off checking the Dumpsters, but it go on deaf ears."

"And?"

"And I thought you could talk to her. She's gonna freeze to death. She's been sitting there all night."

"What makes you think she'll listen to me?"

"You could tell her you got some surveillance going on, and she don't need to butt in."

"That would be a lie."

"What, you never lied before?"

"Okay," I said. "I'll see what I can do."

Half an hour later, I turned the Buick into the RiverEdge Apartments parking lot. Jackie was there, all right, parked in her Chrysler. I pulled up behind her, got out, and rapped on her window.

"Yeah?" Jackie said by way of greeting, not sounding all that happy.

"What are you doing here?"

"I'm waiting for that shit-ass car thief to come out, and then I'm going to put a hole in him big enough to drive a truck through."

I don't know a whole lot about guns, but the cannon resting on the seat next to Jackie looked like it could do the job.

"That's a pretty good idea," I said, "but you look cold. Why don't you let me take over the surveillance for a while?"

"Thanks all the same, but you found him, and now I get to kill him."

"Makes perfect sense to me. I just thought it might be better to kill him when it warms up some. After all, there isn't any real rush. No point sitting out here, catching a cold, just to kill a guy."

"Yeah, but I feel like killing him now. I don't feel like waiting. Besides, I'm not gonna do any business today what with this weather. Only crazy men go out to get their oil changed on a day like this, and I don't need any of that lunatic dick shit. Nope, I might as well sit here. Better than standing on my corner."

She could be right.

"Okay," I said. "Be careful."

"Hunh," Jackie said.

I drove over to the office and told Lula that Jackie was hunkered in for the siege.

"Hunh," Lula said.

Vinnie popped out of his office.

"Well?" Vinnie asked.

We all looked at him. Well what?

Vinnie settled on me. "Where's Mo? Why don't we have Mo in custody? How hard could it be to catch an old man who sells candy?"

"Mo's done a disappearing act," I said. "He's temporarily vanished."

"So where have you looked? You check his apartment? You check his sister? You check his boyfriend?"

The office went suddenly silent.

I found my voice first. "Boyfriend?"

Vinnie smiled. His teeth white and even in his olive complexion. "You didn't know?"

"Oh my God," Connie said, doing the sign of the cross. "Oh my God."

My head was reeling. "Are you sure?" I asked Vinnie. As if I'd doubt Vinnie for a nanosecond when it came to expertise in alternative sexual behavior.

"Moses Bedemier is a flaming fruit," Vinnie said, his face wreathed in happiness, his hands jiggling change in the deep pockets of his pleated polyester slacks. "Moses Bedemier wears ladies' panties."

Vincent Plum, bail bonds. Specializing in sensitivity and political correctness.

I turned to Lula. "I thought you said Mo was a customer."

"Unh-uh. I said I knew him. Sometimes when I was on the corner he'd ride by late at night and ask directions of Jackie or me. He'd want to know where to find Freddie the Frog or Little Lionel. I figure he do some drugs."

"Oh my God," Connie said. "A homosexual and a drug user. Oh my God."

"How do you know?" I asked Vinnie.

"I'd heard rumors. And then I saw him and his significant other having dinner in New Hope a couple months ago."

"How do you know it was a significant other and not just a friend?"

"What, you want details?" Vinnie said, smiling wide, enjoying the moment.

I grimaced and shook my head, no.

Connie squeezed her eyes shut tight.

"Yo ass," Lula said.

"Do you have a name?" I asked Vinnie. "What's this guy look like?"

"The guy was Mo's age. Smaller, slimmer. Soft, like Mo. Dark hair, bald on top. I don't have a name, but I can make some phone calls."

I didn't give much credence to the drug buyer theory, but I wouldn't want it to be said I'd left a stone unturned. When Lula was hooking she'd plied her trade on Stark Street, a mile-long strip of bars and crack houses and row houses converted to airless apartments and rooms to let. It'd be a waste of time for me to canvass Stark Street. No one would talk to me. That left me with two alternatives. Lula was one of them. Ranger was the other.

CHAPTER 4

I could ask Ranger to make inquiries on Mo. Or I could ask Lula. This was a dilemma, being that Ranger would be my first choice, but Lula was here in front of me, on the scent, reading my mind.

"Well?" Lula asked. Shifting her weight. Nervous. Belligerent. Rhino mode. Looking like her feelings would be hurt if I didn't ask her to work with me. Looking like at any moment she might narrow her eyes and squash me like a bug.

So I was beginning to see the wisdom of using Lula. No point to hurting her feelings, right? And probably Lula would be cool with this. I mean, what was the big deal? All she had to do was show Mo's picture to a few drug dealers and hookers. So she wasn't subtle. Hey, was that a crime?

"You have a lot of contacts on Stark Street," I said to Lula. "Maybe you could flash Mo's picture. See if someone can give us a lead."

Lula's face brightened. "You bet. I could do that."

"Yeah," Vinnie said. "Get her out of the office for a while. She makes me nervous."

"You should be nervous," Lula told him. "I'm keeping my eye on your sad ass. You better not trifle with me, mister."

Vinnie set his teeth, and I thought I saw wisps of steam curl out of his ears and evaporate off the top of his head. But maybe it was just my imagination.

"I'll make some phone calls. I'll see if I can get a name for Mo's boyfriend," Vinnie said, retreating into his private lair, slamming the door behind him.

Lula had one arm rammed into her coat. "And I'm gonna get right on this. I'm gonna detect the shit out of this case."

With everyone else in motion, there didn't seem to be much for me to do. I retraced my steps back to my Buick and drove home on autopilot. I pulled into the lot to my apartment building and looked up at my window. I'd left the light burning in my bedroom, and it was all cheerful and welcoming now. A rectangle of comfort floating high above the gray miasma of morning ice smog.

Mr. Kleinschmidt was in the lobby when I swung through the double glass doors.

"Ho," Mr. Kleinschmidt said. "It's the early bounty hunter that catches the worm. Tracking down a ruthless murderer today?"

"Nope. No murderers," I said.

"Drug dealer? Rapist?"

"Nope. Nope."

"Who then? What gets you up and out so early?"

"Actually, I'm looking for Moses Bedemier."

"That's not funny," Mr. Kleinschmidt said. "That's not a good joke. I know Moses Bedemier. Mo would never do anything bad. I think you should look for someone else."

I stepped into the elevator and pushed the second-floor button. I gave Mr. Kleinschmidt a little finger-wave good-bye, but he didn't wave back.

"Why me?" I said to the empty elevator. "Why me?"

I let myself into my apartment and looked in at Rex. He was sleeping in his soup can. Nice and quiet. That's one of the terrific things about having a hamster as a roommate; hamsters keep their thoughts to themselves. If Rex had an opinion about Moses Bedemier, he didn't lay it on me.

I nuked a cup of coffee and settled down to make phone calls.

I started with my cousin Jeanine, who worked at the post office. Jeanine told me Mo's mail was being held, and that Mo hadn't left a forwarding address, nor had he retrieved anything.

I talked to Linda Shantz, Loretta Beeber and Margaret Molinowsky. No one had much to say about Mo, but I found out my archenemy, Joyce Barnhardt, had a drug-resistant yeast infection. That cheered me up some.

At one o'clock I called Vinnie to see if he'd been able to get a name for me. The call was switched to the answering service, and I realized it was Saturday. The office was only open for a half day on Saturday.

I thought about doing something athletic, like going for a run, but when I looked out the living room window it was still January, so I trashed the physical fitness idea.

I returned to the phone and dialed up some more busybodies. I figured it would take me days to go through my list of gossips, and in the meantime I could pretend I was accomplishing something.

By three-thirty my ear felt swollen, and I wasn't sure how much longer I could take being glued to the phone. I was contemplating a nap when someone hammered on my door.

I opened the door and Lula rolled in.

"Outta my way," she said. "I'm so frozen I can't walk straight. My black ass turned blue a half hour ago."

"Do you want hot chocolate?"

"I'm way past hot chocolate. I need alcohol."

I'm not much of a drinker. I'd long ago decided it was best not to muddy the waters of my brain with serious booze. I had a hard enough time making sense when I was sober.

"I haven't got much in the way of alcohol," I told Lula. "Light beer, red wine, mouthwash."

"Pass on that. I just wanted to tell you about Mo, anyway. Carla, the ho on Seventh and Stark, says she saw Mo two days ago. According to Carla, Mo was looking for Shorty O."

I felt my mouth fall open. Mo was on Stark Street two days ago. Holy cow.

"How reliable is Carla?"

"Well she wasn't shaking or nothing today, so I think she could see the picture I showed her," Lula said. "And she wouldn't mess with me."

"What about Shorty O? Do you know him?"

"Everybody knows Shorty O. Shorty's one of those influential people on Stark Street. Middle management. Do some demolition work when there's a need. I would have talked to him, but I couldn't find him."

"Do you think Mo found him?"

"Hard to say."

"Anyone else see Mo?"

"Not that I know of. I asked lots of people, too, but with this weather, people aren't out looking around." Lula stamped her feet and made flapping warm-up motions with her arms. "I gotta go. I'm going home. It's Saturday, and I got a date tonight. I gotta get my hair done. Just because I'm a natural beauty don't mean I don't need extra help sometime."

I thanked Lula and saw her to the elevator. I returned to my apartment and thought about this latest development. Hard to believe Mo was on Stark Street for whatever reason. Still, I wasn't going to totally discount anything . . . no matter how preposterous. Especially since this was my only lead.

I punched the speed-dial number for Ranger and left a message on his machine. If anyone could find Shorty O, it would be Ranger.

Sunday morning I got up at ten. I made hot chocolate and French toast, carried it into the living room and slid the Winnie the Pooh video into the VCR. When Winnie was done having his adventures in the Hundred Acre Wood it was almost noon, and I thought it was time to go to work. Since I didn't have a social life, and I didn't have an office, work time was any time I wanted.

And what I wanted today was to get stupid, spineless Stuart Baggett. Mo was cooking on the back burner, but Stuart wasn't cooking at all.

I showered and dressed and resurrected Stuart's file. He lived with his parents at 10 Applegate Street in Mercerville. I spread my street map on the dining room table and located Applegate. It looked to be about two miles from the mall where Stuart worked. Very convenient.

I've been told there are places in the country where stores close on Sunday. This would never happen in Jersey. We wouldn't stand for it. In Jersey it's part of our constitutional rights to shop seven days a week.

I parked the Buick in the mall lot and diligently ignored the stares from people with less imaginative cars. Since my bank account was at an all-time low, I went straight to the hot dog stand. Best not to detour through the shoe department at Macy's and succumb to temptation.

Two young women were behind the hot dog counter.

"Yes ma'am," one said. "What would you like?"

"I'm looking for Stuart Baggett."

"He doesn't work here anymore."

Oh boy. Minor guilt trip. I got the poor schnook fired. "Gee, that's a shame," I said. "Do you know what happened? Do you know where I can find him?"

"He quit. Closed up early a couple days ago and never came back. Don't know where he is."

A small setback, but not devastating since I still had his home to visit.

Applegate was a pleasant street of well-kept single-family houses and mature trees. The Baggett house was a white Cape with blue shutters and a dark blue door. There were two cars and a kid's bike in the driveway.

Mrs. Baggett answered the door. Stuart was close enough to my age that we might be friends. I thought I'd go with this approach first, saying very little, letting Mrs. Baggett assume the obvious.

"Hi," I said. "I'm looking for Stuart."

There was a moment's hesitation, which might have been concern, or maybe she was just trying to place me. "I'm sorry," she said. "Stuart's not home. Was he supposed to meet you here?"

"No. I just thought I might catch him."

"He's with one of his friends," Mrs. Baggett said. "Moved out yesterday. Said he had a new job, and he was going to share a place with this friend of his."

"Do you have an address or a phone number?"

"No. I don't even have a name. He had some words with his father and stormed off. Would you like to leave a message?"

I gave her my card. "Stuart failed to appear in court. He needs to reschedule his court date as soon as possible. It's very important."

Mrs. Baggett made a distressed little sound. "I don't know what to do with him. He's just gone wild."

"I'd appreciate it if you'd call me if you hear from him."

She nodded her head. "I will. I'll call you."

I could expend a lot of energy looking for Stuart, or I could wait for him to go home. I decided to go with the latter. Mrs. Baggett looked like a responsible, intelligent woman. I felt pretty confident that she'd get back to me. If not I'd make a return visit later in the week.

Ranger called back a little after seven with news that Shorty O had gone south for the winter. No one had seen him in days, and that probably included Mo.

* * *

At eight o'clock I was standing across the street from Uncle Mo's, and I was feeling nervous. Even though I had a key to his apartment, there were some who might regard what I was about to do as breaking and entering. Of course I could always fib, and say Uncle Mo had asked me to look after his things. If it was a judge who was doing the asking I guess my answer might fall into that undesirable area of perjury. Perjury seemed like a good thing to avoid. Although in Jersey, written law often bowed to common sense. Which meant perjury was better than being dispatched to the landfill.

The sky was dark. The moon obscured by cloud cover. Lights were on in houses up and down Mo's street, but Mo's apartment windows were black. A car cruised by and parked three houses away. I was lost in shadow and the driver walked from his car to his house without seeming to notice me. I'd left the Buick on Lindal Street, one block away.

I could see Mrs. Steeger moving in her front room. I was waiting for her to settle before going closer. She peered out her living room window, and my heart stopped dead in my chest. She drew back from the window, and I gasped for air. Little black dots danced in front of my eyes. I clapped a hand to my chest. The woman made my blood run cold.

Headlights swung around the corner, and a car stopped at the Steeger house. The driver beeped, and Mrs. Steeger opened her door and waved. A moment later she was locking up behind herself. I held my breath and willed myself invisible. Mrs. Steeger carefully picked her way along the dark steps and sidewalk to the car. She seated herself next to the driver, slammed the door shut and the car drove off.

My lucky day.

I crossed the street and tried Mo's house key on the candy store door with no success. I walked to the back and tried the same key on the rear entrance. The key didn't work there either.

It had occurred to me while talking to Ranger that due to police interruption, I'd never gotten around to searching Mo's store. I don't know what I expected to find, but it felt like unfinished business.

Since the house keys didn't work on the store doors, I assumed there had to be another set of keys in Mo's apartment. I took the stairs as if I owned the place. When in doubt, always look like you know what you're doing. I pulled a flashlight out of my pocketbook and knocked twice. I called to Uncle Mo. No answer. I unlocked the door, took one step inside and swept a beam of light around the room. Everything seemed to be in order, so I closed the door behind myself and did a fast walk-through of the rest of the apartment. There were no keys lying on open surfaces and no cute little key hooks on any of the walls. There was no evidence that anyone had been in the apartment since my last visit.

The kitchen was small. White metal cupboards over a gray Formica countertop and an old white porcelain sink that had a few black chips showing. The cupboards held a mismatched assortment of glasses, cups, plates and bowls. No keys. I went through the under-the-counter drawers. One dedicated to silverware. One for dish towels. One for plastic wrap, aluminum foil, plastic bags. One for junk. Still no keys.

I took a moment to look at the photos on the wall next to the fridge. Pictures of children. All from the burg. I recognized almost everyone. I searched until I found mine. Twelve years old, eating an ice cream cone. I remembered Mo taking the picture.

I poked in the refrigerator, checking for cleverly hollowed out heads of cabbage and fake cola cans. Not finding any, I moved on to the bedroom.

The double bed was covered with a quilted bedspread, its yellow and brown flowers faded, the cotton material softened from years of service. The bed and nightstand were inexpensive walnut veneer. Uncle Mo lived modestly. Guess there wasn't all that much profit in ice cream cones.

I started with the top bureau drawer and sure enough, there was the key ring consigned to its own compartment in a removable wooden jewelry tray. I pocketed the key ring, closed the drawer and was about to leave when the stack of movie magazines caught my eye. *Premiere, Entertainment Weekly, Soap Opera Digest, Juggs.* Whoa! *Juggs*? Not the sort of reading material one would expect to find in a gay man's bedroom.

I wedged the flashlight under my armpit, sank to the floor and flipped through the first half of *Juggs.* Appalling. I flipped through the second half. Equally appalling and fascinatingly disgusting. The next magazine in the stack had a naked man on the cover. He was wearing a black mask and black socks and his Mr. Happy hung almost to his knees. He looked like he'd been sired by Thunder the Wonder Horse. I was tempted to look inside, but the pages were stuck together, so I moved on. I found a couple magazines that I'd never heard of that were devoted primarily to amateurish snapshots of people in various stages of undress, in a variety of embarrassing poses labeled "Mary and Frank from Sioux City" and "Rebecca Sue in Her Kitchen." There were some more *Entertainment Weeklys*, and on the bottom of the pile there were a couple photographic catalogues, which reminded me that I'd found a couple unopened boxes of film in the fridge.

And this reminded me that I was supposed to be conducting an illegal search, not comparing anatomical features with women wearing crotchless panties and spiked dog collars.

I neatened everything up and crept out of the room, out of the apartment, thinking that Uncle Mo was a very weird guy.

There were two keys on the ring. I tried one of the keys on the back door to the store and struck out. I tried the second key and had to squelch a nervous giggle when the door clicked open. There'd been a part of me that hadn't wanted the keys to work. Probably it was the smart part. The part that knew I wouldn't look good in prison clothes.

The door opened to a narrow hall. Three doors ran off the hall, and the hall opened to the store. I could look the length of the hall and the length of the store, through the front plateglass window, and see lights shining in the house across the street. This meant they could also see lights shining in the store, so I would have to be careful how I used my flashlight. I gave the hall and the store a quick flick of the beam to make sure I was alone. I opened the first door to my right and discovered stairs leading to a basement.

I called, "Hello, anybody down there?"

No one answered, so I closed the door. Hollering into the dark was about as brave as I was going to get on the cellar investigation.

The second door was a lavatory. The third door was a broom closet. I cut the light and took a moment to allow my eyes to adjust. It had probably been two or three years since I'd been in the store, but I knew it well, and I knew nothing had changed. Nothing ever changed at Uncle Mo's.

A counter ran front to rear. The back half of the counter was luncheonette style with five stationary stools. Behind this part of the counter Mo had a small cooktop, a plastic cooler of lemonade, a four-spigot soda dispenser, two milkshake shakers, an ice cream cone dispenser and two hotplates for brewing coffee. The front half of the counter consisted of a display case for tubs of ice cream and another display case devoted to candy.

I prowled around, not sure what I was looking for, but pretty sure I hadn't found it. Nothing seemed out of place. Mo had neatened up before he left. There were no dirty dishes or spoons in the sink. No indication that Mo had been disrupted or left in a rush.

I opened the cash drawer. Empty. Not a nickel. I hadn't found any money in the apartment either.

A shadow cut into the ambient light filtering through the front window, and I crouched low behind the counter. The shadow passed, and I wasted no time scuttling to the back of the store. I held up in the hallway, listening.

Footsteps sounded on the cement walkway. I stopped breathing and watched the doorknob turn. The door didn't open. The door was locked. I heard the rasp of a key and stood rooted to the floor in dumbstruck panic. If it was anyone other than Mo I was in very deep shit.

I quietly took two steps back, listening carefully. The key wasn't working. Maybe it wasn't working because it wasn't a key! Maybe someone else was trying to break into Uncle Mo's!

Damn. What were the chances of two people breaking into Mo's at the same time? I shook my head in disgust. Crime was getting out of hand in Trenton.

I slipped into the bathroom, silently closed the door and held my breath. I heard the tumbler click and the back door swing open. Two footsteps. Someone was standing in the hall, getting used to the dark.

Go for the cash drawer and get this over with, I thought. Take all the friggin' ice cream. Have a party.

Shoes scuffed on the wood floor, and a door opened next to me. This would be the door to the cellar. It was held open long enough for someone to look down into the darkness and then was quietly closed. Whoever was in Mo's store was doing the exact same thing I'd done, and I knew with sickening certainty my door would be opened next. There was no way for me to lock the door, and no window to use for escape.

I had my flashlight in one hand and defense spray in the other. I had a gun in my pocketbook, but I knew from past experience I'd be slow to use it. And besides, I wasn't sure I'd remembered to load the gun. Better to go with the defense spray. I was willing to gas almost anyone.

I heard a hand grasp the bathroom doorknob and in the next instant the door to the bathroom was yanked open. I pressed my thumb against the flashlight's switch, catching angry black eyes in my beam. The plan had been to temporarily blind the intruder, make identification and decide how to act.

The error in the plan was in assuming blindness led to paralysis.

Less than a millisecond after hitting the flashlight ON button, I felt myself fly through the air and slam against the back wall of the lavatory. There was a red flash, fireworks exploded in my brain and then everything went black.

My next memory was of struggling to regain consciousness, struggling to open my eyes, struggling to place my surroundings.

It was dark. Night. I put my hand to my face. My face was sticky. A black stain spread from under my cheek. I dumbly stared at the stain. Blood, I thought. Car crash. No, that wasn't right. Then I remembered. I was at Mo's. I was on my side in the little lavatory, my body impossibly twisted around the toilet, my head under the small sink.

It was very quiet. I didn't move. I listened to the silence and waited for my head to clear. I ran my tongue over my teeth. No teeth were broken. I gingerly touched my nose. My nose seemed okay.

The blood had to be coming from somewhere. I was lying in a pool of it.

I pushed up to hands and knees and saw the source of the blood. A body lying facedown in the narrow hallway. Light from an alley streetlight carried through the store's open back door, enabling me to recognize the man on the floor.

It was the guy who'd pitched me against the wall.

I crept forward and took a closer look, seeing the hole in the back of the man's shirt where the bullet had entered, and a similar hole in the back of his head. The wall to my right had been sprayed with blood and brain and the left half of the dead man's face. His right eye was intact, wide and unseeing. The mouth was open, as if he'd been mildly surprised.

The sound that carved up from my throat was part scream, part gag as I floundered away from the body, arms windmilling out, searching for a handhold where none existed. I sat down hard on the floor, back to the wall, unable to think, breathing hard, only aware that time was passing. I swallowed back bile and closed my eyes, and a thought snaked into the horror. The thought was of hope . . . that this wasn't so bad, so final. That the man could be saved. That a miracle would happen.

I opened my eyes and all hope vanished. The man on the floor was beyond a medical miracle. I had brain gunk and bone fragments stuck to my jeans. My assailant had been murdered, and I'd missed it. Unconscious in the bathroom. The idea was ludicrous.

And the killer. Dear God, where was the killer? My heart gave a painful contraction. For all I knew he was hidden in shadow, watching me struggle. My shoulder bag was on the floor, under the sink. I reached inside and found my gun. The gun wasn't loaded. Dammit, I was such a screwup.

I rose to a crouch and looked through the open back door. The yard was partially illuminated, as was the hallway. I was cold in a way that had nothing to do with the weather. I was bathed in sweat, shivering with fear. I wiped my hands on my jeans. Go for the door, I thought, then run for Ferris Street.

I clenched my teeth and took off, stumbling over the obstructing body. I burst through the door and sprinted the length of the building and across the street. I ran to shadow and held up, gasping for air, searching the neighborhood for movement or for the glint of a gun or belt buckle.

A siren sounded in the distance, and at the end of the street I caught the flash of cop lights. Someone had called the police. A second blue-and-white turned the corner at Lindal. The two cars angled into the curb in front of the store. The uniforms got out and trained a flashlight beam into Mo's front window. I didn't recognize either of the uniforms.

I had myself backed into a corner between stoop and porch, two houses down. I kept my eye on the road and rummaged in my pocketbook, looking for my cell phone. I found the phone and dialed Morelli.

Personal feelings aside, Morelli was a very good cop. I wanted him to be first homicide on the scene.

It was well after midnight when Morelli brought me home. He parked his Toyota in my lot and escorted me into the building. He punched the elevator button and stood silently beside me. Neither of us had spoken a word since we'd left the station. We were both too weary for anything other than the most necessary conversation.

I'd given an on-scene report to Morelli and was ordered to go to St. Francis Hospital to have my head examined, inside and out. I was told I had a concussion and a lump. My scalp was intact. After the hospital, I went home to shower and change my clothes and was brought to the station in a blue-and-white for further questioning. I'd done my best to recall details accurately, with the exception of a small memory lapse concerning the key to Mo's apartment and store and how those two doors happened to swing open for me. No need to burden the police with things that didn't matter. Especially if it might give them the wrong idea about unlawful entry. And then there was the matter of my gun, which happened to no longer be in my pocketbook by the time I got to the police station. Wouldn't want to confuse the issue with that either. Or to be embarrassed by the fact that I'd forgotten to load the miserable thing.

When I closed my eyes I saw the intruder. Heavy-lidded black eyes, dark skin, long dreadlocks, mustache and goatee. A big man. Taller than me. And he'd been strong. And quick. What else? He was dead. Very dead. Shot in the back at close range with a .45.

The motive for the shooting was unknown. Also unknown was why I'd been spared.

Mrs. Bartle, across from Mo's store, had called the police. First, to report seeing a suspicious light through the storefront window, and then a second time when she heard gunshot.

Morelli and I stepped out of the elevator and walked the short distance down the hall to my apartment. I unlocked my door, stepped inside and flipped the light switch. Rex paused on his wheel and blinked at us.

Morelli casually looked into the kitchen. He moved to the living room and lit a table lamp. He sauntered into the bedroom and bath and returned to me. "Just checking," he said.

"What were you checking for?"

"I suppose I was checking for the phantom assailant."

I collapsed into a chair. "I wasn't sure you believed me. I don't exactly have an airtight alibi."

"Honey, you don't have any alibi at all. The only reason I didn't book you for murder is I'm too tired to fill out the paperwork."

I didn't have the energy for indignation. "You know I didn't kill him."

"I don't know anything," Morelli said. "What I have is opinion. And my opinion is that you didn't kill the guy with the dreads. Unfortunately, there are no facts to support that opinion."

Morelli was wearing boots and jeans and a heavy olive drab jacket that looked like army issue. The jacket had lots of pockets and flaps and was slightly worn at the cuffs and collar. By day Morelli looked lean and predatory, but sometimes late at night when his features were softened by exhaustion and eighteen hours of beard growth there were glimpses of a more vulnerable Morelli. I found the vulnerable Morelli to be dangerously endearing. Fortunately, the vulnerable Morelli wasn't showing its face tonight. Tonight Morelli was all tired cop.

Morelli strolled into the kitchen, lifted the lid on my brown bear cookie jar and looked inside. "Where's your thirty-eight? It wasn't on you, and it's not in your cookie jar."

"It's sort of lost." It was lost two houses down and across the street from Mo's store, neatly tucked into an azalea bush. I'd called Ranger when I'd stopped home to shower, and I'd asked him to quietly retrieve the gun for me.

"Sort of lost," Morelli said. "Unh."

I saw him out and locked the door after him. I dragged myself into the bedroom and flopped on the bed. I lay there fully clothed with all the lights blazing and finally fell asleep when I could see the sun shining through my bedroom curtains.

At nine o'clock I opened my eyes to pounding on my apartment door. I lay there for a moment hoping the pounder would go away if I ignored him.

"Open up. It's the police," the pounder yelled.

Eddie Gazarra. My second-best friend all through grade school, now a cop, married to my cousin Shirley.

I rolled out of bed, shuffled to the door and squinted at Gazarra. "What?"

"Jesus," he said. "You look like hell. You look like you slept in those clothes."

My head was throbbing and my eyes felt like they were filled with sand. "It makes it easier in the morning," I said. "Not a lot of fuss."

Gazarra shook his head. "Tsk, tsk, tsk."

I looked down at the white bakery bag hanging from his chunky Polish hand. "Are there doughnuts in that bag?"

"Fuckin' A," Gazarra said.

"Do you have coffee too?"

He held a second bag aloft.

"God bless you," I said. "God bless your children and their children."

Gazarra got a couple plates from the kitchen, grabbed the roll of paper towels and took everything into the dining room. We divided up the doughnuts and coffee and ate in silence until all that was left was a splot of raspberry jelly on the front of Gazarra's uniform.

"So what is this?" I finally asked. "Social call, pity party, show of faith?"

"All of the above," Gazarra said. "Plus a weather report, which you didn't get from me."

"I hope it's warm and sunny."

Gazarra flicked at the mess on his shirtfront with a wad of paper napkin. "There are members of the department who'd like to pin last night's homicide on you."

"That's crazy! I had no motive. I didn't even know that guy."

"Turns out his name is Ronald Anders. Arrested on the eleventh of November for possession and sale of a controlled substance and illegal possession of firearms. Failed to appear in court two weeks later. Recovery never made . . . until last night. Guess who his bondsman is?"

"Vinnie."

"Yes."

Direct hit to the brain. No one had said anything to me about the FTA, including Morelli.

The doughnuts were sitting heavy in my stomach. "How about Morelli? Does Morelli want to charge me?"

Gazarra stuffed the paper coffee cups and napkins into a bag and carted it all off to the kitchen. "I don't know. I'm short on details. What I know is that you might want to get your ducks in a row just in case."

We faced each other at the door.

"You're a good friend," I said to Gazarra.

"Yeah," Gazarra said. "I know."

I closed and locked the door behind him and leaned my forehead against the doorjamb. The backs of my eyeballs hurt and the pain radiated out to the rest of my skull. If ever there was a time for clear thought, this was it, and here I was without a clear thought in my head. I stood a few minutes longer trying to think, but no wondrous revelations, no brilliant deductions burst into my consciousness. After a while I suspected I'd been dozing.

I was debating taking a shower when there was a loud rap on the door. I rolled my eye to the peephole and looked out. Joe Morelli.

Shit.

CHAPTER 5

"Open the door," Morelli said. "I know you're in there. I can hear you breathing."

I figured that was a big fat lie because I'd stopped breathing with the first rap of his knuckles.

Morelli knocked on the door again. "Come on, Stephanie," he said. "Your car's in the lot. I know you're home."

Mr. Wolesky, across the hall, opened his door. "What, you never heard of people in the shower? People sleeping? People going for a walk? I'm trying to watch some TV here. You keep making noise I'm gonna call the cops."

Morelli gave Mr. Wolesky a look that sent Mr. Wolesky scurrying back into his apartment. SLAM, click, click.

Morelli moved out of sight, and I waited with my eye glued to the peephole. I heard the elevator doors open and close, and then everything was quiet. Reprieve. Morelli was leaving.

I didn't know what Morelli wanted, and it seemed prudent not to find out—just in case it involved arresting me. I ran to my bedroom window, looked through the slit between the curtains and peeked down at the parking lot. I watched Morelli leave the building and get into an unmarked car.

I continued to watch, but nothing happened. He wasn't leaving. It looked like he was talking on his car phone. A few minutes went by, and my phone rang. Gosh, I thought, I wonder who that could be? On the odd chance it might be Morelli I let the machine pick it up. No message was left. I looked down into the lot. Morelli wasn't on his phone anymore. He was just sitting there, staking out the building.

I took a fast shower, dressed in clean clothes, fed Rex and went back to the window to check on Morelli. Still there. Rats.

I dialed Ranger's number.

"Yo," Ranger answered.

"It's Stephanie."

"I have something that belongs to you."

"That's a relief," I said, "but that's not my most pressing problem. I've got Joe Morelli sitting out in my parking lot."

"He coming or going?"

"There's a small chance he might want to arrest me."

"Not a good way to start the day, babe."

"I think I can get out the front door without being seen. Can you meet me at Bessie's in half an hour?"

"Be there," Ranger said.

I disconnected, called the office and asked for Lula.

"Your nickel," Lula said.

"It's Stephanie," I told her. "I need a ride."

"Oh boy. Is this more bounty hunter shit?"

"Yeah," I said. "This is bounty hunter shit. I want you to pick me up at my front door in ten minutes. I don't want you to park in the lot. I want you to cruise by the front of the building until you see me standing on the curb."

I blasted my hair with the dryer and did another take-a-look at Morelli. No change. He had to be freezing. Fifteen minutes more, and he'd be back in the building. I zipped myself into my jacket, grabbed my big shoulder bag and took the stairs to the first floor. I quickly crossed the small lobby and exited the front door.

There was no sign of Lula, so I huddled with my back to the building, crunched down inside my coat. Hard to believe Morelli would be here to arrest me, but stranger things have been known to happen. Innocent people were accused of crimes every day. More likely Morelli wanted to do another question session. I couldn't get excited about that either.

I heard Lula before I saw her. To be more specific, I felt the vibrations in the soles of my feet and against my rib cage. The Firebird slid to a stop in front of me, Lula's head bobbing in time to the music, lips moving to the beat. Boombaba boombaba.

I jumped in next to her and motioned to take off. The Firebird sprang to life and rocketed into the stream of traffic.

"Where we going?" Lula shouted.

I adjusted the volume. "Bessie's. I'm meeting Ranger."

"Your Buick on the blink too?"

"The Buick is fine. It's my life that's on the blink. Did you hear about the homicide at Uncle Mo's last night?"

"You mean that you aced Ronald Anders? Sure I heard. Everybody heard."

"I didn't ace him! I was knocked out. Someone killed him while I was unconscious."

"Sure. That's what's going around, but I figured . . . you know, dead or alive, right?"

"Wrong!"

"All right, all right. No cause to go PMS. How come you need a ride to Bessie's?"

"Joe Morelli is camped out in my parking lot, waiting to talk to me, and I don't want to be talked to."

"I guess I could understand that. He got one fine ass, but he's a cop all the same."

Bessie's was a coffee and doughnut shop around the corner from the Social Security offices. It was a scruffy little place with dusty floors and dirty windows, and it was always packed with the chronically unemployed and with worker drones from Social Security. It was the perfect place to get a cheap cup of terrible coffee and to fade away into the huddled masses.

Lula dropped me at the curb, cranked the noise level back to deafening and rumbled off. I elbowed my way to the back of the shop where Ranger was waiting. He had the last stool at the counter with his back to the wall. I never asked how he consistently managed to procure such a position. Sometimes it's best not to know these things.

I took the stool next to him, raising an eyebrow at the coffee and cruller on the counter. "Thought you weren't into internal pollution," I said. Lately Ranger'd been on a health food thing.

"Props," Ranger told me. "Didn't want to look out of place."

I didn't want to burst his fantasy bubble, but the only time Ranger wouldn't look out of place would be standing in a lineup between Rambo and Batman.

"I have a problem," I said to Ranger. "I think I'm in over my head."

"Babe, you've been in over your head since the first day I met you."

I ordered coffee and waited for my cup to arrive. "It's different this time. I might be a suspect in a homicide investigation. The guy on Mo's floor was Ronald Anders. One of Vinnie's skips."

"Tell me about it."

"I went to Uncle Mo's to look around."

"Hold it," Ranger said. "You break into the store?"

"Well, sort of. I had a key. But I guess technically it was an illegal entry."

"That's cool."

"Anyway, I was in the store, and I saw someone pass by the front window, so I went to the back door to leave. Before I could get out I heard footsteps, and then someone trying the lock. I hid in the bathroom. The back door opened and closed. The cellar door opened and closed. And then the door to the bathroom opened, and I was eyeball to eyeball with some big, pissed-off, Rasta-type guy who threw me against the wall and knocked me out. When I came around the guy was dead. What does this mean?"

"It means after you got knocked out someone else arrived and shot Ronald Anders," Ranger said.

"Who? Who would do that?"

We looked at each other, knowing we were both considering the same possibility. Mo.

"Nah," I said. "Impossible."

Ranger shrugged.

"That's a ridiculous idea," I told Ranger. "Mo isn't the sort of man who goes around shooting people."

"Who else could have shot Anders?"

"Anyone."

"That narrows it down." Ranger slid a five onto the counter and stood. "I'll see what I can find."

"My gun?"

He transferred my .38 from his pocket to my shoulder bag. "Not going to do you much good if you don't put bullets in it."

"One more thing," I said. "Could you give me a ride to the office?"

Connie came out of her chair when I blew through the door. "Are you okay? Lula said you actually got knocked out last night."

"Yes, I'm okay. Yes, I got knocked out. No, I didn't kill Ronald Anders."

Vinnie popped out of his office. "Christ, look who's here," he said. "The bounty hunter from hell. I suppose you want your recovery money for whacking Anders."

"I didn't whack Anders!" I shouted.

"Yeah, right," Vinnie said. "Whatever. Just next time try not to shoot your FTA in the back. It doesn't look good."

I gave Vinnie a hand gesture, but he was already back in his office with the door closed.

"Details," Connie said, leaning forward, eyes wide. "I want to know everything."

Truth is, there wasn't much to tell, but I went through the routine one more time.

When I was done Lula gave a disgusted sigh. "That's a pretty lame story," she said. "Cops gonna be after you like flies on a bad bean pie."

"Let me get this straight," Connie said. "You never saw the killer. You didn't smell him or hear him. In fact, you haven't got a teeny-tiny clue who he could be."

"I know the killer came from outside," I said. "And I think Ronald Anders knew the killer. I think Anders let the killer into the store and then turned his back on him."

"A partner?"

"Maybe."

"Maybe it was Old Penis Nose," Lula said. "Maybe Ronald Anders ran a tab and couldn't pay for his Snickers bars, so our man popped him."

"That's disgusting," Connie said. "That's not even funny."

"Hunh," Lula said. "You got a better idea?"

"Yeah," Connie said, "my idea is that you better get to work instead of saying dumb things about Uncle Mo."

"I'd like to get to work," I said, "but I don't know what to do. I'm at a total dead end. I'm a failure as a bounty hunter."

"You're not a failure," Connie said. "You got an apprehension this week. You got Ronald Anders."

"He was dead!"

"Hey, that's the way it goes sometimes." Connie pulled a stack of manila folders from her bottom drawer. "It's just that you're stalled on Mo. You should keep working other cases." She slid a folder from the top of the stack and flipped it open. "Here's a good one. Leroy Watkins. Came in yesterday, and I haven't given it out yet. You could have it if you want."

"He isn't cute, is he?" I asked Connie. "My image is at an all-time low. I'm not taking on any more cases where the FTA is Mr. Popularity."

"I know Leroy," Lula said. "Everybody call him Snake on account of his dick is . . ."

I squinched my eyes closed. "Don't tell me." I looked over at Connie. "What'd Leroy do to get himself arrested?"

"Tried to sell some dope to a narc."

"He ever resist arrest?" I asked.

"Not that I know of," Connie said. "There's nothing on his charge sheet about shooting cops."

I took the file from Connie. If Leroy Watkins was certifiably ugly I might take a crack at it. I flipped to the photo. Yow! He was ugly, all right.

"Okay," I said. "I'll see if I can find him." I glanced over at Connie. "There isn't anything else I should know, is there? Like, was he armed when arrested?"

"Nothing out of the ordinary," Connie said. "A forty-five, a twenty-two and a seven-inch blade."

My voice pitched to incredulity. "Two guns and a knife? Forget it! What do I look like, a suicide waiting to happen?"

We were all quiet for a minute while we considered my chances of success.

"I could go with you," Lula said. "We could be discreet."

Discreet? Lula?

"You think he's dangerous?" Connie asked Lula.

"He ain't no Boy Scout. Don't know if he'd want to shoot us, though. Probably he's just FTA so he could stay on the street and make maximum profit before getting locked down. I know his woman, Shirlene. We could go talk to her."

Talk to his woman. That sounded reasonable. I thought I might be able to handle that. "Okay," I said. "We'll give it a try."

Shirlene lived in a third-floor walk-up at the southern end of Stark Street. The cement stoop was littered with globules of rock salt that had eaten their way through yesterday's ice, leaving a doily of frozen gray slush. The front door to the building was weathered and stood ajar. The small inside hall was steeped in frigid damp.

"Feels like a meat locker in here," I said.

Lula snorted. "That's what it is, all right . . . a meat locker. Plain and simple. That's the trouble with Stark Street. It's all one big meat locker."

We were both panting by the time we got to the third floor.

"I've got to get in better shape," I said to Lula. "I've got to join a gym or something."

"I'm in plenty good shape," Lula said. "It's the altitude that gets me. If it wasn't for the altitude I wouldn't be breathing hard at all." She stared at Shirlene's door. "What are we gonna do if Snake's at home? I figure I should ask, being that you don't like violence except when you're out cold."

"Snake at home? Are you telling me Snake lives here?"

Lula blinked her big duck-egg eyes at me. "You mean you didn't understand that?"

"I thought we were visiting his woman's place."

"Well, yeah," Lula said, "but that happen to be Snake's place too."

"Oh boy."

"Don't worry," Lula said. "That Snake gives us any trouble I'll bust a cap up his ass." She knocked on the door. "I don't take no hard time from no Snake."

No one answered, so Lula knocked louder.

"HEY!" she yelled at the door.

We stood for a moment, listening in utter silence, and then from inside the apartment, inches from the closed door, came the unmistakable ratchet of a pump shotgun.

Lula and I locked eyes for a fraction of a second and shared a simultaneous thought, OH SHIT! We spun on our heels, hurled ourselves down the first flight of stairs and skidded across the second-floor landing.

BOOM! A gun blast blew a two-foot hole in Shirlene's front door, and plaster chunked out of the opposite wall.

"Out of my way!" Lula yelled. "Feet don't fail me!"

I had a head start on the next set of stairs, but Lula missed the first step, slid three steps on her ass and knocked me over like I was a bowling pin. The two of us rolled the rest of the way to the bottom, screaming and swearing until we landed in a heap on the foyer floor.

We scrambled to our feet and almost ripped the front door off its hinges trying to get out. We ran the two and a half blocks to Lula's Firebird, and Lula burned rubber from the curb. Neither of us said anything until we were parked in front of Vinnie's office.

"It wasn't that I was scared," Lula said. "It's just I didn't want to get blood on this here new sweatsuit. You know how hard it is to get blood out of this stuff."

"Yeah," I said, still breathing hard. "Blood is a bitch."

"Okay, so maybe I was a little scared," Lula said. "I mean, hell, that motherfucker would of shot us dead! Shit. What was he thinking of? What's the matter with him?"

"I've got to get a new job," I said to Lula. "I don't like getting shot at."

"I tell you, now that I'm thinking about it, I'm starting to get pissed off. Who the hell does that jerk think he is, anyway? I've got a mind to call him up and tell him what I think."

I handed Lula the file folder. "Be my guest. The phone number's on the first page. And while you're at it, tell him he'd better get his butt over here, because next time someone raps on his door it'll be Ranger."

"Fuckin' A," Lula said. "Ranger'd root that little pecker out. Ranger'd stomp on his miserable ass."

"Boy, I really hate being shot at," I said. "I really *hate* it!"

Lula wrenched her door open. "I'm not taking this shit. I'm not standing still for this kind of treatment."

"Me either," I said, getting caught up in the moment. "That creep needs to be locked up."

"Yeah," Lula said. "And we're just the ones to do it!"

I wasn't sure about that last part, but I let it slide, and Lula and I marched into the office like storm troopers invading Poland.

Connie looked up from her paperwork. "Uh-oh, what's going on?"

"We've just been shot at," Lula said, lower lip protruding a good two inches. "Can you believe it? I mean, I've been caught in drive-bys. I'm used to that shit. This shit was different. This shit was directed at me personally. I didn't like this shit one bit. This shit was offensive, you know what I'm saying?"

Connie raised her eyebrows. "Leroy Watkins?"

"Shot at us through a closed door," I said.

Connie nodded her head. "And?"

"And we ran away," I said. "Lula was worried about bloodstains on her new warm-up suit."

Lula had the file in one hand and Connie's phone in the other. "That Leroy Watkins isn't getting away with this. I'm gonna call up his ass and tell him what I think. I'm gonna tell him I'm not taking this shit."

Lula punched in some numbers and stood hand on hip.

"I want to talk to Leroy," she said into the phone.

Someone responded at the other end, and Lula leaned forward. "What do you mean I can't talk to him? He just almost dropped a cap in me, and now he's not available to talk to me? I'll available his ass."

The phone was returned to Connie after five more minutes of discussion.

"Snake says he didn't know it was us," Lula said. "He said he'd go down to court with us if we come back."

"Who'd he think he was shooting at?" I asked Lula.

"He said he didn't know who he was shooting at. He said it just pays to be careful these days."

"He destroyed his door!"

"Guess a man in Snake's business got to worry."

I grabbed my bag and hung it on my shoulder. "Okay, let's get this over with."

"The filing is starting to get out of hand," Connie said to Lula. "This won't take you all day, will it?"

"Hell no," Lula said. "We'll be back before lunch."

I pulled on gloves but thought twice about a hat. You wear a hat in the morning and you look like a fool for the rest of the day. Not that I looked all that wonderful this morning. It was more that I didn't want to compound the problem. Especially since Morelli was sitting in my parking lot. Just in case the unthinkable happened, and I got arrested . . . I didn't want to have hat hair for my mug shot.

We rumbled off to Stark Street, each of us lost in our own thoughts. My thoughts ran mostly to warm beaches and half-naked men serving me long, cool drinks. From the stony expression on Lula's face I suspected her thoughts ran a lot darker.

Lula pulled up to the curb in front of Shirlene's apartment building and heaved herself out of the car. We stood on the sidewalk and looked up at the third-floor windows.

"He said he wasn't going to shoot at us, right?" I asked, just to be sure.

"That's what he said."

"You believe him?"

Lula shrugged.

Ranger would go in with gun drawn, but that wasn't my style. I felt stupid with a gun in my hand. After all, what purpose did it serve? Was I going to shoot Leroy Watkins if he refused to get in the car with me? I don't think so.

I grimaced at Lula. She grimaced back. We entered the building and slowly climbed the stairs, listening for the shotgun ratchet.

When we got to the third floor, Shirlene was in the dingy hall, staring at her ruined door. Shirlene was medium height, lean and sinewy. Her age would be somewhere between twenty and fifty. She was wearing pink terry cloth bedroom slippers, faded pink warm-up pants that were a size too small and a matching sweatshirt that was dotted with various-hued food stains, none of which looked recent. Her hair was short and chopped. Her mouth turned down at the corners. Her eyes were expressionless. She held a piece of cardboard box in one hand and a hammer in the other.

"Not gonna be able to hammer anything into that cheapskate door," Lula told her. "You need mollies. Only thing gonna hold that cardboard in place is mollies."

"Haven't got any mollies," Shirlene said.

"Where's Leroy?" Lula asked. "He isn't gonna shoot at us again, is he?"

"Leroy's gone," Shirlene said.

"Gone? What do you mean gone?"

"Gone is gone," Shirlene said.

"Where'd he go?"

"Don't know," Shirlene said.

"When will he be back?"

"Don't know that either."

Lula stuffed her fists onto her hips. "Well, what *do* you know?"

"I know I gotta get this door fixed," Shirlene said. "And you're standing here taking up my time."

Lula walked into the front room. "You don't mind if I look around, do you?"

Shirlene didn't say anything. We both knew nothing short of that twelve-gauge pump was going to stop Lula from looking around.

Lula disappeared into the back room for a moment. "You're right," she said to Shirlene. "He's gone. He take any clothes with him? He look like he gonna be gone a long time?"

"He took his gym bag, and you know what he got in there."

I looked over at Lula, eyebrows raised in silent question.

Lula made her hand into a gun shape and aimed it at me.

"Oh," I said.

"My time is valuable," Lula said to Shirlene. "What's the matter with that man, doggin' me like this? He think I haven't got anything better to do than to hike up those stairs?"

I gave Shirlene my card, and Lula and I trudged down the stairs with Lula grumbling the whole way.

"Walk up the stairs, walk down the stairs. Walk up the stairs, walk down the stairs," she said. "Leroy better hope I never catch up with him."

Now that I was back on the street I wasn't all that sad not to have made an apprehension. An apprehension would have meant a trip to the police station. And the police station was the last place I wanted to visit right now.

"I guess we could try some bars," I said with no enthusiasm.

"Snake's not gonna be in a bar at this time of day," Lula said. "Snake's more likely to be hanging around a schoolyard, checking up on his sales force."

That gave me some incentive. "Okay. Let's drive by some schools."

An hour later we were out of schools and still hadn't found Snake.

"Any other ideas?" I asked Lula.

"Who's listed on his bail ticket?"

"Shirlene."

"No one else? No mama?"

"Nope. Just Shirlene."

"I don't know," Lula said. "Usually a man like Snake is out on the street. Even in weather like this he could be on the street." She slowly drove down Stark. "Not nobody out here today. Don't even see anybody we can ask on."

We drove by Jackie's corner, and it was empty too.

"Maybe she's with a client," I said.

Lula shook her head. "Nuh-uh, she isn't with no client. She's in that snooty parking lot, waiting for her man. Bet my life on it."

Lula cruised the block around my apartment building while I checked for Morelli. I didn't see his car, or anything that resembled a cop or a copmobile, so I had Lula drop me at the front door. I entered the lobby cautiously, not completely convinced of Morelli's departure. I did a fast survey and crossed to the stairs. So far, so good. I crept up the stairs, cracked the door at the second floor, peeked out to an empty hallway and sighed in relief. No Morelli.

I couldn't avoid Morelli forever, but I figured if I avoided him long enough he'd find other leads, and eventually I'd be off the hook.

I unlocked my door and was met with the sound of Rex running on his wheel. I bolted the door behind myself, hung my bag and jacket on one of the four coat hooks I'd installed in my tiny foyer and took a left into the kitchen.

The light was blinking on my answering machine. Four messages.

The first was from Morelli. "Call me."

I knew it was Morelli because my nipples contracted at the sound of his voice. His tone held a hint of annoyance. No surprise there.

The second message was just as cryptic. "Leave Mo alone. Or else." A man's voice, muffled. Unrecognizable. Great. Just what I needed. Anonymous threatening messages.

The third was from the Nissan service center telling me I had new points and plugs. The timing had been reset. And my car was ready to be picked up.

The fourth was from my mother. "Stephanie! Are you there? Are you all right? What's this I hear about a shooting? Hello? Hello?"

Good news travels fast in the burg. Bad news travels even faster. And if there's scandal attached, life as we know it comes to a halt until every detail of the tawdry event has been retold, examined, exclaimed over and enhanced.

If I allowed myself to consider what was being said about me at this very moment I'd probably fall over in a faint.

I dialed my parents' number and got a busy signal. I briefly considered whether this absolved me from the obligatory explanatory phone call and decided it didn't.

I made myself a tuna fish, potato chip and pickle sandwich and ate it at the kitchen counter.

I tried calling my mother again. Still busy.

I put Rex in the bathtub while I cleaned his cage. Then I cleaned the tub. Then I cleaned the rest of the bathroom. I ran the vacuum. I damp-mopped the kitchen floor. I scoured some of the crud off the top of the stove. Just in case I was arrested, I didn't want my mother coming into my apartment and finding it dirty.

At three o'clock I gave up with the cleaning and tried another call to my mother. No luck.

I called Sue Ann to get the scoop on myself and to set the record straight. You could always get Sue Ann. Sue Ann had call waiting.

"You ever hear anything about Uncle Mo being . . . odd?" I asked Sue Ann.

"Odd?"

"Romantically."

"You know something!" Sue Ann shouted into the phone. "What is it? What is it? What's the dirt on Uncle Mo? He's having an affair, right?"

"I don't know. I was just wondering. Probably you should forget I said anything."

I disconnected and tried my mother again. Her line was still busy. It was close to four o'clock, and the light was fading. I went to the window and peered down at the parking lot. No sign of Morelli.

"So what do you think?" I asked Rex. "Should I keep trying the phone or should I just take a ride over?"

Rex telepathically suggested that communicating with my mother in person would have the added advantage of being able to scrounge dinner.

I thought this was pretty clever considering Rex had a brain the size of a dried pea.

I grabbed my shoulder bag and my jacket and squinted into the security peephole on my front door. No one in view. I cracked the door and looked out at the hall. Clear. I took the stairs, crossed the small lobby and exited through the rear door to the lot.

The seniors always snapped up all the good slots close to the back entrance, so my Buick was parked at the outer edge, next to the Dumpster.

I could hear a steady drone of cars on St. James, and streetlights had just blinked on. I had almost reached the Buick when a black Jeep Cherokee suddenly wheeled into the lot and rolled to a stop.

The tinted driver's side window slid down and a man wearing a ski mask looked out at me, leveled a .45 and squeezed off two rounds that zinged into the blacktop about six inches from my foot. I stood rooted to the spot, paralyzed by fear and astonishment.

"This is a warning," the man said. "Stop looking for Mo. Next time these bullets will be in your brain." He discharged three rounds into the heavy iron side of the Dumpster. I dove for cover. A fourth round whistled overhead.

The window rolled up, and the car sped out of the lot.

CHAPTER 6

When my heart resumed beating I got to my feet and cautiously looked over the edge of the Dumpster. Mrs. Karwatt was coming toward me, halfway across the lot, picking her way around icy spots on the macadam, clutching a small plastic bag of garbage to her chest.

"Did you see that?" I asked, my voice approaching a level audible only to canines.

"What?"

"That man in the car. He shot at me!"

"No!"

"Didn't you hear it?"

"For goodness' sakes," she said. "Isn't that terrible. I thought it was a backfire. I had my eyes fixed on the ice. Gotta be careful, you know. My sister slipped and broke her hip last winter. Had to put her in a home. Never did recover right. It's not so bad, though. She gets green Jell-O for dessert twice a week at lunchtime."

I ran a shaky finger over the holes in the Dumpster where the bullets had impacted. "This is the second time today someone's shot at me!"

"Getting so a body can't go out of the house," Mrs. Karwatt said. "What with the ice and the shooting. Ever since we put a man on the moon the whole planet's gone to heck in a handbasket."

I was looking for someone to nail for my sorry life, but I didn't think it was fair to lay it all on Neil Armstrong.

Mrs. Karwatt pitched her bag into the Dumpster and headed back to the building. I sort of wanted to go with her, but my knees were shaky, and my feet weren't moving.

I wrenched the door open on the Buick and collapsed onto the seat, hands clutching the wheel. Okay, I said to myself. Get a grip. These were two freak incidents. The first shooting was mistaken identity. And the second shooting was . . . what? A death threat.

SHIT.

I pulled the cell phone out of my shoulder bag and dialed up Morelli.

"Someone just shot at me!" I yelled into the phone at him. "I was getting into my car in my parking lot, and this guy in a ski mask drove up and told me to lay off looking for Mo. And then he shot at me. Warning shots, he said. And then he drove away."

"Are you hurt?"

"No."

"Are you in immediate danger?"

"No."

"Did you make a mess in your pants?"

"Came damn close."

We were silent for a couple beats while we digested all this.

"Did you get his plate number?" Morelli asked. "Can you give me a description of the guy?"

"I was too rattled to think to get the plate. The guy was average build. White. That's all I've got."

"Are you going to be okay?"

"Yeah." I nodded my head in the car. "I feel better now. I just . . . I had to tell somebody."

"While I have you on the phone . . ." Morelli said.

Damn! I forgot I was avoiding Morelli! I snapped the cell phone closed. No sweat, I told myself. No harm done. But probably it's not a good idea to hang out in the lot. That left me with two choices. I could go with my plan to visit my parents, or I could return to my apartment and hide in my coat closet. The coat closet held a lot of appeal short-term, but at some point I'd have to venture out, and by that time I'd most likely have missed dinner.

Go with dinner, I thought. Do the coat closet later.

* * *

My mother wasn't smiling when she opened the door.

"Now what?" she said.

"I didn't do it."

"You used to say that when you were a little girl, and it was always a fib."

"Cross my heart," I said. "I didn't shoot anybody. I accidentally got knocked out, and when I came to I was sharing a hallway with a dead guy."

"You got knocked out!" My mother smacked the heel of her hand against her forehead. "I have to have a daughter who goes around getting herself knocked out."

Grandma Mazur was in line behind my mother.

"Are you sure you didn't pop him one? I could keep a secret, you know."

"I didn't pop him!"

"Well that's a big disappointment," she said. "I had a good story all ready to tell the girls at the beauty parlor."

My father was in the living room, hiding in front of the TV. "Unh," he said, never moving a muscle.

I sniffed the air. "Meat loaf."

"Got a new recipe from Betty Szajack," my mother said. "She puts sliced olives in her meat loaf, and she makes it with soaked bread instead of crackermeal."

The best way to defuse my mother is to talk about food. For thirty years, we've expressed love and anger in terms of gravy and mashed potatoes.

"So are you staying for supper?" my mother wanted to know. "I have spice cake with chocolate mocha icing for dessert."

"Sure," I said. "That would be nice."

I helped Grandma Mazur set the table while my mother finished up in the kitchen. We were about to sit down when the doorbell rang.

"Probably the paperboy trying to juice us out of more money," Grandma said. "I'm wise to his tricks."

I answered the door and found myself looking into Joe Morelli's brown eyes.

He grinned when he saw me. "Surprise."

"What do you want?"

"You asking for the long list or the short list?"

"I don't want any list." I made an attempt to close the door, but he muscled his way into the foyer. "Out!" I said. "This isn't a good time."

He ignored me and strolled into the dining room. "Evening," he said to my mother. He acknowledged my father with a nod of his head, and he winked at my grandmother.

"We're having meat loaf with olives," Grandma Mazur said to Morelli. "You want some? We got plenty."

"I wouldn't want to impose," Morelli said.

This triggered eye rolling on my part.

My mother pulled an extra side chair up next to me and laid out another plate. "We wouldn't think of having you leave without supper," she said to Morelli.

"I'd think of it," I said.

My mother smacked me on the top of my head with a wooden serving spoon. "Miss Fresh Mouth."

Morelli helped himself to two slabs of meat loaf, mashed potatoes, green beans and applesauce. He made polite conversation with my mother and grandmother and discussed sports scores with my father. On the surface Morelli seemed relaxed and smiling, but there were unguarded moments when I caught him watching me with the offhand intensity of a tree toad eyeing a tasty insect.

"So what's going on between you and my granddaughter?" Grandma asked Morelli. "Being that you're here for supper I guess everything's pretty serious."

"Getting more serious by the minute," Morelli said.

"Morelli and I have a working relationship," I said to Grandma. "Nothing more."

Morelli slouched back. "You shouldn't fib to your grandma. You know you're crazy about me."

"Well, listen to that," Grandma said, clearly charmed. "Isn't he the one."

Morelli leaned toward me and lowered his voice. "Speaking of work, I have a matter I'd like to discuss with you in private. I thought maybe we could go for a ride together after the table is cleared."

"Sure," I said. And maybe I'll poke out my eye with the turkey baster.

I gathered the plates together and hauled them off to the kitchen. My mother and Grandma Mazur followed with the serving dishes.

"You go ahead and cut the cake," I told my mother. "I'll get the coffee going."

I waited a moment until I had the kitchen to myself, then I promptly did a quiet exit through the back door. I had no intention of going for a ride that would culminate in a body cavity search. Not that a body cavity search would be a new experience. Morelli had already performed this procedure on me at various ages, with varying degrees of success. The new twist would be that this time the search might be done by a prison matron—and that was even less appealing than falling prey to Morelli.

I was wearing jeans and boots and a flannel shirt over a T-shirt, and my teeth were chattering by the time I'd cut through my parents' backyard and run the two blocks to Mary Lou's house. Mary Lou's been my best friend for as long as I can remember. For six years now she's been more or less happily married to Leonard Stankovic of Stankovic and Sons, Plumbing and Heating. She has two kids and a mortgage and a part-time job as a bookkeeper for an Oldsmobile dealership.

I didn't bother with the formality of knocking on her door. I just barged in and stood there stomping my feet and flapping my arms in her living room, and saying, "D-d-damn it's c-c-cold!"

Mary Lou was on her hands and knees picking up little plastic cars and men that looked like fireplugs. "Maybe it would help if you tried wearing a coat."

"I was at my parents' house and Morelli showed up, and so I had to sneak out the back door."

"I don't buy into that one," Mary Lou said. "If you were with Morelli just now you'd be missing a lot more clothes than your coat."

"This is serious. I'm afraid he might want to arrest me."

Mary Lou's two-year-old, Mikey, toddled in from the kitchen and latched onto Mary Lou's leg dog style.

I thought kids were okay from a distance, but I wasn't all that excited about the way they smelled up close. I suppose when they belong to you it makes a difference.

"You probably should stop shooting guys," Mary Lou said. "You shoot a lot of guys, and eventually the cops get cranky about it."

"I didn't shoot this one. Anyway, I had to sneak out of the house, and I had to leave my coat and everything behind."

Lenny and the four-year-old were sitting in front of the TV watching a rerun of *The Munsters*. Lenny was an okay person but sort of a mouth breather. Mary Lou had always gone for that type, preferring brawn to brain. Not that Lenny was entirely stupid. It's just that you'd never get him confused with Linus Pauling.

Mary Lou dumped the fireplug people into a plastic laundry basket that was filled with toys, and the two-year-old let out a howl. He cried flat out with his hands clasping and unclasping, reaching for who knows what. Mary Lou, I suppose. Or maybe for his toys that were being put away for the night. He cried with his mouth wide open and his eyes scrunched tight, and in between sobs he shrieked, "No, no, no!"

Mary Lou took a graham cracker from her pocket and gave it to Mikey.

Mikey shoved the cracker into his mouth and continued to blubber, chewing and rubbing his face with his fat baby hands. Cracker mush mixed with tears and baby snot worked its way into his hair and onto his face. Brown drool rolled off his chin and stained his shirt.

Mary Lou gave Mikey a "been there, seen this" look. "Mikey's tired," she said.

Like I said before, kids were okay from a distance, but I didn't think they'd ever replace hamsters.

"I need to use your phone to call home," I said to Mary Lou.

She wiped at the mush with her shirttail. "Help yourself."

I dialed from the kitchen, straining to hear over the racket in Mary Lou's living room. "Is Morelli still there?" I asked my mother.

"He just left."

"Are you sure? He's not hanging around outside, is he?"

"I heard his car drive away."

I borrowed a sweatshirt from Mary Lou and ran back to my parents' house. I cut through the backyard and jogged down the driveway to check the street. The street looked clear. No Morelli. I retraced my steps to the kitchen door and let myself in.

"Well," my mother said, "what gives?"

"Never catch me walking out on a hunk like Joe Morelli," Grandma said. "I guess I'd know what to do with a man like that."

I guessed I knew what to do with him too, but probably it was illegal to neuter a cop. "You didn't give him any spice cake to take home, did you?" I asked my mother.

My mother tipped her chin up a fraction of an inch. "I gave him the whole thing. It was the least I could do after you left him sitting here high and dry."

"The whole thing!" I shouted. "How could you do that? I didn't get a single piece!"

"That's what happens when you walk out. And how was I to know where you were? You could have been kidnapped. You could have had a brain seizure and wandered off with amnesia. How was I to know you'd be back and want spice cake?"

"I had reasons for leaving," I wailed. "Perfectly good reasons."

"What reasons?"

"Morelli was going to arrest me . . . maybe."

My mother took a deep breath. "Arrest you?"

"There's a small possibility that I might be a homicide suspect."

My mother made the sign of the cross.

Grandma didn't look nearly so glum. "There was a woman on TV the other day. On one of them talk shows. She said she'd been arrested for smoking dope. She said when you get arrested the cops lock you up in a little cell and then sit around watching you on closed-circuit TV, waiting for you to go to the bathroom. She said there's this stainless steel commode in one corner of your cell, and it hasn't got a toilet seat or anything, and that's where you have to go. And she said the commode faces the TV camera just so they can all get a good view of the whole thing."

My stomach went hollow and little black dots danced in front of my eyes. I wondered if I had enough money in my bank account to buy a ticket to Brazil.

Grandma's expression got crafty. "The woman on TV said what you needed to do before you got arrested was to drink a lot of Kaopectate. She said you needed to get good and plugged up so you could wait until you got out on bail."

I sat down in a chair and put my head between my knees.

"This is what comes of working for your father's cousin," my mother said. "You're a smart girl. You should have a decent job. You should be a schoolteacher."

I thought of Mary Lou's kid with the graham crackers smeared in his hair, and felt better about being a bounty hunter. You see, it could always be worse, I thought. I could be a schoolteacher.

"I need to go home," I said, retrieving my coat from the hall closet. "Lots of work to do tomorrow. Got to get to bed early."

"Here," my mother said, handing me a grocery bag. "Some meat loaf. Enough for a nice sandwich."

I looked in the bag. Meat loaf. No spice cake.

"Thanks," I said to my mother. "Are you sure there isn't any spice cake left?"

"A homicide suspect," my mother said. "How could such a thing happen?"

I didn't know. I wondered the same thing. In fact, I wondered all the way home. I wasn't such a bad person. I only cheated a little on my taxes, and I paid most of my bills. I didn't cuss at old people (at least not to their face). I didn't do drugs. So why was I having such rotten luck? Okay, so I didn't go to church as often as I should, but my mother went regularly. I thought that should count for something.

I rolled Big Blue into the lot. It was late. All the good spots were taken, so I was back by the Dumpster again. What's new. At least it afforded me cover from a drive-by. Maybe I'd park here all the time.

I looked up at my apartment and realized my lights were on. That was weird, because I was almost positive I'd shut them off when I left this afternoon. I got out of the car and walked to the middle of the lot. I looked up at my windows again. The lights were still on. What did this mean? It could mean the lights had been on when I left, and I was suffering from early onset of dementia. Probably I could add a touch of paranoia to the dementia.

A shadowy figure appeared briefly toward the far wall of my living room, and my heart skipped a beat. Someone was in my apartment. I was relieved to be able to rule out the dementia, but I still had a problem. I really didn't want to do my own investigating and get shot at for the third time today. Unfortunately, the alternative was to call the police. Since I was low on Kaopectate, I didn't think calling the police was a good alternative.

The figure reappeared. Long enough for me to decide it was a man. He moved closer to the window, and I was able to see his face.

The face belonged to Morelli.

Of all the nerve. Morelli had broken into my apartment. And that wasn't even the worst of it. He was eating something. I suspected it was spice cake.

"PIG!" I yelled. "Creep!"

He didn't seem to hear. Probably the TV was on.

I did a fast walk around the lot and found Morelli's black Toyota 4×4. I gave the back bumper a kick, and the alarm went off.

Faces appeared in the windows above me while the alarm wailed away.

Mrs. Karwatt on the second floor threw her window open and leaned out. "What's going on out there?"

A shotgun barrel poked from Mr. Weinstein's window. "Whose alarm is that? It's not my Cadillac, is it?"

The only window without a face was mine. I figured that was because Morelli was thundering down the stairs.

I ran to my car with my keys in my hand.

"Stay away from that car, or I'll shoot," Mr. Weinstein shouted.

"It's *my* car," I yelled back.

"The hell it is," Mr. Weinstein said, squinting at me through his inch-thick trifocals. BOOM! Mr. Weinstein fired and took out the windshield on the car next to me.

I bolted across the grass median into the street and streaked for the houses on the other side. I stopped and looked back. Morelli was pacing under the rear overhang, shouting at Mr. Weinstein, obviously afraid to venture out into the lot for fear of getting shot.

I slipped into the shadows between two houses, hopped a backyard fence and came out onto Elm Street. I crossed Elm and repeated the pattern, bringing me to Hartland. I jogged a block up Hartland, crossed Hamilton and plastered myself against the brick wall of an all-night convenience store.

The previous owner of the store had been Joe Echo. He'd sold it in November, and the new Asian owner, Sam Pei, had changed the name to The American Store. I thought the name was appropriate. The American Store contained a sampling of everything an American might need at four times the price. A box of Fig Newtons for $7.50. No matter that there were only twelve in a box. I guess when you needed a Fig Newton in the middle of the night, you damn well didn't care what it cost.

I pulled a knit cap out of my pocket and tugged it down over my ears. The battery was low on my cell phone, so I searched in my shoulder bag for a quarter, found one, dropped it into the pay phone and dialed my number.

Morelli answered on the fourth ring.

I unclenched my teeth enough to get a few words out. "What the hell are you doing in my apartment?"

"Waiting for you," Morelli said.

"What were you eating just now?"

"Spice cake. There's still some left, but you'd better hurry."

I neatly clicked the phone back into the receiver. *"Ugh!"*

I bought a Snickers from Mr. Pei and ate it while I walked. Time to be realistic. Morelli was a lot better at this cops-and-robbers stuff than I was. It seemed to me that if he wanted to arrest me, he would have done it by now. For that matter, if he was serious about bringing me in for further questioning he would have done it. Probably there was no immediate need for the Kaopectate.

So why was Morelli harassing me? Because he wanted something. What did he want? Information that I might be withholding? Maybe he thought he could worm some missing details out of me better under more casual circumstances. Or maybe he wanted to threaten me without witnesses. Or maybe he wanted to ask me for a date.

I turned the corner at Hartland and decided I should talk to Morelli. This was no longer a simple recovery. Mo was still missing. A man had been killed. I'd been threatened. And there were some details I'd neglected to tell Morelli when I'd been questioned at the station. Not to mention the spice cake.

Everything looked status quo when I got to my parking lot. Lights were on in my apartment. Morelli's car hadn't been moved. A small gathering of people were clustered around the Chrysler Mr. Weinstein had used for target practice. Mr. Weinstein was there with a big piece of plastic bagging and a roll of duct tape in his hand.

"Another minute and he would have been driving off in this car, I'm telling you," Mr. Weinstein was saying. "Better a broken windshield than a stolen car."

"Isn't that the truth," Arty Boyt said. "Good thing you had that gun handy."

Everyone else nodded. Good thing, they all said.

I slipped into the building and went to the pay phone at the front of the small lobby. I dropped a quarter and called upstairs.

"It's me again," I said when Morelli answered.

"Where are you?"

"Far away."

"Liar." I could hear the smile in his voice. "I saw you cross the parking lot."

"Why are you stalking me?"

"Cops don't stalk. Cops pursue."

"Okay. Why are you pursuing me?"

"We need to talk," Morelli said.

"That's it? Just talk?"

"You had something else in mind?"

"Nope."

We were both silent for a moment, contemplating the something else.

"Well," I said, "what do you want to talk about?"

"I want to talk about Mo, and I don't want to do it on the phone."

"I heard some people might want to arrest me."

"That's true," Morelli said. "But I'm not one of them."

"I have your word?"

"I won't arrest you tonight. I'd rather not make a blanket statement that covers eternity."

He was waiting with the door open when I got off the elevator.

"You look cold and tired," he said.

"Dodging bullets is exhausting. I don't know how you cops do it day after day."

"I assume you're talking about Mr. Weinstein."

I hung my jacket and my shoulder bag on a wall hook. "I'm talking about everyone. People keep shooting at me." I sliced myself off a big chunk of spice cake and told Morelli about Snake.

"So what do you think?" I asked.

"I think bounty hunters should be tested and licensed. And I think you'd flunk the test."

"I'm learning."

"Yeah," Morelli said. "Let's hope you don't get dead in the process."

Ordinarily I'd consider a remark like that to be an insult, but I'd actually been thinking along the same lines myself. "What's the deal with Uncle Mo?"

"I don't know," Morelli said. "At first I was worried he was dead. Now I don't know what to think."

"What kind of prints did you get from his store?"

"Yours, Mo's and Anders's from the doorknobs in the rear. We didn't bother with the public areas. Two-thirds of the burg would have showed up."

"The neighbors see anything?"

"Only the lady across the street who reported the flashlight." Morelli was slouched against my kitchen counter, arms crossed over his chest. "Any other questions?"

"Do you know who killed Anders?"

"No. Do you?"

I rinsed my plate and put it in the dishwasher. "No." I looked at Morelli. "How did Anders get into the store? I heard him fumbling out there, trying the doorknob. At first I thought he had a key, but the door wouldn't open. So then I decided he must be jimmying the lock."

"There was no sign of forced entry."

"Can we unofficially walk through this?"

"You must be reading my mind," Morelli said.

"I'm not saying any of this to a cop, right?"

"Right."

I poured myself a glass of milk. "This is what I know. The back door to Mo's store was locked. I opened it with a key I got from his apartment. After I was in the store I pulled the door closed. When Ronald Anders tried to get in, the door was locked. At first it sounded like he had a key, but the door wouldn't open. He fiddled with it for a couple minutes, and the door clicked open. Did you find anything on him that he could have used to pick a lock?"

"No."

"Did you find a key to the store on him?"

"No."

I raised my eyebrows.

Morelli raised his eyebrows.

"Either someone needed a set of picks, or else someone lifted a key that doesn't work especially well," I said. "Or maybe someone opened the door with a sticky key, let Ronald Anders into the store, disappeared for a few minutes, returned and killed Anders."

Morelli and I sighed. The logical person to have a sticky key would be Uncle Mo. And it wasn't so far-fetched that Mo would know Anders in light of the fact that Mo had been seen on Stark Street from time to time. Maybe this was drug related. Maybe Mo was buying. Hell, maybe Mo was selling. After perusing Mo's bedtime books I was willing to believe almost anything about him.

"You have anybody talking to the kids who hang at the store?" I asked Morelli. "When you were working vice did you hear anything about drugs coming out of Mo's?"

"Just the opposite," Morelli said. "Mo's was a safe zone. Mo was militant against dope. Everyone knew."

I had another idea. "How militant?" I asked. "Militant enough to kill a dealer?"

Morelli looked at me with his unreadable cop face.

"That would be strange," I said. "Lovable, out-of-shape ice cream guy turns killer. Revenge of the small businessman."

Anders was shot in the back. He'd been carrying a gun, but the gun hadn't been touched. The gun had been found when the police rolled the body. The gun had been stuffed into the waistband of Anders's double-pleated rapper slacks. Whoever got nailed for the murder would have a hard time pleading self-defense.

"Is that it?" I asked Morelli.

"For now."

Morelli was wearing jeans, boots and a long-sleeved driver's shirt with the sleeves pushed up. He had his service pistol clipped to his belt. He grabbed his khaki jacket from one of the wall hooks in the entrance hall and shrugged into it.

"I'd appreciate it if you didn't take any vacations in foreign countries for a couple days," he said.

"Gee, and I have tickets to Monaco."

He gave me a chuck under my chin, smiled and left.

I stared at the closed front door for a moment. A chuck under the chin. What was that? In the past, Morelli had tried to stick his tongue down my throat. Or at the very least he'd make a lewd suggestion. I was suspicious of a chuck under the chin. Now that I thought about it, he'd been a perfect gentleman when he'd brought the pizza. And what about last night? He'd left without so much as a handshake.

I checked myself out in the hall mirror. My hair was still squashed under the knit cap. Not real sexy, but that had never slowed Morelli down before. I pulled the cap off and my hair sprang out. Eek. Good thing I'd left the cap on.

I went back to the kitchen and dialed Ranger.

"Yo," Ranger said.

"Anyone bragging about killing Ronald Anders?"

"No one's bragging about anything these days. The streets are quiet."

"Turf war?"

"Don't know. A couple players are missing. A couple dopers are dead. Got some hot shit going around killing people."

"ODs?"

"That's the way the death certificates read."

"You think something different?"

"Feels dark, babe."

I disconnected and a minute later the phone rang.

"We got a situation on our hands," Lula said.

"A situation?"

"Just got a call from Jackie, and I can't make any sense of what she's saying. Something about how her old man jacked her over again."

"Where is she?"

"She's at the FancyAss Apartments. She's been there day and night, and she sounds flipped out. I told her to wait right where she was, and we'd come fast as we could."

Fifteen minutes later I pulled into the RiverEdge lot. The sky was black and dense above evenly spaced pools of artificial light thrown by the overhead halogen lamps. Jackie had parked her Chrysler on the fringe of one of those pools. The river was a block away, and the ice fog swirled around the lamps and settled on the cars.

Jackie stood beside her car, waving her arms while she yelled at Lula, and Lula was yelling back at Jackie.

"Calm down," Lula was saying. "Calm down!"

"He's dead," Jackie shouted. "Dead, dead, dead. Fucking dead. Dead as a goddamn doorknob. What a bitch!"

I looked at Lula, and Lula gave me an I-don't-know shrug.

"I just got here," Lula said. "I can't get her to say anything besides the motherfucker's dead. Maybe she's too coked up. Maybe we need to get something to slow her down."

"I'm not coked up, you dumb ho," Jackie said. "I'm trying to tell you he's dead, and you're not fucking listening."

I looked around the lot. "Is he dead anywhere nearby?"

I really wanted a no on this one. I'd already had my millennium quota of dead.

"You see that big bush by the Dumpster?" Jackie said.

"Yeah."

"You see that ugly-ass foot sticking out of that big bush?"

Oh boy. She was right. There was a foot sticking out of the bush.

"Shit, Jackie," I said. "You didn't kill that foot, did you?"

"No, I didn't kill that foot. That's what I've been trying to tell you. Someone jacked me over. I've been sitting out here, freezing my ass off, waiting to kill that sonovabitch Cameron Brown, and someone beat me to it. It isn't fair!"

Jackie wheeled off for the Dumpster with Lula and me scrambling to keep up.

"I decided to neaten up the car," Jackie said. "So I come over here with a bag of trash, and I'm throwing it in the Dumpster, and I see something sort of reflecting light. And I look a little harder, and I see it's a watch. And then I see it's attached to a wrist. And I say, Goddamn, I know that watch and that wrist. So I dig around some and look what I come up with. Look what I hauled out of the goddamn garbage."

She stopped at the bush, reached down, grabbed hold of the foot and dragged a man's body out into the open. "Just look at this. He's dead. And if that isn't bad enough, he's frozen solid. This motherfucker is one big frosty Popsicle. It's not even like I get to see him rot. Damn."

Jackie dropped the foot and gave Cameron a good solid kick in the ribs.

Lula and I jumped back and sucked in some air.

"Dang," Lula said.

"That ain't the half of it," Jackie said. "I've been sitting here waiting to shoot him, and that's what I'm going to do."

Jackie opened her coat, pulled a 9mm Beretta out of her sweatpants and drilled half a clip into Cameron Brown. Cameron jumped around some from the impact, but mostly the bullets didn't have much effect—except for putting a bunch of extra holes in various body parts.

"Are you nuts?" Lula yelled. "This guy's dead! You're shooting a dead man!"

"Isn't my fault," Jackie said. "I wanted to shoot him while he was alive, but somebody beat me to it. I'm just making the best of a bad situation."

"You've been drinking," Lula said.

"Damn skippy. Would have froze to death if I didn't have a nip once in a while."

Jackie raised the gun, looking to unload a few more rounds into Cameron.

"Hold on," Lula said. "I hear sirens."

We stood still and listened to the whoop, whoop, whoop.

"Coming this way!" Lula said. "Every man for himself!"

We all ran for our cars and took off at the same time, almost crashing into each other trying to get out of the lot.

CHAPTER 7

Jackie and Lula and I rendezvoused at a Dunkin' Donuts parking lot, about a quarter mile from RiverEdge. We parked our cars side by side and got out to have a huddle.

"I need a doughnut," Jackie said. "I want one of those fancy ones with the colored sprinkles on top."

"You need more than a doughnut," Lula told her. "You need your head examined. You just shot up a dead man. What were you thinking?"

Jackie was rummaging in her pockets, looking for doughnut money. "I guess I got a right to shoot someone if I want to."

"Nuh-uh," Lula said. "There's rules. This man was already dead, and you showed disrespect for the deceased."

"The deceased didn't deserve no respect. He stole my car."

"Everybody deserves respect when they're dead," Lula said. "It's a rule."

"Says who?"

"Says God."

"Oh yeah? Well, God don't know jack-shit about rules. I'm telling you, that's a stupid rule."

Lula had her hands on her hips, and her eyes bugged out of her head. "Don't you talk about God like that, you worthless ho. I'm not gonna stand here and let you blaspheme God."

"Hold it!" I shouted. "What about the police?"

"What about them?" Jackie wanted to know.

"We need to call them."

Jackie and Lula looked at me like I was speaking Klingon.

"Someone killed Cameron Brown before Jackie made Swiss cheese out of him. We can't just leave Brown lying there alongside the Dumpster," I told them.

"No need to worry about that," Lula said. "That place is crawling with cops by now. They'll find Cameron. He's right out there in the open."

"Yeah, but shooting dead people is probably a crime. That makes us accessories if we don't report it."

"I'm not going to the police," Jackie said. "Unh-uh. No way."

"It's the right thing to do," I said.

"The hell," Jackie said. "It's the stupid thing to do."

"Stephanie's right," Lula told Jackie. "It's the dope and the liquor that's stopping you from doing the right thing. Just like it's the dope and the liquor that makes you blaspheme God. You gotta do something for yourself," Lula said to Jackie. "You gotta go to detox."

"Don't need detox," Jackie said.

"Uh-huh," Lula told her.

"Unh-uh."

"Uh-huh."

"I know what you're doing," Jackie said. "You've been trying to get me to detox ever since you got straight. This here's just a trick."

"You bet your ass," Lula said. "And either you go to detox, or we turn you in." Lula looked at me. "Isn't that right?"

"Yeah," I said. "That's right." Seemed like that's what the court would do anyway. Probably the clinic on Perry Street would do it better.

It started with polite rapping on my door. And then when I didn't answer, it turned to pounding. I looked through my peephole and saw Morelli pacing and muttering. He turned and gave my door another shot with his fist.

"Come on, Stephanie," he said. "Wake up. Get out of bed and answer your door."

It was eight-thirty, and I'd been awake for an hour. I'd taken a shower, gotten dressed and had breakfast. I wasn't answering my door because I didn't want to talk to Morelli. I suspected he'd just come from RiverEdge.

I heard him fiddling with the lock. The lock clicked open. Thirty seconds later he had the deadbolt. My front door pushed open but caught on the chain.

"I know you're there," Morelli said. "I can smell your shampoo. Open the door, or I'm coming back with a bolt cutter."

I slid the chain and opened the door. "Now what?"

"We found Cameron Brown."

I opened my eyes wider to simulate surprise. "No!"

"Yes. Frozen solid. And extremely dead. Been dead for days is my guess. Found him next to the Dumpster at the RiverEdge condo complex."

"I'll have to tell Jackie."

"Uh-huh. Funny thing about the body. Looked like whoever killed Brown had him tossed into the Dumpster. And then someone came along last night, dragged the body out of the Dumpster and pumped half a clip into him."

"No!"

"Yes. It gets even funnier. Two of the RiverEdge residents came forward, saying they heard a bunch of women arguing in the lot, late at night, then they heard gunshots. When they looked out their windows what do you suppose they saw?"

"What?"

"Three cars leaving the lot. One of them was an old Buick. They thought it might be powder blue with a white top."

"Did they get a plate? Did they see the women?"

"No."

"Guess that's a tough break for you guys, huh?"

"I thought you might be able to shed some light on the incident."

"Am I talking to you as a cop this morning?"

"Shit," Morelli said. "I don't want to hear this."

"So, is it against the law to shoot someone after he's already dead?"

"Yes, it's against the law."

I made a small grimace. "I thought it would be. Just exactly what law is it against?"

"I don't know," Morelli said. "But I'm sure there's something. I suppose there were extenuating circumstances."

"A woman scorned . . ."

"Is this scorned woman going to come forward?"

"She's going into detox."

"Your job description reads 'bounty hunter,' " Morelli said. "Social worker is a whole different job."

"You want some coffee?"

He shook his head, no. "I've got paperwork. Then I've got an autopsy."

I watched him walk down the hall and disappear into the elevator. Only an idiot would think they could talk to Morelli and not be talking to Morelli the cop. Cops never stopped being cops. It had to be the world's hardest job.

Trenton cops wore more hats than I could name. They were arbitrators, social workers, peacekeepers, baby-sitters and law enforcers. The job was boring, terrifying, disgusting, exhausting and often made no sense at all. The pay was abysmal, the hours were inhuman, the department budget was a joke, the uniforms were short in the crotch. And year after year after year, the Trenton cops held the city together.

Rex was in his soup can, butt side out, half buried under wood shavings, hunkered in for his morning nap. I cracked a walnut and dropped it into his cage. After a moment there was movement under the wood shavings. Rex backed himself out, snatched half of the walnut and carried it into his can. I watched a couple minutes longer, but the show was over.

I checked my pocketbook to make sure I had the essentials . . . beeper, tissues, hair spray, flashlight, cuffs, lipstick, gun with bullets, recharged cell phone, recharged stun gun, hairbrush, gum, pepper spray, nail file. Was I a kick-ass bounty hunter, or what?

I grabbed my keys and stuffed myself into my jacket. First thing on my agenda was a visit to the office. I wanted to make sure Jackie was holding up her part of the bargain.

The sky felt low and forbidding over the parking lot, and the air was as cold as a witch's fadiddy. The lock was frozen on the Buick, and the windshield was coated with ice. I hammered on the lock, but it wouldn't break loose, so I trekked back to my apartment and got some deicer and a plastic scraper. Ten minutes later, I had my door open, the heater going full blast, and I'd chipped a squint hole in the ice on my windshield.

I slid behind the wheel, tested the hole for vision and decided it would do if I didn't drive too fast. By the time I got to Vinnie's I was nice and toasty and could see my entire hood, not to mention the road. Jackie's Chrysler was parked in front of the office. I took the slot behind her and hustled inside.

Jackie was pacing in front of Connie's desk.

"Don't see why I need to do this," Jackie was saying. "It isn't like I can't control myself. It isn't like I couldn't stop if I wanted. I just like to do some once in a while. Don't see what's so wrong about that. Everybody do some once in a while."

"I don't," Connie said.

"Me either," Lula said.

"Me either," I said.

Jackie looked at us one by one. "Hunh."

"You'll be happy when you get straight," Lula said.

"Oh yeah?" Jackie said. "I'm happy now. I'm so goddamn happy I can't hardly stand it. Sometimes I just happy myself into a state."

Connie had her copy of Mo's file on her desk. "We don't get Mo in the next five days and we're going to have to forfeit the bond," she said to me.

I flipped the file open and took another look at the bond agreement and the picture.

Jackie looked over my shoulder. "Hey," she said, "it's Old Penis Nose. You after him? I just saw him."

Everyone turned and stared at Jackie.

"Yep, that's him all right," she said, flicking a false red fingernail against the photo. "Drives a blue Honda. Remember we used to see him on the street sometimes. Saw him coming out of the apartment building on Montgomery. The one next to the mission."

Lula and I looked at each other. Duh.

"He alone?" I asked Jackie.

"I wasn't paying much attention, but I don't remember anyone else."

"I'm gonna drive Jackie over to the clinic on Perry Street," Lula said. "Help her get started."

The problem with the clinic on Perry Street was that it was filled with dopers. Therefore, the street outside was filled with dealers. The dopers came to get their daily dose of methadone, but on the way in and out it was like walking through a controlled-substance supermarket. Easiest place to get dope in any city is always at the meth clinic.

Lula wasn't going along to make sure Jackie got started. Lula was going along to make sure Jackie didn't OD before she even signed the papers.

Lula followed me to my parents' house and waited while I parked the Buick in the driveway. Then she and Jackie dropped me at the Nissan service center.

"Don't let them give you no baloney about that truck," Lula said. "You test-drive it. You tell them you'll bust a cap up their ass if that truck isn't fixed."

"Okay," I said. "Don't worry. Nobody's taking advantage of me."

I waved her off and went in search of the service manager. "So what do you think?" I asked him. "Is the truck in okay shape?"

"We've got it running like a top."

"Excellent," I said, relieved that I didn't have to do any cap busting.

Jackie had seen Mo coming out of an apartment building on the corner of Montgomery and Grant. I wouldn't call it a hot lead, but it was better than nothing, and I thought it deserved a look. Montgomery and Grant were southeast of the burg in an area of Trenton that worked hard at staying prosperous. The apartment building anchored the street, with the rest of the block given over to small businesses. Sal's Café, A&G Appliances, Star Seafood, Montgomery Street Freedom Mission and the Montgomery Street Freedom Church.

I circled the block, looking for a blue Honda. None turned up. The apartment building had its own underground parking, but a key card was required to get past the gate. No problem. I could park on the street and check the garage on foot.

I did three laps around the block, and finally someone pulled out of a desirable space at the curb. I wanted to be on Montgomery, in view of both the front door and the garage entrance. I thought I'd snoop in the garage, take a look at the mailboxes, and then maybe I'd hang out and see if anything interested me.

There were seventy-two mailboxes. None had the name "Moses Bedemier" printed on it. The garage was only a third full. I found two blue Hondas, but none with the correct plate.

I went back to the truck and sat. I watched the people on the street. I watched the cars. I didn't see anyone I knew. At one o'clock I got a sandwich at Sal's Café. I showed Mo's picture and asked if he'd been seen.

The waitress looked at it.

"Maybe," she said. "Looks sort of familiar, but it's hard to say for sure. We get so many people passing through. A lot of older men come in for coffee before the mission opens its doors for breakfast. It started out being for the homeless, but it's used more by seniors who are lonely and strapped for money."

At four I left the pickup and positioned myself just inside the building entrance where I could flash Mo's picture and question the tenants. By seven I was out of tenants and out of luck. Not a single person had recognized Mo's picture.

I bagged the stakeout at eight. I was cold. I was starved. And I was twitchy with pent-up energy. I drove back to the burg, to Pino's Pizzeria.

Two blocks from Pino's I stopped for a stop sign, and sensed seismic activity under the hood. I sat through a few shakes and some rough idle. KAPOW. The truck backfired and stalled. "Son of a bitch!" I yelled out. "Goddamn Japanese piece-of-shit truck. Goddamn lying, cheating, goat-piss mechanic!"

I rested my forehead on the steering wheel for a second. I sounded like my father. This was probably how it felt to go down on the *Titanic.*

I babied the truck into Pino's lot, swiveled from behind the wheel and bellied up to the bar. I ordered a draft beer, a deluxe fried chicken sandwich, a small pepperoni pizza and fries. Failure makes me hungry.

Pino's was a cop hangout. Partly because half of the force lived in the burg, and Pino's was in a convenient location. Partly because Pino had two sons who were cops, and cops supported cops. And partly because the pizza was top of the line. Lots of cheese and grease, a little tomato sauce and great crust. Nobody cared that the roaches in the kitchen were as big as barn cats.

Morelli was at the other end of the bar. He watched me order, but held his distance. When my food arrived he moved to the stool next to me.

"Let me guess," he said, surveying the plates. "You've had a bad day."

I made a so-so gesture with my hand.

He was six hours over on a five o'clock shadow. Even in the darkened barroom I could see the tiny network of lines that appeared around his eyes when he was tired. He slouched with one elbow on the bar and picked at my fries.

"If you had a decent sex life you wouldn't need to gratify yourself like this," he said, his mouth curved into a grin, his teeth white and even against the dark beard.

"My sex life is okay."

"Yeah," Morelli said. "But sometimes it's fun to have a partner."

I moved my fries out of his reach. "Been to any good autopsies lately?"

"Postponed to tomorrow morning. The doc is hoping Cameron Brown will be thawed out by then."

"Know anything on cause of death? Like what kind of bullet did the job?"

"Won't know until tomorrow. Why the interest?"

I had my mouth full of chicken sandwich. I chewed and swallowed and washed it back with beer. "Just curious." Curious because this was the second dead drug dealer I'd stumbled over since starting the Mo search. It was a stretch to think there might be a connection. Still, my radar was emitting a low-level hum.

Morelli looked pained. "You and your girlfriends didn't do him the first time, did you?"

"No!"

He stood and tugged at my hair. "Be careful driving home."

He snagged a brown leather bomber jacket off a hook on the wall at the far end of the bar and left.

I stared after him, dumbstruck. He'd tugged my hair. First a chuck on the chin, and now a tug at my hair. This was a definite put-off. It was one thing for me to snub Morelli. It was an entirely different matter for him to snub me. This was *not* how the game was played.

I rolled out of Pino's at nine-thirty, feeling sulky and suspicious. I stood staring at my truck for a moment before getting in. More misery. My truck wasn't cute anymore. It looked like it needed orthodontia. I'd gotten new points and plugs, but I didn't have money for the bodywork. I slipped behind the wheel and shoved the key in the ignition. The truck started and . . . stalled.

"SHIT!"

My parents' house was only three blocks away. I raced the engine all the way and was relieved to finally be able to let the rotten truck die at the curb.

The Buick sat gloating in the driveway. Nothing was ever wrong with the Buick.

The phone woke me out of a dead sleep. The digital display on my bedside clock read 2 A.M. The voice at the other end was girlish.

"Hi ya," the voice said. "It's Gillian!"

Gillian. I didn't know anyone named Gillian. "You have the wrong number," I told her.

"Oops," she said. "Sorreee. I was looking for Stephanie Plum."

I pushed myself up on an elbow. "This is Stephanie Plum."

"This is Gillian Wurtzer. You gave me your card, and you said I should call you if I saw Uncle Mo."

Now I was fully awake. Gillian, the kid across from Mo's!

Gillian giggled. "My boyfriend was over tonight. You know, helping me with my homework. And he just left. And while we were saying good-bye I noticed there was a light on in the candy store. It must have been the hall light in the back. And I saw someone moving around in there. I couldn't tell if it was Uncle Mo or not, but I thought I should call you anyway."

"Is the light still on?"

"Yes."

"I'm ten minutes away. Keep your eye on the store, but don't go out. I'll be right there."

I was wearing a red flannel nightgown and thick white socks. I pulled on a pair of jeans, shoved my feet into my Doc Martens, grabbed my jacket and my pocketbook and flew down the hall, punching Ranger's number into my cell phone while I ran.

By the time I reached the Buick I'd explained it all to Ranger and had the phone back in my pocketbook. It had begun to drizzle with the temperature hovering at freezing so that every car in the lot sat under a shroud of ice. Déjà vu. I used my nail file to chip the ice away from the door handle and counted to ten in an attempt to lower my blood pressure. When the blood stopped pounding in my ears I used the nail file to carve a six-inch hole in the ice on my windshield. I jumped in the car and took off, driving with my nose practically pressed to the glass.

Please, please, please still be there.

I really wanted to catch Uncle Mo. Not so much for the money as for the curiosity. I wanted to know what was going on. I wanted to know who killed Ronald Anders. And I wanted to know why.

The burg was quiet at this time of night. Houses were dark. Streets were empty of traffic. Streetlights were hazy behind misting rain. I slowly rolled by Mo's store. A light was burning in the back hall, just like Gillian had said. There was no sign of Ranger. No blue Honda parked at the curb. No movement anywhere. I took King and turned into the alley leading to Mo's garage. The garage door was open, and deep in shadow, I could see a car parked in the garage. The car was a Honda.

I cut my lights and angled the Buick so that it was blocking the Honda's exit. I sat for a moment with my window cracked, listening, watching. I silently slipped out of the Buick, walked the length of the alley down King to Ferris and crossed the street. I stood in black shade, behind the Wurtzers' oak, and I waited for Ranger, waited for the store light to be extinguished, for a form to appear.

I glanced at my watch. I'd give Ranger three more minutes. If Ranger wasn't here in three minutes I'd cross the street and cover the back door. I had my gun in one pocket and pepper spray in the other.

Car lights appeared a block down King. When the car reached Ferris the lights in the store blinked out. I took off at a sprint just as Ranger's BMW turned the corner and slid to a stop.

Ranger owned two cars. The first was a black Bronco equipped with a state-of-the-art Bird Dog tracking system. When Ranger was doing a takedown and expected to transport felons he drove the Bronco. When Ranger wasn't responsible for a takedown, he drove a black BMW, limited production 850 Ci. I'd priced the car and found it listed at close to seven figures.

"The lights just went out," I called in a stage whisper. "His car's in the garage. He's going to go out the back door."

Ranger was dressed in black. Black jeans, black shirt, black flak vest with FUGITIVE APPREHENSION AGENT lettered in yellow on the back. His earring shone silver against dark skin. His hair was held back in his usual ponytail. He had his gun in hand when his foot hit the curb. If he'd been after me I'd have wet my pants on the spot.

"I'll take the back," he said, already moving away from me. "You cover the front."

This was fine with me. I was perfectly happy to play second string.

I scooted to one side of the candy shop's front door, pressing myself against the brick front. I had fairly good vision through the window, into the store, and I was in a good position to nab Uncle Mo if he bolted for Ferris Street.

A dog barked in the distance. It was the only sound in the sleeping neighborhood. Ranger was undoubtedly at the back door, but there was no indication of entry or capture. My stomach was clenched in anticipation. I had my lower lip caught between my teeth. Minutes passed. Suddenly the store was flooded with light. I inched to the window and looked inside. I could clearly see Ranger in the back hall. No one else was visible.

Ranger was opening doors just as I had done days ago. He was looking for Mo, and in my gut I knew he wouldn't find him. Mo had slipped away. And it was all my fault. I should have moved sooner. I shouldn't have waited for Ranger.

I turned at the sound of labored breathing and almost collided with Mo. His face was shadowed, but the shadows did little to hide his annoyance.

"You blocked my car," he said. "And now your cohort is nosing around in my store. You keep this up, and you'll ruin everything!"

"You failed to show for your court appearance. I don't know why you decided to run, but it's not a good idea. You should let me drive you to the police station to reschedule."

"I'm not ready. It's too soon. You'll have to talk to my lawyer."

"You have a lawyer?"

"Yes." His eyes locked onto Ranger's Beemer. The door was open, and the keys dangled from the ignition. "Ohhh," he said. "This will do nicely."

"Oh no. Not a good idea."

His mouth tipped up at the corners into an ironic smile. "It looks like the Batmobile."

"It's not the Batmobile. Batman doesn't drive a BMW. And I can't let you go driving off in it. You're going to have to come with me."

Mo was carrying a plastic bag in one hand and a bear-sized can of pepper spray in the other. He narrowed his eyes and pointed the can at me. "Don't make me use this."

I'd seen people get sprayed. It wasn't fun. "Bond is the one in the BMW," I told him. "Happy driving."

"Bond," he repeated. "Of course."

And then he took off.

Ranger rounded the corner at a run and stopped short in the middle of the sidewalk, watching the Beemer's taillights disappear into the night. "Mo?"

I nodded and pulled my collar tight to my neck.

"Probably there's a good reason why you didn't take him down."

"His can of pepper spray was bigger than my can of pepper spray."

We stood there for a few more minutes, squinting into the mist, but Ranger's car didn't reappear.

"I'm going to have to kill him," Ranger said, his voice matter-of-fact.

I thought Ranger might be kidding, but then again . . . maybe not.

I'd once asked Ranger how he could afford such expensive cars, and he said he'd made some good investments. I wasn't sure what he meant by that. A money market account seemed a little tame for Ranger. If I had to venture a guess on the contents of Ranger's portfolio, I'd lean toward running guns to well-connected foreign gunmongers.

"Find anything unusual in the store?" I asked Ranger. Like a dead body.

"Nothing. He must have seen you on the street. Didn't even take the time to make sure the back door was closed. Just cleared out of there."

I filled Ranger in on Cameron Brown and the RiverEdge while we walked back to my car. Then I told him about Jackie seeing Mo on Montgomery Street, coming out of the apartment building. I told Ranger how I'd staked the building out but hadn't come up with anything.

Ranger looked at my bedraggled hair and at the red flannel nightgown hanging under my jacket. "Who are you supposed to be?"

"I was in a hurry."

"You're going to give bounty hunters a bad name you go around looking like that."

I unlocked the passenger door for Ranger, climbed behind the wheel and cranked the engine over. "Where to?"

"Montgomery Street."

That would have been my choice too. I'd listened to the BMW drive away. It had gone southeast, toward Montgomery.

"Nobody home," Ranger said, after walking the underground lot.

"We could wait."

"Babe, I don't know how to break this to you, but we're not exactly inconspicuous. Doing surveillance in this car is like trying to hide a whale in a jelly jar."

Fine by me. I was cold and wet and tired. I wanted to go home and crawl into my nice warm bed and sleep until July.

"Now what?" I asked.

"You can drop me at Twelfth and Major."

No one knew where Ranger lived. I had Norma run a check on him once at the DMV and his address turned out to be an empty lot.

"You aren't really going to kill him, are you?" I asked, nosing the Buick toward Twelfth.

"You steal an eight-fifty Ci, you should be killed."

"It's Uncle Mo."

"Uncle Mo is wacko," Ranger said.

"Yes, but he's my wacko. I'd appreciate it if you didn't kill him until after I log him in and straighten a few things out." Like who killed Ronald Anders.

"Professional courtesy."

"Yeah."

"You have any leads?"

"No."

"We'll work together on this one," Ranger said. "I'll pick you up tomorrow at five."

"Five in the morning?"

"You got a problem with that?"

"Nope. No problem."

Trenton is creepy at three in the morning. Forlorn and subterranean, the pulse of the city checked behind black glass and acid-etched brick. Even the night people, the drunks and the kiddie crews, were tucked away, leaving the occasional fluorescent wash of light to derelict pigeons, walking the sidewalks, pecking at fool's food.

What sort of person would cruise these streets at this hour? Cops, shift workers, evildoers, bounty hunters.

I swung into my lot and cut the engine. Chunks of yellow dotted the big block building in front of me. Mrs. Karwatt, Mrs. Bestler, the DeKune apartment, Mr. Paglionne. Seniors don't waste a lot of time sleeping. Mr. Walesky, across the hall from me, was probably watching TV.

I stepped away from the Buick and heard a car door open and close behind me. My heart did a little tap dance at the sound. I looked to the building entrance and saw two figures move from the shadows. My gun was still in my pocket. I hauled it out and spun around, almost smacking a wiry little guy in the nose with it.

He immediately jumped back a step, hands in the air. "Take it easy," he said.

I had the other two in my peripheral vision. They'd stopped and raised their hands. All three men were wearing ski masks and brown coveralls over their street clothes.

"Who are you?" I asked. "What's going on?"

"We're concerned citizens," the wiry little guy said. "We don't want to hurt you, but if you keep after Mo we're going to have to take action." He reached into his breast pocket and pulled out an envelope. "You're a businesswoman. We understand that. So here's the deal. The money in this envelope represents your fee for bringing Mo in to Vinnie, plus a two-hundred-dollar bonus. Take the money and hop a plane for Barbados."

"Number one, I don't want your money. Number two, I want some answers."

The wiry guy made a come-on signal with his hand, and car lights blinked on behind him. The car rolled forward and the back door opened.

"Get in that car, and I'll shoot," I said.

"I'm unarmed. You wouldn't want to shoot an unarmed man."

He was right there. Not that it mattered. It had been an empty threat to begin with.

I'd set my alarm for four fifty-five and was so startled when it rang that I fell out of bed. I hadn't allowed myself time for a shower, so I brushed my teeth, dressed myself in some clothes I found on the floor from the previous day and staggered downstairs.

Ranger was waiting for me in the lot. He pulled a piece of paper, folded into four sections, from his jacket pocket and gave it to me. "A list of Montgomery Street tenants," he said. "Anything jump out at you?"

I didn't ask how he'd gotten the list. I didn't want to know the details of Ranger's network. I suspected his methods for acquiring information might sometimes involve broken bones and small-caliber bullet holes.

I handed the list back to him. "Don't know any of these people."

"Then we go door-to-door at nine o'clock."

Oh goody.

"In the meantime we'll stake out the lobby and the garage."

The plan was for Ranger to take the lobby and for me to take the garage, to position ourselves at the elevator banks and question the tenants as they left for work. At nine o'clock, after drawing a big zero, we started working the floors.

The first four floors were a washout.

"This doesn't feel hopeful," I said to Ranger. "We've talked to a lot of people, and we haven't even had a nibble."

Ranger shrugged. "People don't notice. Especially in a building like this. No sense of community. And there's another possible reason for no one to have seen him."

"Jackie might have been wrong."

"She's not the most reliable witness."

We walked up a flight and started moving down the hall, knocking on doors, showing Mo's picture. Third door down I got a hit.

The woman was older than most in the building. Sixties, I guessed. Nicely dressed.

"I've seen this man," she said. She studied the photo. "I just don't know . . . Maybe Stanley Larkin. Yes, I think I must have seen him with Stanley."

"Is Larkin's apartment on this floor?" I asked.

"Two doors down on this side. Number five-eleven." Two little frown lines creased her forehead. "You said you were apprehension agents. What does that mean?"

I gave her the minor charge, the missed-a-court-appearance line, and she seemed relieved.

Ranger knocked on Larkin's door, and we both flattened ourselves against the wall so Larkin couldn't see us through the security peephole.

A moment later, Larkin opened the door. "Yes?"

Ranger badged him. "Bond enforcement. May we step inside to ask you a few questions?"

"I don't know," Larkin said. "I don't think so. I mean, what is this all about?"

Larkin was in his late sixties. About five feet, ten inches. Ruddy complexion. Sandy hair, thin on the top.

"It will only take a moment," Ranger said, his hand on Larkin's elbow, gently guiding him back a few steps.

I used the opportunity to step inside and look around. It was a small apartment packed with furniture. Avocado green wall-to-wall carpet. Harvest gold drapes straight from the seventies. I could see the kitchen from where I stood. One juice glass and one cereal bowl in the dish drain. A coffee mug and newspaper on the kitchen table.

Ranger was showing Larkin the picture, asking him about Mo. Larkin was shaking his head.

"No," Larkin said. "I don't know him. Mrs. Greer must have been confused. I have some older men friends. Maybe from a distance one of them might look like this man."

I quietly stepped to the bedroom door. Queen-size bed in the bedroom. Perfectly made with a dark green paisley spread. A few pictures on the dresser in an assortment of silver frames. Night table at bedside with a clock radio.

Ranger handed Stanley Larkin a card. "Just in case," Ranger said. "If you see him, we'd appreciate a call."

"Of course," Stanley said.

"What do you think?" I asked when we were alone in the hall.

"I think we need to finish the building. If no one else places Mo with Larkin, my inclination is to put it on hold. Larkin didn't feel like he had secrets."

CHAPTER 8

Ranger and I went back to the Bronco and stared at the apartment building.

"False alarm," I said. No one else had recognized Mo.

Ranger was silent.

"Sorry about your car."

"It's only a car, babe. I can get a new one."

It occurred to me that it might be significant Ranger had said he could *get* a new Beemer as opposed to *buying* a new Beemer. And it also occurred to me that it might be pointless to suggest filing a police report or informing an insurance company of theft.

"You think we should stake out the building?" I asked.

Ranger looked the length of the street. "We could hang around for a while."

We slouched down, arms crossed over our chests, seat pushed back to give more leg room. Ranger never said anything when we waited like this. Ranger had a conversational potential only slightly greater than Rex's. That was fine by me because I had my own thoughts.

I was bothered that Mo had gone back to the store. Even if the store was the most important thing in my life I'm not sure I'd have risked a visit. Mo was carrying a plastic bag, which could have been filled with anything from underwear to ice cream cones. He also hadn't smelled all that good. He'd smelled musty. And he'd smelled like sweat and dirt. Either he'd been working hard in the garden, or else he was living on the street.

I was still speculating on these possibilities when at twelve o'clock Ranger got us drinks and sandwiches from Sal's.

My sandwich looked like brown bread and grass. "What is this?" I asked.

"Mixed sprouts, shredded carrot, cucumber and raisins."

Raisins! Thank God. I was afraid someone had scooped my sandwich out of the rabbit cage.

"Bedemier has to be staying somewhere," Ranger said. "Did you check out the possibility of a second apartment?"

"Did that first thing. Drew a blank."

"Have you canvassed motels?"

I gave him an openmouthed, goggle-eyed look that said, *Ugh! No!*

"It would pass the time," Ranger said. "Keep us out of trouble."

Ranger's sense of humor.

"Maybe Mo is living on the street. Last time I saw him he smelled like a cave."

"Hard to check on caves," Ranger said. "Easier to check on motels."

"You have any ideas on how you want to do this?"

Ranger pulled a section of the Yellow Pages out of his pocket. "Sal didn't need these," he said. He handed half the pages to me. "You get the first half of the alphabet. Show the picture. Ask about the car. If you find him, don't do anything. Call me."

"What if we zero on this?"

"We enlarge our canvass zone."

I shouldn't have asked.

Half hour later I was behind the wheel of the Buick. I'd rearranged my list according to geography, starting with the closest motels, working my way to Bordentown.

I'd called my father and asked him to please take my pickup back to the Nissan service center. He'd murmured something about throwing good money after bad, and that kids never listened anymore, and then he'd hung up.

By five o'clock I'd gone through two tanks of gas and had struck out from A to J. By five o'clock it had gotten very dark, and I wasn't looking forward to going home. Driving Uncle Sandor's Buick was like rolling along in my own private bomb shelter. Once I parked the bomb shelter in my parking lot, unlocked the door and set foot on the blacktop, I was open season for the Uncle Mo Fan Club.

I didn't feel like being open season on an empty stomach, so I detoured to my parents' house.

My mother was at the door when I pulled up to the curb. "What a nice surprise," she said. "Are you staying for supper? I have a ham in the oven and butterscotch pudding for dessert."

"Did you put pineapple and cloves on the ham?" I asked. "Are there mashed potatoes?"

The pager hooked to my belt started to beep. Ranger's number flashed on the screen.

Grandma came over and took a close look. "Maybe when my Social Security check comes in I'll get one of these gizmos."

From deep in his chair in the living room my father boosted the sound on the TV.

I dialed Ranger's number on the kitchen phone.

"Who are you talking to?" Grandma Mazur wanted to know.

"Ranger."

Grandma's eyes got wide. "The bounty hunter! What does he want?"

"A progress report. Nothing important."

"You should ask him over for dinner."

I put the phone to my chest. "I don't think that's a good idea."

"Tell him we got ham," Grandma said.

"I'm sure he's busy."

My mother looked up from measuring out flour. "Who's busy?"

"Stephanie's boyfriend," Grandma said. "The bounty hunter one. He's on the phone right now."

"And he's too busy to come to dinner?" my mother said. More indignant disbelief than a question. "Whoever heard of such a thing? The man has to eat, doesn't he? Tell him we have plenty of food. Tell him we're setting an extra plate."

"They're setting an extra plate," I told Ranger.

There was a moment of silence at the other end.

"You come from a long line of scary women," Ranger finally said.

Water bubbled up from the boiling potatoes and spattered on the stove. Red cabbage cooked in the two-quart pot. Peas and carrots simmered on the far burner. The kitchen windowpanes were frost-etched on the bottom and steamy on the top. The wall behind the stove had started to sweat.

My mother stabbed at the potatoes. "The potatoes are done," she said.

"I have to go," I told Ranger. "The potatoes are done."

"What'll happen if I don't show up?" Ranger wanted to know.

"Don't ask."

"Shit," Ranger said.

My father is an equal opportunity bigot. He wouldn't deprive a man of his rights. And he's not a hate-filled man. He simply knows in his heart that Italians are superior, that stereotypes were created by God, and if a person is worth anything at all he drives a Buick.

He was now staring at Ranger with the sort of dumbfounded confusion you'd expect of a man whose home had just been firebombed for no good reason.

Ranger was in his black mode today. Double gold studs in his ears, form-fitting long-sleeved black T pushed up to his elbows, black-banded diver's watch at his wrist, black rapper slacks tucked into black combat boots with enough gold chain around his neck to secure bail for murder one.

"Have some ham," Grandma said to Ranger, passing him the plate. "Are you a Negro?" she asked.

Ranger didn't blink an eye. "Cuban."

Grandma looked disappointed. "Too bad," she said. "It would have been something to tell the girls at the beauty parlor I had dinner with a Negro."

Ranger smiled and spooned out potatoes.

I'd decided at an early age to stop being embarrassed over my family. This is yet another advantage to living in Jersey. In Jersey everyone has the right to embarrass themselves with no reflection on anyone else. In fact, embarrassing yourself periodically is almost required.

I could see my mother going through mental gymnastics, searching for a safe subject. "Ranger is an unusual name," she managed. "Is it a nickname?"

"It's a street name," Ranger said. "I was a Ranger in the army."

"I heard about them Rangers on TV," Grandma said. "I heard they get dogs pregnant."

My father's mouth dropped open and a piece of ham fell out.

My mother froze, her fork poised in midair.

"That's sort of a joke," I told Grandma. "Rangers don't get dogs pregnant in real life."

I looked to Ranger for corroboration and got another smile.

"I'm having a hard time finding Mo," I told my mother. "You hear anything at the supermarket?"

My mother sighed. "People don't talk much about Mo. People mostly talk about you."

Grandma mashed her peas into her potatoes. "Elsie Farnsworth said she saw Mo at the chicken place getting a bucket of extra spicy. And Mavis Rheinhart said she saw him going into Giovachinni's Market. Binney Rice said she saw Mo looking in her bedroom window the night before last. Course, two weeks ago Binney was telling everyone Donald Trump was looking in her window."

Ranger declined the butterscotch pudding, not wanting to disrupt the consistency of his blood sugar level. I had two puddings and coffee, choosing to keep my pancreas at peak performance. Use it or lose it is my philosophy.

I helped clear the table and was seeing Ranger to the door when his cell phone chirped. The conversation was short.

"Got a skip in a bar on Stark Street," Ranger said. "Want to ride shotgun?"

Half an hour later we had the Bronco parked in front of Ed's Place. Ed's was standard fare for Stark Street. One room with a couple chipped Formica tables in the front and a bar across the back. The air was stale and smoke-choked, smelling like beer and dirty hair and cold French fries. The tables were empty. A knot of men stood at the bar, forsaking the three bar stools. Eyes swiveled in the dark when Ranger and I walked through the door.

The bartender gave an almost imperceptible nod. His eyes cut to an alcove at one end of the bar. A dented sheet metal sign on the wall by the alcove said GENTS.

Ranger's voice was low at my ear. "Stay here and cover the door."

Cover the door? Moi? Was he kidding? I gave a little finger wave to the men at the bar. No one waved back. I pulled the .38 five-shot out of my pocket and shoved it into the front of my Levi's. This didn't get any waves either.

Ranger disappeared into the alcove. I heard him knock on a door. He knocked again . . . louder. There was the sound of a doorknob being tried, another knock and then the unmistakable sound of a boot kicking in a door.

Ranger burst from the hallway on a run. "Went out the window into the alley."

I followed Ranger into the street. We stopped for a split second, listening for footfalls, and Ranger took off again, through the alley to the back of the bar. I was skidding on ice, kicking at garbage, and I was breathing hard. I caught my toe on a piece of board and went down to one knee. I pulled myself up and swore while I hopped for a few steps until the pain faded.

Ranger and I came out of the alley and hit the cross street. A dark figure ran for the front door of a row house halfway down the block, and we pounded after him. Ranger charged through the front door, and I took the alley two houses down to secure the rear exit. I was gasping for air and fumbling for my pepper spray as I came up to the back door. I had my hand in my pocket when the door flew open, and Melvin Morley III crashed into me.

Morley was as big as a grizzly. He was accused of armed robbery and assault with a deadly weapon. He was drunk as a skunk and didn't smell much better.

We hit the ground with a solid thud. Him on the bottom. Me on top. My fingers reflexively grabbed at his jacket.

"Hey, big boy," I said. Maybe I could distract him with my female charms.

He gave a grunt and flicked me away like I was lint. I rolled back and grabbed hold of his pants leg.

"Help!" I yelled. "HELLLLLLP!"

Morley hauled me up by my armpits and held me at eye level, my feet at least nine inches off the ground. "Dumb white bitch," he said, giving me a couple vicious shakes that snapped my head back.

"F-f-fugitive apprehension agent," I said. "Y-y-you're under arrest."

"Nobody's arresting Morley," he said. "I'll kill anyone who tries."

I flailed my arms and swung my legs, and my toe mysteriously connected with Morley's knee.

"Ouch," Morley yelled.

His big ham hands released me, and he buckled over. I staggered back a couple feet when I hit the ground, knocking into Ranger.

"Hey, big boy?" Ranger said.

"I thought it might distract him."

Morley was curled into a fetal position doing shallow breathing, holding his knee. "She broke my knee," he said on a gasp. "She broke my fucking knee."

"Think it was your boot that distracted him," Ranger said.

A happy accident.

"So if you were standing there the whole time, why didn't you help me?"

"Didn't look like you needed any help, babe. Why don't you run around and get the car while I baby-sit Mr. Morley. He's going to be slow walking."

It was almost ten when Ranger brought me back to my parents' house on High Street. Poochie, Mrs. Crandle's two-hundred-year-old toy poodle, was sitting on the porch across the street, conjuring up one last tinkle before he called it a night. The lights were off next door in Mrs. Ciak's house. Early to bed, early to rise, made old Mrs. Ciak wise. My mother and grandmother obviously didn't feel like they needed any help from a few extra winks, because they were standing with their noses pressed to the glass pane in the storm door, squinting into the darkness at me.

"Probably been standing there since you left," Ranger said.

"My sister is normal," I said. "Always has been."

Ranger nodded. "Makes it all the more confusing."

I waved good-bye to Ranger and headed for the porch.

"There's still some butterscotch pudding left," my mother said when I opened the door.

"Did you shoot anyone?" Grandma wanted to know. "Was there a big to-do?"

"There was a little to-do," I told her. "And we didn't shoot anyone. We almost never shoot people."

My father leaned forward in his chair in the living room. "What's this about shooting?"

"Stephanie didn't shoot anyone today," my mother said.

My father stared at us all for a moment, looking like he might be contemplating the advantages of a six-month tour on an aircraft carrier, and then he returned his attention to the TV.

"I can't stay," I said to my mother. "I just stopped in so you could see everything was okay."

"Okay?" my mother shouted. "You go out in the middle of the night, chasing criminals! How could that possibly be okay? And look at you! What happened to your pants? Your pants have a big hole in them!"

"I tripped."

My mother pressed her lips together. "So do you want pudding, or not?"

"Of course I want pudding."

I opened my eyes to a perfectly black room, and the skin-crawling feeling that I wasn't alone. I had no basis in fact for the feeling. I'd been dragged from sleep by some deep intuition. Possibly the intuition had been triggered by the rustle of clothing or a sweep of air. My heart knocked against my ribs as I waited for movement, for the scent of another person's sweat, for a sign that my fears were true.

I scanned the room but found only familiar shapes. The digital readout on my clock said five-thirty. My eyes cut to my dresser at the sound of a drawer slamming shut, and finally I picked out the intruder.

A pair of sweats sailed through the air and hit me in the head.

"If we're going to work together, you've got to get into shape," the intruder said.

"Ranger?"

"I made you some tea. It's on your nightstand."

I switched the light on. Sure enough, there was a cup of tea steaming on my nightstand. So much for the illusion of Stephanie Plum, keen-sensed bounty hunter.

"I hate tea," I said, sniffing at the noxious brew. I took a sip. YUK! "What *is* this?"

"Ginseng."

"It's weird. It tastes awful."

"Good for your circulation," Ranger said. "Helps oxygenate."

"What are you doing in my bedroom?" Ordinarily I'd be curious as to the mode of entry. With Ranger it was a pointless question. Ranger had ways.

"I'm trying to get you out of bed," Ranger said. "It's late."

"It's five-thirty!"

"I'll be in the living room warming up."

I watched his back disappear through the bedroom door. Was he serious? Warm up for what? I pulled the sweats on and padded out to him. He was doing one-armed push-ups.

"We'll start out with fifty," he said.

I got down on the floor and made an attempt at a push-up. After about five minutes Ranger was finished, and I'd almost done one.

"Okay," Ranger said, jogging in place. "Let's hit the streets."

"I want breakfast."

"We'll do a fast five-mile run, and then we'll come back for breakfast."

A five-mile run? Was he nuts? It was five-thirty in the morning. It was dark out. It was cold. I peeked out the window. It was fucking snowing!

"Great," I said. "Piece of cake."

I zipped myself into a down ski jacket, filled the pockets with tissues and lip balm, pulled on a knit cap, wrapped a scarf around my neck, stuffed my hands into big wool mittens and followed Ranger down the stairs.

Ranger ran effortlessly for several blocks. His stride was steady and measured. His attention directed inward. I struggled beside him . . . nose running, breathing labored, attention directed to surviving the next moment.

We slipped through the gate to the playing field behind the high school and swung onto the track. I dropped back to a walk and applied some lip balm. Ranger lapped me, and I picked it up to a jog. Ranger lapped me a few more times, and then he nudged me off the track, back through the gate to the street.

The sun wasn't yet on the horizon, but the sky had begun to lighten under the snow and the cloud cover. I could see the sheen on Ranger's face, see the sweat soaking through his shirt. His face still bore the same meditative expression. His breathing was even once again, now that he had slowed his pace to mine.

We ran in silence back to my apartment, entering the front door, jogging through the lobby. He took the stairs, and I took the elevator.

He was waiting for me when the doors opened.

"I thought you were behind me," he said.

"I was. Way behind."

"It's all in the attitude," Ranger said. "You want to be tough, you have to live healthy."

"To begin with, I don't want to be tough. I want to be . . . adequate."

Ranger stripped off his sweatshirt. "Adequate is being able to run five miles. How are you going to catch the bad guys if you can't outrun them?"

"Connie gives the bad guys who can run to you. I get the fat, out-of-shape bad guys."

Ranger took a bag out of my refrigerator and dumped a load of stuff from the bag into my blender. He flipped the blender switch and the stuff in the jar turned pink.

"What are you making?" I wanted to know.

"A smoothie." He poured half the smoothie into a big glass and handed it to me.

I took a sip. Not bad. If it was in a much smaller glass and sitting alongside a huge stack of hotcakes drenched in maple syrup, it would be just about tolerable.

"It needs something," I said. "It needs . . . chocolate."

Ranger drank the remaining smoothie. "I'm going home to take a shower and make some phone calls. I'll be back in an hour."

To celebrate our partnership I dressed up like Ranger. Black boots, black jeans, black turtleneck, small silver hoop earrings.

He gave me the once-over when I opened the door to him.

"Smart ass," he said.

I sent him what I hoped was an enigmatic smile.

He was wearing a black leather jacket with fringe running the length of each sleeve. Little blue and black beads were hooked three-quarters down the fringe.

I didn't have any fringe on my black leather jacket. And I didn't have any beads. I had more zippers than Ranger, so I guess it all evened out. I slipped the jacket on and clapped a black Metallica ball cap over my freshly washed hair.

"Now what?" I asked.

"Now we look for Mo."

It was still snowing, but it was cozy in Ranger's Bronco. We cruised the streets, looking for the Batmobile in parking lots and middle-class neighborhoods. At my suggestion we visited some photo stores. Two of the merchants said they recognized Mo but hadn't seen him lately. The snow was still coming down, and traffic was crawling around cars that couldn't make grades.

"Mo's not going to be out in this," Ranger said. "We might as well close up shop for the day."

I wasn't going to argue. It was lunchtime. I was starving, and I didn't want to graze on sprouts and bean curd.

Ranger dropped me at the front door to my building and motored off in four-wheel drive. I took the stairs two at a time, practically ran down the hall and unlocked my door. Everything was quiet and peaceful inside. Rex was sleeping. The refrigerator hummed softly. The snow clacked on the windows. I kicked my shoes off, shuffled out of the black jeans and carted an armload of food into my bedroom. I switched the television on and crawled into bed with the channel changer.

Do I know how to have a good time, or what?

At six-thirty I was coming off a two-hour MTV stint and was approaching a vegetative state. I was trying to choose between a Turner classic and the news when a thought straggled into the front of my brain.

Mo had a lawyer.

Since when? The paperwork I'd been given said he'd waived an attorney. The only one I could think to ask was Joe Morelli.

"Yeah?" Morelli said when he answered the phone.

Just yeah. No hello. "You have a bad day?"

"I didn't have a good day."

"Do you know who Mo is using for a lawyer?"

"Mo waived counsel."

"I ran into him, and he said he had a lawyer."

There was a pause at the other end. "You ran into Mo?"

"He was at the candy store."

"And?"

"And he got away."

"I hear they're hiring at the button factory."

"At least I know he has a lawyer. That's more than you know."

"You got me there," Morelli said. "I'll check with the court tomorrow, but to the best of my knowledge, we haven't been informed of counsel."

A new question to add to the list. Why would Mo get a lawyer? Mo would get a lawyer if he was thinking of turning himself in. Probably there were other reasons, too, but I couldn't think of them.

I went to the window and peered outside. It had stopped snowing, and the streets looked cleared. I paced in my bedroom. I paced in my living room. I went to the dining room table and wrote, "Mo gets a lawyer," on the steno pad. Then I wrote, "Three people think they might have seen Mo on Montgomery Street."

I drew a big round head and filled it with question marks. It was my head.

I did some more pacing. Montgomery Street nagged at me. Hell, I thought, I'll take a ride over there. I haven't got anything else to do.

I got dressed and plowed through the night in the Buick. I parked on Montgomery in almost precisely the same spot I'd parked on previous snooping sessions. I saw precisely the same things. Yellow apartment building, mission, church, appliance store. The only difference was that it was dark now, and it had been light then. Technically it had been dark for the first two hours I'd spent here with Ranger, but I'd been in a sleep-deprived stupor, so it hadn't counted.

Just for kicks, I trained my binoculars on the apartment building, peeping into the lit, undraped windows. I didn't see any nudity, or any murders or any Mo. Peeping isn't all it's cracked up to be.

Lights were out in the mission, but the church next to the mission was getting some traffic. The mission and the church occupied two buildings that were two stories each. They'd been shops at one time. An office supply store and a dry cleaner. The Reverend Bill, a fire-and-brimstone preacher, had bought the buildings five years ago and set up his storefront church. He was one of those hooray for people, let's get back to family values preachers. Every now and then his picture would be in the paper for picketing an abortion clinic or for throwing cow's blood on some woman in a fur coat.

The people entering the church looked normal enough. Nobody carried a picket sign or a bucket of blood. Mostly families. A few single men. I counted twenty-six men, women and children in a half-hour period and then the meeting or the service must have started, because the front door remained closed, and no one else showed up. It wasn't an ethnically diverse group, but that wasn't shocking. The surrounding neighborhood was predominantly white, blue-collar. People usually choose a church that's within their community.

The appliance store and Sal's Café closed at nine. A half hour later, the twenty-six people filed out of the church. I scanned the apartment building windows one more time with the binoculars. I had my eyes glued to the third floor when someone rapped on my passenger-side window.

It was Carl Costanza in cop uniform. He looked in at me and shook his head. I unlocked the door, and Carl took a seat.

"You really need to get a social life," Carl said.

"You sound like my mother."

"We got a complaint about some pervert sitting in a Buick, looking in people's windows with binoculars."

"I'm checking out a Mo sighting."

Costanza reached for the binoculars and looked the building over. "Are you going to be checking it out much longer?"

"No. I'm done. I don't know why I even came back here tonight. I just have this feeling, you know?"

"Nobody ever takes their clothes off in this neighborhood," Costanza said, still going window to window. "Have you talked to Reverend Bill?"

"Not yet."

"You should go do that while I keep an eye on things. I've got a second-floor apartment that looks promising."

"You think Mo might be there?"

"No. I think a naked woman might be there. Come on, sweetheart," Carl crooned, watching the woman in the window, "unbutton your shirt for Uncle Carl."

"You're sick."

"I live to serve," Costanza said.

I crossed the street and tried to peek past the curtains covering the two plate-glass windows in the front of the Freedom Church. I didn't get much mileage from that, so I opened the door and looked inside.

The entire downstairs portion was essentially one large room, set up auditorium style with a bunch of folding chairs arranged in rows and a raised platform set against the back wall. The platform had some blue material tacked to it to make a skirt. A lectern stood in the middle of the platform. I assumed this was the pulpit.

A man was stacking books at one end of the platform. He was medium height, medium weight and had a head like a bowling ball. He wore round tortoiseshell glasses, and had pink scrubbed-clean skin, and looked like he should be saying things like, "Okley dokley, neighbor." I recognized him from his press photos. It was Reverend Bill.

He straightened and smiled when he saw me. His voice was soft and pleasantly melodic. Easy to imagine him in a choir robe. Hard to imagine him throwing cow's blood, but I guess when the moment seizes you . . .

"Of course I know Moses Bedemier," he said affably. "Everyone knows Uncle Mo. He packs one heck of an ice cream cone."

"A couple people have reported seeing him here on Montgomery recently."

"You mean since his disappearance?"

"You know about that?"

"Several of our parishioners are from the burg. Everyone has been concerned. This is pretty strange behavior for a man as stable as Mo Bedemier."

I gave Reverend Bill my card. "If you should see him, I'd appreciate a call."

"Of course." He silently stared at the card, lost in thought, serious. "I hope he's okay."

CHAPTER 9

I didn't want Ranger showing up in my bedroom at the crack of dawn again, so I made sure my windows were locked and the bolt thrown on my front door. Then, to be extra sure, I jury-rigged a tower of pots and pans in front of the door, so that if the door was opened the pots would come crashing down and wake me up. I'd done this once before with a tower of glasses. It had worked like a charm except for the broken glass all over the floor and the necessity of drinking from paper cups until my next paycheck arrived.

I reread my scribblings on the steno pad, but no wondrous revelation jumped off the page at me.

At 5 A.M. the pots clattered to the floor, and I rushed out in my flannel nightshirt to find Ranger smiling in my foyer.

"Hey babe," Ranger said.

I picked my way around the pots and examined my door. The two Yale locks were intact, the bolt was thrown, the chain was attached. My conclusion was that Ranger had knocked the pots over when he slid under the doorjamb.

"I don't suppose it would do me any good to ask how you got in," I said.

"Someday when things are slow we'll have a class in advanced B and E."

"You ever hear of a doorbell?"

Ranger just kept smiling.

Okay, so I wouldn't answer the doorbell. I'd look out the peephole, see Ranger standing there and I'd go back to bed.

"I'm not running," I said. "I went running yesterday. I hated it. I'm not doing it again, ever. Been there, done that."

"Exercise improves your sex life," Ranger said.

I wasn't going to share any embarrassing secrets with Ranger, but my sex life was at an all-time low. You can't improve something that doesn't exist.

"Is it snowing?" I asked.

"No."

"Is it raining?"

"No."

"You aren't going to expect me to drink another one of those smoothies, are you?"

Ranger gave me the once-over. "Wouldn't hurt. You look like Smokey the Bear in that nightgown."

"I do *not* look like Smokey the Bear! All right, so I haven't shaved my legs in a couple days . . . that does not make me look like Smokey the Bear. And I certainly am *not* as fat as Smokey the Bear."

Ranger did more of the smile thing.

I stomped off into the bedroom and slammed the door. I stuffed myself into long johns and sweats, laced up my running shoes and marched back to the foyer where Ranger stood, arms crossed.

"Don't expect me to do this every day," I said to Ranger, teeth clenched. "I'm just doing this to humor you."

An hour later I dragged myself into my apartment and collapsed onto the couch. I thought about the gun on my night table and wondered if it was loaded. And then I thought about using it on Ranger. And then I thought about using it on myself. One more early-morning run and I'd be dead anyway. May as well get it over with now.

"I'm ready for a job at the sanitary products factory," I told Rex, who was hiding in his soup can. "You don't have to be in shape to cram tampons into a box. I could probably blow up to three hundred pounds and still do a good job at the sanitary products plant." I wrenched the shoes off my feet and peeled wet socks away. "Why am I knocking myself out over this? I'm teamed up with a madman, and we're both fixated on finding an old guy who sells ice cream."

Rex backed out of his can and looked at me, whiskers whirring.

"Exactly," I said to Rex. "It's dumb. Dumb, dumb, dumb."

I gave a grunt and got to my feet. I padded into the kitchen and started coffee brewing. At least Ranger hadn't come back with me to supervise breakfast.

"He had to go home on account of the accident," I said to Rex. "Honest to God, I didn't mean to trip him. And I certainly hadn't wanted him to tear the knee out of his sweatsuit when he went down. And of course I'd felt very bad about the pulled groin."

Rex gave me one of those looks that said, Yeah, right.

When I was a little girl I wanted to be a reindeer—the flying kind. I spent a couple years galloping around looking for lichen and fantasizing about boy reindeer. Then one day I saw *Peter Pan* and my reindeer phase was over. I didn't understand the allure of not growing up, because every little girl in the burg couldn't wait to grow up and get boobs and go steady. I did understand that a flying Peter Pan was better than a flying reindeer. Mary Lou had seen *Peter Pan* too, but Mary Lou's ambition was to be Wendy, so Mary Lou and I made a good pair. On most any day we could be seen holding hands, running through the neighborhood singing, "I can fly! I can fly!" If we'd been older this probably would have started rumors.

The Peter Pan stage was actually pretty short-lived because a few months into Peter Pan I discovered Wonder Woman. Wonder Woman couldn't fly, but she had big, fat bulging boobs crammed into a sexy Wondersuit. Barbie was firmly entrenched as role model in the burg, but Wonder Woman gave her a good run for her money. Not only did Wonder Woman spill over her Wondercups but she also kicked serious ass. If I had to name the single most influential person in my life it would have to be Wonder Woman.

All during my teens and early twenties I wanted to be a rock star. The fact that I can't play a musical instrument or carry a tune did nothing to diminish the fantasy. During my more realistic moments I wanted to be a rock star's girlfriend.

For a very short time, while I was working as a lingerie buyer for E. E. Martin, my aspirations ran toward corporate America. My fantasies were of an elegantly dressed woman, barking orders at toadying men while her limo waited at curbside. The reality of E. E. Martin was that I worked in Newark and considered it a good day if no one peed on my shoe in the train station.

I was currently having problems coming up with a good fantasy. I had reverted back to wanting to be Wonder Woman, but it was a cruel fact of life that I was going to have a hard time filling Wonder Woman's Wonderbra.

I popped a frozen waffle into the toaster and ate it cookie style when it was done. I drank two cups of coffee and walked my sore muscles into the bathroom to take a shower.

I stood under the steaming water for a long time, reviewing my mental list of things to do. I needed to call about my pickup. I needed to do laundry and pay some bills. I had to return Mary Lou's sweatshirt. And last but not least, I had to find Uncle Mo.

First thing I called about the pickup.

"It's your carburetor," the service manager of the blue team told me. "We could put a new one in or we could try to rebuild the one you've got. It'd be a lot cheaper to rebuild. Of course there's no guarantee with a rebuild."

"What do you mean it's my carburetor? I just got points and plugs."

"Yeah," he said. "It needed them too."

"And now you're sure it needs a carburetor."

"Yeah. Ninety-five percent sure. Sometimes you get problems like this, and you've got faulty EGR valve operation. Sometimes you've got faulty PCV valve airflow or faulty choke vacuum diaphragm. Could be a defective fuel pump . . . but I don't think that's it. I think you need a new carburetor."

"Fine. Good. Wonderful. Give me a carburetor. How long will it take?"

"Not long. We'll call you."

Next on my list was to stop off at the office and see if anything new had turned up. And while I was there, maybe just for the heck of it I'd run a credit history on Stanley Larkin, the Montgomery Street tenant Ranger and I had questioned.

I threw on a bunch of warm clothes, hustled downstairs, chipped the latest layer of ice off the Buick and rumbled on down to the office.

Lula and Connie were already busy at work. Vinnie's door was closed.

"Is he in?" I asked.

"Haven't seen him," Connie said.

"Yeah," Lula added. "Maybe somebody drove a stake in his heart last night, and he won't be in at all."

The phone rang, and Connie handed it over to Lula. "Someone named Shirlene," Connie said.

I raised my eyebrows to Lula. Shirlene, who was Leroy Watkins's woman?

"Yes!" Lula said when she got off the phone. "We're on a roll! We got ourselves another live one. Shirlene says Leroy came home last night. And then they got into a big fight, and Leroy beat up some on Shirlene and kicked her out to the street. So Shirlene says we could have his ugly ass."

I had my keys in my hand and my coat zipped. "Let's go."

"This is gonna be easy," Lula said when we hit Stark Street. "We're just gonna sneak up on ol' Leroy. Probably he think it gonna be Shirlene at the door. I just hope he don't come to the door too happy, you know what I mean?"

I knew exactly what she meant, and I didn't want to think about it. I parked in front of Leroy's building, and we both sat there in silence.

"Well," Lula finally said. "He probably wouldn't want to ruin his door a second time. Probably he caught it from the landlord. Doors don't grow on trees, you know."

I considered that. "Maybe he isn't even in there," I added. "When was the last Shirlene saw him?"

"Last night."

We did some more sitting.

"We could wait out here for him," Lula said. "Do a stakeout."

"Or we could call."

Lula looked up into the third-story windows. "Calling might be a good idea."

A few more minutes passed.

I took a deep breath. "Okay, let's do it."

"Damn skippy," Lula said.

We paused in the foyer and took stock of the building. A television blaring somewhere. A baby crying. We walked the first flight of stairs slowly, listening as we crept step by step. We stopped on the second-floor landing and took a few deep breaths.

"You aren't gonna hyperventilate, are you?" Lula asked. "I'd hate to have you keel over on me from hyperventilating."

"I'm okay," I told her.

"Yeah," she said. "Me too."

When we got to the third-floor landing neither of us was breathing at all.

We stood there staring at the door that had been patched with cardboard and two slats of stained plywood. I motioned to Lula to stand aside of the door. She jumped to attention and plastered herself against the wall. I did the same on the opposite side.

I rapped on the door. "Pizza delivery," I yelled.

There was no response.

I rapped harder and the door swung open. Lula and I still weren't breathing, and I could feel my blood pounding behind my eyeballs. Neither Lula nor I made a move for a full minute. We just pressed into the wall, not making a sound.

I called out again. "Leroy? It's Lula and Stephanie Plum. Are you there, Leroy?"

After a while Lula said, "I don't think he's here."

"Don't move," I said. "I'm going in."

"Help yourself," Lula said. "I'd go in first, but I don't want to be a hog about this searching shit."

I inched my way into the apartment and looked around. Everything was as I'd remembered. There was no sign of occupancy. I peeked into the bedroom. No one there.

"Well?" Lula asked from the hall.

"Looks empty."

Lula poked her head around the doorjamb. "Too bad. I was looking to do another takedown. I was ready to kick some butt."

I approached the closed bathroom door with my pepper spray in hand. I flipped the door open and jumped back. The door crashed against the wall and Lula dove behind the couch.

I looked into the empty bathroom, and then I looked over at Lula.

Lula picked herself up. "Just testing my reflexes," Lula said. "Trying out new techniques."

"Uh-huh."

"Wasn't that I was scared," she said. "Hell, takes more than a man like Leroy to scare a woman like me."

"You were scared," I said.

"Was not."

"Uh-huh."

"Unh-uh, was not. I'll show you who's scared. And it won't be me. Guess I can open doors too."

Lula stomped over to the closet door and wrenched it open. The door swung wide with Lula glaring straight into the jammed-together coats and other clothes.

The clothes parted and Leroy Watkins, buck naked, sporting a bullet hole in the middle of his forehead, fell out onto Lula.

Lula lost her footing, and the two of them went down to the floor—Leroy, arms outstretched, stiff as a board, looking like Frankenstein from the 'hood, on top of Lula.

"Holy cow," I yelled. "Jesus, Mary and Joseph!"

"Eeeeeeeeee," Lula screamed, flat on her back, arms and legs flailing, with Leroy deadweight on her chest.

I was jumping around, hollering, "Get up. Get up."

And Lula was rolling around, hollering, "Get him off. Get him off."

I grabbed an arm and yanked, and Lula sprang to her feet, shaking herself like a dog in a rainstorm. "Ugh. Gross. Yuk."

We squinted down at Leroy.

"Dead," I said. "Definitely dead."

"You better believe it. Wasn't shot with no BB gun, either. Got a hole in his head about the size of Rhode Island."

"Smells bad."

"Think he pooped in the closet," Lula said.

We both gagged and ran to the window and stuck our heads out for air. When the ringing stopped in my ears I went to the phone and dialed Morelli. "Got a customer for you," I told him.

"Another one?"

He sounded incredulous, and I couldn't blame him. This was my third dead body in the space of a week.

"Leroy Watkins fell out of a closet on top of Lula," I said. "All the king's horses and all the king's men aren't going to put Leroy Watkins together again."

I gave him the address, hung up and went out to the hall to wait.

Two uniforms were the first to arrive. Morelli followed them by thirty seconds. I gave Morelli the details and fidgeted while he checked out the crime scene.

Leroy had been naked and not especially bloody. I thought one possibility was that someone had surprised him in the shower. The bathroom hadn't been covered with gore, but then I hadn't felt inclined to peek behind the drawn shower curtain.

Morelli returned after walking through the apartment and securing the scene. He ushered us down to the second-floor landing, away from the activity, and we went through our story one more time.

Two more uniforms trundled up the stairs. I didn't know either of them. They looked to Joe, and he asked them to wait at the door. A television continued to drone on. The muffled sound of young children arguing carried into the hallway. None of the residents opened a door to snoop on the police activity. I suppose curiosity isn't a healthy character trait in this neighborhood.

Morelli drew the zipper up on my jacket. "I don't need anything else from you . . . for now."

Lula was halfway down the stairs before I even turned around.

"I'm out of here," Lula said. "I got filing to do."

"Cops make her nervous," I told Morelli.

"Yeah," he said. "I know the feeling. They make me nervous too."

"Who do you think did Leroy?" I asked Morelli.

"Anybody could have done Leroy. Leroy's mother could have done Leroy."

"Is it unusual for three dealers to get faded in the space of a week?"

"Not if there's some kind of war going on."

"Is there some kind of war going on?"

"Not that I know of."

A couple suits stopped at the landing. Morelli jerked his thumb toward the next flight of stairs; the men grunted acknowledgment and continued on.

"I need to go," Morelli said. "See you around."

See you around? Just like that? All right, so there was a dead guy upstairs, and the building was crawling with cops. I should be happy Morelli was being so professional. I should be happy I didn't have to fight him off, right? Still, "see you around" felt a little bit like "don't call me, I'll call you." Not that I *wanted* Morelli to call me. It was more that I wondered why he didn't want to. What was wrong with me, anyway? Why wasn't he making serious passes?

"Is something bugging you?" I asked Morelli. But Morelli was already gone, disappeared in the knot of cops on the third-floor landing.

Maybe I should drop a few pounds, I thought, slumping down the stairs. Maybe I should have some red highlights put in my hair.

Lula was waiting for me in the car.

"I guess that wasn't so bad," Lula said. "We didn't get shot at."

"What do you think of my hair?" I asked. "You think I should add some red highlights?"

Lula hauled back and looked at me. "Red would be bitchin'."

I dropped Lula at the office and went home to check my messages and my bank account. There were no messages, and I had a few dollars left in checking. I was almost current on my bills. My rent was paid for the month. If I continued to mooch meals from my mother I could afford highlights. I studied myself in the mirror, fluffing my hair, imagining a radiant new color. "Go for it," I said to myself. Especially since the alternative was to dwell on Leroy Watkins.

I locked up and drove to the mall, where I persuaded Mr. Alexander to work me into his schedule. Forty-five minutes later I was under the dryer with my hair soaked in chemical foam, wrapped in fifty-two squares of aluminum foil. Stephanie Plum, space creature. I was trying to read a magazine, but my eyes kept watering from the heat and fumes. I dabbed at my eyes and looked out through the wide-open arch door and plate-glass windows into the mall.

It was Saturday, and the mall was crowded. Passersby glanced my way. Their stares were emotionless. Empty curiosity. Mothers and children. Kids hanging out. Stuart Baggett. *Holy cow!* It was that little twerp Stuart Baggett at the mall!

Our eyes met and held for a moment. Recognition registered. Stuart mouthed my name and took off. I flipped the dryer hood back and came out of the seat like I was shot from a cannon.

We were on the lower level, sprinting toward Sears. Stuart had a good head start and hit the escalator running. He was pushing people out of his way, apologizing profusely, looking charmingly cute.

I jumped onto the escalator and elbowed my way forward, closing ground. A woman with shopping bags belligerently stood in front of me.

"Excuse me," I said. "I need to get through."

"I got a right to be on this escalator," she said. "You think you own this place?"

"I'm after that kid!"

"You're a kook, that's what you are. Help!" she yelled. "This woman is crazy! This is a crazy woman."

Stuart was off the escalator, moving back down the mall. I held my breath and danced in place, keeping him in view. Twenty seconds later I was off the stairs, running full tilt with the foil flapping against my head, the brown beauty parlor smock still tied at the waist.

Suddenly Stuart was gone, lost in the crowd. I slowed to a walk, scanning ahead, checking side stores. I jogged through Macy's. Scarves, sportswear, cosmetics, shoes. I reached the exit and peered out into the parking lot. No sign of Stuart.

I caught myself in a mirror and stopped dead. I looked like Flypaper Woman meets Alcoa Aluminum. Foilhead does Quaker Bridge Mall. If I saw anyone I knew while I looked like this I'd drop dead on the spot.

I had to pass back through Macy's to get to the mall, including a foray through cosmetics where I might encounter Joyce Barnhardt, queen of the makeover. And after Macy's I still had to negotiate the escalator and main corridor of the mall. This was not something I wanted to do in my present condition.

I'd left my shoulder bag at the beauty parlor, so purchasing a scarf was out of the question. I could rip out the little foil squares wrapped around my hair, but I'd paid sixty dollars to have the squares put on.

I took another look in the mirror. Okay, so I was getting my hair done. What's the big deal? I raised my chin a fraction of an inch. Belligerent. I'd seen my mother and grandmother take this stance a million times. There's no better defense than a steely-eyed offense.

I briskly walked the length of the store and turned to the escalator. A few people stared, but most kept their eyes firmly averted.

Mr. Alexander was pacing at the entrance to the salon. He was looking up and down the mall, and he was muttering. He saw me, and he rolled his eyes.

Mr. Alexander always wore black. His long hair was slicked back in a ducktail. His feet were clad in black patent leather loafers. Gold cross earrings dangled from his earlobes. When he rolled his eyes he pinched his lips together.

"Where did you go?" he demanded.

"After a bail jumper," I said. "Unfortunately, I lost him."

Mr. Alexander tugged a foil packet off my head. "Unfortunately, you should have had your head in the rinse bowl ten minutes ago! That's unfortunate." He waved his hand at one of his underlings. "Miss Plum is done," he said. "We need to rinse her immediately." He removed another foil and rolled his eyes. "Unh," he said.

"What?"

"I'm not responsible for this," Mr. Alexander said.

"What? What?"

Mr. Alexander waved his hand again. "It will be fine," he said. "A little more spectacular than we'd originally imagined."

Spectacular was good, right? I held that thought through the rinse and the comb-out.

"This will be wonderful once you get used to it," Mr. Alexander said from behind a cloud of hair spray.

I squinted into the mirror. My hair was orange. Okay, don't panic. It was probably the lights. "It looks orange," I told Mr. Alexander.

"California sun–kissed," Mr. Alexander said.

I got out of the chair and took a closer look. "My hair is orange!" I shouted. "It's freaking ORANGE!"

It was five when I left the mall. Today was Saturday, and my mother expected me for pot roast at six. "Pity roast" was a more accurate term. Unwed daughter, too pathetic to have a date on a Saturday night, is sucked in by four pounds of rolled rump.

I parked the Buick in front of the house and took a quick look at my hair in the rearview mirror. Not much showed in the dark. Mr. Alexander had assured me I looked fine. Everyone in the salon agreed. I looked fine, they all said. Someone suggested I might want to boost my makeup now that my hair had been "lifted." I took that to mean I was pale in comparison to my neon hair.

My mother opened the door with a look of silent resignation.

My grandmother stood on tippytoes behind my mother, trying to get a better look. "Dang!" Grandma said. "You've got orange hair! And it looks like there's more of it. Looks like one of them clown wigs. How'd you grow all that hair?"

I patted my head. "I meant to have some highlights put in, but the solution got left on too long, so my hair got a little frizzy." And orange.

"I've got to try that," Grandma said. "I wouldn't mind having a big bush of orange hair. Brighten things up around here." Grandma stuck her head out the front door and scanned the neighborhood. "Anybody with you? Any new boyfriends? I liked that last one. He was a real looker."

"Sorry," I said. "I'm alone today."

"We could call him," Grandma said. "We got an extra potato in the pot. It's always nice to have a stud-muffin at the table."

My father hunched in the hall, *TV Guide* dangling from his hand. "That's disgusting," he said. "Bad enough I have to hear crap like this on television, now I have to listen to some old bag talking about stud-muffins in my own home."

Grandma narrowed her eyes and glared at my father. "Who you calling an old bag?"

"You!" my father said. "I'm calling *you* an old bag. You wouldn't know what to do with a stud-muffin if you tripped over one."

"I'm old, but I'm not dead," Grandma said. "And I guess I'd know what to do with a stud-muffin. Maybe I need to go out and get one of my own."

My father's upper lip curled back. "Jesus," he said.

"Maybe I'll join one of those dating services," Grandma said. "I might even get married again."

My father perked up at this. He didn't say anything, but his thoughts were transparent. Grandma Mazur remarried and out of his house. Was it possible? Was it too much to hope for?

I hung my coat in the hall closet and followed my mother into the kitchen. A bowl of rice pudding sat cooling on the kitchen table. The potatoes had already been mashed and were warming in a covered pot on the stove.

"I got a tip that Uncle Mo was seen coming out of the apartment building on Montgomery."

My mother wiped her hands on her apron. "The one next to that Freedom Church?"

"Yeah. You know anyone who lives there?"

"No. Margaret Laskey looked at an apartment there once. She said it had no water pressure."

"How about the church? You know anything about the church?"

"Only what I read in the papers."

"I hear that Reverend Bill is a pip," Grandma said. "They were talking about him in the beauty parlor the other day, and they said he made his church up. And then Louise Buzick said her son, Mickey, knew someone who went to that church once and said Reverend Bill was a real snake charmer."

I thought "snake charmer" was a good description for Reverend Bill.

I felt antsy through dinner, not able to get Mo off my mind. I didn't honestly think Stanley Larkin was the contact, but I did think Mo had been on Montgomery. I'd watched men his age go in and out of the mission and thought Mo would fit right in. Maybe Jackie didn't see Mo coming out of the apartment building. Maybe Jackie saw Mo coming out of the mission. Maybe Mo was grabbing a free meal there once in a while.

Halfway through the rice pudding my impatience got the better of me, and I excused myself to check my answering machine.

The first message was from Morelli. He had something interesting to tell me and would stop by to see me later tonight. That was encouraging.

The second message was more mysterious. "Mo's gonna be at the store tonight," the message said. A girl's voice. No name given. Didn't sound like Gillian, but it could have been one of her friends. Or it could have been a snitch. I'd put out a lot of cards.

I called Ranger and left a message for an immediate callback.

"I have to go," I told my mother.

"So soon? You just got here."

"I have work to do."

"What kind of work? You aren't going out looking for criminals, are you?"

"I got a tip I need to follow up."

"It's nighttime. I don't like you in those bad neighborhoods at night."

"I'm not going to a bad neighborhood."

My mother turned to my father. "You should go with her."

"It's not necessary," I said. "I'll be fine."

"You won't be fine," my mother said. "You get knocked out, and people shoot at you. Look at you! You have orange hair!" She put her hand to her chest and closed her eyes. "You're going to give me a heart attack." She opened her eyes. "Wait while I fix some leftovers to take home."

"Not too much," I said. "I'm going on a diet."

My mother slapped her forehead. "A diet. Unh. You're a rail. You don't need to diet. How will you stay healthy if you diet?"

I paced behind her in the kitchen, watching the leftovers bag fill with packets of meat and potatoes, a jar of gravy, half a green-bean casserole, a jar of red cabbage, a pound cake. Okay, so I'd start my diet on Monday.

"There," my mother said, handing me the bag. "Frank, are you ready? Stephanie is going now."

My father appeared in the kitchen door. "What?"

My mother gave him the long-suffering face. "You never listen to me."

"I always listen. What are you talking about?"

"Stephanie is going out looking for criminals. You should go with her."

I grabbed the leftovers bag and ran for the door, snagging my coat from the hall closet. "I swear I'm not doing anything dangerous," I said. "I'll be perfectly safe."

I let myself out and quickly walked to the Buick. I looked back just before sliding behind the wheel. My mother and grandmother were standing in the doorway, hands clasped in front, faces stern. Not convinced of my safety. My father stood behind them, peering over my grandmother's head.

"The car looks pretty good," he said. "How's it running? You giving it high-test? You got any pings?"

"No pings," I called back.

And then I was gone. On my way to Mo's store. Telling myself I was going to be smarter this time. I wasn't going to get knocked out, and I wasn't going to get faked out. I wasn't going to let Mo get the best of me with pepper spray. As soon as I saw him I was going to give him a snootful of the stuff. No questions asked.

I parked across the street from the store and stared into the black plate-glass window. No light. No activity. No light on in the second-floor apartment. I pulled out and circled surrounding blocks, looking for Ranger's BMW. I tried the alley behind the store and checked the garage. No car. I returned to Ferris. Still no sign of life in the store. I parked a block away on King. Maybe I should try Ranger again. I reached over for my pocketbook. No pocketbook. I closed my eyes in disbelief. In my haste to get away without my father, I'd left my pocketbook behind. No big deal. I'd go back and get it.

I put the car into gear and pulled onto Ferris. I glanced into the store windows one last time as I did a slow drive-by. I saw a shadow move to the rear of the store.

Damn!

I angled the Buick into the curb two houses down and jumped out. I'd like the luxury of having a bag full of bounty hunter loot, like pepper spray and handcuffs, but I wasn't willing to risk losing the opportunity for it. I didn't really want to spray Mo anyway. I wanted to talk to him. I wanted to reason with him. Get some answers. Get him to come back into the system without hurting him.

Stephanie Plum, master of rationalization. Believe whatever the moment calls for.

I jogged to a dark spot across from the store and watched for more movement. My heart gave a lurch when a light flickered briefly. Someone had used a penlight and immediately extinguished it. The information on my answering machine had been right. Mo was in the store.

CHAPTER 10

I sprinted across the street and sought cover in the shadows to the side of the store. I hugged the brick wall, creeping back toward the rear exit, thinking I might barricade the door. I'd stand a better chance of capturing Mo if he had just one avenue of escape.

I took a deep breath and peeked around the building corner. The back door to the store was wide open. I didn't think this was a good sign. Mo wouldn't have left the door open if he was in the store. I feared history had repeated itself, and Mo had flown the coop.

I inched my way to the door and stood there listening. Hard to hear over the pounding of my heart but no footfalls carried to me from the neighborhood. No car engines being started. No doors slamming shut.

I did another deep breath and poked my head into the gaping doorway, squinting into the dark hall that led to the counter area.

I heard the scrape of a shoe from deep inside the store and almost passed out from adrenaline rush. My first instinct was to run away. My second instinct was to shout for help. I didn't follow either of these instincts because the cold barrel of a gun was pressed to my ear.

"Be nice and quiet and walk into the store."

It was the wiry little guy who'd tried to give me money. I couldn't see him, but I recognized the voice. Low and raspy. A smoker's voice. North Jersey accent. Newark, Jersey City, Elizabeth.

"No," I said. "I'm not going into the store."

"I need some help here," the guy with the gun said. "We need to persuade Miss Plum to cooperate."

A second man stepped out of the shadows. He was wearing the requisite ski mask and coveralls. He was taller and heavier. He was shaking a canister of pepper spray. Showing me he knew to make sure the gas is live.

I opened my mouth to scream and was hit with the spray. I felt it suck back to my throat and burn, felt my throat close over. I went down hard to my knees and choked, unable to see, closing my eyes tight to the searing pain, blinded by the spray.

Hands grabbed at me, digging into my jacket, dragging me forward over the doorstep, down the hall. I was thrown to the linoleum at the back of the store, knocking into a teary blur of wall and booth, still unable to catch my breath.

The hands were at me again, wrenching my jacket over my shoulders to form a makeshift straitjacket, binding my arms behind my back and tearing my shirt in the process. I gasped for air and tried to control the fear, tried to ignore the manhandling while I fought the pepper spray. It'll pass, I told myself. You've seen people sprayed before. It passes. Don't panic.

They moved off. Waiting for me to come around. I blinked to see. Three large shapes in the dark. I assumed they were men in ski masks and coveralls.

One of them flashed a penlight in my eyes. "Bet you're not feeling so brave anymore," he said.

I adjusted my jacket and tried to stand but wasn't able to get farther than hands and knees. My nose was running, dripping onto the floor, mixing with drool and tears. My breathing was still shallow, but the earlier panic had passed.

"What's it take?" Jersey City asked me. "We tried to warn you away. We tried to compensate you. Nothing works with you. We're out here trying to do a good deed, and you're being a real pain in the behind."

"Just doing my job," I managed.

"Yeah, well, do your job someplace else."

A match flared in the dark store. It was Jersey City lighting up. He sucked smoke deep into his lungs, let it curl out from his nose. I was still on hands and knees, and the man swooped down and held the glowing tip of the cigarette to the back of my hand. I yelped and jerked my hand away.

"This is just the start," Jersey City said. "We're going to burn you in places that are a lot more painful than the back of your hand. And when we're done you're not going to want to tell anyone about it. And you're not going to want to go chasing after Mo anymore. And if you do . . . we're going to come get you and burn you again. And then maybe we'll kill you."

A door slammed somewhere far off and footsteps sounded on the pavement behind the store. There was an instant of silence while we all listened. And then the back door was opened wide and a shrill voice called into the darkness. "What's going on here?"

It was Mrs. Steeger. Any other time Mrs. Steeger would call the police. Tonight she decided to investigate on her own. Go figure.

"Run!" I yelled to Mrs. Steeger. "Call the police!"

"Stephanie Plum!" Mrs. Steeger said. "I might have known. You come out this instant."

A beam of light played across Mo's backyard. "Who's there?" another voice called. "Mrs. Steeger? Is that you in Mo's backyard?"

Dorothy Rostowski.

A car parked at the curb. Headlights blinked off. The driver's door opened, and a man stepped onto the sidewalk.

"Shit," Jersey City said. "Let's get out of here." He got down on one knee and put his face close to mine. "Get smart," he said. "Because next time we'll make sure nobody saves you."

James Bond would have shown disdain with a clever remark. Indiana Jones would have sneered and said something snotty. The best I could come up with was, "Oh yeah?"

There was scuffling at the back door and some frightened exclamations from Dorothy and Mrs. Steeger.

I dragged myself to my feet and leaned against a booth for support. I was sweating and shivering, and my nose was still running. I wiped my nose on my sleeve and realized my shirt was open and my Levi's were unzipped. I sucked in some air and clenched my teeth. "Damn."

Another deep breath. Come on, Stephanie, get it together. Get yourself dressed and get out there to check on Dorothy and Mrs. Steeger.

I tugged at my jeans, putting a shaking hand to the zipper. My eyes were still watering, and saliva was still pooling in my mouth and I couldn't get the zipper to slide easily. I burst into tears and gave my nose another vicious swipe with my sleeve.

I gathered my shirt together with one hand and lurched toward the back door. Dorothy was standing, arms crossed over her chest. Self-protective. Mrs. Steeger was sitting on the ground. A man squatted in front of her, talking to her. He helped her to her feet and turned to look when I appeared in the doorway. Morelli. Wouldn't you know it.

Morelli raised questioning eyebrows.

"Not now," I said.

I backed up a few paces and sidestepped into the bathroom. I flicked the light on and locked the door. I looked at myself in the rust-rimmed mirror over the sink. Not a pretty sight. I used half a roll of toilet paper to blow my nose. I splashed water on my face and hand and buttoned my shirt. Two of the buttons were missing, but they weren't crucial to modesty.

I did deep breathing, trying to compose myself. I blew my nose some more. I looked at myself again. Not bad except my eyes looked like tomatoes and the cigarette burn was turning into a beauty of a blister.

Morelli had knocked on the door three times, asking if I was okay. My reply each time had been a cranky "Yes! Go away!"

When I finally opened the door, the lights were on in the candy store, and Morelli was behind the counter. I slid onto a stool in front of him, leaned my elbows on the counter and folded my hands.

Morelli set a hot fudge sundae in front of me and gave it a good dose of whipped cream. He handed me a spoon. "Thought this might help."

"Wouldn't hurt," I said, gnawing on my lip, trying hard not to cry. "How's Mrs. Steeger?"

"She's okay. She got shoved out of the way, and it knocked her on her ass."

"Gee, I always wanted to do that."

He gave me the once-over. "Like your hair," he said. "Trying something new?"

I flicked a spoonful of whipped cream at him, but I missed, and it went splat on the wall and slimed its way down to the back counter.

Morelli made a sundae for himself and took the stool next to me. We ate in silence, and when we were done we still sat there.

"So," Morelli finally said. "Let's talk."

I told him about the phone call and the assault and about the attempted payoff.

"Tell me about these men," Morelli said.

"They always wear ski masks and coveralls, and it's always been dark, so I've never been able to get a good look. The eerie part is that I think they're regular people. It's like they're from the community, and they're trying to protect Mo but they've turned violent. Like a lynch mob." I looked down at my hand. "They burned me with a cigarette."

A muscle worked in Morelli's jaw. "Anything else?"

"Under the coveralls they look respectable. Wedding bands on their fingers and nice running shoes. This wiry little guy seems to be the leader."

"How little is he?"

"Maybe five-nine. Got a smoker's voice. I've named him Jersey City because he has a Jersey City accent. The other two were bigger and chunkier."

Morelli covered my hand with his, and we sat some more.

"How did you know I was here?" I asked.

"I accessed your answering machine," Morelli said.

"You know my code?"

"Well . . . yeah."

"You do that a lot? Listen in on my messages?"

"Don't worry," Morelli said. "Your messages aren't that interesting."

"You're scum."

"Yeah," Morelli said. "You've told me that before."

I scraped at a little fudge that was left on the side of the sundae dish. "What did you want to see me about?"

"We got ballistics back on Leroy Watkins. Looks like the same gun that killed Cameron Brown and Ronald Anders also killed Leroy Watkins."

I stopped scraping at the fudge and stared at Morelli.

"Oh boy," I said.

Morelli nodded. "My exact thought."

I shifted on my stool. "Is it me, or is it warm in here?"

"It's warm in here," Morelli said. "Mo must have turned the heat up when he came by to visit."

"Doesn't smell all that good either."

"I wasn't going to mention it. I thought it might be you."

I sniffed at myself. "I don't think it's me." I sniffed at Morelli. "It's not you."

Morelli was off the stool, moving through the store. He got to the hall and stopped. "It's pretty strong in the hall." He opened the cellar door. "Uh-oh."

Now I was off my stool. "What's uh-oh?"

"I think I know this smell," Morelli said.

"Is it dookey?"

"Yeah," Morelli said. "It's dookey . . . among other things." He flipped the light at the top of the stairs.

I stood behind Morelli and decided I should be thankful my nose was still partially clogged. "Somebody should go down and investigate."

Morelli had his gun in his hand. "Stay here," he said.

Which was as good as guaranteeing I'd follow him down.

We crept down together, noting at once that the cellar posed no threat. No bad guys lurking in corners. No nasty-breathed, hairy-handed monsters lying in wait.

"Dirt floor," I said.

Morelli holstered his gun. "A lot of these old cellars have dirt floors."

A couple winter overcoats hung on wall pegs. Bags of rock salt, snow shovels, picks and heavy, long-handled spades lined the wall beside the coats. The furnace rumbled, central in the cellar. A jumble of empty cardboard boxes littered a large portion of the room. The smell of damp cardboard mingled with something more foul.

Morelli tossed some of the boxes to one side. The ground beneath the boxes had been recently disturbed. Morelli became more methodical, moving the boxes with the toe of his boot until he uncovered a patch of dirt that showed black garbage bag peeking through.

"Sometimes people get eccentric when they get old," I said. "Don't want to pay for trash pickup."

Morelli took a penknife from his pocket and exposed more of the plastic. He made a slit in the plastic and let out a long breath.

"What is it?" I asked. As if I didn't know.

"It isn't candy." He turned me around and pushed me toward the stairs. "I've seen enough. Let's leave this to the experts. Don't want to contaminate the scene any more than we already have."

We sat in his car while he called in to the station.

"I don't suppose you'd consider going home to your parents' tonight?" he asked.

"Don't suppose I would."

"I'd rather you didn't go back to your apartment alone."

Me too. "I'll be fine," I said.

A blue-and-white cruised to the curb behind Morelli's 4×4. Eddie Gazarra got out of the car and walked our way. We met him on the street, and we all looked to the store.

"Break out the crime tape," Morelli said.

"Shit," Gazarra said. "I'm not going to like this."

Nobody was going to like this. It was not good etiquette to bury bodies in the basement of a candy store. And it would be especially loathsome to accuse Mo of doing the burying.

Another blue-and-white showed up. Some more homicide cops arrived on the scene. The ID detective came with his tool kit and camera. People started appearing on front porches, standing with arms crossed, checking out the traffic jam. The crowds on the porches grew larger. A reporter stood, hands in pockets, behind the crime tape.

Two hours later I was still sitting in Morelli's car when they brought out the first body bag. The media coverage had grown to a handicam and a half dozen reporters and photographers. Three more body bags were trundled out from the cellar. The photographers hustled for shots. Neighbors left the comfort of their living rooms to return to the porches.

I sidled over next to Morelli. "Is this it?"

"This is it," Morelli said. "Four bodies."

"And?"

"And I can't tell you more than that."

"Any forty-five-caliber bullets embedded in bone?"

Morelli stared at me. Answer enough.

"Anything to implicate Mo?" I asked.

Another stare.

Morelli's eyes moved to a spot behind my left shoulder. I followed his eyes and found Ranger standing inches away.

"Yo," Ranger said. "What's the deal here?"

Morelli looked to the store. "Somebody buried four guys in Mo's cellar. The last one was buried shallow."

And he probably hadn't been buried so long ago, I thought. Like maybe the night Mo stole Ranger's car and smelled like sweat and dirt and something worse.

"I've got to move," Morelli said. "I've got paperwork."

I had to go, too. I felt like someone stuck a pin in me and let out the air. I fished car keys and a tissue out of my pocket. I blew my nose one last time and pumped myself back up for the walk to the car.

"How are you feeling?" I asked Ranger.

"Feeling fine."

"Want to run tomorrow morning?"

He raised an eyebrow, but he didn't ask the question. "See you at six."

"Six is good," I said.

I was halfway home before I picked up the headlights in my rearview mirror. I looked again when I turned off Hamilton. The lights belonged to a black Toyota 4×4. Three antennae. Morelli's car. He was following me home to make sure I was safe.

I gave Morelli a wave, and he beeped the horn. Sometimes Morelli could be okay.

I drove two blocks on St. James and hit Dunworth. I turned into my lot and found a place in the middle. Morelli parked next to me.

"Thanks," I said, locking the car, juggling the food bag.

Morelli got out of his car and looked at the bag. "Wish I could come in."

"I know your type," I said. "You're only interested in one thing, Morelli."

"Got my number, do you?"

"Yes. And you can forget it. You're not getting my leftovers."

Morelli curled his fingers around my jacket collar and pulled me close. "Sweetheart, if I wanted your leftovers you wouldn't have a chance in hell of keeping them."

"That's disgusting."

Morelli grinned, his teeth white against swarthy skin and day-old beard. "I'll walk you to the door."

I turned on my heel. "I can take care of myself, thank you." All huffy. In a snit because Morelli was probably right about the leftovers.

He was still watching when I entered the building and the glass door swung closed behind me. I gave him another wave. He waved back and left.

Mrs. Bestler was in the elevator when I got on. "Going up," she said. "Third floor, lingerie and ladies' handbags."

Sometimes Mrs. Bestler played elevator operator to break up the boredom.

"I'm going to the second floor," I told her.

"Ah," she said. "Good choice. Better dresses and designer shoes."

I stepped out of the elevator, shuffled down the hall, unlocked my door and almost fell into my apartment. I was dead-dog tired. I did a cursory walk through my apartment, checking windows and doors to make sure they were secure, checking closets and shadows.

I dropped my clothes in a heap on the floor, plastered a Band-Aid on my burn and stepped into the shower. Out, damn spot. When I was pink and clean I crawled into bed and pretended I was at Disney World. Stephanie Plum, master of denial. Why deal with the trauma of almost being tortured when I could put it off indefinitely? Someday when the memory was fuzzy at the edges I'd dredge it up and give it attention. Stephanie Plum's rule of thumb for mental health—always procrastinate the unpleasant. After all, I could get run over by a truck tomorrow and never have to come to terms with the attack at all.

I was awakened by the phone at five-thirty.

"Yo," Ranger said. "You still want to run?"

"Yes. I'll meet you downstairs at six." Damned if I was going to let a couple loser men get the better of me. Muscle tone wouldn't help a lot when it came to pepper spray, but it'd give me an edge on attitude. Mentally alert, physically fit would be my new motto.

I pulled on long johns and sweats and laced up my running shoes. I gave Rex fresh water and filled his little ceramic food dish with hamster nuggets and raisins. I did fifteen minutes of stretching and went downstairs.

Ranger was jogging in place when I got to the parking lot. I saw his eyes flick to my hair.

"Don't say it," I warned him. "Don't say a single word."

Ranger held his hands up in a backing-off gesture. "None of my business."

The corners of his mouth twitched.

I stuffed my hands on my hips. "You're laughing at me!"

"You look like Ronald McDonald."

"It's not that bad!"

"You want me to take care of your hairdresser?"

"No! It wasn't his fault."

We ran the usual course in silence. We added an extra block on the way home, keeping the pace steady. Easy for Ranger. Hard for me. I bent at the waist to catch my breath when we pulled up at my building's back door. I was happy with the run. Even happier to have it behind me.

A car roared down the street and wheeled into the parking lot. Ranger stepped in front of me, gun drawn. The car slid to a stop, and Lula stuck her head out.

"I saw him!" she yelled. "I saw him! I saw him!"

"Who?"

"Old Penis Nose! I saw Old Penis Nose! I could of got him, but you're always telling me how I'm not supposed to do nothing, how I'm not authorized. So I tried to call you, but you weren't home. So I drove over here. Where the hell you been at six in the morning?"

"Who's Old Penis Nose?" Ranger wanted to know.

"Mo," I said. "Lula thinks his nose looks like a penis."

Ranger smiled. "Where'd you see him?"

"I saw him on Sixth Street right across from my house. I don't usually get up so early, but I had some intestinal problems. Think it was the burrito I had for supper. So anyway I'm in the bathroom, and I look out the window and I see Mo walking into the building across the street."

"You sure it was Mo?" I asked.

"I got a pretty good look," Lula said. "They got a front light they leave on over there. Must own stock in the electric company."

Ranger beeped the security system off on his Bronco. "Let's move."

"Me too!" Lula yelled, backing into a parking space, cutting her engine. "Hold on for me."

We all piled into Ranger's Bronco, and Ranger took off for Sixth Street.

"I bet Old Penis Nose is gonna pop someone," Lula said. "I bet he's got someone all lined up."

I told Lula about the four bodies in Mo's basement.

"When a man's got a nose looks like a penis he's likely to do anything," Lula said. "It's the sort of thing makes serial killers out of otherwise normal people."

I thought chances were pretty good that Mo was involved in the killing of the men in his cellar. I didn't think his nose had anything to do with it. I thought about Cameron Brown and Leroy Watkins and Ronald Anders. All dead drug dealers. And then I wondered if the men buried in Mo's basement would turn out to be dealers, too. "Maybe Mo's a vigilante," I said. More to hear it said out loud than anything else. And I was thinking that maybe he wasn't alone in his vigilantism. Maybe there was a whole pack of them, running around in ski masks and coveralls, threatening and killing whoever they deemed to be a danger to society.

Lula repeated the word. "Vigilante."

"Someone who takes the law into his own hands," I said.

"Hunh. I guess I know what it means. You're telling me Mo is like Zorro and Robin Hood. Only Old Penis Nose don't just slash a big Z in a man's shirt. Old Penis Nose scatters brains halfway across a room in his pursuit of justice." She paused for a moment, thinking it through. "Probably Zorro blew a few heads apart, too. They don't tell you everything in a movie, you know. Probably after Zorro ruined your shirt he cut off your balls. Or maybe he made a Z on your stomach and all your guts fell out. I heard you could cut open a person's stomach, and his guts could all be hanging out onto the floor and he could live for hours like that."

I was riding shotgun beside Ranger. I slid my eyes in his direction, but he was in his zone, doing eighty between cross streets. Foot to the brake, jerk to a stop, giving the ABS a good test, look both ways. Foot to the floor on the accelerator.

"So what do you think?" Lula asked. "You think Zorro got off on shit like that? Making people look at their guts hanging out?"

My lips parted, but no words came out.

Ranger turned onto Main and then onto Sixth. This was a neighborhood of board and shingle row houses with stoops for porches and sidewalk for front yard. The houses were narrow and dark—sullen patchworks of brown and black and maroon. Originally built for immigrant factory workers, the houses were now predominantly occupied by struggling minorities. Most houses had been converted to rooming houses and apartments.

"Who lives in the house across from you?" Ranger asked Lula.

"A bunch of people," Lula said. "Mostly they come and go. Vanessa Long lives on the first floor, and you never know which of her kids is needing to stay there. Almost always her daughter, Tootie, and Tootie's three kids. Harold sometimes lives there. Old Mrs. Clayton lives on the other side of the hall. There are three rooms on the second floor. Not sure who's in those rooms. They let out weekly. Used to be Earl Bean lived in one, but I haven't seen him lately."

Ranger parked two houses down. "The third floor?"

"Nothing but an attic up there. Crazy Jim Katts lives in it. My guess is Mo was going to see someone on the second floor. It isn't like it's a crack house or anything over there, but when you rent weekly you never know what you get. You probably want to talk to Vanessa. She collects the rent. She knows everything goes on. Her apartment's on the left side when you walk in the door."

Ranger scanned the street. "Mo come in a car?"

"You mean the car he stole from you? Nope. I looked, but I didn't see it. I didn't see any strange cars. Only cars I see were ones that belong."

"You stay here," Ranger said to Lula. He gave an almost imperceptible nod in my direction. "You come with me."

He was wearing black sweatpants and a black hooded sweatshirt. So far as I could tell he'd never broken a sweat during the run. I, on the other hand, started sweating at the quarter-mile mark. My clothes were soaked through, my hair was stuck to my face in ringlets and my legs felt rubbery. I angled out of the car and did a little jig on the sidewalk, trying to keep warm.

"We'll talk to Vanessa," Ranger said. "And we'll look around. You have anything on you?"

I shook my head, no.

"No gun?"

"No gun. Everything's in my pocketbook, and I left my pocketbook at my parents' house."

Ranger looked grim. "Is the gun loaded?"

"I'm not sure."

"Your granny'll be doing target practice, shooting the eyes out of the potatoes."

I tagged after him and made a mental note to get my gun as soon as possible.

The front door to the building was unlocked. The overhead light still on. Inside, the small foyer was dark. Two doors led to the first-floor apartments. Ranger knocked on the left-hand door.

I looked at my watch. Seven forty-five. "It's early," I said.

"It's Sunday," Ranger said. "She'll be getting ready for church. Women need time for their hair."

The door opened the width of the security chain and two inches of face peered out at us.

"Yes?"

"Vanessa?" Ranger asked.

"That's me," she said. "What do you want? If you're looking to rent we're full up."

Ranger badged her. "Bond enforcement," he said. His voice was soft and polite. Respectful. "I'm looking for a man named Moses Bedemier. He was seen entering this house earlier this morning."

"I don't know anybody named Moses Bedemier."

"White man," Ranger said. "In his sixties. Balding. Wearing a gray overcoat. Probably came here looking to buy drugs."

The door closed and the chain snapped off. "I didn't see no jive junkie coming in here, and if I did I'd kick him out on his bony white ass. I've got kids in this house. I don't put up with that kind coming around. I don't put up with drugs in this house."

"Would you mind if we check the upstairs apartments?" Ranger asked.

"Mind? Hell, I'd insist on it," Vanessa said, disappearing into her living room, returning with a set of keys.

She was as wide as Lula, dressed in a red and yellow flowered cotton housecoat with her hair up in rollers. She had a grown daughter and grandchildren, but she didn't look much over thirty. Maybe thirty-five. She knocked on the first door with a vengeance.

KNOCK, KNOCK, KNOCK!

The door opened and a slim young man squinted out at us. "Yuh?"

"You got anybody in here?" Vanessa asked, poking her head around the doorjamb, seeing for herself. "You doing business in here that you shouldn't be doing?"

"No, ma'am. Not me." He shook his head vigorously.

"Hmmm," Vanessa said and moved on to door number two.

Again KNOCK, KNOCK, KNOCK.

The door was jerked open by a fat man wearing briefs and an undershirt. "Jesus fucking Christ," he yelled. "What's a man got to do to get some sleep around here?" He saw Vanessa and took a step back. "Oh, sorry," he said. "Didn't know it was you."

"I'm looking for some nasty white guy," Vanessa said, arms crossed, chin tucked in outraged authority. "You got one in here?"

"Nobody here but me."

We all stood staring at door number three.

CHAPTER 11

Ranger motioned Vanessa to stand to one side, rapped on the door and waited for a response. After a moment he knocked again.

"Got a lady in here," Vanessa said. "Moved in just last week. Name's Gail." She leaned past Ranger. "Gail? It's Vanessa from downstairs, honey. You open the door."

The bolt slid back and a young woman peeked out at us. She was painfully thin, with sleepy eyes and an open sore at the corner of her mouth.

"You have visitors this morning?" Vanessa asked.

The woman hesitated for a couple beats. Probably wondering what she should say. What new trouble was at her doorstep?

Vanessa looked beyond Gail. "There isn't anybody else in there now, is there?"

Gail gave her head a vehement shake. "Unh-uh. And I didn't invite nobody up here either. He just come of his own accord. Honest. It was some crazy white guy looking for my old man."

Vanessa raised a disapproving eyebrow. "I was led to understand you were living alone."

"My old man split on me. I got out of rehab, and he took off. He said he was worrying about things that been happening." She made a gun with her thumb and forefinger. "Now he's gone. Vanished. Poof."

Ranger was hanging loose behind Vanessa. "Name?" he asked Gail.

Gail looked from Vanessa to Ranger to me. More indecision.

"WELL?" Vanessa demanded, loud enough to make Gail jump six inches.

"Elliot Harp," Gail said, the words tumbling out of her mouth. "Everybody call him Harpoon. But I'm not his woman no more. I swear to it." She licked at the sore on her lip. "Is there more?" she asked.

"No," Ranger told her. "Sorry we had to bother you so early in the morning."

Gail nodded once and closed the door very quietly. Click. She was gone.

Ranger thanked Vanessa. Told her how he appreciated her help. Anytime, Vanessa said. And if he ever needed a room, or for that matter, if he ever needed anything at all . . . *anything*, he should remember about her. Ranger assured Vanessa she was unforgettable, and we left on that note.

"Boy," I said when we were out on the street. "Mr. Charm."

"In sweats, too," he said. "You should see me work my magic in leather."

"Where is he?" Lula wanted to know when we were all settled in Ranger's Bronco. "Where's Old Penis Nose?"

"Don't know," I said. "He came here looking for Elliot Harp, but Elliot wasn't at home."

"Elliot Harp's bad news," Lula said. "Mean. Middle management. Must have at least ten kids running for him."

"About that badge you flash," I said to Ranger.

He pulled away from the curb, flicked me a sideways glance. "You want one?"

"Might come in handy."

Ranger shot Lula a look in the rearview mirror. "You know where Elliot lives?"

"So far as I know he lives on Stark. Has a woman there. Junkie ho."

"Gail?"

"Yep. Gail."

"We just talked to Gail. She said Harp split. Says she doesn't know where he is."

"That could be," Lula said. "Lot of that going around."

"If Mo really wants to find Elliot, where will he look next?" I asked.

Ranger turned at Gainsborough and headed back toward the burg. "He'll go to the street. He'll look for Elliot on the corner. Elliot's running scared, but he still needs to do business."

"Elliot won't be on the street now," Lula said. "Maybe around eleven. The corners are always busy after church. After church is time to pick up a ho and get high."

I returned to my apartment for breakfast and a change of clothes. Lula went shopping for something to settle her stomach. And Ranger went home to the Batcave to eat tofu and tree bark. The plan was to rendezvous again at eleven.

The phone was ringing when I walked in the door, and my message light was blinking. Four new messages.

"Where have you been so early in the morning?" my mother wanted to know when I snatched up the phone. "I called an hour ago and nobody was home."

"I went out to run."

"Have you seen the paper?"

"No."

"They found bodies in Mo's basement! Four bodies. Can you imagine?"

"I have to go," I said. "I have to get a paper. I'll call back later."

"You left your pocketbook here."

"I know. Don't let Grandma play with my gun."

"Your grandmother is out to church. Says she needs more of a social life. Says she's going to find herself a man."

I disconnected and played back my messages. My mother, Mary Lou, Connie, Sue Ann Grebek. They were all reporting on the newspaper article. I called next door to Mrs. Karwatt and asked if she had a paper. Yes, she did, she said. And did I hear about the bodies in Mo's basement.

Three minutes later I was back in my kitchen with Mrs. Karwatt's paper, and my phone was ringing again. Lula this time.

"Did you see it?" she shouted. "Old Penis Nose made the paper! Said how he was picked up for carrying and then disappeared, and how he was under suspicion. Newspaper said a source told them the bodies in Mo's cellar could be drug related. Hah!" she said. "You bet your ass."

I read the article, started coffee brewing, took a shower and unplugged my phone after three more calls. This was the biggest thing to hit the burg since Tony the Vig was found dead in his attic, hanging from a crossbeam with his pants down and his hand wrapped around a record-breaking hard-on. Hell, maybe Mo was even bigger than Tony V's wanger.

And the best part of all of this was that I was finally the good guy. No more bullshit about how Uncle Mo would never do anything wrong. The man had a maggot farm in his cellar.

"Looking good," I said to Rex.

I laced up my boots, wrapped a scarf around my neck and went with the black leather jacket. I hopped into the Buick and drove over to my parents' house. Grandma Mazur was taking her coat off in the foyer when I arrived.

"Did you hear about the bodies?" she asked.

"Morelli and I made the discovery," I said.

Grandma's eyes opened wide. "No kidding! Were you there when they dug them up? Are you going to be on TV?"

I retrieved my pocketbook from the hall closet and did a fast check of the contents. "I don't think I'll be on TV."

"Boy," Grandma said, "I sure would have liked to have been there."

"How was church?" I asked.

"Boring," she said. "A big waste of time. We got a bunch of duds in that congregation. Nobody hot to trot. I'm gonna try the bingo hall tonight. I hear they got some live lookers coming to bingo."

Ranger was already parked when I swung into the municipal lot on Woodley. He was dressed in army fatigues and a khaki flight jacket.

"What's up?" I said by way of greeting.

"I got word on one of my FTAs. Earl Forster. Robbed a liquor store and shot the clerk in the foot. Jumped on a three-hundred-thousand-dollar bond. Just got a phone call saying Forster's stopped by to see his girlfriend in New Brunswick. I have a man in place, but I need to be there for the takedown. Can you handle the search for Harp by yourself?"

"No problem. Lula knows what he looks like. She knows his corners."

"Don't get close to him," Ranger said. "Only use him to get to Mo. If Mo and Harp go off together, let Mo put Harp away before you go in. We think Mo might be killing drug dealers. We *know* Harp will kill anybody . . . even female bounty hunters."

Cheery thought for the day.

"If it looks like you can do a takedown, but you need extra help, get me on the cell phone or the pager," Ranger said.

"Be careful," I said to the back of his car as he drove away. No point saying it to his face.

Lula barreled into the lot ten minutes later. "Sorry I'm late," she said. "I got this intestinal problem, you know." She looked around. "Where's Ranger?"

"Had business elsewhere. We're on our own."

If I was doing a serious stakeout with another person, I'd use two cars or have one person on foot with a second car in backup. I suspected this would be more of a ride around and look for a man who didn't show up. And since I had no idea what Harp looked like, I elected to ride with Lula.

It was another gray day with a light rain beginning to fall. Temperatures were in the forties, so nothing was freezing. Lula motored the Firebird out of the lot and headed for Stark Street. We kept our eyes open for the Batmobile, Elliot Harp and bad guys in general. We worked our way down Stark, hit the end of the business district, turned and retraced our route. Lula wove her way through the projects, cruised center city and crossed over to King. When she reached Ferris she drove by Mo's. The store was padlocked and sealed with crime scene tape. We did this circuit two more times. It was raining. Not many people out on the street.

"I'm starving to death," Lula said. "I need a burger. I need fries."

I could see the glow of a fast-food drive-through shining red and yellow through the misting rain. I could feel the force field sucking us forward to the speaker box.

"I want a triple-decker burger," Lula yelled at the box. "I want bacon and cheese and special sauce. I want a large fries, and I want lots of them little ketchup packets. And I want a large chocolate milkshake." She turned to me. "You want something?"

"I'll have the same."

"Double that order," Lula shouted. "And don't forget about the ketchup."

We took the bags of food and parked on Stark Street where we could watch the action. Trouble was, there wasn't much action to watch.

"You ever wonder about him?" Lula asked.

"Who?"

"Ranger."

"What's to wonder?"

"I bet you don't know anything about him," Lula said. "Nobody knows anything about him. I bet you don't even know where he lives."

"I know his address."

"Hah! That vacant lot."

I sipped at my milkshake, and Lula finished up her fries.

"I think we should do some detecting on Ranger," Lula said. "I think someday we should follow his ass."

"Hmm," I said, not feeling especially qualified to follow Ranger's ass.

"In fact, I might follow it tomorrow morning. You run with him every day?"

"Not if I can help it."

"Well if you run with him tomorrow, you call me. I could use some exercise."

After an hour of sitting, I was ready to move on. "This isn't working," I said to Lula. "Just for fun, let's drive over to Montgomery."

Lula drove the length of Stark, looped through the projects one last time and cut across town. We drove back and forth on Montgomery and parked two doors down from Sal's Café.

"Bet they've got doughnuts in there," Lula said.

"What about your intestinal problem? Maybe you want to wait and see how it goes with the burger and fries."

"I suppose you're right, but I sure would like to have some doughnuts."

I had to admit, doughnuts seemed like a pretty good idea on a drizzly day.

"Course there's some advantage to having an intestinal disturbance," Lula said. "Those doughnuts probably wouldn't stay with me long enough to find a home on my ass."

"Better take advantage of the opportunity."

Lula had her purse in her hand. "That's exactly what I'm thinking."

I stayed in the car and watched through the window as Lula picked out a dozen doughnuts.

She handed the doughnuts and the coffees off to me and settled behind the wheel. I chose a Bavarian cream and took a chomp. Lula did the same. She took a second doughnut.

"Have you seen Jackie?" I asked Lula. "Is she still with the program?"

"She's going to the clinic. Problem is, you can make a person do the program, but you can't make them take it serious. Jackie don't believe in herself enough to take the program serious."

"Maybe that will change."

"I sure hope so. I'm lucky because I was born with a positive personality. Even when things aren't looking too good, I don't let myself get beaten down. I just start pushing and shoving. Pretty soon I'm so loud and full of bullshit I just forget about being scared. Jackie wasn't born with such a positive personality. Jackie's more a negative person. She pulls all inside herself."

"Not always," I said. "She was pretty extroverted when it came to drilling holes in Cameron Brown."

Lula gazed into the doughnut box, thinking ahead to doughnut number three. "Yeah. She had a good time on that one. I know it wasn't right what she did to the dead, but I gotta admit, I sort of liked seeing her make old Cameron jump around. She's gotta learn to take charge more like that.

"See, Jackie and me, we've both been beat on a lot. That's the way it is when you haven't got a daddy, and your mama's a crackhead. There's always lots of uncles coming and going and getting high. And when they get high they beat on you.

"Trouble now is that Jackie's still letting people beat on her. She doesn't know she can make it stop. I try to tell her. I tell her to look at me. Nobody's gonna beat on me ever again. I've got self-respect. I'm gonna do something with my life. I might even go to college someday."

"You could do it. Lots of people return to school."

"Fuckin' A," Lula said.

I drank my coffee and looked out the rain-streaked window. Cars drove by in abstract motion. Blurry images and smeary flashes of bright red taillights.

A car pulled out of the underground parking garage across the street. It was a tan sedan with something long and black strapped to the roof. I cracked my window for a better look. Rug, I thought. All rolled up and covered with a plastic tarp.

The driver reached a hand out, checking to see if his cargo was secure. The door opened, and the driver stepped out to make an adjustment.

Suddenly I was at the edge of my seat. "Look at that car with the rug on top!" I hollered, grabbing Lula by the jacket sleeve to get her attention.

"The car at the parking garage?" She put the wipers on and leaned forward to see better. "Holy cow! It's him! It's Old Penis Nose!"

Lula jumped out of the car and took off across the street after Mo. She had a half-eaten Boston creme in her hand, and she was getting pelted with rain and she was yelling, "Stop! Stop in the name of the law!"

Mo's mouth dropped open. A mixture of disbelief and horror registered on his face. He snapped his mouth shut, jumped into his car and took off, burning rubber.

"Get back here!" I hollered at Lula. "He's getting away!"

Lula pulled up and ran back to the Firebird. "Did you see that? He didn't pay no attention to me! I should of shot him. I should of dropped a cap in that old coot."

Hard to do when you're packing a doughnut.

She threw the car into gear, put her foot to the floor and rocketed off after Mo . . . through the intersection, through a red light.

"I see him!" she shouted, giving the wheel a thump with the heel of her hand. "And that isn't no rug on the top of the car. That's something lumpy wrapped in garbage bags. I'm not even gonna tell you what I think is on top of that car."

I'd had the same thought, and the possibility that Elliot Harp was going for his last ride evoked a desire to drive in the opposite direction. I didn't want to find any more dead people. My emotional stability was approaching meltdown. I was doing a pretty good job of denying the attack in the candy store. I was having less success with flashbacks of murdered men.

Mo turned at Slater, and Lula took the corner with two tires touching pavement.

I had my foot braced against the dash. "Slow down! You're going to kill us."

"Don't worry," Lula said. "I know what I'm doing. I've got perfect reflexes. I'm like a cat."

Mo was coming up to Wells Avenue, and I knew where he was going. He was heading for Route 1. No problem, I thought. He can't outrun us with whatever he has on top of his car. Although probably he didn't care much about his cargo by now.

Lula followed Mo onto the ramp, momentarily fell behind when Mo merged into traffic. We caught him easily enough and stuck to his tail.

The dark green plastic was furiously flapping in the wind. Mo had bound the package to the roof of the car by lacing what looked like clothesline through the windows. He changed lanes and the long lumpy object swung side to side under the ropes.

"He don't watch out, he's gonna lose that sucker," Lula said. She beeped her horn at him. "Pull over, Peckernose!" She gave the Firebird some gas and tapped Mo's rear bumper.

I was braced against the dash, and I'd begun chanting under my breath. Holy Mary, mother of God . . . please don't let me die on Route 1 with my hair looking like this.

Lula gave Mo's back bumper another whack. The impact snapped my head and caused Mo to fishtail out of control. He swerved in front of us, a cord snapped loose and a garbage bag whipped off and sailed over our car.

Lula moved in one more time, but before she could make contact the second cord broke, another garbage bag flew away and a body catapulted off Mo's roof and onto the hood of Lula's Firebird, landing with a loud WUMP!

"EEEEEeeeeeh!" Lula and I screamed in unison.

The body bounced once on the hood, and then smacked into the windshield and stuck like a squashed bug, staring in at us, mouth agape, eyes unseeing.

"I got a body stuck to my windshield!" Lula yelled. "I can't drive like this! I can't get my wipers to work. How am I supposed to drive with a dead guy on my wipers?"

The car rocked from lane to lane; the body vaulted off the hood, did a half flip and landed faceup at the side of the road. Lula stomped on the brake and skidded to a stop on the shoulder. We sat there for a moment, hands to our hearts, unable to talk. We turned and looked out the back window.

"Dang," Lula said.

I thought that summed it up.

We looked at each other and did a double grimace. Lula put the Firebird in reverse and cautiously inched back, staying to the shoulder, out of the traffic lane. She stopped and parked a couple feet from the body. We got out of the car and crept closer.

"At least he's got clothes on," Lula said.

"Is it Harp?"

"That would be my guess. Hard to tell with that big hole where his nose used to be."

The drizzle had turned to a driving rain. I pushed wet hair out of my eyes and blinked at Lula. "We should call the police."

"Yeah," Lula said. "That's a good idea. You call the police, and I'll cover the body. I got a blanket in the back."

I ran back to the car and retrieved my pocketbook. I rummaged around some, found my cell phone, flipped it open and punched the on button. A dim light flashed a low-battery message and cut off.

"No juice," I said to Lula. "I must have left the phone on all last night. We'll have to flag someone down."

A dozen cars zoomed past us, spraying water.

"Plan two?" Lula asked.

"We drive to the nearest exit and call the police."

"You gonna leave the body all by itself?"

"I suppose one of us should stay."

"That would be you," Lula said.

An eighteen-wheeler roared by, almost sideswiping us.

"Ditch staying," I told her.

Lula cut her eyes back to Harp. "We could take him with us. We could ram him into the trunk. And then we could drive him to a funeral parlor or something. You know, do a drop-off."

"That would be altering the crime scene."

"Altering, hell. This dead motherfucker fell out of the sky onto the hood of my car! And anyway, he could get run over by a truck if he stays here."

She had a point. Elliot Harp had been in transit when he bounced off the Firebird. And he wouldn't look good with tire tracks across his chest.

"Okay," I said. "We'll take him with us."

We looked down at Elliot. Both of us swallowing hard.

"Guess you should put him in the trunk," Lula said.

"Me?"

"You don't expect *me* to do it, do you? I'm not touching no dead man. I've still got the creeps from Leroy Watkins."

"He's big. I can't get him in the trunk all by myself."

"This whole thing is giving me the runs," Lula said. "I vote we pretend this never happened, and we get our butts out of here."

"It won't be so bad," I said to her, making an effort at convincing myself. "How about your blanket? We could wrap him in the blanket. Then we could pick him up without actually touching him."

"I suppose that'd be all right," Lula said. "We could give it a try."

I spread the blanket on the ground beside Elliot Harp, took a deep breath, hooked my fingers around his belt and rolled him onto the blanket. I jumped back, squeezed my eyes closed tight and exhaled. No matter how much violent death I saw, I would never get used to it.

"I'm gonna definitely have the runs," Lula said. "I can feel it coming on."

"Forget about the runs and help me with this body!"

Lula grabbed hold of the head end of the blanket, and I grabbed hold of the foot end. Harp had full rigor and wouldn't bend, so we put him in the trunk headfirst with his legs sticking out. We carefully closed the lid on Harp's knees and secured the lid with a piece of rope Lula had in her trunk.

"Hold on," Lula said, pulling a red flowered scarf from her coat pocket, tying the scarf on Harp's foot like a flag. "Don't want to get a ticket. I hear the police are real picky about having things sticking out of your trunk."

Especially dead guys.

We pulled into traffic and had gone about a half mile, looking for a place to turn, when I got to worrying about Harp. I wasn't sure how it would go over with the Trenton police if we drove up to the station with a dead drug dealer hanging out of Lula's trunk. They might not understand the decision-making process that led to moving him off the side of the road.

Lula took a jug handle off Route 1 and stopped for a light. "Where're we going?" she wanted to know.

"To the burg. I need to talk to Eddie Gazarra."

Gazarra was a friend first, cop second. Gazarra could be trusted to give me honest advice on the best method of dead body transfer.

A car pulled up behind us at the light. Almost immediately the car went into reverse, backing away from us at high speed. Lula and I stopped watching the rearview mirror and exchanged glances.

"Maybe we should have done a better job of wrapping the blanket around old Elliot's feet," Lula said.

The light changed, and Lula headed south on Route 1. She cut off at Masters Street, preferring to drive a few blocks out of the way rather than chance crossing center city with Elliot. By the time we hit Hamilton Avenue the sky was dark under cloud cover, and the streetlights had blinked on.

Eddie Gazarra lived in a three-bedroom ranch on the fringe of the burg. The house had been built in the sixties. Red brick and white aluminum siding. Postage stamp fenced-in yard. Bugs the Rabbit lived in a wooden hutch at the rear of the yard, banished from the house after eating through the TV cable.

Lula parked in front of the house, and we stared in silence at the black windows.

"Doesn't look like anyone's home," Lula said.

I agreed, but I went to the door anyway. I pressed the doorbell and waited a few seconds. I pressed the doorbell again. I waded into the azaleas, cupped my hands against the living room window and looked inside. Nobody home.

Gus Balog, Eddie's next-door neighbor, stuck his head out his front door. "What's going on? Is that Stephanie Plum?"

"Yes. I'm looking for Eddie."

"Nobody's home. They took the kids out to that new chicken place. Is that your car . . . that red one?"

"It belongs to an associate."

"What's sticking out the trunk? Looks like legs."

"It's just a dummy. You know, like from a department store."

"Don't look like a dummy," Gus said. "Looks like a dead guy. I heard you were looking for Mo. Those aren't Mo's legs, are they?"

I backed out of the azaleas and retreated to the car. "No. They're not Mo's legs." I jumped into the car and slammed the door shut. "Time to leave," I said to Lula.

Lula cruised around a couple blocks. "Well?" she asked.

"I'm thinking. I'm thinking." The problem was that I could only come up with one other person who might be able to help me out. Joe Morelli. Not someone I wanted to see in my present bedraggled condition. And not someone I wanted to owe an additional favor. And not someone I totally trusted to choose me over the Trenton Police Department.

"I'm cold, and I'm wet and I'm sure as anything gonna have the runs any minute now," Lula said. "You better decide what to do pretty soon, or there could be a big mess in the car."

Morelli had recently moved out of his apartment and into a row house on Slater Street. I didn't know any of the details, but the move seemed out of character for Morelli. His previous apartment had been sparsely furnished. Comfortable in a utilitarian sort of way. Minimum maintenance. An entire house for Morelli felt much too domestic. Who would clean it? And what about curtains? Who would pick out curtains?

"Take Chambers and turn left when you get to Slater," I said.

Slater was outside the boundaries of the burg by about a half mile. It was an ethnically mixed neighborhood of modest homes and people scraping to maintain them.

I couldn't remember the number, but I'd know the house. I'd given in to morbid curiosity about a month ago and driven by to check things out. It was brown shingle in the middle of the block. Two stories, small cement front porch. A handyman's special.

We drove two blocks down Slater, and I could see Morelli's car parked at the curb half a block ahead. My stomach gave a nervous little twitch, and I did a panicky review of my options.

"What are you doing making those whimpering sounds?" Lula asked.

"I'm reviewing my options."

"And?"

"I don't have any."

Lula idled at Morelli's back bumper. "Looks like a cop car. Smells like a cop car. . . ."

"Joe Morelli."

"Is this his house?"

"Yeah," I said. "Pull over. I'll only be a minute."

I could see lights shining downstairs, to the rear. Probably coming from the kitchen. I knocked on the door and waited, wondering what sort of reception I'd get, praying Morelli was alone. If he had a woman with him I'd be so embarrassed I'd have to move to Florida.

I heard footsteps to the other side of the door, and the door was opened. Morelli wore thick wool socks and jeans, a black T-shirt and a flannel shirt that was unbuttoned and rolled to his elbows. His eyebrows lifted in surprise. He took in my wet hair and mud-splattered Levi's. His gaze shifted to the red Firebird, which Lula had parked under a streetlight. He shook his head.

"Tell me you don't have legs sticking out of that car."

"Uh, well, actually . . ."

"Christ, Stephanie, this makes four! Four dead bodies. Eight if you count the ones in the cellar."

"It's not my fault!" I stuffed my fists onto my hips. "You think I want to keep finding dead bodies? This is no picnic for me either, you know."

"Who is it?"

"We think it's Elliot Harp. He's got a big hole in the middle of his face, so it's hard to tell for sure."

I told him the story about spotting Mo and following him down Route 1, and how we came to have Elliot Harp rammed into Lula's trunk.

"And?" Morelli said.

"And I brought him here. I thought you might want to have first crack at him." And I thought you might write up the report in a favorable manner that didn't cite me for body snatching. And I thought if I dragged you into this I wouldn't be the brunt of bad cop jokes having to do with tailgate delivery of corpses.

I took a fast peek inside Morelli's house, seeing a wood floor in the small foyer and an old-fashioned wood banister on stairs leading up to the second floor.

Morelli made a one-minute sign to Lula, pulled me inside and shut the door. "You should have left the body on the side of the road. You should have flagged someone down. You should have found a phone and called the police."

"Hello," I said. "Are you listening? I just went through all of that. No one would stop, and I decided it was dangerous to stay at roadside."

Morelli cracked the door and looked out at the Firebird. He closed the door and shook his head again. He looked down at his feet and tried to hide the smile.

"It isn't funny!" I said.

"Whose idea was the flag?"

"Lula's. She didn't want to get a ticket."

The smile widened. "You gotta love her."

"So what should I do with this guy?"

"I'll call the ME's office and have someone meet us at the station. You've driven Harp this far . . . a few more miles won't make much difference."

"I didn't do anything illegal, did I?"

Morelli headed off to the back of the house. "You don't want to know the answer to that."

I followed him down the hall to the kitchen, catching a glimpse of the living room, dining room. The rooms were small, but the ceilings were high with elaborate crown molding. Boxes still sat in all the rooms, waiting to be unpacked. A rug was rolled to one side in the dining room.

Morelli retrieved cross trainers from under the kitchen table and sat down to lace them.

"Nice kitchen," I said. "Reminds me a lot of my parents' house." What about shelf paper, I was thinking. I couldn't imagine Morelli picking out shelf paper.

Morelli looked around like he was seeing the kitchen for the first time. "It needs some work."

"Why did you decide to buy a house?"

"I didn't buy it. I inherited it. My aunt Rose left it to me. She and my uncle Sallie bought this house when they were first married. Sallie died ten years ago, and Aunt Rose stayed on. She died in October. She was eighty-three. They didn't have any kids, and I was a favorite nephew, so I got the house. My sister, Mary, got the furniture." Morelli stood at the table and snagged a jacket that had been draped over a kitchen chair.

"You could sell it."

He shrugged into the jacket. "I thought of that, but I decided to give this a try first. See how it felt."

A horn beeped from outside.

"That's Lula," I said. "She's got the runs."

CHAPTER 12

I directed Lula to the rear of the station so we could unload Elliot in as much privacy as possible. We pulled into the drop-off zone and cut the engine. Morelli parked to the side of the lot. The drop-off is covered by closed-circuit TV, so I knew it was only a matter of minutes before the curious spilled out of the back security door.

Lula and I stood to the front of the Firebird, not wanting to get any closer to Elliot than was absolutely necessary. I was soaked to the skin, and without the car's heater blasting away at me I was cold clear to the bone.

"Funny how life works," Lula said. "All this came about because I ate a bad burrito. It's like God knew what he was doing when he gave me the runs."

I hugged my arms tight to my chest and clenched my teeth to keep them from chattering. "The Lord moves in mysterious ways."

"Exactly my thoughts. Now we know Jackie was right about Old Penis Nose being on Montgomery Street. We even did something good for Elliot. Not that he deserves it, but if it wasn't for us he'd be dumped in the river by now."

The rear door to the building opened and two uniforms stepped out. I didn't know their names, but I'd seen them around. Morelli told them he was going to tie up the drop zone for a few minutes. Told them he'd appreciate it if they kept the traffic down.

The Medical Examiner's pickup arrived and backed in close to the

Firebird. It was a dark blue Ford Ranger with a white cap divided into compartments that reminded me of kennels.

The ID detective said a few words to Morelli and then went to work.

Arnie Rupp, the supervisor of the violent crimes squad, came out and stood hands in pockets, watching the action. A man in jeans, black Trenton PD ball cap and red and black plaid wool jacket stood next to him. Rupp asked the man if he'd completed the paperwork on the Runion job. The man said, not yet. He'd finish it up first thing in the morning.

I stared at the man and little alarms went off in my brain.

The man stared back at me. Noncommittal. Cop face. Unyielding.

Morelli moved into my line of vision. "I'm sending you and Lula home. You both look half drowned, and this will take some time."

"I appreciate it," Lula said, "because I've got an intestinal disturbance."

Morelli lifted my chin a fraction of an inch with his index finger and studied my face. "Are you going to be okay?"

"Sure. I'm f-f-fine."

"You don't look fine. You look like you're down a couple quarts."

"Who's the guy standing next to Arnie Rupp? The guy in the jeans and cop hat and red and black plaid jacket."

"Mickey Maglio. Major Crimes. Robbery detective."

"Remember when I was telling you about the men in the ski masks and coveralls? The leader, the one who burned my hand and offered me money, had a smoker's voice. Jersey City accent. I know you don't want to hear this, but I swear, Maglio sounds just like him. And he's the right height and the right build."

"You never saw his face?"

I shook my head. "No."

"Maglio's a good cop," Morelli said. "He's got three kids and a pregnant wife."

"I don't know," I said. "I could be wrong. I'm c-c-cold. Maybe I'm not thinking right."

Morelli wrapped his arm around me and dragged me toward a waiting squad car. "I'll look into it. In the meantime let's keep it to ourselves."

Lula got dropped off first due to her pressing needs. I rode in silence for the rest of the trip, shivering in the backseat, unable to sort through my thoughts, afraid I'd burst into tears and look like an idiot in front of my cop chauffeur.

I thanked the officer when he pulled up at my door. I scrambled out of the car, ran into the building and took the stairs. The second-floor hall was empty of people but filled with dinner smells. Fried fish from Mrs. Karwatt. Stew from Mr. Wolesky.

My teeth had stopped chattering, but my hands were still shaking, and I had to two-fist the key to get it into the keyhole. I pushed the door open, switched the light on, closed and bolted my door and did a fast security check.

Rex backed out of his soup can and gave me the once-over. He looked startled at my appearance, so I explained my day. When I got to the part about driving Elliot around in Lula's trunk, I burst out laughing. My God, what had I been thinking! It was an absurd thing to do. I laughed until I cried, and then I realized I was no longer laughing. Tears were streaming down my cheeks, and I was sobbing. After a while my nose was running, and my mouth was open but the sobs were soundless.

"Shit," I said to Rex. "This is exhausting."

I blew my nose, dragged myself into the bathroom, stripped and stood under the shower until my skin was scorched and my mind was empty. I got dressed in sweats and cotton socks and cooked my hair into ten inches of red frizz with the hair dryer. I looked like I'd taken a bath with the toaster, but I was way beyond caring. I collapsed onto the bed and instantly fell asleep.

I came awake slowly, my eyes swollen from crying, my mind gauzy and stupid. The clock at bedside said nine-thirty. Someone was knocking. I shuffled into the hall and opened the door without ceremony.

It was Morelli, holding a pizza box and a six-pack.

"You should always look before you open the door," he said.

"I did look."

"You're lying again."

He was right. I hadn't looked. And he was right about being careful.

My eyes locked on the pizza box. "You sure know how to get a person's attention."

Morelli smiled. "Hungry?"

"Are you coming in, or what?"

Morelli dumped the pizza and beer on the coffee table and shrugged out of his jacket. "I'd like to go over the day's events."

I brought plates and a roll of paper towels to the coffee table and sat beside Morelli on the couch. I wolfed down a piece of pizza and told him everything.

By the time I was done, Morelli was on his second beer. "You have any additional thoughts?"

"Only that Gail probably lied to us, so she wouldn't get in trouble with her landlady. Elliot had full rigor when we found him, so he'd been dead awhile. My guess is either Gail told Mo where to find Elliot, or else Elliot was in Gail's room when Mo showed up."

Morelli nodded affirmation. "You're watching the right TV shows," he said. "We ran the plates on the tan car. The car belonged to Elliot Harp."

"Did you find Mo's connection to Montgomery Street?"

"Not yet, but we have men in the neighborhood. The garage was used by a lot of people. It's possible to buy a key card on a monthly basis. No ID necessary. Freedom Church members use the garage. Local merchants use it."

I ate another slice of pizza. I wanted to bring up the topic of Mickey Maglio, but I didn't feel secure about the accusation. Besides, I'd mentioned it once. Morelli was too good a cop to let it slide by and be forgotten.

"So now what?" I asked. "You want to watch some TV?"

Morelli looked at his watch. "Think I'll pass. I should be getting home." He stood and stretched. "Been a long day."

I followed him to the door. "Thanks for helping me dispose of Elliot."

"Hey," Morelli said, punching me lightly on the arm. "What are friends for?"

I blinked. Friends? Morelli and me? "Okay, what's going on?"

"Nothing's going on."

Boy, was that ever the truth. No flirting. No grabbing. Sexist remarks held to a minimum. I narrowed my eyes as I watched him walk to the elevator. There was only one possible explanation. Morelli had a girlfriend. Morelli was enamored with someone else, and I was off the hook.

He disappeared behind the elevator doors, and I retreated into my apartment.

Hooray, I told myself. But I didn't actually feel like hooray. I felt like someone had thrown a party, and I hadn't been included on the guest list. I puzzled on this, trying to determine the cause for my discomfort. The obvious reason, of course, was that I was jealous. I didn't like the obvious reason, so I kept working for another. Finally I gave up in defeat. Truth is, there was unfinished business between Morelli and me. A couple months ago we'd had Buick interruptus, and as much as I hated to admit it, I'd been thinking of him in torrid terms ever since.

And then there was the house move, which seemed so out of character for Morelli the bachelor. But suppose Morelli was thinking of cohabitating? My God, suppose Morelli was thinking of marriage?

I didn't at all like the idea of Morelli getting married. It would wreck my fantasy life, and it would put added pressure on me. My mother would be saying to me . . . Look! Even Joe Morelli is married!

I dropped onto the couch and punched up the television, but there wasn't anything worth seeing. I cleaned the beer cans and pizza off the coffee table. I plugged the telephone back into the wall and reset the answering machine. I tried the television again.

I had a third beer, and when that was done I felt slightly buzzed. Damn Morelli, I thought. He has a lot of nerve getting involved with some other woman.

The more I thought about it, the more annoyed I became. Who was this woman, anyway?

I called Sue Ann Grebek and discreetly asked who the hell Morelli was boffing, but Sue Ann didn't know. I called Mary Lou and my cousin Jeanine, but they didn't know either.

Well, that settles it, I decided. I'll find out for myself. After all, I'm some sort of investigator. I'll simply investigate.

Trouble was, the events of the last two days had me pretty much freaked out. I wasn't afraid of the dark, but I wasn't in love with it either. Well, okay, I was afraid of the dark. So I called Mary Lou back and asked her if she wanted to spy on Morelli with me.

"Sure," Mary Lou said. "Last time we spied on Morelli we were twelve years old. We're due."

I laced up my running shoes, pulled a hooded sweatshirt over the sweatshirt I was wearing and shoved my hair under a black knit cap. I trucked down the hall, down the stairs, and ran into Dillon Ruddick in the lobby. Dillon was the building super and an all-around nice guy.

"I'll give you five dollars if you'll walk me to my car," I said to Dillon.

"I'll walk you for free," Dillon said. "I was just taking the garbage out."

Another advantage to parking by the Dumpster.

Dillon paused at the Buick. "This is a humdinger of a car," he said.

I couldn't argue with that.

Mary Lou was waiting at the curb when I pulled up to her house. She was wearing tight black jeans, a black leather motorcycle jacket, black high-heeled ankle boots and big gold hoop earrings. Evening wear for the well-dressed burg peeper.

"You ever tell anybody I did this, and I'll deny it. And then I'll hire Manny Russo to shoot you in the knee," Mary Lou said.

"I just want to see if he has a woman with him."

"Why?"

I looked over at her.

"Okay," she said. "I know why."

Morelli's car was parked in front. The living room lights were out in his house, but the kitchen light was on, just as it had been earlier in the evening.

A figure moved through the house, up the stairs. A light blinked on in one of the upstairs rooms. The figure returned to the kitchen.

Mary Lou giggled. And then I giggled. Then we slapped ourselves so we'd stop giggling.

"I'm a mother," Mary Lou said. "I'm not supposed to be doing stuff like this. I'm too old."

"A woman's never too old to make an idiot of herself. It goes along with equality of the sexes and potty parity."

"Suppose we find him in the kitchen with a sock on his dick?"

"In your dreams."

This drew more giggles.

I drove around the corner to the paved alley road that intersected the block. I slowly rolled down the single lane, cut my lights and paused at Morelli's backyard. Morelli moved into view through a rear window. At least he was home. He hadn't gone from my house to some hot babe. I continued to the end of the lane and parked the Buick around the corner, on Arlington Avenue.

"Come on," I said to Mary Lou. "Let's take a closer look."

We crept back to Morelli's yard and stood outside the weathered picket fence, hidden in shadow.

After a few moments Morelli once again crossed in front of the window. This time he had the phone to his ear, and he was smiling.

"Look at that!" Mary Lou said. "He's smiling. I bet he's talking to *her*!"

We slipped inside the gate and tippytoed to the house. I flattened myself against the siding and held my breath. I inched closer to the window. I could hear him talking, but I couldn't make out the words. Blah, blah, blah, blah, blah.

A door opened two houses down, and a big black dog bounded into the small yard. He stopped and stood with ears pricked in our direction.

"WOOF!" the dog said.

"Omigod," Mary Lou whispered. "Jesus fucking Christ."

Mary Lou wasn't an animal person.

"WOOF!"

Suddenly this didn't seem like such a good idea. I didn't like the prospect of getting torn to shreds by the hound from hell. And even worse, I didn't want to get caught by Morelli. Mary Lou and I executed a panic-inspired crab scuttle to the back gate and held up just outside Morelli's broken-down fence. We watched the neighbor's dog slowly move to the edge of his yard. He didn't stop. His yard wasn't fenced. He was on the road now, and he was looking directly at us.

Nice dog, I thought. Probably wanted to play. But just in case . . . it might be smart to head for the car. I backed up a few paces, and the dog charged. "YIPES!"

We had two house widths on Rover, and we ran flat out for all we were worth. We were twenty feet from Arlington when I felt paws impact on my back, knocking me off my feet. My hands hit first, then my knees. I belly-whopped onto the blacktop and felt the air whoosh from my lungs.

I braced for the kill, but the dog just stood over me, tongue lolling, tail wagging.

"Good dog," I said.

He licked my face.

I rolled onto my back and assessed the damage. Torn sweats, scraped hands and knees. Large loss of self-esteem. I got to my feet, shooed the dog back home and limped to the car where Mary Lou was waiting.

"You deserted me," I said to Mary Lou.

"It looked like it might turn into one of those sexual things. I didn't want to interfere."

Fifteen minutes later I was in my apartment, dressed in my nightgown, dabbing antiseptic cream on my skinned knees. And I was feeling much better. Nothing like a totally infantile act to put things into perspective.

I stopped dabbing when the phone rang. Not Morelli, I prayed. I didn't want to hear that he'd seen me running from his yard.

I answered with a tentative hello.

Pause on the other end.

"Hello," I repeated.

"I hope that little discussion we had last time meant something to you," the man said. "Because if I find out you've opened your mouth about any of this, I'm going to come get you. And it's not going to be nice."

"Maglio?"

The caller hung up.

I checked all my locks, plugged the battery on my cell phone into the recharger, made sure my gun was loaded and at bedside along with the pepper spray. I cringed at the possibility that Maglio might be involved. It wasn't good to have a cop for an enemy. Cops could be very dangerous people.

The phone rang again. This time I let the machine get it. The call was from Ranger. Just reporting in, he said. Running tomorrow at seven.

I called Lula as promised and registered her for the program.

I was downstairs at seven, but I wasn't in the finest form. I hadn't slept well, and I was feeling tapped out.

"How'd it go yesterday?" Ranger asked.

I gave him the unabridged version, excluding my juvenile visit to Morelli's backyard.

Ranger's mouth tipped at the corners. "You're making this up, right?"

"Wrong. That's what happened. You asked what happened. I told you what happened."

"Okay, let me get this straight. Elliot Harp flew off Mo's car, bounced off the Firebird onto the shoulder of Route 1. You picked Elliot up, and put him in the trunk and drove him to the police station."

"More or less."

Ranger gave a bark of laughter. "Bet that went over big with the boys in blue."

A taxi pulled into the lot, not far from where we were standing, and Lula got out. She was dressed in a pink polar fleece sweatsuit and pink furry earmuffs. She looked like the Energizer rabbit on steroids.

"Lula's going running with us," I told Ranger. "She wants to get in better shape."

Ranger gave Lula the once-over. "You don't keep up, you get left behind."

"Your ass," Lula said.

We took off at a pretty good clip. I figured Ranger was testing Lula. She was breathing hard, but she was close on his heels. She managed until we got to the track, and then she found a seat on the sidelines.

"I don't run in circles," she said.

I sat beside her. "Works for me."

Ranger did a lap and jogged by us without acknowledgment of our presence or lack of.

"So why are you really here?" I asked Lula.

Lula's eyes never left Ranger. "I'm here 'cause he's the shit."

"The shit?"

"Yeah, you know . . . the shit. The king. The cool."

"Do we know anyone else who's the shit?"

"John Travolta. He's the shit, too."

We watched Ranger some, and I could see her point about Ranger being the shit.

"I've been thinking," Lula said. "Suppose there really were superheroes?"

"Like Batman?"

"That's it. That's what I'm saying. It'd be someone who was the shit."

"Are you telling me you think Ranger's a superhero?"

"Think about it. We don't know where he lives. We don't know anything about him."

"Superheroes are make-believe."

"Oh yeah?" Lula said. "What about God?"

"Hmmmm."

Ranger did a couple more laps and veered from the track.

Lula and I jumped off the bench and followed in his footsteps. We collapsed in a heap two miles later, in front of my building.

"Bet you could run forever," Lula said to Ranger, gasping and wheezing. "Bet you got muscles that feel like iron."

"Man of steel," Ranger said.

Lula sent me a knowing look.

"Well, this has been fun," I said to everybody. "But I'm out of here."

"I could use a ride," Lula said to Ranger. "The police still have my car. Maybe you could give me a ride on your way home. Of course I don't want to inconvenience you. I wouldn't want you to go out of your way." She took a momentary pause. "Just exactly where do you live?" she asked Ranger.

Ranger pressed his security remote and the doors clicked open on the Bronco. He motioned to Lula. "Get in."

Ricardo Carlos Mañoso. Master of the two-syllable sentence. Superhero at large.

I hooked Lula by the crook of her arm before she took off. "What's your schedule like today?"

"Like any other day."

"If you get a chance maybe you could check some fast-food restaurants for me. I don't want you to spend all day at it, but if you go out for coffee break or lunch keep your eyes open for Stuart Baggett. He has to be working somewhere in the area. My guess is he'll go to what feels familiar."

An hour later I was on the road, canvassing eateries, doing my part. I figured Lula would stay close to the office, so I took Hamilton Township. I was on Route 33 when my cell phone chirped.

"I found him!" Lula shouted at me. "I took early lunch, and I went to a couple places on account of everyone in the office wanted something different, and I found him! Mr. Cute-as-a-button is serving up chicken now."

"Where?"

"The Cluck in a Bucket on Hamilton."

"You still there?"

"Hell yes," Lula said. "And I didn't let him see me either. I'm holed up in a phone booth."

"Don't move!"

I make lots of mistakes. I try hard not to make the same mistake more than three or four times. This time around, Stuart Baggett would be trussed up like a Christmas goose for his trip to the lockup.

I floored the Buick and roared off for Hamilton Avenue. The money involved in Baggett's capture was now low on my motivating factors list. Baggett had made me look and feel like an idiot. I didn't want revenge. Revenge isn't a productive emotion. I simply wanted to succeed. I wanted to regain some professional pride. Of course, after I restored my professional pride I'd be happy to take the recovery money.

Cluck in a Bucket was a couple blocks past Vinnie's office. It was a brand-new link in a minichain and still in its grand opening stage. I'd driven by and gawked at the big chicken sign but hadn't yet indulged in a bucket of cluck.

I could see the glow from the franchise a block away. The one-story blocky little building had been painted yellow inside and out. At night light spilled from the big plate-glass windows, and a spot played on the seven-foot-tall plastic chicken that was impaled on a rotating pole in the parking lot.

I parked at the back of the Cluck in a Bucket lot and decked myself out in my bounty hunter gear. Cuffs stuffed into one jacket pocket; defense spray in the other. Stun gun clipped to the waistband of my sweats. Smith & Wesson forgotten in the rush, left lying on my bedside table.

Lula was waiting for me just outside the front entrance. "There he is," she said. "He's the one handing out paper chicken hats to the kiddies."

It was Stuart Baggett all right . . . dressed up in a big fat chicken suit, wearing a chicken hat. He did a chicken dance for a family, flapping his elbows, wagging his big chicken butt. He made some squawking sounds and gave each of the kids a yellow-and-red cardboard hat.

"You gotta admit, he makes a cute chicken," Lula said, watching Stuart strut around on his big yellow chicken feet. "Too bad we gotta bust his ass."

Easy for her to say. She didn't have orange hair. I pushed through the front door and crossed the room. I was about ten feet away when Stuart turned and our eyes locked.

"Hello, Stuart," I said.

There was a young woman standing next to Stuart. She was wearing a red-and-yellow Cluck in a Bucket uniform, and she was holding a stack of Cluck in a Bucket giveaway hats. She gave me her best "don't ruin the fun" look and wagged her finger. "His name isn't Stuart," she said. "Today his name is Mr. Cluck."

"Oh yeah?" Lula said. "Well we're gonna haul Mr. Cluck's cute little chicken tushy off to jail. What do you think of that?"

"They're crazy," Stuart said to the Cluck in a Bucket woman. "They're stalkers. They won't leave me alone. They got me fired from my last job because they kept harassing me."

"That's a load of horse pucky," Lula said. "If we were gonna stalk someone it wouldn't be no chicken impersonator working for minimum wage."

"Excuse me," I said, elbowing Lula away from Stuart, turning the force of my most professional smile on the young woman with the hats. "Mr. Baggett is in violation of a bond agreement and needs to reinstate himself with the court."

"Harry," the young woman yelled, waving to a man behind the service counter. "Call the police. We've got a situation here."

"Damn," Lula said. "I hate when people call the police."

"You're ruining everything," Stuart said to me. "Why can't you leave me alone? Who's going to be Mr. Cluck if you take me in?"

I pulled the cuffs out of my pocket. "Don't give me a hard time, Stuart."

"You can't put cuffs on Mr. Cluck!" Stuart said. "What will all these kids think?"

"Wouldn't get my hopes up that they'd give a hello," Lula said. "Isn't like you're Santa Claus. Truth is, you're just some whiny little guy dressed up in a bad suit."

"This isn't a big deal," I said to Stuart as calmly as possible. "I'm going to cuff you and walk you out the door, and if we do it quickly and quietly no one will notice."

I reached out to snap the cuffs on Stuart, and he batted me away with his chicken wing. "Leave me alone," Stuart said, knocking the cuffs out of my hand, sending them sailing across the room. "I'm not going to jail!" He grabbed the mustard and the special-sauce squirters off the condiments counter. "Stand back!" he said.

I had pepper spray and a stun gun, but it seemed like excessive force to use them against a chicken armed with special sauce.

"I haven't got all day," Lula said to Stuart. "I want to get some chicken and go back to work, and you're holding me up. Put those stupid squirters down."

"Don't underestimate these squirters," Stuart said. "I could do a lot of damage with these squirters." He held the red squirter up. "See this? This isn't just any old special sauce. This is extra spicy."

"Oh boy," Lula said. "Think he's been sniffing aerosol from the roach spray."

Lula took a step toward Stuart, and SQUISH, Stuart gave Lula a blast of mustard to the chest.

Lula stopped in her tracks. "What the . . ."

SPLOT! Special sauce on top of the mustard.

"Did you see that?" Lula said, her voice pitched so high she sounded like Minnie Mouse. "He squirted me with special sauce! I'm gonna have to get this jacket dry-cleaned."

"It was your own fault, Fatty," Stuart said. "You made me do it."

"That's it," Lula said. "Out of my way. I'm gonna kill him." She lunged forward, hands reaching for Stuart's chicken neck, slipped on some mustard that had leaked out of Stuart's squirter and went down on her ass.

Stuart took off, shoving his way around tables and customers. I took off after him and caught him with a flying tackle. We both crashed to the floor in a flurry of chicken feathers, Stuart squirting his squirters, and me swearing and grabbing. We rolled around like this for what seemed like an eternity, until I finally got hold of something that wasn't a fake chicken part.

I was breast to breast, on top of Mr. Cluck, twisting his nose in a damn good impression of Moe and Curly, when I felt hands forcefully lifting me off, disengaging my nose hold.

One set of hands belonged to Carl Costanza. The other set of hands belonged to a cop I'd seen around but didn't know on a first-name basis. Both cops were smiling, rocking back on their heels, thumbs stuck into their gun belts.

"I heard about your cousin Vinnie and what he did to that duck," Carl said to me. "Still, I'm surprised to find you on top of a chicken. I always thought you were more like the Mazur side of the family."

I swiped at the gunk on my face. I was covered with mustard, and I had special sauce in my hair. "Very funny. This guy is FTA."

"You got papers?" Carl asked.

I scrounged in my shoulder bag and came up with the bond agreement and the contract to pursue that Vinnie had issued.

"Good enough," Carl said. "Congratulations, you caught yourself a chicken."

I could see the other cop was trying hard not to laugh out loud.

"So what's your problem?" I asked him, feeling sort of aggravated that maybe he was laughing at me.

He held up two hands. "Hey lady, I haven't got a problem. Good bust. Not everyone could have taken that chicken down."

I rolled my eyes and looked at Costanza, but Costanza wasn't entirely successful at controlling his amusement either.

"Good thing we got here before the animal rights people," Costanza said to me. "They wouldn't have been as understanding as us."

I retrieved my cuffs from the other side of the room and clicked them onto Baggett's wrists. Lula had disappeared, of course. I'd resigned myself to the fact that I couldn't expect Lula to share airspace with cops.

"Do you need any help?" Costanza wanted to know.

I shook my head, no. "I can manage. Thanks."

Half an hour later I left the station with my body receipt, happy to escape the cracks about smelling like a barbecue. Not to mention the abuse I took for bringing in a chicken.

A person can take only so much cop humor.

Rex was nosing around in his food cup when I got home, so I gave him a grape and told him about Stuart Baggett. How Stuart had been dressed up in a chicken suit, and how I'd bravely captured him and brought him to justice. Rex listened while he ate the grape, and I think Rex might have smiled when I got to the part about tackling Mr. Cluck, but it's hard to tell about these things with a hamster.

I love Rex a lot, and he has a lot of redeeming qualities, like cheap food and small poop, but the truth is sometimes I pretend he's a golden retriever. I'd never tell this to Rex, of course. Rex has very sensitive feelings. Still, sometimes I long for a big floppy-eared dog.

I fell asleep on the couch, watching Rex run on the wheel. I was awakened by the phone ringing.

"Got a call about my car," Ranger said. "Want to ride along?"

"Sure."

There was a moment of silence. "Were you sleeping?" he asked.

"Nope. Not me. I was just going out the door to look for Mo." Okay, so it was a fib. Better than looking like a slug. Or even worse, better than admitting to the truth, because the truth was that I was becoming emotionally dysfunctional. I was unable to fall asleep in the dark. And if I did fall asleep, it would be only to doze and to wake up to bad dreams. So I was starting to sleep during daytime hours when I had the chance.

My incentive for finding Mo had changed in the last couple of days. I wanted to find Mo so the killing would stop. I couldn't stand seeing any more blown-apart bodies.

I rolled off the couch and into the shower. While in the shower I noticed blisters on my heels as big as quarters. Thank God. I finally had a legitimate excuse to stop running. Eight minutes later, I was dressed and in the hall, with my apartment locked up behind me.

As soon as I climbed into the Bronco I knew this was serious because Ranger was wearing no-nonsense army fatigues and gold post earrings. Also the tear gas gun and the smoke grenades in the backseat were a tip-off.

"What's the deal?" I asked.

"Very straightforward. I got a call from Moses Bedemier. He apologized for borrowing my car. Said it was parked in his garage, and that his neighbor, Mrs. Steeger, had the keys."

I shuddered at the mention of Mrs. Steeger.

"What's that about?" Ranger asked.

"Mrs. Steeger is the Antichrist."

"Damn," Ranger said. "I left my Antichrist gun at home."

"Looks like you brought everything else."

"Never know when you'll need some tear gas."

"If we have to gas Mrs. Steeger, it'll probably ruin my chances of being Miss Burg in the Mayflower Parade."

Ranger turned into the alley from King and stopped at Mo's garage. He got out and tried the door. The door was locked. He walked to the side window and peered in.

"Well?" I asked.

"It's there."

A back curtain was whisked aside and Mrs. Steeger glared out at us from her house.

"Is that her?" Ranger wanted to know.

"Yup."

"One of us should talk to her."

"That would be you," I said.

"Okay, Tex. I don't think Mo's here, but you cover the back just in case. I'll have a word with Mrs. Steeger."

After ten minutes I was stomping my feet to keep warm and beginning to worry about Ranger. I hadn't heard any shots, so that was a good sign. There'd been no screams, no police sirens, no glass breaking.

Ranger appeared at the back door, smiling. He crossed the yard to me. "Did you really tell fibs when you were a kid?"

"Only when it involved matters of life or death."

"Proud of you, babe."

"Has she got the key?"

"Yeah. She's getting her coat on. Taking this key thing very seriously. Says it's the least she could do for Mo."

"The least she could do?"

"Have you read the paper today?"

I shook my head. "No."

"It turns out that all these murders are having a significant impact on crime. Drug sales are way down. Pharmaceutical representatives are booking flights for obscure southern towns."

"Are you telling me Mo is a hero?"

"Let's just say, he isn't despised."

Mrs. Steeger materialized at the back door wearing a coat and hat. She huffed down the porch stairs and across her yard. "Hmmph," she said to me. "Still snooping, I see."

My left eye started to twitch. I put my finger to my eyelid and sank my teeth into my lower lip.

Ranger grinned.

The superhero wasn't afraid of the Antichrist. The superhero thought an eye twitch was funny.

Mrs. Steeger opened the door and stepped back, arms folded over her chest. "I'll lock up when you get your car out," she said to Ranger.

Guess she was worried we'd snitch some jugs of used motor oil.

Ranger handed me the keys to the Bronco. "I'll drive the BMW, and you can follow."

Normally a person would take his cars home. Since Ranger wasn't normal I wasn't sure where we were headed.

I held the tail through center city. Traffic was heavy and people walked head down into the wind on the sidewalks. Ranger turned off State onto Cameron and pulled into a small, attended parking lot. We were behind the state buildings, two blocks from Stark, in an area of quasi-government office buildings. Definitely not residential.

Ranger got out of his car and spoke to the attendant. The attendant smiled and nodded. Friendly. They knew each other.

I parked behind the Beemer and walked over to Ranger. "Are we leaving the cars here?"

"Benny will take care of them while I pick up my mail."

I looked around. "You live here?"

"Office," Ranger said, gesturing to a four-story brick building next to the lot.

"You have an office?"

"Nothing fancy. It helps to keep the businesses straight."

I followed Ranger through the double glass doors into the vestibule. There were two elevators to our left. A tenant directory hung on the wall beside the elevators. I scanned the directory and could find no mention of Ranger.

"You're not listed," I said.

Ranger moved past the elevators to the stairs. "Don't need to be."

I trotted after him. "What businesses are we talking about?"

"Mostly security related. Bodyguard, debris removal, security consultation. Fugitive apprehension, of course."

We rounded the first floor and were working our way up to two. "What's debris removal?"

"Sometimes a landlord wants to clean up his property. I can put together a team to do the job."

"You mean like throwing crack dealers out the window?"

Ranger passed the second floor and kept going. He shook his head. "Only on the lower floors. You throw them out the upper-story windows and it makes too much of a mess on the sidewalk."

He opened the fire door to the third floor, and I followed him down the hall to number 311. He slid a key card into the magnetic slot, pushed the door open and switched the light on.

It was a one-room office with two windows and a small powder room. Beige carpet, cream-colored walls, miniblinds at the windows. Furniture consisted of a large cherry desk with a black leather executive chair behind the desk and two client chairs to the front of the desk. No gun turrets at the windows. No government-issue rockets stacked in the corners. A Mac laptop with a separate Bernoulli drive was plugged in on the desk. Its modem was hooked to the phone line. There was also a multiline phone and answering machine on the desk. Everything was neat. No dust. No empty soda cans. No empty pizza boxes. Thankfully, no dead bodies.

Ranger stooped to pick up the mail that had been delivered through the mail slot. He came up with a handful of envelopes and a couple flyers. He divided the mail into two stacks: garbage and later. He threw the garbage into the wastebasket. The later could wait until later. I guess there hadn't been any *now!* mail.

The red light on the answering machine was going ballistic with blinking. Ranger lifted the lid and popped the incoming tape. He put it in his shirt pocket and replaced the tape with a new one from the top drawer of the desk. No *now!* messages there either, I suppose.

I took a peek at the lavatory. Very clean. Soap. Paper towels. Box of tissues. Nothing personal. "You spend much time here?" I asked Ranger.

"No more than is necessary."

I waited for some elaboration but none was forthcoming. I wondered if Ranger was still interested in Mo now that he had his BMW back.

"Are you feeling vengeful?" I asked Ranger. "Does justice need to be served?"

"He's back on your slate, if that's what you're asking." He killed the light and opened the door to leave.

"Did Mrs. Steeger say anything that might be helpful?"

"She said Mo showed up around nine. Mo told her he'd borrowed a car from someone, and that he'd left the car in his garage for safekeeping until the owner came to retrieve it. Then he gave her the key."

"That's it?"

"That's it."

"Maybe I should have a chat with Mrs. Steeger." I knew it was a long shot, but Mo might come back for his key. Or at least call to see if everything worked out. I wasn't looking forward to spending time with Mrs. Steeger, but if I could get her to arrange a meeting or a phone call between Mo and me it would be worth it.

Ranger checked his door to make sure it was locked. "Gonna explain to her how Mo's crime career is in the toilet, and she should pass him your personal number? The one that guarantees him safe passage to the state spa?"

"Thought it was worth a shot."

"Absolutely," Ranger said. "He didn't want to talk to me about it, but you might have more luck. Are you running tomorrow morning?"

"Gee, I'd love to, but I have blisters."

Ranger looked relieved.

CHAPTER 13

I thought it wouldn't hurt to look professional when I went to see Mrs. Steeger, so I'd dressed in a tailored black suit, white silk shirt, leopard print silk scarf, taupe stockings and heels. I wasn't a master at long division, but I could accessorize with the best of them.

I'd called ahead to tell Mrs. Steeger I was stopping by. Then I'd spent a few moments lecturing myself about attitude. I was an adult. I was a professional. And I looked pretty damn good in my black suit. It was unacceptable that I should be intimidated by Mrs. Steeger. As a final precaution against insecurity, I made sure my .38 was loaded and tucked into my shoulder bag. Nothing like packing a pistol to put spring in a girl's step.

I parked on Ferris Street, got out of the car and sashayed up the sidewalk to Steeger's front porch. I gave the door a couple authoritative knocks and stood back.

Mrs. Steeger opened the door and looked me over. "Are you carrying a gun? I don't want you in my house if you're carrying a gun."

"I'm not carrying a gun," I said. Lie number one. I told myself it was all right to lie since Mrs. Steeger expected it. In fact, she'd probably be disappointed if I told the truth. And hell, I wouldn't want to disappoint Mrs. Steeger.

She led the way into the living room, seated herself in a club chair and motioned me to a corresponding chair on the other side of the coffee table.

The room was compulsively neat, and it occurred to me that Mrs. Steeger had retired while still vital and now had nothing better to do than to polish the polish. Windows were trimmed with white sheers and heavy flowered drapes. Furniture was boxy. Fabric and rug were sensible browns and tans. Mahogany end tables, a dark cherry rocker. Two white Lenox swan nut dishes sat side by side on the coffee table. Nut dishes without nuts. I had a feeling Mrs. Steeger didn't get a lot of company.

She sat there for a moment, poised on the edge of her seat, probably wondering if she was required by burg etiquette to offer me refreshments. I saved her the decision by immediately going into my spiel. I emphasized the fact that Mo was in danger now. He'd put a dent in the pharmaceutical profit margin and not everyone was pleased. Relatives of dead people were unhappy. The pharmaceutical management was bound to be unhappy. Users and abusers were unhappy.

"And Mo isn't good at this," I added. "He isn't a professional hit man." Even as I said it a little voice was whispering . . . eight bodies. How many does it take to make a professional?

I rose and handed Mrs. Steeger my card before she could quiz me on state capitals or ask me to write a book report on *John Quincy Adams, Biography of a Statesman.*

Mrs. Steeger held my card between two fingers. The way you do when you're afraid of cootie contamination. "Just exactly what is it you want me to do?"

"I'd like to talk to Mo. See if I can work something out. Get him back into the system before he gets hurt."

"You want him to call you."

"Yes."

"If I hear from him again I'll pass the message."

I extended my hand. "Thank you."

End of visit.

Neither of us had mentioned the incident in the store. This subject was way beyond our comfort zone. Mrs. Steeger hadn't discovered I was lying about the gun and hadn't threatened to send me to the principal's office, so I considered the entire session a rousing success.

I thought it wouldn't hurt to revisit some neighboring houses. Hopefully the climate would be more receptive now that bodies had been discovered in Mo's basement.

Dorothy Rostowski seemed a good place to start. I knocked on her door and waited while kids shouted inside.

Dorothy appeared with a spoon in her hand. "Making supper," she said. "You want to come in?"

"Thanks, but I've only got a minute. I just wanted to let you know I'm still looking for Mo Bedemier."

I felt the climate shift, and Dorothy's husband came to stand at her side.

"There are a lot of people in this community who'd prefer Mo wasn't found," Rostowski said.

My stomach clenched and for a chilling moment I thought he might pull out a gun or a knife or light up a cigarette and threaten me. My mind raced back to the phone call that had lured me to the candy store. Would I have recognized Dorothy's voice on the phone? Would I have recognized Mrs. Molinowsky's niece, Joyce, or Loretta Beeber, or my cousin Marjorie? And who were those men who were prepared to burn me and possibly kill me? Fathers of kids like these? Neighbors? Schoolmates? Maybe one of them had been Dorothy's husband.

"What we'd really like is for all this to be over, so Mo could come back and reopen the store," Dorothy said. "The kids miss him."

I had a hard time hiding my astonishment. "Mo's suspected of killing eight men!"

"Drug dealers," Dorothy said.

"That doesn't make it okay."

"It makes it better than okay. Mo should get a medal."

"Killing people is wrong."

Dorothy looked down at the floor, studying a spot just in front of her toe. Her voice dropped. "Theoretically I know that's true, but I'm fed up with the drugs and the crime. If Mo wants to take matters in his own hands, I'm not going to rain on his parade."

"I don't suppose you'd call me if you saw Mo in the neighborhood?"

"Don't suppose I would," Dorothy said, still avoiding my eyes.

I crossed the street to talk to Mrs. Bartle.

She met me at the door with her arms crossed over her chest. Not good body language, I thought, taking a mental step backward.

"Is this about Mo?" she asked. "Because I'm going to tell you up front if he was running for president I'd be right there with my vote. It's about time somebody did something about the drug problem in this country."

"He's suspected of killing eight men!"

"Too bad it isn't more. Get rid of every last one of them dope pushers."

On the way home I stopped in to see Connie and Lula. Connie was at her desk. Lula was out like a light on the couch.

"She had a tough morning," I said to Connie. "Went running with Ranger and me. Then she got drilled with special sauce by a chicken."

"So I hear."

Lula opened an eye. "Hmmph." She opened the other eye and took in the suit. "What are you all dressed up for?"

"Business. It's a disguise."

"How's the Mo hunt going?" Connie wanted to know.

"Picking up. Ranger got his car back."

This got Lula to her feet. "Say what?"

I told them about the two visits to Mrs. Steeger. Then I told them about Ranger's office.

"You see," Lula said. "Just like Bruce Wayne. Bruce Wayne had an office."

Connie gave Lula one of her "what the hell are you talking about" looks, so Lula explained her Ranger is a superhero theory.

"First off," Connie said, "Bruce Wayne is Batman, and Batman isn't actually a superhero. Batman's just some neurotic guy in a rubber suit. You have to get nuked or come from another planet to be a real superhero."

"Batman's got his own comic book," Lula said.

Connie wasn't impressed with this logic. "Donald Duck has his own comic book. You think Donald Duck is a superhero?"

"What's the office like?" Lula asked. "Does he have a secretary?"

"No secretary," I said. "It's a one-person office with a desk and a couple chairs."

"We should go over there and snoop around," Lula said. "See what we can find."

Anyone snooping around Ranger's private space would have to have a death wish. "Not a good idea," I told Lula. "Not only would he kill us, but it's also not a nice thing to do. He's not the enemy."

Lula didn't look convinced. "That's all true, but I'd still like to snoop."

"You don't really think he's a superhero," Connie said to Lula. "You think he's hot."

"Damn skippy I do," Lula said. "But that doesn't mean he isn't hiding something. The man has secrets, I'm telling you."

Connie leaned forward. "Secrets could mean lots of things. He could be wanted for murder in twelve states and have assumed a new identity. Even better . . . he could be gay."

"I don't want to think about him being gay," Lula said. "Seems like anymore, all the buff bodies are gay, and all the bad-smelling, rangy men are straight. I find out Ranger's gay and I'm going straight to the freezer section at Shop & Bag. Only men you can count on these days is Ben and Jerry."

Connie and I nodded sympathetically. Used to be I worried about losing my boyfriends to Joyce Barnhardt. Now I had to worry about losing them to her brother, Kevin.

I was curious about Ranger, but I wasn't nearly as curious as Lula. I had bigger fish to fry. I had to find Mo. I had to get my pickup. I had to nail down Joe Morelli's sudden disinterest in me. I was pretty sure it didn't have to do with a shortage of Y chromosomes.

I backtracked to my parents' house, recruited my father to drive the Buick home and zipped off to the garage.

My father didn't say anything on the trip over, but his thoughts were vibrating off the top of his head.

"I know," I said, testily. "I wouldn't be having this trouble if I'd bought a Buick."

The Nissan was parked in a numbered slot in the lot. My father and I cut our eyes to it in silent suspicion.

"You want me to wait?" my father asked.

"Not necessary."

My father cruised off. We'd done this routine before.

Ernie, the service manager, was in the little office attached to the warehouse of bays. He saw me on line and stepped from behind the counter, took my keys from a hook on the wall and pulled my bill. "You talked to Slick about the carburetor?"

"Yes."

Ernie smiled. "We like to keep our customers happy. Don't want you going away without a full explanation."

I was so happy I was practically suicidal. If I had to spend any more time talking to Slick, I was going to slit my throat.

"I'm in sort of a hurry," I said, passing Ernie my credit card. Another lie. I had absolutely nothing to do. I was all dressed up with nowhere to go.

If I was a hotshot detective I'd park myself in a van a couple houses down from the candy store, and I'd watch Mrs. Steeger. Unfortunately, I wasn't a hotshot detective. I didn't have a van. I couldn't afford to buy one. I couldn't afford to rent one. And since everyone in the burg was so nosy, a van probably wouldn't work anyway.

Just for kicks I drove by Morelli's house. Sort of test-driving the pickup. Morelli's car was parked at the curb, and lights were on inside the house. I eased up behind the 4×4 and cut the engine. I checked myself out in the rearview mirror. When a person has orange hair it's best to appraise it in the dark.

"Well, what the hell," I said.

By the time I knocked on Morelli's front door my heart was doing little flutter things in my chest.

Morelli opened the door and grimaced. "If you have another dead guy in your car I don't want to hear about it."

"This is a social call."

"Even worse."

The chest flutterings stopped. "What kind of a crack is that?"

"It's nothing. Forget it. You look frozen. Where's your coat?"

I stepped into the foyer. "I didn't wear a coat. It was warmer when I started out this afternoon."

I followed Morelli back to the kitchen and watched while he filled a cordial glass with amber liquid.

"Here," he said, handing the glass over. "Fastest way to get warm."

I took a sniff. "What is it?"

"Schnapps. My uncle Lou makes it in his cellar."

I tried a teeny taste and my tongue went numb. "I don't know . . ."

Morelli raised eyebrows. "Chicken?"

"I don't see you drinking this stuff."

Morelli took the glass from my hand and tossed the contents down his throat. He refilled the glass and gave it back to me. "Your turn, cupcake."

"To the Pope," I said and drained the glass.

"Well?" Morelli asked. "What do you think?"

I did some coughing and openmouthed wheezing. My throat burned, and liquid fire roiled in my stomach and shot through to every extremity. My scalp started to sweat, and my vagina went into spasm. "Pretty good," I finally said to Morelli.

"Want another?"

I shook my finger in a no motion. "Maybe later."

"What's with the suit?"

I told him about Ranger's car, and about my second trip to speak to Mrs. Steeger. I told him about Dorothy Rostowski and Mrs. Bartle.

"People are nuts," Morelli said. "Freaking nuts."

"So why don't you want this to be a social visit?"

"Forget it."

"It's the hair, isn't it?"

"It's not the hair."

"You're secretly married?"

"I'm not secretly anything."

"Well then, what? What?"

"It's you. You're a walking disaster. A man would have to be a total masochist to be interested in you."

"Okay," I said. "Maybe I will have another schnapps."

He poured two out, and we both threw them back. It was easier this time. Less fire. More glow.

"I'm not a walking disaster," I said. "I can't imagine why you think that."

"Every time I get social with you I end up all by myself, naked, in the middle of the street."

I rolled my eyes. "That only happened once . . . and you weren't naked. You were wearing socks and a shirt."

"I was speaking figuratively. If you want to get specific, what about the time you locked me in a freezer truck with three corpses? What about the time you ran over me with the Buick?"

I threw my hands into the air. "Oh sure, bring up the Buick."

He shook his head, disgusted like. "You're impossible. You're not worth the effort."

I curled my fingers into the front of his T-shirt and hauled him closer. "Not even in your dreams could you imagine how impossible I can be."

We were toe to toe with my breasts skimming his chest, our eyes locked.

"I'll drink to that," Morelli said.

The third schnapps went down smooth as silk. I gave the empty glass to Morelli and licked my lips.

Morelli watched the lip licking, and his eyes darkened and his breathing slowed.

Aha! I thought. This was more like it. Got him interested with the old lip-licking routine.

"Shit," Morelli said. "You did that on purpose."

I smiled. Then he smiled.

It looked to me like his "gotcha" smile. Like the cat that just caught the canary. Like I'd been had . . . again.

Then he closed the space between us, took my face in his hands and kissed me.

The kisses got hotter, and I got hotter and Morelli got hotter. And pretty soon we were all so hot that we needed to get rid of some clothes.

We were half undressed when Morelli suggested we go upstairs.

"Hmmm," I said with lowered eyelids. "What sort of a girl do you think I am?"

Morelli murmured his thoughts on the subject and removed my bra. His hand covered my bare breast, and his fingers played with the tip. "Do you like this?" he asked, gently rolling the nipple between thumb and forefinger.

I pressed my lips together to keep from sinking my teeth into his shoulder.

He tried another variation of the nipple roll. "How about this?"

Oh yeah. That too.

Morelli kissed me again, and next thing we were down on the linoleum floor fumbling with zippers and panty hose.

His finger traced a tiny circle on my silk-and-lace panties, directly over ground zero. My brain went numb, and my body said, YES!

Morelli moved lower and performed the same maneuver with the tip of his tongue, once again finding the perfect spot without benefit of treasure map or detailed instructions.

Now *this* was a superhero.

I was on the verge of singing the Hallelujah Chorus when something crashed outside the kitchen window. Morelli picked his head up and listened. There were some scuffling sounds, and Morelli was on his feet, pulling his jeans on. He had his gun in his hand when he opened the back door.

I was right behind him, my shirt held together by a single button, my panty hose draped over a kitchen chair, my gun drawn. "What is it?" I asked.

He shook his head. "I don't see anything."

"Cats?"

"Maybe. The garbage is tipped over. Maybe it was my neighbor's dog."

I put a hand to the wall to steady myself. "Uh-oh," I said.

"What uh-oh?"

"I don't know how to break this to you, but the floor is moving. Either we're having an earthquake, or else I'm drunk."

"You only had three schnapps!"

"I'm not much of a drinker. And I didn't have supper."

My voice sounded like it was resonating from a tin can, far far away.

"Oh boy," Morelli said. "How drunk are you?"

I blinked and squinted at him. He had four eyes. I hated when that happened. "You have four eyes."

"That's not a good sign."

"Maybe I should go home now," I said. Then I threw up.

I woke up with a blinding headache and my tongue stuck to the roof of my mouth. I was wearing a flannel nightshirt, which I dimly remembered crawling into. I was pretty sure I was alone at the time, although the evening was fuzzy from the third schnapps on.

What I clearly remembered was that a Morelli-induced orgasm had once again eluded me. And I was fairly certain Morelli hadn't fared any better.

He'd done the responsible thing and had insisted I sober up some before I went home. We'd logged a couple miles in the cold air. He'd poured coffee into me, force-fed me scrambled eggs and toast, and then he'd driven me to my apartment building. He'd delivered me to my door, and I think he said good night before the nightshirt crawling-into.

I shuffled into the kitchen, got some coffee going and used it to wash down aspirin. I took a shower, drank a glass of orange juice, brushed my teeth three times. I took a peek at myself in the mirror and groaned. Black circles under bloodshot eyes, pasty hungover skin. Not a nice picture. "Stephanie," I said, "you're no good at drinking."

The headache disappeared at midmorning. By noon I was feeling almost human. I took myself into the kitchen and was standing in front of the refrigerator, staring at the crisper drawer, contemplating the creation of the universe, when the phone rang.

My first thought was that it might be Morelli. My second thought was that I definitely didn't want to talk to him. Let the machine take the message, I decided.

"I know you're there," Morelli said. "You might as well answer. You're going to have to talk to me sooner or later."

Better later.

"I have news on Mo's lawyer."

I snatched at the phone. "Hello?"

"You're going to love this one," Morelli said.

I closed my eyes. I was having a bad premonition on the identity of the lawyer. "Don't tell me."

I could feel Morelli smiling at the other end of the line. "Dickie Orr."

Dickie Orr. My ex-husband. The horse's ass. This was a harpoon to the brain on a day when there was already impaired activity.

Dickie was a graduate of Newark Law. He was with the firm Kreiner and Kreiner in the old Shuman Building, and what he lacked in talent, he compensated for in creative overbilling. He was acquiring a reputation for being a hotshot attorney. I was convinced this was due to his inflated pay schedule rather than his court record. People wanted to believe they got what they paid for.

"When did you learn this?"

"About ten minutes ago."

"Is Mo turning himself in?"

"Thinking about it. Guess he's hired himself a dealmaker."

"He's suspected of murdering eight men. What kind of a deal does he want? Lobster every Friday while he's on death row?"

I got a box of Frosted Flakes from the kitchen cupboard and shoved some into my mouth.

"What are you eating?" Morelli wanted to know.

"Frosted Flakes."

"That's kid cereal."

"So what does Mo want?"

"I don't know. I'm going over to talk to Dickie. Maybe you'd like to tag along."

I ate another fistful of cereal. "Is there a price?"

"There's always a price. Meet you at the coffee shop in the Shuman Building in half an hour."

I considered the state of my hair. "I might be a few minutes late."

"I'll wait," Morelli said.

I could make the Shuman Building in ten minutes if I got all the lights right. It would take at least twenty minutes to do hair and makeup. If I wore a hat I could forgo hair, and that would cut the time in half. I decided the hat was the way to go.

I hit the back door running with a few minutes to spare. I'd gone with taupe eyeliner, a bronze-tone blusher, natural lip gloss and lots of black mascara. The key ingredient to hangover makeup is green concealer for the under-eye bags, covered over with quality liquid foundation. I was wearing my Rangers ball cap, and a fringe of orange frizz framed my face. Orphan Annie, eat your heart out.

I paused for a light at Hamilton and Twelfth and noticed the Nissan was running rough at idle. Two blocks later it backfired and stalled. I coaxed it into the center of the city. Ffft, ffft, ffft, KAPOW! Ffft, ffft, ffft, KAPOW!

A Trans Am pulled up next to me at a light. The Trans Am was filled with high school kids. One of them stuck his head out the passenger-side window.

"Hey lady," he said. "Sounds like you got a fartmobile."

I flipped him an Italian goodwill gesture and pulled the ball cap low on my forehead. When I found a parking space in front of the Shuman Building, I revved the engine, popped the clutch and backed into the parking slot at close to warp speed. The Nissan jumped the curb and rammed a meter. I gnashed my teeth together. Stephanie Plum, rabid woman. I got out and took a look. The meter was fine. The truck had a big dent in the rear bumper. Good. Now the back matched the front. The truck looked like someone had taken a giant pincers to it.

I stormed into the coffee shop, spotted Morelli and stomped over to him. I must have still looked rabid, because Morelli stiffened when he saw me and made one of those unconscious security gestures cops often acquire, surreptitiously feeling to see if their gun is in place.

I tossed my shoulder bag onto the floor and threw myself into the chair across from him.

"I swear I didn't intentionally try to get you drunk," Morelli said.

I squeezed my eyes shut. "Unh."

"Well, okay, so I did," he admitted. "But I didn't mean to get you *that* drunk."

"Take a number."

He smiled. "You have other problems?"

"My car is possessed by the devil."

"You should try my mechanic."

"You have a good mechanic?"

"The best. Bucky Seidler. You remember him from high school?"

"He got suspended for letting a bunch of rats loose in the girls' locker room."

"Yeah. That's Bucky."

"He calm down any?"

"No. But he's a hell of a mechanic."

"I'll think about it."

Morelli thumbed through a stack of cards he kept in his wallet. "Here it is," he said, passing the card over to me. "Mr. Fix It. You can keep the card."

"Bucky Seidler, proprietor."

"Yeah," Morelli said. "And resident crazy man."

I ordered a Coke and French fries. Morelli ordered a Coke and a cheeseburger.

When the waitress left I leaned my elbows on the table. "Do you think Mo could actually have something to bargain?"

"The rumor going around is that Mo is claiming he didn't kill anybody."

"Being an accomplice to murder is the same as pulling the trigger in Jersey."

"If he was cooperative and had something vital to give us . . ." He made a palms-up "who knows" gesture with his hands.

The waitress set the plates on the Formica-topped table and returned with the drinks.

Morelli snitched one of my French fries. "What did you ever see in Dickie Orr?"

I'd asked myself that same question many times and never found a satisfactory answer. "He had a nice car," I said.

Morelli's mouth curved. "Seems like a sound basis for marriage."

I poured ketchup on the fries and started working my way through them. "You ever think about getting married?"

"Sure."

"Well?"

"It's been my sad observation that cops don't make wonderful husbands. In all good conscience, I'd have to marry someone I didn't especially like, so I wouldn't feel crummy about ruining her life."

"So you'd marry someone like me?"

Morelli's face creased into a broad smile. "I hate to admit this, but I actually like you. You're out of the race."

"Jeez," I said. "What a relief."

"Tell me about Dickie."

I drank half the Coke. "Is this the price?"

He nodded. "I've seen Orr in court. Don't know him personally."

"And what's your opinion?"

"Gets a good haircut. Has lousy taste in ties. Big ego. Little dick."

"You're wrong about the dick."

This earned me another smile.

"He cheats on everything from his taxes to his clients to his girlfriends," I told Morelli.

"Anything else?"

"Probably doesn't pay his parking tickets. Used to do some recreational coke. Not sure if he's still into that. Did the deed with Mallory's wife."

Mallory was a uniform who was known for having a higher-than-normal incidence of accidental injuries on his arrest sheets. Uncooperative arrests had a habit of falling down entire flights of stairs while in Mallory's care.

"You sure about Mallory's wife?" Morelli asked.

"Heard it from Mary Lou, who heard it at the beauty parlor."

"Then it must be true."

"I suppose that's the sort of stuff you were looking for?"

"It'll do."

Morelli finished his cheeseburger and Coke and threw a ten onto the table. "Order yourself a piece of pie. I'll come back when I'm done with Dickie."

I jumped from my seat. "You said you'd take me with you!"

"I lied."

"Creep."

"Sticks and stones . . ."

CHAPTER 14

My indignation at being left behind had been mostly show. I hadn't really expected to drag after Morelli when he talked to Dickie. Dickie wouldn't have said anything in front of me.

I ordered coconut cake and decaf coffee. The room was emptying out from the lunch trade. I nursed the cake and the coffee for twenty minutes and paid the bill. There was no sign of Morelli, and I couldn't imagine the confrontation with Dickie as being lengthy, so I thought Morelli might have left me hanging. Wouldn't be the first time. I shrugged into my jacket, hitched my shoulder bag onto my shoulder and was going out the door to the coffee shop when Morelli rounded the corner.

"Thought maybe I got stood up," I said to Morelli.

"Had to wait for Dickie to get off a conference call."

Wind gusted down the street, and we both ducked our heads against it.

"Learn anything?"

"Not much. No address or phone number for Mo. Says Mo calls him."

"You find out what Mo has to trade?"

"Information."

I raised my eyebrows.

"That's all I can tell you," Morelli said.

Morelli was screwing me over again. "Thanks for nothing."

"It's the best I can do."

"Your best isn't very good, is it?"

"Depends." His eyes darkened. Bedroom eyes. "You thought I was pretty hot last night."

"I was drunk."

Morelli curled his fingers into my jacket collar and dragged me closer. "You wanted me bad."

"It was a low point in my life."

His lips skimmed mine. "How about now? Are you at a low point now?"

"I will never again be that low," I said haughtily.

Morelli kissed me like he meant it and released my collar. "Got to get back to work," he said. He crossed the street, angled into his 4×4 and drove off without looking back.

After a moment I realized my mouth was hanging open. I snapped my mouth shut, whipped out my cell phone and called Connie. I told her about Mo and Dickie, and I asked to talk to Lula.

"Hey girlfriend," Lula said.

"Hey yourself. How's it going?"

"It's a little slow. It's more than halfway through the day, and the body count is zip."

"Got a job for you."

"Oh boy. Here it comes."

"Not to worry. It's very tame. I want you to meet me at the entrance to the Shuman Building."

"Now?"

"Now."

Twenty minutes later we were in the elevator.

"What's going on?" Lula wanted to know. "What are we doing here?"

I pushed the button for the third floor. "Mo's hired himself an attorney. The attorney's name is Dickie Orr, and we're on our way to talk to him."

"Okay, but why do you need me? Is this guy dangerous?"

"No. Dickie Orr isn't dangerous. I'm the one who's dangerous. Dickie Orr is my ex-husband, and your job is to keep me from strangling him."

Lula made a low whistle. "This day's just getting better and better."

The offices of Kreiner and Kreiner were at the end of the hall.

There were four names lettered in gold on the office door: Harvey Kreiner, Harvey Kreiner Jr., Steven Owen, Richard Orr.

"So why'd you part ways with this Dickie Orr person?" Lula asked.

"He's a jerk."

"Good enough for me," she said. "I hate him already."

When I was married to Dickie he worked for the district attorney. His career with them was only slightly longer than his career with me. Not enough money came out of either of us, I guess. And after I found him on the dining room table with Joyce Barnhardt I made enough noise to ruin whatever political aspirations he might have had. Our divorce was everything a divorce should be . . . reeking of outrage, filled with loud and lurid accusations. The marriage had lasted less than a year, but the divorce would live on as legend in the burg. After the divorce, when lips loosened in my presence, I learned Dickie's infidelity had stretched far beyond Joyce Barnhardt. During the short tenure of our marriage Dickie had managed to boff half the women in my high school yearbook.

The door with the names opened to a mini lobby with two couches and a coffee table and a modern receptionist desk, all done in pastels. California meets Trenton. The woman behind the desk was upscale help. Very sleek. Pastel dress. Ann Taylor from head to toe.

"Yes," she said. "Can I help you?"

"I'd like to speak to Richard Orr." Just in case the office was too swanky for a guy named Dickie. "Tell him Stephanie is here."

The woman relayed the message and directed me to Dickie's office. The door was open and Dickie stood at his desk when Lula and I appeared on his threshold.

His expression was mildly quizzical . . . which I knew as being expression number seven. Dickie used to practice expressions in front of the mirror. How's this? he'd ask me. Do I look sincere? Do I look appalled? Do I look surprised?

The office was a respectable size with a double window. A realtor would say it was "nicely appointed." Which meant that Dickie had gone with baronial rather than *L.A. Law.* The carpet was a red Oriental. The desk was heavy mahogany antique. The two client chairs were burgundy leather with brass studs. Ultra masculine. The only thing missing was a wolfhound and some hunting trophies. The perfect office for a guy with a big stupid dick.

"This is Lula," I said by way of introduction, approaching the desk. "Lula and I work together."

Dickie inclined his head. "Lula."

"Hunh," Lula said.

"I have a few questions about Mo," I said to Dickie. "For instance, when is he going to turn himself in?"

"That hasn't been determined."

"When it has been determined, I'd like to be informed. I'm working for Vinnie now, and Mo is in violation of his bond agreement."

"Of course," Dickie said. Which meant when cows fly.

I sat in one of his chairs and slouched back. "I understand Mo is talking to the police. I'd like to know what he's got to trade."

"That would be privileged information," Dickie said.

From the corner of my eye I could see Lula morphing into Rhino Woman.

"I hate secrets," Lula said.

Dickie looked over at Lula, and then he looked back at me. "You're kidding, right?"

I smiled. "About Mo's deal . . ."

"I'm not talking about Mo's deal. And you're going to have to excuse me. I have a meeting in five minutes, and I need to prepare."

"How about if I shoot him?" Lula said. "Bet if I shoot him in the foot he tells us everything."

"Not here," I said. "Too many people."

Lula stuck her lower lip out in a pout. "You probably don't want me to beat the crap out of him either."

"Maybe later," I said.

Lula leaned a hand on Dickie's desk. "There's things I can do to a man. You'd probably throw up if I told you about them."

Dickie recoiled from Lula. "This is a joke, right?" He turned to me. "You hire her from Rent-a-thug?"

"Rent-a-thug?" Lula said, eyes big and round. "Excuse me, you little dog turd. I'm a bounty hunter in training. I'm not no rent-a-thug. And I'm not no joke either. You're the joke. You know the saying . . . go fuck yourself? I could make that a possibility for you."

I was back on my feet, and I was smiling because Dickie had gone pale under his tanning-salon tan. "I guess we should go now," I said. "This probably isn't a good place to discuss business. Maybe we can get together another time and share information," I said to Dickie.

Dickie's expression was tight. Not one I'd seen him practice. "Are you threatening me?"

"Hell no," Lula said. "Do we look like the kind of women who'd threaten a man? I don't think so. I don't think I'm the sort of woman looks like she'd threaten some pimple-ass motherfucker like you."

I'm not sure what I'd expected to accomplish by meeting with Dickie, but I felt like I'd gotten my money's worth.

When we were alone in the elevator I turned to Lula. "I think that went well."

"Felt good to me," she said. "We got any more parties to go to?"

"Nope."

"Good deal. I got plans for the rest of the afternoon."

I scooped my car keys out of my pocket. "Have fun. And thanks for riding shotgun."

"See you later," she said.

I drove one block and stopped for a light. The Nissan went into the backfire and stall routine. Stay calm, I told myself. Elevated blood pressure can lead to stroke. My aunt Eleanor'd had a stroke, and it wasn't fun. She called everybody Tootsie and colored her hair with her lipstick.

I restarted the pickup and raced the engine. When the light changed I leaped forward on another backfire. KAPOW! I pulled Morelli's card from my pocket and read the address. Mr. Fix It was on Eighteenth Street, just past the button factory.

"I'm giving you one last chance," I said to the pickup. "Either you shape up, or I'm taking you to Bucky Seidler."

A half a block later it stalled out again. I took it as a sign and made a U-turn. Morelli regularly lied to me, but never about a mechanic. Morelli took his mechanics seriously. I'd give Bucky one shot. If that didn't work, I was going to drive the car off a bridge.

Fifteen minutes later I was chugging down Eighteenth Street, in a part of industrial Trenton that had left prosperity behind. Bucky's garage was a two-bay cinder block structure that sat like an island in a sea of cars. New cars, old cars, smashed cars, rusted cars, cars that had signed on for the vital organ donor program. The bay doors were open. A man in jeans and thermal undershirt stood under a car on the lift in the first bay. He looked out at me as I gasped to a stop on the macadam apron. He wiped his hands on a rag and walked over. He had a butch haircut and a keg of beer hanging over his belt. I hadn't seen him in a while, but I was pretty sure it was Bucky. He looked like the sort of person who'd set rats loose on a bunch of women.

He peered in the window at me. "Stephanie Plum," he said, smiling. "Haven't seen you since high school."

"I'm surprised you recognized me."

"The orange hair threw me for a minute, but then I remembered you from the picture in the paper from when you burned down the funeral home."

"I didn't burn down the funeral home. It was a misprint."

"Too bad," Bucky said. "I thought it was cool. Sounds like you got a car problem."

"It keeps stalling. Joe Morelli suggested I come here. He said you're a good mechanic."

"He gave you a pretty good recommendation, too. Read it on the bathroom wall of Mario's Sub Shop over ten years ago, and I can still remember every word of it."

"I have Mace in my shoulder bag."

"Mostly what I care about is MasterCard."

I sighed. "I've got that too."

"Well," Bucky said, "then let's do business."

I gave him the Nissan's medical history.

Bucky had me run the engine while he looked under the hood.

"Okay," he said. "Been here, done this."

"Can you fix it?"

"Sure."

"How long? How much?"

"Depends on parts."

I'd heard this before.

He jerked his thumb at a bunch of junks lined up against a chain-link fence. "You could pick out one of those to use as a loaner if you want. I got a classic Buick that's a beauty. A fifty-three."

"NO!"

Rex was running on his wheel when I walked through the door. I'd stopped at the supermarket and gotten healthy food for Rex and me.

Fruit, low-fat cottage cheese, potatoes and some of those already washed and peeled thumb-sized carrots in a bag. I said howdy to Rex and gave him a grape. My message light was blinking, so I hit the button and listened while I unpacked the groceries.

Ranger called to say he'd heard about Mo and the lawyer, and that it didn't change my job. It's simple, Ranger said. You get hired to find a man and that's what you do.

Message number two was from Bucky Seidler. "I was able to get the part I needed," Bucky said into the machine. "I'll put it in first thing in the morning. You can pick your car up anytime after ten."

I bit into my lower lip. Lord, I hoped it wasn't another carburetor.

The last call started out with a lot of noise. People talking, and the sort of clatter you hear at an arcade. Then a man came on the line. "I'm watching you, Stephanie," the man said. "I'm watching you have lunch with your cop boyfriend. I was watching you last night, too. Watching you diddle on the kitchen floor. Good to see you decided to do something else besides harassing upstanding citizens. You keep concentrating on banging Morelli and maybe you'll live to be an old lady."

I stared at the machine, unable to breathe. My chest was impossibly tight, and my ears were ringing. I leaned against the refrigerator and closed my eyes. Imagine you're at the ocean, I thought. Hear the surf. Breathe with the surf, Stephanie.

When I got my heart rate under control, I rewound the tape and popped it out of the recorder. I took a blank from the junk drawer next to the refrigerator and slid it into the machine. It was a few minutes after five. I called Morelli to make sure he was home.

" 'Lo," Morelli said.

"You going to be there for a while?"

"Yeah. I just got in."

"Don't go away. I have something you need to hear. I'll be right over."

I dropped the tape into my shoulder bag, grabbed my jacket and locked up behind myself. I got down to the first floor and froze at the door. What if they were out there? Waiting for me. Spying on me. I took a few steps back and exhaled. This wasn't good. It was okay to be afraid, but not okay to let it restrict my life. I moved away from the glass panes and checked my shoulder bag. I had the .38, and it was loaded. My cell phone was charged. My stun gun was charged. I transferred the pepper spray to my jacket pocket. Not good enough. I took the spray out of my pocket and held it in my left hand. Car keys in my right.

I paced in the lobby for a few beats to get the fear under control. When I felt strong, I turned and walked out the door and across the lot to my car. I never broke stride. Never turned my head right or left. But I was listening. I was on the balls of my feet, and I was ready to act if I had to.

I'd chosen a green Mazda as a loaner. It was rusted and dented and reeked of cigarettes, but its performance couldn't be faulted. I checked the interior, stuck the key in the lock, opened the door and slid behind the wheel. I locked the door, immediately cranked the engine over and rolled out of the lot.

No one followed that I could tell, and once I got onto St. James there were too many headlights to distinguish a tail. I had my shoulder bag on the seat alongside me and my pepper spray in my lap. To keep my spirits up I sang "Who's Afraid of the Big Bad Wolf?" all the way to Morelli's house. I parked at the curb and checked the street. No cars. No one on foot. I locked the Mazda, marched to Morelli's front door and knocked. I guess I was still nervous because the knock came out like BAM BAM BAM instead of knock, knock, knock.

"Must have had your Wheaties today," Morelli said when he answered the door.

I pushed past him. "You keep your doors locked?"

"Sometimes."

"They locked now?"

Morelli reached behind him and flipped the Yale lock. "Yep."

I went to the living room window and drew the drapes. "Pull the curtains in the dining room and kitchen."

"What's going on?"

"Just humor me."

I followed him into the kitchen and waited while he adjusted Venetian blinds. When he was done I took the tape out of my shoulder bag. "You have a recorder?"

There was a briefcase sitting on the kitchen table. Morelli opened the briefcase and took out a recorder. He slipped the tape into the recorder and pressed the play button.

Ranger came up first.

"Bad advice," Morelli said.

"That's not what I want you to hear."

The noise blasted out and then the man's voice. Morelli's face showed no expression while he listened to the message. Cop face, I thought. He ran the tape through a second time before shutting the machine off.

"Not Mickey Maglio," he said.

"No." A cop would know better than to have his voice recorded.

"You have any clue you were being followed?"

I shook my head. "No."

"Did you pick up a tail tonight?"

"No."

"There's a record store, grunge shop across from the Shuman Building. It's got some video machines in it. It's a kid hangout. The call probably originated from there. I'll send someone over to ask a few questions."

"Guess the crashing and scuffling we heard didn't come from your neighbor's dog."

"Whoever was out there must have knocked the garbage can over trying to get a better look."

"You don't seem very upset by this."

There were dishes drying in a drainer on the sink. A dinner plate, a cereal bowl, a couple glasses. Morelli grabbed the dinner plate and threw it hard against the opposite wall, where it smashed into a million pieces.

"Okay," I said. "So I was wrong."

"You want to stay for dinner?"

"I don't think that's a good idea."

Morelli made chicken sounds.

"Very adult," I said. "Very attractive."

Morelli grinned.

I paused with my hand on the door handle. "I don't suppose you want to tell me more about your conversation with Dickie."

"No more to tell," Morelli said.

Yeah, right.

"And don't follow me home," I said. "I don't need a bodyguard."

"Who said I was going to follow you home?"

"You have your car keys in your hand, and I know the body language. You look like my mother."

The grin widened. "You sure you don't want an escort?"

"Yes, I'm sure." The only thing worse than being scared out of my wits was having Morelli know it.

Morelli opened the door and glanced at the Mazda. "Looks like you've got one of Bucky's loaners."

"Bucky remembered me from high school. Said you gave me quite a recommendation on the men's room wall at Mario's."

"That was during my reckless youth," Morelli said. "These days I'm the soul of discretion."

It was still early, and I couldn't get excited about going home and fixing dinner for one. The alternatives were Cluck in a Bucket or mooching a meal from my parents. I was afraid I might be recognized and remembered at Cluck in a Bucket, so I opted for family.

My mother looked flustered when she came to the door. "Whose car is that?" she asked.

"It's a loaner from a garage. My car is broken again."

"Hah!" my father said from the dining room.

"We were just sitting down," my mother said. "Roast leg of lamb with mashed potatoes and asparagus."

"Is that Stephanie?" Grandma Mazur hollered from the table. "Have you got your gun? I want to show it around."

"I've got my gun, but you can't see it," I said.

There was a man sitting next to Grandma Mazur.

"This here's Fred," Grandma said. "He's my boyfriend."

Fred nodded to me. "Howdy-do."

Fred looked to be about three hundred years old. Gravity had pulled the skin from the top of his head down to his neck, and Fred had tucked it into his shirt collar.

I took my seat across from Grandma and noticed a set of false teeth neatly placed beside Fred's salad fork.

"Those are my choppers," Fred said. "Got them for free from the VA, but they don't fit right. Can't eat with them in."

"Had to put his lamb through the meat grinder," Grandma said. "That's what the lump of gray stuff is on his plate."

"So," my father said to Fred. "You pretty well fixed?"

"I do okay. I get disability from the army." He tapped a finger against his right eye. "Glass," he said. "World War Two."

"Were you overseas?" my father asked.

"Nope. Lost my eye at Camp Kilmer. I was inspecting my bayonet, and then next thing you know I'd poked my eye out with it."

"The fact he's only got one eye don't slow him down none," Grandma said. "I've seen him handle ten bingo cards and never miss a single call. And he's an artist, too. He hooks rugs. You should see the beautiful rugs he makes. He made one with a picture of a tiger on it."

"I imagine you got a house of your own?" my father asked him.

Fred gummed some of the gray glop. "Nope. I just got a room at Senior Citizens. I sure would like to have a house though. I'd like to marry someone like Sweetie here, and I'd be happy to move right in. I'd be quiet too. You wouldn't hardly know I was here."

"Over my dead body," my father said. "You can take your teeth and get the hell out of here. You're nothing but a goddamn gold digger."

Fred opened his eyes wide in alarm. "I can't get out of here. I haven't had dessert yet. Sweetie promised me dessert. And besides, I don't have a ride back to the Seniors."

"Call him a cab," my father ordered. "Stephanie, go call him a cab. Ellen, wrap up his dessert."

Ten minutes later Fred was on his way.

Grandma Mazur helped herself to a cookie and a second cup of coffee. "There's plenty more where he came from," she said. "Tell you the truth he was kind of old for me anyway. And he was creeping me out with that glass eye . . . the way he'd tap on it all the time. It was okay that he took his teeth out, but I didn't want to see that eye rolling around next to his soup spoon."

The Rangers were playing Montreal, so I stayed to see the game. Watching the game also involved eating a lot of junk food since my father is an even worse junk food addict than I am. By the time the third period rolled around we'd gone through a jar of cocktail wieners, a bag of Chee-tos and a can of cashews and were working on a two-pound bag of M&M's.

When I finally waved good-bye I was considering bulimia.

The upside to lacking self-control was that the threat of masked men paled in comparison to worry over the Chee-tos working their way to my thighs. By the time I remembered to be afraid I was inserting the key in my front door.

My apartment felt relatively safe. Only one phone message, and no cocktail wieners tempting me from cupboard shelves. I punched up the message.

It was from Ranger. "Call me."

I dialed his home number and received a single-word answer. "Go."

"Is this a message?" I asked. "Am I talking to a machine?"

"This is very weird, babe, but I could swear your friend Lula is trying to tail me."

"She thinks you're a superhero."

"Lot of people think that."

"You know how you give everybody that vacant lot as your home address? She thinks that's a little odd. She wants to find out where you live. And by the way, where *do* you live?"

I waited for an answer, but all I heard was a disconnect.

I woke up feeling guilty about the junk food binge, so for penance I cleaned the hamster cage, rearranged the jars in the refrigerator and scrubbed the toilet. I looked for ironing, but there was none. When something needs to be ironed I put it in the ironing basket. If a year goes by and the item is still in the basket I throw the item away. This is a good system since eventually I end up only with clothes that don't need ironing.

Bucky had said my car would be ready at ten. Not that I doubted Morelli or Bucky, but I'd come to regard car repairs with the same sort of cynicism I'd previously reserved for Elvis sightings.

I parked the green Mazda against the garage fence and saw that my pickup was waiting for me in front of one of the open bays. It had been freshly washed and was sparkly clean. It would have been slick if only it didn't have a big crumple in its hood and a big dent in its back bumper.

Bucky sauntered out from the other bay.

I looked at the pickup skeptically. "Is it fixed?"

"Emission control valve needed a doohickey," Bucky said. "Two hundred and thirty dollars."

"Doohickey?"

"That's the technical term," Bucky said.

"Two hundred and thirty dollars sounds high for a doohickey."

"Mr. Fix It don't come cheap."

I drove back to my apartment building without a hitch. No stalls.

No backfires. And no confidence that this would last. The honeymoon period, I thought skeptically.

I returned to my building and parked in my usual Dumpster spot. I cautiously got out of the truck and looked for possible assailants. Finding none, I crossed the lot and swung through the door into the lobby.

Mr. Wexler was in the lobby, waiting for the senior citizens' minibus to pick him up. "You hear about Mo Bedemier?" Mr. Wexler asked. "Isn't he a pip? I tell you, the man's got a lot of jewels. It's about time somebody did something about the drug problem."

"He's suspected of killing a whole bunch of men!"

"Yep. He's on a roll, all right."

The elevator doors opened, and I got in, but I didn't feel like going to my apartment. I felt like striking out at someone.

I got out of the elevator and confronted Mr. Wexler. "Killing is wrong."

"We kill chickens," Mr. Wexler said. "We kill cows. We kill trees. So big deal, we kill some drug dealers."

It was hard to argue with that kind of logic because I like cows and chickens and trees much better than drug dealers.

I got back into the elevator and rode to the second floor. I stood there for a few minutes, trying to talk myself into a relaxing afternoon of doing nothing, but I couldn't sell the idea. I returned to the lobby, stomped over to my truck and wedged myself behind the steering wheel. As long as I was already in a fairly vicious mood I thought I might as well visit Dickie, the little crumb. I wanted to know what he told Morelli.

I parked in a lot a block from Dickie's office, barreled through the lobby and gave his receptionist my power smile.

"I need to have a few words with Dickie," I said. And before she could answer I turned on my heel and stalked off to Dickie's office.

CHAPTER

15

Dickie didn't look happy to see me. In fact, Dickie didn't look happy at all. He was sitting at his desk with his head in his hands and his hair rumpled. This was serious stuff, because Dickie's hair was always perfect. Dickie woke up in the morning with every hair neatly in place. That he was having a bad day did nothing to dampen my spirits.

He jumped in his seat when he saw me. "You! Are you nuts? Are you wacko?" He shook his head. "This is too much. This time you've gone too far."

"What are you talking about?"

"You know what I'm talking about. I'm talking about restraining orders. Harassment charges. Attempts at intimidating an attorney."

"Are you putting that funny white powder in your coffee again?"

"Okay, so I fooled around a little while we were married. Okay, our divorce didn't go smooth as silk. Okay, I know you have some hostile feelings for me." He unconsciously ran his hand through his hair, causing it to stand on end. "That's no reason to turn into the Terminator. Christ, you need help. Have you ever thought of getting some counseling?"

"I get the feeling you're trying to tell me something."

"I'm talking about sending your goon to attack me in my parking lot this morning!"

"Lula attacked you?"

"Not Lula. The other one."

"I don't have another one."

"The big guy," Dickie said. "In the ski mask and coveralls."

"Hold the phone. I've got the picture. That wasn't my goon. And there's more than one. There's a whole pack of them, and they've been threatening me, too. Just exactly what did he say to you?"

"He said Mo didn't need a lawyer, and I was off the case. I said Mo would have to tell that to me personally. And then the guy pulled a gun on me and said that for a lawyer I wasn't very smart at reading between the lines. I told him I was getting smarter with each passing minute. He put the gun away and left."

"He drive away? You get a plate number?"

Dickie's face flushed. "I didn't think."

"Mo's got a fan club," I said. "Concerned citizens."

"This is too weird."

"What was the deal with Mo? What's your contribution here?"

"You're wasting your time. I'm not discussing this with you."

"I know a lot of stuff about you that you probably wouldn't want to get around. I know about your coke habit."

"That's history."

"I know about Mallory's wife."

Dickie was out of his seat. "You were the one who told Morelli!"

"That Mallory is a mean son of a gun. No telling what he'd do if he found out someone was fooling around with his wife. He could plant drugs in your car, Dickie. Then you'd get arrested, and just think what fun that'd be . . . the strip search, the beating you got when you resisted arrest."

Dickie's eyes shrunk into hard, glittery little marbles. I figured his gonads were undergoing a similar transformation.

"How do I know you won't go to Mallory even if I tell you about Mo?" Dickie asked.

"And lose my edge? I might want to blackmail you again."

"Shit," Dickie said. He pushed back in his chair. He stood and paced and returned to his seat. "There's client confidentiality involved here."

"As if you ever cared about client confidentiality." I looked at my watch. "I haven't got a lot of time. I have other things to do. I need to get in touch with the dispatcher before Mallory goes off shift."

"Bitch," Dickie said.

"Dickhead."

His eyes narrowed. "Slut."

"Asshole."

"Fat cow."

"Listen," I said. "I don't have to take this. I got a divorce."

"If I tell you about Mo, you've got to promise to keep your mouth shut."

"My lips are sealed."

He rested his elbows on his desk, laced his fingers together and leaned forward. If it had been a normal-sized desk we would have been nose to nose. Fortunately, the desk was as big as a football field so we still had some space between us.

"First off, Mo didn't do any of the killing. He got mixed up with some bad guys . . ."

"Bad guys? Could you be more specific than that?"

"I don't know any more than that. I'm working as an intermediary. All I'm doing right now is setting up a line of communication."

"And it's these bad guys who did the killing?"

"Mo was fed up with the gangs and the drugs inching closer to his store, and Mo didn't think the cops could do much. He figured the cops were bound up by laws and plea bargaining.

"But Mo knew a lot from listening to the kids. He knew the dealers' names. He knew who specialized in kiddie sales. So Mo started his own little sting. He'd go to the dealer and suggest a partnership."

"Let the dealer work from Mo's store."

"Yes. He'd set up a meeting, usually in his store or garage, someplace else if the dealer was jumpy. Then Mo would give the meeting information to a friend of his. Mo would disappear from the scene and the dealer would be taken care of by this friend. In the beginning, Mo didn't know the dealers were being killed. I guess he thought they'd get roughed up or threatened and that would be the end of it. By the time he figured it out it was late in the game."

"Why'd Mo jump bail?"

"Mo freaked. The gun he was carrying when Gaspick pulled him over was a murder weapon. It had been used to kill a dealer who subsequently floated in on the tide. I guess Mo had bought into some of it by then. Got caught up in the righteousness of being a vigilante. Mo said he never used the gun. In fact, it was empty when he was pulled over. Mo probably felt like John Wayne or something carrying it around. Don't forget we're talking about a shy, nerdy sort of guy who spent his entire life behind the counter of a candy store in the burg."

I felt a painful stab in the midsection. Morelli had withheld that information from me. He'd never told me about the gun connection and the floater. Now it made sense. Now I realized why Morelli was interested in Mo from the very beginning. And why Mo had jumped bail.

"Why has Mo suddenly decided to turn himself in?"

"Just came to his senses, I suppose," Dickie said. "Realized he was getting more and more involved and started to get scared."

"So what's the deal? Mo sells out his friend for a reduced sentence?"

"I suppose, but it hasn't actually gotten to that yet. Like I said, I'm just setting up a line of communication. And I advised Mo of his rights and the consequences of his participation."

"So maybe these ski mask guys aren't protecting Mo anymore. Maybe sentiments have changed and now they're trying to find Mo before I do. . . . Very noble of you to remain as counsel after being threatened."

"Fuck noble," Dickie said. "I'm off this gig."

I dropped a card on Dickie's desk. "Call me if you hear from anyone."

I found myself smiling in the elevator, comforted by the fact that Dickie had been harassed and threatened. I decided to continue the celebration by paying another visit to Mr. Alexander. If Mr. Alexander could make my hair orange, surely he could make it brown again.

"Impossible!" Mr. Alexander said. "I'm totally booked. I would love to help you out, lovey. I really would, but just look at my schedule. I haven't a free moment."

I held some orange frizz between thumb and forefinger. "I can't live like this. Isn't there *anyone* here who can help me?"

"Maybe tomorrow."

"I've got a gun in my pocketbook. I've got pepper spray and an electric gizmo that could turn you into a reading lamp. I'm a dangerous woman, and this orange hair is making me crazy. There's no telling what I might do if I don't get my hair fixed."

The receptionist hastily thumbed down the day page. "Cleo has a cancellation at two o'clock. It was only for a cut, but she might be able to squeeze a color in."

"Cleo is a marvel at color," Mr. Alexander said. "If anyone can help you, it's Cleo."

Three hours later, I was back in my apartment building, and I still had orange hair. Cleo had given it her best shot, but the orange had resisted change. It was a shade darker and perhaps not quite so bright, but it was still basically orange.

Okay, fuck it. So I have orange hair. Big deal. It could be worse. It could be ebola. It could be dengue fever. Orange hair wasn't permanent. The hair would grow out. It wasn't as if I'd wrecked my life.

I was alone in the lobby. The elevator doors opened, and I stepped in, my thoughts turning to Mo. Speaking of someone who'd wrecked his life. If Dickie could be believed, here was a man who'd lived his entire life selling candy to kids and then had snapped in frustration and made some bad choices. Now he was stuck in a labyrinth of judgment errors and terrible crimes.

I considered my own life and the choices I'd made. Until recently those choices had been relatively safe and predictable. College, marriage, divorce, work. Then, through no fault of my own, I didn't have a job. Next thing, I was a bounty hunter, and I'd killed a man. It had been self-defense, but it was still a regrettable act that came creeping back to me late at night. I knew things about myself now, and about human nature, that nice girls from the burg weren't supposed to know.

I traveled the length of the hall, searched for my key and opened my front door. I stepped inside, relieved to be home. Before I had a chance to turn and close the door, I was sent sprawling onto the foyer floor with a hard shove from behind.

There were two of them. Both in masks and coveralls. Both too tall to be Maglio. One of them pointed a gun at me. The other held a lunch bag. It was the sort of soft-sided insulated bag an office worker might use. Big enough for a sandwich, an apple and a soda.

"You make a sound, and I'll shoot you," the guy with the gun said, closing and locking the door. "Shooting you isn't what I want to do, but I'll do it if I have to."

"This isn't going to work," I told him. "Mo is talking to the police. He's telling them all about you. He's naming names."

"Mo should have stuck to selling candy. We'll take care of Mo. What we're doing is for the good of the community . . . for the good of America. We're not going to stop just because an old man got squeamish."

"Killing people is for the good of America?"

"Eliminating the drug scourge."

Oh boy. Scourge removers.

The man carrying the lunch bag jerked me to my feet and shoved me toward the living room. I thought about screaming or simply walking away, but I wasn't sure how these lunatics would act. The one seemed comfortable with his gun. It was possible that he'd killed before, and I suspected killing was like anything else . . . the more you did it, the easier it got.

I was still wearing my jacket, still carrying my shoulder bag, the warning of retaliation ringing in my ears. I still had the blister from my last meeting with Mo's vigilantes, and the thought of being burned again sickened my stomach. "I'm going to give you a chance to leave, before you do something really stupid," I said, working to keep the panic out of my voice.

The guy carrying the lunch bag set it on my coffee table. "You're the stupid one. We keep reasoning with you and warning you, and you refuse to listen. You're still sticking your nose in where it doesn't belong. You and that lawyer you keep visiting. So we figured we'd give you a product demo. Show you the threat firsthand." He removed a small glassine packet from the lunch bag and held it up for me to see. "High-quality boy." The next item to be removed from the carrier was a small bottle of spring water. Then a bottle cap with a wire handle fashioned around it. "The best cooker comes from a wine bottle. Nice and deep. The dopers like this better than a spoon or a soda bottle cap. Do you know what boy is?"

Boy was heroin. Coke was girl. "Yeah, I know what it is."

The man filled the cap with water and mixed in some of the powder from the packet. He pulled a lighter out of his pocket and held it under the cap. Then he produced a syringe from the carrier and filled the syringe with the liquid.

I still had my pocketbook on my shoulder. I ran a shaky hand over the outside, feeling for my .38.

The gunman stepped forward and ripped the bag off my shoulder. "Forget it."

Rex was in his cage on the coffee table. He'd been running on his wheel when we'd come into the room. When the lights flashed on, Rex had paused, whiskers whirring, eyes wide with the expectation of food and attention. After a few moments he'd resumed his running.

The man with the syringe flipped the lid off Rex's cage, reached in and scooped Rex up in his free hand. "Now we get to begin the demonstration."

My heart gave a painful contraction. "Put him back," I said. "He doesn't like strangers."

"We know a lot about you," the man said. "We know you like this hamster. We figure he's like family to you. Now suppose this hamster was a kid. And suppose you thought you were doing all the right things, like feeding that kid good food and helping with his homework and raising him in a neighborhood with a good school. And then somehow, in spite of everything you did, that kid got started experimenting with drugs. How would you feel? Wouldn't you feel like going after the people who were giving him the drugs? And suppose your kid was sold some bad stuff. And your kid died of an overdose. Wouldn't you want to go out there and kill the drug dealer who killed your kid?"

"I'd want him brought to justice."

"The hell you would. You'd want to kill him."

"Are you speaking from personal experience?"

The man with the syringe paused and stared at me. I could see his eyes behind the ski mask, and I guessed my question had hit home.

"I'm sorry," I said.

"Then you understand why we have to do this. It's essential that our work isn't jeopardized. And it's essential that you understand our commitment. We'd prefer not to kill you. We're fair and reasonable people. We have ethics. So, pay attention. This is the last warning. This time we kill the hamster. Next time we kill you."

I felt tears starting behind my eyes. "How can you justify killing an innocent animal?"

"It's a lesson. You ever see anyone die from an overdose? It's not a nice way to go. And it's what's going to happen to you if you don't take a vacation."

Rex's eyes were black and shiny, his whiskers a blur of motion, his little feet treading air, his body squirmy. Not enjoying his confinement.

"Say good-bye," the man with the syringe said. "I'm going to shoot this directly into his heart."

There's a limit to how far a woman can be pushed. I'd been gassed, attacked, stalked by masked men, lied to by Morelli and I'd been swindled by my mechanic. And I'd stayed pretty damn calm through it all. Threatening my hamster brought out a whole new set of rules. Threatening my hamster made me Godzilla. I had no intention of saying good-bye to my hamster.

I blinked back the threat of tears, swiped at my nose and narrowed my eyes. "Listen to me, you two bags of monkey shit," I yelled. "I am not in a good mood. My car keeps stalling. The day before yesterday I threw up on Joe Morelli. I was called a fat cow by my ex-husband. And if that isn't enough . . . my hair is *ORANGE! ORANGE, FOR CHRISSAKE!* And now you have the gall to force yourself into my home and threaten my hamster. Well, you have gone too far. You have crossed the line."

I was shouting and waving my arms, totally out of control. And while I was out of control I was watching Rex, because I knew what would happen if he was held long enough. And when it happened I was going to act.

"So if you want to scare someone, you picked the wrong person," I shrieked. "And don't think I'm going to allow you to harm one hair on that hamster's head!"

And then Rex did what any sensible pissed-off hamster would do. He sank his fangs into his captor's thumb.

The man gave a yelp and opened his fist. Rex dropped onto the floor with a thunk and scurried under the couch. And the guy with the gun swung his weapon in Rex's direction and fired off several rounds reflexively.

I grabbed the table lamp to my right and, keeping the momentum going, smashed the lamp against the gunman's head. The man went down like a bag of sand, and I took off for the door.

I had one foot in the hall when I was grabbed from behind and yanked back into the apartment by the man wielding the syringe. I kicked and clawed at him, the two of us wrestling for our lives in front of the door. My foot connected with his crotch and there was a heart-stopping moment of immobility where I saw his eyes widen in pain, and I thought he might shoot me, or stick me or smack me senseless.

But then he doubled over and tried to suck air, inadvertently backing out the door, into the hall.

The elevator door opened, and Mrs. Bestler jumped out with her walker. Clomp, clomp, clomp with lightning speed, she stomped down the hall and rammed the man, knocking him to his knees.

Mrs. Karwatt's door crashed open, and Mrs. Karwatt trained her .45 on the man on the floor. "What's going on? What did I miss?"

Mr. Kleinschmidt came shuffling down the hall carrying an M-16. "I heard a gunshot."

Mrs. Delgado was right behind Mr. Kleinschmidt. Mrs. Delgado had a cleaver and a blue steel Glock with "sidekick" rubber grips.

Mrs. Karwatt looked at Mrs. Delgado's gun. "Loretta," she said, "you got a new gun."

"Birthday present," Mrs. Delgado said proudly. "My daughter Jean Ann gave it to me. Forty caliber, just like the cops use. More stopping power."

"I've been thinking of getting a new gun," Mrs. Karwatt said. "What kind of kick do you get with that Glock?"

I brought Rex into the bedroom with me for the night. He seemed okay after the evening's trauma. I wasn't sure if the same could be said for me. The police had arrived and unmasked the two men. The man with the needle was a stranger to me. The man who'd held the gun had been a schoolmate. He was married now and had two kids. I'd run into him at the food store a couple weeks ago and had said hello.

I slept through most of the morning and felt pretty decent when I got up. I might not be the most patient woman in the world, or the most glamorous, or the most athletic, but I'm right up there at the top of the line when it comes to resiliency.

I was pouring a second cup of coffee when the phone rang.

It was Sue Ann Grebek. "Stephanie!" she shouted into the phone. "I've got something good!"

"On Mo?"

"Yeah. High-quality vicious rumor. Only one person removed. It might even be true."

"Give it to me!"

"I was just at Fiorello's, and I ran into Myra Balog. You remember

Myra? Went steady with that dork Larry Skolnik all through high school. I never knew what she saw in him. He made weird noises with his nose, and he used to write secret messages on his hands. Like 'S.D.O.B.G.' And then he wouldn't tell anyone what it meant.

"Anyway, I got to talking to Myra, and one thing led to another and we got to talking about Mo. And Myra said that one day Larry told her this really off-the-wall story about Mo. Said Larry swore it was true. Course we don't know what that means, because Larry probably thought he got beamed up a couple times, too."

"So what was the story?"

I sat and stared at the phone for a few minutes after talking to Sue Ann. I didn't like what I had heard, but it made some sense. I thought about what I'd seen in Mo's apartment and pieces of the puzzle started to fit together.

What I needed to do now was to visit Larry Skolnik. So I double-timed down to the lot, stuck the key in the ignition and held my breath. The engine caught and went into a quiet idle. I slowly exhaled, feeling my cynicism giving way to cautious optimism.

Larry Skolnik worked in his father's dry cleaning store on lower Hamilton. Larry was behind the counter when I walked into the store. He'd blimped up by about a hundred pounds since high school, but it wasn't all bad news—his hands were message free. He was an okay person, but if I'd have to take a winger on his social life, I'd say he probably talked to his tie a lot.

He smiled when he saw me. "Hey."

"Hey," I said back.

"You got laundry here?"

"Nope. I came to see you. I wanted to ask you about Uncle Mo."

"Moses Bedemier?" A flush crept into his cheeks. "What about him?"

Larry and I were alone in the store. No one else behind the counter. No one else in front of the counter. Just me and Larry and three hundred shirts.

I repeated the story Sue Ann had told me.

Larry fidgeted with a box of homeless shirt buttons that had been placed by the register. "I tried to tell people, but nobody believed me."

"It's true?"

More fidgeting. He chose a white pearl button and examined it more closely. He made a honking sound in his nose. His face flushed some more. "Sorry," he said. "I didn't mean to honk."

"That's okay. A little stress-related honking never hurt anybody."

"Well, I did it. The story is true," Larry said. "And I'm proud of it. So there."

If he said nah, nah, nah, nah, nah, I was going to smack him.

"I hung around the store a lot," Larry said, looking down into the button box when he talked, poking at the buttons with his finger, making canals in the button collection. "And then when I was seventeen Mo gave me a job sweeping up and polishing the glass in the showcase. It was great. I mean, I was working for Uncle Mo. All the kids wanted a job working for Uncle Mo.

"The thing is, that's how we got to sort of be buddies. And then one day he asked me to . . . um, you know. And I'd never done anything like that before, but I thought what the heck."

He stopped talking and stared aimlessly at the buttons. I waited awhile but Larry just kept quietly looking at the buttons. And it occurred to me that maybe Larry wasn't just weird. Maybe Larry wasn't very smart.

"This is important to me," I finally said. "I need to find Mo. I thought maybe you had some idea where he might be. I thought you might still be in touch."

"Do you really think he killed all those people?"

"I'm not sure. I think he must have been involved."

"I think so too," Larry said. "And I have a theory. I don't have it all put together. But maybe you can make something of it." He forgot about the buttons and leaned forward on the counter. "One time I was paired up with a guy named Desmond, and we got to talking. Sort of one pro to another, if you know what I mean. And Desmond told me how Mo found him.

"See, it's important that Mo can always be finding young guys, because that's what Mo likes."

By the time Larry finished telling me his theory I was just about dancing with excitement. I had a totally off-the-wall connection between Mo and the drug dealers. And I had renewed interest in the second-house idea. Mo had driven Larry to a house in the woods when he'd wanted Larry to do his thing.

There was no guarantee that Mo was still using the same house, but it was a place to start looking. Unfortunately, Larry had always gone to the house during evening hours, and even on a good day, Larry's memory wasn't top of the line. What he remembered was going south and then turning into a rural area.

I thanked Larry for his help and promised to come back with dry cleaning. I hopped into the truck and started it up. I wanted to talk to Vinnie, but Vinnie wouldn't be in the office this early. That was okay. I'd visit the weak link in Mo's chain while I waited for Vinnie.

I parked on the street, across from Lula's apartment. All the row houses looked alike on this block, but Gail's was easy to find. It was the one with the light on over the front stoop.

I went straight to the second floor and knocked on Gail's door. She answered after the second series of knocks. Sleepy-eyed again. A doper.

"Yuh?" she said.

I introduced myself and asked if I could come in.

"Sure," she said. Like who would care.

She sat on the edge of her bed. Hands folded in her lap, fingers occasionally escaping to pick at her skirt. The room was sparsely furnished. Clothes lay in heaps on the floor. A small wood table held a cache of groceries. A box of cereal, half a loaf of bread, peanut butter, a six-pack of Pepsi with two cans missing. A straight-backed chair had been pulled up to the table.

I took the chair for myself and edged it closer to Gail, so we could be friendly. "I need to talk to you about Harp."

Gail grabbed a whole handful of skirt. "I don't know nothin'."

"I'm not a cop. This isn't going to get you into trouble. This is just something I've got to know."

"I already told you."

It wouldn't take much to wear Gail down. Life had already worn her down about as far as she could go. And if that wasn't enough, she'd obviously gotten up early to do some pharmacological experimentation.

"What was the deal with Mo and Elliot? They did business together, didn't they?"

"Yuh. But I didn't have nothin' to do with it. I wouldn't be a party."

It was almost noon when I got to the office.

Lula was shaking a chicken leg at Connie. "I'm telling you, you don't know nothing about fried chicken. You Italians don't have the right genes. You Italians only know about stuff with tomato paste on it."

"You know what you are?" Connie said, pawing through the chicken bucket, settling on a breast. "You're a racist bigot."

Lula chewed off some of the leg meat. "I got a right to be. I'm a minority."

"What? You think Italians aren't minorities?"

"Not anymore. Italians were last year's minorities. Time to move over, baby."

I helped myself to a napkin and a mystery part. "Is Vinnie in?"

"Hey Vinnie," Connie yelled. "Are you in? Stephanie's here."

Vinnie was immediately at the door. "This better be good news."

"I want to know about Mo's boyfriend. The one you saw in New Hope."

"What about him?"

"How do you know they were lovers? Were they kissing? Were they holding hands?"

"No. They were excited. I don't mean like they had a hard-on. I mean like they were charged. And they were looking at pictures of each other. And this other guy was as queer as a three-dollar bill."

"Did you see the pictures?"

"No. I was across the room."

"How do you know they were of Mo and his friend?"

"I guess I don't, but I know they were dirty."

"Must have been one of those psychic things," Lula said. "Like the Great Carnac."

"Hey," Vinnie said. "I know dirty."

No one would argue with that.

"Were you ever able to get a name?" I asked.

"No," Vinnie said. "Nobody knows nothing about Mo. He must not go through the regular channels."

"I need to talk to you in private," I said to Vinnie, motioning him into his office, closing the door behind me. "I have a new network I want you to tap."

Vinnie practically got drooly when I told him where I wanted him to look.

"That Mo!" he said. "Who would have thought?"

I left Vinnie to his task, and I borrowed Connie's phone and dialed Morelli.

"What do you know from my two assailants?" I asked Morelli.

There was a pregnant pause. "We didn't get anything from either of them. They got a lawyer, and they walked."

I sensed there was more. "But?"

"But we did some background checks and came up with an interesting association. If I tell you, you have to promise not to act on it."

"Sure. I promise."

"I don't believe you."

"This must be excellent."

"I'm not telling you over the phone," Morelli said. "Meet me at the luncheonette across from St. Francis."

Morelli ordered a coffee and sandwich at the counter and carried it to the booth. "Been waiting long?"

"A couple minutes."

Morelli ate some of his sandwich. "When I give you this information, you have to promise not to jump out of your seat and act on it. We have men in place. You barge in, and you'll screw everything up."

"If I stay away from the site will you promise to bring me in when Mo comes forward?"

"Yes."

We locked eyes. We both knew he was lying. It wasn't the sort of promise a cop could keep.

"If I'm not present when Mo is captured there's no guarantee Vinnie will get his bond returned."

"I'll make every effort," Morelli said. "I swear, I'll do what I can."

"Just so we have everything straight . . . I know this isn't a gift. You wouldn't be telling me this if I wasn't already in line to get the information from another source." Like Eddie Gazarra or the local paper.

"So I guess you're not treating for dessert."

"What have you got?"

"Both men belonged to the Montgomery Street Freedom Church."

My first reaction was stunned silence. My second was a hoot of laughter. I clapped my hands. "The Montgomery Street Freedom Church! That's perfect."

Morelli ate the rest of his sandwich. "I knew you'd like it."

"It's a natural alliance. Mo wants to get rid of drug dealers, so he goes to the extremist Reverend Bill, and the two of them take vigilantism to a new level. Then, for reasons we aren't sure of, Mo decides to bail out and turn evidence against the good reverend."

Morelli finished his coffee and wiped his mouth with his napkin. "This is all speculation."

And I could speculate one further. I could speculate that this wasn't just about drug dealers.

"Well," I said, "this has been nice, but I need to run. Places to go. People to see."

Morelli wrapped his hand around my wrist and held my palm flat to the table, bringing us nose to nose. "Are you sure there isn't something you want to tell me?"

"I heard Biggie Zaremba had a vasectomy."

"I'm serious, Stephanie. I don't want you messing with this."

"Jesus, Joe, don't you ever stop being a cop?"

"This has nothing to do with being a cop."

I raised an eyebrow. "Oh?"

Another sigh, which sounded a lot like self-disgust. "I don't know why I worry about you. God knows, you can take care of yourself."

"It's because you're Italian. It's chromosomal."

"There's no doubt in my mind," Morelli said, releasing my wrist. "Be careful. Call me if you need help."

"I'm going to go home and wash my hair." I held my hand up. "I swear. Scout's honor. Maybe I'll go shopping."

Morelli stood. "You're hopeless. You were like this as a kid, too."

"What's that supposed to mean?"

"You were nuts. You'd do anything. You used to jump off your father's garage, trying to fly."

"Didn't you ever try to fly?"

"No. Never. I knew I couldn't fly."

"That's because from the day you were born, you had a one-track mind."

Morelli grinned. "It's true. My interests were narrow."

"All you ever thought about was S-E-X. You tricked innocent little girls into your father's garage, so you could look in their underpants."

"Life was a lot simpler back then. Now I have to get them drunk. And, let's be truthful, you were hardly tricked. You practically knocked me over trying to get to the garage."

"You said you were going to teach me to play choo-choo."

The grin widened. "And I kept my word."

The coffee shop door opened, and Vinnie cha-chaed in. Our eyes met, and Vinnie laughed his nasty little laugh and I knew he had something good for me.

CHAPTER 16

I left Morelli and pulled Vinnie outside the coffee shop, so we couldn't be overheard.

"I got an address," Vinnie said, still smiling, knowing his bond was close at hand, pleased to report on a fellow sexual deviant.

A rush of excitement shot from the soles of my feet clear to the roots of my hair. "Tell me!"

"I hit pay dirt with the first phone call. You were right. Moses Bedemier, everyone's favorite uncle, makes dirty movies. Not the kind you can rent in a video store either. These are the real thing! Genuine underground, quality porn.

"He goes under the name M. Bed. And he specializes in discipline. According to my source, you want a good spanking flick, you look for an M. Bed movie." Vinnie shook his head, grinning ear to ear. "I'm telling you the man is famous. He's done a whole series of fraternity initiation films. He did *Tits and Paddles, Gang Spank, Spanky Goes to College*. Real collectors' items. No holds barred. Lots of close-ups. Never fakes anything. That's the difference between the commercial junk and the underground. The underground stuff is real."

"Hold it down, Vinnie," I said. "People are staring."

Vinnie didn't pay any attention. He was waving his hands, and spittle was forming in the corners of his mouth. "The guy is a genius. And his masterpiece is *Bad Boy Bobby and the Schoolmarm*. It's a historical, done in period costume. It's a classic. The best ruler-spanking scene recorded on film."

I thought of Larry Skolnik with dropped drawers and a dunce cap and almost passed out.

"Once you set me in the right direction it was easy," Vinnie said. "I got a friend in the business. Only he does stuff with dogs. He's got a Great Dane that's hung like a bull. And he's got this dog trained to . . ."

I slapped my hands over my ears. *"Ugh! Gross!"*

"Well anyway," Vinnie said. "I was able to find out where Mo makes his movies. This friend of mine uses some of the same actors and actresses as Mo. So he gave me this woman's name. Bebe LaTouch. Heh, heh, heh. Says she's the Dane's favorite."

I felt my upper lip involuntarily curl back and my sphincter muscle tighten.

Vinnie handed me a piece of paper with directions. "I called her up, and according to Bebe, Mo has a house south of here. Off in the woods. She didn't know the address, but she knew how to get there."

This corresponded with the information I'd received from Gail and Larry. Gail told me that Harp had done business with Mo at a location other than the store. She remembered the place because she'd ridden along once when Harp had delivered a "virgin actress."

I took the directions and looked in at Morelli. He was picking at his potato chips and watching me through the door window. I gave him a finger wave and got into the pickup. I rolled the engine over and listened to the idle. Nice and even. No embarrassing backfires. No stalling.

"Thank you, Bucky," I said. And thank God for doohickeys.

I took 206 South for several miles and cut off at White Horse, leading toward Yardville, dropping south again to Crosswicks. At Crosswicks I followed a winding two-lane road to an unmarked cross street where I stopped and checked my map. Everything seemed okay, so I continued on and after about five minutes hit Doyne. I turned right onto Doyne and checked my odometer. After two miles I started looking for a rusty black mailbox at the end of a dirt driveway. I'd passed one house when I'd first made my turn, but nothing now. It was wooded on either side of the road. If Mo was out here, he was well isolated.

At three and a half miles I saw the mailbox. I stopped and squinted through the bare trees at the clapboard bungalow at the end of the driveway. In the summer the bungalow wouldn't be visible. This was the winter, and I could clearly see the carport, and the house. There was a car in the carport, but I had no way of knowing if it belonged to Mo.

I eased down the road about a quarter mile and dialed Ranger's cell phone.

Ranger answered on the fourth ring. "Yo."

"Yo yourself," I said. "I think I have a line on Mo. I'm staking out a bungalow south of Yardville. I need a backup for the takedown."

"Give me directions."

I gave the directions, tapped off on the cell phone and opened the small duffel bag I had on the seat beside me. I was wearing jeans and a turtleneck under my black leather jacket. I took the jacket off, zipped myself into a flak vest and put the jacket back on over the vest. The next item I took out of the duffel was a black nylon webbed gun belt with pouches to hold pepper spray and bludgeoning batons, not to mention my Smith & Wesson. I got out of the truck and strapped on the gun belt, filling the pouches, buckling in my gun. I adjusted the Velcro straps that held my .38 secure to my leg, tucked cuffs into the back of the belt and stuffed two spare nylon cuffs into my jacket pockets.

Now that I knew what Mo was up to I sort of wished I had rubber gloves, too.

I got back into the truck and cracked my knuckles, feeling nervous and stupid, all decked out like SWAT Princess.

I sat there until Ranger rolled to a stop behind me in the Bronco. I walked back to him and saw him smile.

"Looks like you're serious."

"People keep shooting at me."

"That's about as serious as it gets," Ranger said.

He was already wearing his vest. He strapped on his gun belt while I explained the situation.

"This is your takedown," he said. "Do you have a plan?"

"Drive in. Knock on the door. Arrest him."

"You want the front or the back?"

"I want the front."

"I'll leave the Bronco here and circle around through the woods. Give me a couple minutes to get in place, then you do your thing."

It was a long shot that Mo would be in the house. If I'd had more time I'd have set up surveillance. As it was, either we'd scare some poor soul half to death, or we'd risk getting drilled at the door. Then again, maybe Mo really didn't do any of the killing and wasn't all that dangerous.

I gave Ranger a lead and then drove down the driveway, parked behind the car in the carport and walked directly to the bungalow's front door. Shades were drawn in all the windows. I was poised to knock on the door when the door opened, and Mo peered out at me.

"Well," he said, "I guess this is it."

"You don't seem surprised to see me."

"Actually, the sound of a vehicle on my driveway gave me quite a start. But then I realized it was you, and to tell you the truth, I was relieved."

"Afraid it was Reverend Bill?"

"So, you know about Bill." He shook his head. "I'll be happy when this is all cleared up. I don't feel safe here anymore. I don't feel safe anywhere."

I stood just inside the front door and looked around. Two bedrooms, one bath, living room, eat-in kitchen with a back door. The rug was threadbare but clean. The furniture was shabby. Not a lot of clutter. Colors were faded into a blur of neutral nothing. A couch, an overstuffed club chair, a TV and VCR. No dust on the coffee table.

"I imagine you're not safe either," Mo said. "You've been making Bill real nervous."

I did a mental head shake. I'd unwittingly camped out in front of the Freedom Church. Mo and Bill must have been panicked, thinking I was on to them. Sometimes I amazed even myself. How could a person's instincts be so wrong and at the same time so right?

Mo pulled a shade aside and peeked out the front window. "How did you find me?"

"I took a sort of roundabout route through the burg grapevine."

Mo turned back to me, horror etched onto his face. I looked into his eyes and saw his mind racing a million miles an hour.

"That's impossible," he said, anxiety pinching his lips, turning them white. "Nobody in the burg knows about this house."

"Larry Skolnik knows. You remember Larry? The kid who wrote secret messages on his arm. Works in his father's dry cleaning shop now."

I walked to the open bedroom door and looked in. Bed, neatly made. Throw rug on the floor. Bedside table with lamp and clock. The second bedroom was empty. Tracks on the rug from a recent vacuuming. A few indentations in the rug from furniture or whatever. Clearly the room had recently been cleaned out. I checked the bathroom. There was a heavy drape on the small single window. Darkroom, I thought. Mo probably did some stills of his stars. I walked back to the front door.

"I know about the movies," I said to Mo.

He gaped at me. Panicky. Still not believing. I rattled off his list of credits. Asserting my dominance. Letting Mo know that the game was over.

Mo pulled himself together and raised his chin a fraction of an inch. A defensive posture. "Well, what of it? I make art films involving consenting adults."

"Consenting, maybe. Adults is questionable. Does Reverend Bill know about your hobby?"

"Reverend Bill is one of my most devoted fans. Has been for years. Reverend Bill is a firm believer in corporal punishment for bad behavior."

"Then he knows about this house."

"Not the location. And it's not a hobby. I'm a professional filmmaker. I make good money off my films."

"I bet."

"You don't expect me to retire on the money I make selling ice cream cones, do you?" Mo snapped. "You know what the profit is on penny candy? The profit is nothing."

I hoped he didn't expect me to be sympathetic. I was having a hard time not grimacing every time I thought about my picture on his kitchen wall.

He shook his head, the spark of indignant fire sputtering out. Mo collapsing in on himself. "I can't believe this is happening to me. I was making a good living. Putting money away for retirement. I was providing entertainment to a select group of adults. I was employing deserving young people."

I did some mental eye rolling. Moses Bedemier paid street dealers to recruit fresh blood for his porno movies. The street dealers knew the runaways and street kids. They knew the teenagers who still looked healthy and would do most anything to get a new high.

"I made one mistake," Mo said. "One mistake and everything

started to unravel. It was all because of that awful Jamal Brousse." He paced to the window, clearly agitated, peeking around the shade, clasping and unclasping his hands.

"I hope you were careful not to be followed," he said. "Bill is looking for me."

"I wasn't followed." Probably.

Mo kept going, wanting to share his story, I guess, looking slightly dazed that it had all come to this, talking while he continued to pace. Probably he'd been talking and pacing for hours before I arrived, trying to talk himself into calling the police.

"All because of Brousse," he said. "A drug dealer and a purveyor. I made a single unfortunate transaction with him for a young man to model for me. I just wanted some photographs."

He held up and listened. "Bill will kill us both if he finds us here."

There was no doubt in my mind. As soon as Ranger showed up we were moving out. "What about Brousse?" I asked, more to distract myself from thoughts of Reverend Bill arriving before Ranger, than raw curiosity.

"I honored my agreement with Brousse, but he kept coming back at me, making more and more demands. Blackmailing me. I was desperate. I didn't know what to do. I might not make much money from my store, but I have a certain position in the community that I enjoy. Brousse could have ruined everything.

"And then one day Bill stopped in at the store, and I got an idea. Suppose I told Bill about this guy, Jamal Brousse, who was selling drugs to kids. I figured Bill would put a scare into him. Maybe punch him in the nose or something. Maybe scare him enough so he'd go away. Trouble was Bill liked the idea of community justice so much he killed Brousse.

"But Bill made a mistake on Brousse. Dumped him in the river, and Brousse bobbed in to shore two hours later. Bill didn't like that. Said it was messy. I wanted to stop there, but Bill pressed me to give him another name. I finally caved in, and next thing, Bill had killed another dealer and buried him in my cellar. Before I knew it my cellar was full of dead drug dealers. Even after I got arrested, Bill kept up the killing. Only now it was harder to get to the cellar, so we just hid the bodies as best we could. Cameron Brown, Leroy Watkins." Mo shook his head. "Bill was obsessed with the killing. He organized a death squad. And that was so successful Bill started killing not just dealers but hard-core drug users. The death squad learned how to kill the addicts with ODs, so it'd look more natural.

"That's why I hired an attorney. I couldn't be part of all that craziness anymore. They were even talking about killing you. And you wouldn't believe who was taking part in this. Cops, shoe salesmen, grandmothers and schoolteachers. It was insanity. It was like one of those cult things. Like those militia people you see on the television out in Idaho. I even got caught up in it for a while. Carrying a gun. And then that police officer discovered it, and I panicked. It was the gun that had killed Brousse. What was I thinking?"

"Why did you hire a lawyer? Why didn't you just turn yourself in?"

"I'm an old man. I don't want to spend the rest of my life in jail. I guess I hoped if I was cooperative and had a good lawyer I might get off easier. I didn't kill anyone, you know. I just gave Bill some names and set up some meetings."

"You were still participating after you'd gotten a lawyer. You set up Elliot Harp."

"I couldn't get out. I was afraid. I didn't want anyone to know I was talking to the police. As it is, every time I hear a car on the road out there I break into a sweat, thinking it's Bill, and he's found out and come to get me.

"I just wish I'd had some other choice right from the beginning. I feel like I started this in motion. This nightmare."

"There always are choices," Ranger said, laying the barrel of his .44 Magnum alongside Mo's head.

Mo rolled his eyes to look at Ranger. "Where'd you come from? I didn't hear you come in!"

"I come in like the fog on little cat feet."

I looked at Ranger. "Very nice."

"Carl Sandburg," Ranger said. "More or less."

Gravel crunched under tire treads outside, and Mo jumped beside me. "It's him!"

I pulled the shade and looked out. "It's not Reverend Bill."

Ranger and Mo raised their eyebrows at me in silent question.

"You're not going to believe this," I said.

I answered the knock at the door and revealed Lula standing on the stoop, beaming, looking pleased.

"Hey girlfriend," she said. "Vinnie told me all about this hideaway house, and I came out to give you a hand."

Mo's voice cracked. "It's the lunatic in the red Firebird!"

"Hunh," Lula said.

I got Mo's jacket from the hall closet and bundled him into it, at the same time checking him for weapons. I ushered him out the front door and was standing with him on the stoop when I caught the far-off sound of a car on the road. We all paused. The car drew closer. We caught a flash of blue through the trees, and then the vehicle turned into the drive. It was a Ford Econoline van with FREEDOM CHURCH lettered on the side. It stopped halfway to the house, its forward progress halted by Lula's Firebird. The side door to the van slid open and a man in mask and coveralls got out. We stared at each other for a moment, and then he hefted a rocket launcher to his shoulder. There was a flash of fire and a *pfnuffff!* And my truck blew up, its doors shooting off into space like Frisbees.

"That's a warning shot," the man yelled. "We want Mo."

I was speechless. They'd blown up my truck! They'd turned it into a big yellow fireball.

"Look on the bright side," Lula said to me. "You're not going to have to worry about that puppy stalling no more."

"It was fixed!"

Two more men got out of the van. They sighted assault rifles, and we all stumbled back into the house and slammed the door shut.

"If they can blow up a truck, they can blow up a house," Ranger said, pulling car keys from his pocket, handing them to me. "Take Mo out the back door while I pin these guys down. Cut through the woods to my Bronco and get the hell out of here."

"What about you? I'm not going to leave you here!"

The house was peppered with gunshot, and we all hit the deck.

Ranger knocked out window glass and opened fire. "I'll be fine. I'll give you a good start, and then I'll lose myself in the woods." He glanced over at me. "I've done this before."

I grabbed Mo and shoved him toward the back door. Lula ran after us. All of us scuttled in a crouch across the small backyard to the woods while gunfire once again erupted from the driveway. Mo was struggling to run, and Lula was shouting, "Oh shit! Oh shit!"

We slid on our asses down a small embankment, scrambled to our feet and kept going, crashing through dry, viny undergrowth. Not what you'd call a quiet retreat, but quiet didn't matter with World War III going on behind us.

When I thought we'd gone far enough I began curving back toward the road. There was another explosion, and I turned to see a fireball rise to the sky.

"Has to be the bungalow," Lula said.

Her tone was somber. Ominous. Both of us thinking of Ranger.

Mo went down to his knees, his face chalk white, his hand holding his side where a dark stain had begun to spread on his gray coat. A drop of blood hit dry leaves.

"He must have caught one in the house," Lula said.

I tried to hoist Mo back to his feet. "You can make it," I said. "It's not that much farther."

Sirens sounded on the road, and I saw the red flash of police light bars flicker through the trees to my left.

Mo made an effort to stand and collapsed altogether, facedown on the forest floor.

"Run to the road and get help," I told Lula. "I'll stay here."

"You got a gun?"

"Yeah."

"It loaded?"

"Yes. Go!"

She hesitated. "I don't like leaving you."

"Go!"

She swiped at her eyes. "Shit. I'm scared."

She turned and ran. Looked back once and disappeared from view.

I dragged Mo behind a tree, putting the tree trunk between us and the house. I drew my gun and hunkered down.

I really needed to find another job.

It was dark when Lula dropped me off in my parking lot.

"Good thing Morelli and a bunch of cops were following that Freedom Church van," Lula said. "We would have been toast."

"The cops were following the Freedom van. Morelli was following me."

"Lucky you," Lula said.

Mickey's hands were pointing to seven o'clock, but it felt much later. I was tired to the bone, and I had the beginnings of a headache. I shuffled to the elevator and leaned on the button. Thank goodness for elevators, I thought. I'd sleep in the lobby before I'd be able to muster the energy to walk up the stairs.

Lula, Ranger and I had answered questions at police headquarters for what seemed like hours.

Dickie had popped in while I was talking to yet another detective and offered to represent me. I told him I wasn't being charged with anything, but thanks anyway. He seemed disappointed. Probably was hoping he could plea-bargain me into the license plate factory. Keep me away from Mallory. Or maybe he was hoping I'd done something heinous. I could see the headlines: EX-WIFE OF PROMINENT TRENTON ATTORNEY COMMITS HEINOUS CRIME. ATTORNEY SAYS HE ISN'T SURPRISED.

Just before I left the station word came down that Mo was out of surgery and looked pretty good. There'd been a lot of blood lost, but the bullet had entered and exited clean, missing all vital organs. The news had brought a sense of relief and closure. I'd been psyched to that point, hyped on adrenaline. When I finally signed my name to the printed statement of the day's events and realized Mo would make it, the last dregs of energy dribbled out of me.

Rex and I checked out the feast on the coffee table. Rex from his cage. Me from the couch. Bucket of extra-spicy fried chicken, tray of biscuits, container of cole slaw, baked beans. Plus half a chocolate cake, left over from Saturday dinner with my parents.

The Rangers were playing Boston at the Garden, which meant I was wearing my home team white jersey. It was the end of the first period and the Rangers were ahead by a goal.

"This is the life," I said to Rex. "Doesn't get much better than this."

I reached for a piece of chicken and was startled by a knock on my door.

"Don't worry," I said to Rex. "It's probably just Mrs. Bestler."

But I knew it wasn't Mrs. Bestler. Mrs. Bestler never knocked on my door this late at night. No one knocked on my door this late at night. No one who wasn't trouble. It had been a couple weeks since the two masked men had pushed their way into my apartment, but the experience had left me cautious. I'd enrolled in a self-defense class and was careful not to get so tired that my guard was down. Not that the men in the masks were still threatening.

Reverend Bill and the death squad were living rent free, courtesy of the federal government. And that didn't include Mickey Maglio. There'd been cops involved, but he hadn't been one of them. The man who'd burned me had been Reverend Bill's brother-in-law, imported from Jersey City. At least I'd been right about the accent.

Undoubtedly there were some closet vigilantes still at large, but they were keeping a low profile. Some of the wind had gone out of the movement's sails when Mo's secret life was made public information. And whatever vigilante momentum had been left had died a natural death without Reverend Bill acting as catalyst.

I quietly walked to the door and looked out through my peephole. Joe Morelli looked back at me. I should have guessed.

I opened the door to him. "You must have smelled the chicken."

Morelli grinned and rocked back on his heels. "I wouldn't want to impose."

Yeah, right. I got him a beer from the fridge. "Haven't seen you in a while."

"Not since we closed the case on Mo. You never returned my phone calls."

I flopped onto the couch. "Nothing to say."

Morelli took a pull at his beer. "You still pissed off at me for withholding information?"

"Yes. I helped you out with Dickie, and you gave me nothing in return."

"That's not true. I gave you Reverend Bill."

"Only because you knew I'd get it from other sources. I'm glad I ralphed on you that night in your kitchen."

"I suppose that was my fault too?"

"Damn skippy it was." I actually accepted full responsibility, but I had no intention of conveying this to Morelli.

Morelli took a piece of chicken. "Everyone at headquarters is very impressed with you. You were the only one to pick up on the movie angle."

"Thanks to Sue Ann Grebek and her motor mouth. When she told me about Larry Skolnik I thought about Cameron Brown. The Cameron Brown murder never felt right to me. He sold some drugs, but he wasn't a major player. His primary source of income was prostitution. Then Larry and Gail confirmed it. In fact, Larry had already figured most of it out."

The Rangers scored another goal, and we leaned forward to watch the replay.

I'd been reading the papers and talking to Eddie Gazarra, so I knew some of the details on Mo and Reverend Bill. I knew that both of them were coming up to trial. I wasn't sure what would happen to Mo, but Bill was up on seven counts of murder one. Plus, in a late-afternoon raid, the Alcohol, Tobacco and Firearms people hauled enough weapons out of the two Freedom houses on Montgomery Street to fill a five-ton U-Haul. That was way over the limit for anarchist stockpiling.

"I hear you're back to working vice."

Morelli nodded. "I didn't have the wardrobe for homicide. And they actually expected me to shave every day."

"You still living in the house?"

"Yeah. I like it. It's got more space. Lots of closets. Bigger kitchen. Cellar." He leaned close. "It's even got a back door."

I slid him a sideways glance.

He drew a little circle at my temple with his fingertip, and the pitch dropped on his voice. "It's got a backyard, too."

"Backyards are nice."

The fingertip traced down to my collarbone. "Good for summer activities . . . like barbecues."

I hauled back and looked at him. Morelli barbecuing?

"Play your cards right and I might invite you over for a hamburger," Morelli said.

"Just a hamburger?"

"More than a hamburger."

This brought to mind the old adage—be careful what you wish for because you might get it.

Morelli let some smile creep into his voice. "After the hamburger I could show you my garage. Did I mention that I had a garage?"

"Not until now."

"Well, I have a garage, and I know a game . . ."

Oh boy. "I think I know this game."

The smile spread to his eyes. "Yeah?"

"It has to do with . . . transportation. Trains and such."

"I've learned some new routes since the last time we played," he said.

And then his lips brushed the nape of my neck, sending a jolt of fire straight to my doodah.